Timothy Allen

EDWARD ST. AUBYN lives in London with his two children.. His other novels include *On the Edge*, *A Clue to the Exit*, and his latest, *Lost for Words*.

Praise for The Patrick Melrose Novels

"A remarkable cycle of novels . . . The books are written with an utterly idiosyncratic combination of emotional precision, crystalline observation, and black humor, as if one of Evelyn Waugh's wicked satires about British aristos had been mashed up with a searing memoir of abuse and addiction, and injected with Proustian meditations on the workings of memory and time."
—Michiko Kakutani, *The New York Times*

"Stunning, sparkling fiction . . . Unforgettable."
—*The Wall Street Journal*

"One of the great comic writers of our time . . . [A] sprightly, caustic, and harrowing novel sequence."
—*The New York Review of Books*

"Gorgeous, golden prose . . . St. Aubyn is utterly fearless when faced with the task of unpacking and anatomizing the inner lives of characters. No emotion is so subtle and fleeting he can't convey it, or so terrifying or shameful that he can't face it."
—Lev Grossman, *Time*

"One of the most amazing reading experiences I've had in a decade." —Michael Chabon, *Los Angeles Times*

"Parental death, heroin, childhood rape, emotional frigidity, suicide, alcoholism . . . nothing about the plots can prepare you for the rich, acerbic comedy of St. Aubyn's world—or more surprising—its philosophical density." —Zadie Smith, *Harper's Magazine*

"One of the best fictional cycles in contemporary fiction."
—*The Boston Globe*

"I read the five Patrick Melrose novels in five days. When I finished, I read them again."   —Ann Patchett,
The Guardian (London)

"Take P. G. Wodehouse's lighthearted country-house tales of the British aristocracy, then dip them in an acid bath of irony, drug abuse, and general decay, and you have Edward St. Aubyn's Patrick Melrose novels. . . . St. Aubyn's novels fall into that rare category of books that have been highly praised yet are still somehow underrated."   —Scott Stossel,
editor of *The Atlantic*
(The Best Book I Read This Year)

"Highly entertaining and often devastatingly dark . . . The Melrose novels are modern masterworks of social comedy."
—*Bookforum*

"Edward St. Aubyn is probably neck-and-neck with Alan Hollinghurst for the title of 'purest living English prose stylist.'"
—Garth Risk Hallberg, *The Millions*
(Most Anticipated Books of the Year)

"Why did it take me so long to fall in love with the brilliant novels of Edward St. Aubyn?"   —Bret Easton Ellis

"The Melrose novels are a masterwork for the twenty-first century, written by one of the great prose stylists in England."
—Alice Sebold, author of *The Lovely Bones*

"Hilarious and insightful, with a sinister tint and pitch-perfect dialogue . . . St. Aubyn's sentences were the best I read this year. . . . I'm addicted to St. Aubyn."   —Elliott Holt,
author of *You Are One of Them*

PATRICK MELROSE

PATRICK MELROSE

THE NOVELS

Never Mind
Bad News
Some Hope
Mother's Milk
and
At Last

Edward St. Aubyn

PICADOR

Farrar, Straus and Giroux
New York

PATRICK MELROSE. Copyright © 2015 by Edward St. Aubyn. All rights reserved. Printed in the United States of America. For information, address Picador, 175 Fifth Avenue, New York, N.Y. 10010.

picadorusa.com • instagram.com/picador
twitter.com/picadorusa • facebook.com/picadorusa

Picador® is a U.S. registered trademark and is used by Macmillan Publishing Group, LLC, under license from Pan Books Limited.

For book club information, please visit facebook.com/picadorbookclub or email marketing@picadorusa.com.

Grateful acknowledgment is made for permission to reprint excerpts from the following: "Fly Me to the Moon (In Other Words)," words and music by Bart Howard. TRO—©—Copyright 1954 (renewed) by Hampshire House Publishing Corp., New York, NY. Used by permission.
"I Got Plenty o' Nuttin," words and music by George Gershwin, Du Bose Heyward, and Ira Gershwin. Copyright © 1935 (renewed) by Chappell & Co., Inc. (ASCAP). All rights administered by Warner/Chappell North America Ltd.
Excerpt from "Burnt Norton," Part I of *Four Quartets* by T. S. Eliot, copyright © 1936 by Harcourt, Inc., and renewed © 1964 by T. S. Eliot, reprinted by permission of Houghton Mifflin Harcourt Publishing Company.
"Dutch Graves in Bucks County" from *The Collected Poems of Wallace Stevens* by Wallace Stevens, copyright © 1954 by Wallace Stevens and renewed © 1982 by Holly Stevens. Used by permission of Alfred A. Knopf, a division of Random House, Inc.

Designed by Phil Mazzone

The Library of Congress has cataloged the first Picador edition as follows:

Names: St. Aubyn, Edward, 1960– author.
Title: The complete Patrick Melrose novels / Edward St. Aubyn.
Description: First edition. | New York : Picador/Farrar, Straus and Giroux, 2015.
Identifiers: LCCN 2015295911 | ISBN 9781250069603 (trade paperback) | ISBN 9781250069627 (ebook)
Subjects: LCSH: Upper class families—England—Fiction. | Drug addicts—Fiction. | Gloucestershire (England)—Fiction.
Classification: LCC PR6069.T134 A6 2015 | DDC 823'.914—dc23
LC record available at https://lccn.loc.gov/2015295911

Picador Media Tie-in ISBN 978-1-250-30566-4

Our books may be purchased in bulk for promotional, educational, or business use. Please contact your local bookseller or the Macmillan Corporate and Premium Sales Department at 1-800-221-7945, extension 5442, or by email at MacmillanSpecialMarkets@macmillan.com.

Never Mind, Bad News, and *Some Hope* originally published in Great Britain by William Heinemann
Mother's Milk and *At Last* originally published in Great Britain by Picador, an imprint of Pan Macmillan Ltd.

Previously published under the title *The Complete Patrick Melrose Novels* by Picador

First Picador Media Tie-in Edition: May 2018

10 9 8 7 6 5 4 3 2 1

For Eleanor and Lucian

CONTENTS

PATRICK MELROSE

NEVER MIND

I

AT HALF-PAST SEVEN IN the morning, carrying the laundry she had ironed the night before, Yvette came down the drive on her way to the house. Her sandal made a faint slapping sound as she clenched her toes to prevent it from falling off, and its broken strap made her walk unsteadily over the stony, rutted ground. Over the wall, below the line of cypresses that ran along the edge of the drive, she saw the doctor standing in the garden.

In his blue dressing gown, and already wearing dark glasses although it was still too early for the September sun to have risen above the limestone mountain, he directed a heavy stream of water from the hose he held in his left hand onto the column of ants moving busily through the gravel at his feet. His technique was well established: he would let the survivors struggle over the wet stones, and regain their dignity for a while, before bringing the thundering water down on them again. With his free hand he removed a cigar from his mouth, its smoke drifting up through the brown and grey curls that covered the jutting bones of his forehead. He then narrowed the jet of water with his thumb to batter more effectively an ant on whose death he was wholly bent.

Yvette had only to pass the fig tree and she could slip into the house without Dr Melrose knowing she had arrived. His habit, though, was to call her without looking up from the ground just when she thought she was screened by the tree. Yesterday he had talked to her for long enough to exhaust her arms, but not for so long that she might drop the linen. He gauged such things very precisely. He had started by asking her opinion of the mistral, with exaggerated respect for her native knowledge of Provence. By the time he was kind enough to show an interest in her son's job at the shipyard, the pain had spread to her shoulders and started to make sharp forays into her neck. She had been determined to defy him, even when he asked about her husband's back pains and whether they might prevent him from driving the tractor during the harvest. Today he did not call out with the *'Bonjour, chère Yvette'* which inaugurated these solicitous morning chats, and she stooped under the low branches of the fig tree to enter the house.

The chateau, as Yvette called what the Melroses called an old farmhouse, was built on a slope so that the drive was level with the upper floor of the house. A wide flight of steps led down one side of the house to a terrace in front of the drawing room.

Another flight skirted the other side of the house down to a small chapel which was used to hide the dustbins. In winter, water gurgled down the slope through a series of pools, but the gutter which ran beside the fig tree was silent by this time of year, and clogged with squashed and broken figs that stained the ground where they had fallen.

Yvette walked into the high dark room and put down the laundry. She switched on the light and began to divide the towels from the sheets and the sheets from the tablecloths. There were ten tall cupboards piled high with neatly folded linen, none of it now used. Yvette sometimes opened these cupboards to admire this protected collection. Some of the tablecloths had laurel branches and bunches of grapes woven into them in a way that only showed when they were held at certain angles. She would run her finger over the monograms embroidered on the smooth white sheets, and over the coronets encircling the letter 'V' in the corner of the napkins. Her favourite was the unicorn that stood over a ribbon of foreign words on some of the oldest sheets but these too were never used, and Mrs Melrose insisted that Yvette recycle the same poor pile of plain linen from the smaller cupboard by the door.

Eleanor Melrose stormed her way up the shallow steps from the kitchen to the drive. Had she walked more slowly, she might have tottered, stopped, and sat down in despair on the low wall that ran along the side of the steps. She felt defiantly sick in a way she dared not challenge with food and had already aggravated with a cigarette. She had brushed her teeth after vomiting but the bilious taste was still in her mouth. She had brushed her teeth before vomiting as well, never able to utterly crush the optimistic streak in her nature. The mornings had grown cooler since the beginning of September and the air already smelt of autumn, but this hardly mattered to Eleanor who was sweating through the thick layers of powder on her forehead. With each step she pushed her hands against her knees to help her forward, staring down through huge dark glasses at the white canvas shoes on her pale feet, her dark pink raw-silk trousers like hot peppers clinging to her legs.

She imagined vodka poured over ice and all the cubes that had been frosted turning clear and collapsing in the glass and the ice cracking, like a spine in the hands of a confident osteopath. All the sticky, awkward cubes of ice floating together, tinkling, their frost thrown off to the side of the glass, and the vodka cold and unctuous in her mouth.

The drive rose sharply to the left of the steps to a circle of

flat ground where her maroon Buick was parked under an umbrella pine. It looked preposterous, stretched out on its white-
walled tyres against the terraced vines and olive groves behind
it, but to Eleanor her car was like a consulate in a strange city, and
she moved towards it with the urgency of a robbed tourist.

Globules of translucent resin were stuck to the Buick's bonnet. One splash of resin with a dead pine needle inside it was
glued to the base of the windscreen. She tried to pick it off, but
only smeared the windscreen more and made the tips of her fingers sticky. She wanted to get into the car very much, but she
went on scratching compulsively at the resin, blackening her fingernails. The reason that Eleanor liked her Buick so much was
that David never drove it, or even sat in it. She owned the house
and the land, she paid for the servants and the drink, but only
this car was really in her possession.

When she had first met David twelve years ago, she had been
fascinated by his looks. The expression that men feel entitled to
wear when they stare out of a cold English drawing room onto
their own land had grown stubborn over five centuries and per-
fected itself in David's face. It was never quite clear to Eleanor
why the English thought it was so distinguished to have done
nothing for a long time in the same place, but David left her in
no doubt that they did. He was also descended from Charles II
through a prostitute. 'I'd keep quiet about that, if I were you,'
she had joked when he first told her. Instead of smiling, he had
turned his profile towards her in a way she had grown to loathe,
thrusting out his underlip and looking as if he were exercising
great tolerance by not saying something crushing.

There had been a time when she admired the way that David
became a doctor. When he had told his father of his intention,
General Melrose had immediately cut off his annuity, preferring
to use the money to rear pheasants. Shooting men and animals
were the occupations of a gentleman, tending their wounds the

business of middle-class quacks. That was the General's view, and he was able to enjoy more shooting as a consequence of holding it. General Melrose did not find it difficult to treat his son coldly. The first time he had taken an interest in him was when David left Eton, and his father asked him what he wanted to do. David stammered, 'I'm afraid I don't know, sir,' not daring to admit that he wanted to compose music. It had not escaped the General's attention that his son fooled about on the piano, and he rightly judged that a career in the army would put a curb on this effeminate impulse. 'Better join the army,' he said, offering his son a cigar with awkward camaraderie.

And yet, to Eleanor, David had seemed so different from the tribe of minor English snobs and distant cousins who hung around, ready for an emergency, or for a weekend, full of memories that were not even their own, memories of the way their grandfathers had lived, which was not in fact how their grandfathers had lived. When she had met David, she thought that he was the first person who really understood her. Now he was the last person she would go to for understanding. It was hard to explain this change and she tried to resist the temptation of thinking that he had been waiting all along for her money to subsidize his fantasies of how he deserved to live. Perhaps, on the contrary, it was her money that had cheapened him. He had stopped his medical practice soon after their marriage. At the beginning, there had been talk of using some of her money to start a home for alcoholics. In a sense they had succeeded.

The thought of running into David struck Eleanor again. She tore herself away from the pine resin on the windscreen, clambered into the car and drove the unwieldy Buick past the steps and along the dusty drive, only stopping when she was half-way down the hill. She was on her way over to Victor Eisen's so she could make an early start for the airport with Anne, but first she had to straighten herself out. Folded in a cushion under the driver's seat was a half-bottle of Bisquit brandy. In her bag she had the yellow pills for keeping her alert and the white ones for taking away the dread and panic that alertness brought with it. With the long drive ahead of her she took four instead of two of the yellow pills and then, worrying that the double dose might make her jumpy, she took two of the white ones, and drank about half the bottle of brandy to help the pills down. At first she shuddered violently, and then before it even reached her bloodstream, she felt the sharp click of alcohol, filling her with gratitude and warmth.

She subsided into the seat on which she had only been perched, recognizing herself in the mirror for the first time that day. She settled into her body, like a sleepwalker who climbs back into bed after a dangerous expedition. Silent through the sealed windows, she saw black and white magpies burst from the vines, and the needles of the pine trees standing out sharply against the pale sky, swept clean by two days of strong wind. She started the engine again and drove off, steering vaguely along the steep and narrow lanes.

David Melrose, tired of drowning ants, abandoned watering the garden. As soon as the sport lost a narrow focus, it filled him with despair. There was always another nest, another terrace of nests. He pronounced ants 'aunts', and it added zest to his murderous pursuits if he bore in mind his mother's seven haughty sisters, high-minded and selfish women to whom he had displayed his talent on the piano when he was a child.

David dropped the hose on the gravel path, thinking how useless to him Eleanor had become. She had been rigid with terror for too long. It was like trying to palpate a patient's swollen liver when one had already proved that it hurt. She could only be persuaded to relax so often.

He remembered an evening twelve years before, when he had asked her to dinner at his flat. How trusting she was in those days! They had already slept together, but Eleanor still treated him shyly. She wore a rather shapeless white dress with large black polka dots. She was twenty-eight but seemed younger because of the simple cut of her lank blonde hair. He found her pretty in a bewildered, washed-out way, but it was her restlessness that aroused him, the quiet exasperation of a woman who longs to throw herself into something significant, but cannot find what it is.

He had cooked a Moroccan dish of pigeon stuffed with almonds. He served it to her on a bed of saffron rice and then drew back the plate. 'Will you do something for me?' he asked.

'Of course,' she said. 'What?'

He put the plate on the floor behind her chair and said, 'Would you eat your food without using a knife and fork, or your hands, just eat it off the plate?'

'Like a dog, you mean?' she asked.

'Like a girl pretending to be a dog.'

'But why?'

'Because I want you to.'

He enjoyed the risk he was taking. She might have said no and left. If she stayed and did what he wanted, he would capture her. The odd thing was that neither of them thought of laughing.

A submission, even an absurd one, was a real temptation to Eleanor. She would be sacrificing things she did not want to believe in – table manners, dignity, pride – for something she did want to believe in: the spirit of sacrifice. The emptiness of the gesture, the fact that it did not help anybody, made it seem more pure at the time. She knelt down on all fours on the threadbare Persian rug, her hands flattened either side of the plate. Her elbows jutted out as she lowered herself and picked up a piece of pigeon between her teeth. She felt the strain at the base of her spine.

She sat back, her hands resting on her knees, and chewed quietly. The pigeon tasted strange. She looked up a little and saw David's shoes, one pointing towards her along the floor, the other dangling close to her in the air. She looked no higher than the knees of his crossed legs, but bowed down again, eating more eagerly this time, rooting about in the mound of rice to catch an almond with her lips and shaking her head gently to loosen some pigeon from the bone. When she looked up at him at last, one of her cheeks was glazed with gravy and some grains of the yellow rice were stuck to her mouth and nose. All the bewilderment was gone from her face.

For a few moments David had adored her for doing what he had asked. He extended his foot and ran the edge of his shoe gently along her cheek. He was completely captivated by the trust she showed him, but he did not know what to do with it, since it had already achieved its purpose, which was to demonstrate that he could elicit her submission.

The next day he told Nicholas Pratt what had happened. It was one of those days when he made his secretary say that he was busy, and sat drinking in his club, beyond the reach of fevered children and women who pretended their hangovers were migraines. He liked to drink under the blue and gold ceiling of the morning room, where there was always a ripple left by the passage of important men. Dull, dissolute, and obscure members felt buoyed up by this atmosphere of power, as little dinghies bob up and down on their moorings when a big yacht sails out of the harbour they have shared.

'Why did you make her do it?' asked Nicholas, hovering between mischief and aversion.

'Her conversation is so limited, don't you find?' said David.

Nicholas did not respond. He felt that he was being forced to conspire, just as Eleanor had been forced to eat.

'Did she make better conversation from the floor?' he asked.

'I'm not a magician,' said David, 'I couldn't make her amusing, but I did at least keep her quiet. I was dreading having another talk about the agonies of being rich. I know so little about them, and she knows so little about anything else.'

Nicholas chuckled and David showed his teeth. Whatever one felt about David wasting his talents, thought Nicholas, he had never been any good at smiling.

David walked up the right side of the double staircase that led from the garden to the terrace. Although he was now sixty, his hair was still thick and a little wild. His face was astonishingly handsome. Its faultlessness was its only flaw; it was the blueprint of a face and had an uninhabited feeling to it, as if no trace of how its owner had lived could modify the perfection of the lines. People who knew David well watched for signs of decay, but his mask grew more noble each year. Behind his dark glasses, however rigidly he held his neck, his eyes flickered unobserved, assessing the weaknesses in people. Diagnosis had been his most intoxicating skill as a doctor and after exhibiting it he had often lost interest in his patients, unless something about their suffering intrigued him. Without his dark glasses, he wore an inattentive expression, until he spotted another person's vulnerability. Then the look in his eyes hardened like a flexed muscle.

He paused at the top of the stairs. His cigar had gone out and he flung it over the wall into the vines below. Opposite him, the ivy that covered the south side of the house was already streaked with red. He admired the colour. It was a gesture of defiance towards decay, like a man spitting in the face of his torturer. He had seen Eleanor hurrying away early in her ridiculous car. He had even seen Yvette trying to steal into the house without drawing attention to herself. Who could blame them?

He knew that his unkindness to Eleanor was effective only if he alternated it with displays of concern and elaborate apologies for his destructive nature, but he had abandoned these variations because his disappointment in her was boundless. He knew that she could not help him unravel the knot of inarticulacy that he carried inside him. Instead, he could feel it tightening, like a promise of suffocation that shadowed every breath he took.

It was absurd; but all summer long he had been obsessed by the memory of a mute cripple he had seen in Athens airport. This man, trying to sell tiny bags of pistachio nuts by tossing printed advertisements into the laps of waiting passengers, had heaved himself forward, stamping the ground with uncontrollable feet, his head lolling and his eyes rolling upwards. Each time David had looked at the man's mouth twisting silently, like a gasping fish on a river bank, he had felt a kind of vertigo.

David listened to the swishing sound his yellow slippers made as he walked up the last flight of steps to the door that led from the terrace into the drawing room. Yvette had not yet opened the curtains, which saved him the trouble of closing them again. He liked the drawing room to look dim and valuable. A dark red and heavily gilded chair that Eleanor's American grandmother had prised from an old Venetian family on one of her acquisitive sweeps through Europe gleamed against the opposite wall of the room. He enjoyed the scandal connected with its acquisition and, knowing that it ought to be carefully preserved in a museum, he made a point of sitting on it as often as possible. Sometimes, when he was alone, he sat in the Doge's chair, as it was always called, leaning forward on the edge of the seat, his right hand clasping one of the intricately carved arms, striking a pose he remembered from the *Illustrated History of England* he had been given at prep school. The picture portrayed Henry V's superb anger when he was sent a present of tennis balls by the insolent King of France.

David was surrounded by the spoils of Eleanor's matriarchal American family. Drawings by Guardi and Tiepolo, Piazetta and Novelli hung thickly over the walls. An eighteenth-century

French screen, crowded with greyish-brown monkeys and pink roses, divided the long room in half. Partially hidden behind it, from where David stood, was a black Chinese cabinet, its top crowded with neat rows of bottles, and its inner shelves filled with their reinforcements. As he poured himself a drink, David thought about his dead father-in-law, Dudley Craig, a charming, drunken Scotsman who had been dismissed by Eleanor's mother, Mary, when he became too expensive to keep.

After Dudley Craig, Mary had married Jean de Valençay, feeling that if she was going to keep a man, he might as well be a duke. Eleanor had been brought up in a string of houses where every object seemed to have been owned by a king or an emperor. The houses were wonderful, but guests left them with relief, conscious that they were not quite good enough, in the duchess's eyes, for the chairs on which they had sat.

David walked towards the tall window at the end of the room. The only one with its curtain open, it gave a view onto the mountain opposite. He often stared at the bare outcrops of lacerated limestone. They looked to him like models of human brains dumped on the dark green mountainside, or at other times, like a single brain, bursting from dozens of incisions. He sat on the sofa beside the window and looked out, trying to work up a primitive sense of awe.

2

PATRICK WALKED TOWARDS THE well. In his hand he carried a grey plastic sword with a gold handle, and swished it at the pink flowers of the valerian plants that grew out of the terrace wall. When there was a snail on one of the fennel stems, he sliced his sword down the stalk and made it fall off. If he killed a snail he had to stamp on it quickly and then run away, because it went all squishy like blowing your nose. Then he would go back and have a look at the broken brown shell stuck in the soft grey flesh, and would wish he hadn't done it. It wasn't fair to squash the snails after it rained because they came out to play, bathing in the pools under the dripping leaves and stretching out their horns. When he touched their horns they darted back and his hand darted back as well. For snails he was like a grown-up.

One day, when he was not intending to go there, he had been surprised to find himself next to the well and so he decided that the route he had discovered was a secret short cut. Now he always went that way when he was alone. He walked through a terrace of olive trees where yesterday the wind had made the leaves flick from green to grey and grey to green, like running his fingers back and forth over velvet, making it turn pale and dark again.

He had shown Andrew Bunnill the secret short cut and Andrew said it was longer than the other way, and so he told Andrew he was going to throw him down the well. Andrew was feeble and had started to cry. When Andrew flew back to London, Patrick said he would throw him out of the plane. Blub, blub, blub. Patrick wasn't even on the plane, but he told Andrew he would be hiding under the floor and would saw a circle around his chair. Andrew's nanny said that Patrick was a nasty little boy, and Patrick said it was just because Andrew was so wet.

Patrick's own nanny was dead. A friend of his mother's said she had gone to heaven, but Patrick had been there and knew perfectly well that they had put her in a wooden box and dropped her in a hole. Heaven was the other direction and so the woman was lying, unless it was like sending a parcel. His mother cried a lot when nanny was put in the box, she said it was because of her own nanny. That was stupid, because her own nanny was still alive and in fact they had to go and visit her on the train, and it was the most boring thing ever. She had horrible cake with only a tiny bit of jam in the middle and millions of miles of fluff on either side. She always said, 'I know you like this,' which was a lie, because he had told her he didn't the last time. It was called sponge cake and so he had asked was it for having a bath with and his mother's nanny had laughed and laughed and hugged him for ages. It was disgusting because she pressed her cheek next to his and her skin hung down loosely, like that chicken's neck he had seen hanging over the edge of the table in the kitchen.

Why did his mother have to have a nanny anyway? He didn't have one anymore and he was only five. His father said he was a little man now. He remembered going to England when he was three. It was winter and he saw snow for the first time. He could remember standing on the road by a stone bridge and the road was covered in frost and the fields were covered in snow and the sky was shining and the road and the hedges were blazing and he had blue woollen gloves on and his nanny held his hand and they stood still for ages looking at the bridge. He used to think of that often, and the time they were in the back of the car and he had his head in her lap and he looked up at her and she smiled and the sky behind her head was very wide and blue, and he had fallen asleep.

Patrick walked up a steep bank on a path that ran beside a bay tree and emerged next to the well. He was forbidden to play by the well. It was his favourite place to play. Sometimes he climbed onto the rotten cover and jumped up and down, pretending it was a trampoline. Nobody could stop him, nor did they often try. The wood was black where the blistered pink paint had peeled off. It creaked dangerously and made his heart beat faster. He was not strong enough to lift the cover himself, but when it was left open he collected stones and clumps of earth to throw down the shaft. They hit the water with a deep reverberating splash and broke into the blackness.

Patrick raised his sword in triumph as he reached the top of the path. He could see that the cover of the well was pushed back. He started to search about for a good stone, the biggest one he could lift and the roundest he could find. He hunted in the surrounding field and unearthed a reddish stone which he needed both hands to carry. He placed it on the flat surface next to the opening of the well shaft and hoisted himself up until his legs no longer touched the ground and, leaning over as far as he could, looked down at the darkness where he knew the water was hiding. Holding on with his left hand, he pushed the stone over the edge and heard the plunging sound it made and watched the surface break and the disturbed water catch the light of the sky and gleam back at it unreliably. So heavy and black it was more like oil. He shouted down the shaft where the dry bricks turned green and then black. If he leaned over far enough he could hear a damp echo of his own voice.

Patrick decided to climb up the side of the well. His scuffed blue sandals fitted in the gaps between the rocks. He wanted to stand on the ledge beside the open well shaft. He had done it once before, for a dare, when Andrew was staying. Andrew had stood beside the well saying, 'Please don't, Patrick, please come down, *please* don't.' Patrick wasn't scared then, although Andrew was, but now that he was alone he felt dizzy, squatting on the ledge, with his back to the water. He stood up very slowly and as he straightened, he felt the invitation of the emptiness behind him, pulling him backwards. He was convinced that his feet would slip if he moved, and he tried to stop wobbling by clenching his fists and his toes and looking down very seriously at the hard ground around the well. His sword was still resting on the ledge and he wanted to retrieve it in order to make his conquest complete, and so he leaned over carefully, with an enormous effort of will, defying the fear that tried to arrest his limbs, and picked up the sword by its scratched and dented grey blade. Once he got hold of the sword, he bent his knees hesitantly and jumped over the edge, landing on the ground, shouting hooray and making the noise of clashing metal as he slashed about him at imaginary enemies. He whacked a bay leaf with the flat of his sword and then stabbed the air underneath it with a morbid groan, clutching his side at the same time. He liked to imagine an ambushed Roman army about to be smashed to bits by the barbarians, when he arrived, the commander of the special soldiers with purple cloaks, and he was braver than anybody and saved the day from unthinkable defeat.

When he went for a walk in the woods he often thought about Ivanhoe, the hero of one of his favourite comics, who cut down the trees on either side of him as he passed. Patrick had to walk around the pine trees, but he imagined he had the power to carve his own path, striding majestically through the small wood at the end of the terrace on which he stood, felling with a single blow each tree to his right and left. He read things in books and then he thought about them lots. He had read about rainbows in a soppy picture book, but then he had started to see them in the streets in London after it rained, when the petrol from the cars stained the tarmac and the water fanned out in broken purple, blue, and yellow rings.

He didn't feel like going into the wood today and so he decided to jump down all the terraces. It was like flying, but some of the walls were too high and he had to sit on the edge, throw his sword down, and lower himself as far as he could before he dropped. His shoes filled with the dry soil around the vines and he had to take them off twice and hold them upside down to shake out the earth and the pebbles. Nearer the bottom of the valley the terraces became wider and shallower and he could leap over the edge of all the walls. He gathered his breath for the final flight.

Sometimes he managed to jump so far that he felt like Superman practically, and at other times he made himself run faster by thinking about the Alsatian dog that chased him down the beach on that windy day when they had gone to lunch at George's. He had begged his mother to let him go for a walk, because he loved looking at the wind when it exploded the sea, like smashing bottles against rocks. Everyone said not to go too far, but he wanted to be nearer the rocks. There was a sandy path leading to the beach and while he was walking down it a fat, long-haired Alsatian appeared at the top of the hill, barking at him. When he saw it move closer, he started to run, following the twists in the path at first and then jumping straight down the soft slope, faster and faster, until he was taking giant strides, his arms spread out against the wind, rushing down the hill onto the half circle of sand between the rocks, right up to the edge of the highest wave. When he looked up the dog was miles away up on the hill, and he knew it could never catch him because he was so fast. Later he wondered if it had tried.

Patrick arrived panting at the dried-up river bed. He climbed onto a big rock between two clumps of pale green bamboo. When he had taken Andrew there they had played a game that Patrick invented. They both had to stand on the rock and try to push each other off, and on one side they pretended there was a pit full of broken razor blades and on the other there was a tank full of honey. And if you fell to one side you were cut to death in a million places, and on the other you drowned, exhausted by a heavy golden swim. Andrew fell over every time, because he was so utterly wet.

Andrew's father was wet too, in a way. Patrick had been to Andrew's birthday party in London, and there was a huge box in the middle of the drawing room, full of presents for the other children. They all queued up and took a present out of the box and then ran around comparing what they'd got. Unlike them, Patrick hid his present under an armchair and went back to get another one. When he was leaning over the box, fishing out another shiny package, Andrew's father squatted down next to him and said, 'You've already had one haven't you, Patrick?' – not angrily, but in a voice like he was offering Patrick a sweet. 'It isn't fair on the other children if you take their presents, is it?' Patrick looked at him defiantly and said, 'I haven't got one already,' and Andrew's father just looked all sad and utterly wet and said, 'Very well, Patrick, but I don't want to see you taking another one.' And so Patrick got two presents, but he hated Andrew's father because he wanted more.

Patrick had to play the rock game on his own now, jumping from one side of the rock to another, challenging his sense of balance with wild gestures. When he fell over, he pretended it had not happened, although he knew that was cheating.

Patrick looked doubtfully at the rope François had tied for him to one of the nearby trees so that he could swing over the river bed. He felt thirsty and started to climb back up to the house along the path where the tractor worked its way among the vines. His sword had become a burden and he carried it under his arm resentfully. He had heard his father use a funny expression once. He said to George, 'Give him enough rope and he'll hang himself.' Patrick did not know what that meant at first, but he became convinced, with a flash of terror and shame, that they were talking about the rope that François had tied to the tree. That night he dreamt that the rope had turned into one of the tentacles of an octopus and wrapped itself around his throat. He tried to cut it, but he could not because his sword was only a toy. His mother cried a lot when they found him dangling from the tree.

Even when you were awake it was hard to know what grown-ups meant when they said things. One day he had worked out a way of guessing what they were going to do: no meant no, maybe meant perhaps, yes meant maybe and perhaps meant no, but the system did not work, and he decided that maybe everything meant perhaps.

Tomorrow the terraces would be crowded with grape-pickers filling their buckets with bunches of grapes. Last year François had taken him on the tractor. His hands were very strong and hard like wood. François was married to Yvette who had gold teeth you could see when she smiled. One day Patrick was going to have all his teeth made of gold, not just two or three. He sometimes sat in the kitchen with Yvette and she let him taste the things she was cooking. She came up to him with spoons full of tomato and meat and soup and said, '*Ça te plaît?*' And he could see her gold teeth when he nodded. Last year François told him to sit in the corner of the trailer next to two big barrels of grapes. Sometimes when the road was rough and steep he turned around and said, '*Ça va?*' And Patrick shouted back, '*Oui, merci,*' over the noise of the engine and the bumping and squealing of the trailer and the brakes. When they got to the place where the wine was made, Patrick was very excited. It was dark and cool in there, the floor was hosed with water, and there was a sharp smell of juice turning into wine. The room was vast and François took him up a ladder to a high ramp that ran above the wine press and all of the vats. The ramp was made of metal with holes in it and it was a funny feeling being so high up with holes under his feet.

When they got to the wine press Patrick looked down and saw two steel rollers turning in opposite directions with no space in between them. Stained with grape juice, they pressed against each other, spinning loudly. The lower railing of the ramp only came up to Patrick's chin and he felt very close to the wine press. And looking at it, he felt that his eyes were like the grapes, made of the same soft translucent jelly and that they might fall out of his head and get crushed between the two rollers.

As Patrick approached the house, climbing as usual the right-hand flight of the double staircase because it was luckier, he turned into the garden to see if he could find the frog that lived in the fig tree. Seeing the tree frog was very lucky indeed. Its bright green skin was even smoother against the smooth grey skin of the fig tree, and it was hard to find it among the fig leaves which were almost the same colour as itself. In fact, Patrick had only seen the tree frog twice, but he had stood still for ages staring at its sharp skeleton and bulging eyes, like the beads on his mother's yellow necklace, and at the suckers on its front feet that held it motionless against the trunk and, above all, at the swelling sides which enlivened a body as delicate as jewelry, but greedier for breath. The second time he saw the frog, Patrick stretched out his hand and carefully touched its head with the tip of his index finger, and it did not move and he felt that it trusted him.

The frog was not there today and so he climbed wearily up the last flight of steps, pushing against his knees with his hands. He walked around the house to the kitchen entrance and reached up to open the squealing door. He had expected to find Yvette in the kitchen, but she was not there. Bottles of white wine and champagne jostled and clinked as he opened the refrigerator door. He turned back into the larder, where he found two warm bottles of chocolate milk in the corner of the lower shelf. After several attempts he opened one and drank the soothing liquid straight from the bottle, something Yvette had told him not to do. Immediately after drinking he felt violently sad and sat for several minutes on the kitchen counter staring down at his dangling shoes.

He could hear the piano music, muted by distance and closed doors, but he did not pay any attention to it, until he recognized the tune his father had composed for him. He jumped off the counter and ran down the corridor that led to the hall, crossed the hall, and broke into a kind of cantering motion as he entered the drawing room and danced to his father's tune. It was wild music with harsh flurries of high notes superimposed on a rumbling military march. Patrick hopped and skipped between the tables and chairs and around the edge of the piano, only coming to rest when his father ceased to play.

'How are you today, Mr Master Man?' asked his father, staring at him intently.

'All right, thank you,' said Patrick, wondering if it was a trick question. He was out of breath, but he knew he must concentrate because he was with his father. When he had asked what was the most important thing in the world, his father had said, 'Observe everything.' Patrick often forgot about this instruction, but in his father's presence he looked at things carefully, without being sure what he was looking for. He had watched his father's eyes behind their dark glasses. They moved from object to object and person to person, pausing for a moment on each and seeming to steal something vital from them, with a quick adhesive glance, like the flickering of a gecko's tongue. When he was with his father, Patrick looked at everything seriously, hoping he looked serious to anyone who might watch his eyes, as he had watched his father's.

'Come here,' said his father. Patrick stepped closer.

'Shall I pick you up by the ears?'

'No,' shouted Patrick. It was a sort of game they played. His father reached out and clasped Patrick's ears between his forefingers and thumbs. Patrick put his hands around his father's wrists and his father pretended to pick him up by his ears, but Patrick really took the strain with his arms. His father stood up and lifted Patrick until their eyes were level.

'Let go with your hands,' he said.

'No,' shouted Patrick.

'Let go and I'll drop you at the same time,' said his father persuasively.

Patrick released his father's wrists, but his father continued to pinch his ears. For a moment the whole weight of his body was supported by his ears. He quickly caught his father's wrists again.

'Ouch,' he said, 'you said you were going to drop me. *Please* let go of my ears.'

His father still held him dangling in the air. 'You've learned something very useful today,' he said. 'Always think for yourself. Never let other people make important decisions for you.'

'Please let go,' said Patrick. 'Please.' He felt that he was going to cry, but he pushed back his sense of desperation. His arms were exhausted, but if he relaxed them he felt as if his ears were going to be torn off, like the gold foil from a pot of cream, just ripped off the side of his head.

'You *said*,' he yelled, 'you said.'

His father dropped him. 'Don't whimper,' he said in a bored voice, 'it's very unattractive.' He sat down at the piano and started playing the march again, but Patrick did not dance.

He ran from the room, through the hall, out of the kitchen, over the terrace, along the olive grove and into the pine wood. He found the thorn bush, ducked underneath it, and slid down a small slope into his most secret hiding place. Under a canopy of bushes, wedged up against a pine tree which was surrounded by thickets on every side, he sat down and tried to stop the sobs, like hiccups, that snarled his throat.

Nobody can find me here, he thought. He could not control the spasms that caught his breath as he tried to inhale. It was like being caught in sweaters, when he plunged his head in and couldn't find the neck of the sweater and he tried to get out through the arm and it all got twisted and he thought he would never get out and he couldn't breathe.

Why did his father do that? Nobody should do that to anybody else, he thought, nobody should do that to anybody else.

In winter when there was ice on the puddles, you could see the bubbles trapped underneath and the air couldn't breathe: it had been ducked by the ice and held under, and he hated that because it was so unfair and so he always smashed the ice to let the air go free.

Nobody can find me here, he thought. And then he thought, what if nobody can find me here?

3

VICTOR WAS STILL ASLEEP in his room downstairs and Anne wanted him to stay asleep. After less than a year together they now slept in separate rooms because Victor's snoring, and nothing else about him, kept her awake at night. She walked barefoot down the steep and narrow staircase running the tips of her fingers along the curve of the whitewashed walls. In the kitchen she removed the whistle from the spout of the chipped enamel kettle, and made coffee as silently as possible.

There was a tired ebullience about Victor's kitchen, with its bright orange plates and watermelon slices grinning facetiously from the tea towels. It was a harbour of cheap gaiety built up by Victor's ex-wife, Elaine, and Victor had been torn between protesting against her bad taste and the fear that it might be in bad taste to protest. After all, did one notice the kitchen things? Did they matter? Wasn't indifference more dignified? He had always admired David Melrose's certainty that beyond good taste lay the confidence to make mistakes because they were one's own. It was at this point that Victor often wavered. Sometimes he opted for a few days, or a few minutes, of assertive impertinence, but he always returned to his careful impersonation of a gentleman; it was all very well to *épater les bourgeois*, but the excitement was double-edged if you were also one of them. Victor knew that he could never acquire David Melrose's conviction that success was somehow vulgar. Though sometimes he was tempted to believe that David's languor and contempt masked regret for his failed life, this simple idea dissolved in David's overbearing presence.

What amazed Anne was that a man as clever as Victor could be caught with such small hooks. Pouring herself some coffee she felt a strange sympathy for Elaine. They had never met, but she had come to understand what had driven Victor's wife to seek refuge in a full set of Snoopy mugs.

When Anne Moore had been sent by the London bureau of the *New York Times* to interview the eminent philosopher Sir Victor Eisen, he had seemed a little old-fashioned. He had just returned from lunch at the Athenaeum, and his felt hat, darkened by rain, lay on the hall table. He pulled his watch out of his waistcoat pocket with what struck Anne as an archaic gesture.

'Ah, exactly on time,' he said. 'I admire punctuality.'

'Oh, good,' she answered, 'a lot of people don't.'

The interview had gone well, so well in fact that later in the afternoon it moved into his bedroom. From that point on Anne had willingly interpreted the almost Edwardian clothes, the pretentious house and the claret-stained anecdotes as part of the camouflage that a Jewish intellectual would have had to take on, along with a knighthood, in order to blend into the landscape of conventional English life.

During the months that followed she lived with Victor in London, ignoring any evidence that made this mild interpretation look optimistic. Those interminable weekends, for instance, which started with briefings on Wednesday night: how many acres, how many centuries, how many servants. Thursday evening was given over to speculation: he hoped, he really hoped, that the Chancellor wouldn't be there this time; could Gerald still be shooting now that he was in a wheelchair? The warnings came on Friday, during the drive down: '*Don't* unpack your own bags in this house.' '*Don't* keep asking people what they do.' '*Don't* ask the butler how he *feels*, as you did last time.' The weekends only ended on Tuesday when the stalks and skins of Saturday and Sunday were pressed again for their last few drops of sour juice.

In London, she met Victor's clever friends but at weekends the people they stayed with were rich and often stupid. Victor was *their* clever friend. He purred appreciatively at their wine and pictures and they started many of their sentences by saying, 'Victor will be able to tell us . . .' She watched them trying to make him say something clever and she watched him straining himself to be more like them, even reiterating the local pieties: wasn't it splendid that Gerald *hadn't* given up shooting? Wasn't Gerald's mother amazing? Bright as a button and still beavering away in the garden at ninety-two. 'She completely wears me out,' he gasped.

If Victor sang for his supper, at least he enjoyed eating it. What was harder to discount was his London house. He had bought the fifteen-year lease on this surprisingly large white stucco house in a Knightsbridge crescent after selling his slightly smaller but freehold house at a less fashionable address. The lease now had only seven years to run. Anne stoutly ascribed this insane transaction to the absent-mindedness for which philosophers are famous.

Only when she had come down here to Lacoste in July and seen Victor's relationship with David had her loyalty begun to wear away. She started to wonder how high a price in wasted time Victor was prepared to pay for social acceptance, and why on earth he wanted to pay it to David.

According to Victor, they had been 'exact contemporaries', a term he used for anyone of vaguely his own age who had not noticed him at school. 'I knew him at Eton' too often meant that he had been ruthlessly mocked by someone. He said of only two other scholars that they were friends of his at school, and he no longer saw either of them. One was the head of a Cambridge college and the other a civil servant who was widely thought to be a spy because his job sounded too dull to exist.

She could picture Victor in those days, an anxious schoolboy whose parents had left Austria after the First World War, settled in Hampstead, and later helped a friend find a house for Freud. Her images of David Melrose had been formed by a mixture of Victor's stories and her American vision of English privilege. She pictured him, a demigod from the big house, opening the batting against the village cricket team, or lounging about in a funny waistcoat he was allowed to wear because he was in Pop, a club Victor never got into. It was hard to take this Pop thing seriously but somehow Victor managed. As far as she could make out it was like being a college football hero, but instead of making out with the cheerleaders, you got to beat young boys for burning your toast.

When she had met David, at the end of the long red carpet unrolled by Victor's stories, she spotted the arrogance but decided that she was just too American to buy into the glamour of David's lost promise and failure. He struck her as a fraud and she had said so to Victor. Victor had been solemn and disapproving, arguing that on the contrary David suffered from the clarity with which he saw his own situation. 'You mean he *knows* he's a pain in the ass?' she had asked.

Anne moved back towards the stairs, warming her hands with a steaming orange mug covered in purple hearts of various sizes. She would have liked to spend the day reading in the hammock that hung between the plane trees in front of the house, but she had agreed to go to the airport with Eleanor. This American

Girls' Outing had been imposed on her by Victor's unquench-able desire to be associated with the Melroses. The only Mel-rose Anne really liked was Patrick. At five years old he was still capable of a little enthusiasm.

If at first she had been touched by Eleanor's vulnerability, Anne was now exasperated by her drunkenness. Besides, Anne had to guard against her wish to save people, as well as her habit of pointing out their moral deficiencies, especially as she knew that nothing put the English more on edge than a woman having definite opinions, except a woman who went on to defend them. It was as if every time she played the ace of spades, it was beaten by a small trump. Trumps could be pieces of gossip, or insincere remarks, or irrelevant puns, or anything that dispelled the pos-sibility of seriousness. She was tired of the deadly smile on the faces of people whose victory was assured by their silliness.

Having learned this, it had been relatively easy to play along with the tax-exiled English duke, George Watford, who came up from the coast for weekends with the Melroses, wearing shoes that tapered to a quite impossible thinness. His rather wooden face was covered in the thinnest cracks, like the varnish on the Old Masters he had 'shocked the nation' by selling. The English didn't ask much of their dukes in Anne's opinion. All they had to do was hang on to their possessions, at least the very well-known ones, and then they got to be guardians of what other people called 'our heritage'. She was disappointed that this char-acter with a face like a cobweb had not even managed the small task of leaving his Rembrandts on the wall where he found them.

Anne continued to play along until the arrival of Vijay Shah. Only an acquaintance, not a friend of Victor's, they had met ten years before when Vijay, as head of the Debating Society, had invited Victor down to Eton to defend the 'relevance' of philoso-phy. Since then Vijay had cultivated the connection with a bar-rage of arty postcards and they had occasionally met at parties in London. Like Victor, Vijay had been an Eton scholar, but unlike Victor he was also very rich.

Anne felt guilty at first that she reacted so badly to Vijay's appearance. His oyster-coloured complexion and the thick jowls that looked like a permanent attack of mumps were the unhappy setting for a large hooked nose with tufts of intractable hair about the nostrils. His glasses were thick and square but, without them, the raw dents on the bridge of his nose and the weak eyes peering out from the darker grey of their sockets looked worse. His hair was blow-dried until it rose and stiffened like a black meringue on top of his skull. His clothes did nothing to compensate for these natural disadvantages. If Vijay's favourite flared green trousers were a mistake, it was a trivial one compared to his range of lightweight jackets in chaotic tartan patterns, with flapless pockets sewn onto the outside. Still, any clothes were preferable to the sight of him in a bathing suit. Anne remembered with horror his narrow shoulders and their white pustules struggling to break through a thick pelt of wiry black hair.

Had Vijay's character been more attractive his appearance might have elicited pity or even indifference, but spending just a few days with him convinced Anne that each hideous feature had been moulded by internal malevolence. His wide, grinning mouth was at once crude and cruel. When he tried to smile, his purplish lips could only curl and twist like a rotting leaf thrown onto a fire. Obsequious and giggly with older and more powerful people, he turned savage at the smell of weakness, and would attack only easy prey. His voice seemed to be designed exclusively for simpering and yet when they had argued on the night before he left, it had achieved the shrill astringency of a betrayed schoolmaster. Like many flatterers, he was not aware that he irritated the people he flattered. When he had met the Wooden Duke he had poured himself out in a rich gurgling rush of compliments, like an overturned bottle of syrup. She overheard George complaining afterwards to David, 'Perfectly ghastly man your friend Victor brought over. Kept telling me about the plasterwork at Richfield. Thought he must want a job as a guide.' George grunted disdainfully and David grunted disdainfully back.

A little Indian guy being sneered at by monsters of English privilege would normally have unleashed the full weight of Anne's loyalty to underdogs, but this time it was wiped out by Vijay's enormous desire to be a monster of English privilege himself. 'I can't bear going to Calcutta,' he giggled, 'the people, my dear, and the noise.' He paused to let everyone appreciate this nonchalant remark made by an English soldier at the Somme.

The memory of Vijay's ingratiating purr died away as Anne tried to push open her bedroom door, which always stuck on a bulge in the quaintly uneven floor. This was another relic of Elaine, who had refused to change what she called 'the authentic feel of the house'. Now the hexagonal tiles were worn to a paler terracotta where the door scraped them each time it was opened. Afraid of spilling her coffee she let the door stay stuck and edged sideways into the room. Her breasts brushed the cupboard as she passed.

Anne put her coffee mug down on the round marble-topped table with black metal legs which Elaine had carried back in triumph from some junk store in Apt and cunningly used as a bedside table. It was far too high and Anne often pulled the wrong book from the pile of unseen titles above her. Suetonius' *Twelve Caesars*, which David had lent her way back at the beginning of August, kept turning up like a reproach. She had glanced at one or two chapters, but the fact that David had recommended the book made her reluctant to become intimate with it. She knew she really ought to read a bit more of it before dinner so as to have something intelligent to say when she gave it back to him tonight.

All she remembered was that Caligula had planned to torture his wife to find out why he was so devoted to her. What was David's excuse, she wondered.

Anne lit a cigarette. Lying on a pile of pillows and smaller cushions, slurping her coffee and playing with her cigarette smoke, she felt briefly that her thoughts were growing more subtle and expansive. The only thing that compromised her pleasure was the sound of running water in Victor's bathroom.

First, he would shave and wipe the remnants of the shaving cream on a clean towel. Then he would plaster his hair as flat as he could, walk to the foot of the stairs and shout, 'Darling.' After a brief pause he would shout it again in his let's-not-play-foolish-games voice. If she still did not appear he would call out, 'Breakfast.'

Anne had teased him about it just the other day, and said, 'Oh, darling, you shouldn't have.'

'Have what?'

'Made breakfast.'

'I haven't.'

'Oh, I thought when you shouted, "Breakfast," you meant it was ready.'

'No, I meant that I was ready for breakfast.'

Anne had not been far wrong, Victor was indeed in his bathroom downstairs brushing his hair vigorously. But, as always, a few seconds after he stopped the wave of hair which had tormented him since childhood sprang up again.

His pair of ivory hairbrushes had no handles. They were quite inconvenient, but very traditional, like the wooden bowl of shaving soap, which never thickened as satisfactorily as foam from a can. Victor was fifty-seven, but looked younger. Only a drooping in his flesh, a loss of tension around the jaw and the mouth and the tremendous depth of the horizontal lines in his forehead, revealed his age. His teeth were neat and strong and yellow. Though he longed for something more aerodynamic his nose was bulbous and friendly. Women always praised his eyes because their pale grey looked luminous against his slightly pitted olive-brown skin. All in all, strangers were surprised when a rapid and rather fruity lisp emerged from a face which could well have belonged to an overdressed prizefighter.

In pink pyjamas from New & Lingwood, a silk dressing gown, and a pair of red slippers, Victor felt almost sleek. He had walked out of the bathroom, through his simple whitewashed bedroom with its green mosquito netting held in place over the windows by drawing pins, and out into the kitchen, where he hovered, not yet daring to call Anne.

While Victor hesitated in the kitchen, Eleanor arrived. The Buick was too long to twist its way up Victor's narrow drive and she'd had to park it on the edge of a small pine wood at the bottom of the hill. This land did not belong to Victor but his neighbours, the Fauberts, well known in Lacoste for their eccentric way of life. They still used a mule to plough their fields, they had no electricity, and in their large dilapidated farmhouse they lived in just one room. The rest of the house was crowded with barrels of wine, jars of olive oil, sacks of animal feed, and piles of almonds and lavender. The Fauberts had not altered anything since old Madame Faubert died, and she had never changed anything since she arrived as a young bride, half a century before, bearing a glass bowl and a clock.

Eleanor was intrigued by these people. She imagined their austere and fruitful life like a stained-glass window in a medieval church – labourers in the vineyard with grape-filled baskets on their backs. She had seen one of the Fauberts in the Crédit Agricole and he had the sullen air of a man who looks forward to strangling poultry. Nevertheless, she treasured the idea that the

Fauberts were connected to the earth in some wholesome way that the rest of us had forgotten. She had certainly forgotten about being wholesomely connected with the earth herself. Perhaps you had to be a Red Indian, or something.

She tried to walk more slowly up the hill. God, her mind was racing, racing in neutral, she was pouring with sweat and getting flashes of dread through the exhilaration. Balance was so elusive: either it was like this, too fast, or there was the heavy thing like wading through a swamp to get to the end of a sentence. When there were cicadas earlier in the summer it was good. Their singing was like blood rushing in her ears. It was one of those outside inside things.

Just before the top of the hill she stopped, breathed deeply, and tried to muster her scattered sense of calm, like a bride checking her veil in the last mirror before the aisle. The feeling of solemnity deserted her almost immediately and a few yards further on her legs began to shake. The muscles in her cheeks twitched back like stage curtains, and her heart tried to somersault its way out of her chest. She must remember not to take so many of those yellow pills at once. What on earth had happened to the tranquilizers? They seemed to have been drowned by the floodtide of Dexedrine. Oh, my God, there was Victor in the kitchen, dressed like an advertisement as usual. She gave him a breezy and confident wave through the window.

Victor had finally summoned the courage to call Anne, when he heard the sound of feet on the gravel outside and saw Eleanor waving at him eagerly. Jumping up and down, crossing and uncrossing her arms above her head, her lank blonde hair bobbing from side to side, she looked like a wounded marine trying to attract a helicopter.

She formed the word 'Hello' silently and with great exaggeration as if she were speaking to a deaf foreigner.

'It's open,' Victor called.

One really has to admire her stamina, he thought, moving towards the front door.

Anne, primed to hear the cry of 'Breakfast', was surprised to hear 'It's open' instead. She got out of bed and ran downstairs to greet Eleanor.

'How are you? I'm not even dressed yet.'

'I'm wide awake,' said Eleanor.

'Hello, darling, why don't you make a pot of tea,' said Victor. 'Would you like some, Eleanor?'

'No, thanks.'

After making the tea, Anne went up to dress, pleased that Eleanor had arrived early. Nevertheless, having seen her frenzied air and the sweat-streaked face powder, Anne did not look forward to being driven by her, and she tried to think of some way to do the driving herself.

In the kitchen, with a cigarette dangling from her mouth, Eleanor rummaged about in her handbag for a lighter. She still had her dark glasses on and it was hard to make out the objects in the murky chaos of her bag. Five or six caramel-coloured plastic tubs of pills swirled around with spare packets of Player's cigarettes, a blue leather telephone book, pencils, lipstick, a gold powder compact, a small silver hip-flask full of Fernet-Branca, and a dry-cleaning ticket from Jeeves in Pont Street. Her anxious hands dredged up every object in her bag, except the red plastic lighter she knew was in there somewhere. 'God. I must be going mad,' she muttered.

'I thought I'd take Anne to Signes for lunch,' she said brightly.

'Signes? That's rather out of your way, isn't it?'

'Not the way we're going.' Eleanor had not meant to sound facetious.

'Quite,' Victor smiled tolerantly. 'The way you're going it couldn't be closer, but isn't it rather a long route?'

'Yes, only Nicholas's plane doesn't get in until three and the cork forests are so pretty.' It was unbelievable, there was the dry-cleaning ticket again. There must be more than one. 'And there's that monastery to see, but I don't suppose there'll be time. Patrick always wants to go to the Wild West funfair when we drive that way to the airport. We could stop there too.' Rummage, rummage, rummage, pills, pills, pills. 'I must take him one day. Ah, there's my lighter. How's the book going, Victor?'

'Oh, you know,' said Victor archly, 'identity is a big subject.'

'Does Freud come into it?'

Victor had had this conversation before and if anything made him want to write his book it was the desire not to have it again. 'I'm not dealing with the subject from a psychoanalytical point of view.'

'Oh,' said Eleanor, who had lit her cigarette and was prepared to be fascinated for a while, 'I would have thought it was – what's the word? – well, terribly psychological. I mean, if anything's in the mind, it's who you are.'

'I may quote you on that,' said Victor. 'But remind me, Eleanor, is the woman Nicholas is bringing this time his fourth or fifth wife?'

It was no use. She felt stupid again. She always felt stupid with David and his friends, even when she knew it was they who were being stupid. 'She's not his wife,' she said. 'He's left Georgina who was number three, but he hasn't married this one yet. She's called Bridget. I think we met in London, but she didn't make a very strong impression on me.' Anne came downstairs wearing a white cotton dress almost indistinguishable from the white cotton nightgown she had taken off. Victor reflected with satisfaction that she still looked young enough to get away with such a girlish dress. White dresses deepened the deceptive serenity which her wide face and high cheekbones and calm black eyes already gave to her appearance. She stepped lightly into the room. By contrast, Eleanor made Victor think of Lady Wishfort's remark, 'Why I am arrantly flayed; I look like an old peeled wall.'

'OK,' said Anne, 'I guess we can leave whenever you like.

'Will you be all right for lunch?' she asked Victor.

'You know what philosophers are like, we don't notice that kind of thing. And I can always go down to the Cauquière for a rack of lamb with *sauce Béarnaise*.'

'*Béarnaise?* With lamb?' said Anne.

'Of course. The dish which left the poor Due de Guermantes so famished that he had no time to chat with the dying Swann's dubious daughter before hurrying off to dinner.'

Anne smiled at Eleanor and asked, 'Do you get Proust for breakfast round at your house?'

'No, but we get him for dinner fairly often,' Eleanor replied.

After the two women had said goodbye, Victor turned towards the refrigerator. He had the whole day free to get on with his work and suddenly felt tremendously hungry.

4

'GOD, I FEEL AWFUL,' groaned Nicholas, switching on his bed-side table lamp.

'Poor squirrel,' said Bridget sleepily.

'What are we doing today? I can't remember.'

'Going to the South of France.'

'Oh yes. What a nightmare. What time's the plane?'

'Twelve something. It arrives at three something. I think there's an hour difference, or something.'

'For Christ sake, stop saying "something".'

'Sorry.'

'God knows why we stayed so late last night. That woman on my right was utterly appalling. I suppose somebody told her long ago that she had a pretty chin, and so she decided to get another one, and another, and another. You know, she used to be married to George Watford.'

'To who?' asked Bridget.

'The one you saw in Peter's photograph album last weekend with a face like a crème brûlée after the first blow of the spoon, all covered in little cracks.'

'Not everyone can have a lover who's rich *and* beautiful,' said Bridget, sliding through the sheets towards him.

'Oaw, give over, luv, give over,' said Nicholas in what he imagined to be a Geordie accent. He rolled out of bed and, moaning, 'Death and destruction,' crawled histrionically across the crimson carpet towards the open door of the bathroom.

Bridget looked critically at Nicholas's body as he clambered to his feet. He had got a lot fatter in the past year. Maybe older men were not the answer. Twenty-three years was a big difference and at twenty, Bridget had not yet caught the marriage fever that tormented the older Watson-Scott sisters as they galloped towards the thirtieth year of their scatterbrained lives. All Nicholas's friends were such wrinklies and some of them were a real yawn. You couldn't exactly drop acid with Nicholas. Well, you could; in fact, she had, but it wasn't the same as with Barry. Nicholas didn't have the right music, the right clothes, the right attitude. She felt quite bad about Barry, but a girl had to keep her options open.

The thing about Nicholas was that he really was rich and beautiful *and* he was a baronet, which was nice and sort of Jane Austeny. Still, it wouldn't be long before people started saying, 'You can tell he used to be good-looking,' and someone else would intervene charitably with, 'Oh, no, he still is.' In the end she would probably marry him and she would be the fourth Lady Pratt. Then she could divorce him and get half a million pounds, or whatever, and keep Barry as her sex slave and still call herself Lady Pratt in shops. God, sometimes she was so cynical it was frightening.

She knew that Nicholas thought it was the sex that kept them together. It was certainly what had got them together at the party where they first met. Nicholas had been quite drunk and asked her if she was a 'natural blonde'. Yawn, yawn, *what* a tacky question. Still, Barry was in Glastonbury and she'd been feeling a bit restless and so she gave him this heavy look and said, 'Why don't you find out for yourself?' as she slipped out of the room. He thought he *had* found out, but what he didn't know was that she dyed *all* her hair. If you do something cosmetic, you might as well do it thoroughly, that was her motto.

In the bathroom, Nicholas stuck out his tongue and admired its thickly coated surface, still tinged with blackish purple from last night's coffee and red wine. It was all very well to make jokes about Sarah Watford's double chins, but the truth was that unless he held his head up like a Guardsman on parade he had one himself. He couldn't face shaving, but he dabbed on a little of Bridget's make-up. One didn't want to look like the old queen in *Death in Venice*, with rouge trickling down cholera-fevered cheeks, but without a little light powder he had what people called 'a distinctly unhealthy pallor'. Bridget's make-up was rather basic, like her sometimes truly appalling clothes. Whatever one said about Fiona (and one had said some thoroughly unpleasant things in one's time) she did have the most amazing creams and masks sent over from Paris. He sometimes wondered if Bridget might not be (one had to slip into the softening nuances of the French tongue) *insortable*. Last weekend at Peter's she had spent the whole of Sunday lunch giggling like a fourteen-year-old.

And then there was her background. He did not know when the house of Watson and the house of Scott had seen fit to unite their fortunes, but he could tell at a glance that the Watson-Scotts were Old Vicarage material who would kill to have their daughter's engagement in *Country Life*. The father was fond of the races and when Nicholas had taken him and his keen-on-roses wife to *Le Nozze di Figaro* at Covent Garden, Roddy Watson-Scott had said, 'They're under starter's orders,' as the conductor mounted the podium. If the Watson-Scotts were just a little too obscure, at least everyone was agreed that Bridget was flavour of the month and he was a lucky dog to have her.

If he married again he would not choose a girl like Bridget.

Apart from anything else, she was completely ignorant. She had 'done' *Emma* for A-level, but since then, as far as he could make out, she only read illustrated magazines called *Oz* or *The Furry Freak Brothers* supplied to her by a seamy character called Barry. She spent hours poring over pictures of spiralling eyeballs and exploding intestines and policemen with the faces of Doberman pinschers. His own intestines were in a state of bitter confusion and he wanted to clear Bridget out of the bedroom before *they* exploded.

'Darling!' he shouted, or rather tried to shout. The sound came out as a croak. He cleared his throat and spat in the basin.

'You couldn't be an angel and get my glass of orange juice from the dining room, could you? And a cup of tea?'

'Oh, all right.'

Bridget had been lying on her stomach, playing with herself lazily. She rolled out of bed with an exaggerated sigh. God, Nicholas was boring. What was the point of having servants? He treated them better than he treated her. She slouched off to the dining room.

Nicholas sat down heavily on the teak lavatory seat. The thrill of educating Bridget socially and sexually had begun to pall when he had stopped thinking about how wonderfully good he was at it and noticed how little she was willing to learn. After this trip to France he would have to go to Asprey's to get her a going-away present. And yet he did not feel ready for that girl from the Old Masters department of Christie's – a simple string of pearls about her woolly blue neck – who longed to exhaust herself helping a chap to keep his estate intact; a general's daughter used to an atmosphere of discipline. A girl, his thoughts expanded gloomily, who would enjoy the damp little hills of Shropshire's Welsh border, something he had yet to achieve himself despite owning so very many of them and having 'farmer' next to his still unsuccessful candidature for Pratt's club. The Wits never tired of saying, 'But, Nicholas, I thought you owned the place.' He'd made too many enemies to get himself elected.

Nicholas's bowels exploded. He sat there sweating miserably like one of the paranoid wrecks in Bridget's favourite cartoon strips. He could imagine Fattie Poole squealing, 'The man's an absolute cunt, and if they let him in here, I shall have to spend the rest of my life at the Turf.' It had been a mistake to get David Melrose to propose him, but David had been one of his father's best friends, and ten years ago he'd not been as misanthropic or unpopular as he was now, nor had he spent so much time in Lacoste.

The route from Clabon Mews to Heathrow was too familiar to register on Nicholas's senses. He had moved into the soporific phase of his hangover, and felt slightly nauseous. Very tired, he slouched in the corner of the taxi. Bridget was less jaded about foreign travel. Nicholas had taken her to Greece in July and Tuscany in August, and she still liked the idea of how glamorous her life had become.

She disliked Nicholas's English Abroad outfits, particularly the panama hat he had on today and wore tilted over his face to show that he was not in the mood to talk. Nor did she like his off-white wild-silk jacket and the yellow corduroy trousers. She was embarrassed by the shirt with very narrow dark red stripes and a stiff white rounded collar, and by his highly polished shoes. He was a complete freak about shoes. He had fifty pairs, all made for him, and *literally* identical, except for silly details which he treated as world-shatteringly important.

On the other hand, she knew that her own clothes were devastatingly sexy. What could be more sexy than a purple miniskirt and black suede cowboy jacket with tassels hanging all along the arms and across the back? Under the jacket you could see her nipples through the black T-shirt. Her black and purple cowboy boots took half an hour to get off, but they were well worth it, because everybody noticed them.

Since half the time she didn't get the point of one's stories at all, Nicholas wondered whether to tell Bridget about the figs. In any case, he was not sure he wanted her to get the point of the fig story. It had happened about ten years ago, just after David persuaded Eleanor to buy the house in Lacoste. They hadn't married because of Eleanor's mother trying to stop them, and David's father threatening to disinherit him.

Nicholas tipped the brim of his hat. 'Have I ever told you what happened the first time I went to Lacoste?' To make sure the story did not fall flat, he added, 'The place we're going today.'

'No,' said Bridget dully. More stories about people she didn't know, most of them taking place before she was born. Yawn, yawn.

'Well, Eleanor – whom you met at Annabel's, you probably don't remember.'

'The drunk one.'

'Yes!' Nicholas was delighted by these signs of recognition. 'At any rate, Eleanor – who wasn't drunk in those days, just very shy and nervous – had recently bought the house in Lacoste, and she complained to David about the terrible waste of figs that fell from the tree and rotted on the terrace. She mentioned them again the next day when the three of us were sitting outside. I saw a cold look come over David's face. He stuck his lower lip out – always a bad sign, half brutal and half pouting – and said, "Come with me." It felt like following the headmaster to his study. He marched us towards the fig tree with great long strides, Eleanor and I stumbling along behind. When we got there we saw figs scattered all over the stone paving. Some of them were old and squashed, others had broken open, with wasps dancing around the wound or gnawing at the sticky red and white flesh. It was a huge tree and there were a *lot* of figs on the ground. And, then David did this amazing thing. *He told Eleanor to get on all fours and eat all the figs off the terrace.*'

'What, in front of you?' said Bridget, round-eyed.

'Quite. Eleanor *did* look rather confused and I suppose the word is betrayed. She didn't protest, though, just got on with this rather unappetizing task. David wouldn't let her leave a single one. She did once look up pleadingly and say, "I've had enough now, David," but he put his foot on her back and said, "Eat them up. We don't want them going to waste, do we?"'

'Kink-ky,' said Bridget.

Nicholas was rather pleased with the effect his story was having on Bridget. A hit, a palpable hit, he thought to himself.

'What did you do?' asked Bridget.

'I watched,' said Nicholas. 'You don't cross David when he's in that sort of mood. After a while Eleanor looked a little sick and so then I did suggest we collect the rest of the figs in a basket. "You mustn't interfere," said David. "Eleanor can't bear to see the figs wasted when there are starving people in the world. Can you, darling? And so she's going to eat them all up on her own." He grinned at me, and added, "Anyway, she's far too picky about her food, don't you think?"'

'Wow!' said Bridget. 'And you still go and stay with these people?'

The taxi drew up outside the terminal and Nicholas was able to avoid the question. A porter in a brown uniform spotted him immediately and hurried to collect the bags. Nicholas stood transfixed for a moment, like a man under a warm shower, between the grateful cabbie and the assiduous porter, both calling him 'Guv' simultaneously. He always gave larger tips to people who called him 'Guv'. He knew it, and they knew it, it was what was called a 'civilized arrangement'.

Bridget's concentration span was enormously improved by the story about the figs. Even when they had boarded the plane and found their seats, she could still remember what it was she'd wanted him to explain.

'Why do you like this guy anyway? I mean, does he sort of make a habit of ritual humiliation or something?'

'Well, I'm told, although I didn't witness this myself, that he used to make Eleanor take lessons from a prostitute.'

'You're kidding,' said Bridget admiringly. She swivelled round in her seat. 'Kink-ky.'

An air hostess brought two glasses of champagne, apologizing for the slight delay. She had blue eyes and freckles and smiled ingratiatingly at Nicholas. He preferred these vaguely pretty girls on Air France to the absurd ginger-haired stewards and frumpish nannies on English aeroplanes. He felt another wave of tiredness from the processed air, the slight pressure on his ears and eyelids, the deserts of biscuit-coloured plastic around him and the dry acid taste of the champagne.

The excitement radiating from Bridget revived him a little, and yet he had still not explained what attracted him to David. Nor was it a question he particularly wanted to look into. David was simply part of the world that counted for Nicholas. One might not like him, but he was impressive. By marrying Eleanor he had obliterated the poverty which constituted his great social weakness. Until recently the Melroses had given some of the best parties in London.

Nicholas lifted his chin from the cushion of his neck. He wanted to feed Bridget's ingenuous appetite for the atmosphere of perversion. Her reaction to the story about the figs had opened up possibilities he would not know how to exploit, but even the possibilities were stimulating.

'You see,' he said to Bridget, 'David was a younger friend of my father's, and I'm a younger friend of his. He used to come

45

down to see me at school and take me to Sunday lunch at the Compleat Angler.' Nicholas could feel Bridget's interest slipping away in the face of this sentimental portrait. 'But what I think fascinated me was the air of doom he carried around with him. As a boy he played the piano brilliantly and then he developed rheumatism and couldn't play,' said Nicholas. 'He won a scholarship to Balliol but left after a month. His father made him join the army and he left that too. He qualified as a doctor but didn't bother to practise. As you can see, he suffers from an almost heroic restlessness.'

'Sounds like a real drag,' said Bridget.

The plane edged slowly towards the runway, while the cabin crew mimed the inflation of life jackets.

'Even their son is the product of rape.' Nicholas watched for her reaction. 'Although you mustn't tell anyone that. I only know because Eleanor told me one evening, when she was very drunk and weepy. She'd been refusing to go to bed with David for ages because she couldn't bear to be touched by him, and then one evening he rugby tackled her on the stairs and wedged her head between the banisters. In law, of course, there is no such thing as marital rape, but David is a law to himself.'

The engines started to roar. 'You'll find in the course of your life,' boomed Nicholas, and then, realizing that he sounded pompous, he put on his funny pompous voice, 'as I have found in the course of mine, that such people, though perhaps destructive and cruel towards those who are closest to them, often possess a vitality that makes other people seem dull by comparison.'

'Oh, God, gimme a break,' said Bridget. The plane gathered speed and shuddered into the pasty English sky.

5

AS ELEANOR'S BUICK DRIFTED along the slow back roads to Signes the sky was almost clear except for a straggling cloud dissolving in front of the sun. Through the tinted border of the windscreen, Anne saw the cloud's edges curling and melting in the heat. The car had already been caught behind an orange tractor, its trailer loaded with dusty purple grapes; the driver had waved them on magnanimously. Inside the car, the air conditioning gently refrigerated the atmosphere. Anne had tried to prise the keys from her, but Eleanor said that nobody else ever drove her car. Now the soft suspension and streams of cold air made the dangers of her driving seem more remote.

It was still only eleven o'clock and Anne was not looking forward to the long day ahead. There had been an awkward, stale silence since she'd made the mistake of asking how Patrick was. Anne felt a maternal instinct towards him, which was more than she could say for his mother. Eleanor had snapped at her, 'Why do people think they are likely to please me by asking how Patrick is, or how David is? I don't know how they are, only they know.'

Anne was stunned. A long time went by before Anne tried again. 'What did you think of Vijay?'

'Not much.'

'Me neither. Luckily he had to leave earlier than expected.' Anne still did not know how much to reveal about the row with Vijay. 'He was going to stay with that old man they all worship, Jonathan somebody, who writes those awful books with the crazy titles, like *Anemones and Enemies* or *Antics and Antiques*. You know the one I mean?'

'Oh, him, Jesus, he's awful. He used to come to my mother's house in Rome. He would always say things like, "The streets are pullulating with beggars," which made me really angry when I was sixteen. But is that Vijay man rich? He kept talking as if he must be, but he didn't look as if he ever spent any money – not on his clothes anyhow?'

'Oh, yeah,' said Anne, 'he is *so* rich: he is factory-rich, bank-rich. He keeps polo ponies in Calcutta, but he doesn't like polo and never goes to Calcutta. Now that's what I call rich.'

Eleanor was silent for a while. It was a subject in which she felt quietly competitive. She did not want to agree too readily that neglecting polo ponies in Calcutta was what she called rich.

'But stingy as hell,' said Anne to cover the silence. 'That was one of the reasons we had a row.' She was longing to tell the truth now, but she was still unsure. 'Every evening he rang home, which is Switzerland, to chat in Gujarati to his aged mother, and if there was no answer, he'd show up in the kitchen with a black shawl around his frail shoulders, looking like an old woman himself. Finally I had to ask him for some money for the phone calls.'

'And did he pay you?'

'Only after I lost my temper.'

'Didn't Victor help?' asked Eleanor.

'Victor shies away from crass things like money.'

The road had cut into cork forests, and trees with old or

fresh wounds where belts of bark had been stripped from their trunks grew thickly on both sides.

'Has Victor been doing much writing this summer?' asked Eleanor.

'Hardly any. And it's not as if he does anything else when he's at home,' Anne replied. 'You know, he's been coming down here for what? Eight years? And he's never even been over to say hello to those farmers next door.'

'The Fauberts?'

'Right. Not once. They live three hundred yards away in that old farmhouse, with the two cypresses out front. Victor's garden practically belongs to them, but they've never exchanged a word. "We haven't been introduced," is his excuse,' said Anne.

'He's terribly English for an Austrian, isn't he?' smiled Eleanor. 'Oh look, we're coming up to Signes. I hope I can find that funny restaurant. It's in a square opposite one of those fountains that's turned into a mound of wet moss with ferns growing out of it. And inside there are heads of wild boars with polished yellow tusks all over the walls. Their mouths are painted red, so it looks as if they could still charge out from behind the wall.'

'God, how terrifying,' said Anne, drily.

'When the Germans left here,' Eleanor continued, 'at the end of the war, they shot every man in the village, except for Marcel – the one who owns the restaurant. He was away when it happened.'

Anne was silenced by Eleanor's air of crazed empathy. Once they'd found the restaurant, she was at once relieved and a little disappointed that the dark watery square was not more redolent of sacrifice and retribution. The walls of the restaurant were made of blonde plastic moulded to look like planks of pine and there were in fact only two boars' heads in the rather empty room, which was harshly lit by bare fluorescent tubes. After the first course of tiny thrushes full of lead shot and trussed up on pieces of greasy toast, Anne could only toy with the dark depressing stew, loaded onto a pile of overcooked noodles. The red wine was cold and raw and came in old green bottles with no label.

'Great place, isn't it?' said Eleanor.

'It's certainly got atmosphere,' said Anne.

'Look, there's Marcel,' said Eleanor desperately.

'*Ah, Madame Melrose, je ne vous ai pas vue,*' he said, pretending to notice Eleanor for the first time. He hurried round the end of the bar with quick small steps, wiping his hands on the stained white apron. Anne noticed his drooping moustache and the extraordinary bags under his eyes.

Immediately, he offered Eleanor and Anne some cognac. Anne refused despite his claim that it would do her good, but Eleanor accepted, and then returned the offer. They drank another and chatted about the grape harvest while Anne, who could only understand a little of his *midi* accent, regretted even more that she was not allowed to drive.

By the time they got back to the car, the cognac and tranquillizers had come into their own and Eleanor felt her blood tumbling like ball bearings through the veins under her numbed skin. Her head was as heavy as a sack of coins and she closed her eyes slowly, slowly, completely in control.

'Hey,' said Anne, 'wake up.'

'I am awake,' said Eleanor grumpily and then more serenely, 'I'm awake.' Her eyes remained closed.

'Please let me drive.' Anne was ready to argue the point.

'Sure,' said Eleanor. She opened her eyes, which suddenly seemed intensely blue against the pinkish tinge of frayed blood vessels. 'I trust you.'

Eleanor slept for about half an hour while Anne drove up and down the twisting roads from Signes to Marseilles.

When Eleanor woke up, she was lucid again and said, 'Goodness that stew was awfully rich, I did feel a little weighed down after lunch.' The high from the Dexedrine was back; like the theme from *The Valkyrie*, it could not be kept down for long, even if it took a more muted and disguised form than before.

'What's Le Wild Ouest?' said Anne. 'I keep passing pictures of cowboys with arrows through their hats.'

'Oh, we must go, we must go,' said Eleanor in a childish voice. 'It's a funfair but the whole thing is made to look like Dodge City. I've never actually been in, but I'd really like to—'

'Have we got time?' asked Anne sceptically.

'Oh, yes, it's only one-thirty, look, and the airport is only forty-five minutes away. Oh, let's. Just for half an hour. Pl-ea-se?'

Another billboard announced Le Wild Ouest at four hundred metres. Soaring above the tops of the dark pine trees were miniature imitation stagecoaches in brightly coloured plastic hanging from a stationary Ferris wheel.

'This can't be for real,' said Anne. 'Isn't it fantastic? We have to go in.'

They walked through the giant saloon doors of Le Wild Ouest. On either side, the flags of many nations drooped on a circle of white poles.

'Gosh, it's exciting,' said Eleanor. It was hard for her to decide which of the wonderful rides to take first. In the end she chose to go on the stagecoach Ferris wheel. 'I want a yellow one,' she said.

The wheel edged forward as each stagecoach was filled. Eventually, theirs rose above the level of the highest pines.

'Look! There's our car,' squealed Eleanor.

'Does Patrick like this place?' asked Anne.

'He's never been,' said Eleanor.

'You'd better take him soon, or he'll be too old. People grow out of this sort of thing, you know.' Anne smiled.

Eleanor looked massively gloomy for a moment. The wheel started to turn, generating a little breeze. On the upward curve, Eleanor felt her stomach tighten. Instead of giving her a better view of the funfair and the surrounding woods, the motion of the wheel made her feel sick and she stared grimly at the white tips of her knuckles, longing for the ride to be over.

Anne saw that Eleanor's mood had snapped and that she was again in the company of an older, richer, drunker woman.

They got off the ride, and walked through a street of shooting arcades. 'Let's get out of this fucking place,' said Eleanor. 'It's time to collect Nicholas anyhow.'

'So tell me about Nicholas,' said Anne, trying to keep up.

'Oh, you'll find out soon enough.'

6

'SO THIS ELEANOR WOMAN is a real victim, right?' said Bridget. She had fallen asleep after smoking a joint in the loo and she wanted to compensate with a burst of belated curiosity.

'Is every woman who chooses to live with a difficult man a victim?'

Nicholas undid his seatbelt as soon as the plane landed. They were in the second row and could easily get off ahead of the other passengers if, just for once, Bridget did not unsheathe her compact from its blue velvet pouch and admire herself in its powdery little mirror.

'Shall we go,' sighed Nicholas.

'The seatbelt sign is still on.'

'Signs are for sheep.'

'Bahaha-a-a,' bleated Bridget at the mirror, 'I'm a sheep.'

This woman is intolerable, thought Nicholas.

'Well, I'm a shepherd,' he said out loud, 'and don't make me put on my wolf's clothing.'

'Oh, my,' said Bridget, cowering in the corner of her seat, 'what big teeth you have.'

'All the better to bite your head off.'

'I don't think you're my granny at all,' she said with real disappointment.

The plane stopped its creeping progress and there was a general clicking of opening buckles and discarded seatbelts.

'Come on,' said Nicholas, now all businesslike. He very much disliked joining the struggling tourists as they jostled each other down the aisle.

They arrived at the open door of the plane, pale and overdressed, and started to clank their way down a flight of metal steps, caught between the air crew who pretended to be sorry at their departure and the ground crew who pretended to be pleased by their arrival. As she went down the steps, Bridget felt slightly nauseous from the heat and the smell of spent fuel.

Nicholas looked across the tarmac at the long queue of Arabs slowly climbing on board an Air France plane. He thought of the Algerian crisis in '62 and the threat of betrayed colonists parachuting into Paris. The thought petered out as he imagined how far back he would have to begin in order to explain it to Bridget. She probably thought that Algeria was an Italian dress designer. He felt a familiar longing for a well-informed woman in her early thirties who had read history at Oxford; the fact that he had divorced two of them already made little difference to his immediate enthusiasm. Their flesh might hang more loosely on the bone, but the memory of intelligent conversation tormented him like the smell of succulent cooking wafting into a forgotten prison cell. Why was the centre of his desire always in a place he had just deserted? He knew that the memory of Bridget's flesh would betray him with the same easy poignancy if he were now climbing on to the bus with a woman whose conversation he could bear. Theoretically, of course, there were women – he had even had affairs with them – who combined the qualities which he threw into unnecessary competition, but he knew that something inside him would always scatter his appreciation and divide his loyalties.

The doors folded shut and the bus jerked into motion. Bridget sat opposite Nicholas. Under her absurd skirt, her legs were slim and bare and golden. He detached them pornographically from the rest of her body, and found he was still excited by the idea of their availability. He crossed his legs and loosened his entangled boxer shorts through the stiff ridges of his corduroy trousers.

It was only when he considered to whom these golden legs belonged that his fleeting erection seemed a small and inconvenient reward for a state of almost permanent irritation. In fact, scanning the figure above the waist, along the fringed sleeve of her black suede jacket, and up towards the bored and stubborn expression on her face, he felt a spasm of revulsion and estrangement. Why was he taking this ludicrous creature to stay with David Melrose who was, after all, a man of some discernment, not to say a merciless snob?

The terminal building smelled of disinfectant. A woman in blue overalls drifted across the glaring floor, the circular pads of her polishing machine humming as she swung it gently back and forth across the black and brown translucent pebbles trapped in cheap white marble. Still stoned, Bridget lost herself in the flakes of colour as if they were the flint and quartz stars of a white sky.

'What are you staring at?' snapped Nicholas.

'This floor is something else,' said Bridget.

At passport control she could not find her passport but Nicholas refused to start a scene just when they were about to meet Eleanor.

'Rather eccentrically, in this airport one crosses the main lobby before collecting one's luggage,' said Nicholas. 'That's probably where Eleanor will be waiting for us.'

'Wow!' said Bridget. 'If I was a smuggler,' she paused, hoping Nicholas might challenge her, 'this would be my dream airport. I mean, there's this whole lobby where you could slip someone your hand luggage, full of goodies, and then go and fetch your legal luggage for Customs.'

'That's what I admire about you,' said Nicholas, 'your creative thinking. You might have had a brilliant career in advertising; although I think as far as smuggling goes the Marseilles authorities have more pressing problems to wrestle with than any "goodies" you might import in your handbag. I don't know if you're aware of it but . . .'

Bridget had stopped listening. Nicholas was being a wanker again. He always got like this when he was uptight; in fact he was like this all the time except when he was in bed, or with people he wanted to charm. Lagging behind, she stuck her tongue out at him. Nyah, nyah, nyah . . . boring, boring, boring.

Bridget covered her ears and looked down at her dragging feet, while Nicholas strode on alone, pouring sarcasm on ideas increasingly remote from Bridget's tame remarks about smuggling.

Looking up again, Bridget saw a familiar figure. It was Barry leaning against the pillar next to the news-stand. Barry could always sense when he was being looked at and, depending on his mood, attributed this to 'paranoia' or 'ESP'.

'Bridge! Incredible!'

'Barry! All you need is love,' said Bridget, reading out loud the words on Barry's T-shirt and laughing.

'This really is incredible,' said Barry, running his fingers through his long black hair. 'You know I was thinking about you this morning.'

Barry thought about Bridget every morning, but it still struck him as further evidence of mind control that he had not only thought about her today but run into her at the airport as well.

'We're going to Arles for the Progressive Jazz Festival,' said Barry. 'Hey, why don't you come along? It's going to be really fantastic. Bux Millerman is playing.'

'Wow,' breathed Bridget.

'Hey, listen,' said Barry, 'take Etienne's number anyway. That's where I'll be staying and maybe we can like meet up.'

'Yeah,' said Bridget, 'great.'

Barry pulled out a giant Rizla rolling paper and scribbled a number on it. 'Don't smoke it,' he said humorously, 'or we'll never get in touch.'

Bridget gave him the Melrose number because she knew he would not use it, and that this whole meeting-up thing was not going to happen. 'How long have you been here?' she asked.

'Ten days roughly and the only piece of advice I can give you is *don't drink the pink*. That wine is full of chemical shit and the hangover is worse than the comedown off a sulphate binge.'

Nicholas's voice burst in on them. 'What the hell do you think you're doing?' He glared at her. 'You're really pushing your luck, swanning off in the middle of an airport without any warning. I've been dragging round these fucking cases looking for you for the last quarter of an hour.'

'You should get a trolley,' said Barry.

Nicholas stared straight ahead of him as if nobody had spoken. 'Don't ever do this again or I'll snap you like . . . Ah, there's Eleanor!'

'Nicholas, I'm so sorry. We got caught on the Ferris wheel at a funfair and instead of letting us off they sent it round a second time. Can you imagine?'

'So like you, Eleanor, always getting more fun than you bargained for.'

'Well, I'm here now.' Eleanor greeted Nicholas and Bridget with a flat circular wave, like someone polishing a windowpane. 'And this is Anne Moore.'

'Hi,' said Anne.

'How do you do?' said Nicholas, and introduced Bridget.

Eleanor led them towards the car park and Bridget blew a kiss over her shoulder in Barry's direction.

'*Ciao*,' said Barry, jabbing his finger at the confident words on his T-shirt. 'Don't forget.'

'Who was that fascinating-looking man your girlfriend was talking to?' asked Eleanor.

'Oh, just somebody on the plane,' said Nicholas. He was annoyed to find Barry at the airport and for a moment he thought that Bridget might have arranged the meeting. The idea was absurd, but he could not shake it off, and as soon as they were all settled in the car, he hissed at her, 'What were you talking to that chap about?'

'Barry isn't a chap,' said Bridget, 'that's what I like about him, but if you really want to know, he said, "Don't drink the pink, it's full of chemical shit and the hangover is worse than a comedown off a speed binge."'

Nicholas swivelled round and gave her a deadly look.

'He's absolutely right, of course,' said Eleanor. 'Perhaps we should have asked him to dinner.'

7

AFTER HANGING PATRICK FROM his ears and watching him escape from the library, David shrugged, sat down at the piano, and started to improvise a fugue. His rheumatic hands protested at every key he touched. A glass of pastis, like a trapped cloud, stood on top of the piano. His body ached all day long and the pain woke him at night every time he shifted position. Nightmares often woke him as well and made him whimper and scream so loudly that his insomnia overflowed into neighbouring bedrooms. His lungs, also, were shot away and when his asthma flared up he wheezed and rattled, his face swollen by the cortisone he used to appease his constricted chest. Gasping, he would pause at the top of the stairs, unable to speak, his eyes roaming over the ground as if he were searching for the air he desperately needed.

At the age of fifteen his musical talent had attracted the interest of the great piano teacher Shapiro, who took on only one pupil at a time. Unfortunately, within a week, David had contracted rheumatic fever and spent the next six months in bed with hands too stiff and clumsy to practise on the piano. The illness wiped out his chances of becoming a serious pianist and, although pregnant with musical ideas, from then on he claimed to be bored by composition and those 'hordes of little tadpoles' one had to use to record music on paper. Instead, he had hordes of admirers who pleaded with him to play after dinner. They always clamoured for the tune they had heard last time, which he could not remember, until they heard the one he played now, which he soon forgot. His compulsion to amuse others and the arrogance with which he displayed his talent combined to disperse the musical ideas he had once guarded so closely and secretly.

Even while he drank in the flattery he knew that underneath this flamboyant frittering away of his talent he had never overcome his reliance on pastiche, his fear of mediocrity, and the rankling suspicion that the first attack of fever was somehow self-induced. This insight was useless to him; to know the causes of his failure did not diminish the failure, but it did make his self-hatred a little more convoluted and a little more lucid than it would have been in a state of plain ignorance.

As the fugue developed, David attacked its main theme with frustrated repetitions, burying the initial melody under a mud-slide of rumbling bass notes, and spoiling its progress with violent bursts of dissonance. At the piano he could sometimes abandon the ironic tactics which saturated his speech, and visitors whom he had bullied and teased to the point of exasperation found themselves moved by the piercing sadness of the music in the library. On the other hand, he could turn the piano on them like a machine gun and concentrate a hostility into his music that made them long for the more conventional unkindness of his conversation. Even then, his playing would haunt the people who most wanted to resist his influence.

David stopped playing abruptly and closed the lid over the keyboard. He took a gulp of pastis and started to massage his left palm with his right thumb. This massage made the pain a little worse, but gave him the same psychological pleasure as tearing at scabs, probing abscesses and mouth ulcers with his tongue, and fingering bruises.

When a couple of stabs from his thumb had converted the dull ache in his palm into a sharper sensation, he leaned over and picked up a half-smoked Montecristo cigar. One was 'supposed' to remove the paper band from the cigar, and so David left it on. To break even the smallest rules by which others convinced themselves that they were behaving correctly gave him great pleasure. His disdain for vulgarity included the vulgarity of wanting to avoid the appearance of being vulgar. In this more esoteric game, he recognized only a handful of players, Nicholas Pratt and George Watford among them, and he could just as easily despise a man for leaving the band *on* his cigar. He enjoyed watching Victor Eisen, the great thinker, thrashing about in these shallow waters, more firmly hooked each time he tried to cross the line that separated him from the class he yearned to belong to.

David brushed the soft flakes of cigar ash from his blue woollen dressing gown. Every time he smoked he thought of the emphysema that had killed his father, and felt annoyed by the prospect of dying in the same manner.

Under the dressing gown he wore a pair of very faded and much darned pyjamas that had become his on the day his father was buried. The burial had taken place conveniently close to his father's house, in the little churchyard he had spent the last few months of his life staring at through the window of his study. Wearing the oxygen mask which he humorously called his 'gas mask', and unable to negotiate the 'stair drill', he slept in his study, which he renamed the 'departure lounge', on an old Crimean campaign bed left to him by his uncle.

David attended the damp and conventional funeral without enthusiasm; he already knew he had been disinherited. As the coffin was lowered into the ground, he reflected how much of his father's life had been spent in a trench of one sort or another, shooting at birds or men, and how it was really the best place for him.

After the funeral, when the guests had left, David's mother came up to his old bedroom for a moment of private mourning with her son. She said, in her sublime voice, 'I know he would have wanted you to have these,' and placed a pair of carefully folded pyjamas on the bed. When David did not reply, she pressed his hand and closed her faintly blue eyelids for a moment, to show that such things lay too deep for words, but that she knew how much he would prize the little pile of white and yellow flannel from a shop in Bond Street which had gone out of business before the First World War.

It was the same yellow and white flannel that had now grown too hot. David got up from the piano stool and paced about with his dressing gown open, puffing on his cigar. There was no doubt that he was angry with Patrick for running away. It had spoiled his fun. He granted that he had perhaps miscalculated the amount of discomfort he could safely inflict on Patrick.

David's methods of education rested on the claim that childhood was a romantic myth which he was too clear-sighted to encourage. Children were weak and ignorant miniature adults who should be given every incentive to correct their weakness and their ignorance. Like King Chaka, the great Zulu warrior, who made his troops stamp thorn bushes into the ground in order to harden their feet, a training some of them may well have resented at the time, he was determined to harden the calluses of disappointment and develop the skill of detachment in his son. After all, what else did he have to offer him?

For a moment he was winded by a sense of absurdity and impotence; he felt like a farmer watching a flock of crows settle complacently on his favourite scarecrow.

But he pushed on bravely with his original line of thought. No, it was no use expecting gratitude from Patrick, although one day he might realize, like one of Chaka's men running over flinty ground on indifferent feet, how much he owed to his father's uncompromising principles.

When Patrick was born David had been worried that he might become a refuge or an inspiration to Eleanor, and he had jealously set about ensuring that this did not happen. Eleanor eventually resigned herself to a vague and luminous faith in Patrick's 'wisdom', a quality she attributed to him some time before he had learned to control his bowels. She thrust him downstream in this paper boat and collapsed back, exhausted by terror and guilt. Even more important to David than the very natural worry that his wife and his son might grow fond of one another was the intoxicating feeling that he had a blank consciousness to work with, and it gave him great pleasure to knead this yielding clay with his artistic thumbs.

As he walked upstairs to get dressed, even David, who spent most of his day angry or at least irritated, and who made a point of not letting things surprise him, was surprised by the burst of rage that swept over him. What had started as indignation at Patrick's escape turned now into a fury he could no longer control. He strode into his bedroom with his underlip pushed out petulantly and his fists clenched, but he felt at the same time a strong desire to escape his own atmosphere, like a crouching man hurrying to get away from the whirling blades of the helicopter in which he has just landed.

The bedroom he entered had a mock-monastic look, large and white, with bare dark-brown tiles miraculously warm in winter when the underfloor heating was turned on. The only painting on the wall was a picture of Christ wearing the crown of thorns, one of which pierced his pale brow. A trickle of still fresh blood ran down his smooth forehead towards his swimming eyes, which looked up diffidently at this extraordinary headgear as if to ask, 'But is it really *me*?' The painting was a Correggio and

easily the most valuable object in the house, but David had insisted on hanging it in his bedroom, saying sweetly that he would
ask for nothing else.

The brown and gold bedhead, bought by Eleanor's mother,
who was by then the Duchesse de Valençay, from a dealer who
assured her that Napoleon's head had rested against it on at least
one occasion, further compromised the austerity of the room, as
did the dark-green silk Fortuny bedspread, covered in phoenixes
floating up from the fires beneath them. Curtains of the same
fabric hung from a simple wooden pole, at windows which opened
onto a balcony with a wrought-iron balustrade.

David opened these windows impatiently and stepped onto
the balcony. He looked at the tidy rows of vines, the rectangular
fields of lavender, the patches of pinewood, and beyond to the
villages of Bécasse and St-Crau draped over the lower hills. 'Like
a couple of ill-fitting skull-caps,' as he liked to say to Jewish
friends.

He shifted his gaze upward and scanned the long curved
ridge of the mountain which, on a clear day like this, seemed so
close and so wild. Searching for something in the landscape that
would receive his mood and answer it, he could only think again,
as he had so often before, how easy it would be to dominate the
whole valley with a single machine gun riveted to the rail which
he now gripped with both hands.

He was turning back restlessly towards the bedroom when a
movement below the balcony caught the corner of his eye.

Patrick had stayed in his hiding place for as long as he could, but
it was cold in there out of the sun and so he scrambled from under the bush and, with theatrical reluctance, started to walk back
home through the tall dry grass. To sulk alone was difficult. He
felt the need for a wider audience but he wished he didn't. He

dared not punish anyone with his absence, because he was not sure that his absence would be noticed.

He walked along slowly, then curved back to the edge of the wall and stopped to stare at the big mountain on the other side of the valley. The massive formations up on the crest and the smaller ones dotted over its sides yielded shapes and faces as he willed them to appear. An eagle's head. A grotesque nose. A party of dwarfs. A bearded old man. A rocket ship, and countless leprous and obese profiles with cavernous eye sockets formed out of the smoky fluidity his concentration gave to the stone. After a while, he no longer recognized what he was thinking and, just as a shop window sometimes prevents the onlooker from seeing the objects behind the glass and folds him instead in a narcissistic embrace, his mind ignored the flow of impressions from the outside world and locked him into a daydream he could not have subsequently described.

The thought of lunch dragged him back into the present with a strong sense of anxiety. What was the time? Was he too late? Would Yvette still be there to talk to him? Would he have to eat alone with his father? He always recovered from his mental truancy with disappointment. He enjoyed the feeling of blankness, but it frightened him afterwards when he came out of it and could not remember what he had been thinking.

Patrick broke into a run. He was convinced that he had missed lunch. It was always at a quarter to two and normally Yvette would come out and call him, but hiding in the bushes he might not have heard.

When he arrived outside the kitchen, Patrick could see Yvette through the open door, washing lettuce in the sink. He had a stitch in his side from running, and now that he could tell that lunch was some way off he felt embarrassed by his desperate haste. Yvette waved to him from the sink, but he did not want to look hurried, so he just waved back and strolled past the door, as if he had business of his own to attend to. He decided to check once more whether he could find the lucky tree frog before doubling back to the kitchen to sit with Yvette.

Around the corner of the house, Patrick climbed up onto the low wall at the outer edge of the terrace and, a fifteen-foot drop to his left, he balanced his way along with arms spread out. He walked the whole length of the wall and then jumped down again. He was at the top of the garden steps with the fig tree in sight, when he heard his father's voice shouting, *'Don't let me ever see you do that again!'*

Patrick was startled. Where was the voice coming from? Was it shouting at him? He spun around and looked behind him. His heart was beating hard. He often overheard his father shouting at other people, especially his mother, and it terrified him and made him want to run away. But this time he had to stand still and listen because he wanted to understand what was wrong and whether he was to blame.

'Come up here immediately!'

Now Patrick knew where the voice was coming from. He looked up and saw his father leaning over the balcony.

'What have I done wrong?' he asked, but too quietly to be heard. His father looked so furious that Patrick lost all conviction of his own innocence. With growing alarm he tried to work backward from his father's rage to what his own crime might be.

By the time he had climbed the steep stairs to his father's bedroom, Patrick was ready to apologize for anything, but still felt a lingering desire to know what he was apologizing for. In the doorway he stopped and asked again, audibly this time, 'What have I done wrong?'

'Close the door behind you,' said his father. 'And come over here.' He sounded disgusted by the obligation the child had thrust upon him.

As Patrick slowly crossed the floor he tried to think of some way to placate his father. Maybe if he said something clever he'd be forgiven, but he felt extraordinarily stupid and could only think over and over: two times two equals four, two times two equals four. He tried to remember something he had noticed that morning, or anything, anything at all that might persuade his father that he had been 'observing everything'. But his mind was eclipsed by the shadow of his father's presence.

He stood by the bed and stared down at the green bedspread with the bonfire birds on it. His father sounded rather weary when he spoke.

'I'm going to have to beat you.'

'But what have I done wrong?'

'You know perfectly well what you have done,' his father said in a cold, annihilating voice that Patrick found overwhelmingly persuasive. He was suddenly ashamed of all the things he had done wrong. His whole existence seemed to be contaminated by failure.

Moving quickly, his father grabbed Patrick's shirt collar. He sat down on the bed, hoisted Patrick over his right thigh, and removed the yellow slipper from his left foot. Such rapid manoeuvres would normally have made David wince with pain, but he was able to regain his youthful agility in the service of such a good cause. He pulled down Patrick's trousers and underpants and raised the slipper surprisingly high for a man who had trouble with his right shoulder.

The first blow was astonishingly painful. Patrick tried to take the attitude of stoic misery admired by dentists. He tried to be brave but, during the beating, although he at last realized that his father wanted to hurt him as much as possible, he refused to believe it.

The harder he struggled, the harder he was hit. Longing to move but afraid to move, he was split in half by this incomprehensible violence. Horror closed in on him and crushed his body like the jaws of a dog. After the beating, his father dropped him like a dead thing onto the bed.

And he still could not get away. Pushing his palm against Patrick's right shoulder blade, his father was holding him down. Patrick twisted his head around anxiously, but could only see the blue of his father's dressing gown.

'What are you doing?' he asked, but his father did not answer and Patrick was too scared to repeat the question. His father's hand was pushing down on him and, his face squashed into the folds of the bedspread, he could hardly breathe. He stared fixedly up at the curtain pole and the top of the open windows. He could not understand what form the punishment was now taking, but he knew that his father must be very angry with him to be hurting him so much. He could not stand the helplessness that washed over him. He could not stand the unfairness. He did not know who this man was, it could not be his father who was crushing him like this.

From the curtain pole, if he could get up on the curtain pole, he could have sat looking down on the whole scene, just as his father was looking down on him. For a moment, Patrick felt he was up there watching with detachment the punishment inflicted by a strange man on a small boy. As hard as he could Patrick concentrated on the curtain pole and this time it lasted longer, he was sitting up there, his arms folded, leaning back against the wall.

Then he was back down on the bed again feeling a kind of blankness and bearing the weight of not knowing what was happening. He could hear his father wheezing, and the bedhead bumping against the wall. From behind the curtains with the green birds, he saw a gecko emerge and cling motionlessly to the corner of the wall beside the open window. Patrick lanced himself towards it. Tightening his fists and concentrating until his concentration was like a telephone wire stretched between them, Patrick disappeared into the lizard's body.

The gecko understood, because at that very instant it dashed round the corner of the window and out onto the wall. Below he could see the drop to the terrace and the leaves of the Virginia creeper, red and green and yellow, and from up there, close against the wall, he could hold on with suckered feet and hang upside down safely from the eaves of the roof. He scurried onto the old roof tiles which were covered in grey and orange lichen, and then into the trough between the tiles, all the way up to the ridge of the roof. He moved fast down the other slope, and was far away, and nobody would ever find him again, because they wouldn't know where to look, and couldn't know that he was coiled up in the body of a gecko.

'Stay here,' said David, standing up and adjusting his yellow and white pyjamas.

Patrick could not have done anything else. He recognized, dully at first and then more vividly, the humiliation of his position. Face down on the bed, with his trousers bunched around his knees and a strange, worrying wetness at the base of his spine. It made him think he was bleeding. That, somehow, his father had stabbed him in the back.

His father went to the bathroom and came back. With a handful of lavatory paper he wiped away the increasingly cold pool of slime that had started to trickle between Patrick's buttocks.

'You can get up now,' he said.

Patrick could not in fact get up. The memory of voluntary action was too remote and complicated. Impatiently, his father pulled up Patrick's trousers and lifted him off the bed. Patrick stood beside the bed while his father clasped his shoulders, ostensibly to straighten his stance, but it made Patrick think that his father was going to pin his shoulders back and force them together until he was turned inside out and his lungs and heart burst out of his chest.

Instead, David leaned over and said, 'Don't ever tell your mother or anyone else what happened today, or you'll be *very* severely punished. Do you understand?'

Patrick nodded.

'Are you hungry?'

Patrick shook his head.

'Well, I'm starving,' said David chattily. 'You really should eat more, you know. Build up your strength.'

'Can I go now?'

'All right, if you don't want any lunch, you can go.' David was irritated again.

Patrick walked down the drive and as he stared at the toes of his scuffed sandals he saw, instead, the top of his head as if from ten or twelve feet in the air, and he felt an uncomfortable curiosity about the boy he was watching. It was not quite personal, like the accident they saw on the road last year and his mother said not to look.

Back down again, Patrick felt utter defeat. There was no flash of purple cloaks. No special soldiers. No gecko. Nothing. He tried to take to the air again, the way seabirds do when a wave breaks over the rock where they were standing. But he had lost the power to move and stayed behind, drowning.

8

DURING LUNCH DAVID FELT that he had perhaps pushed his disdain for middle-class prudery a little too far. Even at the bar of the Cavalry and Guards Club one couldn't boast about homosexual, paedophiliac incest with any confidence of a favourable reception. Who could he tell that he had raped his five-year-old son? He could not think of a single person who would not prefer to change the subject − and some would behave far worse than that. The experience itself had been short and brutish, but not altogether nasty. He smiled at Yvette, said how ravenous he was, and helped himself to the brochette of lamb and flageolets.

'Monsieur has been playing the piano all morning.'

'And playing with Patrick,' David added piously.

Yvette said they were so exhausting at that age.

'Exhausting!' David agreed.

Yvette left the room and David poured another glass of the Romanée-Conti that he had taken from the cellar for dinner, but had decided to drink on his own. There were always more bottles and it went so well with lamb. 'Nothing but the best, or go without': that was the code he lived by, as long as the 'go without' didn't actually happen. There was no doubt about it, he was a sensualist, and as to this latest episode, he hadn't done anything medically dangerous, just a little rubbing between the buttocks, nothing that would not happen to the boy at school in due course. If he had committed any crime, it was to set about his son's education too assiduously. He was conscious of already being sixty, there was so much to teach him and so little time.

He rang the little bell beside his plate and Yvette came back into the dining room.

'Excellent lamb,' said David.

'Would Monsieur like the tarte Tatin?'

He had no room left, alas, for tarte Tatin. Perhaps she could tempt Patrick to have some for tea. He just wanted coffee. Could she bring it to the drawing room? Of course she could.

David's legs had stiffened and when he rose from his chair he staggered for a couple of steps, drawing in his breath sharply through his teeth. 'God damn,' he said out loud. He had suddenly lost all tolerance for his rheumatic pains and decided to go upstairs to Eleanor's bathroom, a pharmaceutical paradise. He very seldom used painkillers, preferring a steady flow of alcohol and the consciousness of his own heroism.

Opening the cupboard under Eleanor's basin he was struck by the splendour and variety of the tubes and bottles: clear ones and yellow ones and dark ones, orange ones with green caps, in plastic and glass, from half a dozen countries, all urging the consumer not to exceed the stated dose. There were even envelopes marked Seconal and Mandrax, stolen, he imagined, from other people's bathroom cabinets. Rummaging about among the barbiturates and stimulants and anti-depressants and hypnotics, he found surprisingly few painkillers. He had turned up only a bottle of codeine, a few diconol and some distalgesics, when he discovered, at the back of the cupboard, a bottle of sugar-coated opium pellets he had prescribed just two years before, for his mother-in-law, to ease the uncontrollable diarrhoea which accompanied her intestinal cancer. This last act of Hippocratic mercy, long after the end of his brief medical practice, filled him with nostalgia for the healer's art.

On a charmingly quaint label from Harris's in St James's Street, was written: 'The Opium (B.P. 0.6 grains)' and under that, 'Duchesse de Valençay' and finally, 'To be taken as required'. Since there were several dozen pellets left, his mother-in-law must have died before developing an opium habit. A merciful release, he reflected, popping the bottle into the pocket of his houndstooth jacket. It would have been too tiresome if she had been an opium addict on top of everything else.

David poured his coffee into a thin round eighteenth-century china cup, decorated with gold and orange cockerels fighting one another under a gold and orange tree. He took the bottle from his pocket, shook three white pellets into his hand and swallowed them with a gulp of coffee. Excited by the idea of resting comfortably under the influence of opium, he celebrated with some brandy made in the year of his birth, a present to himself which, as he told Eleanor when she paid for a case of it, reconciled him to growing old. To complete the portrait of his contentment he lit a cigar and sat in a deep chair beside the window with a battered copy of Surtees's *Jorrocks' Jaunts and Jollities*. He read the first sentence with familiar pleasure, 'What truebred city sportsman has not in his day put off the most urgent business – perhaps his marriage, or even the interment of his rib – that he might "Brave the morn" with that renowned pack, the Surrey Subscription Fox Hounds?'

When David woke up a couple of hours later, he felt tied down to a turbulent sleep by thousands of small elastic strings. He looked up slowly from the ridges and the valleys of his trousers and focused on his coffee cup. It seemed to have a thin luminous band around its edges and to be slightly raised above the surface of the small round table it lay on. He was disturbed but fascinated when he noticed that one of the gold and orange cockerels was very slowly pecking out the eye of the other. He had not expected to hallucinate. Although extraordinarily free from pain, he was worried by the loss of control that hallucination entailed.

The armchair felt like a cheese fondue as he dragged himself out of it, and walking across the floor reminded him of climbing a sand dune. He poured two glasses of cold coffee and drank them straight down, hoping they would sober him up before Eleanor returned with Nicholas and that girl of his.

He wanted to go for a brisk walk, but could not help stopping to admire the luxurious glow of his surroundings. He became particularly engrossed in the black Chinese cabinet and the colourful figures embossed on its lacquered surface. The palanquin in which an important mandarin lounged shifted forward, and the parasol held above his head by servants in shallow straw hats started to revolve hesitatingly.

David tore himself away from this animated scene and went outside. Before he could find out whether fresh air would dispel his nausea and give him back the control he wanted, he heard the sound of Eleanor's car coming down the drive. He doubled back, grabbed his copy of Surtees, and retreated into the library.

After Anne had been dropped off at Victor's, Nicholas took her place in the front passenger seat. Bridget sprawled in the back sleepily. Eleanor and Nicholas had been talking about people she didn't know.

'I'd almost forgotten how wonderful it is here,' said Nicholas, as they approached the house.

'I've completely forgotten,' said Eleanor, 'and I live here.'

'Oh, Eleanor, what a sad thing to say,' said Nicholas. 'Tell me it isn't true quickly, or I won't enjoy my tea.'

'OK,' said Eleanor, lowering the electric window to flick a cigarette out, 'it isn't true.'

'Good girl,' said Nicholas.

Bridget couldn't think of anything to say about her new surroundings. Through the car window she could see wide steps sweeping down beside a large house with pale blue shutters. Wisteria and honeysuckle climbed and tumbled at various points along the side of the house to break the monotony of the stone. She felt she had seen it all before, and for her it had only the slim reality of a photograph in the flicked pages of a magazine. The dope had made her feel sexy. She was longing to masturbate and felt remote from the chatter going on around her.

'François should come to fetch your bags,' said Eleanor. 'Leave them in the car and he'll bring them later.'

'Oh, it's all right, I can manage the bags,' said Nicholas. He wanted to get Bridget alone in their room for a moment and tell her to 'buck up'.

'No, really, let François do it, he's had nothing to do all day,' said Eleanor, who didn't want to be left alone with David.

Nicholas had to content himself with beaming his unspoken disapproval towards Bridget, who wandered down the steps trying to avoid the cracks between the paving stones, and did not even glance in his direction.

When they arrived in the hall, Eleanor was delighted by David's absence. Perhaps he had drowned in the bath. It was too much to hope. She sent Nicholas and Bridget out onto the terrace and went to the kitchen to ask Yvette for some tea. On the way she drank a glass of brandy.

'Could you bear to make a little light conversation now and again?' said Nicholas as soon as he was alone with Bridget. 'You haven't yet addressed a word to Eleanor.'

'OK, darling,' said Bridget, still trying not to walk on the cracks. She turned towards Nicholas and said in a loud whisper, 'Is this the one?'

'What?'

'The fig tree where he made her eat on all fours.'

Nicholas looked up at the windows above him, remembering the conversations he had overheard from his bedroom the last time he was staying. He nodded, putting his fingers to his lips.

Figs littered the ground underneath the tree. Some were reduced to a black stain and a few pips, but a number had not yet decayed and their purple skins, covered in a dusty white film, were still unbroken. Bridget knelt down like a dog on the ground.

'For God's sake,' snarled Nicholas, leaping over to her side. At that moment the drawing room door opened and Yvette came out, carrying a tray of cakes and cups. She only glimpsed what was going on, but it confirmed her suspicion that rich English people had a strange relationship with the animal kingdom. Bridget rose, smirking.

'*Ah, fantastique de vous revoir, Yvette,*' said Nicholas.

'*Bonjour, Monsieur.*'

'*Bonjour,*' said Bridget prettily.

'*Bonjour, Madame,*' said Yvette stoutly, though she knew that Bridget was not married.

'David!' roared Nicholas over Yvette's head. 'Where have you been hiding?'

David waved his cigar at Nicholas. 'Got lost in Surtees,' he said, stepping through the doorway. He wore his dark glasses to protect him from surprises. 'Hello, my dear,' he said to Bridget, whose name he had forgotten. 'Have either of you seen Eleanor? I caught a glimpse of some pink trousers rounding a corner, but they didn't answer to her name.'

'That's certainly what she was last seen wearing,' said Nicholas.

'Pink suits her so well, don't you think?' said David to Bridget. 'It matches the colour of her eyes.'

'Wouldn't some tea be delicious?' said Nicholas quickly.

Bridget poured the tea, while David went to sit on a low wall, a few feet away from Nicholas. As he tapped his cigar gently and let the ash fall at his feet, he noticed a trail of ants working their way along the side of the wall and into their nest in the corner.

Bridget carried cups of tea over to the two men, and as she turned to fetch her own cup, David held the burning tip of his cigar close to the ants and ran it along in both directions as far as he could conveniently reach. The ants twisted, excruciated by the heat, and dropped down onto the terrace. Some, before they fell, reared up, their stitching legs trying helplessly to repair their ruined bodies.

'What a civilized life you have here,' Bridget sang out as she sank back into a dark-blue deckchair. Nicholas rolled his eyeballs and wondered why the hell he had told her to make light conversation. To cover the silence he remarked to David that he had been to Jonathan Croyden's memorial service the day before.

'Do you find that you go to more memorial services, or more weddings these days?' David asked.

'I still get more wedding invitations, but I find I enjoy the memorials more.'

'Because you don't have to bring a present?'

'Well, that helps a great deal, but mainly because one gets a better crowd when someone really distinguished dies.'

'Unless all his friends have died before him.'

'That, of course, is intolerable,' said Nicholas categorically.

'Ruins the party.'

'Absolutely.'

'I'm afraid I don't approve of memorial services,' said David, taking another puff on his cigar. 'Not merely because I cannot imagine anything in most men's lives that deserves to be celebrated, but also because the delay between the funeral and the memorial service is usually so long that, far from rekindling the spirit of a lost friend, it only shows how easily one can live without him.' David blew on the tip of his cigar and it glowed brightly.

The opium made him feel that he was listening to another man speak.

'The dead are dead,' he went on, 'and the truth is that one forgets about people when they stop coming to dinner. There are exceptions, of course – namely, the people one forgets *during* dinner.'

With his cigar he caught a stray ant which was escaping with singed antennae from his last incendiary raid. 'If you really miss someone, you are better off doing something you both enjoyed doing together, which is unlikely to mean, except in the most bizarre cases, standing around in a draughty church, wearing a black overcoat and singing hymns.'

The ant ran away with astonishing speed and was about to reach the far side of the wall when David, stretching a little, touched it lightly with a surgeon's precision. Its skin blistered and it squirmed violently as it died.

'One should only go to an enemy's memorial service. Quite apart from the pleasure of outlasting him, it is an opportunity for a truce. Forgiveness is so important, don't you think?'

'Gosh, yes,' said Bridget, 'especially getting other people to forgive you.'

David smiled at her encouragingly, until he saw Eleanor step through the doorway.

'Ah, Eleanor,' grinned Nicholas with exaggerated pleasure, 'we were just talking about Jonathan Croyden's memorial.'

'I guess it's the end of an era,' said Eleanor.

'He *was* the last man alive to have gone to one of Evelyn Waugh's parties in drag,' said Nicholas. 'He was said to dress much better as a woman than as a man. He was an inspiration to a whole generation of Englishmen. Which reminds me, after the memorial I met a very tiresome, smarmy Indian who claimed to have visited you just before staying with Jonathan at Cap Ferrat.'

'It must have been Vijay,' said Eleanor. 'Victor brought him over.'

'That's the one,' Nicholas nodded. 'He seemed to know that I was coming here. Perfectly extraordinary as I'd never set eyes on him before.'

'He's desperately fashionable,' explained David, 'and consequently knows more about people he has never met than he does about anything else.'

Eleanor perched on a frail white chair with a faded blue cushion on its circular seat. She rose again immediately and dragged the chair further towards the shade of the fig tree.

'Watch out,' said Bridget, 'you might squash some of the figs.'

Eleanor made no reply.

'It seems a pity to waste them,' said Bridget innocently, leaning over to pick a fig off the ground. 'This one is perfect.' She brought it close to her mouth. 'Isn't it weird the way their skin is purple and white at the same time.'

'Like a drunk with emphysema,' said David, smiling at Eleanor.

Bridget opened her mouth, rounded her lips and pushed the fig inside. She suddenly felt what she later described to Barry as a 'very heavy vibe' from David, 'as if he was pushing his fist into my womb'. Bridget swallowed the fig, but she felt a physical need to get out of the deckchair and move further away from David.

She walked beside the edge of the wall above the garden terrace and, wanting to explain her sudden action, she stretched out her arms, embraced the view, and said, 'What a perfect day.' Nobody replied. Scanning the landscape for something else to say, she glimpsed a slight movement at the far end of the garden. At first she thought it was an animal crouched under the pear tree, but when it got up she saw that it was a child. 'Is that your son?' she asked. 'In the red trousers.'

Eleanor walked over to her side. 'Yes, it's Patrick. Patrick!' she shouted. 'Do you want some tea, darling?'

There was no answer. 'Maybe he can't hear you,' said Bridget.

'Of course he can,' said David. 'He's just being tiresome.'

'Maybe we can't hear him,' said Eleanor. 'Patrick!' she shouted again. 'Why don't you come and have some tea with us?'

'He's shaking his head,' said Bridget.

'He's probably had tea two or three times already,' said Nicholas; 'you know what they're like at that age.'

'God, children are so *sweet*,' said Bridget, smiling at Eleanor. 'Eleanor,' she said in the same tone, as if her request should be granted as a reward for finding children sweet, 'could you tell me which room I'm in because I'd quite like to go up and have a bath and unpack.'

'Of course. Let me show you,' said Eleanor.

Eleanor led Bridget into the house.

'Your girlfriend is very, I believe the word is "vivacious",' said David.

'Oh, she'll do for now,' said Nicholas.

'No need to apologize, she's absolutely charming. Shall we have a real drink?'

'Good idea.'

'Champagne?'

'Perfect.'

David fetched the champagne and reappeared tearing the golden lead from the neck of a clear bottle.

'Cristal,' said Nicholas dutifully.

'Nothing but the best, or go without,' said David.

'It reminds me of Charles Pewsey,' said Nicholas. 'We were drinking a bottle of that stuff at Wilton's last week and I asked him if he remembered Gunter, Jonathan Croyden's unspeakable amanuensis. And Charles roared – you know how deaf he is – "Amanuensis? Bumboy, you mean: *unspeakable bumboy*." Everyone turned round and stared at us.'

'They always do when one's with Charles.' David grinned. It was so typical of Charles, one had to know Charles to appreciate how funny it was.

The bedroom Bridget had been put in was all flowery chintz, with engravings of Roman ruins on every wall. Beside the bed was a copy of Lady Mosley's *A Life of Contrasts*, on top of which Bridget had thrown *Valley of the Dolls*, her current reading. She sat by the window smoking a joint, and watched the smoke drift through the tiny holes in the mosquito net. From below, she could hear Nicholas shout *'unspeakable bumboy'*. They must be reminiscing about their school days. Boys will be boys.

Bridget lifted one foot onto the windowsill. She still held the joint in her left hand, although it would burn her fingers with the next toke. She slipped her right hand between her legs and started to masturbate.

'It just goes to show that being an amanuensis doesn't matter as long as you have the butler on your side,' said Nicholas.

David picked up his cue. 'It's always the same thing in life,' he chanted. 'It's not what you do, it's who you know.'

To find such a ludicrous example of this important maxim made the two men laugh.

Bridget moved over to the bed and spread herself out face down on the yellow bedcover. As she closed her eyes and resumed masturbating, the thought of David flashed over her like a static shock, but she forced herself to focus loyally on the memory of Barry's stirring presence.

9

WHEN VICTOR WAS IN trouble with his writing he had a nervous habit of flicking open his pocket watch and clicking it closed again. Distracted by the noise of other human activities he found it helpful to make a noise of his own. During the contemplative passages of his daydreams he flicked and clicked more slowly, but as he pressed up against his sense of frustration the pace increased.

Dressed this morning in the flecked and bulky sweater he had hunted down ruthlessly for an occasion on which clothes simply didn't matter, he fully intended to begin his essay on the necessary and sufficient conditions of personal identity. He sat at a slightly wobbly wooden table under a yellowing plane tree in front of the house, and as the temperature rose he stripped down to his shirtsleeves. By lunchtime he had recorded only one thought, 'I have written books which I have had to write, but I have not yet written a book which others have to read.' He punished himself by improvising a sandwich for lunch, instead of walking down to La Coquière and eating three courses in the garden, under the blue and red and yellow parasol of the Ricard Pastis company.

Despite himself he kept thinking of Eleanor's puzzled little contribution that morning, 'Gosh, I mean, if anything is in the mind, it's who you are.' If anything is in the mind it's who you are: it was silly, it was unhelpful, but it whined about him like a mosquito in the dark.

Just as a novelist may sometimes wonder why he invents characters who do not exist and makes them do things which do not matter, so a philosopher may wonder why he invents cases that cannot occur in order to determine what must be the case. After a long neglect of his subject, Victor was not as thoroughly convinced that impossibility was the best route to necessity as he might have been had he recently reconsidered Stolkin's extreme case in which 'scientists destroy my brain and body, and then make out of new matter, a replica of Greta Garbo'. How could one help agreeing with Stolkin that 'there would be no connection between me and the resulting person'?

Nevertheless, to think one knew what would happen to a person's sense of identity if his brain was cut in half and distributed between identical twins seemed, just for now, before he had thrown himself back into the torrent of philosophical debate, a poor substitute for an intelligent description of what it is to know who you are.

Victor went indoors to fetch the familiar tube of Bisodol indigestion tablets. As usual he had eaten his sandwich too fast, pushing it down his throat like a sword-swallower. He thought with renewed appreciation of William James's remark that the self consists mainly of 'peculiar motions in the head and between the head and throat', although the peculiar motions somewhat lower down in his stomach and bowels felt at least as personal.

When Victor sat down again he pictured himself thinking, and tried to superimpose this picture on his inner vacancy. If he was essentially a thinking machine, then he needed to be serviced. It was not the problems of philosophy but the problem *with* philosophy that preoccupied him that afternoon. And yet how often the two became indistinguishable. Wittgenstein had said that the philosopher's treatment of a question was like the treatment of a disease. But which treatment? Purging? Leeches? Antibiotics against the infections of language? Indigestion tablets, thought Victor, belching softly, to help break down the doughy bulk of sensation?

We ascribe thoughts to thinkers because this is the way we speak, but persons need not be claimed to be the thinkers of these thoughts. Still, thought Victor lazily, why not bow down to popular demand on this occasion? As to brains and minds, was there really any problem about two categorically different phenomena, brain process and consciousness, occurring simultaneously? Or was the problem with the categories?

From down the hill Victor heard a car door slam. It must be Eleanor dropping Anne at the bottom of the drive. Victor flicked open his watch, checked the time, and snapped it closed again. What had he achieved? Almost nothing. It was not one of those unproductive days when he was confused by abundance and starved, like Buridan's ass, between two equally nourishing bales of hay. His lack of progress today was more profound.

He watched Anne rounding the last corner of the drive, painfully bright in her white dress.

'Hi,' she said.

'Hello,' said Victor with boyish gloom.

'How's it going?'

'Oh, it's been fairly futile exercise, but I suppose it's good to get any exercise at all.'

'Don't knock that futile exercise,' said Anne, 'it's big business. Bicycles that don't go anyplace, a long walk to nowhere on a rubber treadmill, heavy things you don't even *need* to pick up.'

Victor remained silent, staring down at his one sentence. Anne rested her hands on his shoulders. 'So there's no major news on who we are?'

'Afraid not. Personal identity, of course, is a fiction, a pure fiction. But I've reached this conclusion by the wrong method.'

'What was that?'

'Not thinking about it.'

'But that's what the English mean, isn't it, when they say, "He was very philosophical about it"? They mean that someone stopped thinking about something.' Anne lit a cigarette.

'Still,' said Victor in a quiet voice, 'my thinking today reminds me of a belligerent undergraduate I once taught, who said that our tutorials had "failed to pass the So What Test".'

Anne sat down on the edge of Victor's table and eased off one of her canvas shoes with the toe of the other. She liked to see Victor working again, however unsuccessfully. Placing her bare foot on his knee, she said, 'Tell me, Professor, is this *my* foot?'

'Well, some philosophers would say that under certain cir-cumstances,' said Victor, lifting her foot in his cupped hands, 'this would be determined by whether the foot is in pain.'

'What's wrong with the foot being in pleasure?'

'Well,' said Victor, solemnly considering this absurd question, 'in philosophy as in life, pleasure is more likely to be an hallucina-tion. Pain is the key to possession.' He opened his mouth wide, like a hungry man approaching a hamburger, but closed it again, and gently kissed each toe.

Victor released her foot and Anne kicked off the other shoe. 'I'll be back in a moment,' she said, walking out carefully over the warm sharp gravel to the kitchen door.

Victor reflected with satisfaction that in ancient Chinese so-ciety the little game he had played with Anne's foot would have been considered almost intolerably familiar. An unbound foot represented for the Chinese a degree of abandon which genitals could never achieve. He was stimulated by the thought of how intense his desire would have been at another time, in another place. He thought of the lines from *The Jew of Malta*, 'Thou hast committed Fornication: but that was in another country, and besides the wench is dead.' In the past he had been a Utilitarian seducer, aiming to increase the sum of *general* pleasure, but since starting his affair with Anne he had been unprecedentedly faithful. Never physically alluring, he had always relied on his cleverness to seduce women. As he grew uglier and more famous, so the instrument of seduction, his speech, and the instrument of gratification, his body, grew into an increasingly inglorious contrast. The routine of fresh seductions highlighted this aspect of the mind–body problem more harshly than intimacy, and he had decided that perhaps it was time to be in the same country with a living wench. The challenge was not to substitute a mental absence for a physical one.

Anne came out of the house carrying two glasses of orange juice. She gave one to Victor.

'What were you thinking?' she asked.

'Whether you would be the same person in another body,' lied Victor.

'Well, ask yourself, would you be nibbling my toes if I looked like a Canadian lumberjack?'

'If I knew it was *you* inside,' said Victor loyally.

'Inside the steel-capped boots?'

'Exactly.'

They smiled at each other. Victor took a gulp of orange juice. 'But tell me,' he said, 'how was your expedition with Eleanor?'

'On the way back I found myself thinking that everybody who is meeting for dinner tonight will probably have said something unkind about everybody else. I know you'll think it's very primitive and American of me, but why do people spend the evening with people they've spent the day insulting?'

'So as to have something insulting to say about them tomorrow.'

'Why, of course,' gasped Anne. '*Tomorrow is another day.* So different and yet so similar,' she added.

Victor looked uneasy. 'Were you insulting each other in the car, or just attacking David and me?'

'Neither, but the way that everyone else was insulted I knew that we would break off into smaller and smaller combinations, until everyone had been dealt with by everyone else.'

'But that's what charm is: being malicious about everybody except the person you are with, who then glows with the privilege of exemption.'

'If that's what charm is,' said Anne, 'it broke down on this occasion, because I felt that none of us was exempt.'

'Do you wish to confirm your own theory by saying something nasty about one of your fellow dinner guests?'

'Well, now that you mention it,' said Anne, laughing, 'I thought that Nicholas Pratt was a total creep.'

'I know what you mean. His problem is that he wanted to go into politics,' Victor explained, 'but was destroyed by what passed for a sex scandal some years ago and would probably now be called an "open marriage". Most people wait until they've become ministers to ruin their political careers with a sex scandal, but Nicholas managed to do it when he was still trying to impress Central Office by contesting a by-election in a safe Labour seat.'

'Precocious, huh,' said Anne. 'What exactly did he do to deserve his exile from paradise?'

'He was found in bed with two women he was not married to by the woman he was married to, and she decided not to "stand by his side".'

'Sounds like there wasn't any room,' said Anne, 'but like you say, it was bad timing. Back in those days you couldn't go on television and say how it was a "really liberating experience".'

'There may still be,' said Victor with mock astonishment, joining the tips of his fingers pedagogically, to form an arc with his hands, 'certain rural backwaters of Tory England where, even today, group sex is not practised by *all* the matrons on the Selection Committee.'

Anne sat down on Victor's knee. 'Victor, do two people make a group?'

'Only part of a group, I'm afraid.'

'You mean,' said Anne with horror, 'we've been having part-of-a-group sex?' She got up again, ruffling Victor's hair. 'That's awful.'

'I think,' Victor continued calmly, 'that when his political ambitions were ruined so early, Nicholas became rather indifferent to a career and fell back on his large inheritance.'

'He still doesn't make it on to my casualty list,' said Anne. 'Being found in bed with two girls isn't the shower room in Auschwitz.'

'You have high standards.'

'I do and I don't. No pain is too small if it hurts, but any pain is too small if it's cherished,' Anne said. 'Anyhow, he isn't suffering that badly, he's got a stoned schoolgirl with him. She was being moody in the back of the car. Two like her isn't enough, he'll have to graduate to triplets.'

'What's she called?'

'Bridget something. One of those not very convincing English names like Hop-Scotch.'

Anne moved on quickly, she was determined not to let Victor get lost in ruminations about where Bridget might 'fit in'. 'The oddest thing about the day was our visit to Le Wild Ouest.'

'Why on earth did you go there?'

'As far as I could make out we were there because Patrick wants to go, but Eleanor gets priority.'

'You don't think she might have just been checking whether it was an amusing place to take her son?'

'In the Dodge City of arrested development, you gotta be quick on the draw,' said Anne, whipping out an imaginary gun.

'You seem to have entered into the spirit of the place,' said Victor drily.

'If she wanted to take her son there,' Anne resumed, 'he could have come with us. And if she wanted to find out whether it was an "amusing place", Patrick could have told her.'

Victor did not want to argue with Anne. She often had strong opinions about human situations which did not really matter to him, unless they illustrated a principle or yielded an anecdote, and he preferred to concede this stony ground to her, with whatever show of leniency his mood required. 'There isn't anyone at dinner tonight left for us to disparage,' he said, 'except David, and we know what you think of him.'

'That reminds me, I must read at least a chapter of *The Twelve Caesars* so I can give it back to him this evening.'

'Read the chapters on Nero and Caligula,' Victor suggested, 'I'm sure they're David's favourites. One illustrates what happens when you combine a mediocre artistic talent with absolute power. The other shows how nearly inevitable it is for those who have been terrified to become terrifying, once they have the opportunity.'

'But isn't that the key to a great education? You spend your adolescence being promoted from terrified to terrifier, without any women around to distract you.'

Victor decided to ignore this latest demonstration of Anne's rather tiresome attitude towards English public schools. 'The interesting thing about Caligula,' he went on patiently, 'is that he intended to be a model emperor, and for the first few months of his reign he was praised for his magnanimity. But the compulsion to repeat what one has experienced is like gravity, and it takes special equipment to break away from it.'

Anne was amused to hear Victor make such an overtly psychological generalization. Perhaps if people had been dead long enough they came alive for him.

'Nero I dislike for having driven Seneca to suicide,' Victor droned on. 'Although I'm well aware of the hostility that can arise between a pupil and his tutor, it is just as well to keep it within limits,' he chuckled.

'Didn't Nero commit suicide himself, or was that just in *Nero, the Movie?*'

'When it came to suicide he showed less enthusiasm than he had done for driving other people to it. He sat around for a long time wondering which part of his "pustular and malodorous" body to puncture, wailing, "Dead and so great an artist!"'

'You sound like you were there.'

'You know how it is with the books one reads in one's youth.'

'Yeah, that's kinda how I feel about *Francis the Talking Mule,*' said Anne.

She got up from the creaking wicker chair. 'I guess I'd better catch up on "one's youth" before dinner.' She moved over to Victor's side. 'Write me one sentence before we have to go,' she said gently. 'You can do that, can't you?'

Victor enjoyed being coaxed. He looked up at her like an obedient child. 'I'll try,' he said modestly.

Anne walked through the gloom of the kitchen and climbed the twisting stairs. She felt a cool pleasure at being alone for the first time since the early morning and wanted to have a bath straight away. Victor liked to wallow in the tub, controlling the taps with his big toe, and she knew how irrationally disappointed he became if the steaming water ran out during this important ceremony. Besides, if she bathed now she could lie on her bed and read for a couple of hours before going out to dinner.

On top of the books by her bed was *Goodbye to Berlin* and Anne thought how much more fun it would be to reread that rather than dip into the grisly Caesars. From the thought of pre-war Berlin her mind jumped back to the remark she had made about the shower room in Auschwitz. Was she, she wondered, giving in to that English need to be facetious? She felt tainted and exhausted by a summer of burning up her moral resources for the sake of small conversational effects. She felt she had been subtly perverted by slick and lazy English manners, the craving for the prophylactic of irony, the terrible fear of being 'a bore', and the boredom of the ways they relentlessly and narrowly evaded this fate.

Above all it was Victor's ambivalence towards these values that was wearing her down. She could no longer tell whether he was working as a double agent, a serious writer pretending to the Folks on the Hill – of which the Melroses were only rather a tarnished example – that he was a devoted admirer of the effortless nullity of their lives. Or perhaps he was a triple agent, pretending to her that he had not accepted the bribe of being admitted to the periphery of their world.

Defiantly, Anne picked up *Goodbye to Berlin* and headed towards the bathroom.

The sun disappeared early behind the roof of the tall, narrow house. At his table under the plane tree Victor put his sweater back on. He felt safe in the bulk of his sweater with the distant sound of Anne running her bath. He wrote a sentence in his spidery hand, and then another.

IO

IF DAVID HAD AWARDED himself the most important painting in the house, at least Eleanor had secured the largest bedroom. At the far end of the corridor, its curtains were closed all day to protect a host of frail Italian drawings from the draining power of the sun.

Patrick hesitated in the doorway of his mother's bedroom, waiting to be noticed. The dimness of the room made it seem even larger, especially when a breeze stirred the curtains and an unsteady light spread shadows over the stretching walls. Eleanor sat at her desk with her back to Patrick, writing a cheque to the Save the Children Fund, her favourite charity. She did not hear her son come into the room until he stood beside her chair.

'Hello, darling,' she said, with a desperate affection that sounded like a long-distance telephone call. 'What did you do today?'

'Nothing,' said Patrick, looking down at the floor.

'Did you go for a walk with Daddy?' asked Eleanor bravely. She felt the inadequacy of her questions, but could not overcome the dread of having them scantily answered.

Patrick shook his head. A branch swayed outside the window, and he watched the shadow of its leaves flickering above the curtain pole. The curtains billowed feebly and collapsed again, like defeated lungs. Down the corridor a door slammed. Patrick looked at the clutter on his mother's desk. It was covered in letters, envelopes, paper clips, rubber bands, pencils, and a profusion of different-coloured cheque-books. An empty champagne glass stood beside a full ashtray.

'Shall I take the glass down?' he asked.

'What a thoughtful boy you are,' gushed Eleanor. 'You could take it down and give it to Yvette. That would be very kind.'

Patrick nodded solemnly and picked up the glass. Eleanor marvelled at how well her son had turned out. Perhaps people were just born one way or another and the main thing was not to interfere too much.

'Thank you, darling,' she said huskily, wondering what she was meant to have done, as she watched him walk out of the room, gripping the stem of the glass tightly in his right hand.

As Patrick was going down the staircase, he overheard his father and Nicholas talking at the other end of the corridor. Suddenly afraid of falling, he started to walk down the way he used to when he was little, leading with one foot, and then bringing the other down firmly beside it on the same step. He had to hurry in case his father caught up with him, but if he hurried he might fall. He heard his father saying, 'We'll put it to him at dinner, I'm sure he'll agree.'

Patrick froze on the stairs. They were talking about him. They were going to make him agree. Squeezing the stem of the glass fiercely in his hand, he felt a rush of shame and terror. He looked up at the painting hanging on the stairs and imagined its frame hurtling through the air and embedding its sharp corner in his father's chest; and another painting whistling down the corridor and chopping Nicholas's head off.

'I'll see you downstairs in an hour or two,' said Nicholas.

'Right-ho,' said his father.

Patrick heard Nicholas's door close, and he listened intently to his father's footsteps coming down the corridor. Was he going to his bedroom, or coming down the stairs? Patrick wanted to move, but the power to move had deserted him again. He held his breath as the footsteps stopped.

In the corridor David was torn between visiting Eleanor, with whom he was always furious on principle, and going to have a bath. The opium which had taken the edge off the perpetual ache in his body now weakened his desire to insult his wife. After a few moments spent considering the choice he went into his bedroom.

Patrick knew he was not visible from the top of the stairs, but when he heard the footsteps pause he had tried to push back the idea of his father with concentration like a flamethrower. For a long time after David had gone into his bedroom, Patrick did not accept that the danger was over. When he relaxed his grip on the glass, the base and half the stem slipped out of his hand and broke on the step below him. Patrick couldn't understand how the glass had snapped. Removing the rest of the glass from his hand, he saw a small cut in the middle of his palm. Only when he saw it bleed did he understand what had happened and, knowing that he must be in pain, he at last felt the sharp sting of the cut.

He was terrified of being punished for dropping the glass. It had fallen apart in his hand, but they would never believe that, they would say that he'd dropped it. He stepped carefully among the scattered pieces of glass on the steps below and got to the bottom of the stairs, but he did not know what to do with the half glass in his hand, and so he climbed back up three of the steps and decided to jump. He threw himself forward as hard as he could, but tripped as he landed, letting the rest of the glass fly from his hand and shatter against the wall. He lay splayed and shocked on the floor.

When she heard Patrick's screams, Yvette put down the soup ladle, wiped her hands quickly on her apron, and hurried into the hall.

'*Ooh-la-la,*' she said reproachfully, '*tu vas te casser la figure un de ces jours.*' She was alarmed by Patrick's helplessness, but as she drew closer she asked him more gently, '*Où est-ce que ça te fait mal, pauvre petit?*'

Patrick still felt the shock of being winded and pointed to his chest where he had taken the brunt of the fall. Yvette picked him up, murmuring, '*Allez, c'est pas grave,*' and kissed him on the cheek. He went on crying, but less desperately. A tangled sensation of sweat and gold teeth and garlic mingled with the pleasure of being held, but when Yvette started to rub his back, he squirmed in her arms and broke free.

At her desk Eleanor thought, 'Oh God, he's fallen downstairs and cut himself on the glass I gave him. It's my fault again.' Patrick's screaming impaled her on her chair like a javelin, while she considered the horror of her position.

Still dominated by guilt and the fear of David's reprisals, she summoned up the courage to go out onto the landing. At the bottom of the stairs she found Yvette sitting beside Patrick.

'*Rien de cassé, Madame,*' said Yvette. '*Il a eu peur en tombant, c'est tout.*'

'*Merci, Yvette,*' said Eleanor.

It wasn't practical to drink as much as she did, thought Yvette, going to fetch a dustpan and brush.

Eleanor sat down beside Patrick, but a fragment of glass cut into her bottom. 'Ouch,' she exclaimed, and got up again to brush the back of her dress.

'Mummy sat on a piece of glass,' she said to Patrick. He looked at her glumly. 'But never mind about that, tell me about your terrible fall.'

'I jumped down from very high up.'

'With a glass in your hand, darling? That could have been very dangerous.'

'It was dangerous,' said Patrick angrily.

'Oh, I'm sure it was,' said Eleanor, reaching out self-consciously to brush back the fringe of light brown hair from his forehead. 'I'll tell you what we could do,' she said, proud of herself for remembering, 'we could go to the funfair tomorrow, to Le Wild Ouest, would you like that? I went there today with Anne to see if you would like it, and there were lots of cowboys and Indians and rides. Shall we go tomorrow?'

'I want to go away,' said Patrick.

Up in his monk's suite, David hurried next door and turned the bath taps to their full volume, until the thundering water drowned the uncongenial sound of his son. He sprinkled bath salts into the water from a porcelain shell and thought how intolerable it was having no nanny this summer to keep the boy quiet in the evenings. Eleanor hadn't the least idea of how to bring up a child.

After Patrick's nanny had died, there had been a dim procession of foreign girls through the London house. Homesick vandals, they left in tears after a few months, sometimes pregnant, never any more fluent in the English they had come to learn. In the end Patrick was often entrusted to Carmen, the morose Spanish maid who could not be bothered to refuse him anything. She lived in the basement, her varicose veins protesting at every step of the five storeys she seldom climbed to the nursery. In a sense one had to be grateful that this lugubrious peasant had had so little influence on Patrick. Still, it was very tiresome to find him on the stairs night after night, escaped from behind his wooden gate, waiting for Eleanor.

They so often returned late from Annabel's that Patrick had once asked anxiously, 'Who is Annabels?' Everyone in the room had laughed and David could remember Bunny Warren saying, with that simple-hearted tactlessness for which he was almost universally adored, 'She's a very lovely young girl your parents are exceptionally fond of.' Nicholas had seen his chance and said, 'I sospect ze child is experienzing ze sibling rivalry.'

When David came in late at night and found Patrick sitting on the stairs, he would order him back to the nursery, but after he had gone to bed he sometimes heard the floorboards creak on the landing. He knew that Patrick crept into his mother's room to try to extract some consolation from her stupefied back, as she lay curled up and unconscious on the edge of her mattress. He had seen them in the morning like refugees in an expensive waiting room.

David turned off the taps and found that the screaming had stopped. Screaming that only lasted as long as it took to fill a bath could not be taken seriously. David tested the water with a foot. It was far too hot, but he pushed his leg down deeper until the water covered his hairless shin, and started to scald him. Every nerve in his body urged him to step out of the steaming bath, but he called up his deep resources of contempt and kept his leg immersed to prove his mastery over the pain.

He straddled the bath; one foot burning, the other cool against the cork floor. It took no effort for him to revive the fury he had felt an hour earlier when he glimpsed Bridget kneeling under the tree. Nicholas had obviously told that silly bitch about the figs.

Oh, happy days, he sighed, where had they fled? Days when his now bedraggled wife, still freshly submissive and eager to please, had grazed so peacefully among the rotting figs.

David hoisted his other leg over the side of the bath and

plunged it into the water, in the hope that the additional pain would stimulate him to think of the right revenge to take on Nicholas during dinner.

'Why the hell did you have to do that? I'm sure David saw you,' Nicholas snapped at Bridget, as soon as he had heard David's bedroom door close.

'Saw what?'

'You, down on all fours.'

'I didn't have to,' said Bridget sleepily from the bed. 'I only did it because you were so keen to tell me the story, and I thought it might turn you on. It obviously did the first time.'

'Don't be so absurd.' Nicholas stood with his hands on his hips, a picture of disapproval. 'As to your effusive remarks – "What a perfect life you have here",' he simpered, '"What a wonderful view" – they made you sound even more vulgar and stupid than you are.'

Bridget still had trouble in taking Nicholas's rudeness seriously.

'If you're going to be horrid,' she said, 'I'll elope with Barry.'

'And that's another thing,' gasped Nicholas, removing his silk jacket. There were dark sweat rings under the arms of his shirt. 'What was going through your mind – if mind is the right word – when you gave that yob the telephone number here?'

'When I said that we must keep in touch, he asked me for the number of the house I was staying in.'

'You could have lied, you know,' yelped Nicholas. 'There's such a thing as dishonesty.' He paced up and down shaking his head. 'Such a thing as a broken promise.'

Bridget rolled off the bed and crossed the room. 'Just fuck off,' she said, slamming the bathroom door and locking it. She sat on the edge of the bath and remembered that her copy of *Tatler* and, worse, her make-up were in the room next door.

'Open the door, you stupid bitch,' said Nicholas swivelling the doorknob.

'Fuck off,' she repeated. At least she could prevent Nicholas from using the bathroom for as long as possible, even if she only had a bubble bath to amuse her.

II

WHILE HE WAS LOCKED out of the bathroom Nicholas unpacked and filled the most convenient shelves with his shirts; in
the cupboard his suits took up rather more than half the space.
The biography of F. E. Smith that he had already carried with
him to half a dozen houses that summer was placed again on the
table on the right-hand side of the bed. When he was finally allowed access to the bathroom, he distributed his possessions
around the basin in a familiar order, his badger brush to one side
and his rose mouthwash to the other.

Bridget refused to unpack properly. She pulled out a frail-
looking dress of dark-red crushed velvet for tonight, tossed it on
the bed, and abandoned her suitcase in the middle of the floor.
Nicholas could not resist kicking it over, but he said nothing,
conscious that if he was rude to her again straight away she might
cause him difficulties during dinner.

Silently, Nicholas put on a dark-blue silk suit and an old pale-
yellow shirt, the most conventional one he had been able to find
at Mr Fish, and was now ready to go downstairs. His hair smelt
faintly of something made up for him by Trumper's, and his
cheeks of a very simple extract of lime he considered clean and
manly.

Bridget sat at the dressing table, very slowly applying too much black eyeliner.

'We must get downstairs, or we'll be late,' said Nicholas.

'You always say that and then there's nobody there.'

'David is even more punctual than I am.'

'So go down without me.'

'I would rather we went down together,' said Nicholas, with menacing weariness.

Bridget continued to admire herself in the inadequately lit mirror, while Nicholas sat on the edge of the bed and gave his shirtsleeves a little tug to reveal more of his royal cufflinks. Made of thick gold and engraved with the initials E.R., they might have been contemporary, but had in fact been a present to his rakish grandfather, the Sir Nicholas Pratt of his day and a loyal courtier of Edward VII's. Unable to think how he could further embellish his appearance, he got up and wandered around. He drifted back into the bathroom and stole another glance at himself in the mirror. The softening contours of his chin, where the flab was beginning to build up, would undoubtedly profit from yet another suntan. He dabbed a little more lime extract behind his ears.

'I'm ready,' said Bridget.

Nicholas came over to the dressing table and quickly pressed Bridget's powder puff to his cheekbones, and ran it coyly over the bridge of his nose. As they left the room, he glanced at Bridget critically, unable to approve fully of the red velvet dress he had once praised. It carried with it the aura of an antique stall in Kensington Market, and showed up its cheapness glaringly in the presence of other antiques. The red emphasized her blonde hair, and the velvet brought out the glassy blue of her eyes, but the design of the dress, which seemed to have been made for a medieval witch, and the evidence of amateur repairs in the worn material struck him as less amusing than the first time he had seen Bridget in this same dress. It had been at a half Bohemian party in Chelsea given by an ambitious Peruvian. Nicholas and the other social peaks that the host was trying to scale stood together at one end of the room insulting the mountaineer as he scrambled about them attentively. When they had nothing better to do they allowed him to bribe them with his hospitality, on the understanding he would be swept away by an avalanche of invective if he ever treated them with familiarity at a party given by people who really mattered.

Sometimes it was great festivals of privilege, and at other times it was the cringing and envy of others that confirmed one's sense of being at the top. Sometimes it was the seduction of a pretty girl that accomplished this important task and at other times it was down to one's swanky cufflinks.

'All roads lead to Rome,' murmured Nicholas complacently, but Bridget was not curious to know why.

As she had predicted, there was nobody waiting for them in the drawing room. With its curtains drawn, and lit only by pools of urine-coloured light splashed under the dark-yellow lamp-shades, the room looked both dim and rich. Like so many of one's friends, reflected Nicholas.

'Ah, *Extraits de Plantes Marines*,' he said, sniffing the burning essence loudly, 'you know it's impossible to get it now.' Bridget did not answer.

He moved over to the black cabinet and lifted a bottle of Russian vodka out of a silver bucket full of ice cubes. He poured the cold viscous fluid into a small tumbler. 'They used to sell it with copper rings which sometimes overheated and spat burning essence onto the light bulbs. One evening, Monsieur et Madame de Quelque Chose were changing for dinner when the bulb in their dining room exploded, the lampshade caught fire, and the curtains burst into flames. After that, it was taken off the market.'

Bridget showed no surprise or interest. In the distance the

telephone rang faintly. Eleanor so disliked the noise of telephones that there was only one in the house, at a small desk under the back stairs.

'Can I get you a drink?' asked Nicholas, knocking back his vodka in what he considered the correct Russian manner.

'Just a Coke,' said Bridget. She didn't really like alcohol, it was such a crude high. At least that was what Barry said. Nicholas opened a bottle of Coke and poured himself some more vodka, this time in a tall glass packed with ice.

There was a clicking of high heels on the tiles and Eleanor came in shyly, wearing a long purple dress.

'There's a phone call for you,' she said, smiling at Bridget, whose name she had somehow forgotten between the telephone and the drawing room.

'Oh, wow,' said Bridget, 'for me?' She got up, making sure not to look at Nicholas. Eleanor described the route to the phone, and Bridget eventually arrived at the desk under the back stairs. 'Hello,' she said, *'hello?'* There was no answer.

By the time she returned to the drawing room Nicholas was saying, 'Well, one evening, the Marquis and Marquise de Quelque Chose were upstairs changing for a big party they were giving, when a lampshade caught fire and their drawing room was completely gutted.'

'How marvellous,' said Eleanor, with not the faintest idea of what Nicholas had been talking about. Recovering from one of those blank patches in which she could not have said what was going on around her, she knew only that there had been an interval since she was last conscious. 'Did you get through all right?' she said to Bridget.

'No. It's really weird, there was no one there. He must have run out of money.'

The phone rang again, more loudly this time through all the doors that Bridget had left open. She doubled back eagerly.

'Imagine wanting to talk to someone on the phone,' said Eleanor. 'I dread it.'

'Youth,' said Nicholas tolerantly.

'I dreaded it even more in my youth, if that's possible.'

Eleanor poured herself some whisky. She felt exhausted and restless at the same time. It was the feeling she knew better than any other. She returned to her usual seat, a low footstool wedged into the lampless corner beside the screen. As a child, when the screen had belonged to her mother, she had often squatted under its monkey-crowded branches pretending to be invisible.

Nicholas, who had been sitting tentatively on the edge of the Doge's chair, rose again nervously. 'This is David's favourite seat, isn't it?'

'I guess he won't sit in it if you're in it already,' said Eleanor.

'That's just what I'm not so sure of,' said Nicholas. 'You know how fond he is of having his own way.'

'Tell me about it,' said Eleanor flatly.

Nicholas moved to a nearby sofa and sucked another mouthful of vodka from his glass. It had taken on the taste of melted ice, which he disliked, but he rolled it around his mouth, having nothing in particular to say to Eleanor. Annoyed by Bridget's absence and apprehensive about David's arrival, he waited to see which would come through the door. He felt let down when Anne and Victor arrived first.

Anne had replaced her simple white dress with a simple black one and she already held a lighted cigarette. Victor had conquered his anxiety about what to wear and still had on the thick speckled sweater.

'Hi,' said Anne to Eleanor, and kissed her with real affection.

When the greetings were over, Nicholas could not help remarking on Victor's appearance. 'My dear chap, you look as if you're about to go mackerel fishing in the Hebrides.'

'In fact, the last time I wore this sweater,' said Victor, turning around and handing a glass to Anne, 'was when I had to see a student who was floundering badly with his D.Phil. It was called "Abelard, Nietzsche, Sade, and Beckett", which gives you some idea of the difficulties he was running into.'

Does it? thought Eleanor.

'Really, people will stop at nothing to get a doctorate these days.' Victor was warming up for the role he felt was required of him during dinner.

'But how did *your* writing go today?' asked Eleanor. 'I've been thinking all day of you taking a non-psychological approach to identity,' she lied. 'Have I got that right?'

'Absolutely,' said Victor. 'Indeed, I was so haunted by your remark, that if anything is in the mind it's who you are, that I was unable to think of anything else.'

Eleanor blushed. She felt she was being mocked. 'It sounds to me as if Eleanor is quite right,' said Nicholas gallantly. 'How can you separate who we are from who we think we are?'

'Oh, I dare say you can't,' replied Victor, 'once you have decided to consider things in that fashion. But I'm not attempting psychoanalysis, an activity, incidentally, which will seem as quaint as medieval map-making when we have an accurate picture of how the brain works.'

'Nothing a don likes more than bashing another chap's discipline,' said Nicholas, afraid that Victor was going to be a crashing bore during dinner.

'If you can call it a discipline,' chuckled Victor. 'The Unconscious, which we can only discuss when it *ceases* to be unconscious, is another medieval instrument of enquiry which enables the analyst to treat denial as evidence of its opposite. Under these rules we hang a man who denies that he is a murderer, and congratulate him if he says he is one.'

'Are you rejecting the idea that there is an unconscious?' said Anne.

'Are you rejecting the idea that there is an unconscious?' simpered Nicholas to himself in his hysterical American female voice.

'I am saying,' said Victor, 'that if we are controlled by forces we do not understand, the term for that state of affairs is ignorance. What I object to is that we turn ignorance into an inner landscape and pretend that this allegorical enterprise, which might be harmless or even charming, if it weren't so expensive and influential, amounts to a science.'

'But it helps people,' said Anne.

'Ah, the therapeutic promise,' said Victor wisely.

Standing in the doorway, David had been observing them for some time, unnoticed by anyone, except Eleanor.

'Oh, hello, David,' said Victor.

'Hi,' said Anne.

'My dear, so lovely to see you as always,' David answered, turning away from her instantly and saying to Victor, 'Do tell us more about the therapeutic promise.'

'But why don't *you* tell us?' said Victor. 'You're the doctor.'

'In my rather brief medical practice,' said David modestly, 'I found that people spend their whole lives imagining they are about to die. Their only consolation is that one day they're right. All that stands between them and this mental torture is a doctor's authority. And that is the only therapeutic promise that works.'

Nicholas was relieved to be ignored by David, whereas Anne watched with detachment the theatrical way the man set about dominating the room. Like a slave in a swamp full of bloodhounds, Eleanor longed to disappear and she cowered still closer to the screen.

David strode majestically across the room, sat in the Doge's chair and leaned towards Anne. 'Tell me, my dear,' he said, giving a little tug on the stiff silk of his dark-red trousers and crossing his legs, 'have you recovered from your quite unnecessary sacrifice, in going to the airport with Eleanor?'

'It wasn't a sacrifice, it was a pleasure,' said Anne innocently. 'And that reminds me, I've also had the pleasure of bringing back *The Twelve Caesars*. What I mean is that I had the pleasure of reading it and now you have the pleasure of getting it back.'

'So much pleasure in one day,' said David, letting one of the yellow slippers dangle from his foot.

'Right,' said Anne. 'Our cup overfloweth.'

'I've had a delightful day as well,' said David, 'there must be magic in the air.'

Nicholas glimpsed an opportunity to join the conversation without provoking David. 'So what did you think of *The Twelve Caesars?*' he asked Anne.

'Together they would have made a great jury,' said Anne, 'if you like your trials fast.' She turned her thumb towards the floor.

David let out an abrupt, 'Ha,' which showed he was amused. 'They'd have to take turns,' he said, pointing his thumbs down too.

'Absolutely,' said Anne. 'Imagine what would happen if they tried to choose a foreman.'

'And think of the Imperial Thumbache,' said David, twisting his aching thumbs up and down with childish enjoyment.

This happy vein of fantasy was interrupted by Bridget's return. After talking to Barry on the phone, Bridget had smoked another little joint and the colours around her had become very vivid. '*Love* those kinky yellow slippers,' she said to David brightly.

Nicholas winced.

'Do you really like them?' asked David, fixing her genially. 'I'm so pleased.'

David knew intuitively that Bridget would be embarrassed by discussing her phone call, but he had no time to interrogate her now because Yvette came in to announce dinner. Never mind, thought David, I can get her later. In the pursuit of knowledge, there was no point in killing the rabbit before one found out whether its eyes were allergic to shampoo, or its skin inflamed by mascara. It was ridiculous to 'break a butterfly upon a wheel'. The proper instrument for a butterfly was a pin. Stimulated by these consoling thoughts, David rose from his chair and said expansively, 'Let's have dinner.'

Disturbed by a draught from the opening door, the candles in the dining room flickered and animated the painted panels around the walls. A procession of grateful peasants, much appreciated by David, edged a little further along the twisting road that led to the castle gates, only to slip back again as the flames shifted the other way. The wheels of a cart which had been stuck in a roadside ditch, seemed to creak forward, and for a moment the donkey pulling it swelled with dark new muscles.

On the table Yvette had laid out two bowls of rouille for the fish soup, and a sweating green bottle of Blanc de Blancs stood at either end of the table.

On the way from the drawing room to the dining room, Nicholas made one last attempt to extort some enthusiasm for his beleaguered anecdote. It now took place in the residence of the Prince et Princesse de Quelque Chose. 'Whoosh!' he shouted at Anne with an explosive gesture. 'The fifteenth-century tapestries burst into flame and their *hôtel particulier* BURNED TO THE GROUND. The reception had to be cancelled. There was a national scandal, and every bottle of Plantes Marines was banned *worldwide.*'

'As if it wasn't tough enough already being called Quelque Chose,' said Anne.

'But now you can't get it anywhere,' cried Nicholas, exhausted by his efforts.

'Sounds like the right decision. I mean, who wants their peculiar hotel burnt to the ground? Not me!'

Everyone waited to be seated and looked enquiringly at Eleanor. Although there seemed to be no room for doubt, with the women next to David and the men next to her and the couples mixed, she felt a dreadful conviction that she would make a mistake and unleash David's fury. Flustered, she stood there saying, 'Anne . . . would you . . . no, you go there . . . no, I'm sorry . . .'

'Thank God we're only six,' David said in a loud whisper to Nicholas. 'There's some chance she'll crack the problem before the soup gets cold.' Nicholas smirked obediently.

God, I hate grown-up dinner parties, thought Bridget, as Yvette brought in the steaming soup.

'Tell me, my dear, what did you make of the Emperor Galba?' said David to Anne, leaning courteously towards her, to emphasize his indifference to Bridget.

This was the line that Anne had hoped the conversation would not take. Who? she thought, but said, 'Ah, what a character! What *really* interested me, though, was the character of Caligula. Why do you think he was so obsessed with his sisters?'

'Well, you know what they say,' David grinned, 'vice is nice, but incest is best.'

'But what . . .' asked Anne, pretending to be fascinated, 'what's the psychology of a situation like that? Was it a kind of narcissism? The nearest thing to seducing himself?'

'More, I think, the conviction that only a member of his own family could have suffered as he had done. You know, of course, that Tiberius killed almost all of their relations, and so he and Drusilla were survivors of the same terror. Only she could really understand him.'

As David paused to drink some wine, Anne resumed her

impersonation of an eager student. 'Something else I'd love to know is why Caligula thought that torturing his wife would reveal the reason he was so devoted to her?'

'To discover witchcraft was the official explanation, but presumably he was suspicious of affection which was divorced from the threat of death.'

'And, on a larger scale, he had the same suspicion about Roman people. Right?' asked Anne.

'Up to a point, Lord Copper,' said David. He looked as if there were things he knew, but would never divulge. So these were the benefits of a classical education, thought Anne, who had often heard David and Victor talk about them.

Victor had been eating his soup silently and very fast while Nicholas told him about Jonathan Croyden's memorial service. Eleanor had abandoned her soup and lit a cigarette; the extra Dexedrine had put her off her food. Bridget daydreamed resolutely.

'I'm afraid I don't approve of memorial services,' said Victor, pursing his lips for a moment to savour the insincerity of what he was about to say, 'they are just excuses for a party.'

'What's wrong with them,' David corrected him, 'is that they are excuses for such bad parties. I suppose you were talking about Croyden.'

'That's right,' said Victor. 'They say he spoke better than he wrote. There was certainly room for improvement.'

David bared his teeth to acknowledge this little malice. 'Did Nicholas tell you that your friend Vijay was there?'

'No,' said Victor.

'Oh,' said David, turning to Anne persuasively, 'and you never told us why he left so suddenly.' Anne had refused to answer this question on several occasions, and David liked to tease her by bringing it up whenever they met.

'Didn't I?' said Anne, playing along.

'He wasn't incontinent?' asked David.

'No,' said Anne.

'Or worse, in his case, flirtatious?'

'Absolutely not.'

'He was just being himself,' Nicholas suggested.

'That might have done it,' said Anne, 'but it was more than that.'

'The desire to pass on information is like a hunger, and sometimes it is the curiosity, sometimes the indifference, of others that arouses it,' said Victor pompously.

'OK, OK,' said Anne, to save Victor from the silence that might well follow his pronouncement. 'Now it's not going to seem like that big a deal to you sophisticated types,' she added demurely. 'But when I took a clean shirt of his up to his room, I found a bunch of terrible magazines. Not just pornography, much much worse. Of course I wasn't going to ask him to leave. What he reads is his own affair, but he came back and was so rude about my being in his room, when I was only there to take back his lousy shirt, that I kind of lost my temper.'

'Good for you,' said Eleanor timidly.

'What sort of magazines exactly?' asked Nicholas, sitting back and crossing his legs.

'I wish you'd confiscated them,' giggled Bridget.

'Oh, just awful,' said Anne. 'Crucifixion. All kinds of animal stuff.'

'God, how hilarious,' said Nicholas. 'Vijay rises in my estimation.'

'Oh, yeah?' said Anne. 'Well, you should have seen the look on the poor pig's face.'

Victor was a little uneasy. 'The obscure ethics of our relations to the animal kingdom,' he chuckled.

'We kill them when we feel like it,' said David crisply, 'nothing very obscure about that.'

'Ethics is not the study of what we do, my dear David, but what we ought to do,' said Victor.

'That's why it's such a waste of time, old boy,' said Nicholas cheerfully.

'Why do you think it's superior to be amoral?' Anne asked Nicholas.

'It's not a question of being superior,' he said, exposing his cavernous nostrils to Anne, 'it just springs from a desire not to be a bore or a prig.'

'Everything about Nicholas is superior,' said David, 'and even if he *were* a bore or a prig, I'm sure he would be a superior one.'

'Thank you, David,' said Nicholas with determined complacency.

'Only in the English language,' said Victor, 'can one be "a bore", like being a lawyer or a pastry cook, making boredom into a profession – in other languages a person is simply boring, a temporary state of affairs. The question is, I suppose, whether this points to a greater intolerance towards boring people, or an especially intense quality of boredom among the English.'

It's because you're such a bunch of boring old farts, thought Bridget.

Yvette took away the soup plates and closed the door behind her. The candles flickered, and the painted peasants came alive again for a moment.

'What one aims for,' said David, 'is ennui.'

'Of course,' said Anne, 'it's more than just French for our old friend boredom. It's boredom plus money, or boredom plus arrogance. It's I-find-everything-boring, therefore I'm fascinating. But it doesn't seem to occur to people that you can't have a world picture and then not be part of it.'

There was a moment of silence while Yvette came back carrying a large platter of roast veal and vegetables.

'Darling,' said David to Eleanor, 'what a marvellous memory

you have to be able to duplicate the dinner you gave Anne and Victor last time they were here.'

'Oh, God, how awful,' said Eleanor. 'I'm so sorry.'

'Talking of animal ethics,' said Nicholas, 'I gather that Gerald Frogmore shot more birds last year than anyone in England. Not bad for a chap in a wheelchair.'

'Maybe he doesn't like to see things move about freely,' said Anne. She immediately felt the excitement of half wishing she had not made this remark.

'You're not anti-blood sports?' asked Nicholas, with an unspoken 'on top of everything else'.

'How could I be?' asked Anne. 'It's a middle-class prejudice based on envy. Have I got that right?'

'Well, I wasn't going to say so,' said Nicholas, 'but you put it so much better than I could possibly hope to . . .'

'Do you despise people from the middle classes?' Anne asked.

'I don't despise people *from* the middle classes, on the contrary, the further from them, the better,' said Nicholas, shooting one of his cuffs. 'It's people *in* the middle classes that disgust me.'

'Can middle-class people be from the middle class in your sense?'

'Oh, yes,' said Nicholas generously, 'Victor is an outstanding case.'

Victor smiled to show that he was enjoying himself.

'It's easier for girls, of course,' Nicholas continued. 'Marriage is such a blessing, hoisting women from dreary backgrounds into a wider world.' He glanced at Bridget. 'All a chap can really do, unless he's the sort of queer who spends his whole time writing postcards to people who might need a spare man, is to toe the line. And be thoroughly charming and well informed,' he added, with a reassuring smile for Victor.

'Nicholas, of course, is an expert,' David intervened, 'having personally raised several women from the gutter.'

'At considerable expense,' Nicholas agreed.

'The cost of being dragged into the gutter was even higher, wouldn't you say, Nicholas?' said David, reminding Nicholas of his political humiliation. 'Either way, the gutter seems to be where you feel at home.'

'Cor blimey, guv,' said Nicholas in his comical cockney voice. 'When you've gorn down the drain like wot I 'ave, the gutter looks like a bed o' roses.'

Eleanor still found it inexplicable that the best English manners contained such a high proportion of outright rudeness and gladiatorial combat. She knew that David abused this licence, but she also knew how 'boring' it was to interfere with the exercise of unkindness. When David reminded someone of their weaknesses and failures she was torn between a desire to save the victim, whose feelings she adopted as her own, and an equally strong desire not to be accused of spoiling a game. The more she thought about this conflict, the more tightly it trapped her. She would never know what to say because whatever she said would be wrong.

Eleanor thought about her stepfather barking at her mother across the wastes of English silver, French furniture, and Chinese vases that helped to prevent him from becoming physically violent. This dwarfish and impotent French duke had dedicated his life to the idea that civilization had died in 1789. He nonetheless accepted a ten per cent cut from the dealers who sold prerevolutionary antiques to his wife. He had forced Mary to sell her mother's Monets and Bonnards on the ground that they were examples of a decadent art that would never really matter. To him, Mary was the least valuable object in the fastidious museums they inhabited, and when eventually he bullied her to death he felt that he had eliminated the last trace of modernity from his life except, of course, for the enormous income that now came to him from the sales of a dry-cleaning fluid made in Ohio.

Eleanor had watched her mother's persecution with the same vivid silence as she experienced in the face of her own gradual disintegration tonight. Although she was not a cruel person, she remembered being helpless with laughter watching her step-father, by then suffering from Parkinson's disease, lift a forkful of peas, only to find the fork empty by the time it reached his mouth. Yet she had never told him how much she hated him. She had not spoken then, and she would not speak now.

'Look at Eleanor,' said David, 'she has that expression she only puts on when she is thinking of her dear rich dead mother. I'm right, aren't I, darling?' he cajoled her. 'Aren't I?'

'Yes, you are,' she admitted.

'Eleanor's mother and aunt,' said David in the tone of a man reading *Little Red Riding Hood* to a gullible child, 'thought that they could buy human antiques. The moth-eaten bearers of an-cient titles were reupholstered with thick wads of dollars, but,' he concluded with a warm banality which could not altogether conceal his humorous intentions, 'you just can't treat human be-ings like things.'

'Definitely,' said Bridget, amazed to hear herself speak.

'You agree with me?' said David, suddenly attentive.

'Definitely,' said Bridget, who appeared to have broken her silence on somewhat limited terms.

'Maybe the human antiques wanted to be bought,' Anne sug-gested.

'Nobody doubts that,' said David, 'I'm sure they were licking the windowpane. What's so shocking is that after being saved, they dared to rear up on their spindly Louis Quinze legs and start giving orders. The *ingratitude!*'

'Cor!' said Nicholas. 'Wot I wouldn't give for some o' 'em Looey Can's legs – they must be wurf a bob or two.'

Victor was embarrassed on Eleanor's behalf. After all, she was paying for dinner.

Bridget was confused by David. She agreed wholeheartedly with what he had said about people not being things. In fact, once she'd been tripping and had realized with overwhelming clarity that what was wrong with the world was people treating each other like things. It was such a big idea that it was hard to hold on to, but she had felt very strongly about it at the time, and she thought David was trying to say the same thing. She also admired him for being the only person who frightened Nicholas. On the other hand, she could see why he frightened Nicholas.

Anne had had enough. She felt a combination of boredom and rebelliousness which reminded her of adolescence. She could take no more of David's mood, and the way he baited Eleanor, tormented Nicholas, silenced Bridget, and even diminished Victor.

'Sorry,' she murmured to Eleanor, 'I'll be right back.'

In the dim hallway, she pulled a cigarette out of her bag and lit it. The flaming match was reflected in all the mirrors around the hall, and made a sliver of glass shine momentarily at the foot of the stairs. Stooping down to pick up the glass with the tip of her index finger, Anne suddenly knew that she was being watched and, looking up, she saw Patrick sitting on the widest step where the staircase curved. He wore flannel pyjamas with blue elephants on them, but his face looked downcast.

'Hi, Patrick,' said Anne, 'you look so grim. Can't you get to sleep?'

He did not answer or move. 'I just have to get rid of this piece of glass,' said Anne. 'I guess something broke here earlier?'

'It was me,' said Patrick.

'Hang on one second,' she said.

She's lying, thought Patrick, she won't come back.

There was no wastepaper basket in the hall, but she brushed the glass off her finger into a porcelain umbrella stand that bristled with David's collection of exotic canes.

She hurried back to Patrick and sat on the step beneath him. 'Did you cut yourself on that glass?' she asked tenderly, putting her hand on his arm.

He pulled away from her and said, 'Leave me alone.'

'Do you want me to get your mother?' asked Anne.

'All right,' said Patrick.

'OK. I'll go get her right away,' said Anne. Back in the dining room, she heard Nicholas saying to Victor, 'David and I were meaning to ask you before dinner whether John Locke really said that a man who forgot his crimes should not be punished for them.'

'Yes, indeed,' said Victor. 'He maintained that personal identity depended on continuity of memory. In the case of a forgotten crime one would be punishing the wrong person.'

'I'll drink to that,' said Nicholas.

Anne leaned over to Eleanor and said to her quietly, 'I think you ought to go and see Patrick. He was sitting on the stairs asking for you.'

'Thank you,' whispered Eleanor.

'Perhaps it should be the other way round,' said David. 'A man who remembers his crimes can usually be relied upon to punish himself, whereas the law should punish the person who is irresponsible enough to forget.'

'D'you believe in capital punishment?' piped up Bridget.

'Not since it ceased to be a public occasion,' said David. 'In the eighteenth century a hanging was a really good day's outing.'

'Everybody enjoyed themselves: even the man who was being hanged,' added Nicholas.

'Fun for all the family,' David went on. 'Isn't that the phrase everybody uses nowadays? God knows, it's always what *I* aim for, but an occasional trip to Tyburn must have made the task easier.'

Nicholas giggled. Bridget wondered what Tyburn was. Eleanor smiled feebly, and pushed her chair back.

'Not leaving us I hope, darling,' said David.

'I have to . . . I'll be back in a moment,' Eleanor mumbled.

'I didn't quite catch that: you have to be back in a moment?'

'There's something I have to do.'

'Well, hurry, hurry, hurry,' said David gallantly, 'we'll be lost without your conversation.'

Eleanor walked to the door at the same time as Yvette opened it carrying a silver coffee pot.

'I found Patrick on the stairs,' Anne said. 'He seemed kind of sad.'

David's eyes darted towards Eleanor's back as she slipped past Yvette. 'Darling,' he said, and then more peremptorily, 'Eleanor.'

She turned, her teeth locked onto a thumbnail, trying to get a grip that would hold. She often tore at the stunted nails when she was not smoking. 'Yes?' she said.

'I thought that we'd agreed that you wouldn't rush to Patrick each time he whines and blubbers.'

'But he fell down earlier and he may have hurt himself.'

'In that case,' said David with sudden seriousness, 'he may need a doctor.' He rested the palms of his hands on the top of the table, as if to rise.

'Oh, I don't think he's hurt,' said Anne, to restrain David. She had a strong feeling that she would not be keeping her promise to Patrick if she sent him his father rather than his mother. 'He just wants to be comforted.'

'You see, darling,' said David, 'he isn't hurt, and so it is just a sentimental question: does one indulge the self-pity of a child, or not? Does one allow oneself to be blackmailed, or not? Come and sit down – we can at least discuss it.'

Eleanor edged her way back to her chair reluctantly. She knew she would be pinned down by a conversation that would defeat her, but not persuade her.

'The proposition I want to make,' said David, 'is that education should be something of which a child can later say: if I survived that, I can survive anything.'

'That's crazy and wrong,' said Anne, 'and you know it.'

'I certainly think that children should be stretched to the limit of their abilities,' said Victor, 'but I'm equally certain they can't be if they're intensely miserable.'

'Nobody wants to make anybody miserable,' said Nicholas, puffing out his cheeks incredulously. 'We're just saying that it doesn't do the child any good to be mollycoddled. I may be a frightful reactionary, but I think that all you have to do for children is hire a reasonable nanny and put them down for Eton.'

'What, the nannies?' said Bridget giggling. 'Anyway, what if you have a girl?'

Nicholas looked at her sternly.

'I guess that putting things down is your speciality,' said Anne to Nicholas.

'Oh, I know it's an unfashionable view to hold these days,' Nicholas went on complacently, 'but in my opinion nothing that happens to you as a child really matters.'

'If we're getting down to things that don't really matter,' said Anne, 'you're top of my list.'

'Oh, my word,' said Nicholas, in his sports commentator's voice, 'a ferocious backhand from the young American woman, but the line judge rules it out.'

'From what you've told me,' said Bridget, still elated by the thought of nannies in tailcoats, 'nothing much that happened in *your* childhood did matter: you just did what everyone expected.' Feeling a vague pressure on her right thigh, she glanced round at David, but he seemed to be staring ahead, organizing a sceptical expression on his face. The pressure stopped. On her other side, Victor peeled a nectarine with hurried precision.

'It's true,' said Nicholas, making a visible effort at equanimity, 'that my childhood was uneventful. People never remember happiness with the care that they lavish on preserving every detail of their suffering. I remember stroking my cheek against the velvet collar of my overcoat. Asking my grandfather for pennies to throw into that golden pool at the Ritz. Big lawns. Buckets and spades. That sort of thing.'

Bridget could not concentrate on what Nicholas was saying. She felt cold metal against her knee. Looking down, she saw David lifting the edge of her dress with a small silver knife and running it along her thigh. What the fuck did he think he was doing? She frowned at him reproachfully. He merely pressed the point a little more firmly into her thigh, without looking at her.

Victor wiped the tips of his fingers with his napkin, while answering a question which Bridget had missed. He sounded a little bored and not surprisingly, when she heard what he had to say. 'Certainly if the degree of psychological connectedness and psychological continuity have become sufficiently weakened, it would be true to say that a person should look upon his childhood with no more than charitable curiosity.'

Bridget's mind flashed back to her father's foolish conjuring tricks, and her mother's ghastly floral-print dresses, but charitable curiosity was not what she felt.

'Would you like one of these?' said David, lifting a fig from the bowl in the middle of the table. 'They're at their best at this time of year.'

'No, thanks,' she said.

David pinched the fig firmly between his fingers and pushed it towards Bridget's mouth, 'Come on,' he said, 'I know how much you like them.'

Bridget opened her mouth obediently and took the fig between her teeth. She blushed because the table had fallen silent and she knew that everyone was watching her. As soon as she could she took the fig from her mouth and asked David if she could borrow his knife to peel it with. David admired her for the speed and stealth of this tactic and handed over the knife.

Eleanor watched Bridget take the fig with a familiar sense of doom. She could never see David impose his will on anyone without considering how often he had imposed it on her.

At the root of her dread was the fragmented memory of the night when Patrick was conceived. Against her will, she pictured the Cornish house on its narrow headland, always damp, always grey, more Atlantic than earth. He had pushed the hollow base of her skull against the corner of the marble table. When she had broken free he had punched the back of her knees and made her fall on the stairs and raped her there, with her arms twisted back. She had hated him like a stranger and hated him like a traitor. God, how she had loathed him, but when she had become pregnant she had said she would stay if he never, *never* touched her again.

Bridget chewed the fig unenthusiastically. As Anne watched her, she could not help thinking of the age-old question which every woman asks herself at some time or other: do I have to swallow it? She wondered whether to picture Bridget as a collared slave draped over the feet of an oriental bully, or as a rebellious schoolgirl being forced to eat the apple pie she tried to leave behind at lunch. She suddenly felt quite detached from the company around her.

Nicholas struck Anne as more pathetic than he had before. He was just one of those Englishmen who was always saying silly things to sound less pompous, and pompous things to sound less silly. They turned into self-parodies without going to the trouble of acquiring a self first. David, who thought he was the Creature from the Black Lagoon, was just a higher species of this involuted failure. She looked at Victor slumped round-shouldered over the remains of his nectarine. He had not kept up the half-clever banter which he usually felt it his duty to provide. She could remember him earlier in the summer saying, 'I may spend my days doubting doubting, but when it comes to gossip I like *hard* facts.' From then on it had been nothing but hard facts. Today he was different. Perhaps he really wanted to do some work again.

Eleanor's crushed expression no longer moved her either. The only thing that made Anne's detachment falter was the thought of Patrick waiting on the stairs, his disappointment widening as he waited, but it only spurred her on to the same conclusion: that she wanted nothing more to do with these people, that it was time to leave, even if Victor would be embarrassed by leaving early. She looked over to Victor, raising her eyebrows and darting her eyes towards the door. Instead of the little frown she had expected from him, Victor nodded his head discreetly as if agreeing with the pepper mill. Anne let a few moments go by then leaned over to Eleanor and said, 'It's sad, but I think we really must leave. It's been a long day, you must be tired too.'

'Yes,' said Victor firmly, 'I must get up early tomorrow morning and make some progress with my work.' He heaved himself up and started to thank Eleanor and David before they had time to organize the usual protests.

In fact, David hardly looked up. He continued to run his thumbnail around the sealed end of his cigar, 'You know the way out,' he said, in response to their thanks, 'I hope you'll forgive me for not coming to wave goodbye.'

'Never,' said Anne, more seriously than she had intended.

Eleanor knew there was a formula everybody used in these situations, but she searched for it in vain. Whenever she thought of what she was meant to say, it seemed to dash around the corner, and lose itself in the crowd of things she should not say. The most successful fugitives were often the dullest, the sentences that nobody notices until they are not spoken: 'How nice to see you . . . won't you stay a little longer . . . what a good idea . . .'

Victor closed the dining room door behind him carefully,
like a man who does not want to wake a sleeping sentry. He
smiled at Anne and she smiled back, and they were suddenly
conscious of how relieved they were to be leaving the Melroses.
They started to laugh silently and to tiptoe towards the hall.

'I'll just check if Patrick is still here,' Anne whispered.

'Why are we whispering?' Victor whispered.

'I don't know,' Anne whispered back. She looked up the staircase. It was empty. He had obviously grown tired of waiting and
gone back to bed. 'I guess he's asleep,' she said to Victor.

They went out of the front door and up the wide steps towards
their car. The moon was bruised by thin cloud and surrounded by
a ring of dispersed light.

'You can't say I didn't try,' said Anne, 'I was hanging right in
there until Nicholas and David started outlining their educational programme. If some big-deal friend of theirs, like George,
was feeling sad and lonely they would fly back to England and
personally mix the dry martinis and load the shotguns, but when
David's own son is feeling sad and lonely in the room next door,
they fight every attempt to make him less miserable.'

'You're right,' said Victor, opening the car door, 'in the end
one must oppose cruelty, at the very least by refusing to take part
in it.'

'Underneath that New and Lingwood shirt,' said Anne, 'beats
a heart of gold.'

Must you leave so soon? thought Eleanor. *That* was the phrase.
She had remembered it. Better late than never was another
phrase, not really true in this case. Sometimes things were too
late, too late the very moment they happened. Other people
knew what they were meant to say, knew what they were meant
to mean, and other people still – otherer people – knew what the

other people meant when they said it. God, she was drunk. When her eyes watered, the candle flames looked like a liqueur advertisement, splintering into mahogany-coloured spines of light. Not drunk enough to stop the half-thoughts from sputtering on into the night, keeping her from any rest. Maybe she could go to Patrick now. Whatshername had slipped off cunningly just after Victor and Anne left. Maybe they would let her go too. But what if they didn't? She could not stand another failure, she could not bow down another time. And so she did nothing for a little longer.

'If nothing matters, you're top of my list,' Nicholas quoted, with a little yelp of delight. 'One has to admire Victor, who tries so hard to be conventional, for never having an entirely conventional girlfriend.'

'Almost nothing is as entertaining as the contortions of a clever Jewish snob,' said David.

'Very broad-minded of you to have him in your house,' said Nicholas, in his judge's voice. 'Some members of the jury may feel that it is *too* broadminded, but that is not for me to say,' he boomed, adjusting an imaginary wig. 'The openness of English society has always been its great strength: the entrepreneurs and arrivistes of yesterday – the Cecils, for example – become the guardians of stability in a mere three or four hundred years. Nevertheless, there is no principle, however laudable in itself, which cannot be perverted. Whether the openness and the generosity of what the press chooses to call "the establishment" has been abused on this occasion, by welcoming into its midst a dangerous intellectual of murky Semitic origins is for you, and for you alone, to judge.'

David grinned. He was in the mood for fun. After all, what redeemed life from complete horror was the almost unlimited number of things to be nasty about. All he needed now was to ditch Eleanor, who was twitching silently like a beetle on its back, get a bottle of brandy, and settle down to gossip with Nicholas. It was too perfect. 'Let's go into the drawing room,' he said.

'Fine,' said Nicholas, who knew that he had won David over and did not want to lose this privilege by paying any attention to Eleanor. He got up, drained his glass of wine, and followed David to the drawing room.

Eleanor remained frozen in her chair, unable to believe how lucky she was to be completely alone. Her mind rushed ahead to a tender reconciliation with Patrick, but she stayed slumped in front of the debris of dinner. The door opened and Eleanor jumped. It was only Yvette.

'*Oh, pardon, Madame, je ne savais pas que vous étiez toujours là.*'

'*Non, non, je vais justement partir,*' said Eleanor apologetically. She went through the kitchen and up the back stairs to avoid Nicholas and David, walking the whole length of the corridor to see whether Patrick was still waiting for her on the staircase. He was not there. Instead of being grateful that he had already gone to bed, she felt even more guilty that she had not come to console him earlier.

She opened the door to his room gently, excruciated by the whining of the hinge. Patrick was asleep in his bed. Rather than disturb him, she tiptoed back out of the room.

Patrick lay awake. His heart was pounding. He knew it was his mother, but she had come too late. He would not call to her again. When he had still been waiting on the stairs and the door of the hall opened, he stayed to see if it was his mother, and he hid in case it was his father. But it was only that woman who had lied to him. Everybody used his name but they did not know who he was. One day he would play football with the heads of his enemies.

Who the fuck did he think he was? How dare he poke a knife up her dress? Bridget pictured herself strangling David as he sat in his dining-room chair, her thumbs pressing into his windpipe. And then, confusingly, she imagined that she had fallen into his lap, while she was strangling him, and she could feel that he had a huge erection. 'Gross out,' she said aloud, 'totally gross.' At least David was intense, intensely gross, but intense. Unlike Nicholas, who turned out to be a complete cringer, really pathetic. And the others were so boring. How was she meant to spend another second in this house?

Bridget wanted a joint to take the edge off her indignation. She opened her suitcase and took a plastic bag out of the toe of her back-up pair of cowboy boots. The bag contained some dark green grass that she had already taken the seeds and stalks out of, and a packet of orange Rizlas. She sat down at an amusing Gothic desk fitted between the bedroom's two round windows. Sheaves of engraved writing paper were housed under its tallest arch, with envelopes in the smaller arches either side. On the desk's open flap was a black leather pad holding a large piece of blotting paper. She rolled a small joint above it and then brushed the escaped leaves carefully back into her bag.

Turning off the light to create a more ceremonial and private atmosphere, Bridget sat down in the curved windowsill and lit her joint. The moon had risen above the thin clouds and cast deep shadows on the terrace. She sucked a thick curl of smoke appreciatively into her lungs and held it in, noticing how the dull glow of the fig leaves made them look as if they were cut out of old pewter. As she blew the smoke slowly through the little holes in the mosquito net she heard the door open beneath her window.

'Why are blazers so common?' she heard Nicholas ask.

'Because they're worn by ghastly people like him,' David answered.

God, didn't they ever grow tired of bitching about people? thought Bridget. Or, at least, about people she didn't know. Or did she know him? With a little flash of shame and paranoia

Bridget remembered that her father wore blazers. Perhaps they were trying to humiliate her. She held her breath and sat absolutely still. She could see them now, both smoking their cigars. They started to walk down the terrace, their conversation fading as they headed towards the far end. She took another toke on her joint; it had almost gone out, but she got it going again. The bastards were probably talking about her, but she might just be thinking that because she was stoned. Well, she *was* stoned and she did think that. Bridget smiled. She wished she had someone to be silly with. Licking her finger she doused down the side of the joint that was burning too fast. They were pacing back now and she could hear again what they were saying.

'I suppose I would have to answer that,' Nicholas said, 'with the remark that Croyden made – not quoted, incidentally, in his memorial service – when he was found emerging from a notorious public lavatory in Hackney.' Nicholas's voice rose an octave, '"I have pursued beauty wherever it has led me, even to the most unbeautiful places."'

'Not a bad policy,' said David, 'if a little fruitily expressed.'

12

WHEN THEY GOT BACK home, Anne was in a good mood. She flopped down on the brown sofa, kicked off her shoes, and lit a cigarette. 'Everybody knows you've got a great mind,' she said to Victor, 'but what interests me is your slightly less well-known body.'

Victor laughed a little nervously and walked across the room to pour himself a glass of whisky. 'Reputation isn't everything,' he said.

'Come over here,' Anne ordered softly.

'Drink?' asked Victor.

Anne shook her head. She watched Victor drop a couple of ice cubes into his glass.

He walked over to the sofa and sat down beside her, smiling benignly.

When she leaned forward to kiss him, he fished one of the ice cubes out of the glass and, with unexpected swiftness, slipped it down the front of her dress.

'Oh, God,' gasped Anne, trying to keep her composure, 'that's deliciously cool and refreshing. And wet,' she added, wriggling and pushing the ice cube further down under her black dress.

Victor put his hand under her dress and retrieved the ice

cube expertly, putting it in his mouth and sucking it before letting it slip from his mouth back into the glass. 'I thought you
needed cooling off,' he said, putting his palms firmly on each of
her knees.

'Oh, my,' Anne purred, in a southern drawl, 'despite outward
appearances, I can see you're a man of strong appetites.' She lifted
one of her feet onto the sofa and reached out her hand at the
same time to run her fingers through the thick waves of Victor's
hair. She pulled his head gently towards the stretched tendon of
her raised thigh. Victor kissed the white cotton of her underwear
and grazed it like a man catching a grape between his teeth.

Unable to sleep, Eleanor put on a Japanese dressing gown and
retreated to her car. She felt strangely elated in the white leather
interior of the Buick, with her packet of Player's and the bottle
of cognac she retrieved from under the driving seat. Her happiness was complete when she turned on Radio Monte Carlo and
found that it was playing one of her favourite songs: 'I Got Plenty
o' Nuttin'' from *Porgy and Bess*. She mouthed the words silently,
'And nuttin's plenty for me,' dipping her head from side to side,
almost in time with the music.

When she saw Bridget hobbling along in the moonlight with
a suitcase banging against her knee, Eleanor thought, not for the
first time, that she must be hallucinating. What on earth was
the girl doing? Well, it was really very obvious. She was leaving.
The simplicity of the act horrified Eleanor. After years of dreaming about how to tunnel under the guardroom undetected, she
was amazed to see a newcomer walk out through the open gate.
Just going down the drive as if she were free.

Bridget swung her suitcase from one hand to another. She
wasn't sure it would fit on the back of Barry's bike. The whole
thing was a total freakout. She had left Nicholas in bed, snoring

as usual, like an old pig with terminal flu. The idea was to dump her suitcase at the bottom of the drive and go back to fetch it once she had met up with Barry. She swapped hands again. The lure of the Open Road definitely lost some of its appeal if you took any luggage with you.

Two-thirty by the village church, that's what Barry had said on the phone before dinner. She dropped her suitcase into a clump of rosemary, letting out a petulant sigh to show herself she was more irritated than frightened. What if the village didn't have a church? What if her suitcase was stolen? How far was it to the village anyway? God, life was so complicated. She had run away from home once when she was nine, but doubled back because she couldn't bear to think what her parents might say while she was away.

As she joined the small road that led down to the village, Bridget found herself walled in by pines. The shadows thickened until the moonlight no longer shone on the road. A light wind animated the branches of the tall trees. Full of dread, Bridget suddenly came to a stop. Was Barry really a fun person when it came down to it? After making their appointment he had said, 'Be there or be square!' At the time she was so infatuated by the idea of escaping Nicholas and the Melroses that she had forgotten to be annoyed, but now she realized just how annoying it was.

Eleanor was wondering whether to get another bottle of cognac (cognac was for the car because it was so stimulating), or go back to bed and drink whisky. Either way she had to return to the house. When she was about to open the car door she saw Bridget again. This time she was staggering up the drive, dragging her suitcase. Eleanor felt cool and detached. She decided that nothing could surprise her any longer. Perhaps Bridget did this every evening for the exercise. Or maybe she wanted a lift somewhere.

Eleanor preferred to watch her than to get involved, so long as Bridget got back into the house quickly.

Bridget thought she heard the sound of a radio, but she lost it again amid the rustle of leaves. She was shaken and rather embarrassed by her escapade. Plus her arms were about to drop off. Well, never mind, at least she had asserted herself, sort of. She opened the door of the house. It squeaked. Luckily, she could rely on Nicholas to be sleeping like a drugged elephant, so that no sound could possibly reach him. But what if she woke David? *Freak-ee.* Another squeak and she closed the door behind her. As she crept down the corridor she could hear a sort of moaning and then a yelping shout, like a cry of pain.

David woke up with a shout of fear. Why the hell did people say, 'It's *only* a dream'? His dreams exhausted and dismembered him. They seemed to open onto a deeper layer of insomnia, as if he was only lulled to sleep in order to be shown that he could not rest. Tonight he had dreamed that he was the cripple in Athens airport. He could feel his limbs twisted like vine stumps, his wobbling head burrowing this way and that as he tried to throw himself forward, and his unfriendly hands slapping his own face. In the waiting room at the airport all the passengers were people he knew: the barman from the Central in Lacoste, George, Bridget, people from decades of London parties, all talking and reading books. And there he was, heaving himself across the room one leg dragging behind him, trying to say, 'Hello, it's David Melrose, I hope you aren't deceived by this absurd disguise,' but he only managed to moan, or as he grew more desperate, to squeal, while he tossed advertisements for roasted nuts at them with upsetting inaccuracy. He could see the embarrassment in some of their faces, and feigned blankness in others. And he heard George say to his neighbour, 'What a perfectly ghastly man.'

David turned on the light and fumbled for his copy of *Jorrocks*

Rides Again. He wondered whether Patrick would remember. There was always repression, of course, although it didn't seem to work very well on his own desires. He must *try* not to do it again, that really would be tempting fate. David could not help smiling at his own audacity.

Patrick did not wake up from his dream, although he could feel a needle slip under his shoulder blade and push out through his chest. The thick thread was sewing his lungs up like an old sack until he could not breathe. Panic like wasps hovering about his face, ducking and twisting and beating the air.

He saw the Alsatian that had chased him in the woods, and he felt he was running through the rattling yellow leaves again with wider and wider strides. As the dog drew closer and was about to get him, Patrick started adding up numbers out loud, and at the last moment his body lifted off the ground until he was looking down on the tops of the trees, as if at seaweed over the side of a boat. He knew that he must never allow himself to fall asleep. Below him the Alsatian scrambled to a halt in a flurry of dry leaves and picked up a dead branch in its mouth.

BAD NEWS

I

PATRICK PRETENDED TO SLEEP, hoping the seat next to him would remain empty, but he soon heard a briefcase sliding into the overhead compartment. Opening his eyes reluctantly, he saw a tall snub-nosed man.

'Hi, I'm Earl Hammer,' said the man, extending a big freckled hand covered in thick blond hair, 'I guess I'm your seating companion.'

'Patrick Melrose,' said Patrick mechanically, offering a clammy and slightly shaking hand to Mr Hammer.

Early the previous evening, George Watford had telephoned Patrick from New York.

'Patrick, my dear,' he said in a strained and drawling voice, slightly delayed by its Atlantic crossing, 'I'm afraid I have the most awful news for you: your father died the night before last in his hotel room. I've been quite unable to get hold of either you or your mother – I believe she's in Chad with the Save the Children Fund – but I need hardly tell you how I feel; I adored your father, as you know. Oddly enough, he was supposed to be having lunch with me at the Key Club on the day that he died, but of course he never turned up; I remember thinking how unlike him it was. It must be the most awful shock for you. Everybody liked him, you know, Patrick. I've told some of the members there and some of the servants, and they were *very* sorry to hear about his death.'

'Where is he now?' asked Patrick coldly.

'At Frank E. MacDonald's in Madison Avenue: it's the place everyone uses over here, I believe it's awfully good.'

Patrick promised that as soon as he arrived in New York he would call George.

'I'm sorry to be the bringer of such bad news,' said George. 'You're going to need all your courage during this difficult time.'

'Thanks for calling,' said Patrick, 'I'll see you tomorrow.'

'Goodbye, my dear.'

Patrick put down the syringe he had been flushing out, and sat beside the phone without moving. Was it bad news? Perhaps he would need all his courage not to dance in the street, not to smile too broadly. Sunlight poured in through the blurred and caked windowpanes of his flat. Outside, in Ennismore Gardens, the leaves of the plane trees were painfully bright.

He suddenly leaped out of his chair. 'You're not going to get away with this,' he muttered vindictively. The sleeve of his shirt rolled forward and absorbed the trickle of blood on his arm.

'You know, Paddy,' said Earl, regardless of the fact that nobody called Patrick 'Paddy', 'I've made a hell of a lot of money, and I figured it was time to enjoy some of the good things in life.'

It was half an hour into the flight and Paddy was already Earl's good buddy.

'How sensible of you,' gasped Patrick.

'I've rented an apartment by the beach in Monte Carlo, and a house in the hills behind Monaco. *Just a beautiful house,*' said

Earl, shaking his head incredulously. 'I've got an English butler: he tells me what sports jacket to wear – can you believe that? And I've got the leisure time to read the *Wall Street Journal* from cover to cover.'

'A heady freedom,' said Patrick.

'It's *great*. And I'm also reading a real interesting book at the moment, called *Megatrends*. *And* a Chinese classic on the art of war. Are you interested in war at all?'

'Not madly,' said Patrick.

'I guess I'm biased: I was in Vietnam,' said Earl, staring at the horizon through the tiny window of the plane.

'You liked it?'

'Sure did,' Earl smiled.

'Didn't you have any reservations?'

'I'll tell you, Paddy, the only reservations I had about Vietnam were the target restrictions. Flying over some of those ports and seeing tankers deliver oil you *knew* was for the Viet Cong, and not being able to strike them – that was one of the most frustrating experiences of my life.' Earl, who seemed to be in an almost perpetual state of amazement at the things he said, shook his head again.

Patrick turned towards the aisle, suddenly assailed by the sound of his father's music, as clear and loud as breaking glass, but this aural hallucination was soon swamped by the vitality of his neighbour.

'Have you ever been to the Tahiti Club in St Tropez, Paddy? That's a hell of a place! I met a couple of dancers there.' His voice dropped half an octave to match the new tone of male camaraderie. 'I got to tell you,' he said confidentially, 'I love to screw. God, I *love* it,' he shouted. 'But a great body is not enough, you know what I mean? You gotta have that *mental thing*. I was screwing these two dancers: they were *fantastic* women, great bodies, just beautiful, but I couldn't come. You know why?'

'You didn't have that mental thing,' suggested Patrick.

'That's right! I didn't have that *mental thing*,' said Earl.

Perhaps it was that mental thing that was missing with Debbie. He had called her last night to tell her about his father's death.

'Oh, God, that's appalling,' she stammered, 'I'll come over straight away.'

Patrick could hear the nervous tension in Debbie's voice, the inherited anxiety about the correct thing to say. With parents like hers, it was not surprising that embarrassment had become the strongest emotion in her life. Debbie's father, an Australian painter called Peter Hickmann, was a notorious bore. Patrick once heard him introduce an anecdote with the words, 'That reminds me of my best bouillabaisse story.' Half an hour later, Patrick could only count himself lucky that he was not listening to Peter's second-best bouillabaisse story.

Debbie's mother, whose neurotic resources made her resemble a battery-operated stick insect, had social ambitions which were not in her power to fulfill while Peter stood at her side telling his bouillabaisse stories. A well-known professional party planner, she was foolish enough to take her own advice. The brittle perfection of her entertainments turned to dust when human beings were introduced into the airless arena of her drawing room. Like a mountaineer expiring at base camp, she passed on her boots to Debbie, and with them the awesome responsibility: *to climb*. Mrs Hickmann was inclined to forgive Patrick the apparent purposelessness of his life and the sinister pallor of his complexion, when she considered that he had an income of one hundred thousand pounds a year, and came from a family which, although it had done nothing since, had seen the Norman invasion from the winning side. It was not perfect, but it would do. After all, Patrick was only twenty-two.

Meanwhile, Peter continued to weave life into anecdote and to describe grand incidents in his daughter's life to the fast-emptying bar of the Travellers Club where, after forty years of stiff opposition, he had been elected in a moment of weakness which all the members who had since been irradiated by his conversation bitterly regretted.

After Patrick had discouraged Debbie from coming round to see him, he set out for a walk through Hyde Park, tears stinging his eyes. It was a hot dry evening, full of pollen and dust. Sweat trickled down his ribs and broke out on his forehead. Over the Serpentine, a wisp of cloud dissolved in front of the sun, which sank, swollen and red, through a bruise of pollution. On the scintillating water yellow and blue boats bobbed up and down. Patrick stood still and watched a police car drive very fast along the path behind the boathouses. He vowed he would take no more heroin. This was the most important moment in his life and he must get it right. He had to get it right.

Patrick lit a Turkish cigarette and asked the stewardess for another glass of brandy. He was beginning to feel a little jumpy without any smack. The four Valiums he had stolen from Kay had helped him face breakfast, but now he could feel the onset of withdrawal, like a litter of drowning kittens in the sack of his stomach.

Kay was the American girl he had been having an affair with. Last night when he had wanted to bury himself in a woman's body, to affirm that, unlike his father, he was alive, he had chosen to see Kay. Debbie was beautiful (everybody said so), and she was clever (she said so herself), but he could imagine her clicking anxiously across the room, like a pair of chopsticks, and just then he needed a softer embrace.

Kay lived in a rented flat on the outskirts of Oxford, where she played the violin, kept cats, and worked on her Kafka thesis. She took a less complacent attitude towards Patrick's idleness than anyone else he knew. 'You have to sell yourself,' she used to say, 'just to get rid of the damned thing.'

Patrick disliked everything about Kay's flat. He knew she had not put the gold cherubs against the William Morris-styled wallpaper; on the other hand, she had not taken them down. In the dark corridor, Kay had come up to him, her thick brown hair falling on one shoulder, and her body draped in heavy grey silk. She had kissed him slowly, while her jealous cats scratched at the kitchen door.

Patrick had drunk the whisky and taken the Valium she had given him. Kay told him about her own dying parents. 'You have to start looking after them badly before you've got over the shock of how badly they looked after you,' she said. 'I had to drive my parents across the States last summer. My dad was dying of emphysema and my mother, who used to be a ferocious woman, was like a child after her stroke. I was barrelling along at eighty through Utah, looking for a bottle of oxygen, while my mother kept saying with her impoverished vocabulary, "Oh dear, oh my, Papa's not well. Oh my."'

Patrick imagined Kay's father sunk in the back of the car, his eyes glazed over with exhaustion and his lungs, like torn fishing nets, trawling vainly for air. How had his own father died? He had forgotten to ask.

Since his luminous remarks about 'that mental thing', Earl had been speaking about his 'whole variety of holdings' and his love for his family. His divorce had been 'hard on the kids', but he concluded with a chuckle, 'I've been diversifying, and I don't just mean in the business field.'

Patrick was grateful to be flying on Concorde. Not only would he be fresh for the ordeal of seeing his father's corpse, before it was cremated the next day, but he was also halving his conversation time with Earl. They ought to advertise. A simpering voiceover popped into his mind: 'It's because we care, not just for your physical comfort, but for your mental health, that we shorten your conversation with people like Earl Hammer.'

'You see, Paddy,' said Earl, 'I've made very considerable – I mean *big* – contributions to the Republican Party, and I could get just about any embassy I want. But I'm not interested in London or Paris: that's just social shit.'

Patrick drank his brandy in one gulp.

'What I want is a small Latin American or Central American country where the ambassador has control of the CIA on the ground.'

'On the ground,' echoed Patrick.

'That's right,' said Earl. 'But I have a dilemma at this point; a real hard one.' He was solemn again. 'My daughter is trying to make the national volleyball team and she has a series of real important games over the next year. Hell, I don't know whether to go for the embassy or root for my daughter.'

'Earl,' said Patrick earnestly, 'I don't think there's anything more important than being a good dad.'

Earl was visibly moved. 'I appreciate that advice, Paddy, I really do.'

The flight was coming to an end. Earl made some remarks about how you always met 'high-quality' people on Concorde. At the airport terminal Earl took the US citizens' channel, and Patrick headed for the Aliens'.

'Goodbye, friend,' shouted Earl with a big wave, 'see you around!'

'Every parting,' snarled Patrick under his breath, 'is a little death.'

2

'WHAT IS THE PURPOSE of your visit, sir? Business or pleasure?'

'Neither.'

'I'm sorry?' She was a pear-shaped, slug-coloured, shorthaired woman wearing big glasses and a dark blue uniform.

'I'm here to collect my father's corpse,' mumbled Patrick.

'I'm sorry, sir, I didn't catch that,' she said with official exasperation.

'*I'm here to collect my father's corpse,*' Patrick shouted slowly.

She handed back his passport. 'Have a nice day.'

The rage that Patrick had felt after passing through passport control eclipsed his usual terror of Customs (What if they stripped him? What if they saw his arms?).

And so here he was again, slumped in the back of a cab, in a seat often repaired with black masking tape, but still opening occasionally onto small craters of yellow foam, back in a nation that was dieting its way to immortality, while he still dieted his way in the opposite direction.

As his taxi bounced and squeaked along the freeway, Patrick started to register reluctantly the sensations of reentry into New York. There was of course a driver who spoke no English, and whose lugubrious photograph confirmed the suicidal gloom which the back of his neck could only hint at. The neighbouring lanes bore witness to the usual combination of excess and decay. Enormous battered cars with sloppy engines, and black-windowed limos, swarmed into the city, like flies on their favourite food. Patrick stared at the dented hubcap of an old white station wagon. It had seen so much, he reflected, and remembered nothing, like a slick amnesiac reeling in thousands of images and rejecting them instantly, spinning out its empty life under a paler wider sky.

The thought that had obsessed him the night before cut into his trance. It was intolerable: his father had cheated him again. The bastard had deprived him of the chance to transform his ancient terror and his unwilling admiration into contemptuous pity for the boring and toothless old man he had become. And yet Patrick found himself sucked towards his father's death by a stronger habit of emulation than he could reasonably bear. Death was always, of course, a *temptation*; but now it seemed like a temptation to obey. On top of its power to strike a decadent or defiant posture in the endless vaudeville of youth, on top of the familiar lure of raw violence and self-destruction, it had taken on the aspect of conformity, like going into the family business. Really, it had all the options covered.

Acre after acre of tombstones stretched out beside the freeway. Patrick thought of his favourite lines of poetry: 'Dead, long dead, / Long dead!' (How could you beat that?) 'And my heart is a handful of dust, / And the wheels go over my head, / And my bones are shaken with pain, / For into a shallow grave they are thrust, / Only a yard beneath the street,' something, something, 'enough to drive one mad.'

The slippery humming metal of the Williamsburg Bridge re-awakened him to his surroundings, but not for long. He felt queasy and nervous. Another withdrawal in a foreign hotel room; he knew the routine. Except that this was going to be the last time. Or *among* the last times. He laughed nervously. No, the bastards weren't going to get him. Concentration like a flame-thrower. No prisoners!

The trouble was that he always wanted smack, like wanting to get out of a wheelchair when the room was on fire. If you thought about it that much you might as well take it. His right leg twitched up and down rapidly. He folded his arms across his stomach and pinched the collar of his overcoat together. 'Fuck off,' he said out loud, 'just fuck off.'

Into the gorgeous streets. Blocks of light and shadow. Down the avenue, lights turned green all the way. Light and shadow, ticking like a metronome, as they surged over the curve of the earth.

It was late May, it was hot, and he really ought to take off his overcoat, but his overcoat was his defence against the thin shards of glass that passers-by slipped casually under his skin, not to mention the slow-motion explosion of shop windows, the bone-rattling thunder of subway trains, and the heartbreaking passage of each second, like a grain of sand trickling through the hourglass of his body. No, he would not take off his overcoat. Do you ask a lobster to disrobe?

He glanced up and saw that he was on Sixth Avenue. Forty-second Street, Forty-third Street, row after Mies van der Rohe. Who had said that? He couldn't remember. Other people's words drifted through his mind, like the tumbleweed across a windy desert in the opening shots of *They Came from Outer Space*.

And what about all the characters who inhabited him, as if he was a cheap hotel: Gift o' the Gab O'Connor and the Fat Man, and Mrs Garsington, and all the rest of them, longing to push him aside and have their say. Sometimes he felt like a television on which somebody else was changing the channels impatiently and very fast. Well, they could just fuck off as well. This time he was going to fall apart *silently*.

They were getting near the Pierre now. The land of the static electric shock. Doorknobs and lift buttons spitting sparks at a body which had generated its way through miles of thick carpet before forgetting to earth itself. It was here that he had begun his delirious decline on his last visit to New York. From a suite with as much chinoiserie as a person could be expected to take, and a view of the Park from far above the cry of traffic, he had slipped down, via the world-famous seediness of the Chelsea Hotel, and landed in a coffin-sized room at the bottom of a garbage-filled well shaft on Eighth Street, between C and D. From this vantage he had looked back with nostalgia on the hotel he had despised only a few weeks earlier for having a rat in its fridge.

Still, throughout this decline in his accommodation, Patrick had never spent less than five thousand dollars a week on heroin and cocaine. Ninety per cent of the drugs were for him and ten per cent for Natasha, a woman who remained an impenetrable mystery to him during the six months they lived together. The only thing he felt certain about was that she irritated him; but then, who didn't? He continually longed for an uncontaminated solitude, and when he got it he longed for it to stop.

'Hotel,' said the driver.

'About fucking time,' mumbled Patrick.

A grey-coated doorman lifted his cap and held out his hand, while a bellboy hurried out to fetch Patrick's bags. One welcome and two tips later Patrick was stalking sweatily through the long corridor which led to the reception. The tables in the Oval Room were occupied by pairs of lunching women, toying with plates of different-coloured lettuces and ignoring glasses of mineral water. Patrick caught sight of himself in a large gilt mirror, and noticed that, as usual, he looked rather overdressed and extremely ill. There was a disturbing contrast between the care with which the clothes had been assembled and the ease with which the face looked as if it might fall apart. His very long black overcoat, dark blue suit, and thin black and silver tie (bought by his father in the early sixties) seemed to be unrelated to the chaotic tangle of brown hair which surrounded his dead-white and shiny face. The face itself was in a spasm of contradiction. The full lips were pinched inward, the eyes reduced to narrow slits, the nose, which was permanently blocked, forced him to breathe through his open mouth and made him look rather imbecilic; and a frown concentrated his forehead into a vertical crease directly above the nose.

After he had registered, Patrick braced himself to clear as quickly as possible the long gauntlet of welcomes and tips that still lay between him and having a drink in his room. Someone took him to the lift, someone took him up in the lift (that long stale suspense, watching the numbers flicker up to thirty-nine), someone showed him how to turn on the television, someone put his suitcase down on the rack, someone pointed out the bathroom light, someone gave him his room key, and, at last, someone brought him a bottle of Jack Daniel's and a black bucket of frail ice cubes, and four glasses.

He poured himself a full glass over a few cubes of ice. The smell of the bourbon seemed to him infinitely subtle and poignant, and as he gulped down the first burning mouthful, standing by the window, looking out over Central Park, leafy and hot under a paler wider sky, he wanted to cry. It was so fucking beautiful. He felt his sadness and exhaustion fuse with the dissolving and sentimental embrace of the bourbon. It was a moment of catastrophic charm. How could he ever hope to give up drugs? They filled him with such intense emotion. The sense of power they gave him was, admittedly, rather subjective (ruling the world from under the bedcovers, until the milkman arrived and you thought he was a platoon of stormtroopers come to steal your drugs and splatter your brains across the wall), but then again, *life* was so subjective.

He really ought to go to the funeral parlour now, it would be appalling to miss the chance of seeing his father's corpse (perhaps he could rest his foot on it). Patrick giggled and put down his empty glass on the windowsill. He was not going to take any smack. 'I want to make that *absolutely* clear,' he squealed in the voice of Mr Muffet, his old chemistry teacher from school. Walk tall, that was his philosophy, *but get some downers first.* Nobody could give up everything at once, especially (sob, sob) at a time like this. He must go down into that pulsing, burgeoning, monstrous mass of vegetation, the Park, and score. The gaggle of black and Hispanic dealers who hung around the entrance to Central Park opposite his hotel recognized Patrick as a potential customer from some way off.

'Uppers! Downers! Check it out,' said a tall, bruised-looking black man. Patrick walked on.

A hollow-cheeked Hispanic with a scrawny beard jerked his jaw forward and said, 'Wot canna du for ju, my friend?'

'I got goo-ood stuff,' said another black man, wearing shades. '*Check it out.*'

'Have you got any Quaaludes?' drawled Patrick.

'Sure, I got some Quaaludes. I got Lemon 714s – how many you want?'

'How much?'

'Five dollars.'

'I'll take six. And maybe some speed,' Patrick added. This was what they called impulse shopping. Speed was the last thing he wanted, but he didn't like to buy a drug unless he had the capacity to contradict it.

'I got some Beauties, they're phar-ma-ceu-ti-cal.'

'You mean you made them yourself.'

'No, man, pharmaceutical mean they're goo-ood shit.'

'Three of those.'

'Ten dollars each.'

Patrick handed over sixty dollars and took the pills. By this time the other dealers had gathered round, impressed by the easy way that Patrick parted with money.

'Ju English, right?' said the Hispanic.

'Don't bother the man,' said Shades.

'Yes,' said Patrick, knowing what was coming next.

'You got free heroin over there, right?' said the bruised-looking black man.

'That's right,' said Patrick patriotically.

'One day I'm going to come over to Britain and get me some of that free smack,' the bruised-looking man said, looking relieved for a few seconds.

'You do that,' said Patrick, heading back up the steps to Fifth Avenue. 'Bye now.'

'You come back here tomorrow,' said Shades possessively.

'Yeah,' mumbled Patrick, running up the steps. He put the Quaalude in his mouth, summoned a little saliva, and managed to force the pill down. It was an important skill to be able to swallow a pill without anything to drink. People who needed a drink were intolerable, he reflected, hailing a cab.

'Madison Avenue and Eighty-second Street,' he said, realizing that the Quaalude, which was after all a large pill, was stuck halfway down his throat. As the cab sped up Madison Avenue, Patrick twisted his neck into various positions in an attempt to get the pill all the way down.

By the time they reached Frank E. MacDonald's Patrick was stretched out with his neck craned backwards and sideways over the edge of the seat, his hair touching the black rubber floor mat while he squeezed as much saliva as he could from the sides of his dry cheeks and swallowed furiously. The driver looked in the rear-view mirror. Another weirdo.

Patrick eventually dislodged the Quaalude from the ledge it had found just under his Adam's apple, and walked through the tall oak doors of the funeral parlour, dread and absurdity competing inside him. The young woman behind the curved oak counter with Doric half-columns set at either end of its inner panel wore a blue jacket and a grey silk blouse, like an air hostess for a flight into the Afterlife.

'I've come to see the corpse of David Melrose,' said Patrick coldly. She told him to step right into the elevator and go 'straight on up' to the third floor, as if he might be tempted to stop off and see some other corpses on the way.

The lift was a homage to French tapestry-making. Above the buttoned leather bench, on which the bereaved could pause before facing the corpse of their loved one, was an Arcadia of petit point where a courtier pretending to be a shepherd played a flute to a courtier pretending to be a shepherdess.

This was it, the big moment: the corpse of his chief enemy, the ruins of his creator, the body of his dead father; the great weight of all that was unsaid and would never have been said; the pressure to say it now, when there was nobody to hear, and to speak also on his father's behalf, in an act of self-division that might fissure the world and turn his body into a jigsaw puzzle. *This was it.*

The sound that greeted Patrick as the doors of the lift slid open made him wonder if George had organized a surprise party, but the idea was too grotesque, given the difficulty of procuring more than half a dozen people *worldwide* who knew his father at all well and still liked him. He stepped out onto the landing and saw, beyond two Corinthian pillars, a panelled room full of gaily dressed elderly strangers. Men in every variety of lightweight tartan, and women in big white and yellow hats, were drinking cocktails and clutching each other's arms. At the back of the room, into which he wandered uncomprehendingly, was an open tilted coffin lined with white satin, and containing a punctiliously dressed, diminutive man with a diamond tie pin, snow-white hair, and a black suit. On a table beside him Patrick saw a stack of cards saying, 'In Loving Memory of Hermann Newton.' Death was no doubt an overwhelming experience, but it must be even more powerful than he had imagined if it could transform his father into a small Jew with so many amusing new friends.

Patrick's heart thudded into action. He spun round and stormed back to the lift, where he received a static electric shock when he pushed the call button. 'I can't fucking believe it,' he snarled, kicking a Louis XV-styled chair. The lift doors opened to reveal a fat old man with sagging grey flesh, wearing a pair of extraordinary Bermuda shorts and a yellow T-shirt. Hermann had obviously left a No Mourning clause in his will. Or maybe people were just happy to see him dead, thought Patrick. Beside the fat man stood his blowsy wife, also in beachwear, and next to her was the young woman from the reception desk.

'Wrong fucking corpse,' said Patrick, glaring at her.

'Oh, ho. Whoa there,' said the fat man, as if Patrick was over-stating his case.

'Try again,' said Patrick, ignoring the old couple as they waddled past.

He gave the receptionist his special melt-down-and-die stare, with eyebeams as heavy as scaffolding shooting across the space between them and pouring radioactivity into her brain. She seemed unperturbed.

'I'm certain we don't have another party in the building at the moment,' she said.

'I don't want to go to a party,' said Patrick. 'I want to see my father.'

When they had reached the ground floor, the receptionist walked over to the counter where Patrick had first seen her and showed him her list of 'parties' in the building. 'There isn't any name on here except Mr Newton's,' she said smugly, 'that's why I sent you to the Cedar Suite.'

'Perhaps my father isn't dead at all,' said Patrick, leaning towards her; 'that really would be a shock. Maybe it was just a cry for help, what do you think?'

'I'd better go check with our director,' she said, retreating. 'Excuse me just one moment.' She opened a door concealed in one of the panels and slipped behind it.

Patrick leaned against the counter, breathless with rage, among the black and white marble diamonds of the lobby floor. Just like the floor of that hall in Eaton Square. He had only been as high as the old lady's hand. She had clutched her cane, her prominent blue veins flowing down her fingers into a sapphire ring. Blood arrested and clarified. The old lady talked to his mother about their committee, while Patrick got lost in the feeling that he was making the resemblance happen. Now there were days when everything resembled everything else, and the smallest excuse for comparison made one object consume another in a bulimic feast.

What the fuck was going on? Why were his father's *remains* so hard to find? He had no trouble in discovering them in himself, it was only Frank E. MacDonald that was experiencing this difficulty. While Patrick cackled hysterically at this thought, a bald homosexual with a moustache, and a strong sense of the restrained flair he brought with him into the mortuary business, emerged from the panelled door and clicked his way across the black and white diamonds of the lobby floor. Without apology, he told Patrick to step right this way and led him back into the elevator. He pressed the button for the second floor, less near to heaven than Mr Newton, but without the sound of a cocktail party. In the silence of that discreetly lit corridor, the director mincing ahead of him, Patrick began to realize that he had wasted his defences on an impostor and, exhausted by the farce of Mr Newton's wake, he was now dangerously vulnerable to the impact of his father's corpse.

'This is the room,' said the director, playing with his cuff. 'I'll leave you to be alone with him,' he purred.

Patrick glanced into the small, richly carpeted room. *Fucking hell*. What was his father doing in a coffin? He nodded to the director and waited outside the room, feeling a wave of madness rise up inside him. What did it mean that he was about to see his father's corpse? What was it meant to mean? He hovered in the doorway. His father's head was lying towards him and he could not yet see the face, just the grey curls of his hair. They had covered the body with tissue paper. It lay in the coffin, like a present someone had put down halfway through unwrapping.

'It's Dad!' muttered Patrick incredulously, clasping his hands together and turning to an imaginary friend. 'You *shouldn't* have!'

He stepped into the room, filled with dread again, but driven by curiosity. The face, alas, had not been covered in tissue, and Patrick was amazed by the nobility of his father's countenance. Those looks, which had deceived so many people because they were disconnected from his father's personality, were all the more impertinent now that the disconnection was complete. His father looked as if death was an enthusiasm he did not share, but with which he had been surrounded like a priest at a boxing match.

Those bruised, flickering eyes that assessed every weakness, like a teller's fingers counting a stack of banknotes, were now closed. That underlip, so often thrust out before a burst of anger, now contradicted the proud expression into which his features had relaxed. It had been torn open (he must have still been wearing his false teeth) by rage and protest and the consciousness of death.

However closely he tracked his father's life – and he felt the influence of this habit like a pollution in his bloodstream, a poison he had not put there himself, impossible to purge or leech without draining the patient – however closely he tried to imagine the lethal combination of pride and cruelty and sadness which had dominated his father's life, and however much he longed for it not to dominate his own life, Patrick could never follow him into that final moment when he had known he was about to die and he had been right. Patrick had known he was about to die often enough, but he had always been wrong.

Patrick felt a strong desire to take his father's lip in both hands and tear it like a piece of paper, along the gash already made by his teeth.

No, not that. He would not have that thought. The obscene necessity of going over the curtain pole. Not that, he would not have that thought. Nobody should do that to anybody else. He could not be that person. Bastard.

Patrick growled, his teeth bared and clenched. He punched the side of the coffin with his knuckles to bring him round. How should he play this scene from the movie of his life? He straightened himself and smiled contemptuously.

'Dad,' he said in his most cloying American accent, 'you were so fucking sad, man, and now you're trying to make me sad too.' He choked insincerely. 'Well,' he added in his own voice, 'bad luck.'

3

ANNE EISEN TURNED INTO her building, carrying a box of cakes from Le Vrai Pâtisserie. If it had been La Vraie Pâtisserie, as Victor never tired of pointing out, it would have been even *vraie*-er, or *plus vraie*, she thought, smiling at Fred the doorman. Fred looked like a boy who had inherited his older brother's school uniform. The gold-braided sleeves of his brown coat hung down to the knuckles of his big pale hands, whereas his trousers, defeated by the bulk of his buttocks and thighs, flapped high above the pale blue nylon socks that clung to his ankles.

'Hi, Fred,' said Anne.

'Hello, Mrs Eisen. Can I help you with your packages?' said Fred, waddling over.

'Thanks,' said Anne, stooping theatrically, 'but I can still manage two millefeuilles and a pain aux raisins. Say, Fred,' she added, 'I have a friend coming over round four o'clock. He's young and sort of ill-looking. Be gentle with him, his father just died.'

'Oh, gee, I'm sorry,' said Fred.

'I don't think *he* is,' said Anne, 'although he may not know that yet.'

Fred tried to look as if he hadn't heard. Mrs Eisen was a real nice lady, but sometimes she said the weirdest things.

Anne got into the lift and pressed the button for the eleventh floor. In a few weeks it would all be over. No more eleventh floor, no more of Professor Wilson's cane chairs and his African masks and his big abstract I-think-it's-good-but-his-work-never-really-caught-on painting in the drawing room.

Jim Wilson, whose rich wife enabled him to exhibit his rather old-fashioned liberal wares on Park Avenue, no less, had been 'visiting' Oxford since October, while Victor visited Columbia in exchange. Every time Anne and Victor went to a party – and they almost never stopped – she'd needle him about being the visiting professor. Anne and Victor had an 'open' marriage. 'Open', as in 'open wound' or 'open rebellion' or indeed 'open marriage', was not always a good thing, but now that Victor was seventy-six it hardly seemed worth divorcing him. Besides, somebody had to look after him.

Anne got out of the lift and opened the door to apartment 11E, reaching for the light switch, next to the Red Indian blanket that hung in the hall. What the hell was she going to say to Patrick? Although he had turned into a surly and malicious adolescent, and was now a drug-addled twenty-two-year-old, she could still remember him sitting on the stairs at Lacoste when he was five, and she still felt responsible – she knew it was absurd – for not managing to get his mother away from that gruesome dinner party.

Oddly enough, the delusions which had enabled her to marry Victor had really started on that evening. During the next few months Victor immersed himself in the creation of his new book, *Being, Knowing, and Judging*, so easily (and yet so wrongly!) confused with its predecessor, *Thinking, Knowing, and Judging*. Victor's claim that he wanted to keep his students 'on their toes' by giving his books such similar titles had not altogether extinguished Anne's doubts or those of his publisher. Nevertheless, like a masterful broom, his new book had scattered the dust long settled on the subject of identity, and swept it into exciting new piles.

At the end of this creative surge Victor had proposed to Anne. She had been thirty-four and, although she didn't know it at the time, her admiration for Victor was at its peak. She had accepted him, not only because he was imbued with that mild celebrity which is all a living philosopher can hope for, but also because she believed that Victor was a good man.

What the hell was she going to say to Patrick, she wondered as she took a spinach-green majolica plate from Barbara's fabulous collection and arranged the cakes on its irregularly glazed surface.

It was no use pretending to Patrick that she had liked David Melrose. Even after his divorce from Eleanor, when he was poor and ill, David had been no more endearing than a chained Alsatian. His life was an unblemished failure and his isolation terrifying to imagine, but he still had a smile like a knife; and if he had tried to learn (talk about a mature student!) how to please people, his efforts were faintly repulsive to anyone who knew his real nature.

As she leaned over an annoyingly low Moroccan table in the drawing room, Anne felt her dark glasses slip from the top of her head. Perhaps her yellow cotton dress was a little too upbeat for the occasion, but what the hell? Patrick had not seen her recently enough to tell that she had dyed her hair. No doubt Barbara Wilson would have let it go naturally grey, but Anne had to appear on television tomorrow night to talk about 'The New Woman'. While she had been trying to find out what on earth a New Woman might be, she had got a New hairstyle and bought a New dress. It was research and she wanted expenses.

Twenty to four. Dead time until he arrived. Time to light a lethal, cancer-causing cigarette, time to fly in the face of the Surgeon General's advice – as if you could trust a man who was a surgeon and a general at the same time. She called that working both sides of the street. There was no disguising it, though, she *did* feel guilty, but then she felt guilty putting three drops of bath essence into the water instead of two. So what the hell?

Anne had barely lit her mild, light, mentholated, almost entirely pointless cigarette, when the buzzer rang from downstairs.

'Hi, Fred.'

'Oh, hello, Mrs Eisen: Mr Melrose is here.'

'Well, I guess you'd better send him up,' she said, wondering if there wasn't some way they could ever vary this conversation.

Anne went into the kitchen, switched on the kettle, and sprinkled some tea leaves into the Japanese teapot with the wobbly overarching rattan handle.

The doorbell interrupted her and she hurried out of the kitchen to open the front door. Patrick was standing with his back to her in a long black overcoat.

'Hello, Patrick,' she said.

'Hello,' he mumbled, trying to squeeze past her. But she took him by the shoulders and embraced him warmly.

'I'm so sorry,' she said.

Patrick would not yield to this embrace, but slid away like a wrestler breaking an opponent's grip.

'I'm sorry too,' he said, bowing slightly. 'Being late is a bore, but arriving early is unforgivable. Punctuality is one of the smaller vices I've inherited from my father; it means I'll never really be chic.' He paced up and down the drawing room with his hands in his overcoat pockets. '*Unlike* this apartment,' he sneered. 'Who was lucky enough to swap this place for your nice house in London?'

'Victor's opposite number at Columbia, Jim Wilson.'

'God, imagine having an opposite number instead of always being one's own opposite number,' said Patrick.

'Do you want some tea?' asked Anne with a sympathetic sigh.

'Hum,' said Patrick. 'I wonder if I could have a real drink as well? For me it's already nine in the evening.'

'For you it's always nine in the evening,' said Anne. 'What do you want? I'll fix it for you.'

'No, I'll do it,' he said, 'you won't make it strong enough.'

'OK,' said Anne, turning towards the kitchen, 'the drinks are on the Mexican millstone.'

The millstone was engraved with feathered warriors, but it was the bottle of Wild Turkey which commanded Patrick's attention. He poured some into a tall glass and knocked back another Quaalude with the first gulp, refilling the glass immediately. After seeing his father's corpse, he had gone to the Forty-fourth Street branch of the Morgan Guaranty Bank and collected three thousand dollars in cash which now bulged inside an orange-brown envelope in his pocket.

He checked the pills again (lower right pocket) and then the envelope (inside left) and then the credit cards (outer left). This nervous action, which he sometimes performed every few minutes, was like a man crossing himself before an altar – the Drugs; the Cash; and the Holy Ghost of Credit.

He had already taken a second Quaalude after the visit to the bank, but he still felt groundless and desperate and overwrought. Perhaps a third one was overdoing it, but overdoing it was his occupation.

'Does this happen to you?' asked Patrick, striding into the kitchen with renewed energy. 'You see a millstone, and the words "round my neck" ring up like the price on an old cash register. Isn't it humiliating,' he said, taking some ice cubes, 'God, I love these ice machines, they're the best thing about America so far – humiliating that one's thoughts have all been prepared in advance by these idiotic mechanisms?'

'The idiotic ones aren't good,' Anne agreed, 'but there's no need for the cash register to come up with something cheap.'

'If your mind works like a cash register, anything you come up with is bound to be cheap.'

'You obviously don't shop at Le Vrai Pâtisserie,' said Ann, carrying the cakes and tea into the drawing room.

'If we can't control our conscious responses, what chance do we have against the influences we haven't recognized?'

'None at all,' said Anne cheerfully, handing him a cup of tea.

Patrick let loose a curt laugh. He felt detached from what he had been saying. Perhaps the Quaaludes were beginning to make a difference.

'Do you want a cake?' said Anne. 'I bought them to remind us of Lacoste. They're as French as . . . as French letters.'

'That French,' gasped Patrick, taking one of the millefeuilles out of politeness. As he picked it up, the cake oozed cream from its flanks, like pus dribbling from a wound. Christ, he thought, this cake is completely *out of control*.

'It's *alive!*' he said out loud, squeezing the millefeuille rather too hard. Cream spurted out and dropped on to the elaborate brass surface of the Moroccan table. His fingers were sticky with icing. 'Oh, I'm sorry,' he mumbled, putting the cake down.

Anne handed him a napkin. She noticed that Patrick was becoming increasingly clumsy and slurred. Before he had arrived she was dreading the inevitable conversation about his father; now she was worried that it might not take place.

'Have you been to see your father yet?' she asked outright.

'I did see him,' said Patrick without hesitation. 'I thought he was at his best in a coffin – so much less difficult than usual.' He grinned at her disarmingly.

Anne smiled at him faintly, but Patrick needed no encouragement.

'When I was young,' he said, 'my father used to take us to restaurants. I say "restaurants" in the plural, because we never stormed in and out of less than three. Either the menu took too long to arrive, or a waiter struck my father as intolerably stupid, or the wine list disappointed him. I remember he once held a bottle of red wine upside down while the contents gurgled out onto the carpet. "How dare you bring me this filth?" he shouted. The waiter was so frightened that instead of throwing him out, he brought more wine.'

'So you liked being with him in a place he didn't complain about.'

'Exactly,' said Patrick. 'I couldn't believe my luck, and for a while I expected him to sit up in his coffin, like a vampire at sunset, and say, "The service here is intolerable." Then we would have had to go to three or four other funeral parlours. Mind you, the service *was* intolerable. They sent me to the wrong corpse.'

'The wrong corpse!' exclaimed Anne.

'Yes, I wound up at a jaunty Jewish cocktail party given for a Mr Hermann Newton. I wish I could have stayed; they seemed to be having such fun . . .'

'What an appalling story,' said Anne, lighting a cigarette. 'I'll bet they give courses in Bereavement Counselling.'

'Of course,' said Patrick, letting out another quick hollow laugh and sinking back into his armchair. He could definitely feel the influence of the Quaaludes now. The alcohol had brought out the best in them, like the sun coaxing open the petals of a flower, he reflected tenderly.

'I'm sorry?' he said. He had not heard Anne's last question.

'Is he being cremated?' she repeated.

'Yes, that's right,' said Patrick. 'I gather that when people are cremated one never really gets their ashes, just some communal rakings from the bottom of the oven. As you can imagine, I regard that as good news. Ideally, *all* the ashes would belong to somebody else, but we don't live in a perfect world.'

Anne had given up wondering whether he was sorry about

his father's death, and had started wishing he was a little sorrier. His venomous remarks, although they could not affect David, made Patrick look so ill he might have been waiting to die from a snakebite.

Patrick closed his eyes slowly and, after a very long time, slowly opened them again. The whole operation took about half an hour. Another half an hour elapsed while he licked his dry and fascinatingly sore lips. He was really getting something off that last Quaalude. His blood was hissing like a television screen after closedown. His hands were like dumbbells, like dumbbells in his hands. Everything folding inward and growing heavier.

'Hello there!' Anne called.

'I'm so sorry,' said Patrick, leaning forward with what he imagined was a charming smile. 'I'm awfully tired.'

'Maybe you ought to go to bed.'

'No, no, no. Let's not exaggerate.'

'You could lie down for a few hours,' Anne suggested, 'and then have dinner with Victor and me. We're going to a party afterward, given by some ghastly Long Island Anglophiles. Just your kind of thing.'

'It's sweet of you, but I really can't face too many strangers at the moment,' said Patrick, playing his bereavement card a little too late to convince Anne.

'You should come along,' she coaxed. 'I'm sure it will be an example of "unashamed luxury".'

'I can't imagine what that means,' said Patrick sleepily.

'Let me give you the address anyhow,' Anne insisted. 'I don't like the idea of your being alone too much.'

'Fine. Write it down for me before I go.'

He knew he had to take some speed soon or involuntarily take up Anne's offer to 'lie down for a few hours'. He did not want to swallow a whole Beauty, because it would take him on a fifteen-hour megalomaniac odyssey, and he didn't want to be that conscious. On the other hand, he had to get rid of the feeling that he had been dropped into a pool of slowly drying concrete.

'Where's the loo?'

Anne told him how to get there, and Patrick waded across the carpet in the direction she had indicated. Once he had locked the bathroom door Patrick felt a familiar sense of security. Inside a bathroom he could give in to the obsession with his own physical and mental state which was so often compromised by the presence of other people or the absence of a well-lit mirror. Most of the 'quality time' in his life had been spent in a bathroom. Injecting, snorting, swallowing, stealing, overdosing; examining his pupils, his arms, his tongue, his stash.

'O bathrooms!' he intoned, spreading out his arms in front of the mirror. 'Thy medicine cabinets pleaseth me mightily! Thy towels moppeth up the rivers of my blood . . .' He petered out as he took the Black Beauty from his pocket. He was just going to take enough to function, just enough to . . . what had he been about to say? He couldn't remember. My God, it was short-term memory loss again, the Professor Moriarty of drug abuse, interrupting and then obliterating the precious sensations one went to such trouble to secure.

'Inhuman fiend,' he muttered.

The black capsule eventually came apart and he emptied half the contents onto one of the Portuguese tiles around the basin. Taking out one of his new hundred-dollar notes, he rolled it into a tight tube and sniffed up the small heap of white powder from the tile.

His nose stung and his eyes watered slightly but, refusing to be distracted, Patrick resealed the capsule, wrapped it in a Kleenex, put it back in his pocket and then, for no reason he could identify, almost against his will, he took it out again, emptied the rest of the powder onto a tile and sniffed it up as well. The effects wouldn't last so long this way, he argued, inhaling deeply through his nose. It was too sordid to take half of anything. Anyhow, his father had just died and he was entitled to be confused. The main thing, the heroic feat, the proof of his seriousness and his samurai status in the war against drugs, was that he hadn't taken any heroin.

Patrick leaned forward and checked his pupils in the mirror. They had definitely dilated. His heartbeat had accelerated. He felt invigorated, he felt refreshed, in fact he felt rather aggressive. It was as if he had never taken a drink or a drug, he was back in complete control, the lighthouse beams of speed cutting through the thick night of the Quaaludes and the alcohol and the jet lag.

'And,' he said, clasping his lapels with mayoral solemnity, 'last but not least, through the dark shadow, if I might put it thus, of our grief for the passing away of David Melrose.'

How long had he been in the bathroom? It seemed like a lifetime. The fire brigade would probably be forcing the door down soon. Patrick started to clear up hastily. He didn't want to put the shell of the Black Beauty into the waste-paper basket (paranoia!) and so he forced the two halves of the empty capsule down the basin plughole. How was he going to explain his reanimated state to Anne? He splashed some cold water on his face and left it ostentatiously dripping. There was only one thing left to do: that authentic-sounding flush with which every junkie leaves a bathroom, hoping to deceive the audience that crowds his imagination.

'For God's sake,' said Anne when he got back to the drawing room, 'why don't you dry your face?'

'I was just reviving myself with a little cold water.'

'Oh yeah?' said Anne. 'What kind of water was that?'

'Very refreshing water,' he said, wiping his sweaty palms on his trousers as he sat down. 'Which reminds me,' he said, getting up immediately, 'I'd love another drink if I may.'

'Sure,' said Anne resignedly. 'By the way, I forgot to ask, how is Debbie?'

The question filled Patrick with the horror which assailed him when he was asked to consider another person's feelings. How was Debbie? How the fuck should he know? It was hard enough to rescue himself from the avalanche of his own feelings, without allowing the gloomy St Bernard of his attention to wander into other fields. On the other hand the amphetamines had given him an urgent desire to talk and he couldn't ignore the question entirely.

'Well,' he said from the other side of the room, 'she's following in her mother's footsteps, and writing an article about great hostesses. Teresa Hickmann's footsteps, invisible to most people, glow in the dark for her dutiful daughter. Still, we should be grateful that she hasn't modelled her conversational style on her father's.'

Patrick was momentarily lost again in the contemplation of his psychological state. He felt lucid, but not about anything, except his own lucidity. His thoughts, anticipating themselves hopelessly, stuttered in the starting blocks, and brought his feeling of fluency dangerously close to silence. 'But you haven't told me,' he said, tearing himself away from this intriguing mental stammer and at the same time taking his revenge on Anne for asking him about Debbie, 'how is Victor?'

'Oh, fine. He's a grand old man now, a role he's been training for all his life. He gets a lot of attention and he's lecturing on Identity, which, as he says, he can do with his eyes closed. Did you ever read *Being, Knowing, and Judging?*'

'No,' said Patrick.

'Well, I must give you a copy, then,' said Anne, getting up and going to the bookshelves. She took out what looked to Patrick like a tiresomely thick volume from among half a dozen copies of the same book. He liked slim books which he could slip into his overcoat pocket and leave there unread for months. What was the point of a book if you couldn't carry it around with you as a theoretical defence against boredom?

'It's about identity, is it?' he asked suspiciously.

'All you've ever wanted to know but never dared to formulate precisely,' said Anne.

'Goody,' said Patrick, getting up restlessly. He had to pace, he had to move through space, otherwise the world had a dangerous tendency to flatten itself and he felt like a fly crawling up a windowpane looking for a way out of its translucent prison. Anne, thinking he had come to fetch it, handed him the book.

'Oh, eh, thank you,' he said, leaning over to kiss her quickly, 'I'll read it very soon.'

He tried to stuff the book into his overcoat pocket. He had *known* it wasn't going to fit. It was completely fucking useless. Now he had to carry this stupid fat book round with him everywhere. He felt a wave of violent rage. He stared intensely at a waste-paper basket (once a Somalian water jug) and imagined the book spinning towards it like a Frisbee.

'I really ought to be going now,' he said curtly.

'Really? Won't you stay to say hello to Victor?'

'No, I must go,' he said impatiently.

'OK, but let me give you Samantha's address.'

'What?'

'The party.'

'Oh, yes. I doubt I'll come,' said Patrick.

Anne wrote down the address on a piece of paper and handed it to Patrick. 'There you are.'

'Thank you,' said Patrick abruptly, flicking up the collar of his overcoat. 'I'll call you tomorrow.'

'Or see you tonight.'

'Maybe.'

He turned around and hurried towards the door. He had to get outside. His heart seemed to be about to leap out of his chest, like a jack-in-the-box, and he felt that he could only force the lid down for a few seconds more.

'Goodbye,' he called from the door.

'Goodbye,' said Anne.

Down in the sluggish airless lift, past the fat moronic door-man, and into the street. The shock of standing again under the wide pale sky, completely exposed. This must be what the oyster feels when the lemon juice falls.

Why had he left the shelter of Anne's flat? And so rudely. Now she would hate him forever. Everything he did was wrong.

Patrick looked down the avenue. It was like the opening shot of a documentary on overpopulation. He walked down the street, imagining the severed heads of passers-by rolling into the gutter in his wake.

4

HOW COULD HE THINK his way out of the problem when the problem was the way he thought, Patrick wondered, not for the first time, as he slipped reluctantly out of his overcoat and handed it to a brilliantined red-jacketed waiter.

Eating was only a temporary solution. But then all solutions were temporary, even death, and nothing gave him more faith in the existence of an afterlife than the inexorable sarcasm of Fate. No doubt suicide would turn out to be the violent preface to yet another span of nauseating consciousness, of diminishing spirals and tightening nooses, and memories like shrapnel tearing all day long through his flesh. Who could guess what exquisite torments lay ahead in the holiday camps of eternity? It almost made one grateful to be alive.

Only behind a waterfall of brutal and pleasurable sensations, thought Patrick, accepting the leather-clad menu without bothering to glance up, could he hide from the bloodhounds of his conscience. There, in the cool recess of the rock, behind that heavy white veil, he would hear them yelping and snarling confusedly on the river bank, but at least they couldn't tear out his throat with the fury of their reproach. After all, the trail he'd left was not hard to follow. It was littered with the evidence of wasted time and hopeless longing, not to mention those bloodstained shirts, and the syringes whose spikes he had bent in a fit of disgust and then unbent again for one last fix. Patrick drew in his breath sharply and folded his arms over his chest.

'A dry martini. Straight up, with a twist,' he drawled. 'And I'm ready to order.'

A waiter was coming right on over to take his order. Everything was under control.

Most people who were withdrawing and speeding, jet-lagged and cudgelled by Quaaludes, might have lost their interest in food, but Patrick found that all his appetites were operational at all times, even when his loathing of being touched gave his desire for sex a theoretical complexion.

He could remember Johnny Hall saying indignantly of a girlfriend he had recently thrown out, 'She was the kind of girl who came over and ruffled your hair when you'd just had a fix of coke.' Patrick had howled at the horror of such a tactless act. When a man is feeling as empty and fragile as a pane of glass, he does not want to have his hair ruffled. There could be no negotiation between people who thought that cocaine was a vaguely naughty and salacious drug and the intravenous addict who knew that it was an opportunity to experience the arctic landscape of pure terror.

That terror was the price he had to pay for the first heartbreaking wave of pleasure when consciousness seemed to burst out, like white blossoms, along the branches of every nerve. And all his scattered thoughts came rushing together, like loose iron filings as a magnet is held over them and draws them into the shape of a rose. Or – he must stop thinking about it – or like a solution of saturated copper sulphate under the microscope, when it suddenly transforms and crystals break out everywhere on its surface.

He must stop thinking about it – and do it. No! And think

about something else. His father's corpse, for instance. Would that be an improvement? It would get rid of the problem of desire, but hatred could be compulsive too.

Ah, here was the dry martini. If not the cavalry, at least some more ammunition. Patrick drained the cold unctuous liquid in one gulp.

'Would you care for another one, sir?'

'Yes,' said Patrick brusquely.

A more senior waiter in a dinner jacket came over to take Patrick's order.

'Tartare de Saumon Cru, followed by the Steak Tartare,' said Patrick, taking an innocent pleasure in saying 'tartare' twice and pleased to be ordering two adult forms of baby food, already cut up and squished together for him.

A third waiter, with a golden bunch of grapes in his lapel, and a large golden wine-tasting cup dangling from a chain around his neck, was only too ready to bring Patrick a bottle of Corton Charlemagne straight away and to open a bottle of Ducru-Beaucaillou for later on. Everything was under control.

No, he mustn't think about it, or indeed about anything, and especially not about heroin, because heroin was the only thing that really worked, the only thing that stopped him scampering around in a hamster's wheel of unanswerable questions. Heroin was the cavalry. Heroin was the missing chair leg, made with such precision that it matched every splinter of the break. Heroin landed purring at the base of his skull, and wrapped itself darkly around his nervous system, like a black cat curling up on its favourite cushion. It was as soft and rich as the throat of a wood pigeon, or the splash of sealing wax onto a page, or a handful of gems slipping from palm to palm.

The way other people felt about love, he felt about heroin, and he felt about love the way other people felt about heroin: that it was a dangerous and incomprehensible waste of time. What could he say to Debbie? 'Although you know that my hatred for my father, and my love for drugs, are the most important relationships in my life, I want you to know that you come in third.' What woman would not be proud to be 'among the medals' in such a contest?

'Oh, for fuck's sake shut up,' mumbled Patrick out loud, drinking his second dry martini with as little restraint as the first. If things went on this way he would have to call Pierre, his truly wonderful New York dealer. No! He wasn't going to do it, he had sworn that he wasn't going to do it. 555–1726. The number might as well have been tattooed on his wrist. He hadn't rung it since September, eight months ago, but he would never forget the bowel-loosening excitement of those seven digits.

Golden Grapes was back, peeling the heavy yellow lead from the neck of the Corton Charlemagne, and cradling the bottle of claret, while Patrick studied the picture of a white chateau under a flat gold sky. Perhaps with these consolations he would not have to score after dinner, thought Patrick sceptically, sucking a sample of Corton Charlemagne into his mouth.

The first taste made him break into a grin of recognition, like a man who has sighted his lover at the end of a crowded platform. Raising the glass again, he took a large gulp of the pale yellow wine, held it in his mouth for a few seconds, and then let it slide down his throat. Yes, it worked, it still worked. Some things never let him down.

He closed his eyes and the taste rippled over him like an hallucination. Cheaper wine would have buried him in fruit, but the grapes he imagined now were mercifully artificial, like earrings of swollen yellow pearls. He pictured the long sinewy shoots of the vine, dragging him down into the heavy reddish soil. Traces of iron and stone and earth and rain flashed across his palate and tantalized him like shooting stars. Sensations long wrapped in a bottle now unfurled like a stolen canvas.

Some things never let him down. It made him want to cry.

'Would you care to taste the Do-crew Bo-ca-u?'

'Yes,' said Patrick.

Golden Grapes poured the red wine into a ludicrously large glass. Even the smell of it made Patrick see things. Glistening granite. Cobwebs. Gothic cellars.

'That's fine,' he said, without bothering to taste it. 'Pour some now, I'll drink it later.'

Patrick sank back in his chair. Now that the wine distraction was over, the same question returned: would he go to his dealer after dinner, or to his hotel? Perhaps he could go to see Pierre socially. Patrick yelped with laughter at the absurdity of this pretext, but at the same time he felt a tremendous sentimental desire to see the demented Frenchman again. In many ways Pierre was the person Patrick felt closest to.

Pierre had spent eight years in a lunatic asylum under the misapprehension that he was an egg. 'For eight fucking years, man,' he would say, speaking very rapidly in a strong French accent, 'I thought I was an egg. *Je croyais que j'étais un œuf* – it's no fucking joke.' During this time his deserted body was fed, moved, washed, and clothed by nurses who had no idea that they were ministering to an egg. Pierre was let free to shoot about the world on unfettered voyages, in a state of enlightenment which did not require the crass mediation of words and senses. 'I understood everything,' he would say, glaring at Patrick defiantly. '*J'avais une conscience totale.*'

On these voyages, Pierre would occasionally stop by his hospital room and hover with pity and contempt over the as yet unhatched egg of his body. However, after eight years he realized that his body was dying of neglect.

'I had to force myself back into my fucking body; it was horrible. *J'avais un dégoût total.*'

Patrick was fascinated. It reminded him of Lucifer's disgust when he had to squeeze himself into the clammy and confining rings of the serpent's body.

One day the nurses came in with their sponges and their baby food, and found Pierre weak but impatient, sitting on the edge of his bed after almost a decade of inertia and silence.

'OK, I go now,' he snapped.

Tests showed that he was perfectly lucid, perhaps too lucid, and so they discharged him from the hospital with relief.

Only a perpetual flow of heroin and cocaine could now sustain a coarse version of his former glorious insanity. He hovered, but not as lightly as before, on the margins between his body and his fatal nostalgia for disembodiment. In his arm a wound like a volcano cone, a scabrous mound of dried blood and scar tissue, rose up from the soft hollow opposite his elbow. It enabled him to drop the thin spike of his insulin syringes vertically into the vein, never digging for a hit, but leaving open this access to his bloodstream, like an emergency runway, always ready for another speedball to relieve the horror of his incarceration in a jaundiced and inhospitable body he could hardly call his own.

Pierre's routine was perfectly regular. He stayed awake for two and a half days and then, after a big shot of heroin, slept or at least rested for eighteen hours. During his waking periods he sold drugs curtly and efficiently, allowing most of his customers no more than ten minutes in his black-and-white apartment. He also saved himself the inconvenience of people dying in his bathroom by banning injections, a prohibition he soon lifted for Patrick. Throughout the last summer Patrick had tried to keep to the same sleep patterns as Pierre. They often stayed up all night, sitting either side of the horizontal mirror Pierre used as a table, stripped to the waist to save themselves the trouble of rolling their sleeves up and down, shooting up every quarter of an hour and, as they poured with chemical-smelling sweat, talking about their favourite subjects: how to achieve perfect disembodiment; how to witness their own deaths; how to stay in the borderlands, undefined by the identities which their histories tried to thrust upon them; how dishonest and shallow all the straight people were; and, of course, how they could give up drugs if they really wanted to, a condition that had not so far afflicted either of them for very long. Fucking hell, thought Patrick, draining his third glass of white wine and immediately reloading it from the dripping bottle. He *must* stop thinking about it.

With a father like his (sob, sob), Authority Figures and Role Models had always been a problem, but in Pierre he had at last found someone whose example he could follow with unqualified enthusiasm, and whose advice he could bear to take. At least until Pierre had tried to limit him to two grams of coke a day instead of the seven Patrick regarded as indispensable.

'You're fucking crazy, man,' Pierre had shouted at him, 'you go for the rush every time. You kill yourself that way.'

This argument had marred the end of the summer, but in any case it had been time to get rid of the inflamed rashes that covered Patrick's entire body and the burning white ulcers that had suddenly sprouted throughout his mouth, throat, and stomach, and so he had returned to England a few days later to check into his favourite clinic.

'Oh, *les beaux jours*,' he sighed, wolfing down his raw salmon in a few breathless mouthfuls. He drank the last of the white wine, indifferent now to its taste.

Who else was in this ghastly restaurant? Extraordinary that he hadn't looked before; or not so extraordinary, in fact. They wouldn't be calling him in to solve the Problem of Other Minds, although of course the people, like Victor, who thought it was a problem in the first place were famous for being entirely absorbed in the workings of their own minds. Strange coincidence.

He swivelled his eyes around the room with reptilian coldness. He hated them all, every single one, especially that incredibly fat man sitting with the blonde. He must have paid her to mask her disgust at being in his company.

'God, you're repulsive,' muttered Patrick. 'Have you ever considered going on a diet? Yes, that's right, a diet, or hasn't it crossed your mind that you're quite appallingly fat?' Patrick felt vindictively and loutishly aggressive. Alcohol is such a crude high, he thought, remembering the sage pronouncement of his first hash dealer from his schooldays, a zonked-out old hippie bore called Barry.

'If I looked like you,' he sneered at the fat man, 'I'd commit suicide. Not that one needs an incentive.' There was no doubt about it, he was a fattist and a sexist and an ageist and a racist and a straightist and a druggist and, naturally, a snob, but of such a virulent character that nobody satisfied his demands. He defied anyone to come up with a minority or a majority that he did not hate for some reason or another.

'Is everything OK, sir?' asked one of the waiters, mistaking Patrick's mutterings for an attempt to order.

'Yes, yes,' said Patrick. Well, not absolutely everything, he thought, you can't seriously expect anyone to agree to that. In fact the idea of everything being OK made him feel dangerously indignant. Affirmation was too rare a commodity to waste on such a ludicrous statement. He felt like calling the waiter back to correct any false impression of happiness he might have created. But here was another waiter – would they never leave him alone? Could he bear it if they did? – bringing his Steak Tartare. He wanted it spicy, very spicy.

A couple of minutes later, his mouth seared with Tabasco and cayenne pepper, Patrick had already devoured the mound of raw meat and *pommes allumettes* on his plate.

'That's right, dear,' he said in his Nanny voice, 'you get something solid inside you.'

'Yes, Nanny,' he replied obediently. 'Like a bullet, or a needle, eh, Nanny?'

'A bullet, indeed,' he huffed and puffed, 'a needle! Whatever next? You always were a strange boy. No good'll come of it, you mark my words, young man.'

Oh, God, it was starting. The endless voices. The solitary dialogues. The dreadful jabbering that poured out uncontrollably. He gulped down an entire glass of red wine with an eagerness worthy of Lawrence of Arabia, as interpreted by Peter O'Toole, polishing off his glass of lemonade after a thirsty desert crossing. 'We've taken Aqaba,' he said, staring madly into space and twitching his eyebrows expertly.

'Would you care for a dessert, sir?'

At last, a real person with a real question, albeit a rather bizarre question. How was he supposed to 'care for' a dessert? Did he have to visit it on Sundays? Send it a Christmas card? Did he have to feed it?

'Yeah,' said Patrick, smiling wildly, 'I'll have a crème brûlée.'

Patrick stared at his glass. The red wine was definitely beginning to unfold. Pity he had already drunk it all. Yes, it had been beginning to unfold, like a fist opening slowly. And in its palm . . . In its palm, what? A ruby? A grape? A stone? Perhaps similes just shunted the same idea back and forth, lightly disguised, to give the impression of a fruitful trade. Sir Sampson Legend was the only honest suitor who ever sang the praises of a woman. 'Give me your hand, Odd, let me kiss it; 'tis as warm and as soft – as what? Odd, as t'other hand.' Now there was an accurate simile. The tragic limitations of comparison. The lead in the heart of the skylark. The disappointing curvature of space. The doom of time.

Christ, he was really quite drunk. Not drunk enough, though. He poured the stuff in, but it didn't reach the root-confusions, the accident by the roadside, still trapped in the buckling metal after all these years. He sighed loudly, ending in a kind of grunt, and bowing his head hopelessly.

The crème brûlée arrived and he gobbled it down with the same desperate impatience he showed towards all food, but now edged with weariness and oppression. His violent way of eating always left him in a state of speechless sadness at the end of a meal. After several minutes during which he could only stare at the foot of his glass, he summoned enough passion to order some marc de Bourgogne and the bill.

Patrick closed his eyes and let the cigarette smoke drift out of his mouth and up into his nose and out through his mouth again. This was recycling at its best. Of course he could still go to the party Anne had invited him to, but he knew that he wouldn't. Why did he always refuse? Refuse to participate. Refuse to agree. Refuse to forgive. Once it was too late he would long to have gone to this party. He glanced at his watch. Only nine thirty. The time had not yet come, but the moment it did, refusal would turn into regret. He could even imagine loving a woman if he had lost her first.

With reading it was the same thing. As soon as he was deprived of books, his longing to read became insatiable, whereas if he took the precaution of carrying a book with him, as he had this evening, slipping *The Myth of Sisyphus* yet again into his overcoat pocket, then he could be sure that he would not be troubled by a desire for literature.

Before *The Myth of Sisyphus* he had carried round *The Unnamable* and *Nightwood* for at least a year, and for two years before that the ultimate overcoat book, *Heart of Darkness*. Sometimes, driven on by horror at his own ignorance and a determination to conquer a difficult book, or even a seminal text, he would take a copy of something like *Seven Types of Ambiguity* or *The Decline and Fall of the Roman Empire* out of his bookshelves only to find that its opening pages were already covered in spidery and obscure annotations in his own handwriting. These traces of an earlier civilization would have reassured him if he had any recollection at all of the things he had obviously once read, but this forgetfulness made him panic instead. What was the point of an experience if it eluded him so thoroughly? His past seemed to turn to water in his cupped hands and to slip irretrievably through his nervous fingers.

Patrick heaved himself up and walked across the thick red carpet of the restaurant, his head thrown back precariously and his eyes so nearly closed that the tables were dark blurs through the mesh of his eyelashes.

He had made a big decision. He would telephone Pierre and leave it to fate whether he scored or not. If Pierre was asleep then he would not get any smack, but if he was awake it was worth going round to get just enough for a good night's rest. And a little for the morning so he didn't feel sick.

The barman put a telephone down on the mahogany counter, and beside it a second marc. 5...5...5...1...7...2...6. Patrick's heart rate increased; he suddenly felt alert.

'I cannot come to the phone right now, but if you leave . . .'

Patrick slammed the phone down. It was the fucking machine. What was he doing asleep at ten in the evening? It was absolutely intolerable. He picked the phone up and dialled the number again. Should he leave a message? Something subtly coded like 'Wake up, fuckface, I want to score.'

No, it was hopeless. Fate had spoken and he must accept its judgement.

Outside it was surprisingly warm. Nevertheless, Patrick flicked up the collar of his overcoat, scanning the street for a free cab.

He soon spotted a taxi and stepped into the street to hail it.

'The Pierre Hotel,' he said as he climbed inside.

5

WHAT INSTRUMENT COULD HE use to set himself free? Disdain? Aggression? Hatred? They were all contaminated by the influence of his father, the very thing he needed to free himself from. And the sadness he felt, if he paused for a second, had he not learned it from his father's descent into paralysing misery?

After his divorce from Eleanor, David had remained in the south of France, only fifteen miles away from the old house in Lacoste. In his new house, which had no exterior windows, only windows looking onto a central weed-choked courtyard, he lay in bed for days on end wheezing and staring at the ceiling fixedly, without even the energy to cross the room and get the copy of *Jorrocks Rides Again* which had once been able to cheer him up in the most unpromising circumstances.

When Patrick, aged eight or nine, and torn between terror and unfathomable loyalty, visited his father, the enormous silences were only broken for David to express a desire to die, and to issue his final instructions.

'I may not be alive for much longer,' he would gasp, 'and we may not see each other again.'

'No, Daddy, don't say that,' Patrick would plead with him.

And then the old exhortations would come out: observe

everything . . . trust nobody . . . despise your mother . . . effort is vulgar . . . things were better in the eighteenth century.

Impressed by the thought, year after year, that these might be his father's last pronouncements on the world, the distillation of all his wisdom and experience, Patrick paid undue attention to this tiresome set of opinions, despite the overwhelming evidence that they had not got his father very far in the pursuit of happiness. But then that was vulgar too. The whole system worked beautifully, like so many others, after the initial leap of faith.

If his father ever managed to get out of bed, things got worse. They would walk down to the village on a shopping expedition, his father dressed in an old pair of green pyjamas, a short blue overcoat with anchors on the buttons, a pair of dark glasses now tied to a coarse string around his neck, and on his feet the heavy lace-up boots favoured by the local tractor-driving peasants. David had also grown a snow-white beard and always carried with him an orange nylon shopping bag with a tarnished gold handle. Patrick was mistaken for his grandson, and he could remember the shame and horror, as well as the defensive pride, with which he accompanied his increasingly eccentric and depressed father into the village.

'I want to die . . . I want to die . . . I want to die,' muttered Patrick rapidly. It was completely unacceptable. He could not be the person who had been that person. The speed was coming back and bringing with it the menace of lucidity and strong emotion.

They were approaching the hotel and Patrick had to make a quick decision. He leaned forward and said to the driver, 'I've changed my mind, take me to Eighth Street between C and D.'

The Chinese driver looked doubtfully in his rear-view mirror. Avenue D was a far cry from the Pierre Hotel. What sort of man would suddenly veer from one to the other? Only a junkie or an ignorant tourist.

'Avenue D bad place,' he said, testing the second theory.

'I'm relying on that,' said Patrick. 'Just take me there.'

The driver carried on down Fifth Avenue, past the turning for the hotel. Patrick sank back, excited and sick and guilty, but masking the feeling, as usual, with a show of languid indifference.

So what if he had changed his mind? Flexibility was an admirable quality. And nobody was more flexible when it came to giving up drugs, nobody more open to the possibility of taking them after all. He hadn't done anything yet. He could still reverse his decision, or rather reverse his revision. He could still go back.

Plummeting from the Upper to the Lower East Side, from Le Veau Gras to the Bargain Grocery Store on Eighth Street, he could not help admiring the way he ranged freely, or perhaps the word was 'inevitably', between luxury and squalor.

The taxi was approaching Tompkins Square, the beginning of the fun district. It was here that Chilly Willy, his street contact for those annoying occasions on which Pierre was asleep, dragged out his life of perpetual withdrawal. Chilly could only ever get enough smack to keep him looking for more; scavenging enough bags to twitch instead of convulsing, to squeal instead of screaming, he walked in little jerky steps with one limp and nerveless arm dangling by his side, like an old flex from the draughty ceiling. With his good hand, Chilly held up the filthy baggy trousers that were always in danger of slipping down over his emaciated waist. Despite being black, he looked pale and his face was speckled with brown liver spots. His teeth, the four or five that still clung heroically to his gums, were either dark yellow or black, chipped or shattered. He was an inspiration to his community and his customers since nobody could imagine looking as ill as him, however recklessly they lived.

The cab crossed Avenue C and carried on down Eighth Street.

Here he was among the filthy haunches of the city, thought Patrick contentedly.

'Where you want?' asked the Chinaman.

'I want heroin,' said Patrick.

'Heloin,' repeated the driver anxiously.

'That's right,' said Patrick. 'Stop here, this is good.'

Wired Puerto Ricans were pacing about pugilistically on the corner, and black guys with big hats were leaning in doorways. Patrick lowered the window of the taxi, and new friends crowded in from every side.

'What ju wan, man? What ju looking for?'

'Clear tape . . . red tape . . . yellow tape. What you want?'

'Smack,' said Patrick.

'Shit, man, you from the police. You're a policeman.'

'No, I'm not. I'm an Englishman,' Patrick protested.

'Get out the cab, man, we don't sell you nothin' in the cab.'

'Wait here,' said Patrick to the driver. He got out of the taxi. One of the dealers took him by the arm and started to march him round the corner.

'I'm not going any further,' said Patrick as they were about to lose sight of the taxi.

'How much you want?'

'Give me four dime-bags of clear tape,' said Patrick carefully unpeeling two twenty-dollar bills. He kept the twenties in the left trouser pocket, tens in the right trouser pocket, fives and ones in the overcoat pockets. The hundreds remained in their envelope in the inside coat pocket. This way he never tempted anybody with a show of cash.

'I'll give you six for fifty, man. You git one extra bag.'

'No, four is fine.'

Patrick pocketed the four little bags of greaseproof paper, turned around and climbed back into the cab.

'We go hotel now,' said the Chinaman eagerly.

'No, just drive me round the block for a bit. Take me to Sixth and B.'

'What you go lound block for?' The driver mumbled a Chinese curse, but moved off in the right direction.

Patrick had to test the smack he had just bought before he left the area altogether. He tore open one of the bags and poured the powder into the hollow formed in the back of his hand by the tendon of his raised thumb. He raised the tiny quantity of white powder to his nose and sniffed it up.

Oh, God! It was vile. Patrick clutched his stinging nose. Fuck, wank, blast, shit, damn.

It was a hideous cocktail of Vim and barbs. The scouring powder gave that touch of genuine bitterness to the mix, and the barbiturates provided a small thud of sedation. There were some advantages, of course. You could take ten of these bags a day and never become a junkie. You could be arrested with them and not be charged with possession of heroin. Thank God he hadn't shot it up, the Vim afterburn would have scorched his veins. What was he doing scoring off the street? He must be mad. He should have tried to get hold of Chilly Willy and sent him round to Loretta's. At least there were some traces of heroin in her little greaseproof packages.

Still, he wouldn't throw away this rubbish until he knew he could get something better. The cab had arrived at Sixth and C.

'Stop here,' said Patrick.

'I no wai' here,' shouted the driver in a sudden burst of vexation.

'Oh, well, fuck off then,' said Patrick, tossing a ten-dollar bill into the passenger seat and getting out of the cab. He slammed the door and stalked off towards Seventh Street. The taxi screeched away from the kerb. When it had gone, Patrick was conscious of a hush in which his footsteps seemed to ring loudly on the pavement. He was alone. But not for long. On the next corner, a group of about a dozen dealers were standing around outside the Bargain Grocery Store.

Patrick slowed down, and one of the men, spotting him first, detached himself from the group and sauntered across the street with a buoyant and muscular gait. An exceptionally tall black man, he wore a shiny red jacket.

'How you doing?' he asked Patrick. His face was completely smooth, his cheekbones high, and his wide eyes seemingly saturated with indolence.

'Fine,' said Patrick. 'How about you?'

'I'm good. What you looking for?'

'Can you take me to Loretta's?'

'Loretta,' said the black man lazily.

'Sure.' Patrick was frustrated by his slowness and, feeling the book in his overcoat pocket, he imagined whipping it out like a pistol and gunning the dealer down with its ambitious first sentence, 'There is only one really serious philosophical problem: it is suicide.'

'How much you lookin' for?' asked the dealer, reaching nonchalantly behind his back.

'Just fifty dollars' worth,' said Patrick.

There was a sudden commotion on the other side of the street and he saw a half-familiar figure hobbling towards them in an agitated way.

'Don't stick him, don't stick him,' the new character shouted.

Patrick recognized him now: it was Chilly, clutching his trousers. He arrived, stumbling and out of breath. 'Don't stick him,' he repeated, 'he's my man.'

The tall black man smiled as if this was a truly hilarious incident. 'I was going to stick you,' he said, proudly showing Patrick a small knife. 'I didn't know yuz knew Chilly!'

'What a small world,' said Patrick wearily. He felt totally detached from the threat that this man claimed to represent, and impatient to get on with his business.

'That's right,' said the tall man, ever more ebullient. He offered his hand to Patrick, after removing the knife. 'My name's Mark,' he said. 'You ever need anything, ask for Mark.'

Patrick shook his hand and smiled at him faintly. 'Hello, Chilly,' he said.

'Where you been?' asked Chilly reproachfully.

'Oh, over to England. Let's go to Loretta's.'

Mark waved goodbye and lolloped back across the street. Patrick and Chilly headed downtown.

'Extraordinary man,' drawled Patrick. 'Does he always stab people when he first meets them?'

'He's a bad man,' said Chilly. 'You don't wanna hang around him. Why din't you ask for me?'

'I did,' Patrick lied, 'but of course he said you weren't around. I guess he wanted a free hand to stab me.'

'Yeah, he's a bad man,' repeated Chilly.

The two men turned the corner of Sixth Street and Chilly almost immediately led Patrick down a short flight of steps into the basement of a dilapidated brownstone building. Patrick was quietly pleased that Chilly was taking him to Loretta's, instead of leaving him to wait on a street corner.

There was only one door in the basement, reinforced with steel and equipped with a brass flap and a small spyglass. Chilly rang the bell and soon after a voice called out suspiciously, 'Who's that?'

'It's Chilly.'

'How much you want?'

Patrick handed Chilly fifty dollars. Chilly counted the money, opened the brass flap and stuffed it inside. The flap retracted quickly and remained closed for what seemed like a long time.

'You got a bag for me?' asked Chilly, shifting from leg to leg.

'Of course,' replied Patrick magnificently, taking a ten-dollar bill out of his trouser pocket.

'Thanks, man.'

The flap reopened and Patrick clawed out the five little bags. Chilly got one for himself, and the two men left the building with a sense of achievement, counterbalanced by desire.

'Have you got any clean works?' asked Patrick.

'My ole lady got some. You wanna come back to my place?'

'Thanks,' said Patrick, flattered by these multiplying signs of trust and intimacy.

Chilly's place was a room on the second floor of a fire-gutted building. Its walls were blackened by smoke, and the unreliable staircase littered with empty matchbooks, liquor bottles, brown-paper bags, heaps of cornered dust, and balls of old hair. The room itself, only contained one piece of furniture, a mustard-coloured armchair covered in burns, with a spring bursting from the centre of the seat, like an obscene tongue.

Mrs Chilly Willy – if that was her correct title, mused Patrick – was sitting on the arm of this chair when the two men came in. She was a large woman, more masculine in build than her skeletal husband.

'Hi, Chilly,' she said dozily, obviously further from withdrawal than he was.

'Hi,' he said, 'you know my man.'

'Hi, honey.'

'Hello,' beamed Patrick charmingly. 'Chilly said you might have a spare syringe.'

'I might,' she said playfully.

'Is it new?'

'Well, it ain't exactly noo, but I boiled it and everythin'.'

Patrick raised one eyebrow with deadly scepticism. 'Is it *very* blunt?' he asked.

She fished a bundle of loo paper out of her voluminous bra and carefully unwrapped the precious package. At its centre was a threateningly large syringe which a zookeeper would have hesitated to use on a sick elephant.

'That's not a needle, it's a bicycle pump,' Patrick protested, holding out his hand.

Intended for intramuscular use, the spike was worryingly thick, and when Patrick detached the green plastic head that held it he could not help noticing a ring of old blood inside. 'Oh, all right,' he said. 'How much do you want for it?'

'Gimme two bags,' urged Mrs Chilly, wrinkling up her nose endearingly.

It was an absurd price, but Patrick never argued about prices. He tossed two bags into her lap. If the stuff was any good he could always get more. Right now he had to shoot up. He asked Chilly to lend him a spoon and a cigarette filter. Since the light in the main room had failed, Chilly offered him the bathroom, a room without a bath in it, but with a black mark on the floor where there might once have been one. A naked bulb cast a dim yellow light on the insanely cracked basin and the seatless old loo.

Patrick trickled some water into the spoon and rested it at the back of the basin. Tearing open the three remaining packages, he wondered what sort of gear it was. Nobody could claim that Chilly looked well on a diet of Loretta's smack, but at least he wasn't dead. If Mr and Mrs Chilly were planning to shoot it up, there was no reason why he shouldn't. He could hear them whispering next door. Chilly was saying something about 'hurting' and was obviously trying to get the second bag out of his wife. Patrick emptied the three packets into the spoon and heated the solution, the flame from his lighter licking the already blackened underside of the spoon. As soon as it started to bubble, he cut off the heat and put the steaming liquid down again. He tore a thin strip off the cigarette filter, dropped it in the spoon, removed the spike from the syringe, and sucked the liquid up through the filter. The barrel was so thick that the solution barely rose a quarter of an inch.

Dropping his overcoat and jacket on the floor, Patrick rolled up his sleeve and tried to make out his veins in the faint light which gave a hepatic glow to every object that was not already black. Luckily, his track marks formed brown and purple threads, as if his veins were gunpowder trails burned along his arm.

Patrick rolled the sleeve of his shirt tight around his bicep and pumped his forearm up and down several times, clenching and unclenching his fist at the same time. He had good veins and, despite a certain shyness that resulted from his savage treatment of them, he was in a better position than many people whose daily search for a vein sometimes took up to an hour of exploratory digging.

He picked up the syringe and rested its point on the widest section of his track marks, slightly sideways to the scar. With such a long spike there was always a danger that it would go through the vein altogether and into the muscle on the other side, a painful experience, and so he approached the arm at a fairly low angle. At this crucial moment the syringe slipped from his hand and landed on a wet patch of the floor beside the loo. He could hardly believe what had happened. He felt vertiginous with horror and disappointment. There was a conspiracy against his having any fun today. He leaned over, desperate with longing, and picked up the works from the damp patch. The spike wasn't bent. Thank God for that. Everything was all right. He quickly wiped the syringe on his trousers.

By now his heart was beating fast and he felt that visceral excitement, a combination of dread and desire, which always preceded a fix. He pushed the painfully blunt tip of the needle under his skin and thought he saw, miracle of miracles, a globule of blood shoot into the barrel. Not wanting to waste any time with such an unwieldy instrument, he put his thumb on the plunger and pushed it straight down.

He felt a violent and alarming swelling in his arm and recognized immediately that the spike had slipped out of his vein and he had squirted the solution under his skin.

'Shit,' he shouted.

Chilly came shuffling through. 'What's happening, man?'

'I missed,' said Patrick through clenched teeth, pushing the hand of his wounded arm up against his shoulder.

'Oh, man,' croaked Chilly sympathetically.

'Can I suggest you invest in a stronger light bulb?' said Patrick pompously, holding his arm as if it had been broken.

'You shoulda used the flashlight,' said Chilly, scratching himself.

'Oh, thanks for telling me about it,' snapped Patrick.

'You wanna go back and score some more?' asked Chilly.

'No,' said Patrick curtly, putting his coat back on. 'I'm leaving.'

By the time he hit the street Patrick was wondering why he hadn't taken up Chilly's offer. 'Temper, temper,' he muttered sarcastically. He felt weary, but too frustrated to sleep. It was eleven thirty; perhaps Pierre had woken up by now. He had better go back to the hotel.

Patrick hailed a cab.

'You live around here?' asked the driver.

'No, I was just trying to score,' Patrick sighed, posting the bags of Vim and barbs out of the window.

'You wanna score?'

'That's right,' sighed Patrick.

'Shee-eet, I know a better place than this.'

'Really?' said Patrick, all ears.

'Yeah, in the South Bronx.'

'Well, let's go.'

'All right,' laughed the driver.

At last a cab driver who was helpful. An experience like this might put him in a good mood. Perhaps he should write a letter to the Yellow Cab Company. 'Dear sir,' murmured Patrick under his breath, 'I wish to commend in the highest possible terms the initiative and courtesy of your splendid young driver, Jefferson E. Parker. After a fruitless and, to be perfectly frank, infuriating expedition to Alphabet City, this knight errant, this, if I may put it thus, Jefferson Nightingale, rescued me from a very tiresome predicament, and took me to score in the South Bronx. If only more of your drivers displayed the same old-fashioned desire to serve. Yours, et cetera, Colonel Melrose.'

Patrick smiled. Everything was under control. He felt elated, almost frivolous. The Bronx was a bit of a worry for someone who had seen *Bronx Warriors* – a film of unremitting nastiness, not to be confused with the beautifully choreographed violence of the more simply, and more generically named *The Warriors* – but he felt invulnerable. People drew knives on him, but they could not touch him, and if they did he would not be there.

As the cab sped over a bridge Patrick had never crossed before, Jefferson turned his head slightly and said, 'We're gonna be in the Bronx soon.'

'I'll wait in the cab, shall I?' asked Patrick.

'You better lie on the floor,' laughed Jefferson, 'they don't like white people here.'

'On the floor?'

'Yeah, outta sight. If they see you, they gonna smash the windows. Shee-eet, I don't want my windows smashed.'

Jefferson stopped the taxi a few blocks beyond the bridge and Patrick sat down on the rubber floor mat with his back against the door.

'How much you want?' asked Jefferson, leaning over the driver's seat.

'Oh, five bags. And get a couple for yourself,' said Patrick, handing over seventy dollars.

'Thanks,' said Jefferson. 'I'm gonna lock the doors now. You stay outta sight, right?'

'Right,' said Patrick, sliding down further and stretching out on the floor. The bolts of all the doors slithered into place. Patrick wriggled around for some time before curling up in a foetal position with his head on the central hump. After a few moments his hip bone was persecuting his liver and he felt hopelessly tangled up in the folds of his overcoat. He twisted around onto his front, rested his head in his hands, and stared at the grooves in the floor mat. There was quite a strong smell of oil down at this level. 'It gives you a whole new perspective on life,' said Patrick, in the voice of a television housewife.

It was intolerable. Everything was intolerable. He was always getting into these *situations*, always ending up with the losers, the dregs, the Chilly Willys of life. Even at school he had been sent every Tuesday and Thursday afternoons, when the other boys joined their teams and played their matches, to remote playing fields with every variety of sporting misfit: the pale and sensitive musicians, the hopelessly fat Greek boys, and the disaffected cigarette-smoking protesters who regarded physical exertion as hopelessly uncool. As a punishment for their unsporting natures, these boys were forced to make their way round an assault course. Mr Pitch, the overwrought pederast in charge of this unwholesome squad, quivered with excitement and malice as each boy crashed myopically, waddled feebly, or tried to beat the system by running around the wall at the beginning of the course. While the Greeks splattered into the mud, and the music scholars lost their spectacles, and the conscientious objectors made their cynical remarks, Mr Pitch rushed about screaming abuse at them about their 'privileged' lives and, if the opportunity arose, kicking them in the bottom.

What the hell was going on? Had Jefferson gone to fetch some friends so they could beat him up together, or was he simply being abandoned while Jefferson went to get stoned?

Yes, thought Patrick, shifting restlessly, he had hung out with nothing but failures. Living in Paris when he was nineteen, he had fallen in with Jim, an Australian heroin smuggler on the run, and Simon, a black American bank robber just out of prison. He could remember Jim saying, as he had searched for a vein among the thick orange hairs of his forearm, 'Australia's so beautiful in the spring, man. All the little lambs frisking about. You can tell they're just so happy to be alive.' He had pushed the plunger down with a whimsical expression on his face.

Simon had tried to rob a bank while he was withdrawing, but he had been forced to surrender to the police after they had fired several volleys at him. 'I didn't wanna look like no Swiss cheese,' he explained.

Patrick heard the merciful sound of the locks opening again. 'I got it,' said Jefferson huskily. 'Goody,' said Patrick, sitting up.

Jefferson was happy and relaxed as he drove to the hotel. When he had snorted three of the bags Patrick could understand why. Here at last was a powder that contained a little heroin.

Jefferson and Patrick parted with the genuine warmth of people who had exploited each other successfully. Back in his hotel room, lying on the bed with his arms spread out, Patrick realized that if he took the other two bags and turned on the television he could probably fall asleep. Once he had taken heroin he could imagine being without it; when he was without it he could only imagine getting more. But just to see if all the evening's trouble had been completely unnecessary, he decided to call Pierre's number.

As the telephone rang he again wondered what kept him

from suicide. Was it something as contemptible as sentimentality, or hope, or narcissism? No. It was really the desire to know what would happen next, despite the conviction that it was bound to be horrible: the narrative suspense of it all.

'Hallo?'

'Pierre!'

'Who iz this?'

'Patrick.'

'What do you want?'

'Can I come round?'

'OK. How long?'

'Twenty minutes.'

'OK.'

Patrick raised his fist in triumph and sprinted from the room.

6

'PIERRE!'

'*Ça va?*' said Pierre, getting up from his leather office chair. The parched yellow skin of his face was stretched more tautly than ever over the thin nose, high cheekbones, and prominent jaw. He shook hands with Patrick, fixing him with lantern eyes.

The fetid atmosphere of the apartment struck Patrick like the scent of a long-absent lover. The stains of overturned coffee mugs still tattooed the oatmeal carpet in the same places as before, and the familiar pictures of severed heads floating on pieces of jigsaw puzzle, lovingly executed by Pierre with a fine ink pen, made Patrick smile.

'What a relief to see you again!' he exclaimed. 'I can't tell you what a nightmare it is out there, scoring off the streets.'

'You score off the street!' barked Pierre disapprovingly. 'You fucking crazy!'

'But you were asleep.'

'You shoot with tap water?'

'Yes,' admitted Patrick guiltily.

'You crazy,' glared Pierre. 'Come in here, I show you.'

He walked through to his grimy and narrow kitchen. Opening

the door of the big old-fashioned fridge, he took out a large jar of water.

'This is tap water,' said Pierre ominously, holding up the jar. 'I leave it one month and look . . .' He pointed to a diffuse brown sediment at the bottom of the jar. 'Rust,' he said, 'it's a fucking killer! I have one friend who shoot with tap water and the rust get in his bloodstream and his heart . . .' Pierre chopped the air with his hand and said, '*Tak:* it stop.'

'That's appalling,' murmured Patrick, wondering when they were going to do business.

'The water come from the mountains,' said Pierre, sitting down in his swivel chair and sucking water from a glass into an enviably slim syringe, 'but the pipes are full of rust.'

'I'm lucky to be alive,' said Patrick without conviction. 'It's nothing but mineral water from now on, I promise.'

'It's the City,' said Pierre darkly; 'they keep the money for new pipes. They kill my friend. What do you want?' he added, opening a package and piling some white powder into a spoon with the corner of a razor blade.

'Um . . . a gram of smack,' said Patrick casually, 'and seven grams of coke.'

'The smack is six hundred. The coke I make you a price: one hundred a gram instead of one-twenty. Total: thirteen hundred dollar.'

Patrick slipped the orange envelope out of his pocket while Pierre piled another white powder into the spoon and stirred it, frowning like a child pretending to make cement.

Was that nine or ten? Patrick started counting again. When he reached thirteen he tapped the notes together like a shuffled deck of cards and tossed them over to Pierre's side of the mirror where they fanned out extravagantly. Pierre wound a length of rubber around his bicep and gripped it in his teeth. Patrick was pleased to see that he still had the use of the volcano cone in the hollow of his arm.

Pierre's pupils dilated for a moment and then contracted again, like the feeding mouth of a sea anemone.

'OK,' he croaked, trying to give the impression that nothing had happened, but sounding subdued by pleasure, 'I give you what you want.' He refilled the syringe and squirted the contents into a second pinkish glass of water.

Patrick wiped his clammy hands on his trousers. Only the need to make one more tricky negotiation contained his heart-exploding impatience.

'Do you have any spare syringes?' he asked. Pierre could be very awkward about syringes. Their value varied wildly according to how many he had left, and although he was generally helpful to Patrick when he had spent over a thousand dollars, there was always the danger that he would lapse into an indignant lecture on his presumption.

'I give you two,' said Pierre with delinquent generosity.

'Two!' exclaimed Patrick as if he had just witnessed a medieval relic waving from behind its glass case. Pierre took out a pair of pale green scales and measured the quantities Patrick had requested, giving him individual gram packets so that he could keep track of his coke consumption.

'Ever thoughtful, ever kind,' murmured Patrick. The two precious syringes followed across the dusty mirror.

'I get you some water,' said Pierre.

Perhaps he had put more heroin than usual in the speedball. How else could one explain this unaccustomed benevolence?

'Thanks,' said Patrick, slipping hastily out of his overcoat and jacket and rolling up his shirt sleeve. Jesus! There was a black bulge in his skin where he had missed the vein round at Chilly's. He'd better not let Pierre see this sign of his incompetence and desperation. Pierre was such a moral man. Patrick let the sleeve flop down, undid the gold cufflink of his right sleeve, and rolled that up instead. Fixing was the one activity in which he had become truly ambidextrous. Pierre came back with one full and one empty glass, and a spoon.

Patrick unfolded one of the packets of coke. The shiny white paper was imprinted with a pale blue polar bear. Unlike Pierre he preferred to take coke on its own until the tension and fear were unbearable, then he would send in the Praetorian Guard of heroin to save the day from insanity and defeat. He held the packet in a funnel and tapped it gently. Small grains of powder slipped down the narrow valley of paper and tumbled into the spoon. Not too much for the first fix. Not too little either. Nothing was more intolerable than a dissipated, watery rush. He carried on tapping.

'How are you?' asked Pierre, so rapidly that the question seemed like one word.

'Well, my father died the other day and so . . .' Patrick was not sure what to say. He looked at the packet, gave it one more decisive tap, and another flurry of powder joined the small heap already in the spoon. 'And so I'm a little confused at the moment,' he concluded.

'How was he, your father?'

'He was a kitten,' Patrick intoned rhapsodically. 'And he had such artistic hands.' For a moment the water went syrupy and then it dissolved into a clear solution. 'He could have been Prime Minister,' he added.

'He was in politics?' asked Pierre, narrowing his eyes.

'No, no,' Patrick replied, 'it was a sort of joke. In his world – a world of pure imagination – it was better if a person "could have been" Prime Minister than if he *was* Prime Minister: that would have shown vulgar ambition.' There was a faint metallic ringing as he directed the jet of water from his syringe against the side of the spoon.

'*Tu regrettes qu'il est mort?*' asked Pierre shrewdly.

'*Non, absolument pas, je regrette qu'il ait vécu.*'

'*Mais sans lui*, you would not exist.'

'One shouldn't be egotistical about these things,' said Patrick with a smile.

His right arm was relatively unscathed. A few bruises the colour of tobacco stains yellowed his lower forearm, and faded pink puncture marks clustered around the bullseye of his principal vein. He raised the needle and allowed a couple of drops to dribble from its eye. His stomach made a rumbling sound and he felt as nervous and excited as a twelve-year-old in the back of a darkened cinema stretching his arm around a girl's shoulders for the first time.

He aimed the needle at the centre of the existing puncture marks and pushed it almost painlessly under his skin. A thread of blood burst into the barrel and curled around, a private mushroom cloud, luminously red in the clear bitter water. Thank God he had found a vein. His heart rate increased, like the drumbeat of a galley rowing into battle. Holding the barrel firmly between his fingers he pushed the plunger down slowly. Like a film in reverse the blood shot back through the needle towards its source.

Before he felt its effects he smelled the heartbreaking fragrance of the cocaine, and then a few seconds afterward, in a time-lapse frenzy, its cold geometric flowers broke out everywhere and carpeted the surface of his inner vision. Nothing could ever be as pleasurable as this. He clumsily drew back the plunger, filled the barrel with blood, and injected himself a second time. Drunk with pleasure, choking with love, he lurched forward and put the syringe down heavily on the mirror. He would have to flush it out before the blood coagulated, but he couldn't do it straight away. The sensation was too strong. Sound was twisted and amplified until it whistled like the engine of a landing jet.

Patrick sat back and closed his eyes, his lips thrust out like a child waiting for a kiss. Sweat had already broken out high on his forehead, and his armpits dripped every few seconds like defective taps.

Pierre knew exactly what state Patrick was in and disapproved strongly of his unbalanced approach, and the irresponsible way he had put his syringe down without flushing it out. He picked it up and filled it with water so that the mechanism didn't block. Sensing a movement, Patrick opened his eyes and whispered, 'Thank you.'

'You should take smack at the same time,' said Pierre reproachfully; 'it's medicine, man, medicine.'

'I like the rush.'

'But you take too much, you lose control.'

Patrick sat up and looked at Pierre intently. 'I never lose control,' he said, 'I just test its limits.'

'Bullshit,' said Pierre, unimpressed.

'Of course you're right,' smiled Patrick. 'But you know what it's like trying to stay on the edge without falling off it,' he said, appealing to their traditional solidarity.

'I know what it's like,' screeched Pierre, his eyes incandescent with passion. 'For eight years I thought I was an egg, but I had total control, *contrôle total.*'

'I remember,' said Patrick soothingly.

The rush was over, and like a surfer who shoots out of a tube of furling, glistening sea only to peter out and fall among the breaking waves, his thoughts began to scatter before the onset of boundless unease. Only a few minutes after the fix he felt a harrowing nostalgia for the dangerous exhilaration which was already dying out. As if his wings had melted in that burst of light, he felt himself falling towards a sea of unbearable disappointment, and it was this that made him pick up the syringe, finish flushing it out and, despite his shaking hands, begin to prepare another fix.

'Do you think the measure of a perversion is its need to be repeated, its inability to be satisfied?' he asked Pierre. 'I wish my father were around to answer that question,' he added piously.

'Why? He was a junkie?'

'No, no . . .' said Patrick. He wanted to say, 'it was a kind of joke' again, but resisted. 'What sort of man was *your* father?' he asked hastily, in case Pierre followed up his remark.

'He was a *fonctionnaire*,' said Pierre contemptuously, '*Métro, boulot, dodo*. His happiest days were his *service militaire*, and the proudest moment of his life was when the Minister congratulated him for saying nothing. Can you imagine? Each time someone visited the house, which was not often, my father would tell the same story.' Pierre straightened his back, smiled complacently, and wagged his finger. ' "*Et Monsieur le Ministre m'a dit, Vous avez eu raison de ne rien dire.*" When he told that story I used to run from the room. It fill me with disgust, *j'avais un dégoût total.*'

'And your mother?' said Patrick, pleased to have got Pierre off his own parental case.

'What is a woman who is not maternal?' snapped Pierre. 'A piece of furniture with breasts!'

'Quite,' said Patrick, sucking a new solution into his syringe. As a concession to Pierre's medical advice, he had decided to take some heroin rather than further delay the onset of serenity with another chilling shot of cocaine.

'You have to leave all that behind,' said Pierre. 'Parents, all that shit. You have to invent yourself again to become an individual.'

'Right on,' said Patrick, knowing it was best not to argue with Pierre's theories.

'The Americans, they talk all the time about individuality, but they don't have an idea unless everybody else is having the same idea at the same time. My American customers, they always fuck me about to show they are individuals, but they always do it in exactly the same way. Now I have no American customers.'

'People think they are individuals because they use the word "I" so often,' Patrick commented.

'When I died in the hospital,' said Pierre, *j'avais une conscience sans limites*. I knew everything, man, literally *everything*. After that I cannot take seriously the *sociologues et psychologues* who say you are "schizoid" or "paranoid", or "social class two" or "social class three". These people know nothing. They think they know about the human mind, but they know nothing, *absolument rien*.' Pierre glared vehemently at Patrick. 'It's like they put moles in charge of the space programme,' he sneered.

Patrick laughed drily. He had stopped listening to Pierre and started searching for a vein. When he saw a poppy of blood light up the barrel, he administered the injection, and pulled out the syringe, flushing it out efficiently this time.

He was amazed by the strength and smoothness of the heroin. His blood became as heavy as a sack of coins and he sank down appreciatively into his body, resolved again into a single substance after the catapulting exile of the cocaine.

'Exactly,' he whispered, 'like moles . . . God, this is good smack.' He closed his eyelids lingeringly.

'It's pure,' said Pierre. *'Faîtes attention, c'est très fort.'*

'Mm, I can tell.'

'It's medicine, man, medicine,' Pierre reiterated.

'Well, I'm completely cured,' whispered Patrick with a private smile. Everything was going to be all right. A coal fire on a stormy night, rain that could not touch him beating against the windowpane. Streams made of smoke, and smoke that formed into shining pools. Thoughts shimmering on the borders of a languorous hallucination.

He scratched his nose and reopened his eyes. Yes, with the

firm base provided by the heroin, he could play high notes of cocaine all night without cracking altogether.

But he'd have to be alone for that. With good drugs, solitude was not just bearable, it was indispensable. 'It's much more subtle than Persian smack,' he croaked. 'A gentle sustained curve . . . like a, like a polished tortoise shell.' He closed his eyes again.

'It's the strongest smack in the world,' said Pierre simply.

'Ya,' drawled Patrick, 'it's such a bore, one can hardly ever get it in England.'

'You should come and live here.'

'Good idea,' said Patrick amiably. 'By the way, what's the time?'

'One forty-seven.'

'Gosh, I'd better go to bed,' said Patrick, putting the syringes carefully into his inside pocket. 'It's been lovely seeing you again. I'll be in touch very soon.'

'OK,' said Pierre. 'I'm awake tonight, tomorrow, and tomorrow night.'

'Perfect,' said Patrick nodding.

He put on his jacket and overcoat. Pierre got up, undid the four security locks, opened the door, and let him out.

7

PATRICK SLUMPED BACK IN the chair. The tension was deleted from his chest. For a moment he fell quiet. But soon a new character installed itself in his body, forcing his shoulders back and his stomach out, and launching him into another bout of compulsive mimicry.

The Fat Man (pushing back the chair to accommodate his huge stomach): 'I feel compelled to speak, sir, indeed I do. Compelled, sir, is a mild description of the obligation under which I am placed in this matter. My story is a simple one, the story of a man who loved not wisely but too well.' (Wipes a tear from the corner of his eye.) 'A man who ate not from greed, but from passion. Eating, sir – I do not attempt to disguise it – has been my life. Couched in the ruins of this old body are the traces of some of the most exquisite dishes ever cooked. When horses have collapsed beneath my bulk, their legs shattered or their lungs, flooded with their own blood, or I have been forced to renounce the fruitless struggle to intervene between the seat and the steering wheel of a motor car, I have consoled myself with the reflection that my weight has been won, and not merely "put on". Naturally, I have dined in Les Bains and Les Baux, but I have also dined in Quito and Khartoum. And when the ferocious

Yanomami offered me a dish of human flesh, I did not allow prudishness to prevent me from requesting a third helping. Indeed I did not, sir.' (Smiles wistfully.)

Nanny (huffing and puffing): 'Human flesh indeed! Whatever next? You always were a strange boy.'

'Oh, shut up,' screamed Patrick silently, as he paced across the faded green carpet and turned around abruptly.

Gary (raising his eyes to heaven with a charming little sigh): 'My name's Gary, I'll be your waiter tonight. Today's specials include a Dish of Human Flesh, and a sodium-free Frisson of Colombian Cocaine nestling on a bed of "Wild Baby" Chinese White Heroin.'

Pete Bloke: 'Haven't you got any Hovis, then?'

Mrs Bloke: 'Yeah, we want Hovis.'

Hovis Voice-over (theme music from *Coronation Street*): 'It were grand when I were young. I'd go round t' dealer's, buy 'alf an ounce o' coke and four grams o' smack, order round a case o' champagne from Berry Bros., take wench out ta Mirabelle, and still 'ave change from a farthing. Them were the days.'

He was dangerously out of control. Every thought or hint of a thought took on a personality stronger than his own. 'Please, please, please make it stop,' muttered Patrick, getting up and pacing about the room.

Mocking Echo: 'Please, please, please make it stop.'

Nanny: 'I know about the aristocracy and their filthy ways.'

Humpo Languid (laughing disarmingly): 'What filthy ways, Nanny?'

Nanny: 'Oh, no, you won't find Nanny telling tales out of school. My lips are sealed. Whatever would Lady Deadwood think? Rolling stones gather no moss. You mark my words. You always were a strange boy.'

Mrs Garsington: 'Who is in charge here? I wish to speak to the manager immediately.'

Dr McCoy: 'It's life, Jim, but not as we know it.'

Captain Kirk (flicking open his communicator): 'Beam us up, Scotty.'

Patrick opened the packet of heroin and, in too much of a hurry to make another fix, simply tipped some of it onto the glass which protected the surface of the table.

Indignant Eric (knowingly): 'Oh, typical, faced with a problem: take more heroin. Basically, the ultimate self-perpetuating system.'

Pulling a banknote out of his pocket, Patrick sat down and stooped over the table.

Captain Languid: 'I say, Sergeant, shut those fellows up, will you?'

Sergeant: 'Don't worry, sir, we'll bring them under control. They're nothing but a bunch of fuzzywuzzies, black-souled bastards, sir, never seen a Gatling in their miserable, godless lives, sir.'

Captain Languid: 'Well done, Sergeant.'

Patrick sniffed up the powder, threw his head back, and inhaled deeply through his nose.

Sergeant: 'Allow me to take the brunt of the impact, sir.' (Groans, a spear lodged in his chest.)

Captain Languid: 'Oh, thank you . . . um . . .'

Sergeant: 'Wilson, sir.'

Captain Languid: 'Yes, of course. Well done, Wilson.'

Sergeant: 'Only wish I could do the same again, sir. But I'm sorry to say I've been fatally wounded, sir.'

Captain Languid: 'Oh, dear. Well, get that wound seen to, Sergeant.'

Sergeant: 'Thank you, sir, very kind of you. What a wonderful gentleman!'

Captain Languid: 'And if the worst should happen, I'm sure we can get you some sort of posthumous gong. My uncle is the chap in charge of that sort of thing.'

Sergeant (sitting up and saluting, shouts): 'Sir!' (Sinking back.) 'It'll mean a lot to Mrs Wilson and the toddlers, poor little fatherless mites.' (Groans.) 'What . . . a . . . wonderful gentleman.'

George the Barman (polishing a glass meditatively): 'Oh, yes, that Captain Languid, I remember him well. Used to come in here and always ask for nine oysters. Not half a dozen or a dozen, but nine. What a gentleman! They don't make 'em like that anymore. I remember the Fat Man as well. Oh yes, not likely to forget him. We couldn't have him in the bar towards the end, literally couldn't fit him in. What a gentleman, though! One of the old school, didn't go in for all this dieting, dear me, no.'

The Fat Man (standing in an especially enlarged dock at the Old Bailey): 'It has indeed been my misfortune, sir, to live in an age of diets and regimens.' (Wipes a tear from the corner of his eye.) 'They call me the Fat Man, and I am fat enough to flatter myself that the epithet requires no explanation. I stand accused of unnatural appetites and an unnatural degree of appetite. Can I be blamed, sir, if I have filled my cup to the brim, if I have piled the plate of my life high with the *Moules au Menthe Fraîches* of experience (a dish to wake the dead, sir, a dish to charm a king!)? I have not been one of those timid waifs of modern life, I have not been a poor guest at the Feast. Dead men, sir, do not accept the challenge of the Menu Gastronomique at the Lapin Vert when they have scarcely swallowed the last mouthful of the Petit Déjeuner Médiéval at the Château de l'Enterrement. They do not then have themselves driven by ambulance (the natural transport of the bon viveur, sir, the carriage of a king!) to the Sac d'Argent to launch themselves with grim abandon down the Cresta Run of their Carte Royale.' (The violinist from the Café Florian plays in the background.) 'My last days, last days, sir, for I fear that my liver – oh, it has done me valiant service, but now it has grown tired and I have grown tired too; but enough of that – my last days have been clouded with calumny.' (Sound of muffled sobbing in the court.) 'But I do not regret the course, or rather the courses' (sad little laugh) 'I have taken in life, indeed I don't.' (Gathers all his dignity.) 'I have eaten, and I have eaten bravely.'

Judge (with thunderous indignation): 'This case is dismissed. It is a grave miscarriage of justice that it was ever brought to trial and, in recognition of that fact, the court awards the Fat Man a dinner for one at the Pig and Whistle.'

Contented Populace: 'Hooray! Hooray!'

Patrick felt limitless dread. The rotten floorboards of his thoughts gave way one after another until the ground itself seemed no fitter than sodden paper to catch his fall. Maybe it would never stop. 'I'm so tired, so tired,' he said, sitting down on the edge of the bed, but immediately getting up again.

Mocking Echo: 'I'm so tired, I'm so tired.'

Greta Garbo (screaming hysterically): 'I don't want to be alone. I'm sick of being alone.'

Patrick slid down the wall. 'I'm so fucking tired,' he wailed.

Mrs Mop: 'You have a nice fix of coke, dear, perk yourself up a bit.'

Dr Death (taking out a syringe): 'I have just the thing for you. We always use it in cases of bereavement.'

Cleopatra: 'Oh, yes.' (Pouting girlishly.) 'My bluest veins to kiss.'

Mrs Mop: 'Go on, dear, do yourself a favour.'

Cleopatra (hoarsely): 'Go on, you bastard, fuck me.'

This time Patrick had to use his tie. He wound it around his bicep several times and gripped it in his teeth, baring his gums like a snarling dog.

Gift o' the Gab O'Connor (draining a glass of Jameson): 'She took to the leech with rowdy Saxon abandon crying, "I've always wanted to be in two places at once."'

Courtier (excitedly): 'A hit, a palpable hit.'

Captain Kirk: 'Warp factor ten, Mr Sulu.'

Attila the Hun (basso profundo): 'I play football with the heads of my enemies. I ride under triumphal arches, my horse's hooves striking sparks from the cobblestones, the slaves of Rome strewing flowers in my path.'

Patrick fell off the chair and curled up on the floor. The brutality of the rush left him winded and amazed. He shook from the violence of his own heartbeat, like a man cowering under the spinning blades of a helicopter. His limbs were paralysed with tension and he imagined his veins, as thin and brittle as the stems of champagne glasses, snapping if he tried to unbend his arms. Without heroin he would die of a heart attack. 'Just fuck off, the lot of you,' he murmured.

Honest John (shaking his head): 'What a vicious bastard, eh, that Attila. Dear, oh dear. "Wot you staring at?" he said. "Nothing," I said. "Well, don't fucking do it, all right?" he said.' (Shakes his head.) 'Vicious!'

Nanny: 'Nanny says if you don't stop talking in silly voices, the wind will change, and you won't be able to stop.'

Boy (desperately): 'But I want to stop, Nanny.'

Nanny: '"I want" gets nowhere.'

Sergeant: 'Get a grip on yourself, laddie.' (Screaming): 'Quick march! Left, right. Left, right.'

Patrick's legs slid back and forth across the carpet, like a tipped-over wind-up doll.

Short notice in *The Times'* Death Column: 'MELROSE. On 25 May, peacefully, after a happy day in the Pierre Hotel. Patrick, aged 22, loving son of David and Eleanor, will be sadly missed by Attila the Hun, Mrs Mop, Indignant Eric, and his many friends, too numerous to enumerate.'

Gift o' the Gab O'Connor: 'A poor unfortunate soul. If he was not twitching like the severed leg of a galvanized frog, it was only because the mood lay heavy on him, like pennies on the eyelids of the dead.' (Drains a tumbler of Jameson.)

Nanny (older now, her memory no longer what it was): 'I can't get used to it, he was such a lovely little boy. Always called him "my precious pet", I remember. Always said, "Don't forget that Nanny loves you."'

Gift o' the Gab O'Connor (tears rolling down his cheeks): 'And his poor unfortunate arms fit to make a strong man weep. Covered in wounds they were, like the mouths of hungry goldfish crying out for the only thing that would purchase a little peace for his poor troubled heart.' (Drains a tumbler of Jameson.)

Captain Languid: 'He was the sort of chap who stayed in his room a good deal. Nothing wrong with that, of course, except that he paced about the whole time. As I like to say, if one's going to be idle, one should be thoroughly idle.' (Smiles charmingly.)

Gift o' the Gab O'Connor (drinking straight from the bottle now, knee deep in tears, his speech grown more slurred): 'And he was troubled in his mind also. Maybe it was the worry of the freedom killed him? In every situation – and he was always getting himself into situations – he saw the choices stretching out crazily, like the broken blood vessels of tired eyes. And with every action he heard the death cry of all the things he had not done. And he saw the chance to get the vertigo, even in a sky-catching puddle, or the gleaming of a drain on the corner of Little Britain Street. Maddened he was by the terror of forgetting and losing the trail of who he was, and turning in circles, like a foxy bloody foxhound in the middle of the bloody wood.'

Honest John: 'What a prannit, eh? Never did an honest day's work in his life. When did you ever see him help an old lady across the road, or buy a bag of sweets for some deprived kiddies? Never. You gotta be honest.'

The Fat Man: 'He was a man, sir, who did not eat enough, a man who picked at his food, who turned from the cornucopia to the pharmacopoeia of life. In short, sir, the worst kind of scoundrel.'

Gift o' the Gab O'Connor (occasionally surfacing above a lake of tears): 'And the sight of him . . .' (glug, glug, glug) '. . . those torn lips that had never learned to love . . .' (glug, glug, glug) '. . . Those lips that had spoken wild and bitter words . . .' (glug, glug, glug) '. . . torn open by the fury of it, and the knowledge that death was upon him' (glug).

Debbie (stammering): 'I wonder what I'm meant to say?'

Kay: 'I saw him the day it happened.'

'Let me not go mad,' shouted Patrick in a voice that started like his own, but became more like John Gielgud's with the last two words.

The Vicar (looking down soothingly from the pulpit): 'Some of us remember David Melrose as a paedophile, an alcoholic, a liar, a rapist, a sadist, and a "thoroughly nasty piece of work". But, you know, in a situation like that, what Christ asks us to say, and what he would have said himself in his own words is' (pausing) '"But that's not the whole story, is it?"'

Honest John: 'Yes it is.'

The Vicar: 'And that "whole story" idea is one of the most exciting things about Christianity. When we read a book by one of our favourite authors, be he Richard Bach or Peter Mayle, we don't just want to know that it's about a very special seagull, or that it's set in the lovely *campagne*, to use a French word, of Provence; we want the satisfaction of reading all the way to the end.'

Honest John: 'Speak for yourself.'

The Vicar: 'And in very much the same spirit, when we make judgements about other people (and which one of us doesn't?) we have to make sure that we have the "whole story" spread out before us.'

Attila the Hun (basso profundo): 'Die, Christian dog!' (Decapitates the Vicar.)

Vicar's Severed Head (pausing thoughtfully): 'You know, the other day, my young granddaughter came to me and said, "Grandfather, I *like* Christianity." And I said to her (thoroughly puzzled), "Why?" And do you know what she said?'

Honest John: 'Of course we don't, you prannit.'

Vicar's Severed Head: 'She said, "Because it's such a comfort."' (Pauses, and then more slowly and emphatically): '"Because it's such a comfort."'

Patrick opened his eyes and uncurled slowly on the floor. The television stared at him accusingly. Perhaps it could save him or distract him from his own involuntary performance.

Television (snivelling and shivering): 'Turn me on, man. Gimme a turn-on.'

Mr President: 'Ask not what your television can do for you, but what you can do for your television.'

Ecstatic Populace: 'Hooray! Hooray!'

Mr President: 'We shall pay any price, bear any burden, meet any hardship . . .'

Von Trapp Family Singers (ecstatically): 'Climb every mountain!'

Mr President: '. . . support any friend, oppose any foe, to assure the survival and success of television.'

Ecstatic Populace: 'Hooray! Hooray!'

Mr President: 'Let the word go forth from this time and place, that the torch has passed to a new generation of Americans – born in this century, tempered by war, disciplined by a hard and bitter peace, proud of our ancient heritage and unwilling to do anything except watch television.'

'Yes, yes, yes,' thought Patrick, crawling across the floor, 'television.'

Television (shifting restlessly from wheel to wheel): 'Gimme a turn-on, man, I gotta have it.'

Viewer (coolly): 'What you got for me?'

Television (ingratiatingly): 'I got *The Million-Dollar Movie. The Billion-Dollar Man. The Trillion-Dollar Quiz Show.*'

Viewer: 'Yeahyeahyeah, but wot you got *now*?'

Television (guiltily): 'A still of the American flag, and some weirdo in a pale blue nylon suit talkin' about the end of the world. *The Farming Report* should be comin' up real soon.'

Viewer: 'OK, I guess I'll take the flag. But don't push me' (getting out a revolver) 'or I'll blow your fuckin' screen out.'

Television: 'OK, man, just keep cool, OK? The reception isn't too great, but it's a *real* good shot of the flag. I personally guarantee that.'

Patrick switched off the television. When would this dreadful night come to an end? Clambering onto the bed, he collapsed, closed his eyes, and listened intently to the silence.

Ron Zak (his eyes closed, smiling benignly): 'I want you to listen to that silence. Can you hear it?' (Pause.) 'Become part of that silence. That silence is your inner voice.'

Honest John: 'Oh, dear, it's not over yet, eh? Who's this Ron Zak, then? Sounds like a bit of a prannit, to be honest.'

Ron Zak: 'Are you all one with that silence?'

Students: 'We are one with the silence, Ron.'

Ron Zak: 'Good.' (Long pause.) 'Now I want you to use the visualization technique you learned last week to picture a pagoda – that's kind of a Chinese beach house, only in the hills.' (Pause.) 'Good. It's very beautiful, isn't it?'

Students: 'Gee, Ron, it's so neat.'

Ron Zak: 'It's got a beautiful golden roof, and a network of bubbling round pools in the garden. Climb into one of those pools – mm, it feels good – and allow the gatekeepers to wash your body and bring you fresh new robes made of silk and other prestigious fabrics. They feel good, don't they?'

Students: 'Oh, yes, they feel great.'

Ron Zak: 'Good. Now I want you to go into the pagoda.' (Pause.) 'There's somebody in there, isn't there?'

Students: 'Yes, it is the Guide we learned about the week before last.'

Ron Zak (a little irritably): 'No, the Guide is in another room.' (Pause.) 'It's your mum and dad.'

Students (in startled recognition): 'Mum? Dad?'

Ron Zak: 'Now I want you to go over to your mum and say, "Mum, I really love you."'

Students: 'Mum, I really love you.'

Ron Zak: 'Now I want you to embrace her.' (Pause.) 'It feels good, doesn't it?'

Students (they scream, faint, write cheques, embrace each other, burst into tears, and punch pillows): 'It feels so good!'

Ron Zak: 'Now I want you to go over to Dad and say, "You, on the other hand, I cannot forgive."'

Students: 'You, on the other hand, I cannot forgive.'

Ron Zak: 'Take out a revolver and shoot his fuckin' brains out. Bang. Bang. Bang. Bang.'

Students: 'Bang. Bang. Bang. Bang.'

Koenig Spook (terrible creaking of armour): 'Omlet! Ich bin thine Popospook!'

'Oh, for fuck's sake,' shouted Patrick, sitting up and slapping himself across the face, 'stop thinking about it.'

Mocking Echo: 'Stop thinking about it.'

Patrick sat down at the table and picked up the packet of coke. He tapped the packet and an unusually large rock fell into the spoon. Bringing a jet of water down on the cocaine, he heard a silvery ringing where it struck the side of the spoon. The powder flooded and dissolved.

His veins were beginning to shrink from the savage onslaught of the evening but one vein, lower down the forearm, still showed without encouragement. Thick and blue, it snaked its way towards his wrist. The skin was tougher there, and it hurt to break beneath it.

Nanny (singing dreamily to her veins): 'Come out, come out, wherever you are!'

A thread of blood appeared in the barrel.

Cleopatra (gasping): 'Oh, yes, yes, yes, yes, yes.'

Attila the Hun (viciously, through clenched teeth): 'No prisoners!'

Patrick fainted and sank back onto the floor, feeling as if his body had suddenly been filled with wet cement. There was silence as he looked down on his body from the ceiling.

Pierre: 'Look at your body, man, it's fucking rubbish. *Tu as une conscience totale. No limites.*' (Patrick's body accelerates very rapidly. Space turns from blue to dark blue, and from dark blue to black. The clouds are like the pieces of a jigsaw puzzle. Patrick looks down and sees, far below him, the window of his hotel room. Inside the room is a thin white beach surrounded by an intensely blue sea. On the beach children are burying Patrick's body in the sand. Only the head is showing. He thinks he can break the case of sand with a simple movement, but he realizes his mistake when one of the children empties a bucket of wet concrete in his face. He tries to wipe the concrete from his mouth and eyes, but his arms are trapped in a concrete tomb.)

'Jennifer's Diary': 'Patrick Melrose's graveside appeared to be unattended as the coffin was lowered, somewhat roughly, into the ground. However, all was not lost, and in the nick of time, that ever popular, gracious, enchanting, indefatigable couple, Mr and Mrs Chilly Willy, the Alphabet City junkies, on a rare visit uptown, shuffled attractively onto the scene. "Don't sink him, don't sink him, he's my man," cried the inconsolable Chilly Willy. "Where I gonna git a dime bag now?" he wailed. "Did he leave me anything in his will?" asked his grief-stricken wife, who wore a cleverly designed, affordable dress in a superbly colourful floral fabric. Among those who did not attend, claiming that they had never heard of the deceased, were Sir Veridian Gravalaux-Gravalax, Marshal of the Island Kennels, and his cousin the very attractive Miss Rowena Keats-Shelley.'

Honest John: 'I don't think he's going to survive this one, to be honest.'

Indignant Eric (shaking his head incredulously): 'What amazes me is that people think they can come along and, eh, casually, eh, bury people alive.'

Mrs Chronos (carrying a huge hourglass, and wearing a tattered old ball gown): 'Well, I must say, it's nice to be wanted! Not a single part since the fourth act of *The Winter's Tale*' (warmly). 'A play by Bill Shakespeare, of course – a lovely man, by the way, and a close personal friend. As the centuries slipped past I thought, "That's right, just ignore me, I know when I'm not wanted."' (Folds her arms and nods.) 'People think of me as a character actor, but if there's one thing I can't stand, it's being typecast. Anyway,' (little sigh) 'I suppose it's time to say my lines.' (Pulling a face.) 'Frankly, I find them a little bit old fashioned. People don't seem to appreciate that I'm a modern girl.' (Coy laugh.) 'I just want to say one more thing,' (serious now) 'and that's a big "thank you" to all my fans. You kept me going during the lonely years. Thank you for the sonnets, and the letters and the conversations, they mean a lot, they really do. Think of me sometimes, darlings, when your gums go black, and you can't remember someone's name.' (Blows kisses to the audience. Then composes herself, smoothes the folds of her dress, and walks front stage.)

'Since his death cannot be mended,
All our revels now are ended.
Think not harshly of our play
But come again another day.'

Attila the Hun (punches the lid off his coffin, making a sound of growling, snarling, hissing fury, like a leopard being baited through the bars of a cage): 'Raaaarrrrghh!'

Patrick shot bolt upright and banged his head on the leg of the chair. 'Shit, wank, fuck, blast,' he said in his own voice at last.

8

PATRICK LAY ON THE bed like a dead thing. He had parted the curtains for a moment and seen the sun rising over the East River, and it had filled him with loathing and self-reproach.

The sun shone, having no alternative, on the nothing new. That was another first sentence.

Other people's words drifted through his mind. Tumbleweed riding through a desert. Had he already thought that? Had he already said it? He felt bloated and empty at the same time.

Traces of the night's possession surfaced now and again in the slowly simmering scum of his thoughts, and the experience of being so thoroughly and often displaced left him bruised and lonely. Besides, he had almost killed himself.

'Let's not go over that again,' he murmured, like a beleaguered lover who is never allowed to forget an indiscretion.

He winced as he stretched out his aching and sticky arm to check the time on the bedside clock. Five forty-five. He could order a selection of cold meats or a plate of smoked salmon straight away, but it would be another three-quarters of an hour before he could organize that brief moment of affirmation when a trolley rattling with wholesome breakfast food was wheeled into the room.

Then the fruit juice would sweat and separate under its cardboard cap; the bacon and egg, too intimidatingly carnal after all, would grow cold and begin to smell, and the single rose, in its narrow glass vase, would drop a petal on the white tablecloth, while he gulped down some sugary tea and continued to ingest the ethereal food of his syringe.

After a sleepless night, he always spent the hours from five thirty to eight cowering from the gathering roar of life. In London, when the pasty light of dawn had stained the ceiling above the curtain pole, he would listen with vampirish panic to the squealing and rumbling of distant juggernauts, and then to the nearby whining of a milkcart, and eventually to the slamming doors of cars bearing children to school, or real men to work in factories and banks.

It was nearly eleven o'clock in England. He could kill the time until breakfast with a few telephone calls. He would ring Johnny Hall, who was bound to sympathize with his state of mind.

But first he had to have a little fix to keep him going. Just as he could only contemplate giving up heroin when he had already taken some, so he could only recover from the ravages of cocaine by taking more.

After a fix of a moderation that impressed him almost as much as it bored him, Patrick propped up some pillows and installed himself comfortably beside the phone.

'Johnny?'

'Yup.' There was a strained whisper at the other end of the line.

'It's Patrick.'

'What time is it?'

'Eleven.'

'I've only had three hours' sleep in that case.'

'Do you want me to ring back?'

'No, the damage is already done. How are you?'

'Oh, fine. I've had a rather heavy night.'

'Nearly dying, et cetera?' gasped Johnny.

'Yup.'

'Me too. I've been shooting some really disreputable speed, made by a failed chemistry graduate with a shaking hand and a bottle of hydrochloric acid. It's the kind that smells of burnt test tubes when you push the plunger down, and then makes you sneeze compulsively, sending your heart into wild arrhythmic flurries reminiscent of the worst passages of Pound's *Cantos*.'

'As long as your Chinese is good you should be all right.'

'I haven't got any.'

'I have. It's medicine, man, medicine.'

'I'm coming over.'

'To New York?'

'New York! I thought the hesitating, whispering quality of your speech was a combination of my auditory hallucinations and your notorious indolence. It's very disappointing to learn that it has a *real* cause. Why are you there?'

'My father died over here, so I've come to collect his remains.'

'Congratulations. You've achieved half-orphan status. Are they refusing to part with his body? Are they making you put an equal weight of gold in the opposite scales to secure the precious cargo?'

'They haven't billed me for it yet, but if there's even a hint of exaggeration, I'll just leave the rotten thing behind.'

'Good thinking. Are you at all upset?'

'I feel rather haunted.'

'Yes. I remember finding that the ground beneath my feet seemed, if possible, more unreliable than usual, and that my desire to die was, if possible, even greater than before.'

'Yes, there's a lot of that. Plus quite a bad pain in my liver, as if a gravedigger had pushed a shovel under my ribs and stepped on it rather hard.'

'That's what your liver's for, didn't you know?'

'How can you ask that?'

'It's true. Forgive me. So when are we two Olympians going to meet?'

'Well, I should be back tomorrow evening. Could you get some gear, and then I'll come straight round to you from the airport, without having to see the appalling Brian.'

'Of course. Talking of appalling people, I wound up in the flat of some truly idiotic Italians the other night, but they did have some pink crystal coke which made a sound like a glocken-spiel when it dropped into the spoon. Anyhow, I stole the whole lot and locked myself in the bathroom. As you know it takes a lot to ruffle the moronic tranquillity of those doe-eyed Italian dope fiends, but they seemed really pissed off, banging on the door and shouting, "Come out of there, you fucking man, or I kill you. Alessandro, make him come out!"'

'God, how hilarious.'

'Sadly, I think we've said "Ciao" for the last time, or I'd get you some. It was really the stuff to take before pushing the flam-ing longship into the grey waters for the last time.'

'You're making me envious.'

'Well, maybe we'll finally kill ourselves tomorrow night.'

'Definitely. Make sure you get a lot.'

'Yup.'

'OK, I'll see you tomorrow evening.'

'Goodbye.'

'Bye now.'

Patrick hung up the phone with a faint smile on his lips. It al-ways cheered one up talking to Johnny. He immediately dialled a new set of numbers and settled back on the pillows.

'Hello?'

'Kay?'

'Baby! How are you? Hang on, I'll just turn down the music.'

The sound of an exasperated solitary cello grew suddenly muted, and Kay returned to the phone. 'So how are you?' she asked again.

'I haven't managed to get very much sleep.'

'I'm not surprised.'

'Neither am I, I've had about four grams of coke.'

'Oh, God, that's awful. You haven't been taking heroin as well, have you?'

'No, no, no. I've given that up. Just a few tranquillizers.'

'Well, that's something, but why the coke? Think of your poor nose. You can't let it just drop off.'

'My nose is going to be fine. I just felt so depressed.'

'Poor baby, I'm sure you did. Your father dying is the worst thing that could have happened to you. You never got a chance to work things out.'

'We never would have.'

'That's what all sons feel.'

'Mmm . . .'

'I don't like to think of you there alone. Are you seeing anybody nice today, or just morticians?'

'Are you implying that morticians can't be nice?' asked Patrick lugubriously.

'Lord, no, I think they do a wonderful job.'

'I don't really know. I have to collect the ashes, otherwise I'm as free as the wind. I wish you were here.'

'So do I, but I'll, see you tomorrow, won't I?'

'Absolutely. I'll come round straight from the airport.' Patrick lit a cigarette. 'I've been thinking all night,' he continued rapidly, '– if you can call that thinking – about whether ideas come from the continual need to talk, relieved occasionally by the paralysing presence of other people, or if we simply realize in speech what we've already thought.' He hoped this was the kind of question that would distract Kay from the exact details of his return.

'That shouldn't have kept you up,' she laughed. 'I'll tell you the answer tomorrow night. What time do you get in?'

'Around ten,' said Patrick, adding a few hours to the arrival time.

'So I'll see you about eleven?'

'Perfect.'

'Bye, baby. Lots of love.'

'You too. Bye now.'

Patrick put down the phone and made himself another little fix of coke to keep him going. The last fix was still too recent and he had to lie on the bed for a while, sweating, before he could make the next call.

'Hello? Debbie?'

'Darling. I didn't dare call you in case you were asleep.'

'That hasn't been my problem.'

'Well, I'm sorry, I didn't know that.'

'I'm not accusing you of anything. There's no need to be so defensive.'

'I'm not being defensive,' laughed Debbie. 'I was just worried about you. This is ridiculous. I only meant that I've been worried all night about how you were.'

'Ridiculous, I suppose.'

'Oh, please don't let's argue. I wasn't saying *you* were ridiculous. I meant that arguing is ridiculous.'

'Well, I was arguing, and if arguing is ridiculous then I was being ridiculous. My case rests.'

'What case? You always think I'm attacking you. We're not in a courtroom. I'm not your opponent or your enemy.'

Silence. Patrick's head pounded from the effort of not contradicting her. 'So what did you do last night?' he asked at last.

'Well, I was trying to get hold of you for a long time, and then I went to Gregory and Rebecca's dinner thing.'

'Suffering takes place while somebody else is eating. Who said that?'

'It could have been almost anyone,' laughed Debbie.

'It just popped into my mind.'

'Mm. You should try editing some of the things that just pop into your mind.'

'Well, never mind last night, what are you doing tomorrow night?'

'We've been asked to China's thing, but I don't suppose you want to eat and suffer at the same time.' Debbie laughed at her own joke, as was her habit, while Patrick pursued his ruthless policy of never laughing at anything she said, without feeling on this occasion the least trace of meanness.

'What a brilliant remark,' he said drily. 'I won't come along, but nothing could persuade me to stop you from going.'

'Don't be ridiculous, I'll cancel.'

'It sounds as if I had better not stop being ridiculous, or you won't recognize me. I was going to come and see you straight from the airport, but I'll come when you get back from China's. At twelve or one.'

'Well, OK, but I'll cancel if you like.'

'No, no, I wouldn't dream of it.'

'I'd better not go or you'll just use it against me later.'

'We're not in a courtroom. I'm not your opponent or your enemy,' Patrick echoed mockingly.

Silence. Debbie waited until she could make a fresh start, trying to ignore Patrick's impossibly contradictory demands.

'Are you in the Pierre?' she asked brightly.

'If you don't know what hotel I'm in, how could you have rung me?'

'I guessed you were in the Pierre, but I couldn't be sure

since you didn't see fit to tell me,' sighed Debbie. 'Is the room lovely?'

'I think you would like it. There are lots of sachets in the bathroom and a phone next to the loo, so you needn't miss any important calls – an invitation to dinner at China's, for instance.'

'Why are you being so horrid?'

'Am I?'

'I'm going to cancel tomorrow.'

'No, no, *please* don't. It was only a joke. I feel rather mad at the moment.'

'You always feel rather mad,' laughed Debbie.

'Well, my father happens to have died, which makes me feel especially mad.'

'I know, darling, I'm sorry.'

'Plus, I've taken a huge quantity of coke.'

'Was that a good idea?'

'Of course it wasn't a good idea,' yelped Patrick indignantly.

'Do you think your father's death will make you less like him?' Debbie sighed again.

'I'll have the work of two to do now.'

'God, are you sure you wouldn't rather forget the whole thing?'

'Of course I'd rather forget the whole thing,' snapped Patrick, 'but that's not an option.'

'Well, everyone has their cross to bear.'

'Really? What's yours?'

'You,' laughed Debbie.

'Well, be careful or somebody might steal it from you.'

'They'll have to fight for it,' said Debbie affectionately.

'Sweet,' cooed Patrick, wedging the phone between his shoulder and his ear and sitting on the edge of the bed.

'Oh, darling, why do we always argue?' asked Debbie.

'Because we're so in love,' said Patrick haphazardly, as he opened the packet of heroin over the bedside table. He dipped his little finger in the powder, put it to one of his nostrils and inhaled quietly.

'That would seem a strange explanation from anybody else.'

'Well, I hope you're not getting it from anybody else,' said Patrick babyishly, dipping and sniffing several more times.

'Nobody else would dare give it, if they behaved like you,' laughed Debbie.

'It's just that I need you so much,' whispered Patrick, reclining again on the pillows. 'It's frightening if you're addicted to independence like I am.'

'Oh, that's what you're addicted to, is it?'

'Yes. All the other things are illusions.'

'Am I an illusion?'

'No! That's why we argue so much. Do you see?' It sounded good to him.

'Because I'm a *real* obstacle to your independence?'

'To my foolish and misguided desire for independence,' Patrick corrected her gallantly.

'Well, you certainly know how to pay a girl a compliment,' laughed Debbie.

'I wish you were here,' croaked Patrick, dabbing his finger in the white powder again.

'So do I, you must be having a horrible time. Why don't you go and see Marianne? She'll look after you.'

'What a good idea. I'll give her a ring later on.'

'I'd better go now,' sighed Debbie. 'I've got to be interviewed by some silly magazine.'

'What for?'

'Oh, about people who go to lots of parties. I don't know why I agreed to it.'

'Because you're so kind and helpful,' said Patrick.

'Mm . . . I'll call you later. I think you're being very brave and I love you.'

'I love you too.'

'Bye, darling.'

'Bye now.'

Patrick hung up the phone and glanced at the clock. Six thirty-five. He ordered Canadian bacon, fried eggs, toast, porridge, stewed fruit, orange juice, coffee, and tea.

'Is that breakfast for two?' asked the cheerful sounding woman taking the order.

'No, just for one.'

'Wooh, you're sure having a hearty breakfast, honey,' she giggled.

'It's the best way to start the day, don't you find?'

'Sure is!' she agreed.

9

THE SMELL OF DECAYING food had filled the room surprisingly quickly. Patrick's breakfast was devastated without being eaten. A dent in the grey paste of the porridge contained a half-eaten stewed pear; rashers of bacon hung on the edge of a plate smeared with egg yolk, and in the flooded saucer two cigarette butts lay sodden with coffee. A triangle of abandoned toast bore the semicircular imprint of his teeth, and spilled sugar glistened everywhere on the tablecloth. Only the orange juice and the tea were completely finished.

On the television, the Wile E. Coyote, astride an accelerating rocket, crashed explosively into the side of a mountain, while the Road Runner disappeared into a tunnel, emerged at the other side, and receded in a cloud of dust. Watching the Road Runner and the stylized rotundity of the dust in his wake, Patrick was reminded of the early, innocent days of his drug taking, when he had thought that LSD would reveal to him something other than the tyranny of its own effects on his consciousness.

Thanks to his loathing of air conditioning the room was becoming increasingly muggy. Patrick longed to wheel the trolley outside, but the danger of meeting someone in the corridor made him resigned to the growing stench. He had already overheard a conversation about himself between two maids, and although he accepted, theoretically, that it was a hallucination, his strength of mind would not allow him to test this vein of detachment to the extent of opening the door. After all, had one maid not said to the other, 'I told him, "You gonna die, boy, if you go on takin' that shit."' And hadn't the other one replied, "You gotta call the police for your own protection, can't go on livin' like that."'

Wandering into the bathroom, he rolled his right shoulder to ease the pain that was lodged under the shoulder blade. Sceptically but irresistibly, he approached the mirror and noticed that one of his eyelids was drooping much lower than the other, drooping over an inflamed and watering eye. Pulling the skin down he saw the familiar dark yellow of his eyeballs. His tongue was also yellow and thickly coated. Only the purple trenches under his eyes relieved the deadly whiteness of his complexion.

Thank God his father had died. Without a dead parent there was really no excuse for looking so awful. He thought of one of the guiding mottoes of his father's life: 'Never apologize, never explain.'

'What the fuck else is there to do?' muttered Patrick, turning on the taps of his bath and tearing open one of the sachets with his teeth. As he poured the glutinous green liquid into the swirling water he heard, or thought he heard, the ringing of the telephone. Was it the management warning him that the police were on their way up? Whoever it was, the outside world was crashing into his atmosphere, and it filled him with dread. He turned off the taps and listened to the naked ringing of the phone. Why answer? And yet he couldn't bear not to; maybe he was going to be saved.

Sitting on the loo seat, not trusting his own voice, Patrick picked up the phone and said, 'Hello?'

'Patrick, my dear,' drawled a voice from the other end.

'George!'

'Is this a bad time to call?'

'Not at all.'

'I was wondering if you'd like to have lunch with me. It may be the last thing you want to do, of course. You must be feeling perfectly ghastly. It's a terrible shock, you know, Patrick, we all feel that.'

'I do feel a bit wonky, but I'd love to have lunch.'

'I must warn you, I've asked some other people. Charming people, naturally, the nicest sort of Americans. One or two of them have met your father and liked him very much.'

'It sounds perfect,' said Patrick, raising his eyes to the ceiling and grimacing.

'I'm meeting them at the Key Club. Do you know it?'

'No.'

'I think you'll find it amusing in its way. One comes in from the noise and the pollution of New York, and it's quite suddenly like an English country house of a certain sort. God knows whose family they are – I suppose some of the members must have lent them – but the walls are covered in portraits, and the effect is really quite charming. There are all the usual things one would expect to find, like Gentleman's Relish for instance, and strangely enough some things that are nowadays very hard to find in England, like a good Bullshot. Your father and I agreed that we hadn't had such a good Bullshot in years.'

'It sounds heaven.'

'I've asked Ballantine Morgan. I don't know if you've met him. I'm afraid I'm not sure he isn't the most frightful bore, but Sarah has taken to him in a big way and one gets so used to his popping up everywhere that I've asked him to lunch. Oddly enough, I knew someone called Morgan Ballantine once, perfectly charming man; they must be related in some way, but I've never really got to the bottom of it,' said George wistfully.

'Perhaps we'll find out today,' said Patrick.

'Well, I'm not sure I can ask Ballantine again. I have a feeling I must have asked him before, but it's very hard to be sure because one has such trouble listening to his answers.'

'What time shall we meet?'

'About quarter to one in the bar.'

'Perfect.'

'Well, goodbye, my dear.'

'Bye now. See you at quarter to one.' Patrick's voice trailed off.

He turned his bath back on and wandered into the bedroom to pour himself a glass of bourbon. A bath without a drink was like – was like a bath without a drink. Was there any need to elaborate or compare?

A voice on the television spoke excitedly about a complete set of prestigious carving knives, accompanied by an incredible wok, a beautiful set of salad bowls, a book of mouth-watering recipes and, as if this wasn't enough, a machine for cutting vegetables into different shapes. Patrick glazed over as he stared at carrots being sliced, diced, shredded, and cubed.

The mound of shaved ice in which his orange juice had arrived turned out to be completely melted and Patrick, suddenly frustrated, kicked the breakfast trolley and sent it thudding into the wall. He was overwhelmed with despair at the prospect of having no ice in his drink. What was the point of going on? Everything was wrong, everything was hopelessly fucked up. He sat down, defenceless and defeated, on the edge of the bed, the bottle of bourbon held loosely in one hand. He had imagined an icy glass of bourbon resting steamily on the side of the bath, had wagered all his hope on it, but finding that the plan was compromised, nothing stood between him and utter bankruptcy. He drank a gulp straight from the bottle and put it down on the bedside table. It stung his throat and made him shudder.

The clock showed eleven twenty. He must get into action

and prepare himself for the business of the day. Now was the time for speed and alcohol. He must leave the coke behind, or he would spend the whole of lunch shooting up in the loo, as usual.

He got up from the bed and suddenly punched the lampshade, sending the lamp crashing to the carpet. With the bottle of bourbon in his hand, he walked back into the bathroom, where he found the water gently overflowing from the side of the bath and flooding the floor. Refusing to panic or show any surprise, he slowly turned off the water and pushed the sodden bathmat around with his foot, spreading the water into the corners it had not yet reached. He undressed, getting his trousers wet, and tossed his clothes through the open door.

The bath was absurdly hot and Patrick had to pull the plug out and run the cold water before he could climb in. Once he was lying in it, it seemed too cold again. He reached for the bottle of bourbon he had put on the floor beside the bath, and for no reason that he could make out he poured the bourbon from the air and sucked it in as it splashed and trickled over his face.

The bottle was soon empty and he held it under the water, watching the bubbles run out of the neck and then moving it around the bottom of the bath like a submarine stalking enemy ships.

Looking down, he caught sight of his arms and drew in his breath sharply and involuntarily. Among the fading yellow bruises, and the pink threads of old scars, a fresh set of purple wounds clustered around his main veins and at odd points along his arm. At the centre of this unhealthy canvas was the black bulge produced by the missed shot of the night before. The thought that this was his own arm ambushed Patrick quite suddenly, and made him want to cry. He closed his eyes and sank under the surface of the water, breathing out violently from his nose. It didn't bear thinking about.

As he surged out of the water, flicking his head from side to side, Patrick was surprised to hear the phone ring again.

He got out of the bath, and picked up the phone beside the loo. These bathroom phones were really quite useful – perhaps it was China asking him to dinner, begging him to reconsider.

'Yes?' he drawled.

'Hey, Patrick?' said an unmistakable voice on the other end.

'Marianne! How sweet of you to ring.'

'I'm so *sorry* to hear about your father,' said Marianne in a voice that was hesitating but deeply self-assured, whispering but husky. It seemed not to be projected from her body into the world, but to draw the world inside her body; she did not speak so much as swallow articulately. Anyone who listened to her was forced to imagine her long smooth throat, and the elegant S of her body, exaggerated by the extraordinary curve of her spine that made her breasts swell further forward and her bottom further back.

Why had he never been to bed with her? The fact that she had never shown any signs of desire for him had played an unhelpful role, but that might be attributed to her friendship with Debbie. How could she resist him after all, thought Patrick, glancing in the mirror.

Fucking hell. He was going to have to rely on her pity.

'Well, you know how it is,' he drawled sarcastically. 'Death, where is thy sting?'

'Of all the evils in the world which are reproached with an evil character, death is the most innocent of its accusation.'

'Bang on in this case,' said Patrick. 'Who said that anyhow?'

'Bishop Taylor in *The Correct Rules for Holy Dying*,' Marianne disclosed.

'Your favourite book?'

'It's *so* great,' she gasped hoarsely; 'I swear to God, it's the most beautiful prose I've ever read.'

She was clever too. It was really intolerable; he had to have her.

'Will you have dinner with me?' Patrick asked.

'Oh, God, I wish . . .' gasped Marianne, 'but I've got to have dinner with my parents. Do you want to come along?'

'That would be wonderful,' said Patrick, annoyed not to have her to himself.

'Good. I'll let my parents know,' she purred. 'Come on over to their apartment around seven o'clock.'

'Perfect,' said Patrick, and then, unguardedly, 'I adore you.'

'Hey!' said Marianne ambiguously. 'See you later.'

Patrick hung up the phone. He had to have her, he definitely had to have her. She was not merely the latest object on which his greedy desire to be saved had fixed itself; no, she was the woman who was going to save him. The woman whose fine intelligence and deep sympathy and divine body, yes, whose divine body would successfully deflect his attention from the gloomy well shaft of his feelings and the contemplation of his past.

If he got her he would give up drugs forever, or at least have someone really attractive to take them with. He giggled wildly, wrapping a towel around himself and striding back into his bedroom with renewed vigour.

He looked like shit, it was true, but everybody knew that what women really valued, apart from a great deal of money, was gentleness and humour. Gentleness was not his speciality, and he wasn't feeling especially funny, but this was a case of destiny: he had to have her or he would die.

It was time to get practical, to take a Black Beauty and lock the coke in his suitcase. He fished a capsule out of his jacket and swallowed it with impressive efficiency. As he tidied away the coke he could see no reason not to have one last fix. After all, he hadn't had one for almost forty minutes and he would not be having another for a couple of hours. Too lazy to go through the entire ritual, he stuck the needle into an easily accessible vein in the back of his hand and administered the injection.

The effects were certainly growing weaker, he noted, still able to walk around, if a little shakily, with his shoulders hunched high up beside his ears, and his jaw tightly clenched.

It was really unbearable to contemplate being separated from the coke for so long, but he couldn't control himself if he carried supplies with him. The sensible thing to do was to prepare a couple of fixes, one in the rather tired old syringe he had been using all night, its rubber plunger now tending to stick to the sides of the barrel, and the other in the precious untouched syringe. Just as some men wore a handkerchief in their breast pockets to cope with the emergency of a woman's tears, or a sneeze, he often tucked away a couple of syringes into the same pocket to cope with the endlessly renewed emptiness that invaded him. Pip! Pip! Be prepared!

Suffering from yet another aural hallucination, Patrick overheard a conversation between a policeman and a member of the hotel staff.

'Was this guy a regular?'

'Na, he was the holiday-of-a-lifetime type.'

'Ya, ya,' muttered Patrick impatiently. He wasn't that easily intimidated.

He put on a clean white shirt, slipped into his second suit, a dark grey herringbone, stepping into his shoes at the same time as he did up his gold cufflinks. His silver and black tie, unfortunately the only one he had, was flecked with blood, but he managed, by tying it rather too short, to disguise the fact, although he had to tuck the longer strip into his shirt, a practice he despised.

Less easily solved was the problem of his left eye, which had now completely closed, except for an occasional nervous fluttering. He could, with great effort, open it up but only by raising his eyebrows to a position of high indignation. On his way to the

Key Club, he would have to go to the pharmacy and get himself an eyepatch.

His breast pocket was deep enough to conceal the raised plungers of the two syringes, and the bag of smack fitted neatly into the ticket pocket of his jacket. Everything was completely under control, except that he was sweating like a stuck pig and couldn't shake off the sense that he had forgotten something crucial.

Patrick took the chain off the door and glanced back nostalgically at the fetid dark chaos he was leaving behind. The curtains were still closed, the bed unmade, pillows and clothes on the floor, the lamp overturned, the trolley of food rotting in the warm atmosphere, the bathroom flooded and the television, where a man was shouting, 'Come to Crazy Eddie's! The prices are insane,' still flickering.

Stepping out into the corridor, Patrick could not help noticing a policeman standing outside the next-door room.

His overcoat! That was what he had forgotten. But if he doubled back wouldn't it look guilty?

He hovered in the doorway, and then muttered loudly, 'Oh yes, I must . . .' drawing the policeman's attention to himself as he strode back appalled into his room. What were the police doing there? Could they tell what he'd been doing?

His overcoat felt heavy and less reassuring than usual. He mustn't take too long or they would wonder what he was up to.

'You're gonna fry in that coat,' said the policeman with a smile.

'It's not a crime, is it?' asked Patrick, more aggressively than he'd intended.

'Normally,' said the policeman with mock seriousness, 'we'd have to arrest ya, but we got our hands full,' he added with a resigned shrug.

'What happened here?' asked Patrick in his MP-with-the-constituent manner.

'Guy died of a heart attack.'

'The party's over,' said Patrick with a private sense of pleasure.

'There was a party here last night?' The policeman was suddenly curious.

'No, no, I just meant . . .' Patrick felt he was coming from too many directions at once.

'You heard no noises, cries, nothing unusual?'

'No, I heard nothing.'

The policeman relaxed, and ran his hand over his largely bald scalp. 'You're from England, right?'

'That's right.'

'I could tell from the accent.'

'They'll make you a detective soon,' said Patrick boisterously. He waved as he set off down the long carpet of gushing pink and green flower-laden urns, with the policeman's imagined eyebeams burning into his back.

IO

PATRICK SPRANG UP THE steps of the Key Club with unaccustomed eagerness, his nerves squirming like a bed of maggots whose protective stone has been flicked aside, exposing them to the assault of the open sky. Wearing an eyepatch, he hurried gratefully into the gloomy hall of the club, his shirt clinging to his sweating back.

The hall porter took his overcoat in silent surprise and led him down a narrow corridor, its walls covered with memorials to remarkable dogs, horses, and servants, and one or two cartoons bearing witness to the feeble and long-forgotten eccentricities of certain dead members. It really was a temple of English virtues as George had promised.

Ushered into a large panelled room full of green and brown leather armchairs of Victorian design, and huge glossy paintings of dogs holding birds in their obedient mouths, Patrick saw George in the corner, already in conversation with another man.

'Patrick, my dear, how are you?'

'Hello, George.'

'Is there something wrong with your eye?'

'Just a little inflammation.'

'Oh, dear, well, I hope it clears up,' said George sincerely. 'Do you know Ballantine Morgan?' he asked, turning to a small man with weak blue eyes, neat white hair, and a well-trimmed moustache.

'Hello, Patrick,' said Ballantine, giving him a firm handshake. Patrick noticed that he was wearing a black silk tie and wondered if he was in mourning for some reason.

'I was very sorry to hear about your father,' said Ballantine. 'I didn't know him personally, but from everything George tells me it sounds like he was a great English gentleman.'

Jesus Christ, thought Patrick.

'What have you been telling him?' he asked George reproachfully.

'Only what an exceptional man your father was.'

'Yes, I'm pleased to say that he was exceptional,' said Patrick. 'I've never met anybody quite like him.'

'He refused to compromise,' drawled George. 'What was it he used to say? "Nothing but the best, or go without."'

'Always felt the same way myself,' said Ballantine fatuously.

'Would you like a drink?' asked George.

'I'll have one of those Bullshots you spoke about so passionately this morning.'

'Passionately,' guffawed Ballantine.

'Well, there are some things one feels passionately about,' smiled George, looking at the barman and briefly raising his index finger. 'I shall feel quite bereft without your father,' he continued. 'Oddly enough, it was here that we were supposed to be having lunch on the day that he died. The last time I met him we went to a perfectly extraordinary place that has an arrangement of some sort – I can't believe that it's reciprocal – with the Travellers in Paris. The portraits were at least four times life size – we laughed about that a good deal – he was on very good form, although, of course, there was always an undercurrent of disappointment with your father. I think he really enjoyed himself on this last visit. You must never forget, Patrick, that he was very proud of you. I'm sure you know that. Really proud.'

Patrick felt sick.

Ballantine looked bored, as people do when someone they don't know is being discussed. He had a very natural desire to talk about himself, but felt that a little pause was in order.

'Yes,' said George to the waiter. 'We'd like two Bullshots and . . .' He leaned enquiringly towards Ballantine.

'I'll have another martini,' said Ballantine. There was a short silence.

'What a lot of faithful gundogs,' said Patrick wearily, glancing around the room.

'I suppose a lot of the members are keen shots,' said George. 'Ballantine is one of the best shots in the world.'

'Whoa, whoa, whoa,' protested Ballantine, *used* to be the best shot in the world.' He held out his hand to arrest the flow of self-congratulation, but was no more effective than King Canute in the face of another great force of nature. 'What I haven't lost,' he couldn't help pointing out, 'is a gun collection which is probably the greatest in the world.'

The waiter returned with the drinks.

'Would you bring me the book called *The Morgan Gun Collection*?' Ballantine asked him.

'Yes, Mr Morgan,' said the waiter in a voice that suggested he had dealt with this request before.

Patrick tasted the Bullshot and found himself smiling irresistibly. He drank half of it in one gulp, put it down for a moment, picked it up again, and said to George, 'You were right about these Bullshots,' drinking the rest.

'Would you like another one?' asked George.

'I think I will, they're so delicious.'

The waiter weaved his way back to the table with an enormous white volume. On the front cover, visible from some way off, was a photograph of two silver-inlaid pistols.

'Here you are, Mr Morgan,' said the waiter.

'Ahh-aa,' said Ballantine, taking the book.

'And another Bullshot, would you?' said George.

'Yes, sir.'

Ballantine tried to suppress a grin of pride. 'These guns right here,' he said, tapping the front cover of the book, 'are a pair of Spanish seventeenth-century duelling pistols which are the most valuable firearms in the world. If I tell you that the triggers cost over a million dollars to replace, you'll have some idea of what I mean.'

'It's enough to make you wonder if it's worth fighting a duel,' said Patrick.

'The original cleaning brushes alone are worth over a quarter of a million dollars,' chuckled Ballantine, 'so you wouldn't want to fire the pistols too often.'

George looked pained and distant, but Ballantine in his role as the Triumph of Life, performing the valuable task of distracting Patrick from his terrible grief, was unstoppable. He put on a pair of tortoiseshell half-moon spectacles, pushed his head back, and looked condescendingly at his book, while he allowed the pages to flicker past.

'This here,' he said, stopping the flow of pages and holding the book open towards Patrick, 'this is the first Winchester repeating rifle ever manufactured.'

'Amazing,' sighed Patrick.

'When I was shooting in Africa, I brought down a lion with this gun,' admitted Ballantine. 'It took a number of shots – it doesn't have the calibre of a modern weapon.'

'You must have been all the more grateful for the repeating mechanism,' Patrick suggested.

'Oh, I was covered by a couple of reliable hunters,' said Ballantine complacently. 'I describe the incident in the book I wrote about my African hunting trips.'

The waiter returned with Patrick's second Bullshot, and another large book under his arm.

'Harry thought you might want this as well, Mr Morgan.'

'Well, I'll be darned,' said Ballantine with a colloquial twang, craning back in his chair and beaming at the barman. 'I mentioned the book and it falls in my lap. Now that's what I call service!'

He opened the new volume with familiar relish. 'Some of my friends have been kind enough to say that I have an excellent prose style,' he explained in a voice that did not sound as puzzled as it was meant to. 'I don't see it myself, I just put it down as it was. The way I hunted in Africa is a way of life that doesn't exist anymore, and I just told the truth about it, that's all.'

'Yes,' drawled George. 'Journalists and people of that sort write a lot of nonsense about what they call the "Happy Valley Set". Well, I was there a good deal at the time, and I can tell you there was no more unhappiness than usual, no more drunkenness than usual, people behaved just as they did in London or New York.'

George leaned over and picked up an olive. 'We did have dinner in our pyjamas,' he added thoughtfully, 'which I suppose *was* a little unusual. But not because we all wanted to jump into bed with one another, although obviously a good deal of that sort of thing went on, as it always does; it was simply that we had to get up the next day at dawn to go hunting. When we got back in the afternoon, we would have "toasty", which would be a whisky and soda, or whatever you wanted. And then they would say, "Bathy, bwana, bathy time," and run you a bath. After that more "toasty", and then dinner in one's pyjamas. People behaved just as they did anywhere else, although I must say, they did drink a great deal, really a great deal.'

'It sounds like heaven,' said Patrick.

'Well, you know, George, the drinking went with the life-style. You just sweated it all out,' said Ballantine.

'Yes, quite,' said George.

You don't have to go to Africa to sweat too much, thought Patrick.

'This is a photograph of me with a Tanganyikan mountain goat,' said Ballantine, handing Patrick the second book. 'I was told that it was the last potent male of the species, so I can't help having mixed feelings about it.'

God, he's sensitive too, thought Patrick, looking at the photograph of a younger Ballantine, in a khaki hat, kneeling beside the corpse of a goat.

'I took the photographs myself,' said Ballantine casually. 'A number of professional photographers have begged me to tell them my "secret", but I've had to disappoint them – the only secret is to get a fascinating subject and photograph it the best way you know how.'

'Amazing,' mumbled Patrick.

'Sometimes, from a foolish impulse of pride,' Ballantine continued, 'I included myself in the shots and allowed one of the boys to press the trigger – they could do that well enough.'

'Ah,' said George with uncharacteristic verve, 'here's Tom.'

An exceptionally tall man in a blue seersucker suit worked his way through the tables. He had thin but rather chaotic grey hair, and drooping bloodhound eyes.

Ballantine closed the two books and rested them on his knees. The loop of his monstrous vanity was complete. He had been talking about a book in which he wrote about his photographs of the animals he had shot with guns from his own magnificent collection, a collection photographed (alas, not by him) in the second book.

'Tom Charles,' said George, 'Patrick Melrose.'

'I see you've been talking to the Renaissance Man,' said Tom in a dry gravelly voice. 'How are you, Ballantine? Been keeping Mr Melrose up to date on your achievements?'

'Well, I thought he might be interested in the guns,' said Ballantine peevishly.

'The thought he never has, is that somebody might *not* be interested in the guns,' Tom croaked. 'I was sorry to hear about your father, I guess you must be feeling sick at heart.'

'I suppose I am,' said Patrick, caught off balance. 'It's a terrible time for anybody. Whatever you feel, you feel it strongly, and you feel just about everything.'

'Do you want a drink, or do you want to go straight in to lunch?' asked George.

'Let's eat,' said Tom.

The four men got up. Patrick noticed that the two Bullshots had made him feel much more substantial. He could also detect the steady lucid throb of the speed. Perhaps he could allow himself a quick fix before lunch.

'Where are the loos, George?'

'Oh, just through that door in the corner,' said George. 'We'll be in the dining room, up the stairs on the right.'

'I'll see you there.'

Patrick broke away from the group and headed for the door that George had pointed out. On the other side he found a large cool room of black and white marble, shiny chrome fittings, and mahogany doors. At one end of a row of basins was a pile of starched linen with 'Key Club' sewn into the corner in green cotton, and, beside it, a large wicker basket for discarding the used towels.

With sudden efficiency and stealth, he picked up a towel,

filled a glass with water, and slipped into one of the mahogany cubicles.

There was no time to waste and Patrick seemed to put the glass down, drop the towel, and take off his jacket in one gesture.

He sat on the loo seat and put the syringe carefully on the towel in his lap. He rolled his sleeve up tightly on his bicep to act as a makeshift tourniquet and, while he frantically clenched and unclenched his fist, removed the cap of the syringe with the thumb of his other hand.

His veins were becoming quite shy, but a lucky stab in the bicep, just below his rolled-up sleeve, yielded the gratifying spectacle of a red mushroom cloud uncurling in the barrel of the syringe.

He pushed the plunger down hard and unrolled his shirt as fast as he could to allow the solution a free passage through his bloodstream.

Patrick wiped the trickle of blood from his arm and flushed out the syringe, also squirting its pinkish water into the towel.

The rush was disappointing. Although his hands were shaking and his heart was pounding, he had missed that blissful fainting sensation, that heartbreaking moment, as compressed as the autobiography of a drowning man, but as elusive and intimate as the smell of a flower.

What was the fucking point of shooting coke if he wasn't going to get a proper rush? It was intolerable. Indignant and yet anxious about the consequences, Patrick took out the second syringe, sat down on the loo again, and rolled up his sleeve. The strange thing was that the rush seemed to be getting stronger, as if it had been dammed up against his shirt sleeve and had taken unusually long to reach his brain. In any case he was now committed to a second fix and, with a combination of bowel-loosening excitement and dread, he tried to put the spike back in exactly the same spot as before.

As he rolled down his sleeve this time, he realized that he had made a serious mistake. This was too much. Only far too much was enough. But this was more than enough.

Too overwhelmed to flush it out, he only managed to put the cap back on the precious new syringe and drop it on the floor. He slumped against the back wall of the cubicle, his head hanging to one side, gasping and wincing like an athlete who has just crossed the finishing line after losing a race, the prickle of fresh sweat breaking out all over the surface of his skin, and his eyes tightly closed while a rapid succession of scenes flashed across his inner vision: a bee crashing drunkenly into the pollen-laden pistils of a flower; fissures spreading over the concrete of a disintegrating dam; a long blade cutting strips of flesh from the body of a dead whale; a barrel of gouged-out eyes tumbling stickily between the cylinders of a wine press.

He forced his eyes open. His inner life was definitely *in decline* and it would be more cautious to go upstairs and face the confusing effects of other people than sink any further into this pool of discrete and violent imagery.

The aural hallucinations that afflicted Patrick as he groped his way along the wall towards the line of basins were not yet organized into words, but consisted of twisting strands of sound and an eerie sense of space, like amplified breathing.

He mopped his face and emptied the glass of bloody water down the drain. Remembering the second syringe, he quickly tried to clean it out, watching the reflection of the door in the mirror in case somebody came in. His hands shook so badly it was hard to hold the needle under the tap.

It must have been ages since he left the others. They were probably ordering the bill by now. Short of breath, but with insane urgency, he stuffed the wet syringe back into his breast pocket and hurried back through the bar, into the hall, and up the main staircase.'

In the dining room he saw George, Tom, and Ballantine still reading the menu. How long had he kept them waiting, politely postponing their lunch? He moved clumsily towards the table, the strands of curving, twisting sound bending the space around him.

George looked up.

'Ziouuu . . . Ziouuu . . . Ziouuu . . .' he asked. 'Chok-chok-chok-chok,' said Ballantine, like a helicopter.

'Aioua. Aioua,' Tom suggested.

What the fuck were they trying to tell him? Patrick sat down and mopped his face with the pale pink napkin.

'Sot,' he said in a long elastic whisper. 'Chok-chok-chok,' Ballantine replied.

George was smiling, but Patrick listened helplessly as the sounds streamed past him like a photograph of brake lights on a wet street.

'Ziou . . . Ziou . . . Ziou . . . Aiou. Aiou. Chokchok-chok.'

He sat astonished in front of the menu, as if he had never seen one before. There were pages of dead things – cows, shrimps, pigs, oysters, lambs – stretched out like a casualty list, accompanied by a brief description of how they had been treated since they died – skewered, grilled, smoked, and boiled. Christ, if they thought he was going to eat these things they must be mad.

He had seen the dark blood from the neck of a sheep gushing into the dry grass. The busy flies. The stench of offal. He had heard the roots tearing as he eased a carrot out of the ground. Any living man squatted on a mound of corruption, cruelty, filth, and blood.

If only his body would turn into a pane of glass, the fleshless interval between two spaces, knowing both but belonging to neither, then he would be set free from the gross and savage debt he owed to the rest of nature.

'Ziou . . . Ziou . . . wan?' asked George.

'Um . . . I'll . . . um, eh just,' Patrick felt remote from his own voice, as if it was coming out of his feet. 'I'll . . . um, eh, have . . . another . . . Bullshot . . . late   breakfast . . . eh . . . not really hungry.'

The effort of saying these few words left him breathless.

'Chok-chok-chok-chok,' objected Ballantine. 'Aioua sure. Aioua ziou?' asked Tom.

What was he saying 'Ziou' for? The fugue was growing more complicated. Before long George would be saying 'Chok' or 'Aioua', and then where would he stand? Where would any of them stand?

'Justanothershot,' gasped Patrick, 'really.' Mopping his brow again, he stared fixedly at the stem of his wineglass which, caught by the sun, cast a fractured bone of light onto the white tablecloth, like an X-ray of a broken finger. The twisting echoing sounds around him had started to die down to the faint hiss of an untuned television. It was no longer incomprehension but a kind of sadness, like an enormously amplified postcoital gloom, that cut him off from what was happening around him. 'Martha Boeing,' Ballantine was saying, 'told me that she was experiencing dizzy spells on the drive up to Newport and that her doctor told her to take along these small French cheeses to eat on the journey – evidently it was some kind of protein deprivation.'

'I can't imagine that Martha's malnutrition is too severe,' said Tom.

'Well,' remarked George diplomatically, 'not everybody has to be driven to Newport as often as she does.'

'I mention it because I,' said Ballantine with some pride, 'was getting the same symptoms.'

'On the same journey?' asked Tom.

'The exact same journey,' Ballantine confirmed.

'Well, that's Newport for you,' said Tom; 'sucks the protein right out of you. Only sporting types can make it there without medical assistance.'

'But *my* doctor,' said Ballantine patiently, 'recommended peanut butter. Martha was sorta doubtful about it, and said that these French cheeses were so great because you could just peel them off and pop them in your mouth. She wanted to know how you were supposed to eat the peanut butter. "With a spoon," I said, "like caviar."' Ballantine chuckled. 'Well, she had no answer to that,' he concluded triumphantly, 'and I believe she's going to be switching to peanut butter.'

'Somebody ought to warn Sun-Pat,' said Tom.

'Yes, you must be careful,' drawled George, 'or you'll start a run on this butter of yours. Once these Newport people take to something, there's really no stopping them. I remember Brooke Rivers asking me where I had my shirts made, and the next time I ordered some they told me there was a two-year waiting list. They told me there had been a perfectly extraordinary surge in American orders. Well, of course, I knew who that was.'

A waiter came to take the orders and George asked Patrick if he was absolutely sure that he didn't want 'something solid'.

'Absolutely. Nothing solid,' Patrick replied.

'I never knew your father to lose his appetite,' said George.

'No, it was the one thing about him that was reliable.'

'Oh, I wouldn't go that far,' protested George. 'He was an awfully good pianist. Used to keep one up all night,' he explained to the others, 'playing the most spellbinding music'

Pastiche and parody and hands twisted like old vine stumps, thought Patrick.

'Yes, he could be very impressive at the piano,' he said out loud.

'And in conversation,' George added.

'Mm . . .' said Patrick. 'It depends what you find impressive. Some people don't like uninterrupted rudeness, or so I'm told.'

'Who *are* these people?' asked Tom, looking around the room with mock alarm.

'It is true,' said George, 'that I once or twice had to tell him to stop being quite so argumentative.'

'And what did he do?' asked Ballantine, thrusting his chin forward to get more of his neck out of its tight collar.

'Told me to bugger off,' replied George tersely.

'Hell,' said Ballantine, seeing an opportunity for wisdom and diplomacy. 'You know, people argue about the darnedest things. Why, I spent an entire weekend trying to persuade my wife to dine in Mortimer's the evening we got back to New York. "I'm all Mortimered out," she kept saying, "can't we go someplace else?" Of course she couldn't say where.'

'Of course she couldn't,' said Tom, 'she hasn't seen the inside of another restaurant in fifteen years.'

'All Mortimered out,' repeated Ballantine, his indignation tinged with a certain pride at having married such an original woman.

A lobster, some smoked salmon, a crab salad, and a Bullshot arrived. Patrick lifted the drink greedily to his lips and then froze, hearing the hysterical bellowing of a cow, loud as an abattoir in the muddy liquid of his glass.

'Fuck it,' he murmured, taking a large gulp.

His defiance was soon rewarded with the vivid fantasy that a hoof was trying to kick its way out of his stomach. He remembered, when he was eighteen, writing to his father from a psychiatric ward, trying to explain his reasons for being there, and receiving a short note in reply. Written in Italian, which his father knew he could not understand, it turned out, after some research, to be a quotation from Dante's *Inferno*: 'Consider your descent / You were not made to live among beasts / But to pursue virtue and knowledge.' What had seemed a frustratingly sublime response at the time, struck him with a fresh sense of relevance now that he was listening to the sound of howling, snuffling cattle and felt, or thought he felt, another blow on the inner wall of his stomach.

As his heart rate increased again and a new wave of sweat prickled his skin, Patrick realized that he was going to be sick.

'Excuse me,' he said, getting up abruptly.

'Are you all right, my dear?' said George.

'I feel rather sick.'

'Perhaps we should get you a doctor.'

'I have the best doctor in New York,' said Ballantine. 'Just mention my name and . . .'

Patrick tasted a bitter surge of bile from his stomach. He swallowed stubbornly and, without time to thank Ballantine for his kind offer, hurried out of the dining room.

On the stairs Patrick forced down a second mouthful of vomit, more solid than the first. Time was running out. Wave after wave of nausea heaved the contents of his stomach into his mouth with increasing velocity. Feeling dizzy, his vision blurred by watering eyes, he fumbled down the corridor, knocking one of the hunting prints askew with his shoulder. By the time he reached the cool marble sanctuary of the lavatories, his cheeks were as swollen as a trumpeter's. A member of the club, admiring himself with that earnestness reserved for mirrors, found that the ordinary annoyance of being interrupted was soon replaced by alarm at being so close to a man who was obviously about to vomit.

Patrick, despairing of reaching the loo, threw up in the basin next to him, turning the taps on at the same time.

'Jesus,' said the member, 'you could have done that in the john.'

'Too far,' said Patrick, throwing up a second time. 'Jesus,' repeated the man, leaving hastily.

Patrick recognized traces of last night's dinner and, with his stomach already empty, knew that he would soon be bringing up that sour yellow bile which gives vomiting its bad name.

To encourage the faster disappearance of the vomit he twirled his finger in the plughole and increased the flow of water with his other hand. He longed to gain the privacy of one of the cubicles before he was sick again. Feeling queasy and hot, he abandoned the not yet entirely clean basin and staggered over to one of the mahogany cubicles. He hardly had time to slide the brass lock closed before he was stooped over the bowl of the loo convulsing fruitlessly. Unable to breathe or to swallow, he found himself trying to vomit with even more conviction than he had tried to avoid vomiting a few minutes earlier.

Just when he was about to faint from lack of air he managed to bring up a globule of that yellow bile he had been anticipating with such dread.

'Fucking hell,' he cursed, sliding down the wall. However often he did it, being sick never lost its power to surprise him.

Shaken by coming so close to choking, he lit a cigarette and smoked it through the bitter slime that coated his mouth. The question now, of course, was whether to take some heroin to help him calm down.

The risk was that it would make him feel even more nauseous.

Wiping the sweat from his hands, he gingerly opened the packet of heroin over his lap, dipped his little finger into it, and sniffed through both nostrils. Not feeling any immediate ill effects, he repeated the dose.

Peace at last. He closed his eyes and sighed. The others could just fuck off. He wasn't going back. He was going to fold his wings and (he took another sniff) relax. Where he took his smack was his home, and more often than not that was in some stranger's bog.

He was so tired; he really must get some sleep. Get some

sleep. Fold his wings. But what if George and the others sent somebody to look for him and they found the sick-spattered basin and hammered on the door of the cubicle? Was there no peace, no resting place? Of course there wasn't. What an absurd question.

II

'I'M HERE TO COLLECT the remains of David Melrose,' said
Patrick to the grinning young man with the big jaw and the mop
of shiny chestnut hair.

'Mr . . . David . . . Melrose,' he mused, as he turned the pages
of a large leather register.

Patrick leaned over the edge of the counter, more like a
grounded pulpit than a desk, and saw, next to the register, a cheap
exercise book marked 'Almost Dead'. That was the file to get on;
might as well apply straight away.

Escaping from the Key Club had left him strangely elated.
After passing out for an hour in the loo, he had woken refreshed but unable to face the others. Bolting past the doorman like a criminal, he had dashed round the corner to a
bar, and then walked on to the funeral parlour. Later he would
have to apologize to George. Lie and apologize as he always
did or wanted to do after any contact with another human
being.

'Yes, sir,' said the receptionist brightly, finding the page. 'Mr
David Melrose.'

'I have come not to praise him, but to bury him,' Patrick declared, thumping the table theatrically.

'Bu-ry him?' stammered the receptionist. 'We under-stood that party was to be cre-mated.'

'I was speaking metaphorically.'

'Metaphorically,' repeated the young man, not quite reassured. Did that mean the customer was going to sue or not?

'Where are the ashes?' asked Patrick.

'I'll go fetch them for you, sir,' said the receptionist. 'We have you down for a box,' he added, no longer as confident as he'd sounded at first.

'That's right,' said Patrick. 'No point in wasting money on an urn. The ashes are going to be scattered anyway.'

'Right,' said the receptionist with uncertain cheerfulness. Glancing sideways he quickly rectified his tone. 'I'll attend to that right away, sir,' he said in an unctuous and artificially loud singsong, setting off promptly towards a door concealed in the panelling.

Patrick looked over his shoulder to find out what had provoked this new eagerness. He saw a tall figure he recognized without immediately being able to place him.

'We're in an industry where the supply and the demand are *bound* to be identical,' quipped this half-familiar man.

Behind him stood the bald, moustachioed director who had led Patrick to his father's corpse the previous afternoon. He seemed to wince and smile at the same time.

'We've got the one resource that's never going to run out,' said the tall man, obviously enjoying himself.

The director raised his eyebrows and flickered his eyes in Patrick's direction.

Of course, thought Patrick, it was that ghastly man he'd met on the plane.

'Goddamn,' whispered Earl Hammer, 'I guess I still got something to learn about PR.' Recognizing Patrick, he shouted 'Bobby!' across the chequered marble hall.

'Patrick,' said Patrick.

'Paddy! Of course. That eyepatch was unfamiliar to me. What happened to you anyway? Some lady give you a black eye?' Earl guffawed, pounding over to Patrick's side.

'Just a little inflammation,' said Patrick. 'Can't see properly out of that eye.'

'That's too bad,' said Earl. 'What are you doing here anyhow? When I told you on the plane that I had been diversifying my business interests, I bet you never guessed that I was in the process of acquiring New York's premier funeral parlour.'

'I hadn't guessed that,' confessed Patrick. 'And I don't suppose you guessed that I was coming to collect my father's remains from New York's premier funeral parlour.'

'Hell,' said Earl, 'I'm sorry to hear that. I'll bet he was a fine man.'

'He was perfect in his way,' said Patrick.

'My condolences,' said Earl, with that abrupt solemnity that Patrick recognized from the discussion about Miss Hammer's volleyball prospects.

The receptionist returned with a simple wooden box about a foot long and eight inches high.

'It's so much more compact than a coffin, don't you think?' commented Patrick.

'There's no way of denying that,' Earl replied.

'Do you have a bag?' Patrick asked the receptionist.

'A bag?'

'Yes, a carrier bag, a brown-paper bag, that sort of thing.'

'I'll go check that, sir.'

'Paddy,' said Earl, as if he had been giving the matter some thought, 'I want you to have a ten per cent discount.'

'Thank you,' said Patrick, genuinely pleased.

'Don't mention it,' said Earl.

The receptionist returned with a brown-paper bag that was

already a little crumpled, and Patrick imagined that he'd had to empty out his groceries hastily in order not to fail in front of his employer.

'Perfect,' said Patrick.

'Do we charge for these bags?' asked Earl, and then, before the receptionist could answer, he added, 'Because this one's on me.'

'Earl, I don't know what to say.'

'It's nothing,' said Earl. 'I have a meeting right now, but I would be honoured if you would have a drink with me later.'

'Can I bring my father?' asked Patrick, raising the bag.

'Hell, yes,' said Earl, laughing.

'Seriously, though, I'm afraid I can't. I'm going out to dinner tonight and I have to fly back to England tomorrow.'

'That's too bad.'

'Well, it's a great regret to me,' said Patrick with a wan smile, as he headed quickly for the door.

'Goodbye, old friend,' said Earl, with a big wave.

'Bye now,' said Patrick, flicking up the collar of his overcoat before he ventured into the rush hour street.

In the black-lacquered hall, opposite the opening doors of the elevator, an African mask gawked from a marble-topped console table. The gilded aviary of a Chippendale mirror gave Patrick a last chance to glance with horror at his fabulously ill-looking face before turning to Mrs Banks, Marianne's emaciated mother, who stood vampirishly in the elegant gloom.

Opening her arms so that her black silk dress stretched from her wrists to her knees, like bat's wings, she cocked her head a little to one side, and exclaimed with excrutiated sympathy, 'Oh, Patrick, we were so sorry to hear your news.'

'Well,' said Patrick, tapping the casket he held under his arm, 'you know how it is: ashes to ashes, dust to dust. What the Lord giveth he taketh away. After what I regard, in this case, as an un-naturally long delay.'

'Is that . . . ?' asked Mrs Banks, staring round-eyed at the brown-paper bag.

'My father,' confirmed Patrick.

'I must tell Ogilvy we'll be one more for dinner,' she said with peals of chic laughter. That was Nancy Banks all over, as maga-zines often pointed out after photographing her drawing room, so daring but so *right*.

'Banquo doesn't eat meat,' said Patrick, putting the box down firmly on the hall table.

Why had he said Banquo? Nancy wondered, in her husky inner voice which, even in the deepest intimacy of her own thoughts, was turned to address a large and fascinated audience. Could he, in some crazy way, feel responsible for his father's death? Because he had wished for it so often in fantasy? God, she had become good at this after seventeen years of analysis. After all, as Dr Morris had said when they were talking through their affair, what was an analyst but a former patient who couldn't think of anything better to do? Sometimes she missed Jeffrey. He had let her call him Jeffrey during the 'letting-go pro-cess' that had been brought to such an abrupt close by his sui-cide. Without even a note! Was she really meeting the challenges of life, as Jeffrey had promised? Maybe she was 'incompletely analysed'. It was too dreadful to contemplate.

'Marianne's dying to see you,' she murmured consolingly as she led Patrick into the empty drawing room. He stared at a ba-roque escritoire cascading with crapulous putti.

'She got a phone call the moment you arrived and couldn't get out of answering it,' she added.

'We have the whole evening . . .' said Patrick. And the whole night, he thought optimistically. The drawing room was a sea of pink lilies, their shining pistils accusing him of lust. He was dangerously obsessed, dangerously obsessed. And his thoughts, like a bobsleigh walled with ice, would not change their course until he had crashed or achieved his end. He wiped his hands sweatily on his trousers, amazed to have found a preoccupation stronger than drugs. 'Ah, there's Eddy,' exclaimed Nancy.

Mr Banks strode into the room in a chequered lumberjack shirt and a pair of baggy trousers. 'Hello,' he said with his rapid little blur, 'I was tho thorry to hear about your fawther. Marianne says that he was a wemarkable man.'

'You should have heard the remarks,' said Patrick.

'Did you have a very difficult relationship with him?' asked Nancy encouragingly.

'Yup,' Patrick replied.

'When did the twouble stawt?' asked Eddy, settling down on the faded orange velvet of a bow-legged marquise.

'Oh, June the ninth, nineteen-o-six, the day he was born.'

'That early?' smiled Nancy.

'Well, we're not going to resolve the question of whether his problems were congenital or not, at least not before dinner; but even if they weren't, he didn't delay in acquiring them. By all accounts, the moment he could speak he dedicated his new skill to hurting people. By the age of ten he was banned from his grandfather's house because he used to set everyone against each other, cause accidents, force people to do things they didn't want to.'

'You make him sound evil in a rather old-fashioned way. The satanic child,' said Nancy sceptically.

'It's a point of view,' said Patrick. 'When he was around, people were always falling off rocks, or nearly drowning, or bursting into tears. His life consisted of acquiring more and more victims for his malevolence and then losing them again.'

'He must have been charming as well,' said Nancy.

'He was a kitten,' said Patrick.

'But wouldn't we now say that he was just wery disturbed?' asked Eddy.

'So what if we did? When the effect somebody has is destructive enough the cause becomes a theoretical curiosity. There are some very nasty people in the world and it is a pity if one of them is your father.'

'I don't think that people noo so much about how to bring up kids in those days. A lot of parents in your fawther's generation just didn't know how to express their love.'

'Cruelty is the opposite of love,' said Patrick, 'not just some inarticulate version of it.'

'Sounds right to me,' said a husky voice from the doorway.

'Oh, hi,' said Patrick, swivelling around in his chair, suddenly self-conscious in Marianne's presence.

Marianne sailed towards him across the dim drawing room, its floorboards creaking underfoot, and her body tipped forward at a dangerous angle like the figurehead on the prow of a ship.

Patrick rose and wrapped his arms around her with greed and desperation.

'Hey, Patrick,' she said, hugging him warmly. 'Hey,' she repeated soothingly when he seemed reluctant to let go. 'I'm so sorry. Really, really sorry.'

Oh, God, thought Patrick, this is where I want to be buried.

'We were just tawking about how parents sometimes don't know how to express their love,' lisped Eddy.

'Well, I guess I wouldn't know about that,' said Marianne with a cute smile.

Her back as curved as a negress's, she walked towards the drinks tray with awkward and hesitating grace, as if she were a mermaid only recently equipped with human legs, and helped herself to a glass of champagne.

'Does anybody wanna a glass of this,' she stammered, craning her neck forward and frowning slightly, as if the question might contain hidden depths.

Nancy declined. She preferred cocaine. Whatever you said about it, it wasn't fattening. Eddy accepted and Patrick said he wanted whisky.

'Eddy hasn't really gotten over *his* father's death,' said Nancy to nudge the conversation on a little.

'I never really told my fawther how I felt,' explained Eddy, smiling at Marianne as she handed him a glass of champagne.

'Neither did I,' said Patrick. 'Probably just as well in my case.'

'What would you have said?' asked Marianne, fixing him intently with her dark blue eyes.

'I would have said . . . I can't say . . .' Patrick was bewildered and annoyed by having taken the question seriously. 'Never mind,' he mumbled, and poured himself some whisky.

Nancy reflected that Patrick was not really pulling his weight in this conversation.

'They fuck you up. They don't mean to but they do,' she sighed.

'Who says they don't mean to?' growled Patrick.

'Philip Larkin,' said Nancy, with a glassy little laugh.

'But what was it about your father that you couldn't get over?' Patrick asked Eddy politely.

'He was kind of a hero to me. He always noo what to do in any situation, or at least what he wanted to do. He knew how to handle money and women; and when he hooked a three-hundred-pound marlin, the marlin always lost. And when he bid for a picture at auction, he always got it.'

'And when *you* wanted to sell it again you always succeeded,' said Nancy humorously.

'Well, you're *my* hero,' stammered Marianne to her father, 'and I don't want to get over it.'

Fucking hell, thought Patrick, what do these people do all day, write scripts for *The Brady Bunch*? He hated happy families with their mutual encouragement, and their demonstrative affection, and the impression they gave of valuing each other more than other people. It was utterly disgusting.

'Are we going out to dinner together?' Patrick asked Marianne abruptly.

'We could have dinner here.' She swallowed, a little frown clouding her face.

'Would it be frightfully rude to go out?' he insisted. 'I'd like to talk.'

The answer was clearly yes, as far as Nancy was concerned, it would be frightfully rude. Consuela was preparing the scallops this very minute. But in life, as in entertaining, one had to be flexible and graceful and, in this case, some allowances should be made for Patrick's bereavement. It was hard not to be insulted by the implication that she was handling it badly, until one considered that his state of mind was akin to temporary insanity.

'Of course not,' she purred.

'Where shall we go?' asked Patrick.

'Ah . . . there's a small Armenian restaurant I really really like,' Marianne suggested.

'A small Armenian restaurant,' Patrick repeated flatly.

'It's so great,' gulped Marianne.

12

UNDER A CERULEAN DOME dotted with dull-gold stars Marianne and Patrick, in a blue velveteen booth of their own, read the plastic-coated menus of the Byzantium Grill. The muffled rumble of a subway train shuddered underfoot and the iced water, always so redundant and so quick to arrive, trembled in the stout ribbed glasses. Everything was shaking, thought Patrick, molecules dancing in the tabletop, electrons spinning, signals and soundwaves undulating through his cells, cells shimmering with country music and police radios, roaring garbage trucks and shattering bottles; his cranium shuddering like a drilled wall, and each sensation Tabasco-flicked onto his soft grey flesh.

A passing waiter kicked Patrick's box of ashes, looked round and apologized. Patrick refused his offer to 'check that for you' and slid the box further under the table with his feet.

Death should express the deeper being rather than represent the occasion for a new role. Who had said that? The terror of forgetting. And yet here was his father being kicked around by a waiter. A new role, definitely a new role.

Perhaps Marianne's body would enable him to forget his father's corpse, perhaps it contained a junction where his obsession with his father's death and his own dying could switch tracks and hurtle towards its new erotic destination with all of its old morbid élan. What should he say? What could he say?

Angels, of course, made love without obstruction of limb or joint, but in the sobbing frustration of human love-making, the exasperating substitution of ticklishness for interfusion, and the ever-renewed drive to pass beyond the mouth of the river to the calm lake where we were conceived, there would have been, thought Patrick, as he pretended to read the menu but in fact fixed his eyes on the green velvet that barely contained Marianne's breasts, an adequate expression of the failure of words to convey the confusion and intensity he felt in the wake of his father's death.

Besides, not having fucked Marianne was like not having read the *Iliad* – something else he had been meaning to do for a long time.

Like a sleeve caught in some implacable and uncomprehending machine, his need to be understood had become lodged in her blissful but dangerously indifferent body. He would be dragged through a crushing obsession and spat out the other end without her pulse flickering or her thoughts wandering from their chosen paths.

Instead of her body saving him from his father's corpse, their secrets would become intertwined; half the horizon formed by his broken lip, half by her unbroken lips. And this vertiginous horizon, like an encircling waterfall, would suck him away from safety, as if he stood on a narrow column of rock watching the dragging water turn smooth around him, seeming still as it turned to fall, falling everywhere.

Jesus, thought Marianne, why had she agreed to have dinner with this guy? He read the menu like he was staring at a ravine from a high bridge. She couldn't bear to ask him another question about his father, but it seemed wrong to make him talk about anything else.

The whole evening could turn into a major drag. He was in some drooling state between loathing and desire. It was enough to make a girl feel guilty about being so attractive. She tried to avoid it, but she had spent too much of her life sitting opposite hangdog men she had nothing in common with, their eyes burning with reproach, and the conversation long congealed and mouldy, like something from way way *way* back in the icebox, something you must have been crazy to have bought in the first place.

Vine leaves and hummus, grilled lamb, rice, and red wine. At least she could eat. The food here was really good. Simon had brought her here first. He had a gift for finding the best Armenian restaurants in any city in the world. Simon was so so clever. He wrote poems about swans and ice and stars, and it was tough to know what he was trying to say, because they were so indirect without really being very suggestive. But he was a genius of savoir faire, especially in the Armenian-restaurant department. One day Simon had said to her in his faintly Brooklyn stammer, 'Some people have certain emotions. I don't.' Just like that. No swans, no ice, no stars, nothing.

They had made love once and she had tried to absorb the essence of his impudent, elusive genius, but when it was over he had gone into the bathroom to write a poem, and she'd lain in bed feeling like an ex-swan. Of course it was wrong to want to change people, but what else could you possibly want to do with them?

Patrick aroused a reforming zeal akin to carpet bombing. Those slit eyes and curling lips, that arrogant way he arched one of his eyebrows, the stooped, near-foetal posture, the stupid self-destructive melodrama of his life – which of these could not be cheerfully cast aside? But then what would be left if you threw out the rotten stuff? It was like trying to imagine bread without the dough.

There he was, drooling at her again. The green velvet dress

was obviously a big hit. It made her angry to think of Debbie, who was ragged and crazy with love of this sleaze-ball (Marianne had made the mistake of calling him a 'temporary aberration' at the beginning, but Debbie had forgiven her now that she wished it was true), of Debbie being rewarded with this would-be infidelity, no doubt as generalized as his insatiable appetite for drugs.

The trouble with doing something you didn't like was that it made you conscious of all the things that you should be doing instead. Even going to the movies for the first performance of the afternoon failed to provoke the sense of burning urgency she felt right now. The untaken photographs, the call of the dark room, the sting of unwritten thank-you letters which had left her untroubled until now, all crowded in and gave an even more desperate air to the conversation she was having with Patrick.

Condemned to the routine of dismissing men, she sometimes wished (especially tonight) that she didn't arouse emotions she could do nothing to satisfy. Naturally a *tiny* part of her wanted to save them, or at least stop them trying so hard.

Patrick had to acknowledge that the conversation was going pretty badly. Every line he threw to the quayside slipped back heavily into the filthy harbour. She might as well have had her back turned to him, but then nothing excited him more than a turned back. Each mute appeal, disguised by a language as banal as it was possible to imagine, made him more conscious of how little experience he had of saying what he meant. If he could speak to her in another voice, or with another intention – to deceive or to ridicule, for example – then he could wake from this tongue-tied nightmare.

Thick, black and sweet, the coffee arrived. Time was running out. Couldn't she see what was going on? Couldn't she read between the lines? And so what if she could? Perhaps she liked to see him suffer. Perhaps she didn't even like that about him.

Marianne yawned and complained of tiredness. All the signs are good at this point, thought Patrick sarcastically. She's dying for it, *dying* for it. Yes means yes, maybe means yes, perhaps means yes, and no of course means yes as well. He knew how to read women like an open book.

Outside in the street, Marianne kissed him goodbye, sent her love to Debbie, and grabbed a cab.

Patrick stormed down Madison Avenue with his father on his arm. The brown-paper bag occasionally crashed into a passer-by who was unwise enough not to get out of the way.

By the time he reached Sixty-first Street, Patrick realized that it was the first time he had been alone with his father for more than ten minutes without being buggered, hit, or insulted. The poor man had had to confine himself to blows and insults for the last fourteen years, and insults alone for the last six.

The tragedy of old age, when a man is too weak to hit his own child. No wonder he had died. Even his rudeness had been flagging towards the end, and he had been forced to introduce a note of repulsive self-pity to ward off any counterattack.

'Your trouble,' snarled Patrick, as he swept past the doorman of his hotel, 'is that you're mentally ill.'

'You mustn't say those things to your poor old father,' he murmured, shaking imaginary heart pills into a bunched and twisted palm.

Bastard. Nobody should do that to anybody else.

Never mind, never tell.

Stop thinking about it right now.

'Right now,' said Patrick out loud.

Death and destruction. Buildings swallowed by flame as he passed. Windows shattering at a glance. An inaudible jugular-bursting scream. No prisoners.

'Death and destruction,' he muttered. Christ, he was really anxious now, really very *fucking anxious*.

Patrick imagined sliding a chainsaw through the neck of the lift operator. Wave after wave of shame and violence, ungovernable shame and violence.

If thy head offend thee, cut it off. Incinerate it and trample it into ash. No prisoners, no pity. Tamburlaine's black tent. My favourite colour! It's so chic.

'Which floor, sir?'

What are you staring at, fuckface?

'Thirty-nine.'

Steps. Over-associative. Over-accelerated. Sedation. Scalpel. Patrick flicked out his hand. Anaesthetic first, surely, Doctor?

Surely: the adverb of a man without an argument. Scalpel first, anaesthetic afterward. The Dr Death Method. You know it makes sense.

Whose idea was it to put him on the thirty-ninth floor? What were they trying to do? Drive him mad? Hide under the sofa. Must hide under the sofa.

Nobody can find me there. What if nobody finds me there? What if they do?

Patrick burst into the room, dropped the brown-paper bag, and threw himself onto the floor. He rolled over towards the sofa, lay on his back, and tried to squirm underneath the skirt of the sofa.

What was he doing? He was going mad. Can't get under the sofa anymore. Too big now. Six foot two. No longer a child.

Fuck that. He lifted the sofa into the air and insinuated his body underneath it, lowering it again onto his chest.

And he lay there in his overcoat and his eyepatch, with the sofa covering him up to his neck, like a coffin built for a smaller man.

Dr Death: 'This is just the sort of episode we had hoped to avoid. Scalpel. Anaesthetic' Patrick flicked out his hand.

Not that again. Quickly, quickly, a fix of smack. More of the speed capsules must be dissolving in his stomach. There was an explanation for everything.

'There isn't a bin in the world that wouldn't take you for free,' he sighed in the voice of an affectionate but dishonest hospital matron, as he wriggled from under the sofa and got up slowly to his knees.

He slipped out of his now rather crumpled and fluff-covered overcoat and crawled towards the box of ashes on all fours, watching it carefully as if it might pounce.

How could he get into the box? Get into the box, take out the ashes and empty them down the loo. What better resting place could there be for his father than a New York sewer, among the albino wildlife and tons of shit?

He examined the bevelled cedarwood for a gap or a screw which would enable him to pry the casket open, but only found a thin gold plaque taped to the seamless base in a tiny plastic bag.

In fury and frustration, Patrick leaped to his feet and jumped up and down on the box. It was made of sturdier wood than he had imagined and withstood the assault without a creak. Could he order a chainsaw from room service? He remembered no mention of it on the menu.

Drop it out of the window and watch it shatter on the pavement? He would probably kill someone without denting the box.

With one last effort Patrick kicked the impregnable casket across the floor, where it hit the metal wastepaper basket with a hollow clang and came to a rest.

With admirable swiftness and efficiency, Patrick prepared and administered an injection of heroin. His eyelids clicked closed. And half opened again, cool and inert.

If only it could always be like this, the calm of the initial hit. But even in this voluptuous Caribbean tranquillity there were too many snapped trees and flayed roofs to let him relax. There was always an argument to win, or a feeling to fight off. He glanced at the box. Observe Everything. Always think for yourself. Never let other people make important decisions for you.

Patrick scratched himself lazily. Well, at least he didn't care so much.

13

PATRICK HAD TRIED TO sleep, but tattered rags of speed still trailed through his consciousness and kept him charging forward. He rubbed his eye compulsively, obsessed with the stye that tickled his eyeball with each blink. The jelly they had given him at the pharmacy was of course completely useless. Nevertheless, he squirted a large amount into his eye and his vision blurred like a greased camera. The eyepatch had left a diagonal dent across his forehead, and he only stopped rubbing his eye to scratch the dent with the same desperate irritation. He wanted to scratch out his eye and peel off his face to end the terrible itchiness that had erupted from his failed attempt to sleep, but knew that it was only the surface play of a more fundamental unease: itching powder in the first pair of nappies, sniggering faces around the hospital cot.

He rolled off the bed, loosening his tie. The room was stiflingly hot, but he loathed the meat-locker cold of the air conditioning. What was he, a carcass on a hook? A corpse in a morgue? Better not to ask.

It was time to check his drugs, to review his troops and see what chance he had of making it through another night and getting onto the plane the next morning at nine thirty.

He sat down at the desk, taking the heroin and pills out of his coat pockets and the coke from an envelope in his suitcase. He had about one and a half out of the seven grams of coke, about a fifth of a gram of heroin, one Quaalude, and one Black Beauty. If he wasn't going to sleep but abandon himself to shooting coke, then there was only enough for two or three hours. It was eleven o'clock now and even with exemplary self-restraint, whatever that was, he would be left with the agony of the comedown in the deadest part of the night. There was enough heroin, just. He was still OK from the fix he'd had after dinner. If he had one at three in the morning and one just before getting on the plane, he'd be able to last until he got to Johnny Hall's. Thank God for Concorde. On the other hand, more coke meant more smack to control the danger of heart attack and insanity, and so he should try to avoid scoring again, or he'd be too out of it for Customs.

The sensible thing to do was to try to divide the coke into two halves, taking the first now and the second after he had gone out to a nightclub or bar. He would try to stay out until three and take the amphetamines just before returning, so that the lift from the speed would cushion the coke comedown after the second bout of fixing. The Black Beauty had about a fifteen-hour life, or maybe a twelve-hour life on the second day, which meant that the effect would be wearing off at about three in the afternoon New York time – eight o'clock London time: just when he could expect to arrive at Johnny's and get some more gear.

Brilliant! He really ought to be in charge of a multinational company or a wartime army to find an outlet for these planning skills. The Quaalude was a freefloating agent. He could use it to cope with the boredom of the plane flight, or give it to some chick in the Mudd Club so as to get her into bed. The incident with Marianne had left him bruised, like a bad dry martini. He wanted to strike back at the female sex and also to satisfy the desires that Marianne had inflamed.

So, he could have a fix of coke now. Yes, yes, yes. He wiped his clammy hands on his trousers, and began to prepare the solution. His bowels loosened at the thought, and all the longing that a man bestows on a woman who is betraying him, and whose betrayal deepens his longing and enslaves him as her fidelity never could, all the impatience and desperation of waiting while flowers wither in his hands, assailed him. It was love, there was no other word for it.

Like an incompetent bullfighter who cannot find the angle for a kill, Patrick stabbed at his veins without bringing blood into the barrel. Trying to calm himself down, he breathed deeply and reintroduced the needle into his arm, moving it slowly clockwise to find an angle that would break the wall of the vein without going through the other side. As he made this arc, he teased the plunger upward with his thumb.

At last a small thread of blood galloped into the barrel and circled round. Patrick held the syringe as still as possible and pushed down the plunger. The mechanism was stiff and he immediately pulled the plunger back. He felt a sharp pain in his arm. He had lost the vein! He had lost the fucking vein. He was in the muscle. There was only about twenty seconds before the blood coagulated and then he would be shooting a heart-arresting clot into his bloodstream. But if he didn't shoot it up the fix would be ruined. Heat could miraculously reliquify the blood in a solution of heroin, but it would spoil the coke. Almost weeping with frustration, Patrick didn't know whether to push deeper or withdraw the needle. Taking a gamble, he retracted the syringe slightly and flattened it at the same time. More blood curled into the barrel and, with hysterical gratitude, he pushed the plunger down as hard as he could. It was insane to shoot up so quickly, but he couldn't take the risk of the blood coagulating.

When he tried to draw the plunger back a second time to make sure he got all the coke that was still lurking in the barrel, he found the mechanism stuck and realized that he had slipped out of the vein again.

He whipped the spike out of his arm and, struggling against a flood of promiscuous lucidity, tried to fill the barrel with water before the blood dried. His hands shook so badly that the syringe clinked on the side of the glass. Jesus, it was strong. Once he had sucked in the water, he put the syringe down, too high to flush it out.

Clasping his arm so that the fist was couched under his chin, he rocked back and forth on the edge of his chair and tried to disperse the pain. But he could not shake off the sense of intimate violation that came with every botched fix. The walls of his veins were perforated again and again by the thin steel he had stuck into them, torturing his body to gratify his mind.

The coke was marauding through his system, like a pack of white wolves, spreading terror and destruction. Even the brief euphoria of the rush had been eclipsed by the fear that he had shot up a blood clot. Next time he would inject himself in the back of his hand where he could still see the veins clearly. The good old-fashioned pain of puncturing that tough skin and probing the tiny delicate bones was less spooky than the horror of missed invisible veins. At least he wasn't fixing in his groin. Gouging around unsuccessfully among those elusive veins could make one question the whole intravenous method of absorbing drugs.

In fact, it was at times like this, in the wake of missed veins, overdoses, minor heart attacks, and fainting fits, that his vicious addiction to needles, quite apart from drugs, made him want to bend spikes and post syringes down drains. It was only the certainty that these quarrels were always lost and merely committed him to the tedious search for new works, or the humiliation of fishing the old ones out from under the wet Kleenexes, slimy yogurt pots, and limp potato peel of the bin liner, that prevented Patrick from destroying his syringes straight away.

This needle fever had a psychological life of its own. What better way to be at once the fucker and the fucked, the subject and the object, the scientist and the experiment, trying to set the spirit free by enslaving the body? What other form of self-division was more expressive than the androgynous embrace of an injection, one arm locking the needle into the other, enlisting pain into the service of pleasure and forcing pleasure back into the service of pain?

He had injected whisky, watching his burned vein turn black under the skin, just to satisfy the needle fever. He had dissolved cocaine in Perrier because the tap was too far away for his imperious desire. Brain like a bowl of Rice Krispies – snap! crackle! pop! – and a disturbing effervescence in the valves of his heart. He had woken up after passing out for thirty hours, the syringe, still half full of smack, hanging loosely from his arm, and started again, with that cold annihilating will, the ritual that had nearly killed him.

Patrick could not help wondering, after his failure to capture Marianne, if a syringe would not have been a better intermediary than his conversation. It made him sentimental to think of Natasha saying in her hoarse whisper, 'Baby, you're so good, you always hit the vein,' a trickle of dark blood flowing from her pale arm as it dangled over the edge of the chair.

He'd shot her up the first time they'd met. She had sat on the sofa with her knees raised, and proffered her arm trustingly. He sat beside her on the floor, and when he gave her the fix, her knees fell open, gathering light in the heavy folds of her black silk trousers, and he was overwhelmed with tenderness as she fell back and sighed, her eyes closed and her face glowing, 'Too much . . . pleasure . . . too much.'

What was sex next to this compassionate violence? Only this violence could break open a world constrained by the hidden cameras of conscience and vanity.

After that, their relationship had decayed from injection to intercourse, from dazzled recognition to chat. Still, thought Patrick, dazed by the solid-looking objects around him, as he got up from his chair and out of his trance, he had to believe that somewhere out there was a girl willing to trade her body for a couple of drinks and a Quaalude. And he was going to begin his search at the Mudd Club. After one more quick fix.

An hour later, Patrick managed with some difficulty to leave the hotel. He sprawled in the back of the cab as it rumbled downtown. Those pencils of steel, chrome fans, and crystal towers that seemed to burst like pure soprano notes from a prima donna's hideous, pockmarked face, were muffled by darkness. Crossword puzzles of lit and unlit offices slipped by cluelessly. Two lit offices down – call it 'no' – and five across. Five-letter word beginning with 'o'. Oran . . . one . . . order. Call it order. No order. The building disappeared in the back window. Did everyone play this game? The land of the free and the home of the brave, where people only did something if everyone else did too. Had he already thought that? Had he already said that?

As usual, there was a crowd outside the Mudd Club. Patrick slipped to the front where two black men and a fat, bearded white man stood behind a twisted red cord and decided who to let in. He greeted the bouncers in a tired drawl. They always let him in. Perhaps it was because he assumed that they would; or because he didn't really care if they did; or, of course, because he looked rich and likely to order a lot of drinks.

Patrick went straight upstairs where, instead of the live music that was blaring from a small stage on the ground floor, tapes played continuously while videos of spectacular but familiar events – time-lapse flowers suddenly blossoming, Hitler thumping the podium at Nuremberg and then embracing himself in an ecstasy of approval, early attempts at human flight crashing, disintegrating and plummeting from bridges – radiated from a dozen television screens into every angle of the dark room. Just before he stepped inside, a slim sulky girl with short white hair and violet contact lenses slipped past him down the stairs. Dressed all in black, her white make-up and discontented but symmetrical features made her look like a junkie doll. She even had a black silk tourniquet around her thin bicep. Sweet! He watched her. She was not leaving, just switching rooms. He would check her out later.

The Talking Heads pulsed from every speaker. 'The centre is missing,' gasped David Byrne, and Patrick could not help agreeing with him. How did they know exactly what he was feeling? It was spooky.

A shot of a cheetah chasing an antelope through the African bush flickered onto all the screens at once. Patrick pressed himself against the wall as if he had been thrown back by the centrifugal force of a spinning room. He felt waves of weakness and exhaustion when the real state of his body broke through the guard of drugs. The last fix of coke had petered out on the journey down and he might have to take that Black Beauty sooner than scheduled.

The antelope was brought down in a cloud of dust. Its legs twitched for a while as the cheetah ate into its neck. At first the event seemed to shatter and dissipate among all the screens, and then, as the shot closed in, the kill multiplied and gathered force. The room still seemed to Patrick to be throwing him backward, as if rejection and exclusion, the companions of any social contact, had been turned into a physical force. Sometimes the startling contentment of a smack rush caused him to believe that the universe was indifferent rather than hostile, but such a touching faith was bound to be betrayed and seemed especially remote now, as he rested with flattened palms against the wall of the room.

Naturally, he still thought of himself in the third person, as a character in a book or a movie, but at least it was still the third person singular. 'They' hadn't come to get him yet tonight, the bacteria of voices that had taken over the night before. In the presence of the absence, in the absence of the presence, Tweedledee and Tweedledum. Life imitating bad literary criticism. Dis/inte/gration. Exhausted and febrile. Business as usual. Funny business as usual.

Like a man in the spinning barrel of a funfair, Patrick unglued himself laboriously from the wall. Under the shimmering blue light of the televisions, cool customers sprawled uncomfortably on the bench of soft grey cushions that ran around the edge of the room. Patrick walked towards the bar with the care of a driver trying to convince a policeman that he is sober.

'Doctor said his liver looked like a relief map of the Rockies,' said a thick-necked, jocular man leaning on the bar.

Patrick winced and immediately felt a needle-sharp twinge in his side. Absurdly suggestible, must try to calm down. In a parody of detachment, he swivelled his eyes around the room with the small staccato movements of a predatory lizard.

Sprawling on the cushion nearest to the bar was a guy in a red and yellow kilt, a studded belt, army boots, a black leather jacket, and thunderbolt earrings. He looked as if he'd had too many Tuinals. Patrick thought of the black flash of the Tuinal rush, burning the arm like scouring powder; strictly an emergency measure. The look struck him as outmoded; after all, it was six years since the punk summer of '76 when he'd sat on the fire escape at school in the sweltering heat, smoking joints, listening to 'White Riot', and shouting 'destroy' over the rooftops. Next to the kilted punk were two nervous New Jersey secretaries perched on the edge of their seats in tight trousers that cut into their soft bellies. They transferred red lipstick to their all-white cigarette butts with promising zeal, but were too hideous to be considered for the task of consoling him for Marianne's indifference. With his back slightly turned to them, a commodity broker in a dark suit (or was he an art dealer?) was talking to a man who compensated for his near-baldness with a long wispy curtain of grey hair emerging from the last productive follicles at the back of his skull. They looked as if they were keeping in touch with the desperate state of youth, checking out the new-wave kids, spotting the latest inflections of rebellious fashion.

On the other side of the room, a pretty girl with the ever-popular poor look, a black sweater over a simple second-hand skirt, held hands with a man in a T-shirt and jeans. They stared obediently at one of the TV screens, two glasses of beer at their feet. Beyond them, a group of three people talked excitedly. One man in a cobalt-blue suit and thin tie, and another in a primary-red suit and thin tie, bracketed a hook-nosed girl with long black hair and a pair of leather jodhpurs. From the far reaches of the room, Patrick could make out the gleam of chains.

Hopeless, completely hopeless. The only remotely pretty girl in the room was physically linked to another man. They weren't even having an argument. It was disgusting.

He checked his pockets again, crossing himself devoutly. The smack, the speed, the cash, and the Quaalude. One could never be too paranoid − or could one? The coke was back in the hotel with the credit cards. He ordered a bourbon on the rocks, fished out the Black Beauty, and swallowed it with the first gulp. Two hours ahead of schedule, but never mind. Rules were made to be broken. Which meant, if that was a rule, that sometimes they should be observed. Mind sputtering on. Circular thinking. So tired.

A shot of David Bowie sitting drunkenly in front of a serried bank of television screens flickered onto the club's television screens, only to be replaced by the famous shot of Orson Welles walking through the hall of mirrors in Charles Foster Kane's Floridian castle. Multiplying images of multiplication.

'I suppose you think that's clever,' sighed Patrick, like a disappointed schoolmaster.

'I'm sorry?'

Patrick turned around. It was the man with the curtain of long grey hair.

'Just talking to myself,' muttered Patrick. 'I was thinking that the images on the screen were empty and out of control.'

'Maybe they are intended to be images about emptiness,' said the man solemnly. 'I think that's something the kids are very much in touch with right now.'

'How can you be in touch with emptiness?' asked Patrick.

'By the way, my name's Alan. Two Beck's,' he said to the waiter. 'What's yours?'

'Bourbon.'

'I mean your name.'

'Oh, eh, Patrick.'

'Hi.' Alan extended his hand. Patrick shook it reluctantly. 'What are headlights flaring on the road?' asked Alan as if it were a riddle.

Patrick shrugged his shoulders.

'Headlights flaring on the road,' Alan replied with admirable calm.

'That's a relief,' said Patrick.

'Everything in life is a symbol of itself.'

'That's what I was afraid of,' said Patrick, 'but luckily words are too slippery to communicate that.'

'They must communicate that,' Alan affirmed. 'It's like when you're screwing you gotta think of the person you're with.'

'I suppose so,' said Patrick sceptically, 'as long as you put them in a different situation.'

'If the screens here show other ways of making images, other screens, mirrors, cameras, you can call that self-reflection emptiness or you can call it honesty. It announces that it can only announce itself.'

'But what about Batman?' said Patrick. 'That's not about the nature of the television medium.'

'At some level it is.'

'Somewhere below the Batcave.'

'That's right,' said Alan encouragingly, 'somewhere below the Batcave. That's what a lot of the kids feel: the cultural emptiness.'

'I'll take your word for it,' said Patrick.

'*I* happen to think that there's still news of Being worth telling,' said Alan, picking up the bottles of Beck's. 'Whitman's love is more precious than money,' he beamed.

Fucking hell, thought Patrick.

'Do you want to join us?'

'No, in fact I was just going,' said Patrick. 'Frightfully bad jet lag.'

'OK,' said Alan unperturbed.

'So long.'

'Bye now.'

Patrick drained his glass of bourbon to convince Alan that he was really leaving, and headed for the downstairs room.

He really wasn't doing too well. Not only had he failed to pick up a chick, but he'd had to ward off this loony faggot. What a pickup line, 'Whitman's love is more precious than money.' Patrick let out a short burst of laughter on the stairs. At least down here he might be able to track down that violet-eyed punk. He had to have her. She was definitely the lucky woman destined to share his hotel bed for the last few hours before he left the country.

The atmosphere downstairs was very different from the carpeted bar above. On the stage, musicians in black T-shirts and torn jeans produced a heavily strumming wall of sound which the lead singer's voice tried unsuccessfully to scale. The long bare room, once a warehouse, had no decorations or fancy lights, only a heroic sense of its own rawness. In this loud darkness, Patrick made out blue and pink spiked hair, zebra, leopard and tiger prints, tight black trousers and pointy shoes, exotics and tramps leaning against the walls sniffing powders, solitary dancers with closed eyes and nodding heads, robotic couples, and small groups of jumping and crashing bodies nearer the stage.

Patrick stood on tiptoe trying to find the violet-eyed junkie doll. She was nowhere to be seen, but he soon became distracted by the back of a blonde girl in a homemade chiffon dress and a black leather jacket. Wandering casually past her he glanced around. 'You must be fucking joking,' he muttered vehemently. He felt angry and betrayed, as if her face were a broken promise.

How could he have been so disloyal? He was after the violet-eyed junkie doll. Debbie had once screamed at him in the middle of an argument, 'Do you know what love is, Patrick? Do you have the faintest idea?' And he'd said wearily, 'How many guesses do I get?'

Patrick doubled back and, checking from side to side, weaved his way across the room, and took up a position against the wall.

There she was! With her back to a column and her hands behind her, as if she were tied to a stake, she looked up at the musicians with reverent curiosity. Patrick concentrated madly and imagined her sliding across the floor towards the magnetic field of his chest and stomach. Frowning ferociously, he cast a neurone net over her body and hauled her in like a heavy catch. He whipped mental lassoes around the column she stood beside, and brought her staggering across the floor like a bound slave. Finally, he closed his eyes, took flight, and projected his desire through the room, covering her neck and breasts with kisses.

When he opened his eyes she was gone. Maybe he should have tried conversation. He looked around him indignantly. Where the hell was she? His psychic powers were failing, even though the resurgence of the speed was giving his incompetence a renewed intensity.

He must have her. He must have her, or someone else. He needed contact, skin to skin, muscle to muscle. Above all, he needed the oblivious moment of penetration when, for a second, he could stop thinking about himself. Unless, as too often happened, the appearance of intimacy unleashed a further disembodiment and a deeper privacy. Never mind that. Even if sex sentenced him to an exile which, on top of the usual melancholy, contained the additional irritation of another person's dumb reproach, the conquest was bound to be exhilarating. Or was it? Who was left to him? Beautiful women were always with someone, unless you happened to catch them in the split second between inconsolable loss and consolation, or in the taxi that was taking them from their principal lover to one of the secondary ones. And if you had a beautiful woman, they always kept you waiting, kept you doubting, because it was the only time they could be sure that you were thinking about them.

Having worked himself up into a state of some bitterness, Patrick strode over to the bar.

'Jack Daniel's on the rocks,' he said to the barman. As he drew back, Patrick checked the girl to his left. She was slightly plump, dark-haired, and marginally pretty. She looked back at him steadily, a good sign.

'Aren't you hot in that coat?' she asked. 'It is May, you know.'

'Incredibly hot,' Patrick admitted with a half-smile, 'but I'd feel flayed without it.'

'It's like a defence mechanism,' said the girl.

'Yes,' drawled Patrick, feeling that she had not captured the full subtlety and poignancy of his overcoat. 'What's your name?' he asked as casually as possible.

'Rachel.'

'Mine's Patrick. Can I offer you a drink?' Christ, he sounded like a parody of someone making conversation. Everything had taken on a threatening or facetious aspect that made it harder than ever to climb down from the position of an observer. Perhaps she would experience the crushing dullness as a reassuring ritual.

'Sure. I'd like a beer. A Dos Equis.'

'Fine,' said Patrick, catching the barman's attention. 'So what kind of work do you do?' he went on, practically vomiting at the effort of making ordinary conversation and feigning an interest in somebody else.

'I work in a gallery.'

'Really?' said Patrick, hoping he sounded impressed. He seemed to have lost all control over his voice.

'Yeah, but I really wanna start a gallery of my own.'

Here we go again, thought Patrick. The waiter who thinks he's an actor, the actor who thinks he's a director, the taxi driver who thinks he's a philosopher. All the signs are good at this point, the deal is about to happen, there's a lot of interest from the record companies . . . a city full of phoney aggressive fantasists and, of course, a few genuinely unpleasant people with power.

'Only, I need the financial backing,' she sighed.

'Why do you want to start out on your own?' he asked, concerned and yet encouraging.

'I don't know if you're familiar with Neo-Objective art, but I think it's going to be really major,' said Rachel. 'I know a lot of the artists and I'd like to get their careers started while everybody else is still ignoring them.'

'I'm sure that won't be for long.'

'That's why I gotta move quickly.'

'I'd love to see some Neo-Objective art,' said Patrick earnestly.

'I could arrange that,' said Rachel, looking at him in a new light. Was this the financial backing she had been waiting for? His overcoat might be weird, but it looked expensive. It might be kinda cool to have an eccentric English backer who wasn't going to breathe down her neck.

'I do a little collecting,' Patrick lied. 'By the way, would you like a Quaalude?'

'I don't really do drugs,' said Rachel, wrinkling her nose.

'Neither do I,' said Patrick. 'I just happen to have one floating around. Somebody gave it to me ages ago.'

'I don't need to get high to have fun,' said Rachel coolly.

She's on for it, she's definitely on for it, thought Patrick. 'You're so right,' he said, 'it spoils the magic – makes people unreal.' His heartbeat accelerated; he'd better clinch the deal. 'Do you want to come back to my hotel? I'm staying at the Pierre.'

The Pierre, thought Rachel; all the signs were good. 'Sure,' she smiled.

14

TWO THIRTY ACCORDING TO the clock next to the St Christopher medallion. That gave him about five hours. More than enough, more than a lifetime's worth of conversation with Rachel. He smiled at her vaguely. What could he tell her? That his father had just died? That he was a drug addict? That he was leaving for the airport in five hours? That his girlfriend really wouldn't mind? He certainly didn't want to ask her any more questions about herself. Nor did he want to hear her views on Nicaragua.

'I'm feeling kinda hungry,' said Rachel uneasily.

'Hungry?'

'Yeah, I got this craving for chilli.'

'Well, I'm sure we can get you some on room service,' said Patrick, who knew perfectly well that there was no chilli on the Pierre's all-night menu and would have disapproved if there had been.

'But there's this diner where they make like the greatest chilli in the entire world,' said Rachel, sitting up eagerly. 'I *really* wanna go there.'

'Right,' said Patrick patiently. 'What's the address?'

'Eleventh Avenue and Thirty-eighth.'

'I'm sorry about this,' said Patrick to the driver, 'we've changed our minds. Could we go to Eleventh Avenue and Thirty-eighth Street instead?'

'Eleventh and Thirty-eighth?' repeated the driver.

'Yup.'

The diner was a ribbed silver caravan with TRY OUR FAMOUS CHILI AND TACOS in red neon outside. It was an offer that Rachel could not resist. A green neon chilli flashed cutely next to a yellow sombrero.

When the giant oval plate arrived loaded with chilli-flavoured minced meat, refried beans, guacamole, and sour cream, topped with bright orange Cheddar and accompanied by speckled ochre tortilla shells, Patrick lit a cigarette in the hope of drawing a veil of thin blue smoke over the pungent heap of spicy food. He took another sip of insipid coffee and sat back as far as possible in the corner of the red plastic bench. Rachel was clearly a nervous overeater, stuffing herself before he stuffed her, or perhaps, very persuasively, trying to put him off sex altogether by wreaking havoc on her digestive system, and saturating her breath with the torrid stench of cheese and chilli.

'Uh-hum,' said Rachel appreciatively, 'I love this food.'

Patrick raised an eyebrow slightly but made no comment.

She piled the chilli into the tortilla, smeared some guacamole on top, and patted down the sour cream with the back of her fork. Finally, she took a pinch of Cheddar between her fingers and sprinkled it on top.

The tortilla flopped open and chilli flooded onto her chin. Giggling, she lifted it with her index finger and forced it back into her mouth.

'Delicioso,' she commented.

'It looks disgusting,' said Patrick sullenly.

'You should try some.'

She stooped over the plate and found ingenious angles from which to snap at the collapsing tortilla. Patrick rubbed his eye.

It was itching wildly again. He stared out of the window but was drawn back into the arena of its reflections. The tulip-red bar stools on their chrome stems, the hatch into the kitchen, the old man hunched over a cup of coffee and, of course, Rachel like a pig in a trough. It reminded him of the famous painting by whatshisname. Memory getting burned out. The terror of forgetting everything. Hooper . . . Hopper. Got it. Life in the old dog.

'Finished?' asked Patrick.

'They make a great banana split here,' said Rachel saucily, still chomping her last mouthful of chilli.

'Well, don't restrain yourself,' said Patrick. 'Will one be enough?'

'Don't you want one too?'

'No, I do not,' said Patrick pompously.

Soon a long glass dish arrived on which scoops of chocolate, vanilla, and strawberry ice cream were bracketed by the two halves of a banana, buried under rippling waves of whipped cream and decorated with beads of pink and green candy. Red maraschino cherries ran down the centre like a row of clown's buttons.

Patrick's leg twitched up and down involuntarily as he watched Rachel exhume bits of banana from the mound of brightly coloured creams.

'I've given up dairy products,' she said, 'but I allow myself these binges sometimes.'

'So it seems,' said Patrick stiffly.

He was overcome with loathing and contempt. The girl was completely out of control. Whereas drugs were at least amenable to advertising: life on the edge, exploring the inner Congo, the heart of darkness, outstaring death, returning with the scars and medals of a haunting knowledge, Coleridge, Baudelaire, Leary . . . ; and even if this advertising seemed horribly false to anyone who had taken drugs at all seriously, it wasn't possible even to pretend that there was anything heroic about an eating problem. And yet there was something unsettlingly familiar about Rachel's obsessive greed and ridiculous dishonesty.

'Can we go now?' snapped Patrick.

'Yeah, OK,' said Rachel timidly.

He ordered the check, threw down a twenty-dollar bill before it arrived, and wriggled out of the booth. Another fucking taxi drive, he thought.

'I feel kinda nau-tious,' complained Rachel, as they went up in the hotel elevator.

'I'm not surprised,' said Patrick severely, 'I feel nauseous and I was only watching.'

'Hey, you're pretty hos-tel.'

'I'm sorry,' said Patrick, 'I'm awfully tired.' Better not lose her now.

'Me too,' said Rachel.

Patrick unlocked the door, and switched on the lights.

'Sorry about the mess.'

'You should see my apartment.'

'Maybe I will,' said Patrick, 'and all that Neo-Objective art.'

'Definitely,' said Rachel. 'Can I use the bathroom?'

'Of course.'

Time to mix a quick fix, thought Patrick, as he heard the lock slide closed on the bathroom door. He fished the coke from his suitcase and the smack from his inner left pocket, took the spoon from the back of the bottom drawer, and retrieved the half-bottle of Evian he had hidden, with unnecessary caution, behind the curtain. There might not be many more opportunities, and he'd better make a strong speedball to reduce the number of fixes to a minimum. He mixed the smack and coke together, dissolved them and drew the solution into the syringe.

He was ready, but how long did he have before Rachel

emerged from the bathroom? With his hearing strained, like a man listening to his footsteps on a creaking staircase, he concentrated on the sounds coming from the bathroom. The muffled noise of vomiting, followed by a little rasping cough, reassured him that there would be time for a fix.

Taking no risks, he stuck the spike into a thick vein in the back of his hand. The smell of cocaine assailed him and he felt his nerves stretching like piano wires. The heroin followed in a soft rain of felt hammers playing up his spine and rumbling into his skull.

He groaned contentedly and scratched his nose. It was so pleasurable, so fucking pleasurable. How could he ever give up? It was love. It was coming home. It was Ithaca, the end of all his storm-tossed wanderings. He dropped the syringe into the top drawer, staggered across the room, and sprawled on the bed.

Peace at last. The mingling lashes of half-closed eyes, the slow reluctant flutter of folding wings; his body pounded by felt hammers, pulses dancing like sand on a drum; love and poison evacuating his breath in a long slow exhalation, fading into a privacy he could never quite remember, nor for a moment forget. His thoughts shimmered like a hesitating stream, gathering into pools of discrete and vivid imagery.

He pictured his feet walking through a damp London square, his shoes sealing wet leaves darkly to the pavement. In the square, the heat from a heap of smouldering leaves syruped the air, and billows of yellow smoke skewed the sunlight like a broken wheel, its spokes scattered among the balding plane trees. The lawn was littered with dead branches, and from the railings he watched the sad and acrid ceremony, his eyes irritated by the smoke.

Patrick blinked back into the present, scratching his eye. He focused on the painting of a Normandy beach that hung above his desk. Why didn't the women in long dresses and the straw-hatted men walk into the sea? Was it the sheer gaiety of the parasols that detained them on the beach, or a sentence they must complete before disrobing their flesh in the indifferent water?

Everything was dying, every lifted stone revealed its bed of blind white maggots. He must leave the dank rotting earth and the all-consuming sea, and head for the mountains. 'I hail you, great mountains!' he chanted under his breath. 'Lofty! Alone! Serene! Good for jumping off!'

Patrick giggled feebly. The coke had already sputtered out. He was really beginning to feel rather ghastly. There was only enough for two more good fixes of coke and then he would be condemned to an accelerating agony of disappointment. The speed was perhaps only temporarily eclipsed by the heroin, but even so its performance was bound to be enormously reduced after he'd been awake for so long. The sensible thing to do in a situation like this, when one's body was a battleground strewn with the carnage of internarcotic wars, was to take the last Quaalude that Rachel had so high-mindedly refused, and try to have a nap on the plane. There was definitely an argument for getting some sleep; namely, that when he woke up the impact of the drugs would be stronger.

As usual, his liver ached as if he'd had a rugby ball kicked under his ribcage. His desire for drugs, like the fox hidden under the Spartan's tunic, gnawed at his entrails. The double vision which afflicted him if he didn't blink constantly had grown worse, and the two images of each object were drifting further apart.

These complaints and the general feeling that his body was held together with paper clips and safety pins and would tear apart at the slightest strain, filled him with remorse and terror. It was always now, on the dawn of the third day, that he was filled with a disgusted desire to stop taking drugs, but he knew that the first hints of lucidity and withdrawal would bring an even greater horror of their absence.

Patrick was surprised to see Rachel standing miserably at the end of his bed. She had faded quickly from his memory while she threw up in the bathroom, losing her individuality and simply becoming Other People, someone who might interrupt his fix, or his contemplation of the rush.

'I feel so bloated,' she complained, clasping her stomach.

'Why don't you lie down?' croaked Patrick.

Rachel sank onto the bed and crawled to the far end, groaning as she collapsed on the pillows.

'Come here,' said Patrick in what he hoped was a tender voice.

Rachel rolled over slightly and lay sideways. He leaned towards her, hoping she had brushed her teeth and wondering when he had last brushed his own, and kissed her. The difficult angle meant that their noses clashed and then, in their haste to overcome this awkwardness, their teeth clashed too.

'Jesus, it's like being twelve years old,' said Patrick.

'I'm sorry,' said Rachel.

He sat back with his head in one hand and ran the other hand over Rachel's knitted white dress. She looked drained and nervous. There was a bulge in her lower abdomen which had not been visible when she was standing up. Patrick skirted the bulge and brushed the back of his fingers gently over her hip and thigh.

'I'm sorry,' Rachel repeated, 'I can't go through with this, I'm too nervous. Maybe we can spend some time together, get to know each other.'

Patrick disengaged his hand and flopped back onto the bed.

'Of course,' he said flatly, glancing at the bedside clock. Four fifty. They had about two hours and forty minutes to 'get to know each other'.

'When I was younger I used to fall into bed with anyone,' Rachel whined, 'but it always left me feeling empty.'

'Even after a plate of chilli and a banana split?' said Patrick. If he wasn't going to fuck her, he might as well torment her.

'You're a really hos-tel person,' said Rachel, 'do you know that? Do you have a problem with women?'

'Men, women, dogs: I don't discriminate,' said Patrick, 'they all piss me off.'

He rolled off the bed and went over to the desk. Why had he brought this tiresome lump of lard back to his room? It was intolerable, everything was intolerable.

'Look, I don't want to argue with you,' said Rachel. 'I know you're disappointed, I just need you to help me relax.'

'Relaxing isn't my speciality,' said Patrick, putting the coke and spoon into his trouser pocket and reaching to the back of the drawer to find the second syringe.

Rachel got off the bed and came over to Patrick's side.

'We're both real tired,' she said; 'let's go to bed and get some sleep. Maybe in the morning things'll seem different,' she said coyly.

'Will they?' asked Patrick. Her hand was burning into his back. He didn't want to be touched by her or by anybody else. He wriggled away, waiting for the opportunity to leave her.

'What's in this box?' asked Rachel, with a renewed effort at cheerfulness, touching the casket on top of the television.

'My father's ashes.'

'Your father's ashes.' She gulped, retracting her hand. 'That makes me feel weird.'

'I wouldn't worry about it,' said Patrick. 'I think it counts as hand luggage, don't you?'

'I guess,' said Rachel, puzzled by this line of argument. 'God, I mean, I really feel weird about this. Your father is in the room with us. Maybe I sensed that before.'

'Who knows? Anyway, he can keep you company while I'm in the bathroom. I may be some time.'

'This is heavy,' said Rachel, round-eyed.

'Don't be alarmed. He was a charming man, everybody said so.'

Patrick left Rachel in the bedroom and locked the bathroom door behind him. She sat on the edge of the bed, looking anxiously at the casket, as if she expected it to move. She took this golden opportunity to use the breathing exercises she dimly remembered from her two yoga classes, but after a couple of minutes she grew bored and still wanted to leave. The trouble was that she lived way over in Brooklyn. The cab ride was going to be ten–twelve dollars, and she would only arrive a couple of hours before she had to struggle to the gallery on the subway. If she stayed here she might get some sleep and some breakfast. She snuggled up with the breakfast menu and, after the initial excitement and guilt of seeing how many wonderful things there were to eat, she was overcome by tiredness.

Patrick lay in the bathtub, one leg dangling over the edge of the bath, blood trickling from his arm. He'd put all the coke in one last fix and, blasted by the rush, had fallen off the edge of the bath. Now he stared at the chrome shower rail and the glossy white ceiling, drawing shallow breaths through his gritted teeth, as if a girder had collapsed on his chest. Dark patches of sweat stained his shirt, and his nostrils were powdered with heroin. He had pressed the packet straight to his nose, and now it lay crumpled and empty on his neck.

With his left hand he ground the spike of the syringe against the side of the bath. He had to stop shooting up – especially now that he had run out of gear.

All the harm he'd done crowded in on him at once, like a troupe of fallen angels in a medieval painting, goading him towards hell with red-hot pitchforks, their sniggering and malicious faces surrounding him with ugliness and despair. He felt the irresistible desire to make an eternal resolution, to make the devout and impossible promise never to take a drug again. If he survived now, if he was allowed to survive, he would never shoot up again.

In this grave predicament, his fervour outweighed the knowledge of his dishonesty, even though he already detected, like distant gunfire, the disturbing feeling that something was missing. He had run out of gear. One syringe was destroyed and the other blocked with blood. It was just as well, but it was infinitely sad. Soon enough, his synapses would be screaming like starving children, and every cell in his body tugging pathetically at his sleeve.

Patrick moved his leg down tentatively and hoisted himself upright. Nearly died again. Always a shock to the system. Better take that Quaalude. He heaved himself up, nearly fainted and, leaning heavily on the wall like an old man, stepped carefully out of the bath. His coat was lying on the floor (he'd often thought of asking his tailor to put flaps in the sleeves) and he very slowly picked it up, very slowly took out the Quaalude, put it in his mouth, and washed it down with a little water.

Dazed, Patrick sat down on the loo and unhooked the phone. 555–1726.

'I cannot come to the phone right now, but if you leave . . .' Fuck, he wasn't in.

'Pierre, it's Patrick. I just rang to say goodbye,' he lied. 'I'll be in touch the *moment* I get back to New York. Bye now.'

Next, he rang Johnny Hall in London to make sure there would at least be something waiting for him when he arrived. The phone rang a few times. Maybe Johnny could meet him at the airport. It rang a few more times. Jesus Christ, he wasn't in either. It was intolerable.

Patrick tried to hook the phone back, missing several times before he got it on the receiver. He was as weak as a child. Noticing that the syringe was still in the bath he picked it up wearily, wrapped it in loo paper and threw it in the waste-paper basket under the basin.

In the bedroom, Patrick found Rachel stranded on the bed, snoring erratically. If he were in love, he thought. But couldn't finish. The flame play of disturbed water under a bridge's arch, a muffled echo, a kiss. Snow sliding from his boots in front of the stove, blood swelling back into his fingertips. If he were in love.

As it was, white-bellied and heavy breathing, she looked to Patrick like a beached whale.

Packing was easy if you rolled everything into one ball, stuffed it in the suitcase, sat on it, and did up the zip. He had to undo the zip again to squeeze Victor's book in. 'I think I'm an egg, therefore I am an egg,' he squealed in Pierre's French accent. Putting on his last clean shirt, he went back into the bathroom to call the reception.

'Hello?' he drawled.

'Yes, sir, how may I help you?'

'I'd like a limo at seven thirty, please. A big one with black windows,' he added childishly.

'I'll arrange that for you, sir.'

'And prepare my bill, will you?'

'Yes, sir. Shall I send a bellboy to collect your baggage?'

'In about quarter of an hour, thank you.' Everything was under control. He finished dressing, put on his eyepatch, and sat in the armchair waiting for the man to collect his bag. Should he leave a note for Rachel? 'I do not think I shall ever forget our evening together', or 'Let's do this again sometime soon'. Sometimes silence was more eloquent.

There was a faint knock on the door. The bellboy was about sixty, small, bald, and dressed in the hotel's plainest grey uniform.

'There's only one bag.'

'Roight, sir,' he said in an Irish accent.

They walked down the corridor, Patrick a little stooped to protect his liver, and lopsided from the pain in his back.

'Life's not just a bag of shit,' said Patrick conversationally, 'but a leaky one. You can't help being touched by it, don't you find?'

'I believe dat's what a lot of people feel about it,' the other man replied in a lilting and agreeable tone. And then he came to a halt and put Patrick's bag down.

'And there will be rivers of blood. And de wicked shall be drowned,' he intoned. 'Nor shall de high places be spared.'

'One of your own prophecies?' asked Patrick suavely.

'It's in de Boible,' said the bellboy. 'And de bridges shall be swept away,' he promised, pointing to the ceiling and then swatting an invisible fly. 'And men shall say that de end of de world cometh upon them.'

'And they shall have a point,' said Patrick, 'but I really must be going.'

'Roight you are,' said the bellboy, still excited. 'I'll be meeting you at the reception.' He scuttled off towards the service elevator. Try as one might to live on the edge, thought Patrick, getting into the other lift, there was no point in competing with people who believed what they saw on television.

The bill for two thousand one hundred and fifty-three dollars was larger than even Patrick had expected. He was secretly pleased. Capital erosion was another way to waste his substance, to become as thin and hollow as he felt, to lighten the burden of undeserved good fortune, and commit a symbolic suicide while he still dithered about the real one. He also nursed the opposite fantasy that when he became penniless he would discover some incandescent purpose born of his need to make money. On top of the hotel bill, he must have spent another two or two and a half thousand on taxis, drugs, and restaurants, plus six thousand for the air tickets. That brought the total to over ten thousand dollars, and the funeral expenses were on their way. He felt like a gameshow winner. How irritating if it had been eight and a half or nine. Ten thousand in two days. Nobody could say he didn't know how to have fun.

Patrick tossed his American Express card onto the counter without bothering to verify the bill.

'Oh, by the way,' he yawned, 'I'll sign the form, but could you leave the total open? A friend of mine is still in the room. She may want breakfast; in fact, I'm sure she will. She can order anything she likes,' he added munificently.

'O-kay.' The receptionist hesitated, wondering whether to make an issue of the double occupancy. 'She'll be leaving the room by noon, will she?'

'I suppose so. She works, you see,' said Patrick as if this were rather exceptional. He signed the credit-card form.

'We'll send a copy of the total to your home address.'

'Oh, I wouldn't bother to do that,' said Patrick, yawning again. He noticed the bellboy standing nearby with his bag. 'Hello,' he smiled. 'Rivers of blood, eh?'

The bellboy looked at him with servile incomprehension. Maybe he'd imagined the whole thing. Might be a good idea to get some sleep.

'I hope you enjoyed your stay with us,' said the receptionist, handing Patrick a copy of the bill in an envelope.

'Enjoyed isn't the word,' said Patrick with his most charming smile, 'I loved it.' He refused the envelope with a little frown. 'Oh my God,' he suddenly exclaimed, 'I've forgotten something in the room.' He turned to the bellboy. 'There's a wooden box on top of the television; you couldn't go and fetch it for me, could you? And the brown-paper bag would be very useful too.'

How could he have forgotten the box? No need to call Vienna for an interpretation. What would they have done on the bleak Cornish estuary where his father had asked to have his ashes scattered? He would have had to bribe a local crematorium to give him some of their spare sweepings.

The bellboy returned ten minutes later. Patrick stubbed out his cigarette and took the brown-paper bag from him. The two of them walked together towards the revolving doors.

'The young lady was wondering where you were going,' said the bellboy.

'What did you say?'

'I said I thought it was de airport.'

'And what did she say?'

'I wouldn't loik to repeat it, sir,' said the bellboy respectfully.

So much for that, thought Patrick, spinning through the doors. Slash. Burn. Move on. Out into the scintillating light, under a paler wider sky, his eyeballs drilled like a Roman statue.

Across the street he saw a man, his left arm severed at the wrist, a slight rawness where the bone was most prominent, a four days' unshaven, bitter face, yellow lenses, curling lip, lank hair, stained raincoat. The stump twitched upward in brisk involuntary jerks. Heavy smoker. Hater of the world. *Mon semblable.* Other people's words.

Still, there were some important differences. Patrick distributed banknotes to the doorman and the bellboy. The driver opened the door for him and he climbed into the back with his brown-paper bag. He sprawled across the black leather seat, closed his eyes, and pretended to sleep.

SOME HOPE

I

PATRICK WOKE UP KNOWING he had dreamed but unable to remember the contents of his dream. He felt the familiar ache of trying to track something that had just disappeared off the edge of consciousness but could still be inferred from its absence, like a whirlwind of scrap paper left by the passage of a fast car.

The obscure fragments of his dream, which seemed to have taken place beside a lake, were confused with the production of *Measure for Measure* he had seen the night before with Johnny Hall. Despite the director's choice of a bus depot as the setting for the play, nothing could diminish the shock of hearing the word 'mercy' so many times in one evening.

Perhaps all his problems arose from using the wrong vocabulary, he thought, with a brief flush of excitement that enabled him to throw aside the bedcovers and contemplate getting up. He moved in a world in which the word 'charity', like a beautiful woman shadowed by her jealous husband, was invariably qualified by the words 'lunch', 'committee', or 'ball'. 'Compassion' nobody had any time for, whereas 'leniency' made frequent appearances in the form of complaints about short prison sentences. Still, he knew that his difficulties were more fundamental than that.

He was worn out by his lifelong need to be in two places at

once: in his body and out of his body, on the bed and on the curtain pole, in the vein and in the barrel, one eye behind the eyepatch and one eye looking at the eyepatch, trying to stop observing by becoming unconscious, and then forced to observe the fringes of unconsciousness and make darkness visible; cancelling every effort, but spoiling apathy with restlessness; drawn to puns but repelled by the virus of ambiguity; inclined to divide sentences in half, pivoting them on the qualification of a 'but', but longing to unwind his coiled tongue like a gecko's and catch a distant fly with unwavering skill; desperate to escape the self-subversion of irony and say what he really meant, but really meaning what only irony could convey.

Not to mention, thought Patrick, as he swung his feet out of bed, the two places he wanted to be tonight: at Bridget's party and *not* at Bridget's party. And he wasn't in the mood to dine with people called Bossington-Lane. He would ring Johnny and arrange to have dinner with him alone. He dialled the number but immediately hung up, deciding to call again after he had made some tea. He had scarcely replaced the receiver when the phone rang. Nicholas Pratt was ringing to chastise him for not answering his invitation to Cheatley.

'No need to thank me,' said Nicholas Pratt, 'for getting you invited to this glittering occasion tonight. I owe it to your dear Papa to see that you get into the swim of things.'

'I'm drowning in it,' said Patrick. 'Anyhow, you prepared the way for my invitation to Cheatley by bringing Bridget down to Lacoste when I was five. Even then one could tell she was destined to command the heights of society.'

'You were much too badly behaved to notice anything as important as *that*,' said Nicholas. 'I remember you once in Victoria Road giving me a very sharp kick in the shins. I hobbled through the hall, trying to hide my agony so as not to upset your sainted mother. How is she, by the way? One never sees her these days.'

'It's amazing, isn't it? She seems to think there are better things to do than going to parties.'

'I always thought she was a little peculiar,' said Nicholas wisely.

'As far as I know she's driving a consignment of ten thousand syringes to Poland. People say it's marvellous of her, but I still think that charity begins at home. She could have saved herself the journey by bringing them round to my flat,' said Patrick.

'I thought you'd put all that behind you,' said Nicholas.

'Behind me, in front of me. It's hard to tell, here in the Grey Zone.'

'That's rather a melodramatic way to talk at thirty.'

'Well, you see,' sighed Patrick, 'I've given up everything, but taken nothing up instead.'

'You could make a start by taking my daughter up to Cheatley.'

'I'm afraid I can't,' lied Patrick, who couldn't bear Amanda Pratt. 'I'm getting a lift from someone else.'

'Oh, well, you'll see her at the Bossington-Lanes',' said Nicholas. 'And we'll see each other at the party.'

Patrick had been reluctant to accept his invitation to Cheatley for several reasons. One was that Debbie was going to be there. After years of trying to thrust her away, he was bewildered by his sudden success. She, on the other hand, seemed to enjoy falling out of love with him more than anything else about their long affair. How could he blame her? He ached with unspoken apologies.

In the eight years since his father's death, Patrick's youth had slipped away without being replaced by any signs of maturity, unless the tendency for sadness and exhaustion to eclipse hatred and insanity could be called 'mature'. The sense of multiplying alternatives and bifurcating paths had been replaced by a quayside desolation, contemplating the long list of missed boats. He had been weaned from his drug addiction in several clinics, leaving promiscuity and party-going to soldier on uncertainly, like troops which have lost their commander. His money, eroded by extravagance and medical bills, kept him from poverty without enabling him to buy his way out of boredom. Quite recently, to his horror, he had realized he would have to get a job. He was therefore studying to become a barrister, in the hope that he would find some pleasure in keeping as many criminals as possible at large.

His decision to study the law had got him as far as hiring *Twelve Angry Men* from a video shop. He had spent several days pacing up and down, demolishing imaginary witnesses with withering remarks, or suddenly leaning on furniture and saying with mounting contempt, 'I put it to you that on the night of . . .' until he recoiled, and, turning into the victim of his own cross-examination, collapsed in a fit of histrionic sobs. He had also bought some books, like *The Concept of Law, Street on Tort*, and *Charlesworth on Negligence*, and this pile of law books now competed for his attention with old favourites like *Twilight of the Idols* and *The Myth of Sisyphus*.

As the drugs had worn off, a couple of years earlier, he had started to realize what it must be like to be lucid all the time, an unpunctuated stretch of consciousness, a white tunnel, hollow and dim, like a bone with the marrow sucked out. 'I want to die, I want to die, I want to die,' he found himself muttering in the middle of the most ordinary task, swept away by a landslide of regret as the kettle boiled or the toast popped up.

At the same time, his past lay before him like a corpse waiting to be embalmed. He was woken every night by savage nightmares; too frightened to sleep, he climbed out of his sweat-soaked sheets and smoked cigarettes until the dawn crept into the sky, pale and dirty as the gills of a poisonous mushroom. His flat in Ennismore Gardens was strewn with violent videos which were a shadowy expression of the endless reel of violence that played in his head. Constantly on the verge of hallucination, he walked on ground that undulated softly, like a swallowing throat.

Worst of all, as his struggle against drugs grew more successful, he saw how it had masked a struggle not to become like his father. The claim that every man kills the thing he loves seemed to him a wild guess compared with the near certainty of a man turning into the thing he hates. There were of course people who didn't hate anything, but they were too remote from Patrick for him to imagine their fate. The memory of his father still hypnotized him and drew him like a sleepwalker towards a precipice of unwilling emulation. Sarcasm, snobbery, cruelty, and betrayal seemed less nauseating than the terrors that brought them into existence. What could he do but become a machine for turning terror into contempt? How could he relax his guard when beams of neurotic energy, like searchlights weaving about a prison compound, allowed no thought to escape, no remark to go unchecked.

The pursuit of sex, the fascination with one body or another, the little rush of an orgasm, so much feebler and more laborious than the rush of drugs, but like an injection, constantly repeated because its role was essentially palliative – all this was compulsive enough, but its social complications were paramount: the treachery, the danger of pregnancy, of infection, of discovery, the pleasures of theft, the tensions that arose in what might otherwise have been very tedious circumstances; and the way that sex merged with the penetration of ever more self-assured social circles where, perhaps, he would find a resting place, a living equivalent to the intimacy and reassurance offered by the octopus embrace of narcotics.

As Patrick reached for his cigarettes, the phone rang again.

'So, how are you?' said Johnny.

'I'm stuck in one of those argumentative daydreams,' said Patrick. 'I don't know why I think intelligence consists of proving that I can have a row all on my own, but it would be nice just to grasp something for a change.'

'*Measure for Measure* is a very argumentative play,' said Johnny.

'I know,' said Patrick. 'I ended up theoretically accepting that people have to forgive on a "judge not that ye be not judged" basis, but there isn't any emotional authority for it, at least not in that play.'

'Exactly,' said Johnny. 'If behaving badly was a good enough reason to forgive bad behaviour, we'd all be oozing with magnanimity.'

'But what is a good enough reason?' asked Patrick.

'Search me. I'm more and more convinced that things just happen, or don't just happen, and there's not much you can do to hurry them along.' Johnny had only just thought of this idea and was not convinced of it at all.

'Ripeness is all,' groaned Patrick.

'Yes, exactly, another play altogether,' said Johnny.

'It's important to decide which play you're in before you get out of bed,' said Patrick.

'I don't think anyone's heard of the one we're in tonight. Who are the Bossington-Lanes?'

'Are they having you for dinner too?' asked Patrick. 'I think we're going to have to break down on the motorway, don't you? Have dinner in the hotel. It's so hard facing strangers without drugs.'

Patrick and Johnny, although they now fed on grilled food and mineral water, had a well-established nostalgia for their former existence.

'But when we took gear at parties, all we saw was the inside of the loos,' Johnny pointed out.

'I know,' said Patrick. 'Nowadays when I go into the loos I say to myself, "What are you doing here? You don't take drugs anymore!" It's only after I've stormed out that I realize I wanted to have a piss. By the way, shall we drive down to Cheatley together?'

'Sure, but I have to go to an NA meeting at three o'clock.'

'I don't know how you put up with those meetings,' said Patrick. 'Aren't they full of ghastly people?'

'Of course they are, but so is any crowded room,' said Johnny.

'But at least I'm not required to believe in God to go to this party tonight.'

'I'm sure if you were you'd find a way,' laughed Johnny. 'What is a strain is being forced into the lobster pot of good behaviour while being forced to sing its praises.'

'Doesn't the hypocrisy get you down?'

'Luckily, they have a slogan for that: "Fake it to make it."'

Patrick made a vomiting sound. 'I don't think that dressing the Ancient Mariner as a wedding guest is the solution to the problem, do you?'

'It's not like that, more like a roomful of Ancient Mariners deciding to have a party of their own.'

'Christ!' said Patrick. 'It's worse than I thought.'

'You're the one who wants to dress as a wedding guest,' said Johnny. 'Didn't you tell me that the last time you were banging your head against the wall and begging to be released from the torment of your addiction, you couldn't get that sentence about Henry James out of your mind: "He was an inveterate diner-out and admitted to accepting one hundred and fifty invitations in the winter of 1878," or something like that?'

'Hmm,' said Patrick.

'Anyhow, don't you find it hard not to take drugs?' asked Johnny.

'Of course it's hard, it's a fucking nightmare,' said Patrick. Since he was representing stoicism against therapy, he wasn't going to lose the chance to exaggerate the strain he was under.

'Either I wake up in the Grey Zone,' he whispered, 'and I've forgotten how to breathe, and my feet are so far away I'm not sure I can afford the air fare; or it's the endless reel of lazy decapitations, and kneecaps stolen by passing traffic, and dogs fighting over the liver I quite want back. If they made a film of my inner life, it would be more than the public could take. Mothers would scream, "Bring back *The Texas Chainsaw Massacre*, so we can have some decent family entertainment!" And all these joys accompanied by the fear that I'll forget everything that's ever happened to me, and all the things I've seen will be lost, as the Replicant says at the end of *Blade Runner*, "like tears in rain".'

'Yeah, yeah,' said Johnny, who'd often heard Patrick rehearse fragments of this speech. 'So why don't you just go ahead?'

'Some combination of pride and terror,' said Patrick, and then, changing the subject quickly, he asked when Johnny's meeting ended. They agreed to leave from Patrick's flat at five o'clock.

Patrick lit another cigarette. The conversation with Johnny had made him nervous. Why had he said, 'Some combination of pride and terror'? Did he still think it was uncool to admit to any enthusiasm, even in front of his greatest friend? Why did he muzzle new feelings with old habits of speech? It might not have been obvious to anyone else, but he longed to stop thinking about himself, to stop strip-mining his memories, to stop the introspective and retrospective drift of his thoughts. He wanted to break into a wider world, to learn something, to make a difference. Above all, he wanted to stop being a child without using the cheap disguise of becoming a parent.

'Not that there's much danger of that,' muttered Patrick, finally getting out of bed and putting on a pair of trousers. The days when he was drawn to the sort of girl who whispered, 'Be careful, I'm not wearing any contraception,' as you came inside her, were almost completely over. He could remember one of them speaking warmly of abortion clinics. 'It's quite luxurious while you're there. A comfortable bed, good food, and you can tell all your secrets to the other girls because you know you're not going to meet them again. Even the operation is rather exciting. It's only afterwards that you get really depressed.'

Patrick ground his cigarette into the ashtray and walked through to the kitchen.

And why did he have to attack Johnny's meetings? They were simply places to confess. Why did he have to make everything so harsh and difficult? On the other hand, what was the point of going somewhere to confess if you weren't going to say the one thing that mattered? There were things he'd never told anyone and never would.

2

NICHOLAS PRATT, STILL WEARING his pyjamas, waddled back to the bedroom of his house in Clabon Mews, squeezing the letters he had just collected from the doormat and scrutinizing the handwriting on the envelopes to see how many 'serious' invitations they might contain. At sixty-seven his body was as 'well preserved' as his memoirs were 'long awaited'. He had met 'everybody', and had a 'fund of marvellous stories', but discretion had placed its gallant finger on his half-opened lips and he had never started the book which he was widely known to be working on. It was not unusual in what he called the 'big world', namely among the two or three thousand rich people who recognized his name, to hear anxious men and women 'dreading to think' how they had turned out in 'Nicholas's book'.

Collapsing on his bed, where he nowadays slept alone, he was about to test his theory that he had only received three letters that were really worth opening, when he was interrupted by the ringing of the phone.

'Hello,' he yawned.

'Ni-ko-la?' said a brisk woman's voice, pronouncing the name as if it were French. 'It's Jacqueline d'Alantour.'

'*Quel honneur*,' simpered Nicholas in his appalling French accent.

'How are you, darling? I r-ring because Jacques and I are staying at Cheet-lai for Sonny's birthday, and I thought you might be going there too.'

'Of course I am,' said Nicholas sternly. 'In fact, as the patron saint of Bridget's social triumph, I'm meant to be there already. It was I, after all, who introduced little Miss Watson-Scott, as she was then, into the beau monde, as *it* was then, and she has not forgotten her debt to Uncle Nicholas.'

'R-remind me,' said Jacqueline, 'was she one of the ladies you married?'

'Don't be absurd,' said Nicholas, pretending to take offence. 'Just because I've had six failed marriages, there's no need to invent more.'

'But Ni-ko-la, seriously, I r-ring in case you want to come with us in the car. We have a driver from the embassy. It will be more fun – no? – to go down together, or up together – this English "up" and "down" *c'est vraiment* too much.'

Nicholas was enough of a man of the world to know that the French ambassador's wife was not being entirely altruistic. She was offering him a lift so as to arrive at Cheatley with an intimate friend of Bridget's. Nicholas, for his part, would bring fresh glamour to that intimacy by arriving with the Alantours. They would enhance each other's glory.

'Up or down,' said Nicholas, 'I'd adore to come with you.'

Sonny Gravesend sat in the library at Cheatley dialling the familiar digits of Peter Porlock's number on his radio telephone. The mystical equation between property and person which had so long propped up Sonny's dim personality was worshipped nowhere more ardently than at Cheatley. Peter, George Watford's eldest son, was Sonny's best friend and the only person he really trusted when he wanted sound advice about farming or sex. Sonny sat back in his chair and waited for Peter to wade through the vast rooms of Richfield to the nearest telephone. He looked at the fireplace, above which hung the painting that Robin Parker was taking so long to authenticate as a Poussin. It had been a Poussin when the fourth Earl bought it and, as far as Sonny was concerned, it still was. Nevertheless, one had to get an 'expert opinion'.

'Sonny?' bawled Peter.

'Peter!' Sonny shouted back. 'Sorry to interrupt you again.'

'Quite the opposite, old boy, you've saved me from showing round the Gay London Bikers my old housemaster sent down to gawp at the ceilings.'

'Slaving away as usual,' said Sonny. 'Makes it all the more annoying when one reads the sort of rubbish they put in the papers this morning: "ten thousand acres . . . five hundred guests . . . Princess Margaret . . . party of the year." Sounds as if we're *made* of money, whereas the reality, as nobody knows better than you, with your Gay London Bikers, is that we never stop slaving to keep the rain out.'

'Do you know what one of my tenants said to me the other day after my famous appearance on the box?' Peter adopted his standard yokel accent. ' "Saw you on the television, m'lord, pleading poverty, as usual." Damned cheek!'

'It's quite funny, actually.'

'Well, he's really a splendid fellow,' said Peter. 'His family have been tenants of ours for three hundred years.'

'We've got some like that. One lot have been with us for twenty generations.'

'Shows an amazing lack of initiative when you think of the conditions we keep them in,' said Peter mischievously.

Both men guffawed, and agreed that that was just the sort of thing one shouldn't say during one's famous television appearances.

'What I really rang about,' said Sonny, more seriously, 'is this business with Cindy. Bridget, of course, wouldn't have her, on the grounds that we didn't know her, but I've spoken to David Windfall this morning and, since his wife's ill, he's agreed to bring Cindy along. I hope he'll be discreet.'

'David Windfall? You must be joking!' said Peter.

'Well, I know, but I made out that I was longing to meet her, rather than the truth, namely that all my Historic Houses Association and Preservation of Rural England meetings have been one long thrash in the sack with Cindy.'

'I'm glad you didn't tell him that,' said Peter wisely.

'The thing is, and I need hardly tell you to keep this under your hat, the thing is, Cindy's pregnant.'

'Are you sure it's yours?'

'Apparently there's no doubt about it,' said Sonny.

'I suppose she's blackmailing you,' said Peter loyally.

'No, no, no, that's not it at all,' said Sonny, rather put out. 'The thing is, I haven't had "conjugal relations" with Bridget for some time, and I'm not sure anyway, given her age, that it would be a good idea to try and have another child. But, as you know, I'm very keen to have a son, and I thought that if Cindy has a boy . . .' Sonny trailed off, uncertain of Peter's reaction.

'Golly,' said Peter, 'but you'd have to marry her if he was going to inherit. It's one of the penalties of being a peer,' he added with a note of noble stoicism.

'Well, I know it sounds awfully mercenary to chuck Bridget at this stage of the game,' Sonny admitted, 'and of course it's bound to be misrepresented as a sexual infatuation, but one does feel some responsibility towards Cheatley.'

'But think of the expense,' said Peter, who had grave doubts that the divorce could be achieved in time. 'And, besides, is Cindy the right girl for Cheaters?'

'She'll be a breath of fresh air,' said Sonny breezily, 'and, as you know, all the things are in trust.'

'I think,' said Peter with the measured authority of a consultant advising his patient to have surgery, 'we'd better have lunch in Buck's next week.'

'Good idea,' said Sonny. 'See you tonight.'

'Very much looking forward to it,' said Peter. 'Oh, and, by the way, happy birthday.'

Kitty Harrow, at home in the country, lay in bed propped up by a multitude of pillows, her King Charles spaniels hidden in the troughs of her undulating bedspread, and a ravaged breakfast tray abandoned beside her like an exhausted lover. Under a pink satin lampshade, bottles of contradictory medicines crowded the inlaid surface of her bedside table. Her hand rested on the telephone she used ceaselessly every morning between eleven o'clock and lunchtime, or, as on this occasion, until the hairdresser arrived at twelve thirty to rebuild those cliffs of grey hair against which so many upstarts had dashed themselves in vain. When she had found Robin Parker's name in the large red leather address book that was spread open on her lap, she dialled his number and waited impatiently.

'Hello,' said a rather peevish voice.

'Robin, my darling,' warbled Kitty, 'why aren't you here already? Bridget has unloaded some perfectly ghastly people on me, and you, my only ally, are still in London.'

'I had to go to a drinks party last night,' simpered Robin.

'A party in London on a Friday night!' protested Kitty. 'It's the most antisocial thing I've ever heard. I do think people are inconsiderate, not to say cruel. I practically never go to London these days,' she added with a real note of pathos, 'and so I rely terribly on my weekends.'

'Well, I'm coming to the rescue,' said Robin. 'I ought to be leaving for Paddington in five minutes.'

'Thank God,' she continued, 'you'll be here to protect me. I had an obscene telephone call last night.'

'Not again,' sighed Robin.

'He made the most perfectly revolting suggestions,' confided Kitty. 'And so before putting the phone down I said to him, "Young man, I should have to see your face before I allowed you to do any of those things!" He seemed to think I was encouraging him, and rang back the very next minute. I insist on answering the phone myself in the evenings: it's not fair on the servants.'

'It's not fair on you either,' Robin warned her.

'I've been haunted,' growled Kitty, 'by what you told me about those cocks the prudish Popes snapped off the classical statues and stored in the Vatican cellars. I'm not sure *that* wasn't an obscene phone call.'

'That was history of art,' giggled Robin.

'You know how fascinated I am by people's families,' said Kitty. 'Well, now, whenever I think about them, and the dark secrets they all have lurking under the surface, I can't help picturing those crates hidden in the Vatican cellars. You've corrupted my imagination,' she declared. 'Did you know what a dreadful effect you have on people?'

'My conversation will be completely chaste this evening,' threatened Robin. 'But I really ought to be going to the station now.'

'Goodbye,' cooed Kitty, but her need to talk was so imperious that she added conspiratorially, 'Do you know what George Watford told me last night? – he at least was a familiar face. He said that three-quarters of the people in his address book are dead. I told him not to be so morbid. Anyway, what could be more natural at his age: he's well into his eighties.'

'My dear, I'm going to miss my train,' said Robin.

'I used to suffer terribly from train fever,' said Kitty considerately, 'until my wonderful doctor gave me a magic pill, and now I just float on board.'

'Well, I'm going to have to sprint on board,' squealed Robin.

'Goodbye, my dear,' said Kitty, 'I won't delay you a moment longer. Hurry, hurry, hurry.'

Laura Broghlie felt her existence threatened by solitude. Her mind became 'literally blank', as she had told Patrick Melrose during their week-long affair. Five minutes alone, or off the telephone, unless it was spent in the company of a mirror and a great deal of make-up, was more literal blankness than she could stand.

It had taken her ages to get over Patrick's defection. It was not that she had liked him particularly – it never occurred to her to like people while she was using them, and when she had finished using them, it would clearly have been absurd to start liking them – but it was such a *bore* getting a new lover. Being married put some people off, until she made it clear that it was no impediment from her point of view. Laura was married to Angus Broghlie, who was entitled by ancient Scottish custom to call himself 'The Broghlie'. Laura, by the same token, could call herself 'Madame Broghlie', a right she seldom exercised.

Eventually, after a whole fortnight without a lover, she had managed to seduce Johnny Hall, Patrick's best friend. Johnny wasn't as good as Patrick because he worked during the day. Still, as a journalist he could often 'work on a story at home', which was when, they could spend the whole day in bed.

Some subtle questioning had established that Johnny didn't

yet know about her affair with Patrick, and she had sworn Johnny
to secrecy about their own affair. She didn't know whether to be
insulted by Patrick's silence or not, but she intended to let Patrick
know about Johnny whenever it would cause maximum confusion. She knew that Patrick still found her sexy, even if he had
reservations about her personality. Even she had reservations
about her personality.

When the phone rang, Laura raised her head and wriggled
across the bed.

'Don't answer it,' moaned Johnny, but he knew he was in a
weak position, having left the room earlier to talk to Patrick. He
lit a cigarette.

Laura turned to him and stuck her tongue out, hooking her
hair behind her ear as she picked up the phone. 'Hello,' she said,
suddenly serious.

'Hi.'

'China! God, your party was *so* great,' gasped Laura, pinching
her nose with her thumb and index finger and raising her eyes to
the ceiling. She had already analysed with Johnny what a failure
it had been.

'Did you really think it was a success?' China asked sceptically.

'Of course it was, darling, everybody loved it,' said Laura,
grinning at Johnny.

'But everybody got stuck in the downstairs room,' China
whined. 'I really hated it.'

'One always hates one's own parties,' said Laura sympathetically, rolling onto her back and stifling a yawn.

'But you really did like it,' pleaded China. 'Promise.'

'Promise,' said Laura, crossing her fingers, her legs, and finally her eyes. Suddenly convulsed with silent giggles, she raised
her feet in the air and rocked on the bed.

Johnny watched, amazed by her childishness, faintly contemptuous of the mocking conspiracy into which he was being

drawn, but charmed by the contortions of her naked body. He sank back against the pillows, scanning the details which might explain, but only confirmed the mystery of his obsession: the small dark mole on the inner slope of her hip bone, the surprisingly thick golden hair on her forearm, the high arch of her pale feet.

'Is Angus with you?' sighed China.

'No, he's going straight from Scotland to the party. I have to collect him in Cheltenham. It's such a bore, I don't see why he can't get a taxi.'

'Save, save, save,' said China.

'He looked so good on paper,' said Laura, 'but when it comes down to it, he's completely obsessed with whether a cheap-day return is refundable if you don't use the second half, and other fascinating problems of that kind. It makes one long for an extravagant lover.' She allowed one of her knees to flop sideways on the bed.

Johnny took a long drag on his cigarette and smiled at her.

China hesitated and then, spurred on by the thought that Laura's praise of her party might not have been entirely sincere, she said, 'You know there's a rumour going around that you're having an affair with Patrick Melrose.'

'Patrick Melrose,' said Laura, as if she were repeating the name of a fatal disease, 'you must be joking.' She raised her eyebrows at Johnny and putting her hand over the mouthpiece whispered, 'Apparently I'm having an affair with Patrick.'

He flicked up one of his eyebrows and stubbed out his cigarette.

'Who on earth told you that?' she asked China.

'I shouldn't really tell you, but it was Alexander Politsky.'

'Him, I don't even know him.'

'Well, he thinks he knows about you.'

'How pathetic,' said Laura. 'He just wants to get in with you by pretending he knows all about your friends.' Johnny knelt in front of Laura and, catching both her feet, eased her legs apart.

'He said he found out from Ali Montague,' China insisted.

Laura drew in her breath sharply. 'Well, that just proves it's a lie,' she sighed. 'Anyway, I don't even fancy Patrick Melrose,' she added, digging her nails into Johnny's arms.

'Oh, well, you know better than me whether you're having an affair with him or not,' China concluded. 'I'm glad you're not, because personally I find him really tricky . . .'

Laura held the phone in the air so Johnny could hear. 'And,' continued China, 'I can't stand the way he treated Debbie.'

Laura put the phone back to her ear. 'It was disgusting, wasn't it?' she said, grinning at Johnny, who leaned down to bite her neck. 'But who are you going to the party with?' she asked, knowing that China was going alone.

'I'm not going with anybody, but there's someone called Morgan Ballantine,' China put on an unconvincing American accent to pronounce his name, 'who is going to be there, and I'm quite keen on him. He's supposed to have just inherited two hundred and forty million dollars and an amazing gun collection,' she added casually, 'but that's not really the point, I mean, he's *really* sweet.'

'He may be worth two hundred and forty million dollars, but is he going to spend it?' asked Laura, who had bitter experience of how misleading these figures could be. 'That's the real question,' she said, propping herself up on one elbow and effortlessly ignoring the caresses she had found so breathtaking moments before. Johnny stopped and leaned over, partly from curiosity, but also to disguise the fact that his sexual efforts could not compete with the mention of such a large sum of money.

'He did say something rather sinister the other day,' China admitted.

'What?' asked Laura eagerly.

'Well, he said, "I'm too rich to lend money." A friend of his had gone bankrupt, or something.'

'Don't touch him,' said Laura, in her special serious voice. 'That's the kind of thing Angus says. You think it's all going to be private planes, and the next thing you know he's asking for a doggy bag in a restaurant, or implying that *you* ought to be doing the cooking. It's a complete nightmare.'

'That reminds me,' said China, rather annoyed that she had given so much away. 'We played a wonderful game after you left last night. Everybody had to think of the things people were least likely to say, and someone came up with one for Angus: "Are you sure you won't have the lobster?"'

'Very funny,' said Laura drily.

'By the way, where are you staying?' asked China.

'With some people called Bossington-Lane.'

'Me too,' exclaimed China. 'Can I have a lift?'

'Of course. Come here about twelve thirty and we can go out to lunch.'

'Perfect,' said China. 'See you later.'

'Bye, darling,' Laura trilled. 'Stupid cow,' she said, putting the phone down.

All her life men had rushed around Cindy, like the citizens of Lilliput with their balls of string, trying to tie her down so she wouldn't wreck their little lives, but now she was thinking of tying herself down voluntarily.

'Hello?' she purred in her soft Californian accent. 'Can I speak with David Windfall, please?'

'Speaking,' said David.

'Hi there, I'm Cindy Smith. I guess Sonny already talked to you about tonight.'

'He certainly did,' said David, flushing to a deeper shade of raspberry than usual.

'I hope you've got your Sonny and Bridget invitation, 'cause I sure don't have one,' said Cindy with disarming candour.

'I've got mine in the bank,' said David. 'One can't be too careful.'

'I know,' said Cindy, 'that's a valuable item.'

'You realize you'll have to pretend to be my wife,' said David.

'How far am I meant to go?'

David, quivering, sweating, and blushing at the same time, took refuge in the bluffness for which he was well known. 'Only until we get past the security people,' he said.

'Anything you say,' Cindy replied meekly. 'You're the boss.'

'Where shall we meet?' asked David.

'I've got a suite in the Little Soddington House Hotel. That's in Gloucestershire, right?'

'I certainly hope so, unless it's moved,' said David, more pompously than he'd intended.

Cindy giggled. 'Sonny didn't tell me you were so funny,' she said. 'We could have dinner together at my hotel, if you'd like.'

'Splendid,' said David, already scheming to get out of the dinner party Bridget had put him in. 'About eight?'

Tom Charles had ordered a car to take him down to the country. It was extravagant, but he was too old to fool around with trains and suitcases. He was staying at Claridge's, as usual, and one of the nicest things about it was the wood fire that was subsiding brightly in the grate while he finished his frugal breakfast of tea and grapefruit juice.

He was on his way to stay with Harold Greene, an old friend from the IMF days. Harold had said to bring a dinner jacket because they were going to a neighbour's birthday party. He'd got the low-down on the neighbour, but all Tom could remember was that he was one of those Englishmen with plenty of 'background' and not a hell of a lot going on in the foreground. If you weren't unduly impressed by these 'background' types they said you were 'chippy', but in fact nothing could make you feel less 'chippy' than contemplating a lifetime wasted in gossip, booze, and sexual intrigue.

Harold was not like that at all; he was a mover and shaker. He was on the Christmas-card lists of grateful presidents and friendly senators – as was Tom – but like everybody else on this rainy island he liked the 'background' types too much.

Tom picked up the phone to ring Anne Eisen. Anne was an old friend and he was looking forward to driving down with her to Harold's, but he had to know what time to send the car to collect her. Her number was engaged and so Tom hung up crisply and continued reading the pile of English and American newspapers he'd ordered with his breakfast.

3

TONY FOWLES WAS WHAT Bridget called an 'absolute genius' when it came to colours and fabrics. He confessed to 'having a crush on ash colours at the moment,' and she had agreed to have the interior of the tent done in grey. Her initial misgivings about this bold idea were swept aside by Tony's remark that Jacqueline d'Alantour, the French Ambassador's wife, was 'so correct that she's never really *right*'.

Bridget wondered how far one could be incorrect without being wrong, and it was in this grey area that Tony had become her guide, increasing her dependency on him until she could hardly light a cigarette without his assistance, and had already had a row with Sonny about wanting to have him at her side during dinner.

'That appalling little man shouldn't be coming at all,' said Sonny, 'let alone sitting next to you. I need hardly remind you that we're having Princess Margaret for dinner and that every one of the men has a better claim to be by your side than that . . .' Sonny spluttered, 'that popinjay.'

What was a popinjay anyway? Whatever it was, it was so unfair, because Tony was her guru and her jester. People who knew how funny he was – and one only had to hear his story about hurrying through the streets of Lima clutching bolts of fabric during a bread riot to practically die laughing – didn't perhaps realize how wise he was also.

But where was Tony? He was supposed to meet her at eleven o'clock. One could worship him for all sorts of things, but punctuality wasn't one of them. Bridget looked around at the wastes of grey velvet that lined the inside of the tent; without Tony, her confidence faltered. One end of the tent was dominated by a hideous white stage on which a forty-piece band, flown over from America, would later play the 'traditional New Orleans jazz' favoured by Sonny. The industrial heaters that roared in every corner still left the atmosphere numbingly cold.

'Obviously, I'd rather that my birthday was in June instead of gloomy old February,' Sonny was fond of saying, 'but one can't choose when one's born.'

The shock of not having planned his own birth had given Sonny a fanatical desire to plan everything else. Bridget had tried to keep him out of the tent on the grounds that it should be a 'surprise', but since this word was for him roughly equivalent to 'terrorist outrage', she had failed. She had, on the other hand, managed to keep secret the astonishing cost of the velvet, communicated to her by a honking Sloane with a laugh like a death rattle, who had said that it came to 'forty thousand, plus the dreaded'. Bridget had thought 'the dreaded' was a technical decorating term until Tony explained that it was VAT.

He had also said that the orange lilies would make a 'riot of colour' against the soft grey background, but now that they were being arranged by a team of busy ladies in chequered blue overalls, Bridget could not help thinking they looked more like dying embers in a huge heap of ash.

Just as this heretical thought was entering her mind, Tony swept into the tent dressed in a baggy earth, ash, and grape sweater, a pair of beautifully ironed jeans, white socks, and brown moccasins with surprisingly thick soles. He had wrapped a white silk scarf around his throat after he felt, or thought he felt, a tickle. 'Tony! At last,' Bridget dared to point out.

'I'm sorry,' croaked Tony, laying his hand on his chest and frowning pathetically. 'I think I'm coming down with something.'

'Oh, dear,' said Bridget, 'I hope you won't be too ill for to-night.'

'Even if they had to wheel me in on a life-support machine,' he replied, 'I wouldn't miss it for the world. I know the artist is supposed to stand outside his creation, paring his fingernails,' he said, looking down at his fingernails with affected indifference, 'but I don't feel my creation is finished until it's filled with living fabric.'

He paused and stared at Bridget with hypnotic intensity, like Rasputin about to inform the Tsarina of his latest inspiration. 'Now, I know what you're thinking,' he assured her. 'Not enough colour!'

Bridget felt a searchlight shining into the recesses of her soul. 'The flowers haven't changed it as much as I thought they would,' she confessed.

'And that's why I've brought you these,' said Tony, pointing to a group of assistants who had been waiting meekly until they were called forward. They were surrounded by large cardboard boxes.

'What are they?' asked Bridget, apprehensive.

The assistants started to open the tops of the boxes. 'I thought tents, I thought poles, I thought ribbons,' said Tony, who was always ready to explain his imaginative processes. 'And so I had these specially made. It's a sort of regimental-maypole theme,' he explained, no longer able to contain his excitement. 'It'll look stunning against the pearly texture of the ash.'

Bridget knew that 'specially made' meant extremely expensive. 'They look like ties,' she said, peering into a box.

'Exactly,' said Tony triumphantly. 'I saw Sonny wearing a rather thrilling green and orange tie. He told me it was a regimental tie and I thought, that's it: the orange will pick up the lilies and lift the whole room.' Tony's hands flowed upward and outward. 'We'll tie the ribbons to the top of the pole and bring them over to the sides of the tent.' This time his hands flowed outwards and downward.

These graceful balletic gestures were enough to convince Bridget that she had no choice.

'It sounds wonderful,' she said. 'But put them up quickly, we haven't much time.'

'Leave it to me,' said Tony serenely.

A maid came to tell Bridget that there was a phone call for her. Bridget waved goodbye to Tony, and hurried out of the tent through the red-carpeted tunnel that led back to the house. Smiling florists arranged wreaths of ivy around the green metal hoops that supported the canvas.

It was strange, in February, not to give the party in the house, but Sonny was convinced that his 'things' would be imperilled by what he called 'Bridget's London friends'. He was haunted by his grandfather's complaint that his grandmother had filled the house with 'spongers, buggers, and Jews', and, while he recognized the impossibility of giving an amusing party without samples from all these categories, he wasn't about to trust them with his 'things'.

Bridget walked across the denuded drawing room, and picked up the phone.

'Hello?'

'Darling, how are you?'

'Aurora! Thank God it's you. I was dreading another virtual stranger begging to bring their entire family to the party.'

'Aren't people *awful*?' said Aurora Donne in that condescending voice for which she was famous. Her large liquid eyes and creamy complexion gave her the soft beauty of a Charolais cow, but her sniggering laughter, reserved for her own remarks, was more reminiscent of a hyena. She had become Bridget's best friend, instilling her with a grim and precarious confidence in exchange for Bridget's lavish hospitality.

'It's been a nightmare,' said Bridget, settling down in the spindly caterer's chair that had replaced one of Sonny's things. 'I can't believe the cheek of some of these people.'

'You don't have to tell me,' said Aurora. 'I hope you've got good security.'

'Yes,' said Bridget. 'Sonny's got the police, who were supposed to be at a football match this afternoon, to come here instead and check everything. It makes a nice change for them. They're going to form a ring around the house. Plus, we've got the usual people at the door, in fact, someone called "Gresham Security" has left his walkie-talkie by the phone.'

'They make such a fuss about royalty,' said Aurora.

'*Don't*,' groaned Bridget. 'We've had to give up two of our precious rooms to the private detective and the lady-in-waiting. It's such a waste of space.'

Bridget was interrupted by the sound of screaming in the hall.

'You're a filthy little girl! And nothing but a burden to your parents!' shouted a woman with a strong Scottish accent. 'What would the Princess say if she knew that you dirtied your dress? You filthy child!'

'Oh dear,' said Bridget to Aurora, 'I do wish Nanny wasn't quite so horrid to Belinda. It's rather terrible, but I never dare say anything to her.'

'I know,' said Aurora sympathetically, 'I'm absolutely terrified of Lucy's nanny. I think it's because she reminds one of one's own nanny.'

Bridget, who had not had a 'proper' nanny, wasn't about to reveal this fact by disagreeing. She had made a special effort, by way of compensation, to get a proper old-fashioned nanny for seven-year-old Belinda. The agency had been delighted when they found such a good position for the vicious old bag who'd been on their books for years.

'The other thing I dread is my mother coming tonight,' said Bridget.

'Mothers can be so critical, can't they?' said Aurora.

'Exactly,' said Bridget, who in fact found her mother tiresomely eager to please. 'I suppose I ought to go off and be nice to Belinda,' she added with a dutiful sigh.

'Sweet!' cooed Aurora.

'I'll see you tonight, darling.' Bridget was grateful to get rid of Aurora. She had a million and one things to do and besides, instead of giving her those transfusions of self-confidence for which she was, well, almost employed (she didn't have a bean), Aurora had recently taken to implying that she would have handled the arrangements for the party better than Bridget.

Given that she had no intention of going up to see Belinda it was quite naughty to have used her as an excuse to end the conversation. Bridget seldom found the time to see her daughter. She could not forgive her for being a girl and burdening Sonny with the anxiety of having no heir. After spending her early twenties having abortions, Bridget had spent the next ten years having miscarriages. Successfully giving birth had been complicated enough without having a child of the wrong gender. The doctor had told her that it would be dangerous to try again, and at forty-two she was becoming resigned to having one child, especially in view of Sonny's reluctance to go to bed with her.

Her looks had certainly deteriorated over the last sixteen years of marriage. The clear blue eyes had clouded over, the candlelit glow of her skin had sputtered out and could only be partially rekindled with tinted creams, and the lines of her body, which had shaped so many obsessions in their time, were now deformed by accumulations of stubborn fat. Unwilling to betray Sonny, and unable to attract him, Bridget had allowed herself to go into a mawkish physical decline, spending more and more time thinking of other ways to please her husband – or rather not to displease him, since he took her efforts for granted but lavished his attention on the slightest failure.

She ought to get on with the arrangements, which, in her case, meant worrying, since all the work had been delegated to somebody else. The first thing she decided to worry about was the walkie-talkie on the table beside her. It had clearly been lost by some hopeless security man. Bridget picked the machine up and, curious, switched it on. There was a loud hissing sound and then the whinings of an untuned radio.

Interested to see if she could make anything intelligible emerge from this melee of sound, Bridget got up and walked around the room. The noises grew louder and fainter, and sometimes intensified into squeals, but as she moved towards the windows, darkened by the side of the marquee that reared up wet and white under the dull winter sky, she heard, or thought she heard, a voice. Pressing her ear close to the walkie-talkie she could make out a crackling, whispering conversation.

'The thing is, I haven't had conjugal relations with Bridget for some time . . .' said the voice at the other end, and faded again. Bridget shook the walkie-talkie desperately, and moved closer to the window. She couldn't understand what was going on. How could it be Sonny she was listening to? But who else could claim that he hadn't had 'conjugal relations' with her for some time?

She could make out words again, and pressed the walkie-talkie to her ear with renewed curiosity and dread.

'To chuck Bridget at this . . . it's bound to be . . . but one does feel some responsibility towards . . .' Interference drowned the conversation again. A prickling wave of heat rushed over her body. She must hear what they were saying, what monstrous plan they were hatching. Who was Sonny talking to? It must be Peter. But what if it wasn't? What if he talked like this to everyone, everyone except her?

'All the things are in trust,' she heard, and then another voice saying: 'Lunch . . . next week.' Yes, it was Peter. There was more crackling, and then, 'Happy birthday.'

Bridget sank down in the window seat. She raised her arm and almost flung the walkie-talkie against the wall, but then lowered it again slowly until it hung loosely by her side.

4

JOHNNY HALL HAD BEEN going to Narcotics Anonymous meetings for over a year. In a fit of enthusiasm and humility he found hard to explain, he had volunteered to make the tea and coffee at the Saturday three o'clock meeting. He recognized many of the people who took one of the white plastic cups he had filled with a tea bag or a few granules of instant coffee, and struggled to remember their names, embarrassed that so many of them remembered his.

After making the tea Johnny took a seat in the back row, as usual, although he knew that it would make it harder for him to speak, or 'share', as he was urged to say in meetings. He enjoyed the obscurity of sitting as far away as possible from the addict who was 'giving the chair'. The 'preamble' – a ritual reading of selections from 'the literature', explaining the nature of addiction and NA – washed over Johnny almost unnoticed. He tried to see if the girl sitting in the front row was pretty, but couldn't see enough of her profile to judge.

A woman called Angie had been asked by the secretary to do the chair. Her stumpy legs were clad in a black leotard, and her hair hid two-thirds of her raddled and exhausted face. She had been invited down from Kilburn to add a touch of grit to a Chelsea meeting which dwelt all too often on the shame of burgling one's parents' house, or the difficulty of finding a parking space.

Angie said she had started 'using', by which she meant taking drugs, in the sixties, because it was 'a gas'. She didn't want to dwell on the 'bad old days', but she had to tell the group a little bit about her using to put them in the picture. Half an hour later, she was still describing her wild twenties, and yet there was clearly some time to go before her listeners could enjoy the insight that she had gleaned from her regular attendance of meetings over the last two years. She rounded off her chair with some self-deprecating remarks about still being 'riddled with defects'. Thanks to the meetings she had discovered that she was totally insane and completely addicted to everything. She was also 'rampantly co-dependent', and urgently needed individual counselling in order to deal with lots of 'childhood stuff', Her 'relationship', by which she meant her boyfriend, had discovered that living with an addict could create a lot of extra hassles, and so the two of them had decided to attend 'couples counselling'. This was the latest excitement in a life already packed with therapeutic drama, and she was very hopeful about the benefits.

The secretary was very grateful to Angie. A lot of what she had shared, he said, was relevant for him too. He'd 'identified one hundred per cent', not with her using because his had been very different – he had never used needles or been addicted to heroin or cocaine – but with 'the feelings'. Johnny could not remember Angie describing any feelings, but tried to silence the scepticism which made it so difficult for him to participate in the meetings, even after the breakthrough of volunteering to make the tea. The secretary went on to say that a lot of childhood stuff had been coming up for him too, and he had recently discovered that although nothing unpleasant had happened to him in child-hood, he'd found himself smothered by his parents' kindness and that breaking away from their understanding and generosity had become a real issue for him.

With these resonant words the secretary threw the meeting open, a moment that Johnny always found upsetting because it put him under pressure to 'share'. The problem, apart from his acute self-consciousness and his resistance to the language of 'recovery', was that sharing was supposed to be based on 'identification' with something that the person who was doing the chair had said, and it was very rare for Johnny to have any clear recollection of what had been said. He decided to wait until somebody else's identification identified for him the details of Angie's chair. This was a hazardous procedure because most of the time people identified with something that had not in fact been said in the chair.

The first person to speak from the floor said that he'd had to nurture himself by 'parenting the child within'. He hoped that with God's help – a reference that always made Johnny wince – and the help of the Fellowship, the child within would grow up in a 'safe environment'. He said that he too was having problems with his relationship, by which he meant his girlfriend, but that hopefully, if he worked his Step Three and 'handed it over', everything would be all right in the end. He wasn't in charge of the results, only the 'footwork'.

The second speaker identified one hundred per cent with what Angie had said about her veins being 'the envy of Kilburn', because his veins had been the envy of Wimbledon. There was general merriment. And yet, the speaker went on to say, when he had to go to the doctor nowadays for a proper medical reason, they couldn't find a vein anywhere on his body. He had been doing a Step Four, 'a fearless and searching moral inventory', and it had brought up a lot of stuff that needed looking at. He had heard someone in a meeting saying that she had a fear of success and he thought that maybe this was his problem too. He was in a lot of pain at the moment because he was realizing that a lot of his 'relationship problems' were the result of his 'dysfunctional family'. He felt unlovable and consequently he was unloving, he concluded, and his neighbour, who recognized that he was in the presence of feelings, rubbed his back consolingly.

Johnny looked up at the fluorescent lights and the white polystyrene ceiling of the dingy church-hall basement. He longed to hear someone talk about their experiences in ordinary language, and not in this obscure and fatuous slang. He was entering the stage of the meeting when he gave up daydreaming and became increasingly anxious about whether to speak. He constructed opening sentences, imagined elegant ways of linking what had been said to what he wanted to say, and then, with a thumping heart, failed to announce his name quickly enough to win the right to speak. He was particularly restless after the show of coolness he always felt he had to put on in front of Patrick. Talking to Patrick had exacerbated his rebellion against the foolish vocabulary of NA, while increasing his need for the peace of mind that others seemed to glean from using it. He regretted agreeing to have dinner alone with Patrick, whose corrosive criticism and drug nostalgia and stylized despair often left Johnny feeling agitated and confused.

The current speaker was saying that he'd read somewhere in the literature that the difference between 'being willing' and 'being ready' was that you could sit in an armchair and be willing to leave the house, but you weren't entirely ready until you had on your hat and overcoat. Johnny knew that the speaker must be finishing, because he was using Fellowship platitudes, trying to finish on a 'positive' note, as was the custom of the obedient recovering addict, who always claimed to bear in mind 'newcomers' and their need to hear positive notes.

He must do it, he must break in now, and say his piece.

'My name's Johnny,' he blurted out, almost before the previous speaker had finished. 'I'm an addict.'

'Hi, Johnny,' chorused the rest of the group.

'I have to speak,' he said boldly, 'because I'm going to a party this evening, and I know there'll be a lot of drugs around. It's a big party and I just feel under threat, I suppose. I just wanted to come to this meeting to reaffirm my desire to stay clean today. Thanks.'

'Thanks, Johnny,' the group echoed.

He'd done it, he'd said what was really troubling him. He hadn't managed to say anything funny, clever, or interesting, but he knew that somehow, however ridiculous and boring these meetings were, having taken part in one would give him the strength not to take drugs at the party tonight and that he would be able to enjoy himself a little bit more.

Glowing with goodwill after speaking, Johnny listened to Pete, the next speaker, with more sympathy than he'd been able to muster at the beginning of the meeting.

Someone had described recovery to Pete as 'putting your tie around your neck instead of your arm'. There was subdued laughter. When he was using, Pete had found it easy to cross the road because he didn't care whether he was run over or not, but in early recovery he'd become fucking terrified of the traffic (subdued laughter) and walked for miles and miles to find a zebra crossing. He'd also spent his early recovery making lines out of Coleman's mustard powder and wondering if he'd put too much in the spoon (one isolated cackle). He was 'in bits' at the moment because he had broken up with his relationship. She'd wanted him to be some kind of trout fisherman, and he'd wanted her to be a psychiatric nurse. When she'd left she'd said that she still thought he was the 'best thing on two legs'. It had worried him that she'd fallen in love with a pig (laughter). Or a centipede (more laughter). Talk about pushing his shame buttons! He'd been on a 'Step Twelve Call' the other day, by which he meant a visit to an active addict who had rung the NA office, and the guy was in a dreadful state, but frankly, Pete admitted, he had wanted what the other guy had more than the other guy wanted what he had. That was the insanity of the disease! 'I came to this programme on my knees,' concluded Pete in a more pious tone, 'and it's been suggested that I remain on them' (knowing grunts, and an appreciative, 'Thanks, Pete').

The American girl who spoke after Pete was called Sally. 'Sleeping at night and staying awake during the day' had been 'a real concept' for her when she 'first came round'. What she wanted from the programme was 'wall-to-wall freedom', and she knew she could achieve that with the help of a 'Loving Higher Power'. At Christmas she'd been to a pantomime to 'celebrate her inner child'. Since then she'd been travelling with another member of the Fellowship because, like they said in the States, 'When you're sick together, you stick together.'

After the group had thanked Sally, the secretary said that they were in 'Newcomer's Time' and that he would appreciate it if people would respect that. This announcement was almost always followed by a brief silence for the Newcomer who either didn't exist, or was too terrified to speak. The last five minutes would then be hogged by some old hand who was 'in bits' or 'just wanted to feel part of the meeting'. On this occasion, however, there was a genuine Newcomer in the room, and he dared to open his mouth.

Dave, as he was called, was at his first meeting and he didn't see how it was supposed to stop him taking drugs. He'd been about to go, actually, and then someone had said about the mustard and the spoon and making lines, and like he'd thought he was the only person to have ever done that, and it was funny hearing someone else say it. He didn't have any money, and he couldn't go out because he owed money everywhere: the only reason he wasn't stoned was that he didn't have the energy to steal anymore. He still had his TV, but he had this thing that he was controlling it, and he was afraid of watching it now because last night he'd been worried that he'd been putting the bloke on TV off by staring at him. He couldn't think what else to say.

The secretary thanked him in the especially coaxing voice he used for Newcomers whose distress formed his own spiritual nourishment, an invaluable opportunity to 'give it away' and 'pass on the message'. He advised Dave to stick around after the meeting and get some phone numbers. Dave said his phone had been cut off. The secretary, afraid that magical 'sharing' might degenerate into mere conversation, smiled firmly at Dave and asked if there were any more Newcomers.

Johnny, somewhat to his surprise, found himself caring about what happened to Dave. In fact, he really hoped that these people, people like him who had been hopelessly dependent on drugs, obsessed with them, and unable to think about anything else for years, would get their lives together. If they had to use this obscure slang in order to do so, then that was a pity but not a reason to hope that they would fail.

The secretary said that unless there was somebody who urgently needed to share, they were out of time. Nobody spoke, and so he stood up and asked Angie to help him close the meeting. Everybody else stood up as well and held hands.

'Will you join me in the Serenity Prayer,' asked Angie, 'using the word "God" as you understand him, her, or it. God,' she said to kickstart the prayer, and then when everyone was ready to join in, repeated, 'God, grant me the serenity to accept the things I cannot change, The courage to change the things I can, And the wisdom to know the difference.'

Johnny wondered as usual to whom he was addressing this prayer. Sometimes when he got chatting to his 'fellow addicts' he would admit to being 'stuck on Step Three'. Step Three made the bold suggestion that he hand his will and his life over to God 'as he understood him'.

At the end of the meeting, Amanda Pratt, whom he hadn't noticed until then, came up to him. Amanda was the twenty-two-year-old daughter of Nicholas Pratt by his most sensible wife, the general's daughter with the blue woolly and the simple string of pearls he used to dream gloomily of marrying when he was going out with Bridget.

Johnny did not know Amanda well, but he somehow knew this story about her parents. She was eight years younger than him, and to Johnny she was not a drug addict at all, just one of those neurotic girls who had taken a bit of coke or speed to help her dieting, and a few sleeping pills to help her sleep, and, worst of all, when these pitiful abuses had started to become unpleasant, she had stopped them. Johnny, who had wasted his entire twenties repeating the same mistakes, took a very condescending view of anybody who came to the end of their tether before him, or for less good reasons.

'It was so funny,' Amanda was saying rather louder than Johnny would have liked, 'when you were sharing about going to a big party tonight, I knew it was Cheatley.'

'Are you going?' asked Johnny, already knowing the answer.

'Oh, ya,' said Amanda. 'Bridget's practically a stepmother, because she went out with Daddy just before he married Mummy.'

Johnny looked at Amanda and marvelled again at the phenomenon of pretty girls who were not at all sexy. Something empty and clinging about her, a missing centre, prevented her from being attractive.

'Well, we'll see each other tonight,' said Johnny, hoping to end the conversation.

'You're a friend of Patrick Melrose, aren't you?' asked Amanda, immune to the finality of his tone.

'Yes,' said Johnny.

'Well, I gather he spends a lot of time slagging off the Fellowship,' said Amanda indignantly.

'Can you blame him?' sighed Johnny, looking over Amanda's shoulder to see if Dave was still in the room.

'Yes, I do blame him,' said Amanda. 'I think it's rather pathetic, actually, and it just shows how sick he is: if he wasn't sick, he wouldn't need to slag off the Fellowship.'

'You're probably right,' said Johnny, resigned to the familiar tautologies of 'recovery'. 'But listen, I have to go now, or I'll miss my lift down to the country.'

'See you tonight,' said Amanda cheerfully. 'I may need you for an emergency meeting!'

'Umm,' said Johnny. 'It's nice to know you'll be there.'

5

ROBIN PARKER WAS HORRIFIED to see, through the pebble spectacles which helped him to distinguish fake Poussins from real ones, but could not, alas, make him a safe driver, that an old woman had moved into 'his' compartment during the ordeal he had just undergone of fetching a miniature gin and tonic from the squalid buffet. Everything about the train offended him: the plastic 'glass', the purple-and-turquoise upholstery, the smell of diesel and dead skin, and now the invasion of his compartment by an unglamorous personage wearing an overcoat that only the Queen could have hoped to get away with. He pursed his lips as he squeezed past an impossible pale-blue nanny's suitcase that the old woman had left cluttering the floor. Picking up his copy of the *Spectator*, a Perseus's shield against the Medusa of modernity, as he'd said more than once, he lapsed into a daydream in which he was flown *privately* into Gloucestershire from Zurich or possibly Deauville, with someone really glamorous. And as he pretended to read, passing through Charlbury and Moreton-in-Marsh, he imagined the clever and subtle things he would have said about the Ben Nicholsons on the wall of the cabin.

Virginia Watson-Scott glanced nervously at her suitcase, knowing it was in everybody's way. The last time she'd been on a train, a kind young man had hoisted it into the luggage rack without sparing a thought for how she was going to get it down again. She'd been too polite to say anything, but she could remember tottering under the weight as the train drew in to Paddington. Even so, the funny-looking gentleman opposite might at least have offered.

In the end she'd decided not to pack the burgundy velvet dress she'd bought for the party. She had lost her nerve, something that would never have happened when Roddy was alive, and fallen back on an old favourite that Sonny and Bridget had seen a hundred times before, or would have seen a hundred times if they asked her to Cheatley more often.

She knew what it was, of course: Bridget was embarrassed by her. Sonny was somehow gallant and rude at the same time, full of old-fashioned courtesies that failed to disguise his underlying contempt. She didn't care about him, but it did hurt to think that her daughter didn't want her around. Old people were always saying that they didn't want to be a burden. Well, she *did* want to be a burden. It wasn't as if she would be taking the last spare room, just one of Sonny's cottages. He was always boasting about how many he had and what a terrible responsibility they were.

Bridget had been such a nice little girl. It was that horrible Nicholas Pratt who had changed her. It was hard to describe, but she had started to criticize everything at home, and look down her nose at people she'd known all her life. Virginia had only met Nicholas once, thank goodness, when he had taken her and Roddy to the opera. She had said to Roddy afterwards that Nicholas wasn't her cup of tea at all, but Roddy had said that Bridget was a sensible girl and she was old enough now to make her own decisions.

'Oh, do come on,' said Caroline Porlock. 'We promised to arrive early and lend moral support.'

Moral support, thought Peter Porlock, still dazed from his conversation with Sonny that morning, was certainly what Cheatley needed.

They headed down the drive past placid deer and old oaks. Peter reflected that he was one of those Englishmen who could truly claim that his home was his castle, and wondered whether that was the sort of thing to say during one's famous television appearances. On balance, he decided, as Caroline whizzed the Subaru through the honey-coloured gateposts, probably not.

Nicholas Pratt lounged in the back of the Alantours' car. This is how the world should be seen, he thought: through the glass partition of a limousine.

The rack of lamb had been excellent, the cheeses flown in from France that morning, delicious, and the 1970 Haut Brion, '*très buvable*', as the ambassador had modestly remarked.

'*Et la comtesse, est-elle bien née?*' asked Jacqueline, returning to the subject of Bridget, so that her husband could savour the details of her background.

'*Pas du tout*,' answered Nicholas in a strong English accent.

'Not quite from the top basket!' exclaimed Jacques d'Alantour, who prided himself on his command of colloquial English.

Jacqueline was not quite from the top basket herself, reflected Nicholas, which was what gave that rather hungry quality to her fascination with social standing. Her mother had been the daughter of a Lebanese arms dealer, and had married Phillipe du Tant, a penniless and obscure baron who had neither been able to spoil her like her father, nor to save her from being spoilt. Jacqueline had not been born so much as numbered, somewhere in the

Union des Banques Suisses. With the slightly sallow complexion and downturned mouth she had inherited from her mother, she could have done without the frighteningly prominent nose that her father had settled on her; but already famous as an heiress from an early age, she appeared to most people as a photograph come to life, a name made flesh, a bank account personified.

'Is that why you didn't marry her?' teased Jacqueline.

'I'm quite *bien né* enough for two,' replied Nicholas grandly. 'But, you know, I'm not the snob I used to be.'

The ambassador raised his finger in judgement. 'You are a better snob!' he declared, with a witty expression on his face.

'There are so many varieties of snobbism,' said Jacqueline, 'one cannot admire all of them.'

'Snobbery is one of the things one should be most discriminating about,' said Nicholas.

'Some things, like not tolerating stupid people, or not having pigs at one's table, are not snobbish at all, they are simply common sense,' said Jacqueline.

'And yet,' said the wily ambassador, 'sometimes it is necessary to have pigs at one's table.'

Diplomats, thought Nicholas, long made redundant by telephones, still preserved the mannerisms of men who were dealing with great matters of state. He had once seen Jacques d'Alantour fold his overcoat on a banister and declare with all the emphasis of a man refusing to compromise over the Spanish Succession, 'I shall put my coat *here*.' He had then placed his hat on a nearby chair and added with an air of infinite subtlety, 'But my hat I shall put *here*. Otherwise it may fall!' as if he were hinting that on the other hand some arrangement could be reached over the exact terms of the marriage.

'If they are at one's table,' concluded Jacqueline tolerantly, 'they are no longer pigs.'

Obeying the law that people always loathe those they have wronged, Sonny found himself especially allergic to Bridget after his conversation with Peter Porlock, and went as far as the nursery to avoid her.

'Dada! What are you doing here?' asked Belinda.

'I've come to see my favourite girl,' boomed Sonny.

'What a lucky girl you are,' cooed Nanny, 'a busy man like your father coming to see you on a day like this!'

'That's all right, Nanny,' said Sonny. 'I'll take over.'

'Yes, sir,' said Nanny unctuously.

'Well,' said Sonny, rubbing his hands together, 'what have you been up to?'

'We were reading a book!'

'What's the story about?' asked Sonny.

'It's a school trip,' said Belinda rather shyly.

'And where do they go?'

'To the wax museum.'

'Madame Tussaud's?'

'Yes, and Tim and Jane are very naughty and they stay behind and hide, and when it's night-time all the wax people come to life, and then they start to dance with each other like real people, and they make friends with the children. Will you read it to me, Dada, please?'

'But you've just read it,' said Sonny, puzzled.

'It's my favourite story, and it's better if you read it. *Please*,' pleaded Belinda.

'Of course I will. I'd be delighted,' said Sonny with a little bow, as if he'd been asked to address an agricultural fair. Since he was in the nursery he might as well create a good impression. Besides, he was jolly fond of Belinda and there was no harm in underlining the fact. It was awful to think this way, but one had to be practical and plan ahead and think of Cheatley. Nanny would be a useful character witness if there was a fuss about custody. One could be sure that this unexpected swoop into the nursery would be branded on her memory. Sonny installed himself in an old battered armchair and Belinda, hardly believing her luck, sat in his lap and rested her head against the soft cashmere of his bright red sweater.

'All the children in Tim and Jane's class were very excited,' boomed Sonny. 'They were going on a trip to London . . .'

'It's too bad your not being able to come,' said David Windfall to his wife, slipping a couple of condoms into the inside pocket of his dinner jacket, just in case.

'Have fun, darling,' gasped Jane, longing for him to leave.

'It won't be fun without you,' said David, wondering whether two condoms were enough.

'Don't be silly, darling, you'll forget about me on the motorway.'

David couldn't be bothered to contradict the truth of this assertion.

'I hope you feel better tomorrow,' he said instead. 'I'll call you first thing.'

'You're an angel,' said his wife. 'Drive carefully.'

Johnny had called to say that he would take his own car after all, and so Patrick left London alone, relieved to get away before it was dark. He marvelled at the feverish excitement he had once been able to put into partygoing. It had been based on the hope, never yet fulfilled, that he would stop worrying and stop feeling pointless once the movie of his life took on the appearance of flawless glamour. For this to work, though, he would have had to allow the perspective of a stranger leafing through the filled pages of his diary to eclipse his own point of view, and he would have had to believe, which was far from being the case, that if he got enough reflected glory he could be spared the trouble of seeking out any of his own. Without this snobbish fever he was stranded under the revolving ceiling fan of his own consciousness, taking shallow breaths to get as little oxygen as possible into a brain apparently unable to manufacture anything but dread and regret.

Patrick rewound Iggy Pop's 'The Passenger' for the third time. His car shot down the hill towards the viaduct suspended between the factories and houses of High Wycombe. Released from the trance of the music, a fragment of the dream he'd forgotten that morning came back to him. He could picture an obese Alsatian flinging itself against a padlocked gate, the rattling of the gate. He'd been walking along the path next to a garden, and the dog had been barking at him through the green chicken wire that so often marks the boundary of a French suburban garden.

His car swept up the hill on the other side of the viaduct while the introductory notes of the song strummed through the speakers. Patrick contorted his face, preparing to sing along with Iggy, starting to shout out the familiar words half a beat too early. The smoke-filled car sped tunelessly on into the gathering darkness.

One of the reservations Laura had about her personality was that she sometimes got this thing about leaving her flat. She couldn't get through the door, or if she did she had to double back, she just *had* to. Lost and forgotten objects surfaced in her bag the moment she stepped back inside. It had grown worse since her cat died. Making sure the cat had water and food before she went out, and making sure it didn't follow her into the corridor, had helped a lot.

She had just sent China off to fetch the car with the excuse that the bags were too bulky to carry far, but really so that China didn't witness the propitiatory ritual that enabled Laura to get out of the flat. She had to walk out backwards – it was ridiculous, she knew it was ridiculous – and touch the top of the door frame as she went through. There was always the danger of one of her neighbours finding her reversing out of her flat on tiptoe with her arms outstretched, and so she glanced down the corridor first to check that it was clear.

'We could play a game in the car,' China had said. 'The person you'd least like to sit next to at dinner.'

'We've played that before,' Laura had complained.

'But we could play it from other people's point of view.'

'Oh, I hadn't thought of that,' Laura had said.

Anyhow, thought Laura as she locked her front door, Johnny was China's ex-boyfriend and so at least she could have some fun on the drive down, asking about his habits and about how much China missed him.

Alexander Politsky, whose extreme Englishness derived from his being Russian, was perhaps the last man in England to use the term 'old bean' sincerely. He was also widely acknowledged to have the best collection of shoes in the country. A pair of pre-First World War Lobb riding boots given to him by 'a marvellous old boulevardier and *screaming* queen who was rather a friend of my father's' were only brought out on special occasions when the subject of boots or shoes arose spontaneously in the conversation.

He was driving Ali Montague down to the Bossington-Lanes', where they were both staying. Ali, who had known Bill

Bossington-Lane for forty years, had described him and his wife as 'the sort of people one never sees in London. They just don't travel well.'

Someone once asked Bill if he still had his beautiful manor house. 'Beautiful manor house?' he said. 'We've still got the old dump, if that's what you mean.' 'By the way,' Ali continued, 'did you see that thing in Dempster about tonight? After all the usual rubbish about the best shoot in England, and ten thousand acres and Princess Margaret, there was Bridget saying, "I'm just having a few people round to celebrate my husband's birthday." She just can't get it right, can she?'

'Ugh,' groaned Alexander, 'I can't stand that woman. I mean, I almost don't mind being patronized by Princess Margaret, and no doubt will be tonight—'

'You should be so lucky,' interjected Ali. 'Do you know, I think I *prefer* parties given by people I don't like.'

'But,' Alexander continued, unperturbed, 'I won't be patronized by Bridget Gravesend, née Watson-Spot or whatever it was.'

'Watson-Spot,' laughed Ali. 'Oddly enough I knew the father *slightly* in another lifetime. He was called Roddy Watson-Scott, frightfully stupid and jolly and rather used-car salesman, but nice. As you know I'm *not* a snob, but you didn't have to be a snob to drop that man.'

'Well, there you are,' said Politsky. 'I don't want to be patronized by the daughter of a used-car salesman. After all, my family used to be able to walk from Moscow to Kiev on their own land.'

'It's no use telling me about these foreign places,' said Ali. 'I'm afraid I just don't know where Kiev is.'

'All you need to know is that it's a very long way from Moscow,' said Alexander curtly. 'Anyway, it sounds as if Bridget'll get her comeuppance with this Cindy Smith affair.'

'What I can't understand is why Cindy's gone for Sonny,' said Ali.

'He's the key to the world she wants to penetrate.'

'Or be penetrated *by*,' said Ali.

Both men smiled.

'By the way, are you wearing pumps this evening?' asked Alexander casually.

With her fist, Anne Eisen rubbed the Jaguar's back window and got nowhere; the dirty fog on the other side stood its ground.

The driver glanced in the rear-view mirror disapprovingly.

'Do you know where we are?' asked Tom.

'Sure,' said Anne. 'We're out of our minds.' She spaced the words slowly and evenly. 'That's where we are. We're on our way to see a lot of museum pieces, arrogant snobs, airheads, and feudal boondockers . . .'

'Harold tells me that Princess Margaret is coming.'

'And thick Krauts.' Anne added this last item to her list with satisfaction.

The Jaguar turned left and crept down to the end of a long drive where the lights of an Elizabethan manor glowed through the fog. They had arrived at Harold Greene's, their host for the weekend.

'Wow!' said Anne. 'Get a load of this: fifty rooms, and I'll bet all of them are haunted.'

Tom, picking up a battered leather case from the floor, was not impressed. 'It's a Harold-type house,' he said, 'I'll give you that. He had one just like it years ago in Arlington, when we were young and saving the world.'

6

BRIDGET HAD TOLD HER mother to get a taxi at the station and not to worry because she would pay, but when Virginia Watson-Scott arrived at Cheatley she was too embarrassed to ask and so she paid herself, although seventeen pounds plus a pound for the driver was no small sum.

'If orchids could write novels,' Tony Fowles was saying when Virginia was shown into Bridget's little sitting room, 'they would write novels like Isabel's.'

'Oh, hello, Mummy,' sighed Bridget, getting up from the sofa where she'd been drinking in Tony's words. The Valium had helped to muffle the impact of overhearing Sonny's telephone call, and Bridget was slightly shocked but pleased by her ability to enter into the trance of habit and to be distracted by Tony's witty conversation. Nevertheless the presence of her mother struck her as an additional and unfair burden.

'I thought I was so well organized,' she explained to her mother, 'but I've still got a million and one things to do. Do you know Tony Fowles?'

Tony got up and shook hands. 'Pleased to meet you,' he said.

'It's nice to be in proper countryside,' said Virginia, nervous of silence. 'It's become so built-up around me.'

'I know,' said Tony. 'I love seeing cows, don't you? They're so natural.'

'Oh yes,' said Virginia, 'cows are nice.'

'My trouble,' Tony confessed, 'is that I'm so aesthetic. I want to rush into the field and arrange them. Then I'd have them glued to the spot so they looked perfect from the house.'

'Poor cows,' said Virginia, 'I don't think they'd like that. Where's Belinda?' she asked Bridget.

'In the nursery, I imagine,' said Bridget. 'It's a bit early, but would you like some tea?'

'I'd rather see Belinda first,' Virginia replied, remembering that Bridget had asked her to come at teatime.

'All right, we'll go and have tea in the nursery,' said Bridget. 'I'm afraid your room is on the nursery floor anyhow – we're so crowded with Princess Margaret and everything – so I can show you your room at the same time.'

'Righty-ho,' said Virginia. It was a phrase Roddy had always used, and it drove Bridget mad.

'Oh,' she couldn't help groaning, 'please don't use that expression.'

'I must have caught it from Roddy!'

'I know,' said Bridget. She could picture her father in his blazer and his cavalry twills saying 'righty-ho' as he put on his driving gloves. He had always been kind to her, but once she had learned to be embarrassed by him she had never stopped, even after he died.

'Let's go up, then,' sighed Bridget. 'You'll come with us, won't you?' she pleaded with Tony.

'Aye-aye,' said Tony, saluting, 'or aren't I allowed to say that?'

Bridget led the way to the nursery. Nanny, who had been in the middle of scolding Belinda for being 'overexcited', set off to make tea in the nursery kitchen, muttering, 'Both parents in one day,' with a mixture of awe and resentment.

'Granny!' said Belinda, who liked her grandmother. 'I didn't know you were coming!'

'Didn't anyone tell you?' asked Virginia, too pleased with Belinda to dwell on this oversight.

Tony and Bridget moved over to the tattered old sofa at the far end of the room.

'Roses,' said Tony reproachfully, sitting down.

'Aren't they sweet together?' asked Bridget, watching Belinda on Virginia's knee, peering into her grandmother's bag to see if there were sweets in it. For a moment Bridget could remember being in the same position and feeling happy.

'Sweet,' confirmed Tony, 'or sweets anyway.'

'You old cynic,' said Bridget.

Tony put on an expression of wounded innocence. 'I'm not a cynic,' he moaned. 'Is it my fault that most people are motivated by greed and envy?'

'What motivates you?' asked Bridget.

'Style,' said Tony bashfully. 'And love for my friends,' he added, softly patting Bridget's wrist.

'Don't try to butter me up,' said Bridget.

'Who's being a cynic now?' gasped Tony.

'Look what Granny brought me,' said Belinda, holding out a bag of lemon sherbets, her favourite sweets.

'Would you like one?' she asked her mother.

'You mustn't give her sweets,' said Bridget to Virginia. 'They're frightfully bad for her teeth.'

'I only bought a quarter of a pound,' said Virginia. 'You used to like them too as a girl.'

'Nanny disapproves terribly, don't you, Nanny?' asked Bridget, taking advantage of the reappearance of Nanny with a tea tray.

'Oh yes,' said Nanny, who hadn't in fact heard what was being discussed.

'Sweets rot little girls' teeth,' said Bridget.

'Sweets!' cried Nanny, able to focus on the enemy at last. 'No sweets in the nursery except on Sundays!' she thundered.

Belinda ran through the nursery door and out into the corridor. 'I'm not in the nursery anymore,' she chanted.

Virginia put her hand over her mouth to make a show of concealing her laughter. 'I didn't want to cause any trouble,' she said.

'Oh, she's a lively one,' said Nanny cunningly, seeing that Bridget secretly admired Belinda's rebelliousness.

Virginia followed Belinda out into the corridor. Tony looked critically at the old tweed skirt she wore. Stylish it was not. He felt licensed by Bridget's attitude to despise Virginia, without forgoing the pleasure of despising Bridget for not being more loyal to her mother, or stylish enough to rise above her.

'You should take your mum shopping for a new skirt,' he suggested.

'Don't be so rude,' said Bridget.

Tony could smell the weakness in her indignation. 'That maroon check gives me a headache,' he insisted.

'It is ghastly,' admitted Bridget.

Nanny brought over two cups of tea, and a plate of Jaffa Cakes.

'Granny's going to keep the sweets for me,' said Belinda, coming back into the nursery. 'And I have to ask her if I want one.'

'It seemed to us like a good compromise,' Virginia explained.

'And she's going to read me a story before dinner,' said Belinda.

'Oh, I meant to tell you,' said Bridget absently, 'you've been asked to dinner at the Bossington-Lanes'. I couldn't refuse, they made such a fuss about needing extra women. It'll be so stuffy here with Princess Margaret, you'll be much more at home over there. They're neighbours of ours, frightfully nice.'

'Oh,' said Virginia. 'Well, if I'm needed I suppose . . .'

'You don't *mind*, do you?' asked Bridget.

'Oh no,' said Virginia.

'I mean, I thought it would be nicer for you, more relaxed.'

'Yes, I'm sure I'll be more relaxed,' said Virginia.

'I mean, if you really don't want to go I could still cancel them I suppose, although they'll be frightfully angry at this stage.'

'No, no,' said Virginia. 'I'd love to go, you mustn't cancel them now. They sound very nice. Will you excuse me a moment?' she added, getting up and opening the door that led to the other rooms on the nursery floor.

'Did I handle that all right?' Bridget asked Tony.

'You deserve an Oscar.'

'You don't think it was unkind of me? It's just that I don't think I can handle P.M. and Sonny *and* my mother all at once.'

'You did the right thing,' Tony reassured her. 'After all, you couldn't very well send either of *those* two to the Bossington-Lanes'.'

'I know, but I mean, I was thinking of her too.'

'I'm sure she'll be happier there,' said Tony. 'She seems a nice woman but she's not very . . .' he searched for the right word, '. . . social, is she?'

'No,' said Bridget. 'I know the whole P.M. thing would make her terribly tense.'

'Is Granny upset?' asked Belinda, coming to sit down next to her mother.

'What on earth makes you ask that?'

'She looked sad when she left.'

'That's just the way she looks when her face relaxes,' said Bridget inventively.

Virginia came back into the nursery, stuffing her handkerchief up the sleeve of her cardigan.

'I went into one of the rooms for a moment and saw my suitcase there,' she said cheerfully. 'Is that where I'm sleeping?'

'Hmm,' said Bridget, picking up her cup of tea and sipping it slowly. 'I'm sorry it's rather poky, but after all it's only for one night.'

'Just for one night,' echoed Virginia, who'd been hoping to stay for two or three.

'The house is incredibly full,' said Bridget. 'It's such a strain on . . . on everybody.' She tactfully swallowed the word 'servants' in Nanny's presence. 'Anyhow, I thought you'd like to be near Belinda.'

'Oh, of course,' said Virginia. 'We can have a midnight feast.'

'A midnight feast,' spluttered Nanny who could contain herself no longer. 'Not in *my* nursery!'

'I thought it was Belinda's nursery,' said Tony waspishly.

'I'm in charge,' gasped Nanny, 'and I can't have midnight feasts.'

Bridget could remember the midnight feast her mother had made to cheer her up on the night before she went to boarding school. Her mother had pretended that they had to hide from her father, but Bridget later found out that he had known all about it and had even gone to buy the cakes himself. She suppressed this sentimental memory with a sigh and got up when she heard the noise of cars at the front of the house. She craned out of one of the small windows in the corner of the nursery.

'Oh God, it's the Alantours,' she said. 'I suppose I have to go down and say hello to them. Tony, will you be an angel and help me?' she asked.

'As long as you leave me time to put on my ball gown for Princess Margaret,' said Tony.

'Can I do anything?' asked Virginia.

'No, thanks. You stay here and unpack. I'll order you a taxi to go to the Bossington-Lanes'. At about seven thirty,' said Bridget calculating that Princess Margaret would not yet have come down for a drink. 'My treat, of course,' she added.

Oh, dear, thought Virginia, more money down the drain.

7

PATRICK HAD BOOKED HIS room late and so had been put in the annexe of the Little Soddington House Hotel. With the letter confirming his reservation the management had enclosed a brochure featuring a vast room with a four-poster bed, a tall marble fireplace, and a bay window opening onto wide views of the ravishing Cotswolds. The room Patrick was shown into, with its severely pitched ceiling and view onto the kitchen yard, boasted a full complement of tea-making facilities, instant-coffee sachets, and tiny pots of longlife milk. The miniature floral pattern on its matching waste-paper basket, curtains, bedspread, cushions, and Kleenex dispenser seemed to shift and shimmer.

Patrick unpacked his dinner jacket and threw it onto the bed, throwing himself down after it. A notice under the glass of the bedside table said: 'To avoid disappointment, residents are advised to book in the restaurant in advance.' Patrick, who had been trying to avoid disappointment all his life, cursed himself for not discovering this formula earlier.

Was there no other way he could stop being disappointed? How could he find any firm ground when his identity seemed to begin with disintegration and go on to disintegrate further? But perhaps this whole model of identity was misconceived. Perhaps identity was not a building for which one had to find foundations, but rather a series of impersonations held together by a central intelligence, an intelligence that knew the history of the impersonations and eliminated the distinction between action and acting.

'Impersonation, sir,' grunted Patrick, thrusting out his stomach and waddling towards the bathroom, as if he were the Fat Man himself, 'is a habit of which I cannot approve, it was the ruination of Monsieur Escoffier . . .' He stopped.

The self-disgust that afflicted him these days had the stagnancy of a malarial swamp, and he sometimes missed the cast of jeering characters that had accompanied the more dramatic disintegrations of his early twenties. Although he could conjure up some of these characters, they seemed to have lost their energy, just as he had soon forgotten the agony of being a ventriloquist's dummy and replaced it with a sense of nostalgia for a period that had made up for some of its unpleasantness with its intensity.

'Be absolute for death', a strange phrase from *Measure for Measure*, returned to him while he bared his teeth to rip open a sachet of bath gel. Perhaps there was something in this half-shallow, half-profound idea that one had to despair of life in order to grasp its real value. Then again, perhaps there wasn't. But in any case, he pondered, squeezing the green slime from the sachet and trying to get back to his earlier line of thought, what was this central intelligence, and just how intelligent was it? What was the thread that held together the scattered beads of experience if not the pressure of interpretation? The meaning of life was whatever meaning one could thrust down its reluctant throat.

Where was Victor Eisen, the great philosopher, when he needed him most? How could he have left the doubtless splendid *Being, Knowing, and Judging* (or was it *Thinking, Knowing, and Judging*?) behind in New York when Anne Eisen had generously given him a copy during his corpse-collecting trip?

On his most recent visit to New York, he'd been back to the funeral parlour where, years before, he had seen his father's body. The building was not as he remembered it at all. Instead of the grey stone facade, he saw soft brown brick. The building was much smaller than he expected and when he was driven inside by curiosity he found that there was no chequered black-and-white marble floor, and no reception desk where he expected to see one. Perhaps it had been changed, but even so, the scale was wrong, like places remembered from childhood and dwarfed by the passage of time.

The strange thing was that Patrick refused to alter his memory of the funeral parlour. He found the picture he had evolved over the years more compelling than the facts with which he was presented on revisiting the place. This picture was more suitable to the events that had occurred within the disappointing building. What he must remain true to was the effort of interpretation, the thread on which he tried to hang the scattered beads.

Even involuntary memory was only the resurfacing of an old story, something that had definitely once been a story. Impressions that were too fleeting to be called stories yielded no meaning. On the same visit to New York he had passed a red-and-white funnel next to some roadworks, spewing steam into the cold air. It felt nostalgic and significant, but left him in a state of nebulous intensity, not knowing whether he was remembering an image from a film, a book, or his own life. On the same walk he had dropped into a sleazy hotel in which he had once lived and found that it was no longer a hotel. The thing he was remembering no longer existed but, blind to the refurbished lobby, he continued to imagine the Italian with the scimitar tie-pin accusing him of trying to install his girlfriend Natasha as a prostitute, and to imagine the frenetic wallpaper covered in scratchy red lines like the frayed blood vessels of exhausted eyes.

What could he do but accept the disturbing extent to which

memory was fictional and hope that the fiction lay at the service of a truth less richly represented by the original facts?

The house in Lacoste, where Patrick had spent most of his childhood, was now separated by only a few vines from a nasty suburb. Its old furniture had been sold and the redundant well filled in and sealed. Even the tree frogs, bright green and smooth against the smooth grey bark of the fig trees had gone, poisoned, or deprived of their breeding ground. Standing on the cracked terrace, listening to the whining of a new motorway, Patrick would try to hallucinate the faces that used to emerge from the smoky fluidity of the limestone crags, but they remained stubbornly hidden. On the other hand, geckos still flickered over the ceilings and under the eaves of the roof, and a tremor of unresolved violence always disturbed the easy atmosphere of holidays, like the churning of an engine setting the gin trembling on a distant deck. Some things never let him down.

The phone rang, and Patrick picked it up hastily, grateful for the interruption. It was Johnny saying that he'd arrived, and suggesting that they meet in the bar at eight thirty. Patrick agreed and, released from the hamster's wheel of his thoughts, got up to turn off the bathwater.

David Windfall, florid and hot from his bath, squeezed into dinner jacket trousers that seemed to strain like sausage skins from the pressure of his thighs. Beads of sweat broke out continually on his upper lip and forehead. He wiped them away, glancing at himself in the mirror; although he looked like a hippopotamus with hypertension he was well satisfied.

He was going to have dinner with Cindy Smith. She was world-famously sexy and glamorous, but David was not intimidated because he was charming and sophisticated and, well, English. The Windfalls had been making their influence felt in Cumbria for centuries before Miss Smith popped onto the scene, he reassured himself as he buttoned up the over-tight shirt on his already sweating neck. His wife was in the habit of buying him seventeen-and-a-half-inch collars in the hope that he would grow thin enough to wear them. This trick made him so indignant that he decided that she deserved to be ill and absent and, if everything went well, betrayed.

He still hadn't told Mrs Bossington-Lane that he wouldn't be going to her dinner. He decided, as he choked himself on his bow tie, that the best way to handle it was to seek her out at the party and claim that his car had broken down. He just hoped that nobody else he knew would be having dinner in the hotel. He might try to use this fear to persuade Cindy to dine in his room. His thoughts panted on optimistically.

It was Cindy Smith who occupied the magnificent bedroom advertised in the brochure of the hotel. They'd told her it was a suite, but it was just a semi-large bedroom without a separate seating area. These old English houses were so uncomfortable. She'd only seen a photograph of Cheatley from the outside, and it looked real big, but there'd better be underfloor heating and a whole lot of private bathrooms, or she couldn't even face her own plan to become the independently wealthy ex-Countess of Gravesend.

She was taking a long-term view and looking ahead two or three years. Looks didn't last forever and she wasn't ready for religion yet. Money was kind of a good compromise, staked up somewhere between cosmetics and eternity. Besides, she liked Sonny, she really did. He was cute, not to look at, God no, but aristocratic cute, old-fashioned out-of-a-movie cute.

Last year in Paris all the other models had come back to her suite in the Lotti – now there was a real suite – and each one of them, except a couple who chickened out, had done her fake orgasm, and Cindy's was voted Best Fake Orgasm. They'd pretended the champagne bottle was an Oscar and she'd made an acceptance speech thanking all the men without whom it wouldn't have been possible. Too bad she'd mentioned Sonny, seeing how she was going to marry him. Whoops!

She'd drunk a bit too much and put her father on the list also, which was probably a mistake 'cause all the other girls fell silent and things weren't so much fun after that.

Patrick arrived downstairs before Johnny, and ordered a glass of Perrier at the bar. Two middle-aged couples sat together at a nearby table. The only other person in the bar, a florid man in a dinner jacket, obviously going to Sonny's party, sat with folded arms, looking towards the door.

Patrick took his drink over to a small book-lined alcove in the corner of the room. Scanning the shelves, his eye fell on a volume called *The Journal of a Disappointed Man*, and next to it a second volume called *More Journals of a Disappointed Man*, and finally, by the same author, a third volume entitled *Enjoying Life*. How could a man who had made such a promising start to his career have ended up writing a book called *Enjoying Life*? Patrick took the offending volume from the shelf and read the first sentence that he saw: 'Verily, the flight of a gull is as magnificent as the Andes!'

'Verily,' murmured Patrick.

'Hi.'

'Hello, Johnny,' said Patrick, looking up from the page. 'I've just found a book called *Enjoying Life*.'

'Intriguing,' said Johnny, sitting down on the other side of the alcove.

'I'm going to take it to my room and read it tomorrow. It might save my life. Mind you, I don't know why people get so fixated on happiness, which always eludes them, when there are so many other invigorating experiences available, like rage, jealousy, disgust, and so forth.'

'Don't you want to be happy?' asked Johnny.

'Well, when you put it like *that*,' smiled Patrick.

'Really you're just like everyone else.'

'Don't push your luck,' Patrick warned him.

'Will you be dining with us this evening, gentlemen?' asked a waiter.

'Yes,' replied Johnny, taking a menu, and passing one on to Patrick who was too deep in the alcove for the waiter to reach.

'I thought he said, "Will you be dying with us?"' admitted Patrick, who was feeling increasingly uneasy about his decision to tell Johnny the facts he had kept secret for thirty years.

'Maybe he did,' said Johnny. 'We haven't read the menu yet.'

'I suppose "the young" will be taking drugs tonight,' sighed Patrick, scanning the menu.

'Ecstasy: the non-addictive high,' said Johnny.

'Call me old fashioned,' blustered Patrick, 'but I don't like the sound of a non-addictive drug.'

Johnny felt frustratingly engulfed in his old style of banter with Patrick. These were just the sort of 'old associations' that he was supposed to sever, but what could he do? Patrick was a great friend and he wanted him to be less miserable.

'Why do you think we're so discontented?' asked Johnny, settling for the smoked salmon.

'I don't know,' lied Patrick. 'I can't decide between the onion soup and the traditional English goat's cheese salad. An analyst once told me I was suffering from a "depression on top of a depression".'

'Well, at least you got on top of the first depression,' said Johnny, closing the menu.

'Exactly,' smiled Patrick. 'I don't think one can improve on the traitor of Strasbourg whose last request was that he give the order to the firing squad himself. Christ! Look at that girl!' he burst out in a half-mournful surge of excitement.

'It's whatshername, the model.'

'Oh, yeah. Well, at least now I can get obsessed with an unobtainable fuck,' said Patrick. 'Obsession dispels depression: the third law of psychodynamics.'

'What are the others?'

'That people loathe those they've wronged, and that they despise the victims of misfortune, and . . . I'll think of some more over dinner.'

'I don't despise the victims of misfortune,' said Johnny. 'I am worried that misfortune is contagious, but I'm not secretly convinced that it's deserved.'

'Look at her,' said Patrick, 'pacing around the cage of her Valentino dress, longing to be released into her natural habitat.'

'Calm down,' said Johnny, 'she's probably frigid.'

'Just as well if she is,' said Patrick. 'I haven't had sex for so long I can't remember what it's like, except that it takes place in that distant grey zone beneath the neck.'

'It's not grey.'

'Well, there you are, I can't even remember what it looks like, but I sometimes think it would be nice to have a relationship with my body which wasn't based on illness or addiction.'

'What about work and love?' asked Johnny.

'You know it's not fair to ask me about work,' said Patrick reproachfully, 'but my experience of love is that you get excited thinking that someone can mend your broken heart, and then you get angry when you realize that they can't. A certain economy creeps into the process and the jewelled daggers that used to pierce one's heart are replaced by ever-blunter penknives.'

'Did you expect Debbie to mend your broken heart?'

'Of course, but we were like two people taking turns with a bandage – I'm afraid to say that her turns tended to be a great deal shorter. I don't blame anyone anymore – I always mostly and rightly blamed myself . . .' Patrick stopped. 'It's just sad to spend so long getting to know someone and explaining yourself to them, and then having no use for the knowledge.'

'Do you prefer being sad to being bitter?' asked Johnny.

'Marginally,' said Patrick. 'It took me some time to get bitter. I used to think I saw things clearly when we were going out. I thought, she's a mess and I'm a mess, but at least I know what kind of mess I am.'

'Big deal,' said Johnny.

'Quite,' sighed Patrick. 'One seldom knows whether perseverance is noble or stupid until it's too late. Most people either feel regret at staying with someone for too long, or regret at losing them too easily. I manage to feel both ways at the same time about the same object.'

'Congratulations,' said Johnny.

Patrick raised his hands, as if trying to quiet the roar of applause.

'But why is your heart broken?' asked Johnny, struck by Patrick's unguarded manner.

'Some women,' said Patrick, ignoring the question, 'provide you with anaesthetic, if you're lucky, or a mirror in which you can watch yourself making clumsy incisions, but most of them spend their time tearing open old wounds.' Patrick took a gulp of Perrier. 'Listen,' he said, 'there's something I want to tell you.'

'Your table is ready, gentlemen,' a waiter announced with gusto. 'If you'd care to follow me into the dining room.'

Johnny and Patrick got up and followed him into a brown-carpeted dining room decorated with portraits of sunlit salmon and bonneted squires' wives, each table flickering with the light of a single pink candle.

Patrick loosened his bow tie and undid the top button of his shirt. How could he tell Johnny? How could he tell anyone? But if he told no one, he would stay endlessly isolated and divided against himself. He knew that under the tall grass of an apparently untamed future the steel rails of fear and habit were already laid. What he suddenly couldn't bear, with every cell in his body, was to act out the destiny prepared for him by his past, and slide obediently along those rails, contemplating bitterly all the routes he would rather have taken.

But which words could he use? All his life he'd used words to distract attention from this deep inarticulacy, this unspeakable emotion which he would now have to use words to describe. How could they avoid being noisy and tactless, like a gaggle of children laughing under the bedroom window of a dying man? And wouldn't he rather tell a woman, and be engulfed in maternal solicitude, or scorched by sexual frenzy? Yes, yes, yes. Or a psychiatrist, to whom he would be almost obliged to make such an offering, although he had resisted the temptation often enough. Or his mother, that Mrs Jellyby whose telescopic philanthropy had saved so many Ethiopian orphans while her own child fell into the fire. And yet Patrick wanted to tell an unpaid witness, without money, without sex, and without blame, just another human being. Perhaps he should tell the waiter: at least he wouldn't be seeing him again.

'There's something I have to tell you,' he repeated, after they had sat down and ordered their food. Johnny paused expectantly, putting down his glass of water from an intuition that he had better not be gulping or munching during the next few minutes.

'It's not that I'm embarrassed,' Patrick mumbled. 'It's more a question of not wanting to burden you with something you can't really be expected to do anything about.'

'Go ahead,' said Johnny.

'I know that I've told you about my parents' divorce and the drunkenness and the violence and the fecklessness . . . That's not really the point at all. What I was skirting around and not saying is that when I was five—'

'Here we are, gentlemen,' said the waiter, bringing the first courses with a flourish.

'Thank you,' said Johnny. 'Go on.'

Patrick waited for the waiter to slip away. He must try to be as simple as he could.

'When I was five, my father "abused" me, as we're invited to call it these days—' Patrick suddenly broke off in silence, unable to sustain the casualness he'd been labouring to achieve. Switchblades of memory that had flashed open all his life reappeared and silenced him.

'How do you mean "abused"?' asked Johnny uncertainly. The answer somehow became clear as he formulated the question.

'I . . .' Patrick couldn't speak. The crumpled bedspread with the blue phoenixes, the pool of cold slime at the base of his spine, scuttling off over the tiles. These were memories he was not prepared to talk about.

He picked up his fork and stuck the prongs discreetly but very hard into the underside of his wrist, trying to force himself back into the present and the conversational responsibilities he was neglecting.

'It was . . .' he sighed, concussed by memory.

After having watched Patrick drawl his way fluently through every crisis, Johnny was shocked at seeing him unable to speak, and he found his eyes glazed with a film of tears. 'I'm so sorry,' he murmured.

'Nobody should do that to anybody else,' said Patrick, almost whispering.

'Is everything to your satisfaction, gentlemen?' said the chirpy waiter.

'Look, do you think you could leave us alone for five minutes so we can have a conversation?' snapped Patrick, suddenly regaining his voice.

'I'm sorry, sir,' said the waiter archly.

'I can't stand this fucking music,' said Patrick, glancing around the dining room aggressively. Subdued Chopin teetered familiarly on the edge of hearing.

'Why don't they turn the fucking thing off, or turn it up?' he snarled. 'What do I mean by abused?' he added impatiently. 'I mean sexually abused.'

'God, I'm sorry,' said Johnny. 'I'd always wondered why you hated your father quite so much.'

'Well, now you know. The first incident masqueraded as a punishment. It had a certain Kafkaesque charm: the crime was never named and therefore took on great generality and intensity.'

'Did this go on?' asked Johnny.

'Yes, yes,' said Patrick hastily.

'What a bastard,' said Johnny.

'That's what I've been saying for years,' said Patrick. 'But now I'm exhausted by hating him. I can't go on. The hatred binds me to those events and I don't want to be a child anymore.' Patrick was back in the vein again, released from silence by the habits of analysis and speculation.

'It must have split the world in half for you,' said Johnny.

Patrick was taken aback by the precision of this comment.

'Yes. Yes, I think that's exactly what happened. How did you know?'

'It seemed pretty obvious.'

'It's strange to hear someone say that it's obvious. It always seemed to me so secret and complicated.' Patrick paused. He felt that although what he was saying mattered to him enormously, there was a core of inarticulacy that he hadn't attacked at all. His intellect could only generate more distinctions or define the distinctions better.

'I always thought the truth would set me free,' he said, 'but the truth just drives you mad.'

'Telling the truth might set you free.'

'Maybe. But self-knowledge on its own is useless.'

'Well, it enables you to suffer more lucidly,' argued Johnny.

'Oh, ya, I wouldn't miss that for the world.'

'In the end perhaps the only way to alleviate misery is to become more detached about yourself and more attached to something else,' said Johnny.

'Are you suggesting I take up a hobby?' laughed Patrick. 'Weaving baskets or sewing mailbags?'

'Well, actually, I was trying to think of a way to avoid those two particular occupations,' said Johnny.

'But if I were released from my bitter and unpleasant state of mind,' protested Patrick, 'what would be left?'

'Nothing much,' admitted Johnny, 'but think what you could put there instead.'

'You're making me dizzy . . . Oddly enough there was something about hearing the word mercy in *Measure for Measure* last night that made me imagine there might be a course that is neither bitter nor false, something that lies beyond argument. But if there is I can't grasp it; all I know is that I'm tired of having these steel brushes whirring around the inside of my skull.'

Both men paused while the waiter silently cleared away their plates. Patrick was puzzled by how easy it had been to tell another person the most shameful and secret truth about his life. And yet he felt dissatisfied; the catharsis of confession eluded him. Perhaps he had been too abstract. His 'father' had become the codename for a set of his own psychological difficulties and he had forgotten the real man, with his grey curls and his wheezing chest and his proud face, who had made such clumsy efforts in his closing years to endear himself to those he had betrayed.

When Eleanor had finally gathered the courage to divorce David, he had gone into a decline. Like a disgraced torturer whose victim has died, he cursed himself for not pacing his cruelty better, guilt and self-pity competing for mastery of his mood. David had the further frustration of being defied by Patrick who, at the age of eight, inspired by his parents' separation, refused one day to give in to his father's sexual assaults. Patrick's transformation of himself from a toy into a person shattered his father, who realized that Patrick must have known what was being done to him.

During this difficult time, David went to visit Nicholas Pratt in Sister Agnes, where he was recovering from a painful operation on his intestine following the failure of his fourth marriage. David, reeling from the prospect of his own divorce, found Nicholas lying in bed drinking champagne smuggled in by loyal friends, and only too ready to discuss how one should never trust a bloody woman.

'I want someone to design me a fortress,' said David, for whom Eleanor was proposing to build a small house surprisingly close to her own house in Lacoste. 'I don't want to look out on the fucking world again.'

'Completely understand,' slurred Nicholas, whose speech had become at once thicker and more staccato in his postoperative haze. 'Only trouble with the bloody world is the bloody people in it,' he said. 'Give me that writing paper, would you?'

While David paced up and down the room, flouting the hospital rules by smoking a cigar, Nicholas, who liked to surprise his friends with his amateur draughtsmanship, made a sketch worthy of David's misanthropic ecstasy.

'Keep the buggers out,' he said when he had finished, tossing the page across the bedclothes.

David picked it up and saw a pentagonal house with no windows on the outside and a central courtyard in which Nicholas had poetically planted a cypress tree, flaring above the low roof like a black flame.

The architect who was given this sketch took pity on David and introduced a single window into the exterior wall of the drawing room. David locked the shutters and stuffed crunched-up copies of *The Times* into the aperture, cursing himself for not sacking the architect when he first visited him in his disastrously converted farmhouse near Aix, with its algae-choked swimming pool. He pressed the window closed on the newspaper and then sealed it with the thick black tape favoured by those who wish to gas themselves efficiently. Finally a curtain was drawn across the window and only reopened by rare visitors who were soon made aware of their error by David's rage.

The cypress tree never flourished and its twisted trunk and grey peeling bark writhed in a dismal parody of Nicholas's noble vision. Nicholas himself, after designing the house, was too busy ever to accept an invitation. 'One doesn't have fun with David Melrose these days,' he would tell people in London. This was a polite way to describe the state of mental illness into which David had degenerated. Woken every night by his own screaming nightmares, he lay in bed almost continuously for seven years, wearing those yellow-and-white flannel pyjamas, now worn through at the elbows, which were the only things he had inherited from his father, thanks to the generous intervention of his mother who had refused to see him leave the funeral empty-handed. The most enthusiastic thing he could do was to smoke a cigar, a habit his father had first encouraged in him, and one he had passed on to Patrick, among so many other disadvantages, like a baton thrust from one wheezing generation to the next. If David left his house he was dressed like a tramp, muttering to himself in giant supermarkets on the outskirts of Marseilles. Sometimes in winter he wandered about the house in dark glasses, trailing a Japanese dressing gown, and clutching a glass of pastis, checking again and again that the heating was off so that he didn't waste any money. The contempt that saved him from complete madness drove him almost completely mad. When he emerged from his depression he was a ghost, not improved but diminished, trying to tempt people to stay in the house that had been designed to repel their unlikely invasion.

Patrick stayed in this house during his adolescence, sitting in the courtyard, shooting olive stones over the roof so that they at least could be free. His arguments with his father, or rather his one interminable argument, reached a crucial point when Patrick said something more fundamentally insulting to David than David had just said to him, and David, conscious that he was growing slower and weaker while his son grew faster and nastier, reached into his pocket for his heart pills and, shaking them into his tortured rheumatic hands, said with a melancholy whisper, 'You mustn't say those things to your old Dad.'

Patrick's triumph was tainted by the guilty conviction that his father was about to die of a heart attack. Still, things were not the same after that, especially when Patrick was able to patronize his disinherited father with a small income, and cheapen him with his money as Eleanor had once cheapened him with hers. During those closing years Patrick's terror had largely been eclipsed by pity, and also by boredom in the company of his 'poor old Dad'. He had sometimes dreamed that they might have an honest conversation, but a moment in his father's company made it clear that this would never happen. And yet Patrick felt there was something missing, something he wasn't admitting to himself, let alone telling Johnny.

Respecting Patrick's silence, Johnny had eaten his way through most of his corn-fed chicken by the time Patrick spoke again.

'So, what can one say about a man who rapes his own child?'

'I suppose it might help if you could see him as sick rather than evil,' Johnny suggested limply. 'I can't get over this,' he added, 'it's really awful.'

'I've tried what you suggest,' said Patrick, 'but then, what is evil if not sickness celebrating itself? While my father had any power he showed no remorse or restraint, and when he was poor and abandoned he only showed contempt and morbidity.'

'Maybe you can see his actions as evil, but see *him* as sick. Maybe one can't condemn another person, only their actions . . .' Johnny hesitated, reluctant to take on the role of the defence. 'Maybe he couldn't stop himself anymore than you could stop yourself taking drugs.'

'Maybe, maybe, maybe,' said Patrick, 'but I didn't harm anyone else by taking drugs.'

'Really? What about Debbie?'

'She was a grown-up, she could choose. I certainly gave her a hard time,' Patrick admitted. 'I don't know, I try to negotiate truces of one sort or another, but then I run up against this unnegotiable rage.' Patrick pushed his plate back and lit a cigarette. 'I don't want any pudding, do you?'

'No, just coffee.'

'Two coffees, please,' said Patrick to the waiter who was now theatrically tight-lipped. 'I'm sorry I snapped at you earlier, I was in the middle of trying to say something rather tricky.'

'I was only trying to do my job,' said the waiter.

'Of course,' said Patrick.

'Do you think there's any way you can forgive him?' asked Johnny.

'Oh, yes,' said the waiter, 'it wasn't that bad.'

'No, not you,' laughed Johnny.

'Sorry I spoke,' said the waiter, going off to fetch the coffee. 'Your father, I mean.'

'Well, if that absurd waiter can forgive me, who knows what chain reaction of absolution might not be set in motion?' said Patrick. 'But then neither revenge nor forgiveness change what happened. They're sideshows, of which forgiveness is the less attractive because it represents a collaboration with one's persecutors. I don't suppose that forgiveness was uppermost in the minds of people who were being nailed to a cross until Jesus, if not the first man with a Christ complex still the most successful, wafted onto the scene. Presumably those who enjoyed inflicting cruelty could hardly believe their luck and set about popularizing the superstition that their victims could only achieve peace of mind by forgiving them.'

'You don't think it might be a profound spiritual truth?' asked Johnny.

Patrick puffed out his cheeks. 'I suppose it might be, but as far as I'm concerned, what is meant to show the spiritual advantages of forgiveness in fact shows the psychological advantages of thinking you're the son of God.'

'So how do you get free?' asked Johnny.

'Search me,' said Patrick. 'Obviously, or I wouldn't have told you, I think it has something to do with telling the truth. I'm only at the beginning, but presumably there comes a point when you grow bored of telling it, and that point coincides with your "freedom".'

'So rather than forgive you're going to try and talk it out.'

'Yes, narrative fatigue is what I'm going for. If the talk cure is our modern religion then narrative fatigue must be its apotheosis,' said Patrick suavely.

'But the truth includes an understanding of your father.'

'I couldn't understand my father better and I still don't like what he did.'

'Of course you don't. Perhaps there is nothing to say except, "What a bastard." I was only groping for an alternative because you said you were exhausted by hatred.'

'I am, but at the moment I can't imagine any kind of liberation except eventual indifference.'

'Or detachment,' said Johnny. 'I don't suppose you'll ever be indifferent.'

'Yes, detachment,' said Patrick, who didn't mind having his vocabulary corrected on this occasion. 'Indifference just sounded cooler.'

The two men drank their coffee, Johnny feeling that he had been drawn too far away from Patrick's original revelation to ask, 'What actually happened?'

Patrick, for his part, suspected that he had left the soil of his own experience, where wasps still gnawed at the gaping figs and he stared down madly onto his own five-year-old head, in order to avoid an uneasiness that lay even deeper than the uneasiness of his confession. The roots of his imagination were in the Pagan South and the unseemly liberation it had engendered in his father, but the discussion had somehow remained in the Cotswolds being dripped on by the ghosts of England's rude elms. The opportunity to make a grand gesture and say, 'This thing of darkness I acknowledge mine,' had somehow petered out into ethical debate.

'Thanks for telling me what you've told me,' said Johnny.

'No need to get Californian about it, I'm sure it's nothing but a burden.'

'No need to be so English,' said Johnny. 'I *am* honoured. Any time you want to talk about it I'm available.'

Patrick felt disarmed and infinitely sad for a moment. 'Shall we head off to this wretched party?' he said.

They walked out of the dining room together, passing David Windfall and Cindy Smith.

'There was an unexpected fluctuation in the exchange rate,' David was explaining. 'Everyone panicked like mad, except for me, the reason being that I was having a tremendously boozy lunch with Sonny in his club. At the end of the day I'd made a huge amount of money from doing absolutely nothing while everybody else had been very badly stung. My boss was absolutely livid.'

'Do you get on well with your boss?' asked Cindy who really couldn't have cared less.

'Of course I do,' said David. 'You Americans call it "internal networking", we just call it good manners.'

'Gee,' said Cindy.

'We'd better go in separate cars,' said Patrick, as he walked through the bar with Johnny, 'I might want to leave early.'

'Right,' said Johnny, 'see you there.'

8

SONNY'S INNER CIRCLE, THE forty guests who were dining at Cheatley before the party, hung about in the Yellow Room, unable to sit down before Princess Margaret chose to.

'Do you believe in God, Nicholas?' asked Bridget, introducing Nicholas Pratt into the conversation she was having with Princess Margaret.

Nicholas rolled his eyeballs wearily, as if someone had tried to revive a tired old piece of scandal.

'What intrigues me, my dear, is whether he still believes in *us*. Or have we given the supreme schoolmaster a nervous breakdown? In any case, I think it was one of the Bibescos who said, "To a man of the world, the universe is a suburb."'

'I don't like the sound of your friend Bibesco,' said Princess Margaret, wrinkling her nose. 'How can the universe be a suburb? It's too silly.'

'What I think he meant, ma'am,' replied Nicholas, 'is that sometimes the largest questions are the most trivial, because they cannot be answered, while the seemingly trivial ones, like where one sits at dinner,' he gave this example while raising his eyebrows at Bridget, 'are the most fascinating.'

'Aren't people funny? I don't find where one sits at dinner

fascinating at all,' lied the Princess. 'Besides, as you know,' she went on, 'my sister is the head of the Church of England, and I don't like listening to atheistic views. People think they're being so clever, but it just shows a lack of humility.' Silencing Nicholas and Bridget with her disapproval, the Princess took a gulp from her glass of whisky. 'Apparently it's on the increase,' she said enigmatically.

'What is, ma'am?' asked Nicholas.

'Child abuse,' said the Princess. 'I was at a concert for the NSPCC last weekend, and they told me it's on the increase.'

'Perhaps it's just that people are more inclined to wash their dirty linen in public nowadays,' said Nicholas. 'Frankly I find *that* tendency much more worrying than all this fuss about child abuse. Children probably didn't realize they were being abused until they had to watch it on television every night. I believe in America they've started suing their parents for bringing them up badly.'

'Really?' giggled the Princess. 'I must tell Mummy, she'll be fascinated.'

Nicholas burst out laughing. 'But seriously, ma'am, the thing that worries me isn't all this child abuse, but the appalling way that people spoil their children these days.'

'Isn't it dreadful?' gasped the Princess. 'I see more and more children with absolutely no discipline at all. It's frightening.'

'Terrifying,' Nicholas confirmed.

'But I don't think that the NSPCC were talking about *our* world,' said the Princess, generously extending to Nicholas the circle of light that radiated from her presence. 'What it really shows is the emptiness of the socialist dream. They thought that every problem could be solved by throwing money at it, but it simply isn't true. People may have been poor, but they were happy because they lived in real communities. My mother says that when she visited the East End during the Blitz she met more people there with real dignity than you could hope to find in the entire corps diplomatique.'

'What I find with beautiful women,' said Peter Porlock to Robin Parker as they drifted towards the dining room, 'is that, after one's waited around for ages, they all arrive at once, as buses are supposed to do. Not that I've ever waited around for a bus, except at that British Heritage thing in Washington. Do you remember?'

'Yes, of course,' said Robin Parker, his eyes swimming in and out of focus, like pale blue goldfish, behind the thick lenses of his glasses. 'They hired a double-decker London bus for us.'

'Some people said "coals to Newcastle",' said Peter, 'but I was jolly pleased to see what I'd been missing all these years.'

Tony Fowles was full of amusing and frivolous ideas. Just as there were boxes at the opera where you could hear the music but not see the action, he said that there should be soundproof boxes where you could neither hear the music nor see the action, but just look at the other people with very powerful binoculars.

The Princess laughed merrily. Something about Tony's effete silliness made her feel relaxed, but all too soon she was separated from him and placed next to Sonny at the far end of the table.

'Ideally, the number of guests at a private dinner party,' said Jacques d'Alantour, raising a judicious index finger, 'should be more than the graces and less than the muses! But this,' he said, spreading his hands out and closing his eyes as if words were about to fail him, 'this is something absolutely extraordinary.'

Few people were more used than the ambassador to looking at a dinner table set for forty, but Bridget smiled radiantly at him, while trying to remember how many muses there were supposed to be.

'Do you have any politics?' Princess Margaret asked Sonny.

'Conservative, ma'am,' said Sonny proudly.

'So I assumed. But are you *involved* in politics? For myself I don't mind who's in government so long as they're good at governing. What we must avoid at all costs is these windscreen wipers: left, right, left, right.'

Sonny laughed immoderately at the thought of political windscreen wipers.

'I'm afraid I'm only involved at a very local level, ma'am,' he replied. 'The Little Soddington bypass, that sort of thing. Trying to make sure that footpaths don't spring up all over the place. People seem to think that the countryside is just an enormous park for factory workers to drop their sweet papers in. Well, those of us who live here feel rather differently about it.'

'One needs someone responsible keeping an eye on things at a local level,' said Princess Margaret reassuringly. 'So many of the things that get ruined are little out-of-the-way places that one only notices once they've already been ruined. One drives past thinking how nice they must have once been.'

'You're absolutely right, ma'am,' agreed Sonny.

'Is it venison?' asked the Princess. 'It's hard to tell under this murky sauce.'

'Yes, it is venison,' said Sonny nervously. 'I'm awfully sorry about the sauce. As you say, it's perfectly disgusting.' He could remember checking with her private secretary that the Princess liked venison.

She pushed her plate away and picked up her cigarette lighter. 'I get sent fallow deer from Richmond Park,' she said smugly. 'You have to be on the list. The Queen said to me, "Put yourself on the list," so I did.'

'How very sensible, ma'am,' simpered Sonny.

'Venison is the one meat I rr-eally don't like,' Jacques d'Alantour admitted to Caroline Porlock, 'but I don't want to create a diplomatic incident, and so . . .' He popped a piece of meat into his mouth, wearing a theatrically martyred expression which Caroline later described as being 'a bit much'.

'Do you like it? It's venison,' said Princess Margaret leaning over slightly towards Monsieur d'Alantour, who was sitting on her right.

'Really, it is something absolutely mar-vellous, ma'am,' said the ambassador. 'I did not know one could find such cooking in your country. The sauce is extremely subtle.' He narrowed his eyes to give an impression of subtlety.

The Princess allowed her views about the sauce to be eclipsed by the gratification of hearing England described as 'your country', which she took to be an acknowledgement of her own feeling that it belonged, if not legally, then in some much more profound sense, to her own family.

In his anxiety to show his love for the venison of merry old England, the ambassador raised his fork with such an extravagant gesture of appreciation that he flicked glistening brown globules over the front of the Princess's blue tulle dress.

'I am prostrated with horr-rror!' he exclaimed, feeling that he was on the verge of a diplomatic incident.

The Princess compressed her lips and turned down the corners of her mouth, but said nothing. Putting down the cigarette holder into which she had been screwing a cigarette, she pinched her napkin between her fingers and handed it over to Monsieur d'Alantour.

'Wipe!' she said with terrifying simplicity.

The ambassador pushed back his chair and sank to his knees obediently, first dipping the corner of the napkin in a glass of water. While he rubbed at the spots of sauce on her dress, the Princess lit her cigarette and turned to Sonny.

'I thought I couldn't dislike the sauce more when it was on my plate,' she said archly.

'The sauce has been a disaster,' said Sonny, whose face was now maroon with extra blood. 'I can't apologize enough, ma'am.'

'There's no need for *you* to apologize,' she said.

Jacqueline d'Alantour, fearing that her husband might be performing an act inconsistent with the dignity of France, had risen and walked around the table. Half the guests were pretending not to have noticed what was going on and the other half were not bothering to pretend.

'What I admire about P.M.,' said Nicholas Pratt, who sat on Bridget's left at the other end of the table, 'is the way she puts everyone at their ease.'

George Watford, who sat on Bridget's other side, decided to ignore Pratt's interruption and to carry on trying to explain to his hostess the purpose of the Commonwealth.

'I'm afraid the Commonwealth is completely ineffectual,' he said sadly. 'We have nothing in common, except our poverty. Still, it gives the Queen some pleasure,' he added, glancing down the table at Princess Margaret, 'and that is reason enough to keep it.'

Jacqueline, still unclear about what had happened, was amazed to find that her husband had sunk even deeper under the table and was rubbing furiously at the Princess's dress.

'*Mais tu es complètement cinglé*,' hissed Jacqueline. The sweating ambassador, like a groom in the Augean stables, had no time to look up.

'I have done something unpardonable!' he declared. 'I have splashed this wonder-fool sauce on Her Royal Highness's dress.'

'Ah, ma'am,' said Jacqueline to the Princess, girl to girl, 'he's so clumsy! Let me help you.'

'I'm quite happy to have your husband do it,' said the Princess. 'He spilled it, he should wipe it up! In fact, one feels he might have had a great career in dry cleaning if he hadn't been blown off course,' she said nastily.

'You must allow us to give you a new dress, ma'am,' purred Jacqueline, who could feel claws sprouting from her fingertips. '*Allez*, Jacques, it's enough!' She laughed.

'There's still a spot here,' said Princess Margaret bossily, pointing to a small stain on the upper edge of her lap.

The ambassador hesitated.

'Go on, wipe it up!'

Jacques dipped the corner of the napkin back into his glass of water, and attacked the spot with rapid little strokes.

'*Ah, non, mais c'est vraiment insupportable*,' snapped Jacqueline.

'What is "*insupportable*",' said the Princess in a nasal French accent, 'is to be showered in this revolting sauce. I needn't remind you that your husband is Ambassador to the Court of St James's,' she said as if this were somehow equivalent to being her personal maid.

Jacqueline bobbed briefly and walked back to her place, but only to grab her bag and stride out of the room.

By this time the table had fallen silent.

'Oh, a silence,' declared Princess Margaret. 'I don't approve of silences. If Noël were here,' she said, turning to Sonny, 'he'd have us all in stitches.'

'Nole, ma'am?' asked Sonny, too paralysed with terror to think clearly.

'Coward, you silly,' replied the Princess. 'He could make one laugh for hours on end. It's the people who could make one laugh,' she said, puffing sensitively on her cigarette, 'whom one really misses.'

Sonny, already mortified by the presence of venison at his table, was now exasperated by the absence of Noël. The fact that Noël was long dead did nothing to mitigate Sonny's sense of failure, and he would have sunk into speechless gloom had he not been saved by the Princess, who found herself in a thoroughly good mood after asserting her dignity and establishing in such a spectacular fashion that she was the most important person in the room.

'Remind me, Sonny,' she said chattily, 'do you have any children?'

'Yes, indeed, ma'am, I have a daughter.'

'How old is she?' asked the Princess brightly.

'It's hard to believe,' said Sonny, 'but she must be seven by now. It won't be long before she's at the blue-jean stage,' he added ominously.

'Oh,' groaned the Princess, making a disagreeable face, a muscular contraction that cost her little effort, 'aren't they dreadful? They're a sort of uniform. And so scratchy. I can't imagine why one would want to look like everyone else. I know I don't.'

'Absolutely, ma'am,' said Sonny.

'When my children got to that stage,' confided the Princess, 'I said, "For goodness' sake, don't get those dreadful blue jeans," and they very sensibly went out and bought themselves some green trousers.'

'Very sensible,' echoed Sonny, who was hysterically grateful that the Princess had decided to be so friendly.

Jacqueline returned after five minutes, hoping to give the

impression that she had only absented herself because, as one mistress of modern manners has put it, 'certain bodily functions are best performed in private'. In fact she had paced about her bedroom furiously until she came to the reluctant conclusion that a show of levity would in the end be less humiliating than a show of indignation. Knowing also that what her husband feared most, and had spent his career nimbly avoiding, was a diplomatic incident, she hastily applied some fresh lipstick and breezed back into the dining room.

Seeing Jacqueline return, Sonny experienced a fresh wave of anxiety, but the Princess ignored her completely and started telling him one of her stories about 'the ordinary people of this country' in whom she had 'enormous faith' based on a combination of complete ignorance about their lives and complete confidence in their royalist sympathies.

'I was in a taxi once,' she began in a tone that invited Sonny to marvel at her audacity. He duly raised his eyebrows with what he hoped was a tactful combination of surprise and admiration. 'And Tony said to the driver, "Take us to the Royal Garden Hotel," which, as you know, is at the bottom of our drive. And the driver said – ' the Princess leaned forward to deliver the punch line with a rough little jerk of her head, in what might have been mistaken by a Chinaman for a Cockney accent – '"I know where *she* lives."' She grinned at Sonny. 'Aren't they wonderful people?' she squawked. 'Aren't they marvellous people?'

Sonny threw back his head and roared with laughter. 'What a splendid story, ma'am,' he gasped. 'What wonderful people.'

The Princess sat back in her chair well satisfied; she had charmed her host and lent a golden touch to the evening. As to the clumsy Frenchman on her other side, she wasn't going to let him off the hook so easily. After all, it was no small matter to make a mistake in the presence of the Queen's sister. The constitution itself rested on respect for the Crown, and it was her duty (oh, how she sometimes wished she could lay it all aside! How, in fact, she sometimes did, only to scold more severely those who thought she was serious), yes, it was her *duty* to maintain that respect. It was the price she had to pay for what other people foolishly regarded as her great privileges.

Next to her the ambassador appeared to be in a kind of trance, but under his dumb surface he was composing, with the fluency of an habitual dispatch writer, his report for the Quai d'Orsay. The glory of France had not been diminished by his little gaffe. Indeed, he had turned what might have been an awkward incident into a triumphant display of gallantry and wit. It was here that the ambassador paused for a while to think of something clever he might have said at the time.

While Alantour pondered, the door of the dining room opened slowly, and Belinda, barefooted, in a white nightdress, peered around the edge of the door.

'Oh, look, it's a little person who can't sleep,' boomed Nicholas.

Bridget swivelled around and saw her daughter looking pleadingly into the room.

'Who is it?' the Princess asked Sonny.

'I'm afraid it's my daughter, ma'am,' replied Sonny, glaring at Bridget.

'Still up? She should be in bed. Go on, tuck her up immediately!' she snapped.

Something about the way she had said 'tuck her up' made Sonny momentarily forget his courtly graces and feel protective towards his daughter. He tried again to catch Bridget's eye, but Belinda had already come into the room and approached her mother.

'Why are you still up, darling?' asked Bridget.

'I couldn't sleep,' said Belinda. 'I was lonely because everyone else is down here.'

'But this is a dinner for grown-ups.'

'Which one's Princess Margaret?' asked Belinda, ignoring her mother's explanation.

'Why don't you get your mother to present you to her?' suggested Nicholas suavely. 'And then you can go to bed like a good little girl.'

'OK,' said Belinda. 'Can someone read me a story?'

'Not tonight, darling,' said her mother. 'But I'll introduce you to Princess Margaret.' She got up and walked the length of the table to Princess Margaret's side. Leaning over a little, she asked if she could present her daughter.

'No, not now, I don't think it's right,' said the Princess. 'She ought to be in bed, and she'll just get overexcited.'

'You're quite right, of course,' said Sonny. 'Honestly, darling, you must scold Nanny for letting her escape.'

'I'll take her upstairs myself,' said Bridget coldly.

'Good girl,' said Sonny, extremely angry that Nanny, who after all cost one an absolute bomb, should have shown him up in front of the Princess.

'I'm very pleased to hear that you've got the Bishop of Cheltenham for us tomorrow,' said the Princess, grinning at her host, once the door was firmly closed on his wife and daughter.

'Yes,' said Sonny. 'He seemed very nice on the phone.'

'Do you mean you don't know him?' asked the Princess.

'Not as well as I'd like to,' said Sonny, reeling from the prospect of more royal disapproval.

'He's a saint,' said the Princess warmly. 'I really think he's a saint. And a wonderful scholar: I'm told he's happier speaking in Greek than in English. Isn't it marvellous?'

'I'm afraid my Greek's a bit rusty for that sort of thing,' said Sonny.

'Don't worry,' said the Princess, 'he's the most modest man in the world, he wouldn't dream of showing you up; he just gets into these Greek trances. In his mind, you see, he's still chatting away to the apostles, and it takes him a while to notice his surroundings. Isn't it fascinating?'

'Extraordinary,' murmured Sonny.

'There won't be any hymns, of course,' said the Princess.

'But we can have some if you like,' protested Sonny.

'It's Holy Communion, silly. Otherwise I'd have you all singing hymns to see which ones I liked best. People always seem to enjoy it, it gives one something to do after dinner on Saturday.'

'We couldn't have managed that tonight in any case,' said Sonny.

'Oh, I don't know,' said the Princess, 'we might have gone off to the library in a small group.' She beamed at Sonny, conscious of the honour she was bestowing on him by this suggestion of deeper intimacy. There was no doubt about it: when she put her mind to it she could be the most charming woman in the world.

'One had such fun practising hymns with Noël,' she went on. 'He would make up new words and one would die laughing. Yes, it might have been rather cosy in the library. I do so *hate* big parties.'

9

PATRICK SLAMMED THE CAR door and glanced up at the stars, gleaming through a break in the clouds like fresh track marks in the dark blue limbs of the night. It was a humbling experience, he thought, making one's own medical problems seem so insignificant.

An avenue of candles, planted on either side of the drive, marked the way from the car park to the wide circle of gravel in front of the house. Its grey porticoed facade was theatrically flattened by floodlights, and looked like wet cardboard, stained by the sleet that had fallen earlier in the afternoon.

In the denuded drawing room, the fireplace was loaded with crackling wood. The champagne being poured by a flushed barman surged over the sides of glasses and subsided again to a drop. As Patrick headed down the hooped canvas tunnel that led to the tent, he heard the swell of voices rising, and sometimes laughter, like the top of a wave caught by the wind, splashing over the whole room. A room, he decided, full of uncertain fools, waiting for an amorous complication or a practical joke to release them from their awkward wanderings. Walking into the tent, he saw George Watford sitting on a chair immediately to the right of the entrance.

'George!'

'My dear, what a nice surprise,' said George, wincing as he clambered to his feet. 'I'm sitting here because I can't hear anything these days when there's a lot of noise about.'

'I thought people were supposed to lead lives of *quiet* desperation,' Patrick shouted.

'Not quiet enough,' George shouted back with a wan smile.

'Oh, look there's Nicholas Pratt,' said Patrick, sitting down next to George.

'So it is,' said George. 'With him one has to take the smooth with the smooth. I must say I never really shared your father's enthusiasm for him. I miss your father, you know, Patrick. He was a very brilliant man, but never happy, I think.'

'I hardly ever think of him these days,' said Patrick.

'Have you found something you enjoy doing?' asked George.

'Yes, but nothing one could make a career out of,' said Patrick.

'One really has to try to make a contribution,' said George. 'I can look back with reasonable satisfaction on one or two pieces of legislation that I helped steer through the House of Lords. I've also helped to keep Richfield going for the next generation. Those are the sorts of things one is left hanging on to when all the fun and games have slipped away. No man is an island – although one's known a surprising number who own one. Really a surprising number, and not just in Scotland. But one really must try to make a contribution.'

'Of course you're right,' sighed Patrick. He was rather intimidated by George's sincerity. It reminded him of the disconcerting occasion when his father had clasped his arm, and said to him, apparently without any hostile intention, 'If you have a talent, use it. Or you'll be miserable all your life.'

'Oh, look, it's Tom Charles, over there taking a drink from the waiter. He has a jolly nice island in Maine. Tom!' George called out. 'I wonder if he's spotted us. He was head of the IMF at one time, made the best of a frightfully hard job.'

'I met him in New York,' said Patrick. 'You introduced us at that club we went to after my father died.'

'Oh, yes. We all rather wondered what had happened to you,' said George. 'You left us in the lurch with that frightful bore Ballantine Morgan.'

'I was overwhelmed with emotion,' said Patrick.

'I should think it was dread at having to listen to another of Ballantine's stories. His son is here tonight. I'm afraid he's a chip off the old block, as they say. Tom!' George called out again.

Tom Charles looked around, uncertain whether he'd heard his name being called. George waved at him again. Tom spotted them, and the three men greeted each other. Patrick recognized Tom's bloodhound features. He had one of those faces that ages prematurely but then goes on looking the same forever. He might even look young in another twenty years.

'I heard about your dinner,' said Tom. 'It sounds like quite something.'

'Yes,' said George. 'I think it demonstrates again that the junior members of the royal family should pull their socks up and we should all be praying for the Queen during these difficult times.'

Patrick realized he was not joking.

'How was your dinner at Harold's?' asked George. 'Harold Greene was born in Germany,' he went on to explain to Patrick. 'As a boy he wanted to join the Hitler Youth – smashing windows and wearing all those thrilling uniforms: it's any boy's dream – but his father told him he couldn't because he was Jewish. Harold never got over the disappointment, and he's really an anti-Semite with a veneer of Zionism.'

'Oh, I don't think that's fair,' said Tom.

'Well, I don't suppose it is,' said George, 'but what is the point of reaching this idiotically advanced age if one can't be unfair?'

'There was a lot of talk at dinner about Chancellor Kohl's claim that he was "very shocked" when war broke out in the Gulf.'

'I suppose it was shocking for the poor Germans not to have started the war themselves,' George interjected.

'Harold was saying over dinner,' continued Tom, 'that he's surprised there isn't a United Nations Organisation called UNUC because "when it comes down to it they're no bloody use at all".'

'What I want to know,' said George, thrusting out his chin, 'is what chance we have against the Japanese when we live in a country where "industrial action" means going on strike. I'm afraid I've lived for too long. I can still remember when this country counted for something. I was just saying to Patrick,' he added, politely drawing him back into the conversation, 'that one has to make a contribution in life. There are too many people in this room who are just hanging around waiting for their relations to die so that they can go on more expensive holidays. Sadly, I count my daughter-in-law among them.'

'Bunch of vultures,' growled Tom. 'They'd better take those holidays soon. I don't see the banking system holding up, except on some kind of religious basis.'

'Currency always rested on blind faith,' said George.

'But it's never been like this before,' said Tom. 'Never has so much been owed by so many to so few.'

'I'm too old to care anymore,' said George. 'Do you know, I was thinking that if I go to heaven, and I don't see why I shouldn't, I hope that King, my old butler, will be there.'

'To do your unpacking?' suggested Patrick.

'Oh, no,' said George. 'I think he's done quite enough of that sort of thing down here. In any case, I don't think one takes any luggage to heaven, do you? It must be like a perfect weekend, with no luggage.'

Like a rock in the middle of a harbour, Sonny stood stoutly near the entrance of the tent putting his guests under an obligation to greet him as they came in.

'But this is something absolutely marvellous,' said Jacques d'Alantour in a confidential tone, spreading his hands to encompass the whole tent. As if responding to this gesture the big jazz band at the far end of the room struck up simultaneously.

'Well, we try our best,' said Sonny smugly.

'I think it was Henry James,' said the ambassador, who knew perfectly well that it was and had rehearsed the quotation, unearthed for him by his secretary, many times before leaving Paris, 'who said: "this richly complex English world, where the present is always seen, as it were in profile, and the past presents a full face."'

'It's no use quoting these French authors to me,' said Sonny. 'All goes over my head. But, yes, English life is rich and complex – although not as rich as it used to be with all these taxes gnawing away at the very fabric of one's house.'

'Ah,' sighed Monsieur d'Alantour sympathetically. 'But you are putting on a "brave face" tonight.'

'We've had our tricky moments,' Sonny confessed. 'Bridget went through a mad phase of thinking we knew nobody, and invited all sorts of odds and sods. Take that little Indian chap over there, for instance. He's writing a biography of Jonathan Croyden. I'd never set eyes on him before he came down to look at some letters Croyden wrote to my father, and blow me down, Bridget asked him to the party over lunch. I'm afraid I lost my temper with her afterwards, but it really was a bit much.'

'Hello, my dear,' said Nicholas to Ali Montague. 'How was your dinner?'

'Very *county*,' said Ali.

'Oh, dear. Well, ours was really *tous ce qu'il y a de plus chic*, except that Princess Margaret rapped me over the knuckles for expressing "atheistic views".'

'Even I might have a religious conversion under those circumstances,' said Ali, 'but it would be so hypocritical I'd be sent straight to hell.'

'One thing I am sure of is that if God didn't exist, nobody would notice the difference,' said Nicholas suavely.

'Oh, I thought of you a moment ago,' said Ali. 'I overheard a couple of old men who both looked as if they'd had several riding accidents. One of them said, "I'm thinking of writing a book," and the other one replied, "Jolly good idea." "They say everyone has a book in them," said the would-be author. "Hmm, perhaps I'll write one as well," his friend replied. "Now you're stealing my idea," said the first one, really quite angrily. So naturally I wondered how your book was getting along. I suppose it must be almost finished by now.'

'It's very difficult to finish an autobiography when you're leading as thrilling a life as I am,' said Nicholas sarcastically. 'One constantly finds some new nugget that has to be put in, like a sample of your conversation, my dear.'

'There's always an element of cooperation in incest,' said Kitty Harrow knowingly. 'I know it's supposed to be fearfully taboo, but of course it's always gone on, sometimes in the very best families,' she added complacently, touching the cliff of blue-grey hair that towered over her small forehead. 'I remember my own father standing outside my bedroom door hissing, "You're completely hopeless, you've got no sexual imagination."'

'Good God!' said Robin Parker.

'My father was a marvellous man, very magnetic.' Kitty rolled her shoulders as she said this. 'Everybody adored him. So, you see, I *know* what I'm talking about. Children give off the most enormous sexual feeling; they set out to seduce their parents. It's all in Freud, I'm told, although I haven't read his books myself. I remember my son always showing me his little erection. I don't think parents should take advantage of these situations, but I can quite see how they get swept along, especially in crowded conditions with everybody living on top of each other.'

'Is your son here?' asked Robin Parker.

'No, he's in Australia,' Kitty replied sadly. 'I begged him to take over running the farm here, but he's mad about Australian sheep. I've been to see him twice, but I really can't manage the plane flight. And when I get there I'm not at all keen on that way of life, standing in a cloud of barbecue smoke being bored to death by a sheepshearer's wife – one doesn't even get the sheepshearer. Fergus took me to the coast and *forced* me to go snorkelling. All I can say is that the Great Barrier Reef is the most vulgar thing I've ever seen. It's one's worst nightmare, full of frightful loud colours, peacock blues, and impossible oranges all higgledy-piggledy while one's mask floods.'

'The Queen was saying only the other day that London property prices are so high that she doesn't know how she'd cope without Buckingham Palace,' Princess Margaret explained to a sympathetic Peter Porlock.

'How are you?' Nicholas asked Patrick.

'Dying for a drink,' said Patrick.

'Well you have all my sympathy,' yawned Nicholas. 'I've never been addicted to heroin, but I had to give up smoking cigarettes, which was quite bad enough for me. Oh, look, there's Princess

Margaret. One has to be so careful not to trip over her. I suppose you've already heard what happened at dinner.'

'The diplomatic incident.'

'Yes.'

'Very shocking,' said Patrick solemnly.

'I must say, I rather admire P.M.,' said Nicholas, glancing over at her condescendingly. 'She used a minor accident to screw the maximum amount of humiliation out of the ambassador. Somebody has to uphold our national pride during its Alzheimer years, and there's no one who does it with more conviction. Mind you,' said Nicholas in a more withering tone, *'entre nous,* since I'm relying on them to give me a lift back to London, I don't think France has been so heroically represented since the Vichy government. You should have seen the way Alantour slid to his knees. Although I'm absolutely devoted to his wife who, behind all that phoney chic, is a genuinely malicious person with whom one can have the greatest fun, I've always thought Jacques was a bit of a fool.'

'You can tell him yourself,' said Patrick as he saw the ambassador approaching from behind.

'Mon cher Jacques,' said Nicholas, spinning lightly round, 'I thought you were absolutely brilliant! The way you handled that tiresome woman was faultless: by giving in to her ridiculous demands you showed just how ridiculous they were. Do you know my young friend Patrick Melrose? His father was a very good friend of mine.'

'René Bollinger was such heaven,' sighed the Princess. 'He was a really great ambassador, we all absolutely adored him. It makes it all the harder to put up with the mediocrity of these two,' she added, waving her cigarette holder towards the Alantours, to whom Patrick was saying goodbye.

'I hope we didn't dr-rive away your young friend,' said Jacqueline. 'He seemed very nervous.'

'We can do without him even if I am a great advocate of diversity,' said Nicholas.

'You?' laughed Jacqueline.

'Absolutely, my dear,' Nicholas replied. 'I firmly believe that one should have the widest possible range of acquaintances, from monarchs right down to the humblest baronet in the land. With, of course, a sprinkling of superstars,' he added, like a great chef introducing a rare but pungent spice into his stew, 'before they turn, as they inevitably do, into black holes.'

'*Mais il est vraiment* too much,' said Jacqueline, delighted by Nicholas's performance.

'One's better off with a title than a mere name,' Nicholas continued. 'Proust, as I'm sure you're aware, writes very beautifully on this subject, saying that even the most fashionable commoner is bound to be forgotten very quickly, whereas the bearer of a great title is certain of immortality, at least in the eyes of his descendants.'

'Still,' said Jacqueline a little limply, 'there have been some very amusing people without titles.'

'My dear,' said Nicholas, clasping her forearm, 'what would we do without them?'

They laughed the innocent laughter of two snobs taking a holiday from that need to appear tolerant and open-minded which marred what Nicholas still called 'modern life', although he had never known any other kind.

'I feel the royal presence bearing down on us,' said Jacques uncomfortably. 'I think the diplomatic course is to explore the depths of the party.'

'My dear fellow, you are the depths of the party,' said Nicholas.

'But I quite agree, you shouldn't expose yourself to any more petulance from that absurd woman.'

'*Au revoir,*' whispered Jacqueline.

'*A bientôt,*' said Jacques, and the Alantours withdrew and separated, taking the burden of their glamour to different parts of the room.

Nicholas had hardly recovered from the loss of the Alantours when Princess Margaret and Kitty Harrow came over to his side.

'Consorting with the enemy,' scowled the Princess.

'They came to me for sympathy, ma'am,' said Nicholas indignantly, 'but I told them they'd come to the wrong place. I pointed out to him that he was a clumsy fool. And as to his absurd wife, I said that we'd had quite enough of her petulance for one evening.'

'Oh, did you?' said the Princess, smiling graciously.

'Good for you,' chipped in Kitty.

'As you saw,' boasted Nicholas, 'they slunk off with their tails between their legs. "I'd better keep a low profile," the ambassador said to me. "You've got a low enough profile already," I replied.'

'Oh, how marvellous,' said the Princess. 'Putting your sharp tongue to good use, I approve of that.'

'I suppose this'll go straight into your book,' said Kitty. 'We're all terrified, ma'am, by what Nicholas is going to say about us in his book.'

'Am I in it?' asked the Princess.

'I wouldn't dream of putting you in, ma'am,' protested Nicholas. 'I'm far too discreet.'

'You're allowed to put me in it as long as you say something nice,' said the Princess.

'I remember you when you were five years old,' said Bridget. 'You were so sweet, but rather standoffish.'

'I can't imagine why,' said Patrick. 'I remember seeing you kneeling down on the terrace just after you arrived. I was watching from behind the trees.'

'Oh God,' squealed Bridget. 'I'd forgotten that.'

'I couldn't work out what you were doing.'

'It was very shocking.'

'I'm unshockable,' said Patrick.

'Well, if you really want to know, Nicholas had told me it was something your parents did: your father making your mother eat figs off the ground, and I was rather naughtily acting out what he'd told me. He got frightfully angry with me.'

'It's nice to think of my parents having fun,' said Patrick.

'I think it was a power thing,' said Bridget, who seldom dabbled in deep psychology.

'Sounds plausible,' said Patrick.

'Oh God, there's Mummy, looking terribly lost,' said Bridget. 'You wouldn't be an angel and talk to her for a second, would you?'

'Of course,' said Patrick.

Bridget left Patrick with Virginia, congratulating herself on solving her mother problem so neatly.

'So how was your dinner here?' said Patrick, trying to open the conversation on safe ground. 'I gather Princess Margaret got showered in brown sauce. It must have been a thrilling moment.'

'I wouldn't have found it thrilling,' said Virginia. 'I know how upsetting it can be getting a stain on your dress.'

'So you didn't actually see it,' said Patrick.

'No, I was having dinner with the Bossington-Lanes,' said Virginia.

'Really? I was supposed to be there. How was it?'

'We got lost on the way there,' sighed Virginia. 'All the cars were busy collecting people from the station, so I had to go by taxi. We stopped at a cottage that turned out to be just at the bottom of their drive and asked the way. When I said to Mr

Bossington-Lane, "We had to ask the way from your neighbour in the cottage with the blue windows," he said to me, "That's not a neighbour, that's a tenant, and what's more he's a sitting tenant and a damned nuisance."'

'Neighbours are people you can ask to dinner,' said Patrick.

'That makes me his neighbour, then,' laughed Virginia. 'And I live in Kent. I don't know why my daughter told me they needed spare ladies, there were nothing but spare ladies. Mrs Bossington-Lane told me just now that she's had apologies from all four gentlemen who didn't turn up, and they all said they'd broken down on the motorway. She was very put out, after all the trouble she'd been to, but I said, "You've got to keep your sense of humour."'

'I thought she looked unconvinced when I told her I'd broken down on the motorway,' said Patrick.

'Oh,' said Virginia, clapping her hand over her mouth. 'You must have been one of them. I'd forgotten you said you were supposed to have dinner there.'

'Don't worry,' smiled Patrick. 'I just wish we'd compared stories before all telling her the same one.'

Virginia laughed. 'You've got to keep your sense of humour,' she repeated.

'What is it, darling?' asked Aurora Donne. 'You look as if you've seen a ghost.'

'Oh, I don't know,' sighed Bridget. 'I just saw Cindy Smith with Sonny – and I remember saying that we couldn't ask her because we didn't know her, and thinking it was odd of Sonny to make a thing of it – and now she's here and there was something familiar about the way they stood together, but I'm probably just being paranoid.'

Aurora, presented with the choice of telling a friend a painful

truth which could do her no possible good, or reassuring her, felt no hesitation in taking the first course for the sake of 'honesty', and the pleasure of seeing Bridget's enjoyment of her expensive life, which Aurora had often told herself she would have handled better, spoiled.

'I don't know whether I should tell you this,' said Aurora. 'I probably shouldn't.' She frowned, glancing at Bridget.

'What?' Bridget implored her. 'You've got to tell me.'

'No,' said Aurora. 'It'll only upset you. It was stupid of me to mention it.'

'You *have* to tell me now,' said Bridget desperately.

'Well, of course you're the last to know – one always is in these situations, but it's been fairly common knowledge . . .' Aurora lingered suggestively on the word 'common' which she had always been fond of, 'that Sonny and Miss Smith have been having an affair for some time.'

'God,' said Bridget. 'So that's who it is. I knew something was going on . . .' She suddenly felt very tired and sad, and looked as if she was going to cry.

'Oh, darling, don't,' said Aurora. 'Chin up,' she added consolingly.

But Bridget was overwhelmed and went up with Aurora to her bedroom and told her all about the telephone call she'd overheard that morning, swearing her to a secrecy to which Aurora swore several other people before the evening was out. Bridget's friend advised her to 'go on the warpath', thinking this was the policy likely to yield the largest number of amusing anecdotes.

'Oh, do come and help us,' said China who was sitting with Angus Broghlie and Amanda Pratt. It was not a group that Patrick had any appetite to join.

'We're making a list of all the people whose fathers aren't really their fathers,' she explained.

'Hmm, I'd do anything to be on it,' groaned Patrick. 'Anyway, it would take far too long to do in one evening.'

David Windfall, driven by a fanatical desire to exonerate himself from the blame of bringing Cindy Smith and making his hostess angry, rushed up to his fellow guests to explain that he had just been obeying orders, and it wasn't really his idea. He was about to make the same speech to Peter Porlock when he realized that Peter, as Sonny's best friend, might view it as faint-hearted, and so he checked himself and remarked instead on 'that dreadful christening' where they had last met.

'Dreadful,' confirmed Peter. 'What's the vestry for, if it isn't to dump babies along with one's umbrella and so forth? But of course the vicar wanted all the children in the church. He's a sort of flower child who believes in swinging services, but the purpose of the Church of England is to be the Church of England. It's a force of social cohesion. If it's going to get evangelical we don't want anything to do with it.'

'Hear, hear,' said David. 'I gather Bridget's very upset about my bringing Cindy Smith,' he added, unable to keep away from the subject.

'Absolutely furious,' laughed Peter. 'She had a blazing row with Sonny in the library, I'm told: audible above the band and the din, apparently. Poor Sonny, he's been locked in there all evening,' grinned Peter, nodding his head towards the door. 'Stole in there to have a *tête-à-tête*, or rather a *jambe-à-jambe*, I should imagine, with Miss Smith, then the blazing row, and now he's stuck with Robin Parker trying to cheer himself up by having his Poussin authenticated. The thing is for you to stick to your story. You met Cindy, wife couldn't come, asked her instead, foolishly

didn't check, nothing to do with Sonny. Something along those lines.'

'Of course,' said David who had already told a dozen people the opposite story.

'Bridget didn't actually see them at it, and you know how women are in these situations: they believe what they want to believe.'

'Hmm,' said David, who'd already told Bridget he was just obeying orders. He winced as he saw Sonny emerging from the library nearby. Did Sonny know that he'd told Bridget?

'Sonny!' squealed David, his voice slipping into falsetto.

Sonny ignored him and boomed, 'It is a Poussin!' to Peter.

'Oh, well done,' said Peter, as if Sonny had painted it himself. 'Best possible birthday present to find that it's the real thing and not just a "school of"—'

'The trees,' said Robin, slipping his hand inside his dinner jacket for a moment, 'are unmistakable.'

'Will you excuse us?' Sonny asked Robin, still ignoring David. 'I have to have a word with Peter in private.' Sonny and Peter went into the library and closed the door.

'I've been a bloody fool,' said Sonny. 'Not least for trusting David Windfall. That's the last time I'm having him under my roof. And now I've got a wife crisis on my hands.'

'Don't be too hard on yourself,' said Peter needlessly.

'Well, you know, I was driven to it,' said Sonny, immediately taking up Peter's suggestion. 'I mean, Bridget's not having a son and everything has been frightfully hard. But when it comes to the crunch I'm not sure I'd like life here without the old girl running the place. Cindy has got some very peculiar ideas. I'm not sure what they are, but I can sense it.'

'The trouble is it's all become so complicated,' said Peter. 'One doesn't really know where one stands with women. I mean, I was reading about this sixteenth-century Russian marriage-guidance thing, and it advises you to beat your wife lovingly so as not to render her permanently blind or deaf. If you said that sort of thing nowadays they'd string you up. But, you know, there's a lot in it, obviously in a slightly milder form. It's like the old adage about native bearers: "Beat them for no reason and they won't give you a reason to beat them."'

Sonny looked a little bewildered. As he later told some of his friends, 'When it was all hands on deck with the Bridget crisis, I'm afraid Peter didn't really pull his weight. He just waffled on about sixteenth-century Russian pamphlets.'

'It was that lovely judge Melford Stevens,' said Kitty, 'who said to a rapist, "I shall not send you to prison but back to the Midlands, which is punishment enough." I know one isn't meant to say that sort of thing, but it is rather marvellous, isn't it? I mean England used to be full of that sort of wonderfully eccentric character, but now everybody is so grey and goody-goody.'

'I frightfully dislike this bit,' said Sonny, struggling to keep up the appearance of a jovial host. 'Why does the band leader introduce the musicians, as if anyone wanted to know their names? I mean, one's given up announcing one's own guests, so why should these chaps get themselves announced?'

'Couldn't agree with you more, old bean,' said Alexander Politsky. 'In Russia, the grand families had their own estate band, and there was no more question of introducing them than there was of presenting your scullion to a grand duke. When we went shooting and there was a cold river to cross, the beaters would lie in the water and form a sort of bridge. Nobody felt they had to know their names in order to walk over their heads.'

'I think that's going a bit far,' said Sonny. 'I mean, walking over their heads. But, you see, that's why we didn't have a revolution.'

'The reason you didn't have a revolution, old bean,' said Alexander, 'is because you had two of them: the Civil War and the Glorious one.'

'And on cornet,' said Joe Martin, the band leader, '"Chilly Willy" Watson!'

Patrick, who had been paying almost no attention to the introductions, was intrigued by the sound of a familiar name. It certainly couldn't be the Chilly Willy he'd known in New York. He must be dead by now. Patrick glanced round anyway to have a look at the man who was standing up in the front row to play his brief solo. With his bulging cheeks and his dinner jacket he couldn't have been less reminiscent of the street junkie whom Patrick had scored from in Alphabet City. Chilly Willy had been a toothless, hollow-cheeked scavenger, shuffling about on the edge of oblivion, clutching on to a pair of trousers too baggy for his cadaverous frame. This jazz musician was vigorous and talented, and definitely black, whereas Chilly, with his jaundice and his pallor, although obviously a black man, had managed to look yellow.

Patrick moved towards the edge of the bandstand to have a closer look. There were probably thousands of Chilly Willys and it was absurd to think that this one was 'his'. Chilly had sat down again after playing his solo and Patrick stood in front of him frowning curiously, like a child at the zoo, feeling that talking was a barrier he couldn't cross.

'Hi,' said Chilly Willy, over the sound of a trumpet solo.

'Nice solo,' said Patrick.

'Thanks.'

'You're not . . . I knew someone in New York called Chilly Willy!'

'Where'd he live?'

'Eighth Street.'

'Uh-huh,' said Chilly. 'What did he do?'

'Well, he . . . sold . . . he lived on the streets really . . . that's why I knew it couldn't be you. Anyway, he was older.'

'I remember you!' laughed Chilly. 'You're the English guy with the coat, right?'

'That's right!' said Patrick. 'It is you! Christ, you look well. I practically didn't recognize you. You play really well too.'

'Thanks. I was always a musician, then I . . .' Chilly made a diving motion with his hand, glancing sideways at his fellow musicians.

'What happened to your wife?'

'She OD'd,' said Chilly sadly.

'Oh, I'm sorry,' said Patrick, remembering the horse syringe she had carefully unwrapped from the loo paper and charged him twenty dollars for. 'Well, it's a miracle you're alive,' he added.

'Yeah, everything's a miracle, man,' said Chilly. 'It's a fuckin' miracle we don't melt in the bath like a piece of soap.'

'The Herberts have always had a weakness for low life,' said Kitty Harrow. 'Look at Shakespeare.'

'They were certainly scraping the barrel with him,' said Nicholas. 'Society used to consist of a few hundred families all of whom knew each other. Now it just consists of one: the Guinnesses. I don't know why they don't make an address book with an especially enlarged G spot.'

Kitty giggled.

'Oh, well, I can see that you're an entrepreneur *manqué*,' said Ali to Nicholas.

'That dinner at the Bossington-Lanes' was beyond anything,' said Ali Montague to Laura and China. 'I knew we were in trouble when our host said, "The great thing about having daughters is that you can get them to fag for you." And when that great horsy girl of his came back she said, "You can't argue with Daddy, he used to have exactly the same vital statistics as Muhammad Ali, except he was a foot and a half shorter."'

Laura and China laughed. Ali was such a good mimic.

'The mother's absolutely terrified,' said Laura, 'because some friend of Charlotte's went up to "the Metrop" to share a flat with a couple of other county gals, and the first week she fell in with someone called "Evil John"!'

They all howled with laughter.

'What really terrifies Mr Bossington-Lane,' said Ali, 'is Charlotte getting an education.'

'Fat chance,' said Laura.

'He was complaining about a neighbour's daughter who had "a practically unheard of number of Os".'

'What, three?' suggested China.

'I think it was five and she was going on to do an A level in history of art. I asked him if there was any money in art, just to get him going.'

'And what did he say?' asked China.

Ali thrust out his chin and pushed a hand into his dinner jacket pocket with a thumb resting over the edge.

'"Money?" he boomed. "Not for most of them. But you know, one's dealing with people who are too busy struggling with the meaning of life to worry about that sort of thing. Not that one isn't struggling a bit oneself!" I said I thought the meaning of life included a large income. "And capital," he said.'

'The daughter is impossible,' grinned Laura. 'She told me a really boring story that I couldn't be bothered to listen to, and then ended it by saying, "Can you imagine anything worse than having your barbecue sausage stolen?" I said, "Yes, easily." And she made a dreadful honking sound and said, "Well, obviously, I didn't mean *literally*."'

'Still, it's nice of them to have us to stay,' said China provocatively.

'Do you know how many of those horrid porcelain knick-knacks I counted in my room?' Ali asked with a supercilious expression on his face to exaggerate the shock of the answer he was about to give.

'How many?' asked Laura.

'One hundred and thirty-seven.'

'A hundred and thirty-seven,' gasped China.

'And, apparently, if one of them moves, she knows about it,' said Ali.

'She once had everyone's luggage searched because one of the knick-knacks had been taken from the bedroom to the bathroom or the bathroom to the bedroom, and she thought it was stolen.'

'It's quite tempting to try and smuggle one out,' said Laura.

'Do you know what's rather fascinating?' said Ali, hurrying on to his next insight. 'That old woman with the nice face and the ghastly blue dress was Bridget's mother.'

'No!' said Laura. 'Why wasn't she at dinner here?'

'Embarrassed,' said Ali.

'How awful,' said China.

'Mind you, I do see what she means,' said Ali. 'The mother *is* rather Surrey Pines.'

'I saw Debbie,' said Johnny.

'Really? How was she looking?' asked Patrick.

'Beautiful.'

'She always looked beautiful at big parties,' said Patrick. 'I must talk to her one of these days. It's easy to forget that she's just another human being, with a body and a face and almost certainly a cigarette, and that she may well no longer be the same person that I knew.'

'How have you been feeling since dinner?' asked Johnny.

'Pretty weird to begin with, but I'm glad we talked.'

'Good,' said Johnny. He felt awkward not knowing what more to say about their earlier conversation, but not wanting to pretend it had never happened. 'Oh, I thought of you during my meeting,' he said with artificial brightness. 'There was this man who had to switch off his television last night because he thought he was putting the presenters off.'

'Oh, I used to get that,' said Patrick. 'When my father died in New York one of the longest conversations I had (if I is the right pronoun in this case) was with the television set.'

'I remember you telling me,' said Johnny.

The two men fell silent and stared at the throng that struggled under wastes of grey velvet with the same frantic but restricted motion as bacteria multiplying under a microscope.

'It takes about a hundred of these ghosts to precipitate one flickering and disreputable sense of identity,' said Patrick. 'These are the sort of people who were around during my childhood: hard dull people who seemed quite sophisticated but were in fact as ignorant as swans.'

'They're the last Marxists,' said Johnny unexpectedly. 'The last people who believe that class is a total explanation. Long after that doctrine has been abandoned in Moscow and Peking it will continue to flourish under the marquees of England. Although most of them have the courage of a half-eaten worm,' he continued, warming to his theme, 'and the intellectual vigour of dead sheep, they are the true heirs to Marx and Lenin.'

'You'd better go and tell them,' said Patrick. 'I think most of them were expecting to inherit a bit of Gloucestershire instead.'

'Every man has his price,' said Sonny tartly. 'Wouldn't you agree, Robin?'

'Oh, yes,' said Robin, 'but he must make sure that his price isn't too low.'

'I'm sure most people are very careful to do that,' said Sonny, wondering what would happen if Robin blackmailed him.

'But it's not just money that corrupts people,' said Jacqueline d'Alantour. 'We had the most wonder-fool driver called Albert. He was a very sweet, gentle man who used to tell the most touching story you could imagine about operating on his goldfish. One day, when Jacques was going shooting, his loader fell ill and so he said, "I'll have to take Albert." I said, "But you can't, it will kill him, he adores animals, he won't be able to bear the sight of all that blood." But Jacques insisted, and he's a very stubborn man, so there was nothing I could do. When the first few birds were shot, poor Albert was in agony,' Jacqueline covered her eyes theatrically, 'but then he started to get interested,' she parted her fingers and peeped out between them. 'And now,' she said, flinging her hands down, 'he subscribes to the *Shooting Times*, and has every kind of gun magazine you can possibly imagine. It's become quite dangerous to drive around with him because every time there's a pigeon, which in London is every two metres, he says, "Monsieur d'Alantour would get that one." When we go through Trafalgar Square, he doesn't look at the road at all, he just stares at the sky, and makes shooting noises.'

'I shouldn't think you could eat a London pigeon,' said Sonny sceptically.

'Patrick Melrose? You're not David Melrose's son, by any chance?' asked Bunny Warren, a figure Patrick could hardly remember, but a name that had floated around his childhood at a time when his parents still had a social life, before their divorce.

'Yes.'

Bunny's creased face, like an animated sultana, raced through half a dozen expressions of surprise and delight. 'I remember you as a child, you used to take a running kick at my balls each time I came to Victoria Road for a drink.'

'I'm sorry about that,' said Patrick. 'Oddly enough, Nicholas Pratt was complaining about the same sort of thing this morning.'

'Oh, well, in his case . . .' said Bunny with a mischievous laugh.

'I used to get to the right velocity,' Patrick explained, 'by starting on the landing and running down the first flight of stairs. By the time I reached the hall I could manage a really good kick.'

'You don't have to tell me,' said Bunny. 'Do you know, it's a funny thing,' he went on in a more serious tone, 'hardly a day passes without my thinking of your father.'

'Same here,' said Patrick, 'but I've got a good excuse.'

'So have I,' said Bunny. 'He helped me at a time when I was in an extremely wobbly state.'

'He helped to put me *into* an extremely wobbly state,' said Patrick.

'I know a lot of people found him difficult,' admitted Bunny, 'and he may have been at his most difficult with his children – people usually are – but I saw another side of his personality. After Lucy died, at a time when I really couldn't cope at all, he took care of me and stopped me drinking myself to death, listened with enormous intelligence to hours of black despair, and never used what I told him against me.'

'The fact that you mention his not using anything you said against you is sinister enough.'

'You can say what you like,' said Bunny bluntly, 'but your father probably saved my life.' He made an inaudible excuse and moved away abruptly.

Alone in the press of the party, Patrick was suddenly anxious to avoid another conversation, and left the tent, preoccupied by what Bunny had said about his father. As he hurried into the now-crowded drawing room, he was spotted by Laura, who stood with China and a man Patrick did not recognize.

'Hello, darling,' said Laura.

'Hi,' said Patrick, who didn't want to be waylaid.

'Have you met Ballantine Morgan?' said China.

'Hello,' said Patrick.

'Hello,' said Ballantine, giving Patrick an annoyingly firm handshake. 'I was just saying,' he continued, 'that I've been lucky enough to inherit what is probably the greatest gun collection in the world.'

'Well, I think,' said Patrick, 'I was lucky enough to see a book about it shown to me by your father.'

'Oh, so you've read *The Morgan Gun Collection*,' said Ballantine.

'Well, not from cover to cover, but enough to know how extraordinary it was to own the greatest gun collection in the world and be such a good shot, as well as write about the whole thing in such beautiful prose.'

'My father was also a very fine photographer,' said Ballantine.

'Oh, yes, I knew I'd forgotten something,' said Patrick.

'He was certainly a multitalented individual,' said Ballantine.

'When did he die?' asked Patrick.

'He died of cancer last year,' said Ballantine. 'When a man of my father's wealth dies of cancer, you know they haven't found a cure,' he added with justifiable pride.

'It does you great credit that you're such a fine curator of his memory,' said Patrick wearily.

'Honour thy father and thy mother all thy days,' said Ballantine.

'That's certainly been my policy,' Patrick affirmed.

China, who felt that even Ballantine's gargantuan income might be eclipsed by his fatuous behaviour, suggested that they dance.

'I'd be pleased to,' said Ballantine. 'Excuse us,' he added to Laura and Patrick.

'What a ghastly man,' said Laura.

'You should have met his father,' said Patrick.

'If he could get that silver spoon out of his mouth—'

'He would be even more pointless than he already is,' said Patrick.

'How are you, anyway, darling?' Laura asked. 'I'm pleased to see you. This party is really getting on my nerves. Men used to tell me how they used butter for sex, now they tell me how they've eliminated it from their diet.'

Patrick smiled. 'You certainly have to kick a lot of bodies out there before you find a live one,' he said. 'There's a blast of palpable stupidity that comes from our host, like opening the door of a sauna. The best way to contradict him is to let him speak.'

'We could go upstairs,' said Laura.

'What on earth for?' smiled Patrick.

'We could just fuck. No strings.'

'Well, it's something to do,' said Patrick.

'Thanks,' said Laura.

'No, no, I'm really keen,' said Patrick. 'Although I can't help thinking it's a terrible idea. Aren't we going to get confused?'

'No strings, remember?' said Laura, marching him towards the hall.

A security guard stood at the foot of the staircase. 'I'm sorry, no one goes upstairs,' he said.

'We're staying here,' said Laura, and something indefinably arrogant about her tone made the security man step aside.

Patrick and Laura kissed, leaning against the wall of the attic room they had found.

'Guess who I'm having an affair with?' asked Laura as she detached herself.

'I dread to think. Anyhow, why do you want to discuss it just now?' Patrick mumbled as he bit her neck.

'He's someone you know.'

'I give up,' sighed Patrick who could feel his erection dwindling.

'Johnny.'

'Well, that's put me right off,' said Patrick.

'I thought you might want to steal me back.'

'I'd rather stay friends with Johnny. I don't want more irony and more tension. You never really understood that, did you?'

'You love irony and tension, what are you talking about?'

'You just go round imagining everybody's like you.'

'Oh, fuck off,' said Laura. 'Or as Lawrence Harvey says in *Darling*, "Put away your Penguin Freud."'

'Look, we'd better just part now, don't you think?' said Patrick. 'Before we have a row.'

'God, you're a pain,' said Laura.

'Let's go down separately,' said Patrick. The flickering flame of his lighter cast a dim wobbling light over the room. The lighter went out, but Patrick found the brass doorknob and, opening the door cautiously, allowed a wedge of light to cross the dusty floorboards.

'You go first,' he whispered, brushing the dust from the back of her dress.

'Bye,' she said curtly.

IO

PATRICK CLOSED THE DOOR gratefully and lit a cigarette. Since his conversation with Bunny there'd been no time to think, but now the disturbing quality of Bunny's remarks caught up with him and kept him in the attic.

Even when he had gone to New York to collect his ashes, Patrick had not been completely convinced by the simple solution of loathing his father. Bunny's loyalty to David made Patrick realize that his real difficulty might be in acknowledging the same feelings in himself.

What had there been to admire about his father? The music he had refused to take the risk of recording? And yet it had sometimes broken Patrick's hearts to hear it. The psychological insight he had habitually used to torment his friends and family, but which Bunny claimed had saved his life? All of David's virtues and talents had been double-edged, but however vile he had been he had not been deluded, most of the time, and had accepted with some stoicism his well-deserved suffering.

It was not admiration that would reconcile him to his father, or even the famously stubborn love of children for their parents, able to survive far worse fates than Patrick's. The greenish faces of those drowning figures clinging to the edge of the *Medusa*'s raft haunted his imagination, and he did not always picture them *from* the raft, but often as enviably closer to it than he was. How many choked cursing? How many slipped under silently? How many survived a little longer by pressing on the shoulders of their drowning neighbours?

Something more practical made him rummage about for a reason to make peace. Most of Patrick's strengths, or what he imagined were his strengths, derived from his struggle against his father, and only by becoming detached from their tainted origin could he make any use of them.

And yet he could never lose his indignation at the way his father had cheated him of any peace of mind, and he knew that however much trouble he put into repairing himself, like a once-broken vase that looks whole on its patterned surface but reveals in its pale interior the thin dark lines of its restoration, he could only produce an illusion of wholeness.

All Patrick's attempts at generosity ran up against his choking indignation while, on the other hand, his hatred ran up against those puzzling moments, fleeting and always spoiled, when his father had seemed to be in love with life and to take pleasure in any expression of freedom, or playfulness, or brilliance. Perhaps he would have to settle for the idea that it must have been even worse being his father than being someone his father had attempted to destroy.

Simplification was dangerous and would later take its revenge. Only when he could hold in balance his hatred and his stunted love, looking on his father with neither pity nor terror but as another human being who had not handled his personality especially well; only when he could live with the ambivalence of never forgiving his father for his crimes but allowing himself to be touched by the unhappiness that had produced them as well as the unhappiness they had produced, could he be released, perhaps, into a new life that would enable him to live instead of merely surviving. He might even enjoy himself.

Patrick grunted nervously. Enjoy himself? He mustn't let his optimism run away with him. His eyes had adjusted to the dark and he could now make out the chests and boxes that surrounded the small patch of floor he had been pacing around. A narrow half window giving onto the roof and gutter caught the murky brown glow of the floodlights at the front of the house. He lit another cigarette and smoked it, leaning against the windowsill. He felt the usual panic about needing to be elsewhere, in this case downstairs where he couldn't help imagining the carpets being hoovered and the caterers' vans loaded, although it had only been about one thirty when he came upstairs with Laura. But he stayed in the attic, intrigued by the slightest chance of release from the doldrums in which his soul had lain breathless for so long.

Patrick opened the window to throw his cigarette onto the damp roof. Taking a last gulp of smoke, he smiled at the thought that David probably would have shared his point of view about their relationship. It was the kind of trick that had made him a subtle enemy, but now it might help to end their battle. Yes, his father would have applauded Patrick's defiance and understood his efforts to escape the maze into which he had placed him. The thought that he would have wanted him to succeed made Patrick want to cry.

Beyond bitterness and despair there was something poignant, something he found harder to admit than the facts about his father's cruelty, the thing he had not been able to say to Johnny: that his father had wanted, through the brief interludes of his depression, to love him, and that he had wanted to be able to love his father, although he never would.

And why, while he was at it, continue to punish his mother?

She had not done anything so much as failed to do anything, but he had put himself beyond her reach, clinging on to the adolescent bravado of pretending that she was a person he had nothing in common with at all, who just happened to have given birth to him; that their relationship was a geographical accident, like that of being someone's neighbour. She had frustrated her husband by refusing to go to bed with him, but Patrick would be the last person to blame her for that. It would probably be better if women arrested in their own childhood didn't have children with tormented misogynist homosexual paedophiles, but nothing was perfect in this sublunary world, thought Patrick, glancing up devoutly at the moon which was of course hidden, like the rest of the sky during an English winter, by a low swab of dirty cloud. His mother was really a good person, but like almost everybody she had found her compass spinning in the magnetic field of intimacy.

He really must go downstairs now. Obsessed by punctuality and dogged by a heart-compressing sense of urgency, Patrick was still incapable of keeping a watch. A watch might have soothed him by challenging his hysteria and pessimism. He would definitely get a watch on Monday. If he was not going to have an epiphany to take with him from the attic, the promise of a watch might at least represent a shimmering of hope. Wasn't there a single German word meaning 'shimmering of hope'? There was probably a single German word meaning, 'Regeneration through Punctuality, Shimmering of Hope, and Taking Pleasure in the Misfortune of Others'. If only he knew what it was.

Could one have a time-release epiphany, an epiphany without realizing it had happened? Or were they always trumpeted by angels and preceded by temporary blindness, Patrick wondered, as he walked down the corridor in the wrong direction.

Turning the corner, he saw that he was in a part of the house he had never seen before. A threadbare brown carpet stretched down a corridor that ended in darkness.

'How the fuck do you get out of this fucking house?' he cursed.

'You're going the wrong way.'

Patrick looked to his right and saw a girl in a white nightie sitting on a short flight of stairs.

'I didn't mean to swear,' he said. 'Or rather, I did mean to, but I didn't know you'd overhear me.'

'It's all right,' she said, 'Daddy swears all the time.'

'Are you Sonny and Bridget's daughter?'

'Yes. I'm Belinda.'

'Can't you get to sleep?' asked Patrick, sitting down on the stairs next to her. She shook her head. 'Why not?'

'Because of the party. Nanny said if I said my prayers properly I'd go to sleep, but I didn't.'

'Do you believe in God?' asked Patrick.

'I don't know,' said Belinda. 'But if there is a God he's not very good at it.'

Patrick laughed. 'But why aren't you at the party?' he asked.

'I'm not allowed. I'm meant to go to bed at nine.'

'How mean,' said Patrick. 'Do you want me to smuggle you down?'

'Mummy would see me. And Princess Margaret said I had to go to bed.'

'In that case we must definitely smuggle you down. Or I could read you a story.'

'Oh, that would be nice,' said Belinda, and then she put her fingers to her lips and said, 'Shh, there's someone coming.'

At that moment Bridget rounded the corner of the corridor and saw Patrick and Belinda together on the stairs.

'What are you doing here?' she asked Patrick.

'I was just trying to find my way back to the party and I ran into Belinda.'

'But what were you doing here in the first place?'

'Hello, Mummy,' interrupted Belinda.

'Hello, darling,' said Bridget, holding out her hand.

'I came up here with a girl,' Patrick explained.

'Oh God, you're making me feel very old,' said Bridget. 'So much for the security.'

'I was just going to read Belinda a story.'

'Sweet,' said Bridget. 'I should have been doing that years ago.' She picked Belinda up in her arms. 'You're so heavy, nowadays,' she groaned, smiling at Patrick firmly, but dismissively.

'Well, good night,' said Patrick, getting up from the stairs.

'Night,' yawned Belinda.

'I've got something I have to tell you,' said Bridget, as she started to carry Belinda down the corridor. 'Mummy is going to stay at Granny's tonight, and we'd like you to come along as well. There won't be any room for Nanny, though.'

'Oh good, I hate Nanny.'

'I know, darling,' said Bridget.

'But why are we going to Granny's?'

Patrick could no longer hear what they were saying as they went round the corner of the corridor.

Johnny Hall had been curious to meet Peter Porlock ever since Laura told him that Peter had needlessly paid for one of her abortions. When Laura introduced them, Peter wasted no time in swearing Johnny to secrecy about this 'dreadful Cindy and Sonny thing'.

'Of course I've known about it for ages,' he began.

'Whereas I had no idea,' David Windfall chipped in, 'even when Sonny asked me to bring her.'

'That's funny,' said Laura, 'I thought everybody knew.'

'Some people may have suspected, but nobody knew the details,' said Peter proudly.

'Not even Sonny and Cindy,' mocked Laura.

David, who was already apprised of Peter's superior knowledge, drifted off and Laura followed.

Left alone with Johnny, Peter tried to correct any impression of frivolity he might have given by saying how worried he was about his 'ailing papa' to whom he had not bothered to address a word all evening. 'Are your parentals still alive?' he asked.

'And kicking,' said Johnny. 'My mother would have managed to give an impression of mild disappointment if I'd become the youngest Prime Minister of England, so you can imagine what she feels about a moderately successful journalist. She reminds me of a story about Henry Miller visiting his dying mother with a pilot friend of his called Vincent. The old woman looked at her son and then at Vincent and said, "If only I could have a son like you, Vincent."'

'Look here, you won't leak anything I've said to the press, will you?' asked Peter.

'Alas, the editorial pages of *The Times* aren't yet given over entirely to love-nest scandals,' said Johnny contemptuously.

'Oh, *The Times*,' murmured Peter. 'Well, I know it's frightfully unfashionable, but I still think one should practise filial loyalty. It's been frightfully easy for me: my mother was a saint and my father's the most decent chap you could hope to meet.'

Johnny smiled vaguely, wishing Laura had charged Peter double.

'Peter!' said a concerned Princess Margaret.

'Oh, ma'am, I didn't see you,' said Peter, bowing his head briefly.

'I think you should go to the hall. I'm afraid your father isn't at all well, and he's being taken off by ambulance.'

'Good God,' said Peter. 'Please excuse me, ma'am, I'll go immediately.'

The Princess, who had announced in the hall that she would tell Peter herself, and forced her lady-in-waiting to intercept other well-wishers on the same mission, was thoroughly impressed by her own goodness.

'And who are you?' she asked Johnny in the most gracious possible manner.

'Johnny Hall,' said Johnny, extending a hand.

The republican omission of ma'am, and the thrusting and unacceptable invitation to a handshake, were enough to convince the Princess that Johnny was a man of no importance.

'It must be funny having the same name as so many other people,' she speculated. 'I suppose there are hundreds of John Halls up and down the country.'

'It teaches one to look for distinction elsewhere and not to rely on an accident of birth,' said Johnny casually.

'That's where people go wrong,' said the Princess, compressing her lips, 'there is no accident in birth.'

She swept on before Johnny had a chance to reply.

Patrick walked down towards the first floor, the hubbub of the party growing louder as he descended past portraits by Lely and Lawrence and even a pair, dominating the first-floor landing, by Reynolds. The prodigious complacency which the Gravesend genes had carried from generation to generation, without the usual interludes of madness, diffidence or distinction, had defied the skills of all these painters, and, despite their celebrity, none of them had been able to make anything appealing out of the drooping eyelids and idiotically arrogant expressions of their sitters.

Thinking about Belinda, Patrick started half-consciously to

walk down the stairs as he had in moments of stress when he was her age, leading with one foot and bringing the other down firmly beside it on the same step. As he approached the hall he felt an overwhelming urge to cast himself forward onto the stone floor, but stopped instead and held onto the banister, intrigued by this strange impulse, which he could not immediately explain.

Yvette had told him many times about the day he had fallen down the stairs at Lacoste and cut his hand. The story of his screams and the broken glass and Yvette's fear that he had cut a tendon had installed themselves in his picture of childhood as an accepted anecdote, but now Patrick could feel the revival of the memory itself: he could remember imagining the frames of the pictures flying down the corridor and embedding themselves in his father's chest, and decapitating Nicholas Pratt. He could feel the despairing urge to jump down the stairs to hide his guilt at snapping the stem of the glass by squeezing it so tightly. He stood on the stairs and remembered everything.

The security guard looked at him sceptically. He'd been worried ever since he allowed Patrick and Laura to go upstairs. Laura's coming down on her own and claiming that Patrick was still in their room had strengthened his suspicions. Now Patrick was behaving very eccentrically, trailing one leg as he came down the stairs, staring at the ground. He must be on drugs, thought the security guard angrily. If he had his way he'd arrest Patrick and all the other rich cunts who thought they were above the law.

Patrick, noticing the expression of hostility on the security guard's face, surfaced into the present, smiled weakly, and walked down the final steps. Across the hall, through the windows on either side of the open front door, he could see a flashing blue light.

'Are the police here?' Patrick asked.

'No, it's not the police,' said the security guard sadly. 'Ambulance.'

'What happened?'

'One of the guests had a heart attack.'

'Do you know who it was?' said Patrick.

'Don't know his name, no. White-haired gentleman.' Cold air swept into the hall through the open door. Snow was falling outside. Noticing Tom Charles standing in the doorway, Patrick went over to his side.

'It's George,' said Tom. 'I think he had a stroke. He was very weak, but he could still talk, so I hope he'll be all right.'

'So do I,' said Patrick, who had known George all his life and suddenly realized that he would miss him if he died. George had always been friendly to him, and he urgently wanted to thank him. 'Do you know which hospital they're taking him to?'

'Cheltenham Hospital for tonight,' answered Tom. 'Sonny wants to move him to a clinic, but this ambulance is from the hospital, and I guess the priority is to keep him alive rather than to get him a more expensive room.'

'Quite,' said Patrick. 'Well, I hope King won't be unpacking for him tonight,' he added.

'Don't forget he's travelling light,' said Tom. 'Heaven is the ideal country weekend without any luggage.'

Patrick smiled. 'Let's go and see him tomorrow before lunch.'

'Good idea,' said Tom. 'Where are you staying?'

'The Little Soddington House Hotel,' said Patrick. 'Do you want me to write it down?'

'No,' said Tom, 'with a name like that I may never shake it off.'

'I think it was Talleyrand,' suggested Jacques d'Alantour, pouting a little before his favourite quotation, 'who said,' he paused, '"Doing and saying nothing are great powers, but they should not be abused."'

'Well, nobody could accuse you of doing and saying nothing this evening,' said Bridget.

'Nevertheless,' he continued, 'I shall speak to the Princess about this matter, which I hope will not become known as *"l'affaire Alantour"*.' He chuckled. 'And I hope we can get the bull out of the china shop.'

'Do what you like,' said Bridget. 'I'm past caring.'

Monsieur d'Alantour, too pleased with his new plan to notice his hostess's indifference, bowed and turned on his heels.

'When the Queen's away, I become regent and head of the Privy Council,' Princess Margaret was explaining with satisfaction to Kitty Harrow.

'Ma'am,' said Monsieur d'Alantour, who after considerable thought had worked out the perfect formula for his apology.

'Oh, are you still here,' said the Princess.

'As you can see . . .' said the ambassador.

'Well, shouldn't you be setting off now? You've got a very long journey ahead of you.'

'But I'm staying in the house,' he protested.

'In that case we shall see quite enough of each other tomorrow without spending the whole evening chattering,' said the Princess, turning her back on him.

'Who's that man over there?' she asked Kitty.

'Ali Montague, ma'am,' said Kitty.

'Oh, yes, I recognize the name. You can present him to me,' said Princess Margaret, heading off in Ali's direction.

The ambassador stood in consternation and silence while Kitty presented Ali Montague to Princess Margaret. He was wondering whether he was facing another diplomatic incident or merely the extension of the previous diplomatic incident.

'Oh,' said Ali Montague boldly, 'I love the French. They're treacherous, cunning, two-faced – I don't have to make an effort there, I just fit in. And further down in Italy, they're cowards as well, so I get on even better.'

The Princess looked at him mischievously. She was in a good mood again and had decided that Ali was being amusing.

Alexander Politsky later sought out Ali to congratulate him on 'handling P.M. so well'.

'Oh, I've had my fair share of royalty,' said Ali suavely. 'Mind you, I didn't do nearly so well with that dreadful Amanda Pratt. You know how ghastly all those people become when they're "on the programme" and go to all those meetings. Of course, they do save people's lives.'

Alexander sniffed and looked languidly into the middle distance. 'I've been to them myself,' he admitted.

'But you never had a drink problem,' protested Ali.

'I like heroin, cocaine, nice houses, good furniture, and pretty girls,' said Alexander, 'and I've had all of them in large quantities. But you know, they never made me happy.'

'My word, you're hard to please, aren't you?'

'Frankly, when I first went along I thought I'd stick out like a pair of jeans on a Gainsborough, but I've found more genuine love and kindness in those meetings than I've seen in all the fashionable drawing rooms of London.'

'Well, that's not saying much,' said Ali. 'You could say the same thing about Billingsgate fish market.'

'There isn't one of them,' said Alexander, throwing his shoulders back and closing his eyelids, 'from the tattooed butcher upward, whom I wouldn't drive to Inverness at three in the morning to help.'

'To Inverness? From where?' asked Ali.

'London.'

'Good God,' exclaimed Ali. 'Perhaps I should try one of those meetings, next time I have a spare evening. But the point is, would you ask your tattooed butcher to dinner?'

'Of course not,' said Alexander. 'But only because he wouldn't enjoy it.'

'Anne!' said Patrick. 'I didn't expect to see you here.'

'I know,' said Anne Eisen, kissing him warmly. 'It's not my kind of scene. I get nervous in the English countryside with everybody talking about killing animals.'

'I'm sure there isn't any of that sort of thing in Sonny's part of the world,' said Patrick.

'You mean, there isn't anything alive for miles around,' said Anne. 'I'm here because Sonny's father was a *relatively* civilized man – he noticed that there was a library in the house as well as a boot room and a cellar. He was a sort of friend of Victor's, and used to ask us to stay for weekends sometimes. Sonny was just a kid in those days but even then he was a pompous creep. Jesus,' sighed Anne, surveying the room, 'what a grim bunch. Do you think they keep them in the deep freeze at Central Casting and thaw them out for big occasions?'

'If only,' said Patrick. 'Unfortunately I think they own most of the country.'

'They've only just got the edge on an ant colony,' said Anne, 'except that they don't do anything useful. You remember those ants in Lacoste, they were always tidying up the terrace for you. Talking of doing something useful, what are you planning to do with your life?'

'Hmm,' said Patrick.

'Jesus Christ!' said Anne. 'You're guilty of the worst sin of all.'

'What's that?'

'Wasting time,' she replied.

'I know,' said Patrick. 'It was a terrible shock to me when I realized I was getting too old to die young anymore.'

Exasperated, Anne changed the subject. 'Are you going to Lacoste this year?' she asked.

'I don't know. The more time passes the more I dislike that place.'

'I've always meant to apologize to you,' said Anne, 'but you used to be too stoned to appreciate it. I've felt guilty for years for not doing anything when you were waiting on the stairs one evening during one of your parents' godawful dinner parties, and I said I'd get your mother for you, but I couldn't, and I should have gone back, or stood up to David, or something. I always felt I'd failed you.'

'Not at all,' said Patrick. 'On the contrary, I remember your being kind. When you're young it makes a difference to meet people who are kind, however rarely. You'd imagine they're buried under the routine of horror, but in fact incidents of kindness get thrown into sharp relief.'

'Have you forgiven your father?' asked Anne.

'Oddly enough you've caught me on the right evening. A week ago I would have lied or said something dismissive, but I was just describing over dinner exactly what I had to forgive my father.'

'And?'

'Well,' said Patrick, 'over dinner I was rather against forgiveness, and I still think that it's detachment rather than appeasement that will set me free, but if I could imagine a mercy that was purely human, and not one that rested on the Greatest Story Ever Told, I might extend it to my father for being so unhappy. I just can't do it out of piety. I've had enough near-death experiences to last me a lifetime, and not *once* was I greeted by a white-robed figure at the end of a tunnel – or only once and he turned out to be an exhausted junior doctor in the emergency ward of the Charing Cross Hospital. There may be something to this idea that you have to be broken in order to be renewed, but renewal doesn't have to consist of a lot of phoney reconciliations!'

'What about some genuine ones?' said Anne.

'What impresses me more than the repulsive superstition that I should turn the other cheek, is the intense unhappiness my father lived with. I ran across a diary his mother wrote during the First World War. After pages of gossip and a long passage about how marvellously they'd managed to keep up the standards at some large country house, defying the Kaiser with the perfection of their cucumber sandwiches, there are two short sentences: "Geoffrey wounded again", about her husband in the trenches, and "David has rickets", about her son at his prep school. Presumably he was not just suffering from malnutrition, but being assaulted by paedophiliac schoolmasters and beaten by older boys. This very traditional combination of maternal coldness and official perversion helped to make him the splendid man he turned into, but to forgive someone, one would have to be convinced that they'd made some effort to change the disastrous course that genetics, class, or upbringing proposed for them.'

'If he'd changed the course he wouldn't need forgiving,' said Anne. 'That's the whole deal with forgiving. Anyhow, I don't say you're wrong not to forgive him, but you can't stay stuck with this hatred.'

'There's no point in staying stuck,' Patrick agreed. 'But there's even less point in pretending to be free. I feel on the verge of a great transformation, which may be as simple as becoming interested in other things.'

'What?' said Anne. 'No more father-bashing? No more drugs? No more snobbery?'

'Steady on,' gasped Patrick. 'Mind you, this evening I had a brief hallucination that the world was real . . .'

'"An hallucination that the world was real" – you oughta be Pope.'

'Real,' Patrick continued, 'and not just composed of a series of effects – the orange lights on a wet pavement, a leaf clinging to the windscreen, the sucking sound of a taxi's tyres on a rainy street.'

'Very wintery effects,' said Anne.

'Well, it is February,' said Patrick. 'Anyway, for a moment the world seemed to be solid and out there and made up of things.'

'That's progress,' said Anne. 'You used to belong to the the-world-is-a-private-movie school.'

'You can only give things up once they start to let you down. I gave up drugs when the pleasure and the pain became simultaneous and I might as well have been shooting up a vial of my own tears. As to the naive faith that rich people are more interesting than poor ones, or titled people more interesting than untitled ones, it would be impossible to sustain if people didn't also believe that they became more interesting by association. I can feel the death throes of that particular delusion, especially as I patrol this room full of photo opportunities and feel my mind seizing up with boredom.'

'That's your own fault.'

'As to my "father-bashing",' said Patrick, ignoring Anne's comment, 'I thought of him this evening without thinking about his influence on me, just as a tired old man who'd fucked up his life, wheezing away his last years in that faded blue shirt he wore in the summer. I pictured him sitting in the courtyard of that horrible house, doing *The Times'* crossword, and he struck me as more pathetic and more *ordinary*, and in the end less worthy of attention.'

'That's what I feel about my dreadful old mother,' said Anne. 'During the Depression, which for some of us never ended, she used to collect stray cats and feed them and look after them.

The house would be full of cats. I was just a kid, so naturally I'd get to love them, and play with them, but then in the autumn my crazy old mother would start muttering, "They'll never make it through the winter, they'll never make it through the winter." The only reason they weren't going to make it through the winter was that she'd soak a towel in ether and drop it in the old brass washing machine and pile the cats in afterward, and when they'd "fallen asleep" she'd turn on the washing machine and drown the poor buggers. Our whole garden was a cat cemetery, and you couldn't dig a hole or play a game without little cat skeletons turning up. There was a terrible scratching sound as they tried to get out of the washing machine. I can remember standing by the kitchen table – I was only as high as the kitchen table – while my mother loaded them in and I'd say, "Don't, please don't," and she'd be muttering, "They'll never make it through the winter." She was ghastly and quite mad, but when I grew up I figured that her worst punishment was to be herself and I didn't have to do anything more.'

'No wonder you get nervous in the English countryside when people start talking about killing animals. Perhaps that's all identity is: seeing the logic of your own experience and being true to it. If only Victor was with us now!'

'Oh, yes, poor Victor,' said Anne. 'But he was looking for a non-psychological approach to identity,' she reminded Patrick with a wry smile.

'That always puzzled me,' he admitted. 'It seemed like insisting on an overland route from England to America.'

'If you're a philosopher, there is an overland route from England to America,' said Anne.

'Oh, by the way, did you hear that George Watford had a stroke?'

'Yeah, I'm sorry to hear that. I remember meeting him at your parents.'

'It's the end of an era,' said Patrick.

'It's the end of a party as well,' said Anne. 'Look, the band is going home.'

When Robin Parker asked Sonny if they could have 'a private word' in the library, Sonny not only felt that he'd spent his entire birthday party having difficult interviews in that wretched room, but also that, as he'd suspected (and he couldn't help pausing here to congratulate himself on his perspicacity), Robin was going to blackmail him for more money.

'Well, what is it,' he said gruffly, once again sitting at his library desk.

'It isn't a Poussin,' said Robin, 'so I really don't want to authenticate it. Other people, including experts, might think it was, but I *know* it isn't.' Robin sighed. 'I'd like my letter back and of course I'll return the . . . fee,' he said, placing two thick envelopes on the table.

'What are you blathering about?' asked Sonny, confused.

'I'm not blathering,' said Robin. 'It's not fair on Poussin, that's all,' he added with unexpected passion.

'What's Poussin got to do with it?' thundered Sonny.

'Nothing, that's just what I object to.'

'I suppose you want more money.'

'You're wrong,' said Robin. 'I just want some part of my life not to be compromised.' He held out his hand for the certificate of authentication.

Furious, Sonny took a key out of his pocket and opened the top drawer of his desk, and tossed the letter over to Robin. Robin thanked him and left the room.

'Tiresome little man,' muttered Sonny. It really wasn't his day. He'd lost his wife, his mistress, and his Poussin. Buck up, old boy, he thought to himself, but he had to admit that he felt decidedly wobbly.

Virginia was sitting on a frail gold chair by the drawing-room door, waiting anxiously for her daughter and granddaughter to come downstairs and start the long drive back to Kent. Kent was ever such a long way, but she completely understood Bridget's wanting to get out of this bad atmosphere, and she'd encouraged her to bring Belinda along. She couldn't hide from herself, although she felt a little guilty about it, that she quite liked being *needed*, and having Bridget close to her again, even if it took a crisis like this one. She'd already got her overcoat and her essentials; it didn't matter about her suitcase, Bridget had said they could send for that later. She didn't want to draw attention to herself: the overcoat was suspicious enough.

The party was thinning out and it was important to leave before there were too few people, or Sonny might start badgering Bridget. Bridget's nerves had never been strong, she'd always been a little frightened as a girl, never wanted to put her head under water, that sort of thing, things only a mother could know. Bridget might be intimidated and lose her resolve if Sonny was there booming at her, but she knew that what her daughter needed, after this Cindy Smith affair, was a good rest and a good think. She'd already asked Bridget if she wanted her old room back – it was a marvel how the human mind worked, as Roddy had been fond of remarking – but it had only seemed to annoy Bridget, who'd said, 'Honestly, Mummy, I don't know, we'll think about that later.' On reflection, it was probably better to give that room to Belinda, and put Bridget in the nice spare room with the bathroom en suite. There was plenty of room now that she was alone.

Sometimes a crisis was good for a marriage, not all the time of course, or it wouldn't really be a crisis. There'd been that one time with Roddy. She hadn't said anything, but Roddy had known she knew, and she'd known he knew she knew, and that had been enough to end it. He'd bought her that ring and said it was their second engagement ring. He was such an old softie, really. Oh dear, there was a man bearing down on her. She had no idea who he was but he was obviously going to talk to her. That was the last thing she needed.

Jacques d'Alantour was too tormented to go to sleep and, although Jacqueline had warned him that he'd had enough to drink, too melancholy to resist another glass of champagne.

Charm was his speciality, everyone knew that, but since '*l'affaire Alantour*', as he now called it, he had entered a diplomatic labyrinth which seemed to require more charm and tact than it was reasonable to ask of a single human being. Virginia, who was, after all, his hostess's mother, played a relatively clear role in the campaign he was launching to regain Princess Margaret's favour.

'Good evening, dear lady,' he said with a deep bow.

Foreign manners, thought Virginia. What Roddy used to call 'a hand-kissing sell-your-own-mother type'.

'Am I right in assuming that you are the mother of our charming hostess?'

'Yes,' said Virginia.

'I am Jacques d'Alantour.'

'Oh, hello,' said Virginia.

'May I get you a glass of champagne?' asked the ambassador.

'No, thank you, I don't like to have more than two. Anyway, I'm on a diet.'

'A diet?' asked Monsieur d'Alantour, seeing an opportunity to prove to the world that his diplomatic skills were not dead. 'A diet?' he repeated with bewilderment and incredulity. 'But w-h-y?' he lingered on the word, to emphasize his astonishment.

'The same reason as everyone else, I suppose,' said Virginia drily.

Monsieur d'Alantour sat down next to her, grateful to get the weight off his legs. Jacqueline was right, he'd drunk too much champagne. But the campaign must continue!

'When a lady tells me she is on a diet,' he said, his gallantry a little slurred, but his fluency, from years of making the same speech (which had been a great success with the German Ambassador's wife in Paris) undiminished, 'I always clasp her breast so,' he held his cupped hand threateningly close to Virginia's alarmed bosom, 'and say, "But now I think you are exactly the right weight!" If I were to do this to you,' he continued, 'you would not be shocked, would you?'

'Shocked,' gulped Virginia, 'isn't the word. I'd be—'

'You see,' Monsieur d'Alantour interrupted, 'it's the most natural thing in the world!'

'Oh, goodness,' said Virginia, 'there's my daughter.'

'Come on, Mummy,' said Bridget, 'Belinda's already in the car, and I'd rather not run into Sonny.'

'I know, darling, I'm just coming. I can't say it's been a pleasure,' she said to the ambassador stiffly, hurrying after her daughter.

Monsieur d'Alantour was too slow to catch up with the hastening women, but stood mumbling, 'I can't express sufficiently . . . my deepest sentiments . . . a most distinguished gathering.'

Bridget moved so much faster than her guests that they had no time to compliment her or waylay her. Some thought that she was following George Watford to hospital, everyone could tell that she was on important business.

When she got into the car, a four-wheel-drive Subaru that Caroline Porlock had persuaded her to buy, and saw Belinda asleep and seatbelted in the back, and her mother sitting beside her with a warm and reassuring smile, Bridget felt a wave of relief and remorse.

'I've treated you dreadfully sometimes,' she suddenly said to her mother. 'Snobbishly.'

'Oh no, darling, I understand,' said her mother, moved but practical.

'I don't know what came over me sending you to dinner with those dreadful people. Everything gets turned upside down. I've been so anxious to fit in with Sonny's stupid, pompous life that everything else got squeezed out. Anyway, I'm glad the three of us are together.'

Virginia glanced back at Belinda to make sure she was asleep.

'We can have a good long talk tomorrow,' she said, squeezing Bridget's hand, 'but we should probably get started now, we've got a long way to go.'

'You're right,' said Bridget who suddenly felt like crying but busied herself with starting the car and joining the queue of departing guests who choked up her drive.

There was still a gentle snowfall as Patrick left the house behind him, steaming breath twisting around the upturned collar of his overcoat. Footprints crisscrossed his path, and the gravel's black and brown chips shone wetly among the bright patches of snow. Patrick's ears rang from the noise of the party and his eyes, bloodshot from smoke and tiredness, watered in the cold air, but when he reached his car he wanted to go on walking a little longer, and so he climbed over a nearby gate and jumped into a field of unbroken snow. A pewter-coloured ornamental lake lay at the end of the field, its far bank lost in a thick fog.

His thin shoes grew wet as he crunched across the field and his feet soon felt cold, but with the compelling and opaque logic of a dream the lake drew him to its shore.

As he stood in front of the reeds which pierced the first few yards of water, shivering and wondering whether to have his last cigarette, he heard the sound of beating wings emerging from the other side of the lake. A pair of swans rose out of the fog, concentrating its whiteness and giving it shape, the clamour of their wings muffled by the falling snow, like white gloves on applauding hands.

Vicious creatures, thought Patrick.

The swans, indifferent to his thoughts, flew over fields renewed and silenced by the snow, curved back over the shore of the lake, spread their webbed feet, and settled confidently onto the water.

Standing in sodden shoes Patrick smoked his last cigarette. Despite his tiredness and the absolute stillness of the air, he felt his soul, which he could only characterize as the part of his mind that was not dominated by the need to talk, surging and writhing like a kite longing to be let go. Without thinking about it he picked up the dead branch at his feet and sent it spinning as far as he could into the dull grey eye of the lake. A faint ripple disturbed the reeds.

After their useless journey the swans drifted majestically back into the fog. Nearer and noisier, a group of gulls circled overhead, their squawks evoking wilder water and wider shores.

Patrick flicked his cigarette into the snow, and not quite knowing what had happened, headed back to his car with a strange feeling of elation.

MOTHER'S MILK

AUGUST 2000

I

WHY HAD THEY PRETENDED to kill him when he was born? Keeping him awake for days, banging his head again and again against a closed cervix; twisting the cord around his throat and throttling him; chomping through his mother's abdomen with cold shears; clamping his head and wrenching his neck from side to side; dragging him out of his home and hitting him; shining lights in his eyes and doing experiments; taking him away from his mother while she lay on the table, half-dead. Maybe the idea was to destroy his nostalgia for the old world. First the confinement to make him hungry for space, then pretending to kill him so that he would be grateful for the space when he got it, even this loud desert, with only the bandages of his mother's arms to wrap around him, never the whole thing again, the whole warm thing all around him, being everything.

The curtains were breathing light into their hospital room. Swelling from the hot afternoon, and then flopping back against the French windows, easing the glare outside.

Someone opened the door and the curtains leapt up and rippled their edges; loose paper rustled, the room whitened, and the shudder of the roadworks grew a little louder. Then the door clunked and the curtains sighed and the room dimmed.

'Oh, no, not more flowers,' said his mother.

He could see everything through the transparent walls of his fish-tank cot. He was looked over by the sticky eye of a splayed lily. Sometimes the breeze blew the peppery smell of freesias over him and he wanted to sneeze it away. On his mother's nightgown spots of blood mingled with streaks of dark orange pollen.

'It's so nice of people . . .' She was laughing from weakness and frustration. 'I mean, is there any room in the bath?'

'Not really, you've got the roses in there already and the other things.'

'Oh, God, I can't bear it. Hundreds of flowers have been cut down and squeezed into these white vases, just to make us happy.' She couldn't stop laughing. There were tears running down her face. 'They should have been left where they were, in a garden somewhere.'

The nurse looked at the chart.

'It's time for you to take your Voltarol,' she said. 'You've got to control the pain before it takes over.'

Then the nurse looked at Robert and he locked on to her blue eyes in the heaving dimness.

'He's very alert. He's really checking me out.'

'He is going to be all right, isn't he?' said his mother, suddenly terrified.

Suddenly Robert was terrified too. They were not together in the way they used to be, but they still had their helplessness in common. They had been washed up on a wild shore. Too tired to crawl up the beach, they could only loll in the roar and the dazzle of being there. He had to face facts, though: they had been separated. He understood now that his mother had already been on the outside. For her this wild shore was a new role, for him it was a new world.

The strange thing was that he felt as if he had been there before. He had known there was an outside all along. He used to think it was a muffled watery world out there and that he lived at the heart of things. Now the walls had tumbled down and he could see what a muddle he had been in. How could he avoid getting in a new muddle in this hammeringly bright place? How could he kick and spin like he used to in this heavy atmosphere where the air stung his skin?

Yesterday he had thought he was dying. Perhaps he was right and this was what happened. Everything was open to question, except the fact that he was separated from his mother. Now that he realized there was a difference between them, he loved his mother with a new sharpness. He used to be close to her. Now he longed to be close to her. The first taste of longing was the saddest thing in the world.

'Oh, dear, what's wrong?' said the nurse. 'Are we hungry, or do we just want a cuddle?'

The nurse lifted him out of the fish-tank cot, over the crevasse that separated it from the bed and delivered him into his mother's bruised arms.

'Try giving him a little time on the breast and then try to get some rest. You've both been through a lot in the last couple of days.'

He was an inconsolable wreck. He couldn't live with so much doubt and so much intensity. He vomited colostrum over his mother and then in the hazy moment of emptiness that followed, he caught sight of the curtains bulging with light. They held his attention. That's how it worked here. They fascinated you with things to make you forget about the separation.

Still, he didn't want to exaggerate his decline. Things had been getting cramped in the old world. Towards the end he was desperate to get out, but he had imagined himself expanding back into the boundless ocean of his youth, not exiled in this harsh land. Perhaps he could revisit the ocean in his dreams, if it weren't for the veil of violence that hung between him and the past.

He was drifting into the syrupy borders of sleep, not know-ing whether it would take him into the floating world or back to the butchery of the birth room.

'Poor Baba, he was probably having a bad dream,' said his mother, stroking him. His crying started to break up and fade.

She kissed him on the forehead and he realized that although they didn't share a body any more, they still had the same thoughts and the same feelings. He shuddered with relief and stared at the curtains, watching the light flow.

He must have been asleep for a while, because his father had arrived and was already locked on to something. He couldn't stop talking.

'I looked at some more flats today and I can tell you, it's re-ally depressing. London property is completely out of control. I'm leaning back towards plan C.'

'What's plan C? I've forgotten.'

'Stay where we are and squeeze another bedroom out of the kitchen. If we divide it in half, the broom cupboard becomes his toy cupboard and the bed goes where the fridge is.'

'Where do the brooms go?'

'I don't know – somewhere.'

'And the fridge?'

'It could go in the cupboard next to the washing machine.'

'It won't fit.'

'How do you know?'

'I just know.'

'Anyway . . . we'll work it out. I'm just trying to be practical. Everything changes when you have a baby.'

His father leant closer, whispering, 'There's always Scotland.'

He had come to be practical. He knew that his wife and son were drowning in a puddle of confusion and sensitivity and he was going to save them. Robert could feel what he was feeling.

'God, his hands are so tiny,' said his father. 'Just as well, really.'

He raised Robert's hand with his little finger and kissed it.
'Can I hold him?'

She lifted him towards his father. 'Watch out for his neck, it's very floppy. You have to support it.'

They all felt nervous.

'Like this?' His father's hand edged up his spine, took over from his mother, and slipped under Robert's head. Robert tried to keep calm. He didn't want his parents to get upset.

'Sort of. I don't really know either.'

'Ahh . . . how come we're allowed to do this without a licence? You can't have a dog or a television without a licence. Maybe we can learn from the maternity nurse – what's her name?'

'Margaret.'

'By the way, where is Margaret going to sleep on the night before we go to my mother's?'

'She says she's perfectly happy on the sofa.'

'I wonder if the sofa feels the same way.'

'Don't be mean, she's on a "chemical diet".'

'How exciting. I hadn't seen her in that light.'

'She's had a lot of experience.'

'Haven't we all?'

'With babies.'

'Oh, babies.' His father scraped Robert's cheek with his stubble and made a kissing sound in his ear.

'But we adore him,' said his mother, her eyes swimming with tears. 'Isn't that enough?'

'Being adored by two trainee parents with inadequate housing? Thank goodness he's got the backup of one grandmother who's on permanent holiday, and another who's too busy saving the planet to be entirely pleased by this additional strain on its resources. My mother's house is already too full of shamanic rattles and "power animals" and "inner children" to accommodate anything as grown-up as a child.'

'We'll be all right,' said his mother. 'We're not children any more, we're parents.'

'We're both,' said his father, 'that's the trouble. Do you know what my mother told me the other day? A child born in a developed nation will consume two hundred and forty times the resources consumed by a child born in Bangladesh. If we'd had the self-restraint to have two hundred and thirty-nine Bangladeshi children, she would have given us a warmer welcome, but this gargantuan Westerner, who is going to take up acres of landfill with his disposable nappies, and will soon be clamouring for a personal computer powerful enough to launch a Mars flight while playing tic-tac-toe with a virtual buddy in Dubrovnik, is not likely to win her approval.' His father paused. 'Are you all right?' he asked.

'I've never been happier,' said his mother, wiping her glistening cheeks with the back of her hand. 'I just feel so empty.'

She guided the baby's head towards her nipple and he started to suck. A thin stream from his old home flooded his mouth and they were together again. He could sense her heartbeat. Peace shrouded them like a new womb. Perhaps this was a good place to be after all, just difficult to get into.

That was about all that Robert could remember from the first few days of his life. The memories had come back to him last month when his brother was born. He couldn't be sure that some of the things hadn't been said last month, but even if they had been, they reminded him of when he was in hospital; so the memories really belonged to him.

Robert was obsessed with his past. He was five years old now. Five years old, not a baby like Thomas. He could feel his infancy disintegrating, and among the bellows of congratulation that accompanied each little step towards full citizenship he heard the whisper of loss. Something had started to happen as he became dominated by talk. His early memories were breaking off, like slabs from those orange cliffs behind him, and crashing into an all-consuming sea which only glared back at him when he tried to look into it. His infancy was being obliterated by his childhood. He wanted it back, otherwise Thomas would have the whole thing.

Robert had left his parents, his little brother and Margaret behind, and he was wobbling his way across the rocks towards the clattering stones of the lower beach, holding in one of his outstretched hands a scuffed plastic bucket decorated with vaulting dolphins. Brilliant pebbles, fading as he ran back to show them off, no longer tricked him. What he was looking for now were those jelly beans of blunted glass buried under the fine rush of black and gold gravel on the shore. Even when they were dry they had a bruised glow. His father told him that glass was made of sand, so they were halfway back to where they came from.

Robert had arrived at the shoreline now. He left his bucket on a high rock and started the hunt for wave-licked glass. The water foamed around his ankles and as it rushed down the beach he scanned the bubbling sand. To his astonishment he could see something under the first wave, not one of the pale green or cloudy white beads, but a rare yellow gem. He pulled it out of the sand, washed the grit from it with the next wave and held it up to the light, a little amber kidney between his finger and thumb. He looked up the beach to share his excitement, but his parents were huddled around the baby, while Margaret rummaged in a bag.

He could remember Margaret very well now that she was back. She had looked after him when he was a baby. It was different then because he had been his mother's only child. Margaret liked to say that she was a 'general chatterbox' but in fact her

449

only subject was herself. His father said that she was an expert on 'the theory of dieting'. He was not sure what that was but it seemed to have made her very fat. To save money his parents weren't going to have a maternity nurse this time but they had changed their minds just before coming to France. They almost changed them back when the agency said that Margaret was the only one available at such short notice. 'I suppose she'll be an extra pair of hands,' his mother had said. 'If only they didn't come with the extra mouth,' said his father.

Robert had first met Margaret when he came back from the hospital after being born. He woke up in his parents' kitchen, jiggling up and down in her arms.

'I've changed His Majesty's nappy so he'll have a nice dry botty,' she said.

'Oh,' said his mother, 'thank you.'

He immediately felt that Margaret was different from his mother. Words drained out of her like an unplugged bath. His mother didn't really like talking but when she did talk it was like being held.

'Does he like his little cot?' said Margaret.

'I don't really know, he was with us in the bed last night.'

A quiet growl came out of Margaret. 'Hmmm,' she said, 'bad habits.'

'He wouldn't settle in his cot.'

'They never will if you take them into the bed.'

'"Never" is a long time. He was inside me until Wednesday evening; my instinct is to have him next to me for a while – do things gradually.'

'Well, I don't like to question your instincts, dear,' said Margaret, spitting the word out the moment it formed in her mouth, 'but in my forty years of *experience* I've had mothers thank me again and again for putting the baby down and leaving it in the cot. I had one mother, she's an Arab lady, actually, nice enough,

rang me only the other day in Botley and said, "I wish I'd listened to you, Margaret, and not taken Yasmin into the bed with
me. I can't do anything with her now." She wanted me back, but
I said, "I'm sorry, dear, but I'm starting a new job next week, and
I shall be going to the south of France for July to stay with the
baby's grandmother."'

Margaret tossed her head and strutted about the kitchen, a
downpour of crumbs tickling Robert's face. His mother said
nothing, but Margaret rumbled on.

'I don't think it's fair on the baby, apart from anything else –
they like to have their own little cot. Of course, I'm used to having
sole charge. It's usually *me* has them during the night.'

His father came into the room and kissed Robert on the
forehead.

'Good morning, Margaret,' he said. 'I hope you got some
sleep, because none of the rest of us did.'

'Yes, thank you, your sofa's quite comfortable, actually; not
that I shall be complaining when I have a room of my own at
your mother's.'

'I should hope not,' said his father. 'Are you all packed and
ready to go? Our taxi is coming any minute now.'

'Well, I haven't exactly had time to *un*pack, have I? Except for
my sun hat. I got that out in case it's blazing at the other end.'

'It's always blazing at the other end. My mother wouldn't
stand for anything less than catastrophic global warming.'

'Hmmm, we could do with a bit of global warming in Botley.'

'I wouldn't make that sort of remark if you want a good room
at the Foundation.'

'What's that, dear?'

'Oh, my mother's made a "Transpersonal Foundation".'

'Is the house not going to be yours, then?'

'No.'

'Do you hear that?' said Margaret, her waxen pallor looming

over Robert and spraying shortbread in his face with renewed vigour.

Robert could sense his father's irritation.

'He's far too cool to be worried about all that,' said his mother.

Everyone started to move about at the same time. Margaret, wearing her sun hat, took the lead, Robert's parents struggling behind with the luggage. They were taking him outside, where the light came from. He was amazed. The world was a birth room screaming with ambitious life. Branches climbing, leaves flickering, cumulonimbus mountains drifting, their melting edges curling in the light-flooded sky. He could feel his mother's thoughts, he could feel his father's thoughts, he could feel Margaret's thoughts.

'He loves the clouds,' said his mother.

'He can't see the clouds, dear,' said Margaret. 'They can't focus at his age.'

'He might still be looking at them without seeing them as we do,' said his father.

Margaret grunted as she got into the humming taxi.

He was lying still in his mother's lap, but the land and sky were slipping by outside the window. If he got involved in the moving scene he thought he was moving too. Light flashed on the windowpanes of passing houses, vibrations washed over him from all directions, and then the canyon of buildings broke open and a wedge of sunlight drifted across his face, turning his eyelids orange-pink.

They were on their way to his grandmother's house, the same house they were staying in now, a week after his brother's birth.

2

ROBERT WAS SITTING IN the window sill of his bedroom, playing with the beads he had collected on the beach. He had been
arranging them in every possible combination. Beyond his mosquito net (with its bandaged cut) was a mass of ripe leaves belonging to the big plane tree on the terrace. When the wind moved
through the leaves it made a sound like lips smacking. If a fire
broke out, he could climb out of the window and down those convenient branches. On the other hand, a kidnapper could climb up
them. He never used to think about the other hand; now he
thought about it all the time. His mother had told him that when
he was a baby he loved lying under that plane tree in his cot.
Thomas was lying there now, bracketed by his parents.

Margaret was leaving the next day – thank God, as his father
said. His parents had given her an extra day off, but she was already back from the village, bearing down on them with a deadly
bulletin. Robert waddled across the room pretending to be
Margaret and circled back to the window. Everyone said he did
amazing imitations; his headmaster went further and said that it
was a 'thoroughly sinister talent which I hope he will learn to
channel constructively.' It was true that once he was intrigued
by a situation, as he was by Margaret being back with his family,

he could absorb everything he wanted. He pressed against the mosquito net to get a better view.

'Ooh, it's that hot,' said Margaret, fanning herself with a knitting magazine. 'I couldn't find any of the cottage cheese in Bandol. They didn't speak a word of English in the supermarket. "Cottage cheese," I said, pointing to the house on the other side of the street, "cottage, you know, as in house, only smaller," but they still couldn't make head or tail of what I was saying.'

'They sound incredibly stupid,' said his father, 'with so many helpful clues.'

'Hmmm. I had to get some of the French cheeses in the end,' said Margaret, sitting down on the low wall with a sigh. 'How's the baby?'

'He seems very tired,' said his mother.

'I'm not surprised in this heat,' said Margaret. 'I think I must have got sunstroke on that boat, frankly. I'm done to a crisp. Give him plenty of water, dear. It's the only way to cool them down. They can't sweat at that age.'

'Another amazing oversight,' said his father. 'Can't sweat, can't walk, can't talk, can't read, can't drive, can't sign a cheque. Foals are standing a few hours after they're born. If horses went in for banking, they'd have a credit line by the end of the week.'

'Horses don't have any use for banking,' said Margaret.

'No,' said his father, exhausted.

In a moment of ecstatic song the cicadas drowned out Margaret's voice, and Robert felt he could remember exactly what it was like being in that cot, lying under the plane trees in a cool green shade, listening to the wall of cicada song collapse to a solitary call and escalate again to a dry frenzy. He let things rest where they fell, the sounds, the sights, the impressions. Things resolved themselves in that cool green shade, not because he knew how they worked, but because he knew his own thoughts and feelings without needing to explain them. And if he wanted to play with his thoughts, nobody could stop him. Just lying there in his cot, they couldn't tell whether he was doing anything dangerous. Sometimes he imagined he was the thing he was looking at, sometimes he imagined he was in the space in between, but the best was when he was just looking, without being anyone in particular or looking at anything in particular, and then he floated in the looking, like the breeze blowing without needing cheeks to blow or having anywhere particular to go.

His brother was probably floating right now in Robert's old cot. The grown-ups didn't know what to make of floating. That was the trouble with grown-ups: they always wanted to be the centre of attention, with their battering rams of food, and their sleep routines and their obsession with making you learn what they knew and forget what they had forgotten. Robert dreaded sleep. He might miss something: a beach of yellow beads, or grasshopper wings like sparks flying from his feet as he crunched through the dry grass.

He loved it down here at his grandmother's house. His family only came once a year, but they had been every year since he was born. Her house was a Transpersonal Foundation. He didn't really know what that was, and nobody else seemed to know either, even Seamus Dourke, who ran it.

'Your grandmother is a wonderful woman,' he had told Robert, looking at him with his dim twinkly eyes. 'She's helped a lot of people to connect.'

'With what?' asked Robert.

'With the other reality.'

Sometimes he didn't ask grown-ups what they meant because he thought it would make him seem stupid; sometimes it was because he knew they were being stupid. This time it was both. He thought about what Seamus had said and he didn't see how there could be more than one reality. There could only be different states of mind with reality housing all of them. That's what he had told his mother, and she said, 'You're so brilliant, darling,' but she wasn't really paying attention to his theories like she used to. She was always too busy now. What they didn't understand was that he really wanted to know the answer.

Back under the plane tree, his brother had started screaming. Robert wished someone would make him stop. He could feel his brother's infancy exploding like a depth charge in his memory. Thomas's screams reminded Robert of his own helplessness: the ache of his toothless gums, the involuntary twitching of his limbs, the softness of the fontanelle, only a thumb's thrust away from his growing brain. He felt that he could remember objects without names and names without objects pelting down on him all day long, but there was something he could only dimly sense: a world before the wild banality of childhood, before he had to be the first to rush out and spoil the snow, before he had even assembled himself into a viewer gazing at the white landscape through a bedroom window, when his mind had been level with the fields of silent crystal, still waiting for the dent of a fallen berry.

He had seen Thomas's eyes expressing states of mind which he couldn't have invented for himself. They reared up from the scrawny desert of his experience like brief pyramids. Where did they come from? Sometimes he was a snuffling little animal and then, seconds later, he was radiating an ancient calm, at ease with everything. Robert felt that he was definitely not making up these complex states of mind, and neither was Thomas. It was just that Thomas wouldn't know what he knew until he started to tell himself a story about what was happening to him. The trouble was that he was a baby, and he didn't have the attention span to tell himself a story yet. Robert was just going to have to do it for him. What was an older brother for? Robert was already caught in a narrative loop, so he might as well take his little

brother along with him. After all, in his way, Thomas was helping Robert to piece his own story together.

Outside, he could hear Margaret again, taking on the cicadas
and getting the upper hand.

'With the breast-feeding you've got to build yourself up,' she
started out reasonably enough. 'Have you not got any Digestive
biscuits? Or Rich Tea? We could have a few of those right away,
actually. And then you want to have a nice big lunch, with lots of
carbohydrates. Not too many vegetables, they'll give him wind.
Nice bit of roast beef and Yorkshire pudding is good, with
some roast potatoes, and then a slice or two of sponge cake at
tea time.'

'Good God, I don't think I can manage all that. In my book it
says grilled fish and grilled vegetables,' said his tired, thin, elegant
mother.

'*Some* vegetables are all right,' grumbled Margaret. 'Not onions
or garlic, though, or anything too spicy. I had one mother had a
curry on my day off! The baby was howling its head off when I got
back. "Save me, Margaret! Mummy's set my little digestive system on fire!" Personally, I always say, "I'll have the meat and two
veg, but don't worry too much about the veg."'

Robert had stuffed a cushion under his T-shirt and was tottering around the room pretending to be Margaret. Once his
head was jammed full of someone's words he had to get them
out. He was so involved in his performance that he didn't notice
his father coming into the room.

'What are you doing?' asked his father, half knowing already.

'I was just being Margaret.'

'That's all we need – another Margaret. Come down and
have some tea.'

'I'm that stuffed already,' said Robert, patting his cushion.
'Daddy, when Margaret leaves, I'll still be here to give Mummy

bad advice about how to look after babies. And I won't charge you anything.'

'Things are looking up,' said his father, holding out his hand to pull Robert up. Robert groaned and staggered across the floor and the two of them headed downstairs, sharing their secret joke.

After tea Robert refused to join the others outside. All they did was talk about his brother and speculate about his state of mind. Walking up the stairs, his decision grew heavier with each step, and by the time he reached the landing he was in two minds. Eventually, he sank to the floor and looked down through the banisters, wondering if his parents would notice his sad and wounded departure.

In the hall, angular blocks of evening light slanted across the floor and stretched up the walls. One piece of light, reflected in the mirror, had broken away and trembled on the ceiling. Thomas was trying to comment. His mother, who understood his thoughts, took him over to the mirror and showed him where the light bounced off the glass.

His father came into the hall and handed a bright red drink to Margaret.

'Ooh, thank you very much,' said Margaret. 'I shouldn't really get tipsy on top of my sunstroke. Frankly, this is more of a holiday for me than a job, with you being so involved and that. Oh, look, Baby's admiring himself in the mirror.' She leant the pink shine of her face towards Thomas.

'You can't tell whether you're over here or over there, can you?'

'I think he knows that he's in his body rather than stuck to a piece of glass,' said Robert's father. 'He hasn't read Lacan's essay on the mirror stage yet, that's when the real confusion sets in.'

'Ooh, well, you'd better stick to Peter Rabbit, then,' chuckled Margaret, taking a gulp of the red liquid.

'Much as I'd love to join you outside,' said his father, 'I have a million important letters to answer.'

'Ooh, Daddy's going to be answering his important letters,' said Margaret, breathing the red smell into Thomas's face. 'You'll just have to content yourself with Margaret and Mummy.'

She swung her way towards the front door. The lozenge of light disappeared from the ceiling and then flickered back. Robert's parents stared at each other silently.

As they stepped outside, he imagined his brother feeling the vast space around him.

He stole halfway down the stairs and looked through the doorway. A golden light was claiming the tops of the pines and the bone-white stones of the olive grove. His mother, still barefoot, walked over the grass and sat under their favourite pepper tree. Crossing her legs and raising her knees slightly, she placed his brother in the hammock formed by her skirt, still holding him with one hand and stroking his side with the other. Her face was dappled by the shadow of the small bright leaves that dangled around them.

Robert wandered hesitantly outside, not sure where he belonged. Nobody called him and so he turned round the corner of the house as if he had always meant to go down to the second pond and look at the goldfish. Glancing back, he saw the stick with sparkly wheels that Margaret had bought his brother at the little carousel in Lacoste. The stub of the stick had been planted in the ground near the pepper tree. The wheels spun in the wind, gold and pink and blue and green. 'It's the colour and the movement,' said Margaret when she bought it, 'they love that.' He had snatched it from the corner of his brother's pram and run around the carousel, making the wheels turn. When he was swishing it through the air he somehow broke the stick and everyone got upset on his brother's behalf because he never really got the chance to enjoy his sparkly windmill before it was broken. Robert's father had asked him a lot of questions, or rather the same question in a lot of different ways, as if it would do him good to admit that he had broken it on purpose. Do you think you're jealous? Do you think you're angry that he's getting all the attention and the new toys? Do you? Do you? Do you? Well, he had just said it was an accident and wouldn't budge. And it really was an accident, but it so happened that he did hate his brother, and he wished that he didn't. Couldn't his parents remember what it was like when it was just the three of them? They loved each other so much that it hurt when one of them left the room. What had been wrong with having just him on his own? Wasn't he enough? Wasn't he good enough? They used to sit on the lawn, where his brother was now, and throw each other the red ball (he had hidden it; Thomas wasn't going to get that as well) and whether he caught it or dropped it, they had all laughed and everything was perfect. How could they want to spoil that?

Maybe he was too old. Maybe babies were better. Babies were impressed by pretty well anything. Take the fish pond he was throwing pebbles into. He had seen his mother carrying Thomas to the edge of the pond and pointing to the fish, saying, 'Fish.' It was no use trying that sort of thing with Robert. What he couldn't help wondering was how his brother was supposed to know whether she meant the pond, the water, the weeds, the clouds reflected on the water, or the fish, if he could see them. How did he even know that 'Fish' was a thing rather than a colour or something that you do? Sometimes, come to think of it, it was something to do.

Once you got words you thought the world was everything that could be described, but it was also what couldn't be described. In a way things were more perfect when you couldn't describe anything. Having a brother made Robert wonder what it had been like when he only had his own thoughts to guide him. Once you locked into language, all you could do was shuffle the greasy pack of a few thousand words that millions of people had used before. There might be little moments of freshness, not because the life of the world has been successfully translated but because a new life has been made out of this thought stuff. But before the thoughts got mixed up with words, it wasn't as if the dazzle of the world hadn't been exploding in the sky of his attention.

Suddenly, he heard his mother scream.

'What have you done to him?' she shouted.

He sprinted round the corner of the terrace and met his father running out of the front door. Margaret was lying on the lawn, holding Thomas sprawled on her bosom.

'It's all right, dear, it's all right,' said Margaret. 'Look, he's even stopped crying. I took the fall, you see, on my bottom. It's my training. I think I may have broken my finger, but there's no need to worry about silly old Margaret as long as no harm has come to the baby.'

'That's the first sensible thing I've ever heard you say,' said his mother, who never said anything unkind. She lifted Thomas out of Margaret's arms and kissed his head again and again. She was taut with anger, but as she kissed him tenderness started to drown it out.

'Is he all right?' asked Robert.

'I think so,' said his mother.

'I don't want him to be hurt,' Robert said, and they walked back into the house together, leaving Margaret talking on the ground.

The next morning, they were all hiding from Margaret in his parents' bedroom. Robert's father had to drive Margaret to the airport that afternoon.

'I suppose we ought to go down,' said his mother, closing the poppers of Thomas's jumpsuit, and lifting him into her arms.

'No,' howled his father, throwing himself onto the bed.

'Don't be such a baby.'

'Having a baby makes you more childish, haven't you noticed?'

'I haven't got time to be more childish, that's a privilege reserved for fathers.'

'You would have time if you were getting any competent help.'

'Come on,' said Robert's mother, reaching out to his father with her spare hand.

He clasped it lightly but didn't move.

'I can't decide which is worse,' he said, 'talking to Margaret, or listening to her.'

'Listening to her,' Robert voted. 'That's why I'm going to do my Margaret imitation all the time after she's gone.'

'Thanks a lot,' said his mother. 'Look, even Thomas is smiling at such a mad idea.'

'That's not smiling, dear,' grumbled Robert, 'that's wind tormenting his little insides.'

They all started laughing and then his mother said, 'Shhh, she might hear us,' but it was too late, Robert was determined to entertain them. Swinging his body sideways to lubricate the forward motion, he rocked over to his mother's side.

'It's no use trying to blind me with science, dear,' he said, 'I can tell he doesn't like that formula you're giving him, even if it is made by organic goats. When I was in Saudi Arabia – she was a princess, actually – I said to them, "I can't work with this formula, I have to have the Cow and Gate Gold Standard," and they said to me, "With all your experience, Margaret, we trust you completely," and they had some flown out from England in their private jet.'

'How do you remember all this?' asked his mother. 'It's ter-rifying. I told her that we didn't have a private jet.'

'Oh, money was no object to them,' Robert went on, with a proud little toss of his head. 'One day I remarked, you know, quite *casually*, on how nice the Princess's slippers were, and the next thing I knew there was a pair waiting for me in my bed-room. The same thing happened with the Prince's camera. It was quite embarrassing, actually. Every time I did it, I'd say to myself, "Margaret, you must learn to keep your mouth shut."'

Robert wagged his finger in the air, and then sat down on the bed next to his father and carried on with a sad sigh.

'But then it would just pop out, you know: "Ooh, that's a lovely shawl, dear; lovely soft fabric," and sure enough I'd find one spread out on my bed that evening. I had to get a new suitcase in the end.'

His parents were trying not to make too much noise but they had hopeless giggles. As long as he was performing they hardly paid any attention to Thomas at all.

'Now it's even harder for us to go down,' said his mother, joining them on the bed.

'It's impossible,' said his father, 'there's a force field around the door.'

Robert ran up to the door and pretended to bounce back. 'Ah,' he shouted, 'it's the Margaret field. There's no way through, Captain.'

He rolled around on the floor for a while and then climbed back onto the bed with his parents.

'We're like the dinner guests in *The Exterminating Angel*,' said his father. 'We might be here for days. We might have to be res-cued by the army.'

'We've got to pull ourselves together,' said his mother. 'We must try to end her visit on a kind note.'

None of them moved.

'Why do you think it's so hard for us to leave?' asked his father. 'Do you think we're using Margaret as a scapegoat? We feel guilty that we can't protect Thomas from the basic suffering of life, so we pretend that Margaret is the cause – something like that.'

'Let's not complicate it, darling,' said his mother. 'She's the most boring person we've ever met and she's no good at looking after Thomas. That's why we don't want to see her.'

Silence. Thomas had fallen asleep, and so there was a general agreement to keep quiet. They all settled comfortably on the bed. Robert stretched out and rested his head on his folded hands, scanning the beams of the ceiling. Familiar patterns of stains and knots emerged from the woodwork. At first he could take or leave the profile of the man with the pointed nose and the helmet, but soon the figure refused to be dissolved back into the grain, acquiring wild eyes and hollow cheeks. He knew the ceiling well, because he used to lie underneath it when it was his grandmother's bedroom. His parents had moved in after his grandmother was taken to the nursing home. He still remembered the old silver-framed photograph that used to be on her desk. He had been curious about it because it was taken when his grandmother had been only a few days old. The baby in the picture was smothered in pelts and satin and lace, her head bound in a beaded turban. Her eyes had a fanatical intensity that looked to him like panic at being buried in the immensity of her mother's shopping.

'I keep it here,' his grandmother had told him, 'to remind me of when I had just come into the world and I was closer to the source.'

'What source?' he asked.

'Closer to God,' she said shyly.

'But you don't look very happy,' he said.

'I think I look as if I haven't forgotten yet. But in a way

you're right, I don't think I've ever really got used to being on the material plane.'

'What material plane?'

'The Earth,' she said.

'Would you rather live on the moon?' he had asked.

She smiled and stroked his cheek and said, 'You'll understand one day.'

Instead of the photograph, there was a changing mat on the desk now, with a stack of nappies next to it and a bowl of water.

He still loved his grandmother, even if she was not leaving them the house. Her face was a cobweb of creases earned from trying so hard to be good, from worrying about really huge things like the planet, or the universe, or the millions of suffering people she had never met, or God's opinion of what she should do next. He knew his father didn't think she was good, and discounted how badly she wanted to be. He kept telling Robert that they must love his grandmother 'despite everything'. That was how Robert knew that his father didn't love her any more.

'Will he remember that fall for the rest of his life?' Robert asked, staring at the ceiling.

'Of course not,' said his father. 'You can't remember what happened to you when you were a few weeks old.'

'Yes I can,' said Robert.

'We must all reassure him,' said his mother, changing the subject as if she didn't want to point out that Robert was lying. But he wasn't lying.

'He doesn't need reassuring,' said his father. 'He wasn't actually hurt, and so he can't tell that he shouldn't be bouncing off Margaret's floundering body. We're the ones who are freaked out, because we know how dangerous it was.'

'That's why he needs reassuring,' said his mother, 'because he can tell that we're upset.'

'Yes, at that level,' his father agreed, 'but in general babies live in a democracy of strangeness. Things happen for the first time all the time – what's surprising is things happening again.'

Babies are great, thought Robert. You can invent more or less anything about them because they never answer back.

'It's twelve o'clock,' his father sighed.

They all struggled with their reluctance, but the effort to escape seemed to drag them deeper into the quicksand of the mattress. He wanted to delay his parents just a little longer.

'Sometimes,' he began dreamily in his Margaret voice, 'when I'm stopped at home for a couple of weeks between jobs, I get itchy fingers. I'm that keen to lay my hands on another baby.' He grabbed hold of Thomas's feet and made a devouring sound.

'Gently,' said Robert's mother.

'He's right, though,' said his father, 'she's got a baby habit. She needs them more than they need her. Babies are allowed to be unconscious and greedy, so she uses them for camouflage.'

After all the moral effort they had put in to conceding another hour of their lives to Margaret, they felt cheated when they found that she wasn't waiting for them downstairs. His mother went off to the kitchen and he sat with his father on the sofa with Thomas between them. Thomas fell silent and became absorbed in staring at the picture on the wall immediately above the sofa. Robert moved his head down beside Thomas's and as he looked up he could tell from the angle that Thomas couldn't see the picture itself, because of the glass that protected it. He remembered being fascinated by the same thing when he was a baby. As he looked at the image reflected in the glass, it drew him deeper into the space behind him. In the reflection was the doorway, a brilliant and perfect miniature, and through the doorway the still smaller, but in fact larger, oleander bush outside, its flowers tiny pink lights on the surface of the glass. His attention was funnelled towards the vanishing point of sky between the oleander branches, and then his imagination expanded into the real sky beyond it, so that his mind was like two cones tip to tip. He was there with Thomas, or rather, Thomas was there with him, riding to infinity on that little patch of light. Then he noticed that the flowers had disappeared and a new image filled the doorway.

'Margaret's here,' he said.

His father turned around while Robert watched her plaintive bulk roll towards them. She came to a halt a few feet away from them.

'No harm done,' she said, half asking.

'He seems OK,' said his father.

'This won't affect my reference, will it?'

'What reference?' asked his father.

'Oh, I see,' said Margaret, half wounded, half angry, all dignified.

'Shall we have lunch?' said his father.

'I shan't be needing any lunch, thank you very much,' said Margaret.

She turned towards the staircase and began her laborious climb.

Suddenly, Robert couldn't bear it any longer.

'Poor Margaret,' he said.

'Poor Margaret,' said his father. 'What will we do without her?'

3

ROBERT WAS WATCHING AN ant disappear behind the sweating bottle of white wine on the stone table. The condensation suddenly streaked down the side of the bottle, smoothing the beaded surface in its wake. The ant reappeared, magnified through the pale green glass, its legs knitting frantically as it sampled a glittering grain of sugar spilt by Julia when she had sweetened her coffee after lunch. The sound of the cicadas billowed around them in and out of time with the limp flapping of the canvas awning over their heads. His mother was having a siesta with Thomas, and Lucy was watching a video, but he had stayed behind, despite Julia almost forcing him to join Lucy.

'Most people wait for their parents to die with a mixture of tremendous sadness and plans for a new swimming pool,' his father was saying to Julia. 'Since I'm going to have to renounce the swimming pool, I thought I might ditch the sadness as well.'

'But couldn't you pretend to be a shaman and keep this place?' said Julia.

'Alas, I'm one of the few people on the planet with absolutely no healing powers. I know that everyone else has just discovered their inner shaman, but I remain trapped in my materialistic conception of the universe.'

'There's such a thing as hypocrisy, you know,' said Julia. 'There's a shop round the corner from me called the Rainbow Path, I could get you a drum and some feathers.'

'I can already feel the power surging into my fingertips,' said his father, yawning. 'I, too, have a special gift to offer the tribe. I didn't realize until now that I have incredible psychic powers.'

'There you go,' said Julia encouragingly, 'you'll be running the place in no time.'

'I have enough trouble looking after my family without saving the world.'

'Looking after children can be a subtle way of giving up,' said Julia, smiling at Robert sternly. 'They become the whole ones, the well ones, the postponement of happiness, the ones who won't drink too much, give up, get divorced, become mentally ill. The part of oneself that's fighting against decay and depression is transferred to guarding them from decay and depression. In the meantime one decays and gets depressed.'

'I disagree,' said his father, 'when you're just fighting for yourself it's defensive and grim.'

'Very useful qualities,' Julia interrupted him. 'That's why it's important not to treat children too well – they won't be able to compete in the real world. If you want your children to become television producers, for instance, or chief executives, it's no use filling their little heads with ideas of trust and truth-telling and reliability. They'll just end up being somebody's secretary.'

Robert decided to ask his mother whether this was true, or whether Julia was being – well, like Julia. She came to stay every year with Lucy, her quite stuck-up daughter a year older than Robert. He knew his mother wasn't wild about Julia, because she was an old girlfriend of his father's. She felt a little bit jealous of her, but also a little bit bored. Julia didn't know how to stop wanting people to think she was clever. 'Really clever people are just thinking aloud,' his mother had told him, 'Julia is thinking about what she sounds like.'

Julia was always trying to throw Robert and Lucy together. The day before, Lucy had tried to kiss him. That was why he didn't want to watch a video with her. He doubted that his front teeth would survive another collision like that. The theory that it was good for him to spend time with children of his own age, even if he didn't like them, ground on. Would his father ask a woman to tea just because she was forty?

Julia was playing with the sugar again, spooning it back and forth in the bowl.

'Since divorcing Richard,' she said, 'I get these horrible moments of vertigo. I suddenly feel as if I don't exist.'

'I get that!' said Robert, excited that they had chosen a subject he knew something about.

'At your age,' said Julia, 'I think that's very pretentious. Are you sure you haven't just heard grown-ups talking about it?'

'No,' he said, in his dazed by injustice voice, 'I get it all on my own.'

'I think you're being unfair,' said his father to Julia. 'Robert has always had a capacity for horror well beyond his years. It doesn't interfere with his being a happy child.'

'Well, it does, actually,' he corrected his father, 'when it's going on.'

'Ah, when it's going on,' his father conceded with a gentle smile.

'I see,' said Julia, resting her hand on Robert's. 'In that case, welcome to the club, darling.'

He didn't want to be a member of Julia's club. He felt prickly all over his body because he wanted to take his hand away but didn't want to be rude.

'I always thought children were simpler than us,' said Julia, removing her hand and placing it on his father's forearm. 'We're like ice-breakers crashing our way towards the next object of desire.'

'What could be simpler than crashing one's way towards the next object of desire?' asked his father.

'*Not* crashing one's way towards it.'

'That's renunciation – not as simple as it looks.'

'It's only renunciation if you have the desire in the first place,' said Julia.

'Children have plenty of desire in the first place,' said his father, 'but I think you're right, it's essentially one desire: to be close to the people they love.'

'The normal ones want to watch *Raiders of the Lost Ark* as well,' said Julia.

'We're more easily distracted,' said his father, ignoring her last remark, 'more used to a culture of substitution, more easily confused about exactly who we do love.'

'Are we?' said Julia, smiling. 'That's nice.'

'Up to a point,' said his father.

He didn't really know what they were talking about now, but Julia seemed to have cheered up. Substitution must be something pretty wonderful. Before he got the chance to ask what it meant, a voice, a caring Irish voice, called out.

'Hello? Hello?'

'Oh, Christ,' muttered his father, 'it's the boss.'

'Patrick!' said Seamus warmly, walking towards them in a shirt covered in palm trees and rainbows. 'Robert,' he greeted him, ruffling his hair vigorously. 'Pleased to meet you,' he said to Julia, fixing her with his candid blue eyes and his firm handshake. Nobody could accuse him of not being friendly.

'Oh, it's a lovely spot here,' he said, 'lovely. We often sit out here after a session, with everyone laughing or crying, or just being with themselves, you know. This is definitely a power point, a place of tremendous release. That's right,' he sighed, as if agreeing with someone else's wise insight, 'I've seen people let go of a lot of stuff here.'

'Talking of "letting go of a lot of stuff",' his father handed the phrase back to Seamus, held by the corner like someone else's used handkerchief, 'when I opened the drawer of my bedside table I found it so full of "Healing Drum" brochures that there was no room for my passport. There are also several hundred copies of *The Way of the Shaman* in my wardrobe which are getting in the way of the shoes.'

'The Way of the Shoes,' said Seamus, letting out a great roar of healthy laughter, 'now that would be a good title for a book about, you know, staying grounded.'

'Do you think that these signs of institutional life,' continued his father coldly, rapidly, 'could be removed before we come down here on holiday? After all, my mother does want the house to return each August to its incarnation as a family home.'

'Of course, of course,' said Seamus. 'I apologize, Patrick. That'll be Kevin and Anette. They were going through a very powerful personal process, you know, before going back to Ireland on holiday, and they obviously weren't thorough enough in getting things ready for you.'

'Are you also going back to Ireland?' his father asked.

'No, I'll be in the cottage through August,' said Seamus. 'The Pegasus Press have asked me to write a short book about the shamanic work.'

'Oh, really,' said Julia, 'how fascinating. Are you a shaman yourself?'

'I had a look at the book that was in the way of my shoes,' said his father, 'and some obvious questions spring to mind. Have you spent twenty years being the disciple of a Siberian witch doctor? Have you gathered rare plants under the full moon during the brief summer? Have you been buried alive and died to the world?

Have your eyes watered in the smoke of campfires while you muttered prayers to the spirits who might help you to save a dying man? Have you drunk the urine of caribou who have grazed on outcrops of *Amanita muscaria* and journeyed into other worlds to solve the mystery of a difficult diagnosis? Or did you study in Brazil with the *ayahuascaras* of the Amazon basin?'

'Well,' said Seamus, 'I trained as a nurse with the Irish National Health.'

'I'm sure that was an adequate substitute for being buried alive,' said his father.

'I worked in a nursing home for many years, doing the basics, you know: washing patients who were covered in their own faeces and urine; spoon-feeding old people who couldn't feed themselves any more.'

'Please,' said Julia, 'we've only just finished our lunch.'

'That was my reality at the time,' said Seamus. 'I sometimes wondered why I hadn't gone on to university and got the medical qualifications, but looking back I'm grateful for those years in the nursing home – they've helped to keep me grounded. When I discovered the Holotropic Breathwork and went to California to study with Stan Grof, I met some pretty out-there people, you know. I remember one particular lady, wearing a sunset-coloured dress, and she stood up and said, "I am Tamara from the Vega system, and I have come to the Earth to heal and to teach." Well, at that point, I thought about the old people in the home in Ireland and I was grateful to them for keeping my feet firmly planted on the ground.'

'Is holo . . . whatever you called it, a shamanic thing?' asked Julia.

'No, not really. That's what I was doing before I got into the shamanic work, but it all ties in, you know. It gets people in touch with that something beyond, that other dimension. When people touch that, it can trigger a radical change in their lives.'

'But I don't understand why this counts as a charity. People pay to come here, don't they?' said Julia.

'They do, they do,' said Seamus, 'but we recycle the profits, you see, so as to give scholarships to students like Kevin and Anette who are learning the shamanic work. And they've started to bring groups of inner-city kids from the estates in Dublin. We let them attend the courses for free, you know, and it's a wonderful thing to see the transformations. They love the trance music and the drumming. They come up to me and say, "Seamus, this is incredible, it's like tripping without the drugs," and they take that message back to the inner city and start up shamanic groups of their own.'

'Do we need a charity for tripping?' asked his father. 'Of all the ills in the world, the fact that there are a few people who are not tripping seems a wild hole to plug. Besides, if people want to trip, why not give them a strong dose of acid, instead of messing about with drums?'

'You can tell he's a barrister,' said Seamus amiably.

'I'm all for people having hobbies,' said his father. 'I just think they should explore them in the comfort of their own homes.'

'Sadly, Patrick,' said Seamus, 'some homes are not that comfortable.'

'I know the feeling,' said his father. 'Which reminds me, do you think we could clear out some of those books, advertisements, brochures, bric-a-brac'

'Surely,' said Seamus, 'surely.'

His father and Seamus got up to leave and Robert realized that he was going to be left alone with Julia.

'I'll help,' he said, following them round the terrace. His father led the way into the hall and stopped almost immediately.

'These fluttering leaflets,' he said, 'advertising other centres, other institutes, healing circles, advanced drumming courses – they're really wasted on us. In fact, this whole noticeboard,' he continued, unhooking it from the wall, 'despite its attractive cork surface and its multicoloured drawing pins, might as well not be here.'

'No problem,' said Seamus, embracing the notice-board.

Although his father's manner remained supremely controlled, Robert could feel that he was intoxicated with rage and contempt. Seamus clouded over when Robert tried to make out what he was feeling, but eventually he groped his way to the terrible conclusion that Seamus pitied his father. Knowing that he was in charge, Seamus could afford to indulge the fury of a betrayed child. His repulsive pity saved him from feeling the impact of Patrick's fury, but Robert found himself caught between the punchbag and the punch and, feeling frightened and useless, he slipped out of the front door, while his father marched Seamus on to the next offence.

Outside, the shadow of the house was spreading to the flower beds on the edge of the terrace, indicating to some effortless part of his mind that the middle of the afternoon had arrived. The cicadas scratched on. He could see without looking, hear without listening; he was aware that he was not thinking. His attention, which usually bounced from one thing to another, was still. He pushed to test its resistance but he didn't push too hard, knowing that he could probably make himself pinball around again if he tried. His mind was glazed over, like a pond drowsily repeating the pattern of the sky.

The funny thing was that by imagining a pond he had started disturbing the trance it was being compared to. Now he wanted to go to the pond at the top of the steps, a stone semicircle of water at the end of the drive, where the goldfish would be hiding under a shield of reflection. That was right; he didn't want to go round the house with his father and Seamus, he wanted to scatter bread on the water to see if he could make that slippery Catherine wheel of orange fish break the surface. He ran into the kitchen and grabbed a piece of old bread before sprinting up the steps to the pond.

His father had told him that in winter the source gushed out of the pipe and thundered down among the darting fish; it over-flowed into the lower ponds and eventually into the stream that ran along the crease of the valley. He wished he could see that one day. By August the pond was only half full. The algae-bearded pipe dripped into greenish water. Wasps and hornets and drag-onflies crowded its warm dusty surface, resting on the water-lily pads for a safer drink. The goldfish were invisible unless tempted by food. The best method was to rub two pieces of stale bread together until they disintegrated into fine dry crumbs. Pellets of bread just sank, but the crumbs were held on the surface like dust. The most beautiful fish, the one he really wanted to see, had red and white patches on its skin. The others were all shades of orange, apart from a few small black ones which must either turn orange later on, or die out, because there were no big black ones.

He broke the bread and grated the two halves, watching a rain of light crumbs land on the water and spread out. Nothing happened.

The truth was that he had only seen the swirling frenzy of fish once, and since then either nothing had happened or a soli-tary fish fed lazily under the wobbling sinking crumbs.

'Fish! Fish! Fish! Come on! Fish! Fish! Fish!'

'Are you calling to your power animal?' said a voice behind him.

He stopped abruptly and swung round. Seamus was standing there, smiling at him benevolently, his tropical shirt blazing in the sun.

'Fish! Fish! Fish!' Seamus called.

'I was just feeding them,' mumbled Robert.

'Do you feel you have a special connection with fish?' Seamus asked him, leaning in closer. 'That's what a power animal is, you know. It helps you on your journey through life.'

'I just like them being fish,' said Robert. 'They don't have to do anything for me.'

'Now fish, for instance, bring us messages from the depths, from under the surface of things.' Seamus wriggled his hand through the air. 'Ah, it's a magical land here,' said Seamus, pushing his elbows back and twisting his neck from side to side with his eyes closed. 'My own personal power point, you know, is up there in the little wood, by the bird bath. Do you know the spot? It was your grandmother first pointed it out to me, it was a special place for her too. The first time I did a journey here, that's where I connected with the non-ordinary reality.'

Robert suddenly realized, and as he realized it he also saw its inevitability, that he loathed Seamus.

Seamus cupped his hands around his mouth and howled, 'Fish! Fish! Fish!'

Robert wanted to kill him. If he had a car he would run him over. If he had an axe he would cut him down.

He heard the upper door of the house being opened, and then the mosquito door squeaking open as well and out came his mother, holding Thomas in her arms.

'Oh, it's you. Hello, Seamus,' said his mother politely. 'We were half asleep, and I couldn't work out why a travelling fishmonger was bellowing outside the window.'

'We were, you know, invoking the fish,' said Seamus.

Robert ran over to his mother. She sat down with him on the low wall around the edge of the pond, away from where Seamus was standing, and tilted Thomas so he could see the water. Robert really hoped the fish didn't come to the surface now, or Seamus would probably think he had made it happen with his special powers. Poor Thomas, he might never see the orange swirl, he might never see the big fish with red and white patches. Seamus was taking away the pond and the wood and the bird bath and the whole landscape from him. In fact, when you thought about it, Thomas had been attacked by his own grandmother from the moment he was born. She wasn't a grandmother at all; more like a stepmother in a fairy tale, cursing him in his cot. How could she have shown Seamus the bird bath in the wood? He patted Thomas's head protectively. Thomas started to laugh, his surprisingly deep gurgling laugh, and Robert realized that his brother didn't really know about these things that were driving Robert crazy, and that he needn't know, unless Robert told him.

4

JOSH PACKER WAS A boy in Robert's class at school. He had decided (all on his own) that they were best friends. Nobody else could understand why they were inseparable, least of all Robert. If he could have broken away from Josh for long enough he would definitely have made another best friend, but Josh followed Robert round the playground, copied out his spelling tests, and dragged him back to his house for tea. All Josh did outside school was watch television. He had sixty-five channels, whereas Robert only had the free ones. Josh's parents were very rich, so he often had amazing new toys before anyone else had even heard of them. For his last birthday he had been given a real electric jeep, with a DVD player and a miniature television. He drove it round the garden, squashing the flowers and trying to run over Arnie, his dog. Eventually, he crashed into a bush and he and Robert sat in the rain watching the miniature television. When he came round to Robert's flat he said how pathetic the toys were and complained that he was bored. Robert tried to make up games with him but he didn't know how to make things up. He just pretended to be a television character for about three seconds, and then fell over and shouted, 'I'm dead.'

Jilly, Josh's mother, had telephoned the day before to say that she and Jim had rented a fabulous house in Saint-Tropez for the whole of August, and why didn't Robert's family come over for a day of fun and games. His parents said it would be good for him to spend a day with someone of his own age. They said it would be an adventure for them as well, because they had only met Josh's parents once, at the school sports day. Even then Jim and Jilly were too busy making rival movies of Josh's races to talk much. Jilly showed them how her videocam could make the whole thing go in slow motion, which wasn't really necessary as Josh came in last anyway.

Now that they were actually on their way, Robert's father was ranting at the wheel of the car. He seemed to be much grumpier since Julia had left. He couldn't believe that they were spending a day of their precious holiday in a traffic jam, in a heatwave, crawling into this 'world-famous joke of a town'.

Robert was sitting next to Thomas, who was in his old baby chair facing the wrong way, with only the stained fabric of the back seat to entertain him. Robert made barking noises as he climbed Thomas's leg with a small toy dog. Thomas couldn't have been less interested. Why should he be? thought Robert. He hasn't seen a real dog yet. Mind you, if he was only curious about things he'd seen before, he'd still be trapped in a whirlpool of birth-room lights.

When they finally found the right street, Robert was the one who spotted the tilted script of '*Les Mimosas*' scrawled across a rustic tile. They thrummed down the ribbed concrete to a parking lot already congested with Jim's private motor show: a black Range Rover, a red Ferrari and an old cream convertible with cracked leather seats and bulbous chrome fenders. His father found a space for their Peugeot next to a giant cactus, its serrated tongues sticking out in every direction.

'A neo-Roman villa decorated by a disciple of Gauguin's syphilitic twilight,' said his father. 'What more could one ask?' He slipped into his golden advertising voice, 'Situated in St Tro-pay's most prestigious gated community, only six hours' drive from Brigitte Bardot's legendary pet cemetery—'

'Sweetheart,' interrupted his mother.

There was a tap on the window.

'Jim!' said his father warmly, as he wound down the window.

'We're just off to buy some inflatables for the pool,' said Jim, lowering the videocam with which he'd been filming their arrival. 'Does Robert want to come along?'

Robert glanced at Josh slumped in the back of the Range Rover. He could tell that he was playing with his GameBoy.

'No, thanks,' he said. 'I'll help unpack the car.'

'You've got him well trained, haven't you?' said Jim. 'Jilly's poolside, catching some rays. Just follow the garden path.'

They walked through a whitewashed colonnade daubed with Pacific murals, and down a spongy lawn towards the pool, per-fectly concealed under a flotilla of inflatable giraffes, fire en-gines, footballs, racing cars, hamburgers, Mickeys, Minnies and Goofys, his father lopsided by the baby chair in which Thomas still slept, and his mother like a mule, her sides bulging with bags. Jilly lay stunned on a white and yellow sunbed, flanked by two glistening strangers, all three of them in wigs of Walkman and mobile-phone wires. His father's shadow roused Jilly as it fell across her baking face.

'Hi, there!' she said, unhooking her headphones. 'I'm sorry, I was in a world of my own.'

She got up to greet her guests, but was soon staggering back-wards, staring at Thomas, a hand sprawled over her heart.

'Oh, my God,' she gasped, 'your new one is beautiful. I'm sorry, Robert,' she dug her long shiny nails into his shoulders to help steady him, 'I don't want to fan the flames of sibling rivalry, but your little brother is something really special. Aren't you a spe-cial one?' she said, swooping down towards Thomas. 'He's going to make you dead jealous,' she warned his mother, 'with all the girls throwing themselves at his feet. Look at those eyelashes! Are you going to have another one? If mine looked like that, I'd have at least six. I sound greedy, don't I? But I can't help it, he's so love-ly. He's made me forget myself, I haven't introduced you to Christine and Roger yet. As if they cared. Look at them, they're in a world of their own. Go on, wake up!' She pretended to kick Roger. 'Roger's a business partner of Jim's,' she filled them in, 'and Christine's from Australia. She's four months pregnant.'

She shook Christine awake.

'Oh, hi,' said Christine, 'have they arrived?'

Jilly introduced everybody.

'I was just telling them about the pregnancy,' she explained to Christine.

'Oh, yeah. Actually, I think we're in major denial about it,' said Christine. 'I just feel a little heavier, that's all, as if I'd drunk four litres of Evian, or something. I mean, I don't even feel sick in the mornings. The other day Roger said, "Do you wanna go skiing in January? I've got to be in Switzerland on business any-way," and I said, "Sure, why not?" We'd both forgotten that that's the week I'm supposed to be giving birth!'

Jilly hooted with laughter and rolled her eyes skywards.

'I mean, is that absent-minded, or what?' said Christine. 'Mind you, pregnancy really does your brain in.'

'Look at them,' said Jilly, pointing to Robert's mother and father, 'they're absolutely gobsmacked – they're loving parents.'

'So are we,' protested Christine. 'You know how we are with Megan. Megan's our two-year-old,' she explained to the guests. 'We've left her with Roger's mother. She's just discovered rage – you know the way they discover emotions and then work them for all they're worth, until they get on to the next one.'

'How interesting,' said Robert's father, 'so you don't think emotions have anything to do with how a child is feeling – they're just layers in an archaeological dig. When do they discover joy?'

'When you take them to Legoland,' said Christine.

Roger woke up groggily, clasping his earpiece.

'Oh, hi. Sorry, I've got a call.'

He got up and started to pace the lawn.

'Have you brought your nanny?' asked Jilly.

'We haven't got one,' said Robert's mother.

'That's brave,' said Jilly. 'I don't know what I'd do without Jo. She's only been with us a week and she's already part of the family. You can dump your lot on her, she's marvellous.'

'We quite like looking after them ourselves,' said his mother.

'Jo!' shouted Jilly. 'Jo-o-euh!'

'Tell them it's a mixed leisure portfolio,' said Roger. 'Don't give them any more details at this stage.'

'Jo!' Jilly called again. 'Lazy bitch. She spends the whole day gawping at *Hello!* magazine and eating Ben & Jerry's ice cream. A bit like her employer, you might say, hem-hem, but it's costing me a fortune, whereas *she's* getting paid.'

'I don't care what they told Nigel,' said Roger, 'it's none of their bloody business. They can keep their noses out of it.'

Jim came striding down the lawn, glowing with successful shopping. Tubby Josh followed behind, a tangle of dragging feet. Jim got out a foot-pump and unfolded the plastic skin of another inflatable on the flagstones next to the pool.

'What did you get him?' asked Jilly, staring furiously at the house.

'You know he had his heart set on the ice-cream cone,' said Jim, pumping up a strawberry Cornetto. 'And I got him the Lion King.'

'And the machine gun,' said Josh pedantically.

'Inland Revenue,' said Jim to Robert's father, jerking his chin towards Roger, 'breathing down his neck. He may want some legal advice over lunch.'

'I don't work when I'm on holiday,' said his father.

'You don't work much when you're not on holiday,' said Robert's mother.

'Oh dear, do I detect marital conflict?' said Jim, filming the strawberry Cornetto as it unwrinkled on the ground.

'Jo!' screamed Jilly.

'I'm here,' called a big freckly girl in khaki shorts emerging from the house. The words 'Up For It' danced on the front of her T-shirt as she bobbed down the lawn.

Thomas woke up screaming. Who could blame him? The last thing he knew he had been in the car with his lovely family, and now he was surrounded by shouting strangers with blacked-out eyes; a nervous herd of monsters jostling brightly in the chlorinated air, another one swelling at his feet. Robert couldn't stand it either.

'Who's a hungry young man?' said Jo, leaning in on Thomas. 'Oh, he's beautiful, isn't he?' she said to Robert's mother. 'He's an old soul, you can tell.'

'Get these two parked in front of a video,' said Jilly, 'so we can have a bit of peace and quiet. And send Gaston down with a bottle of rosé. You'll love Gaston,' she told Robert's mother. 'He's a genius. A real old-fashioned French chef. I've put on about three stone since we arrived, and that was only a week ago. Never mind. We've got Heinrich coming to the rescue this afternoon – he's the personal trainer, great big German hunk, gives you a proper old workout. You should join me, help to get your figure back after the pregnancy. Not that you don't look great.'

'Is that what you want,' his mother asked Robert, 'to watch a video?'

'Yeah, sure,' he said, desperate to get away.

'It's difficult to see how he could swim,' admitted his father, 'with all the inflatable food in the pool.'

'Come on!' said Jo, sticking a hand out on each side. She seemed to think that Josh and Robert were going to take a hand each and skip up the hill with her.

'Isn't anybody going to hold my hand?' howled Jo, in a fit of mock blubbing.

Josh joined his pudgy palm with hers, but Robert managed to stay free, following at a little distance, fascinated by Jo's pouting khaki bottom.

'We're entering the video cave,' said Jo, making spooky noises. 'Right! What are you two going to watch? And I don't want any fighting.'

'*The Adventures of Sinbad*,' shouted Josh.

'Again! Crikey!' said Jo, and Robert couldn't help agreeing with her. He liked to watch a good video five or six times, but when he knew all the dialogue by heart and each shot was like a drawer full of identical socks, he started to feel a twinge of reluctance. Josh was different. He started out with a sort of sullen greed for a new video and only developed real enthusiasm somewhere around the twentieth viewing. Love, an emotion he didn't throw around lightly, was reserved for *The Adventures of Sinbad*, now seen over a hundred times, far too many of them with Robert. Videos were Josh's daydreams, Robert's daydream was solitude. How could he escape from the video cave? When you're a child nobody leaves you alone. If he ran away now, they would send out a search party, round him up and entertain him to death. Maybe he could just lie there and think while Josh's borrowed imagination flickered on the wall. The whine of the rewind was slowing down and Josh had collapsed back into the dent already made by his breakfast viewing and resumed munching the bright orange cheese puffs scattered on the table next to him. Jo started the tape, switched off the light and left discreetly. Josh was no fast-forward vandal: the warning about video piracy, the pre-views of films he had already seen, the plugs for merchandised toys he had already discarded and the message from the Video Standards Authority were not allowed to rush past like so many ugly suburbs before a train breaks out into the bovine melan-choly of true countryside; they were appreciated in their own right, granted their own dignity, which suited Robert fine, since the rubbish now pouring from the screen was too familiar to make any impact on his attention at all.

He closed his eyes and let the pool-side inferno dissipate. After a few hours of other people, he had to get the pile-up of impressions out of him one way or another; by doing imperson-ations, or working out how things worked, or just trying to empty his mind. Otherwise the impressions built up to a critical density and he felt as if he was going to explode.

Sometimes, when he was lying in bed, a single word like 'fear' or 'infinity' flicked the roof off the house and sucked him into the night, past the stars that had been bent into bears and ploughs, and into a pure darkness where everything was annihilated ex-cept the feeling of annihilation. As the little capsule of his intel-ligence disintegrated, he went on feeling its burning edges, its fragmenting hull, and when the capsule flew apart he was the bits flying apart, and when the bits turned into atoms he was the fly-ing apart itself, growing stronger instead of fading, like an evil energy defying the running out of everything and feeding on waste, and soon enough the whole of space was a waste-fuelled rush and there was no place in it for a human mind; but there he was, still feeling.

He would reel down the corridor to his parents' bedroom, choking. He would do anything to make it stop, sign any con-tract, take any vow, but he knew it was useless, he knew that he had seen something true, that he couldn't change it, only ignore it for a while, cry in his mother's arms, and let her put the roof back on and introduce him to some kinder words.

It was not that he was unhappy. It was just that he had seen something and sometimes it was truer than anything else. He first saw it when his grandmother had a stroke. He hadn't wanted to abandon her but she could hardly speak and so he had spent a lot of time imagining what she was feeling. Everybody said you had to be loyal, so he stuck at it. He held her hand for a long time and she gripped his. He didn't like it but he didn't let go. He could tell that she was frightened. Her eyes were dimmed. Part of her was relieved: she had always had trouble communicating, now nobody expected her to make the effort. Part of her was already gone, back to the source, perhaps, or at least far from the material plane about which she had such chronic doubts. What he could get close to was the part of her that was left behind wondering, now that she couldn't help keeping them, if she wanted all those secrets after all. Illness had blown her apart like a dandelion clock. He had wondered if he would end up like that, a few seeds sticking to a broken stem.

'This is my favourite bit,' said Josh, love-struck. Pirates were boarding Sinbad's ship. The ship's parrot flew in the face of the meanest-looking pirate. He staggered around disoriented and was effortlessly tipped overboard by Sinbad's men. Shot of pleased parrot squawking.

'Hmm,' said Robert. 'Listen, I'll be back in a minute.'

Josh paid no attention to his departure. Robert scanned the corridor for Jo, but she was not there. He retraced the route they had come in by, and when he got to the garden door, saw that the grown-ups were no longer around the pool. He slipped outside and hooked round to the back of the house. The tailored lawn petered out to a carpet of pine needles and a couple of big dustbins. He sat down and leant back against the ridged bark of the pine, unsupervised.

He wondered who was wasting the most time by spending a day with the Packers, not counting the Packers themselves who were always wasting more time than anybody, and usually had a film to prove it. Thomas was only sixty days old, so it was the biggest waste of time for him, because one day was one-sixtieth of his life, whereas his father, who was forty, was wasting the smallest proportion of his life. Robert tried to work out what proportion of their lives a day was for each of them. The calculations were hard to hold in his mind, so he imagined different sizes of wheels in a clock. Then he wondered how to include the opposite facts: that Thomas had his whole life ahead of him, whereas his parents had quite a lot of theirs behind them, so that one day was less wasteful for Thomas because he had more days left. That created a new set of wheels – red instead of silver – his father's spinning round and Thomas's turning with a stately infrequent click. He still had to include the different qualities of suffering and the different benefits for each of them, but that made his machine fantastically complicated and so, in one salutary sweep, he decided that they were all suffering equally, and that none of them had got anything out of it at all, making the value of the day a nice fat zero. Hugely relieved, he got back to visualizing the rods connecting the two sets of wheels. It all looked quite like the big steam engine in the Science Museum, except that paper came out at one end with a figure for the units of waste. It turned out, when he read the figures, that he was wasting more time than anyone else. He was horrified by this result, but at the same time quite pleased. Then he heard Jo's dreadful voice calling his name.

For a moment he froze with indecision. The trouble was that hiding only made the search party more frantic and furious. He decided to act casual and amble round the corner just in time to hear Jo bawling his name for the second time.

'Hi,' he said.

'Where have you been? I've been looking for you everywhere.'

'You can't have been, or you would have found me,' he said.

'Don't get smart with me, young man,' said Jo. 'Have you been fighting with Josh?'

'No,' he said. 'How could anyone fight with Josh? He's just a blob.'

'He's not a blob, he's your best friend,' said Jo.

'No he isn't,' he said.

'You *have* been fighting,' said Jo.

'We haven't,' he insisted.

'Well, anyway, you can't just go off like that.'

'Why not?'

'Because we all worry about you.'

'I worry about my parents when they go away, but that doesn't stop them,' he remarked. 'Nor should it.'

He was definitely winning this argument. In an emergency, his father could send Robert to court on his behalf. He imagined himself in a wig, bringing the jury round to his way of seeing things, but then Jo squatted down in front of him and looked searchingly into his eyes.

'Do your parents go away a lot?' she asked.

'Not really,' he said, but before he could tell her that they had never both been out of the house for more than about three hours, he found himself swept into her arms and crushed against the words 'Up For It', without fully understanding what they meant. He had to tuck his shirt in again after she had pulled it out of his trousers with her consoling back rub.

'What does "Up For It" mean?' he asked when he got his breath back.

'Never you mind,' she said, round-eyed. 'Come on! Lunch time!'

She marched him into the house. He couldn't exactly refuse to hold her hand now that they were practically lovers.

A man in an apron was standing beside the lunch table.

'Gaston, you're spoiling us rotten,' said Jilly reproachfully. 'I'm putting on a stone just looking at these tarts. You should have your own television programme. Vous sur le television, Gaston, make you beaucoup de monnaie. Fantastique!'

The table was crowded with bottles of pink wine, two of them empty, and a variety of custard tarts: a custard tart with bits of ham in it, a custard tart with bits of onion in it, a custard tart with curled-up tomatoes on it and a custard tart with curled-up courgettes on it.

Only Thomas was safe, breast-feeding.

'So you've rounded up the stray,' said Jilly. She whipped her hand in the air and burst into song. 'Round 'em up! Bring 'em in! Raw-w h-ide!'

Robert felt prickles of embarrassment breaking out all over his body. It must be desperate being Jilly.

'He's used to being alone a lot, is he?' said Jo, challenging his mother.

'Yes, when he wants to be,' said his mother, not realizing that Jo thought he might as well be living in an orphanage.

'I was just telling your parents they ought to take you to see the real Father Christmas,' said Jilly, dishing out the food. 'Concorde from Gatwick in the morning, up to Lapland, snowmobiles waiting, and whoosh, you're in Father Christmas's cave twenty minutes later. He gives the children a present, then back on Concorde and home in time for dinner. It's in the Arctic Circle, you see, which makes it more real than mucking about in Harrods.'

'It sounds very educational,' said his father, 'but I think the school fees will have to take priority.'

'Josh would murder us if we didn't take him,' said Jim.

'I'm not surprised,' said his father.

Josh made the sound of a massive explosion and punched the air.

'Smashing through the sound barrier,' he shouted.

'Which one of these tarts do you fancy?' Jilly asked Robert.

They all looked equally disgusting.

He glanced at his mother with her copper hair spiralling down towards the suckling Thomas, and he could feel the two of them blending together like wet clay.

'I want what Thomas is having,' he said. He hadn't meant to say it out loud, it just slipped out.

Jim, Jilly, Roger, Christine, Jo and Josh brayed like a herd of donkeys. Roger looked even angrier when he was laughing.

'Mine's a breast-milk,' said Jilly, raising her glass drunkenly.

His parents smiled at him sympathetically.

'I'm afraid you're on solids now, old man,' said his father. 'I've got used to wishing I was younger, but I didn't expect you to start quite yet. You're still supposed to be wishing you were older.'

His mother let him sit on the edge of her chair and kissed him on the forehead.

'It's perfectly normal,' Jo reassured his parents, who she knew had hardly ever seen a child. 'They're not usually that direct about it, that's all.' She allowed herself a last hiccup of laughter.

Robert tuned out of the babble around him and gazed at his brother. Thomas's mouth was busy and then quiet and then busy, massaging the milk from their mother's breast. Robert wanted to be there, curled up in the hub of his senses, before he knew about things he had never seen – the length of the Nile, the size of the moon, what they wore at the Boston Tea Party – before he was bombarded by adult propaganda, and measured his experi-

ence against it. He wanted to be there too, but he wanted to take
his sense of self with him, the sneaky witness of the very thing
that had no witnesses. Thomas was not witnessing himself doing things, he was just doing them. It was an impossible task to
join him there as Robert was now, like somersaulting and standing still at the same time. He had often brooded on that idea and
although he didn't end up thinking he could do it, he felt the
impossibility receding as the muscles of his imagination grew
more tense, like a diver standing on the very edge of the board
before he springs. That was all he could do: drop into the atmosphere around Thomas, letting his desire for observation peel
away as he got closer to the ground where Thomas lived, and
where he had once lived as well. It was hard to do it now, though,
because Jilly was on to him again.

'Why don't you stay here with us, Robert?' she suggested. 'Jo
could drive you back tomorrow. You'd have more fun playing
with Josh than going home and being dead jealous of your baby
brother.'

He squeezed his mother's leg desperately.

Eventually Gaston returned, distracting Jilly with the dessert, a slimy mound of custard in a puddle of caramel.

'Gaston, you're ruining us,' wailed Jilly, slapping his incorri-
gible, egg-beating wrist.

Robert leant in close to his mother. '*Please* can we go now,' he
whispered in her ear.

'Right after lunch,' she whispered back.

'Is he pleading with you?' said Jilly, wrinkling her nose.

'As a matter of fact he is,' said his mother.

'Go on, let him have a sleep-over,' insisted Jilly.

'He'll be well looked after,' said Jo, as if this was some kind of
novelty.

'I'm afraid we can't. We have to go and see his grandmother

in her nursing home,' said his mother, not mentioning that they were going there in three days' time.

'It's funny,' said Christine, 'Megan doesn't seem to feel any jealousy yet.'

'Give her a chance,' said his father, 'she's only just discovered rage.'

'Yeah,' laughed Christine. 'Maybe it's because I'm not really owning my pregnancy.'

'That must help,' sighed his father. Robert could tell that his father was now viciously bored. Immediately after lunch, they left the Packers with an urgency rarely seen outside a fire brigade.

'I'm starving,' he said, as their car climbed up the driveway.

They all burst out laughing.

'I wouldn't dream of criticizing your choice of friend,' said his father, 'but couldn't we just get the video instead.'

'I didn't choose him,' Robert protested, 'he just . . . stuck to me.'

He spotted a restaurant by the roadside where they had a late lunch of extremely excellent pizzas and salad and orange juice. Poor Thomas had to have milk again. That was all he ever got, milk, milk, milk.

'My favourite was the London house speech,' said Robert's father. He put on a very silly voice, not particularly like Jilly's but like her attitude. '"It looked huge when we bought it, but by the time we put in the guest suite and the exercise room and the sauna and the home office and the cinema, you know, there really wasn't that much room."'

'Room for what?' asked his father, amazed. 'Room for room. This is the room room, for having room in. Next time we climb onto our coat hangers in London to sleep like a family of bats, let's appreciate that we're not just a few bedrooms away from real civilization, but a room room away.

'"I said to Jim,"' his father continued imitating Jilly, '"I hope we can afford this, because I like the lifestyle – the restaurants, the holidays, the shopping – and I'm not going to give them up. Jim assures me that we can afford both."

'And this was the killer,' said his father – '"He knows that if we can't afford it, I'll divorce him." She's unfucking-believable. She isn't even attractive.'

'She is amazing,' said his mother. 'But I felt in their own quiet way that Christine and Roger had a lot to offer too. When I said that I used to talk to my children when I was pregnant, she said' – his mother put on a shrill Australian accent – '"Hang on! A baby is after the birth. I'm not going to talk to my pregnancy. Roger would have me committed."'

Robert imagined his mother talking to him when he had been sealed up in her womb. Of course he wouldn't have known what her blunted syllables were meant to mean, but he was sure he would have felt a current flowing between them, the contraction of a fear, the stretch of an intention. Thomas was still close to those transfusions of feeling; Robert was getting explanations instead. Thomas still knew how to understand the silent language which Robert had almost lost as the wild margins of his mind fell under the sway of the verbal empire. He was standing on a ridge, about to surge downhill, getting faster, getting taller, getting more words, getting bigger and bigger explanations, cheering all the way. Now Thomas had made him glance backwards and lower his sword for a moment while he noticed everything that he had lost as well. He had become so caught up in building sentences that he had almost forgotten the barbaric days when thinking was like a splash of colour landing on a page. Looking back, he could still see it: living in what would now feel like pauses: when you first open the curtains and see the whole landscape covered in snow and you catch your breath and pause before breathing out again. He couldn't get the whole thing back, but maybe he wouldn't rush down the slope quite yet, maybe he would sit down and look at the view.

'Let's get out of this sorry town,' said his father, chucking back his small cup of coffee.

'I've just got to change him first,' said his mother, gathering up a bulging bag covered in sky-blue rabbits.

Robert looked down at Thomas, slumped in his chair, staring at a picture of a sailing boat, not knowing what a picture was and not knowing what a sailing boat was, and he could feel the drama of being a giant trapped in a small incompetent body.

5

WALKING DOWN THE LONG, easily washed corridors of his grandmother's nursing home, the squeak of the nurse's rubber soles made his family's silence seem more hysterical than it was. They passed the open door of a common room where a roaring television masked another kind of silence. The crumpled, paper-white residents sat in rows. What could be making death take so long? Some looked more frightened than bored, some more bored than frightened. Robert could still remember from his first visit the bright geometry decorating the walls. He remembered imagining the apex of a long yellow triangle stabbing him in the chest, and the sharp edge of that red semicircle slicing through his neck.

This year they were taking Thomas to see his grandmother for the first time. She wouldn't be able to say much, but then neither would Thomas. They might get on really well.

When they went into the room, his grandmother was sitting in an armchair by the window. Outside, too close to the window, was the thick trunk of a slightly yellowing poplar tree and beyond it, the bluish cypress hedge that hid part of the car park. Noticing the arrival of her family, his grandmother organized her face into a smile, but her eyes remained detached from the process, frozen in bewilderment and pain. As her lips broke open he saw her blackened and broken teeth. They didn't look as if they could manage anything solid. Perhaps that was why her body seemed so much more wasted than when he had last seen her.

They all kissed his grandmother's soft, rather hairy face. Then his mother held Thomas close to his grandmother and said, 'This is Thomas.'

His grandmother's expression wavered as she tried to negotiate between the strangeness and the intimacy of his presence. Her eyes made Robert feel as if she was scudding through an overcast sky, breaking briefly into clear space and then rushing back through thickening veils into the milky blindness of a cloud. She didn't know Thomas and he didn't know her, but she seemed to have a sense of her connection with him. It kept disappearing, though, and she had to fight to get it back. When she was about to speak, the effort of working out what to say in these particular circumstances wiped her out. She couldn't remember who she was in relation to all the people in the room. Tenacity didn't work any more; the harder she grasped at an idea, the faster it shot away.

Finally, uncertainly, she wrapped her fingers around something, looked up at his father and said, 'Does . . . he . . . like me?'

'Yes,' said Robert's mother instantly, as if this was the most natural question in the world.

'Yes,' said his grandmother, the pool of despair in her eyes flooding back into the rest of her face. It wasn't what she had meant to ask, but a question which had broken through. She sank back into her chair.

After what he had heard that morning Robert was struck by her question, and by the fact that it seemed to be addressed to his father. On the other hand, he was not surprised that his mother had answered it instead of him.

That morning he had been playing in the kitchen while his mother was upstairs packing a bag for Thomas. He hadn't noticed that the monitor was still on, until he heard Thomas waking up with a few short cries, and his mother going into Thomas's bedroom and talking to him soothingly. Before he could gauge whether she was even sweeter to Thomas when he was not around, his father's voice came blasting over the receiver.

'I can't believe this fucking letter.'

'What letter?' asked his mother.

'That scumbag Seamus Dourke is trying to get Eleanor to make the gift of this property absolute during her lifetime. I had arranged for the solicitor to put it on an elastic band of debt. In her will the debt is waived and the house is transferred irrevocably to the charity, but during her lifetime the charity has been lent the value of this property, and if she recalls the debt the place returns to her. She agreed to set things up that way on the grounds that she might get ill and need the money to look after herself, but needless to say, I also hoped she would come to her senses and realize that this joke charity was doing a lot of harm to us and no good to anyone else, except Seamus. Talk about the luck of the Irish. There he was, a National Health nurse changing bedpans in County Meath, until my mother airlifted him from the Emerald Isle and made him the sole beneficiary of an enormous tax-free income from a New Age hotel masquerading as a charity. It makes me sick, completely sick.'

His father was shouting by now.

'Sweetheart, you're ranting,' said his mother. 'Thomas is getting upset.'

'I have to rant,' said his father, 'I've just seen this letter. She was always a lousy mother, but I thought she might take a holiday towards the end of her life, feel that she'd achieved enough by way of betrayal and neglect, and that it was time to have a break, play with her grandchildren, let us stay in the house, that sort of thing. What really terrifies me is realizing how much I loathe her. When I read this letter, I tried to loosen my shirt so that I could breathe, but then I realized it was already loose enough, I just felt as if a noose was tightening around my neck, a noose of loathing.'

'She's a confused old woman,' said Robert's mother.

'I know.'

'And we're seeing her later today.'

'I know,' said his father, much more quietly now, almost inaudibly. 'What I really loathe is the poison dripping from generation to generation. My mother felt disinherited because of her stepfather getting all her mother's money, and now, after thirty years of consciousness-raising workshops and personal-growth programmes, she has found Seamus Dourke to stand in for her stepfather. He's really just the incredibly willing instrument of her unconscious. It's the monotony that drives me mad. I'd rather cut my throat than inflict the same thing on my children.'

'You won't,' his mother answered.

'If you can imagine anything . . .'

Robert had leant closer to the monitor, trying to make out his father's fading voice, only to hear it growing louder behind him as his parents made their way downstairs.

'. . . the result would be my mother,' his father was saying.

'King Lear and Mrs Jellyby,' his mother laughed.

'On the heath,' said his father, 'a quick rut between the feeble tyrant and the fanatical philanthropist.'

He had run from the kitchen, not wanting his parents to know that he had heard their conversation on the monitor. He sat on the knowledge all morning, but when his grandmother had stared at his father, as if she was talking about him, and asked, 'Does he like me?' Robert couldn't help having the mad idea that she had overheard the same conversation as him.

Although he didn't understand everything his father had said that morning, he understood enough to feel cracks opening in the ground. And now, in the silence that followed his grandmother's shrewd unintentional question, he could feel her misery, and he could feel his mother's desire for harmony, and he could feel the strain in his father's self-restraint. He wanted to do something to make everything all right.

His grandmother was taking about half an hour to ask if Thomas had been christened yet.

'No,' said his mother, 'we're not having a formal christening. The trouble is that we don't really think that children are steeped in sin, and a lot of the ceremony seems to be based on the idea that they're fallen and need to be saved.'

'Yes,' said his grandmother. 'No.'

Thomas started to shake the tiny silver dumbbell he had rediscovered in the creases of his chair. It made a strange high tinkling sound as he waved it jerkily around his head. Soon enough, he banged it against his forehead. After a delay in which he seemed to be trying to work out what had happened, he started to cry.

'He doesn't know whether he hit himself or whether the dumbbell hit him,' said Robert's father.

His mother took sides against the dumbbell and said, 'Naughty dumbbell,' kissing Thomas's forehead.

Robert hit himself on the side of the head and fell off his grandmother's bed theatrically. Thomas wasn't as amused as he had hoped he would be.

His grandmother held her arms out in pleading sympathy, as if Thomas was expressing something that she felt as well, but didn't want to be reminded of. Robert's mother lifted Thomas gently into his grandmother's lap. Seduced by the novelty of his position, Thomas stopped crying and looked searchingly at his grandmother. She seemed to be calmed by his presence. He sat on her lap, giving her what she needed, and they sank together into speechless solidarity. The rest of the family fell silent as well, not wanting to show up the non-speakers. Robert felt his father hovering over his grandmother, resisting saying what was on his mind. In the end it was his grandmother who spoke, not quite fluently but much better than before, as if her speech, abandoning the hopelessly blocked highway of longing, had stolen out under cover of darkness and silence.

'I want you to know,' she said, 'that I'm very . . . unhappy . . . at not being able to communicate.'

His mother reached out and touched her knee.

'It must be horrible for you,' said his father.

'Yes,' said his grandmother, staring at the faraway floor.

Robert didn't know what to do. His father hated his own mother. He couldn't join him and he couldn't condemn him. His grandmother had done her family some wrong, but she was suffering horribly. Robert could only fall back on how things were before they had been darkened by his father's disappointment. Those cloudless days when he was just meant to love his grandmother; he was not sure they had ever existed, but he was sure they didn't exist now. It was still too unfair to gang up against his frightened grandmother, even if she was leaving the house to Seamus.

He hopped down from the bed and sat on the arm of his grandmother's chair, taking her hand in his, like he used to when she first fell ill. That way she could tell him things without having to speak, her thoughts flooding into him in pictures.

The bridges were burnt and broken and everything his grandmother wanted to say got banked up on one side of a ravine, never taking form, never moving on. She felt a perpetual pressure, a scratching behind her eyeballs, like a dog pleading to be let in, a fullness that could only escape in tears and sighs and jagged gestures.

Under the bruise of feeling there was a brutal instinct to stay alive, like a run-over snake thrashing on a hot road, or blind roots pumping sap into a bleeding stump.

Why was she being tortured? They had sewn her into a sack and thrown her into the bottom of a boat, chains wrapped around her feet. She must have done something very bad to be teased by the oarsmen as they rowed her out into the bay. Something very bad which she couldn't remember.

He tried to break off. It was too much. He didn't let go of her hand, he just tried to close down, but it was impossible to break the connection completely.

He noticed that his grandmother was crying. She gave his hand a squeeze.

'I am . . . no.' She couldn't say it. A carefully threaded thought unstrung itself and scattered across the floor. She couldn't get it back. Something opaque clung to her all the time. Her head had been sealed in a dirty plastic bag; she wanted to tear it off but her hands were tied.

'I . . . am,' she tried again. 'Brave. Yes.'

The evening light was on the other side of the building and the room was growing dimmer. They were all lost for words, except for Thomas who had none to lose. He leant against his grandmother's arms, looking at her with his cool objective gaze. His example balanced the atmosphere. They sat in the fading light of the almost peaceful room, feeling sympathetic and a little bored. Robert's grandmother sank into a quieter anguish, like someone deep in the broken springs of a chair, watching a dust storm coat the world in a blunt grey film.

After knocking on the door and not waiting for a reply, a nurse squeaked in with a trolley of food and slid a clattering tray onto the mobile table next to the bed. Robert's mother lifted Thomas back into her arms, while his father wheeled the table into position and removed the tin hood from the main dish. The sweaty grey fish and leaky ratatouille might have made a greedy man pause, but for his grandmother, who would rather have starved to death anyway, all food was equally unwelcome, and so she gave Robert's hand a last squeeze and broke the circuit which had introduced so many violent pictures into his imagination, and picked up her fork with the strange flat obedience of despair. She manoeuvred a flake of fish onto her fork and began to lift it towards her mouth. Then she stopped and lowered the fork again, staring at his father.

'I can't . . . find my mouth,' she said with emergency precision.

His father looked frustrated, as if his mother had found a trick to stop him from being angry with her, but Robert's mother immediately picked up the fork and smiled and said, 'Can I help you, Eleanor?' in the most natural way.

His grandmother's shoulders crumpled a little further at the thought that it had come to that. She nodded and his mother started to feed her, still holding Thomas on her other arm. His father, temporarily frozen, came to his senses and took Thomas from Robert's mother.

After a few more mouthfuls his grandmother shook her head and said, 'No,' and leant back in her chair exhausted. In the silence that followed, his father handed Thomas back to his mother and sat down next to his grandmother.

'I hesitate to mention this,' said his father, pulling a letter out of his pocket.

'I think you should keep on hesitating,' said his mother quickly.

'I can't,' he said to her, 'hesitate any longer.' He turned back to Robert's grandmother. 'Brown and Stone have written to me saying that you intend to make an outright gift of Saint-Nazaire to the Foundation. I just want to say that I think that leaves you very exposed. You can barely afford to stay here and if you needed any more medical care you would go broke very quickly.'

Robert hadn't thought his grandmother could look any more

unhappy, but somehow her features managed to yield a fresh impression of horror.

'I . . . really . . . I . . . really . . . no.'

She covered her face with her hands and screamed.

'I really do object . . .' she wailed.

His mother put her arm around his grandmother without glancing at his father. His father put the letter back in his pocket and looked at his shoes with perfect contempt.

'It's all right,' said his mother. 'Patrick just wants to help you, he's worried that you may give too much away too soon, but nobody's questioning that you can do what you like with the Foundation. The lawyers only told him because you've asked him to help you in the past.'

'I . . . need . . . to rest now,' said his grandmother.

'We'll leave, then,' said his mother.

'Yes.'

'I'm sorry I've upset you,' sighed his father. 'I just don't see what the hurry is: Saint-Nazaire is going to the Foundation in your will anyway.'

'I think we should drop this subject,' said his mother.

'Fine,' he agreed.

Robert's grandmother allowed herself to be kissed by each of them in turn. Robert was the last to say goodbye to her.

'Don't . . . leave me,' she said.

'Now?' he asked, confused.

'No . . . don't . . . no.' She gave up.

'I won't,' he said.

Any discussion of their visit to the nursing home seemed too hazardous, and they started the drive home in silence. Soon enough, though, his father's determination to talk took over. He tried to keep things general, he tried to keep away from the subject of his mother.

'Hospitals are very shocking places,' he said, 'full of poor de-

luded fools who aren't looking for groundless celebrity or obscene quantities of money, but think the point of life is to help
other people. Where do they get these ideas from? We must send
them on an empowerment weekend workshop with the Packers.'

Robert's mother smiled.

'I'm sure Seamus could organize it, give it a shamanic angle,'
said his father, dragged irresistibly out of his orbit. 'Mind you,
although hospitals may be awash with cheerful saints, I would
rather shoot myself in the head than experience the erosion of
self we witnessed this afternoon.'

'I thought Eleanor did very well,' said his mother. 'I was very
moved when she said that she was brave.'

'What can drive a man mad is being forced to have the emotion which he is forbidden to have at the same time,' said his father. 'My mother's treachery forced me to be angry, but then her
illness forced me to feel pity instead. Now her recklessness
makes me angry again but her bravery is supposed to smother
my anger with admiration. Well, I'm a simple sort of a fellow,
and the fact is that I remain *fucking angry*,' he shouted, banging
the steering wheel.

'Who is King Lear?' asked Robert from the back seat.

'Did you overhear our conversation this morning?' asked his
mother.

'Yes.'

'Eavesdropping,' said his father.

'No I wasn't,' he objected. 'You left the monitor on.'

'Oh, yes,' said his mother, 'so I did. Anyway, it hardly matters
now, does it, darling?' she asked his father sweetly. 'Since you're
screaming that you're "fucking angry" at the top of your voice.'

'King Lear,' said his father, 'is a petulant tyrant in Shakespeare
who gives everything away and is then surprised when Goneril
and Regan – or Seamus Dourke, as I prefer to think of them –
refuse him the care he requires and boot him out.'

'And who's Mrs Jellybean?'

'Jellyby. She's a compulsive do-gooder who writes indignant letters about orphans in Africa, while her own children fall into the fireplace at the other end of the drawing room.'

'And what's a rut?'

'Well, the idea is that if you combined these two characters you would get someone like Eleanor.'

'Oh,' said Robert, 'it's quite complicated.'

'Yes,' said his father. 'The thing is that Eleanor is trying to buy herself a front-row seat in heaven by giving all her money to "charity" but, as you can see, she has in fact bought herself a ticket to hell.'

'I don't think it's that clever to turn Robert against his grandmother,' said his mother.

'I don't think it was that clever of her to make it inevitable.'

'You're the one who feels betrayed – she's your mother.'

'She's lied to all of us,' his father insisted. 'At every stage she told me that such and such a thing was destined for Robert, but one by one these little concessions to family feeling were ripped from their pedestals and sucked into the black hole of the Foundation.'

Robert's mother let some time pass in silence and then said, 'Well, at least we didn't have *my* mother to stay this year.'

'Yes, you're right,' said his father, 'we must cultivate gratitude.'

The atmosphere settled down a little after this moment of harmony. They climbed the lane towards the house. The sunset was simple that evening, without clouds to make mountains and chambers and staircases, just a clear pink light around the hill tops, and an edge of moon hanging in the darkening sky. As they rumbled down the rough drive, Robert felt a sense of home which he knew he must learn to set aside. Why was his grandmother causing so much trouble? The scramble for a front-row seat in heaven seemed unbearably expensive. He looked at Thomas in his baby chair and wondered if he was closer to 'the source' than the rest of them, and whether it was a good thing if he was. His grandmother's impatience to be reabsorbed into a luminous anonymity suddenly filled him with the opposite impatience: to live as distinctively as he could before time nailed him to a hospital bed and cut out his tongue.

AUGUST 2001

6

BY DAY, WHEN PATRICK heard the echoing bark of the unhappy dog on the other side of the valley, he imagined his neighbour's shaggy Alsatian running back and forth along the split-cane fence of the yard in which he was trapped, but now, in the middle of the night, he thought instead of all the space into which the rings of yelping howling sound were expanding and dissipating. The crowded house compressed his loneliness. There was no one he could go to, except possibly, or rather impossibly (or, perhaps, possibly), Julia, back again after a year.

As usual, he was too tired to read and too restless to sleep. The tower of books on his bedside table seemed to provide for every mood, except the mood of agitated despair he was invariably in. *The Elegant Universe* made him nervous. He didn't want to read about the curvature of space when he was already watching the ceiling shift and warp under his exhausted gaze. He didn't want to think about the neutrinos streaming through his flesh – it seemed vulnerable enough already. He had started but finally had to abandon Rousseau's *Confessions*. He had all the persecution mania he could handle without importing any more. A novel pretending to be the diary of one of Captain Cook's officers on his first voyage to Hawaii was too well researched to bear any resemblance to life. Weighed down by the tiny variations of emblems on the Victualling Board's biscuits, Patrick had started to feel thoroughly depressed, but when a second narrative, written by a descendant of the first narrator, living in twenty-first-century Plymouth and taking a holiday in Honolulu, had set up a ludic counterpoint with the first narrative, he thought he was going to go mad. Two works of history, one a history of salt and the other a history of the entire world since 1500 BC, competed for a place at the bottom of the pile.

Also as usual, Mary had gone to sleep with Thomas, leaving Patrick split between admiration and abandonment. Mary was such a devoted mother because she knew what it felt like not to have one. Patrick also knew what it felt like, and as a former beneficiary of Mary's maternal overdrive, he sometimes had to remind himself that he wasn't an infant any more, to argue that there were real children in the house, not yet horror-trained; he sometimes had to give himself a good talking-to. Nevertheless, he waited in vain for the maturing effects of parenthood. Being surrounded by children only brought him closer to his own childishness. He felt like a man who dreads leaving harbour, knowing that under the deck of his impressive yacht there is only a dirty little twin-stroke engine: fearing and wanting, fearing and wanting.

Kettle, Mary's mother, had arrived that afternoon and, as usual, immediately found a source of friction with her daughter.

'How was your flight?' asked Mary politely.

'Ghastly,' said Kettle. 'There was an awful woman next to me on the plane who was terribly proud of her breasts, and kept sticking them in her child's face.'

'It's called breast-feeding, Mummy,' said Mary.

'Thank you, darling,' said Kettle. 'I know it's all the rage now, but when I was having children the talk was of getting one's figure back. A clever woman was the one who went to a party look-ing as if she'd never been pregnant, not the one with her breasts hanging out, at least not for breast-feeding.'

As usual, the bottle of Tamazepam squatted on his bedside table. He definitely had a Tamazepam problem, namely, that it wasn't strong enough. The side effects, the memory loss, the dehy-dration, the hangover, the menace of nightmarish withdrawals, all that worked beautifully. It was just the sleep that was miss-ing. He went on swallowing the pills in order not to confront the withdrawal. He remembered, in the distant past, a leaflet saying not to take Tamazepam for more than thirty consecutive days. He had been taking it every night for three years in larger and larger doses. He would be 'perfectly happy', as people said when they meant the opposite, to suffer horribly, but he never seemed to find the time. Either it was one of the children's birthdays, or he was appearing in court, already hung-over, or some other enormous duty required the absence of hallucination and high anxiety. Tomorrow, for instance, his mother was coming to lunch. Both mothers at once: not an occasion for bringing on any addi-tional psychosis.

And yet he still cherished the days when additional psychosis had been his favourite pastime. His second year at Oxford was spent watching the flowers pulse and spin. It was during that summer of alarming experiments that he had met Julia. She was the younger sister of a dull man on the same staircase in Trinity. Patrick, already in the early stages of a mushroom trip, had been hurriedly refusing his invitation to tea, when he saw through the half-open door a neck-twistingly pretty girl hugging her knees in the window seat. He veered towards a 'quick cup of tea' and spent the next two hours staring idiotically at the unfairly lovely Julia, with her rose-pink cheeks and dark blue eyes. She wore a raspberry T-shirt which showed her nipples, and faded blue jeans frayed open a few inches under the back pocket and above her right knee. He swore to himself that when she was old enough he would seduce her, but she pre-empted his timid resolution by seducing him the same evening. They had made time-lapse, slow-motion and technically illegal (she was only sixteen the following week) love. They had fallen upwards, disappeared down rabbit holes, watched clocks go anticlockwise and run away from policemen who weren't chasing them. When they went to Greece he helped to stash the acid in his favourite hiding place: between her legs. He thought that things would cascade from one adventure to another, but now the stammering ecstasy of their love-making seemed like a miracle of freedom belonging to a lost world. Nothing had ever been as spontaneously intimate again, especially not, he kept reminding himself, conversation with the harder, drier Julia who was staying with him now. And yet, there she was, just down the corridor, bruised but still pretty. Should he go? Should he risk it? Should they mount a joint retrospective? Would the intensity come back once their bodies intertwined? The idea was insane. He would have to walk past Robert, the insomniac observation-freak, past the ferocious Kettle, past Mary, who hovered like a dragonfly over the surface of sleep in case she missed the slightest inflection of her baby's distress, and then into Julia's room (the corner of her door scraped the floor), which had probably already been invaded by her daughter Lucy anyway. He was paralysed, as usual, by equal and opposite forces.

Everything was as usual. That was depression: being stuck, clinging to an out-of-date version of oneself. During the day, when he played with the children, he was very close to being what he appeared to be, a father playing with his children, but at night he was either aching with nostalgia or writhing with self-rejection. His youth had sprinted away in its Nike Air Max trainers (only Kettle's youth still wore winged sandals), leaving a swirl of dust and a collection of fake antiques. He tried to remind himself what his youth had really been like, but all he could remember was the abundance of sex and the sense of potential greatness, replaced, as his view closed in on the present, by the disappearance of sex and the sense of wasted potential. Fearing and wanting, fearing and wanting. Perhaps he should take another twenty milligrams of Tamazepam. Forty milligrams, as long as he drank a lot of red wine for dinner, sometimes purchased a couple of hours of sleep; not the gorgeous oblivion which he craved, but a sweaty, turbulent sleep laced with nightmares. Sleep, in fact, was the last thing he wanted if it was going to usher in those dreams: strapped to a chair in the corner of the room watching his children being tortured while he screamed curses at the torturer, or begged him to stop. There was also a diet version, the Nightmare Lite, in which he threw himself in front of his sons just in time to have his body shredded by gunfire, or dismembered by ravenous traffic. When he wasn't woken by these shocking images, he dozed off dreamlessly, only to wake a few minutes later, gasping for air. The price he paid for the sedation he needed to drop off, was that his breathing seized up, until an emergency unit in his back brain sent a screaming ambulance to his frontal lobes and jolted him back into consciousness.

His dreams, dreadful enough in their own right, were almost always accompanied by a defensive analytic sequel. Johnny, his child-psychologist friend, had said this was 'lucid dreaming', in which the dreamer acknowledged that he was dreaming. What was he protecting his children from? His own sense of being tortured, of course. The in-dream dream seminars always reached such reasonable conclusions.

He was obsessed, it was true, with stopping the flow of poison from one generation to the next, but he already felt that he had failed. Determined not to inflict the causes of his suffering

on his children, he couldn't protect them from the consequences.
Patrick had buried his own father twenty years ago and hardly
ever thought about him. At the peak of his kindness David had
been rude, cold, sarcastic, easily bored; compulsively raising the
hurdle at the last moment to make sure that Patrick cracked his
shins. It would have been too flagrant for Patrick to become a
disastrous father, or to get a divorce, or to disinherit his children; instead they had to live with the furious, sleepless consequence of those things. He knew that Robert had inherited his
midnight angst and refused to believe that there was a midnight-
angst gene which furnished the explanation. He remembered
talking endlessly about his insomnia at a time when Robert had
wanted to copy everything about him. He also saw, with a mixture of guilt and satisfaction and guilt about the satisfaction, the
gradual shift in Robert from empathy and loyalty towards hatred and contempt for Eleanor and her philanthropic cruelty.

One great relief was that they wouldn't be seeing the Packers
this year. Josh had been taken out of school for three weeks and
lost the habit of pretending that he and Robert were best friends.
During that period of heady freedom, Patrick and Robert had
run into Jilly in Holland Park and found out that she was getting
a divorce from Jim.

'The glitter's off the diamond,' she admitted. 'But at least
I get to keep the diamond,' she added with a triumphant little
hoot. 'It's awful about Roger being sent to prison. Hadn't you
heard? It's an open prison, one of the posh ones. Still, it isn't great,
is it? They got him for fraud and tax evasion. Basically, for doing
what everyone else does, but not getting away with it. Christine's
in bits, with the two kids and everything. She can't even afford a
nanny. I said to her, "Get a divorce, it really bucks you up." Mind
you, I forgot she wouldn't be getting a huge settlement. I don't
know how much it *does* buck you up without a fortune thrown
in. I sound awful, don't I? But you've got to be realistic. The

doctor's put me on these pills; I can't stop talking. You'd better just walk away, or I'll have you pinned down here all day listening to me wittering on. It's funny, though, thinking of us last year, all sat around the pool in St Trop, having the time of our lives, and now everyone going their separate ways. Still, we've got the children, haven't we? That's the main thing. Don't forget that Josh is still your best friend,' she shouted at Robert as they left.

Thomas had started speaking over the last year. His first word was 'light', followed soon afterwards by 'no'. All those atmospheres evaporated and got so convincingly replaced, it was hard to remember the beginning, when he was speaking not so much to tell a story as to see what it was like to come out of silence into words. Amazement was gradually replaced by desire. He was no longer amazed by seeing, for instance, but by seeing what he wanted. He spotted a broom hundreds of yards down the street, before the rest of them could even see the sweeper's fluorescent jacket. Hoovers hid behind doors in vain; desire had given him X-ray vision. Nobody could wear a belt for long if he was in the room, it was commandeered for an obscure game in which Thomas, looking solemn, waved the buckle around, humming like a machine. If they ever made it out of London, his parents sniffed the flowers and admired the view, Robert looked for good climbing trees, and Thomas, who wasn't yet far enough from nature to have turned it into a cult, hurtled across the lawn towards the limp coils of a hose lying almost invisibly in the uncut grass.

At his first birthday party last week, Thomas had been attacked for the first time, by a boy called Eliot. A commotion suddenly drew Patrick's attention to the other side of the drawing room. Thomas, who was walking along unsteadily with his wooden rabbit on a string, had just been pushed over by a bruiser from his playgroup, and had the string wrenched from his hand.

He let out a cry of indignation and then burst into tears. The thug wandered off triumphantly with the undulating rabbit clattering behind him on uneven wheels.

Mary swooped down and lifted Thomas off the ground. Robert went over to check that he was all right, on the way to recapture the rabbit.

Thomas sat on Mary's lap and soon stopped crying. He looked thoughtful, as if he was trying to introduce the novelty of being attacked into his frame of reference. Then he wriggled off Mary's knee and back down to the ground.

'Who was that dreadful child?' said Patrick. 'I don't think I've ever seen such a sinister face. He looks like Chairman Mao on steroids.'

Before Mary could answer, the bruiser's mother came over.

'I'm sorry about that,' she said. 'Eliot is so competitive, just like his dad. I hate to repress all that drive and energy.'

'You're relying on the penal system for that,' said Patrick.

'He should try knocking me over,' said Robert, practising his martial arts moves.

'Let's not go global with this rabbit thing,' said Patrick.

'Eliot,' said the bruiser's mother, in a special false voice, 'give Thomas his rabbit back.'

'No,' growled Eliot.

'Oh, dear,' said his mother, delighted by his tenacity.

Thomas had transferred his focus to the fire tongs which he was dragging noisily out of their bucket. Eliot, convinced that he must have stolen the wrong thing, abandoned the rabbit and headed for the tongs. Mary picked up the string of the rabbit and handed it to Thomas, leaving Eliot revolving next to the bucket, unable to decide what he should be fighting for. Thomas offered the rabbit string to Eliot who refused it and waddled over to his mother with a cry of pain.

'Don't you want the tongs?' she asked coaxingly.

Patrick hoped he would handle things more wisely with Thomas than he had with Robert, not infuse him with his own anxieties and preoccupations. The hurdles were always raised at the last moment. He was so tired now. The hurdles always raised . . . of course . . . he would think that . . . he was chasing his tail now . . . the dog was barking on the other side of the valley . . . the inner and outer worlds ploughing into each other . . . he was almost falling asleep . . . perchance to dream . . . fuck that. He sat up and finished the thought. Yes, even the most enlightened care carried a shadow. Even Johnny (but then, he was a child psychologist) reproached himself for making his children feel that he really understood them, that he knew what they were feeling before they knew themselves, that he could read their unconscious impulses. They lived in the panoptic prison of his sympathy and expertise. He had stolen their inner lives. Perhaps the kindest thing Patrick could do was to break up his family, to offer his children a crude and solid catastrophe. All children had to break free in the end. Why not give them a hard wall to kick against, a high board to jump from. Christ, he really must get some rest.

After midnight, the wonderful Dr Zemblarov was never far from his thoughts. A Bulgarian who practised in the local village, he spoke in extremely rapid, heavily accented English. 'In our culture, we have only this,' he would say, signing an elaborate prescription, '*la pharmacologie*. If we lived in the *Pacifique*, maybe we could dance, but for us there is only the chemical manipulation. When I go back to Bulgaria, for example, I take *de l'amphetamine*. I drive I drive I drive, I see my family, I drive I drive I drive, and I come back to Lacoste.' The last time Patrick had hesitantly asked for more Tamazepam, Dr Zemblarov reproached him for being so shy. '*Mais il faut toujours demander*. I take it myself when I travel. *L'administration* want to limit us to thirty days, so I will put "one in the evening and one at night", which naturally is not true, but it will avoid you to come here so often. I will also give you Stilnox, which is from another family – the hypnotics! We also have the barbiturate family,' he added with an appreciative smile, his pen hovering over the page.

No wonder Patrick was always tired, and could only offer short bursts of child care. Today, Thomas had been in pain. Some more teeth were bullying their way through his sore gums, his cheeks were red and swollen and he was rushing about looking for distractions. In the evening, Patrick had finally contributed a quick tour of the house. Their first stop was the socket in the wall under the mirror. Thomas looked at it longingly and then anticipated his father by saying, 'No, no, no, no, no.' He shook his head earnestly, piling up as many 'no's as he could between him and the socket, but desire soon washed away the little dam of his conscience, and he lunged towards the socket, improvising a plug with his small wet fingers. Patrick swept him off his feet and hauled him further down the corridor. Thomas shouted in protest, planting a couple of sharp kicks in his father's testicles.

'Let's go and see the ladder,' gasped Patrick, feeling it would be unfair to offer him anything much less dangerous than electrocution. Thomas recognized the word and calmed down, knowing that the frail, paint-spattered aluminium ladder in the boiler room had its own potential for injury and death. Patrick held him lightly by the waist while he monkeyed up the steps, almost pulling the ladder back on them. As he was lowered to the ground, Thomas burst into a drunken run, reeling his way towards the boiler. Patrick caught him and prevented him from crashing into the water tank. He was completely exhausted by now. He'd had enough. It wasn't as if he hadn't contributed to the baby care. Now he needed a holiday. He staggered back into the drawing room, carrying his wriggling son.

'How are you?' asked Mary.

'Done in,' said Patrick.

'I'm not surprised, you've had him for a minute and a half.'

Thomas hurtled towards his mother, buckling at the last minute. Mary caught him before his head hit the floor and put him back on his feet.

'I don't know how you cope without a nanny,' said Julia.

'I don't know how I would cope with one. I've always wanted to look after the children myself.'

'Motherhood takes some people that way,' said Julia. 'I must say, it didn't in my case, but then I was so *young* when I had Lucy.'

To show that she too went mad in the sun-drenched south, Kettle had come down to dinner wearing a turquoise silk jacket and a pair of lemon-yellow linen trousers. The rest of the household, still wearing their sweat-stained shirts and khaki trousers, left her just where she wanted to be, the lonely martyr to her own high standards.

Thomas slapped his hands over his face as she came in.

'Oh, it's too sweet,' said Kettle. 'What's he doing?'

'Hiding,' said Mary.

Thomas whipped his hands away and stared at the others with his mouth wide open. Patrick reeled back, thunderstruck by his reappearance. It was Thomas's new game. It seemed to Patrick the oldest game in the world.

'It's so relaxing having him hide where we can all see him,' said Patrick. 'I dread the moment when he feels he has to leave the room.'

'He thinks we can't see him because he can't see us,' said Mary.

'I must say, I do sympathize,' said Kettle. 'I rather wish people saw things exactly as I do.'

'But you know that they don't,' said Mary.

'Not always, darling,' said Kettle.

'I'm not sure that it's a story of the self-centred child and the well-adjusted adult,' Patrick had made the mistake of theorizing.

'Thomas knows that we don't see things as he does, otherwise he wouldn't be laughing. The joke is the shift in perspective. He expects us to flow into his point of view when he covers his face, and back into our own when he whips his hands away. We're the ones who are stuck.'

'Honestly, Patrick, you always make everything so intellectual,' Kettle complained. 'He's just a little boy playing a game. Apropos of hiding,' she said, in the manner of someone taking the wheel from a drunken driver, 'I remember going to Venice with Daddy before we were married. We were trying to be discreet because one was expected to make an effort in those days. Well, of course the first thing that happened was that we ran into Cynthia and Ludo at the airport. We decided to behave rather like Thomas and pretend that if we didn't look at them they couldn't see us.'

'Was it a success?' asked Patrick.

'Not at all. They shouted our names across the airport at the top of their voices. I would have thought it was perfectly obvious that we didn't want to be spotted, but tact was never Ludo's forte. Anyway, we made all the right noises.'

'But Thomas does want to be spotted, that's his big moment,' said Mary.

'I'm not saying it's exactly the same situation,' said Kettle, with a little splutter of irritation.

'What are the "right noises"?' Robert had asked Patrick on the way into dinner.

'Anything that comes out of Kettle,' he replied, half hoping she would hear.

It didn't help that Julia was so unfriendly to Mary, not that it would have helped if she had been friendly. His loyalty to Mary was not in question (or was it?); what was in question was whether he could last without sex for one more second. Unlike the riotous appetites of adolescence, his present cravings had a tragic tinge, they were cravings for the appetites, metacravings, wanting to want. The question now was whether he would be able to sustain an erection, rather than whether he could ever get rid of the damn thing. At the same time the cravings had to cultivate simplicity, they had to collapse into an object of desire, in order to hide their tragic nature. They were not cravings for things which he could get, but for capacities which he would never have back. What would he do if he did get Julia? Apologize for being exhausted, of course. Apologize for being tied up. He was having (get it off your chest, dear, it'll do you good) a midlife crisis, and yet he wasn't, because a midlife crisis was a cliché, a verbal Tamazepam made to put an experience to sleep, and the experience he was having was still wide awake – at three thirty in the fucking morning.

He didn't accept any of it: the reduced horizons, the fading faculties. He refused to buy the pebble spectacles his Magoo-standard eyesight pleaded for. He loathed the fungus which seemed to have invaded his bloodstream, blurring everything. The impression of sharpness which he still sometimes gave was a simulation. His speech was like a jigsaw puzzle he had done a hundred times, he was just remembering what he had done before. He didn't make fresh connections any more. All that was over.

From down the corridor, he heard Thomas starting to cry. The sound sandpapered his nerves. He wanted to console Thomas. He wanted to be consoled by Julia. He wanted Mary to be consoled by consoling Thomas. He wanted everyone to be all right. He couldn't bear it any longer. He threw the bedclothes aside and paced the room.

Thomas soon settled down, but his cries had set off a reaction which Patrick could no longer control. He was going to go to Julia's room. He was going to turn the narrow allotment of his life into a field of blazing poppies. He opened the door slowly, lifting it on its hinges so that it didn't whine. He pulled it closed again with the handle held down so that it didn't click. He released the tongue slowly into the groove. The corridor was glowing with child-friendly light. It was as bright as a prison yard. He walked down it, heel-to-toe, all the way to the end, to Lucy's partially open door. He wanted to check first that she was still in her room. Yes. Fine. He doubled back to Julia's door. His heart was thumping. He felt terrifyingly alive. He leant close to the door and listened.

What was he going to do next? What would Julia do if he went into her room? Call the police? Pull him into bed whispering, 'What took you so long?' Perhaps it was a little tactless to wake her at four in the morning. Maybe he should make an appointment for the following evening. His feet were getting cold, standing on the hexagonal tiles.

'Daddy.'

He turned around and saw Robert, pale and frowning in the doorway of his bedroom.

'Hi,' whispered Patrick.

'What are you doing?'

'Good question,' said Patrick. 'Well, I heard Thomas crying ...' That much was true. 'And I wondered if he was all right.'

'But why are you standing outside Julia's room?'

'I didn't want to disturb Thomas if he had gone back to sleep,' Patrick explained. Robert was too intelligent for this rubbish, but perhaps he was a shade too young to be told the truth. In a couple of years Patrick could offer him a cigar and say, 'I'm having this rather awkward *mezzo del camin* thing, and I need a quick affair to buck me up.' Robert would slap him on the back and say, 'I completely understand, old man. Good luck and happy hunting.' In the meantime, he was six years old and the truth had to be hidden from him.

As if to save Patrick from his predicament, Thomas let out another wail of pain.

'I think I'd better go in,' said Patrick. 'Poor Mummy has been up all night.'

He smiled stoically at Robert. 'You'd better get some sleep,' he said, kissing him on the forehead.

Robert turned back into his room, unconvinced.

The safety plug in Thomas's cluttered room cast a faint orange glow across the floor. Patrick picked his way towards the bed into which Mary carried Thomas every night out of his hated cot, and lowered himself onto the mattress, pushing half a dozen soft toys onto the floor. Thomas writhed and twisted, trying to find a comfortable position. Patrick lay on his side, teetering on the edge of the bed. He certainly wasn't going to get any sleep in this precarious sardine tin, but if he could just let his mind glide along, he might get some rest; if he could go omnogogic, gaining the looseness of dreams without their tyranny, that would be something. He was just going to forget about the Julia incident. What Julia incident?

Perhaps Thomas wouldn't be a wreck when he grew up. What more could one ask?

He was beginning to glide along in half-thoughts . . . quarter-thoughts, counting down . . . down.

Patrick felt a violent kick land on his face. The warm metallic rush of blood flooded his nose and the roof of his mouth.

'Jesus,' he said, 'I think I've got a nosebleed.'

'Poor you,' mumbled Mary.

'I'd better go back to my room,' he whispered, rolling backwards onto the floor. He replaced Thomas's velveteen bodyguards and clambered to his feet. His knees hurt. He probably had arthritis. He might as well move into his mother's nursing home. Wouldn't that be cosy?

He slouched back down the corridor, pressing his nostril with the knuckle of his index finger. There were spots of blood on his pyjamas: so much for the field of poppies. It was five in the morning now, too late for one half of life and too early for the other. No prospect of sleep. He might as well go downstairs, drink a gallon of healthy, organic coffee and pay some bills.

7

KETTLE, WEARING DARK GLASSES and an enormous straw hat, was already sitting at the stone table. Using her expired boarding pass as a bookmark, she closed her copy of James Pope-Hennessy's biography of Queen Mary and put it down next to her plate.

'It's like a dream,' said Patrick, easing his mother's wheelchair into position, 'having you both here at the same time.'

'Like . . . a . . . dream,' said Eleanor, generalizing.

'How are you, my dear?' asked Kettle, bristling with indifference.

'Very . . .'

The effort that Eleanor put into producing, after some time, a high-pitched 'well' gave an impression of something quite different, as if she had seen herself heading towards 'mad' or 'miserable' and just managed to swerve at the last moment. Her radiant smile uncovered the dental bomb site Patrick had so often begged her to repair. It was no use: she was not about to waste money on herself while she could still draw a charitable breath. The tiny amount of spare income she had left was being saved up for Seamus's sensory-deprivation tanks. In the meantime she was well on her way to depriving herself of the sensation of eating. Her tongue curled and twisted among shattered crags, searching forlornly for a whole tooth. There were several no-go areas too sensitive for food to enter.

'I'm going to help with the lunch,' said regretful, duty-bound Patrick, bolting across the lawn like a swimmer hurrying to the surface after too long a dive.

He knew that it was not really his mother he needed to escape but the poisonous combination of boredom and rage he felt whenever he thought about her. That, however, was a long-term project. 'It may take more than one lifetime,' he warned himself in a voice of simpering tenderness. Just looking at the next few minutes, he needed to put as many literal-minded yards between himself and his mother as he could manage. That morning, in the nursing home, he had found her sitting by the door with her bag on her knees, looking as if she had been ready for hours. She handed him a faint pencil-written note. It said that she wanted to transfer Saint-Nazaire to the Foundation straight away and not, as things stood, after her death. He had managed to postpone things last year, but could he manage it again? The note said she 'needed closure' and wanted his help and his 'blessing'. Seamus's rhetoric had left its fingerprints all over the prose. No doubt he had a closure ritual lined up, a Native American trance dance which would close its own closure with a macrocosmic and microcosmic, a father sky and mother earth, a symbolic and actual, an immediate and eternal booting out of Patrick and his family from Saint-Nazaire. At the centre of a dogfight of contradictory emotions, Patrick could sometimes glimpse his longing to get rid of the fucking place. At some point he was going to have to drop the whole thing, he was going to have to come back to Saint-Nazaire for a healing-drum weekend, to ask Seamus to help him let go of his childhood home, to put the 'trans' into what seemed so terribly personal.

As he crossed from the terrace into the olive grove, Patrick imagined himself extolling to a group of neo-shamen and neo-shawomen the appropriateness, the challenge, and 'I never would have believed this possible, but I have to use the word "beauty", of coming back to this property in order to achieve closure in the letting-go process (sighs of appreciation). There was a time when I resented and, yes, I must admit, hated Seamus and the Foundation and my own mother, but my loathing has been miraculously transformed into gratitude, and I can honestly say (little catch in his throat) that Seamus has been not only a wonderful teacher and drum guide, but also my truest friend (the pitter-patter of applause and rattles).'

Patrick ditched his little fantasy with a sarcastic yelp and sat down on the ground with his back to the house, leaning against the knotted grey trunk of an old bifurcating olive tree that he had used all his life to hide and to think. He had to keep reminding himself that Seamus was not a straightforward crook who had cheated a little old lady out of her money. Eleanor and Seamus had corrupted each other with the extravagance of their good intentions. Seamus might have continued to do some good, changing bedpans in Navan – the only town in Ireland to be spelt the same way backwards – and Eleanor could have lived on Ryvita and given her income to the blind, or to medical research, or to the victims of torture, but instead they had joined forces to produce a monument of pretension and betrayal. Together they were going to save the world. Together they were going to heighten consciousness by dumbing down an already dangerously dumb constituency. Whatever good there was in Seamus was being destroyed by Eleanor's pathological generosity, and whatever good had been in Eleanor was being destroyed by Seamus's inane vision.

What had turned Eleanor into such a goody-goody? Patrick felt that Eleanor's loathing for her own mother was at the root of her overambitious altruism. Eleanor had told him the story of being taken by her mother to her first big party. It took place in Rome just after the Second World War. Eleanor was a fifteen-year-old girl back for the holidays from her boarding school in Switzerland. Her mother, a rich American and a dedicated snob, had divorced Eleanor's dissolute, charming and untitled father and married a dwarfish and ill-tempered French duke, Jean de Valencay, obsessed with questions of rank and genealogy. On the tattered stage of a near-communist Republic, and entirely subsidized by his wife's recent industrial wealth, he was all the keener to insist on the antiquity of his bloodline. On the night of the party, Eleanor sat in her mother's immense Hispano-Suiza, parked next to a bombed-out building, round the corner from the glowing windows of Princess Colonna's house. Her stepfather had been taken ill but, languishing in an ornate Renaissance bed which had been in his family since his wife bought it for him the month before, he made his wife swear that she wouldn't enter the Princess's house until after the Duchessa di Dino, over whom she had precedence. Precedence, it turned out, meant that her mother had to arrive late. They waited in the car. In the front, next to the driver, was a footman, periodically sent round to check if the inferior Duchessa had arrived. Eleanor was a shy and idealistic girl, happier talking to the cook than to the guests who were being cooked for, but she was still quite impatient and curious about the party.

'Can't we just go? We're not even Italian.'

'Jean would kill me,' said her mother.

'He can't afford to,' said Eleanor.

Her mother froze with fury. Eleanor regretted what she had just said, but also felt a twinge of adolescent pride at giving precedence to honesty over tact. She looked out of the glass cage of her mother's car and saw a tramp stumbling towards them in torn brown clothes. As he grew closer, she saw the skeletal sharpness of his face, the outsized hunger in his eyes. He shuffled up to the car and tapped on the window, pointing pleadingly to his mouth, raising his hands in prayer, pointing again to his mouth.

Eleanor looked over at her mother. She was staring straight ahead, waiting for an apology.

'We've got to give him some money,' said Eleanor. 'He's starving.'

'So am I,' said her mother, without turning her head. 'If this Italian woman doesn't show up soon, I'm going to go crazy.'

She tapped the glass separating her from the front seat and waved impatiently at the footman.

When they eventually got inside the house, Eleanor spent the party in her first flush of philanthropic fever. Her rejection of her mother's values fused with her idealism to produce an in-toxicating vision of herself as a barefoot saint: she was going to dedicate her life to helping others, as long as they weren't related to her. A few years later, her mother speeded Eleanor along the path of self-denial by allowing herself to be bullied, as she lay dying of cancer, into leaving almost all of her vast fortune out-right to Eleanor's stepfather. He had protested that the original will, in which he only had the use of her fortune during his life-time, was an insult to his honour since it implied that he might cheat his stepdaughters by disinheriting them. He, in turn, broke the promise he had made to his dying wife and left the loot to his nephew. Eleanor was by then too implicated in her spiritual quest to admit how bewildered she was about the loss of all that money. The resentment was being passed on to Pat-rick, carefully preserved like one of the antiques which Jean loved to collect at his wife's expense. Her mother had liked dukes whereas Eleanor liked would-be witch doctors, but regardless of the social decline the essential formula remained the same: rip off the children for the sake of some cherished self-image, the grande dame, or the holy fool. Eleanor had pushed on to the next generation the parts of her experience she wanted to get rid of: divorce, betrayal, mother-hatred, disinheritance; and clung to an idea of herself as part of the world's salvation, the Aquarian Age, the return to primitive Christianity, the revival of shamanism – the terms shifted over the years, but Eleanor's role remained the same: heroic, optimistic, visionary, proud of its humility. The result of her psychological apartheid was to keep both the rejected and aspirant parts of herself frozen. On the night of that Roman party, she had borrowed some money from a family friend and dashed outside to find the starving tramp whose life she was going to save. A few corners later, she found that the streets had not recovered as quickly from six years of war as the merrymakers she had left behind. She couldn't help feeling conspicuous among the rats and the rubble, dressed in her sky-blue ball gown with a large banknote gripped in her eager fist. Shadows shifted in a doorway, and a splash of fear sent her shivering back to her mother's car.

Fifty-five years later, Eleanor still hadn't worked out a realistic way to act on her desire to be good. She still missed the feast without relieving the famine. When things went wrong, and they always did, the bad experiences were not allowed to inform the passionate teenager; they were exiled to the bad-experience dump. A secret half of Eleanor grew more bitter and suspicious, so that the visible half could remain credulous and eager. Before Seamus there had been a long procession of allies. Eleanor handed her life over to them with complete trust and then, within a few hours of their last moment of perfection, they were suddenly rejected, and never mentioned again. What exactly they had done to deserve exile was never mentioned either. Illness was producing a terrifying confluence of the two selves which Eleanor had gone to such trouble to keep apart. Patrick was curious to know whether the cycle of trust and rejection would remain intact. After all, if Seamus crossed over into the shadows, Eleanor might want to dismantle the Foundation as vehemently as she had wanted to set it up. Maybe he could delay things for another year. There he was, still hoping to hang on to the place.

Patrick could remember wandering around the rooms and gardens of his grandmother's half-dozen exemplary houses. He had watched a world-class fortune collapse into the moderate wealth that his mother and his aunt Nancy enjoyed from a relatively minor inheritance they received before their mother caved in to the lies and bullying of her second husband. Eleanor and Nancy looked rich to some people, living at good addresses, one in London and one in New York, each with a place in the country, and neither of them needing to work, or indeed shop, wash, garden or cook for themselves, but in the history of their own family they were surviving on loose change. Nancy, who still lived in New York, combed the catalogues of the world's auction houses for images of the objects she should have owned. On the last occasion Patrick visited her on 69th Street, she had scarcely offered him a cup of tea before getting out a sleek black catalogue from Christie's, Geneva. It had just arrived and inside was a photograph of two lead jardinières, decorated with gold bees almost audibly buzzing among blossoming silver branches. They had been made for Napoleon.

'We didn't even used to comment on them,' said Nancy bitterly. 'Do you know what I'm saying? There were so many beautiful things. They used to just sit on the terrace in the rain. A million and a half dollars, that's what the little nephew got for Mummy's garden tubs. I mean, wouldn't you like to have some of these things to give to your children?' she asked, carrying over a new set of photograph albums and catalogues, to syncopate the sale price with the sentimental significance of what had been lost.

She went on decanting the poison of her resentment into him for the next two hours.

'It was thirty years ago,' he would point out from time to time.

'But the little nephew sells something of Mummy's every week,' she growled in defence of her obsession.

The continuing drama of deception and self-deception made Patrick violently depressed. He was only really happy when Thomas first greeted him with a burst of uncomplicated love, throwing open his arms in welcome. Earlier that morning, he had carried Thomas around the terrace, looking for geckos behind the shutters. Thomas grabbed every shutter as they passed, until Patrick unhooked it and creaked it open. Sometimes a gecko shot up the wall towards the shelter of a shutter on the upper floor. Thomas pointed, his mouth rounded with surprise. The gecko was the trigger to the real event, the moment of shared excitement. Patrick tilted his head until his eyes were level with Thomas's, naming the things they came across. 'Valerian . . . Japonica . . . Fig tree,' said Patrick. Thomas stayed silent until he suddenly said, 'Rake!' Patrick tried to imagine the world from Thomas's point of view, but it was a hopeless task. Most of the time, he couldn't even imagine the world from his own point of view. He relied on nightfall to give him a crash course in the real despair that underlay the stale, remote, patchily pleasurable days. Thomas was his antidepressant, but the effect soon wore off as Patrick's lower back started to ache and he caved in to his terror of early death, of dying before the children were old enough to earn a living, or old enough to handle the bereavement. He had no reason to believe that he would die prematurely; it was just the most flagrant and uncontrollable way of letting his children down. Thomas had become the great symbol of hope, leaving none for anyone else.

Thank goodness Johnny was coming later in the month. Patrick felt sure that he was missing something which Johnny could illuminate for him. It was easy to see what was sick, but it was so difficult to know what it meant to be well.

'Patrick!'

They were after him. He could hear Julia calling his name. Perhaps she could come and join him behind the olive tree, give him a very quick blow job, so that he felt a little lighter and calmer during lunch. What a great idea. Standing outside her door last night. The tangle of shame and frustration. He clambered to his feet. Knees going. Old age and death. Cancer. Out of his private space into the confusion of other people, or out of the confusion of his private space into the effortless authority of his engagement with others. He never knew which way it would go.

'Julia. Hi, I'm over here.'

'I've been sent to find you,' said Julia, walking carefully over the rougher ground of the olive grove. 'Are you hiding?'

'Not from you,' said Patrick. 'Come and sit here for a few seconds.'

Julia sat down next to him, their backs against the forking trunk.

'This is cosy,' she said.

'I've been hiding here since I was a child. I'm surprised there isn't a dent in the ground,' said Patrick. He paused and weighed up the risks of telling her.

'I stood outside your door last night at four in the morning.'

'Why didn't you come in?' said Julia.

'Would you have been pleased to see me?'

'Of course,' she said, leaning over and kissing him briefly on the lips.

Patrick felt a surge of excitement. He could imagine pretending to be young, rolling around among the sharp stones and the fallen twigs, laughing manfully as mosquitoes fed on his naked flesh.

'What stopped you?' asked Julia.

'Robert. He found me hesitating in the corridor.'

'You'd better not hesitate next time.'

'Is there going to be a next time?'

'Why not? You're bored and lonely; I'm bored and lonely.'

'God,' said Patrick, 'if we got together, there would be a ter-rifying amount of boredom and loneliness in the room.'

'Or maybe they have opposite electrical charges and they'd cancel each other out.'

'Are you positively or negatively bored?'

'Positively,' said Julia. 'And I'm absolutely and positively lonely.'

'You may have a point, then,' smiled Patrick. 'There's some-thing very negative about *my* boredom. We're going to have to conduct an experiment under strictly controlled conditions to see whether we achieve a perfect elimination of boredom or an overload of loneliness.'

'I really should drag you back to lunch now,' said Julia, 'or everyone will think we're having an affair.'

They kissed. Tongues. He'd forgotten about tongues. He felt like a teenager hiding behind a tree, experimenting with real kissing. It was bewildering to feel alive, almost painful. He felt his pent-up longing for closeness streaming through his hand as he placed it carefully on her belly.

'Don't get me going now,' she said, 'it's not fair.'

They climbed groaning to their feet.

'Seamus had just arrived when I came to get you,' said Julia, brushing the dust off her skirt. 'He was explaining to Kettle what went on during the rest of the year.'

'What did Kettle make of that?'

'I think she's decided to find Seamus charming so as to an-noy you and Mary.'

'Of course she has. It's only because you've got me all flus-tered that I hadn't worked that out already.'

They made their way towards the stone table, trying not to

smile too much or to look too solemn. Patrick felt himself sliding back under the microscope of his family's attention. Mary smiled at him. Thomas threw out his arms in welcome. Robert gazed at him with his intimidating, knowledgeable eyes. He picked up Thomas and smiled at Mary, thinking, 'A man may smile and smile and be a villain.' Then he sat down next to Robert, feeling as he did when he defended an obviously guilty client in front of a famously difficult judge. Robert noticed everything. Patrick admired his intelligence, but far from short-circuiting his depression as Thomas did, Robert made him more aware of the subtle tenacity of the destructive influence that parents had on their children – that he had on his children. Even if he was an affectionate father, even if he wasn't making the gross mistakes his parents had made, the vigilance he invested in the task created another level of tension, a tension which Robert had picked up. With Thomas he would be different – freer, easier, if one could be free and easy while feeling unfree and uneasy. It was all so hopeless. He really must get a decent night's sleep. He poured himself a glass of red wine.

'It's good to see you, Patrick,' said Seamus, rubbing him on the back.

Patrick felt like punching him.

'Seamus has been telling me all about his workshops,' said Kettle. 'I must say they sound absolutely fascinating.'

'Why don't you sign up for one?' said Patrick. 'It's the only way you'll see the place in the cherry season.'

'Ah, the cherries,' said Seamus. 'Now, they're something really special. We always have a ritual around the cherries – you know, the fruits of life.'

'It sounds very profound,' said Patrick. 'Do the cherries taste any better than they would if you experienced them as the fruits of a cherry tree?'

'The cherries . . .' said Eleanor. 'Yes . . . no . . .' She rubbed out the thought hastily with both hands.

'She loves the cherries. They're grand, aren't they?' said Seamus, clasping Eleanor's hand in his reassuring grip. 'I always take her a bowl in the nursing home, freshly picked, you know.'

'A handsome rent,' said Patrick, draining his glass of wine.

'No,' said Eleanor, panic-stricken, 'no rent.'

Patrick realized he was upsetting his mother. He couldn't even go on being sarcastic. Every avenue was blocked. He poured himself another glass of wine. One day he was going to have to drop the whole thing, but just for now he was going to go on fighting; he couldn't stop himself. Fight with what, though? If only he hadn't gone to such trouble to make his mother's folly legally viable. She had handed him, without any sense of irony, the task of disinheriting himself, and he had carried it out carefully. He had sometimes thought of putting a hidden flaw in the foundations. He had sat in the multi-jurisdictional meetings with *notaires* and solicitors, discussing ways of circumventing the forced inheritance of the Napoleonic code, the best way to form a charitable foundation, the tax consequences and the accountancy procedures, and he had never done anything except refine the plan to make it stronger and more efficient. The only way out was that elastic band of debt which Eleanor was now proposing to snip. He had really put it in for her protection. He had tried to set aside the hope that she would take advantage of it, but now that he was about to lose that hope, he realized that he had been cultivating it secretly, using it to keep him at a small but fatal distance from the truth. Saint-Nazaire would soon be gone for ever and there was nothing he could do about it. His mother was an unmaternal idiot and his wife had left him for Thomas. He still had one reliable friend, he sobbed silently, splashing more red wine into his glass. He was definitely going to get drunk and insult Seamus, or maybe he wasn't. In the end, it was even harder to behave badly than to behave well. That was the trouble with not being a psychopath. Every avenue was blocked.

A scene was unfolding around him, no doubt, but his attention was so submerged that he could hardly make out what was going on. If he clawed his way up the slippery well shaft, what would he find anyway, except Kettle extolling Queen Mary's child-rearing methods, or Seamus radiating Celtic charisma? Patrick looked over the valley, a gauntlet of memory and association. In the middle of the view was the Mauduits' ugly farmhouse, its two big acacia trees still growing in the front yard. When he was a child he had often played with the oafish Marcel Mauduit. They used to fashion spears out of the pale green bamboos that flanked the stream at the bottom of the valley. They flung them at little birds which managed to leave several minutes before the bamboo clattered onto the abandoned branch. When Patrick was six years old Marcel invited him to watch his father beheading a chicken. There was nothing more curious and amusing than watching a chicken run around in silly circles looking for its head, Marcel explained. You really had to see it for yourself. The boys waited in the shade of the acacia trees. An old hatchet was stuck at a handy angle among the crisscross cuts on the surface of a brownish plane tree stump. Marcel danced around like an Indian with a tomahawk, pretending to decapitate his enemies. In the distance, Patrick could hear the panic in the chicken coop. By the time Marcel's father arrived, gripping a hen by the neck, her wings beating uselessly against his vast belly, Patrick was beginning to side with her. He wanted this one to get away. He could see that she knew what was going on. She was held down sideways, her neck stuck over the edge of the stump. Monsieur Mauduit brought the hatchet down so that her head flopped neatly at his feet. Then he put the rest of her quickly on the ground and, with an encouraging pat, set her off on a frantic dash for freedom, while Marcel jeered and laughed and pointed. Elsewhere, the hen's eyes stared at the sky and Patrick stared at her eyes.

With his fourth glass of wine, Patrick found his imagination tilting towards Victorian melodrama. Dark scenes formed of their own accord, but he did nothing to stop them. He saw the bloated figure of a drowned Seamus floating in the Thames. His mother's wheelchair seemed to have lost control and was bouncing down the coastal path towards a Dorset cliff. Patrick noted the magnificent National Trust backdrop as she pitched forwards over the edge. One day he really must drop the whole thing, get real, get contemporary, accept the facts, but just for the moment he would go on imagining himself putting the last touches to a forged will, while Julia, seated on the edge of his desk, bemused him with the complexity of her undergarments. Just for now, he would have another little splash of wine.

Thomas leant forward in Mary's lap, and with her usual perfect intuition, she immediately handed him a biscuit. He sank back on her chest convinced, as he was hundreds of times a day, that he would never need something without being given it. Patrick scanned himself for jealousy, but it wasn't there. There was plenty of dark emotion but no rivalry with his infant son. The trick was to keep up a high level of loathing for his own mother, leaving no room to feel jealous of Thomas getting the solid foundations his father so obviously lacked. Thomas leant forwards a second time and, with an enquiring murmur, held out his biscuit to Julia, offering her a bite. Julia looked at the wet and blunted biscuit, made a face and said, 'Yuk. No thank you very much.'

Patrick suddenly realized that he couldn't make love to someone who missed the point of Thomas's generosity so completely. Or could he? Despite his revulsion, he felt his lust running on, not unlike a beheaded chicken. He had now achieved the pseudo-detachment of drunkenness, the little hillock before the swamps of self-pity and memory loss. He saw that he really must get well, he couldn't go on this way. One day he was going to drop the whole thing, but he couldn't do that until he was ready, and he couldn't control when he would be ready. He could, however, get ready to be ready. He sank back in his chair and agreed at least to that: his business for the rest of the month was to get ready to be ready to be well.

8

'HOW ARE YOU?' ASKED Johnny, lighting a cheap cigar.

The flaring match brought a patch of colour into the black and white landscape cast by the moonlight. The two men had come outside after dinner to talk and smoke. Patrick looked at the grey grass and then up at a sky bleached of stars by the violence of the moon. He didn't know where to begin. The previous evening he had somehow managed to transcend the 'Yuk' incident, stealing into Julia's bed after midnight and staying there until five in the morning. He had slept with Julia in a speculative haze which his impulsiveness and greed failed to abolish. Too busy asking himself what adultery felt like, he had almost forgotten to notice what Julia felt like. He wondered what it meant to be back inside a woman who, apart from the relatively faint reality of her limbs and skin, was above all a site of nostalgia. What it certainly did not mean was Time Regained. Being a pig in the trough of a disreputable emotion turned out to fall short of the spontaneous timelessness of involuntary memory and associative thinking. Where were the uneven cobblestones and silver spoons and silver doorbells of his own life? If he stumbled across them, would floating bridges spring into being, with their own strange sovereignty, belonging to neither the original nor the repeated, the past nor the fugitive present, but to some kind of enriched present capable of englobing the linearity of time? He had no reason to think so. He felt deprived not only of the ordinary magic of intensified imagination, but of the even more ordinary magic of immersion in his own physical sensations. He wasn't going to scold himself for a lack of particularity in experiencing his sexual pleasure. All sex was prostitution for both participants, not always in the commercial sense, but in the deeper etymological sense that they stood in for something else. The fact that this was sometimes done so effectively that there were weeks or months in which the object of desire and the person one happened to be in bed with seemed identical could not prevent the underlying model of desire from beginning to drift away, sooner or later, from its illusory home. The strangeness of Julia's case was that she stood in for herself, as she had been twenty years ago, a pre-drift lover.

'Sometimes a cigar is just a cigar,' said Johnny, realizing that Patrick didn't want to answer his question.

'When's that?' said Patrick.

'Before you light it – after that, it's a symptom of unreconstructed orality.'

'I wouldn't be having this cigar unless I'd given up smoking,' said Patrick. 'I want to make that absolutely clear.'

'I completely understand,' said Johnny.

'One of the burdens of being a child psychologist,' said Patrick, 'is that if you ask someone how they are, they tell you. Instead of saying that I feel fine, I have to give you the real answer: *not* fine.'

'Not fine?'

'Bad, chaotic, terrified. My emotional life seems to cascade into wordlessness in every direction, not only because Thomas hasn't taken up words yet and Eleanor has already been abandoned by them, but also, internally, I feel the feebleness of everything I can control surrounded by the immensity of everything I can't control. It's very primitive and very strong. There's no wood left for the fire that keeps the wild animals at bay, that sort of thing. But also something even more confusing – the wild animals are a part of me that's winning. I can't stop them from destroying me without destroying them, but I can't destroy them without destroying myself. Even that makes it sound too organized. It's really more like a cartoon of cats fighting: a spinning blackness with exclamation marks flying off it.'

'You sound as if you have a good grasp of what's going on,' said Johnny.

'That should be a strength, but since I'm trying to communicate how little grasp I have of what's going on, it's a hindrance.'

'It's not a hindrance to your telling me about the chaos. It's only a hindrance if you're trying to manifest it.'

'Perhaps I do want to manifest it, so that it takes some concrete form, instead of it being this enormous state of mind.'

'I'm sure it does take some concrete form.'

'Hmm . . .'

Patrick scanned the concrete forms, the insomnia, the heavy drinking, the bouts of overeating, the constant longing for solitude which, if achieved, made him desperate for company, not to mention (or should he mention it? He felt the heavy gravitational field of confession surrounding Johnny) last night's adulterous incident.

He could remember only a few hours ago concluding that it had been a mistake, and beginning to imagine the mature discussion he was going to have with Julia. Now that the tide of alcohol was rising again, he was becoming more and more convinced that he had simply gone to bed with the wrong attitude. He must do better. He would do better.

'I must do better,' said Patrick.

'Do what better?'

'Oh, everything,' said Patrick vaguely.

He certainly wasn't going to tell Johnny, and then have his inflamed appetites placed in some pathological context or, worse, in a therapeutic programme. On the other hand, what was the point of his friendship with Johnny if it wasn't truthful? They had been friends for thirty years. Johnny's parents had known his parents. They knew each other's lives in depth. If Patrick had been wondering whether to commit suicide, he would have asked Johnny's opinion. Maybe he could shift the conversation away from his own mental health and onto one of their favourite topics: the way that time was grinding down their generation. Their shorthand for this process was 'the retreat from Moscow', thanks to the vivid picture they both had of the straggling survivors of Napoleon's army limping, bloodstained and bootless, through a landscape of frozen horses and dying men. Out of professional curiosity, Johnny had recently attended a reunion dinner of their year at school. He reported back to Patrick. The captain of the First XI was now a crack-head. The most brilliant student of their year was buried in the middle ranks of the civil service. Gareth Williams couldn't come because he was in a mental hospital. Their most 'successful' contemporary was the head of a merchant bank who, according to Johnny, 'failed to register on the authenticity graph'. That was the graph that Johnny cared about, the one that would determine whether, in his own eyes, he ended up in a roadside ditch or not.

'I'm sorry to hear that you've been feeling bad,' said Johnny, before Patrick could get him onto the safe ground of collective disappointment, sell-out and loss.

'I slept with Julia last night,' said Patrick.

'Did that make you feel better?'

'It made me wonder if I was feeling better. It was perhaps just a little bit too cerebral.'

'That's what you "must do better".'

'Exactly. I didn't know whether to tell you. I thought I might have to stop if we worked out exactly what was going on.'

'You've worked it out already.'

'Up to a point. I know that Thomas is making me revisit my own infancy in a way that Robert never did. Maybe it's the prominence of that old prop, a mother who needs mothering, which has lent so much authenticity to this revival. In any case, a deep sense of ancestral gloom stalks the night, and I would rather spend it with Julia who, instead of the primal chaos I feel on my own, offers the relatively innocuous death of youth.'

'It all sounds very allegorical – Primal Chaos and the Death of Youth. Sometimes a woman is just a woman.'

'Before you light her up?'

'No, no, that's a cigar,' said Johnny.

'Honestly, there are no easy answers. Just when you think you've worked something out . . .'

Patrick could hear the whining of a mosquito in his right ear. He turned his head and blew smoke in its direction. The sound stopped.

'Obviously, I would love to have real, embodied, fully present experiences – especially of sex,' Patrick went on, 'but, as you've pointed out, I'm taking refuge in an allegorical realm where everything seems to represent a well-known syndrome or conflict. I remember complaining to my doctor about the side effects of the Ribavirin he prescribed for me. "Oh, yes, that's known," he said with a kind of tremendous, uninfectious calm. Mind you, when I told him about a side effect that wasn't known, he dismissed it by saying, "I've never heard of that before." I think I'm trying to be like him, to immunize myself against experience by concentrating on phenomena. I keep thinking, "That's known," when in fact I feel the opposite, that it's alien and menacing and out of control.'

Patrick felt a sharp sting. 'Fucking mosquitoes,' he said, slapping the back of his neck rather too hard. 'I'm being eaten alive.'

'I've never heard of that before,' said Johnny sceptically.

'Oh, it's *known*,' Patrick assured him. 'It's quite standard among the highlanders of Papua New Guinea. The only question is whether they make you eat yourself alive.'

Johnny let this prospect drown in silence.

'Listen,' said Patrick, leaning forward, and speaking more rapidly than before, 'I'm not in any serious doubt that everything I'm going through at the moment corresponds with the texture of my infancy in some way. I'm sure that my midnight angst resembles some free fall I felt in my cot when, for my own good, and so as to save me from becoming a manipulative little monster, my parents did exactly what suited them and ignored me. As you know, my mother only paves the road to hell with the best intentions, so we can assume that my father was the advocate of the character-building advantages of a willbreaking upbringing. But how can I really know and what good would it do me to find out?'

'Well, for a start, you're not using your powers of persuasion to keep Mary away from Thomas. Without any sense of connection with your own infancy, you almost certainly would be. It's true that the hardest maps to draw up are the very early ones, the first two years. We can only work with inferences. If, for example, someone had an acute intolerance of being kept waiting, felt a perpetual hunger which eating turned into a bloated despair, and was kept awake by hypervigilance . . .'

'Stop! Stop!' sobbed Patrick. 'It's all true.'

'That would imply a certain quality of early care,' Johnny went on, 'different from the kind of omnipotent fantasy world that Eleanor wants to perpetuate with her "non-ordinary reality" and her "power animals". We are always "the veils that veil us from ourselves", but looking into infancy, with no memories and no established sense of self, it's *all veils*. If the privation is bad enough, there's nobody there to have the insights. It's a question of reinforcing the best false self you can lay your hands on – the authenticity project is not an option. But that's not your case. I think you can afford to lose control, to go into the free fall. If the past was going to destroy you it already would have.'

'Not necessarily. It might have been waiting for just the right moment. The past has all the time in the world. It's only the future which is running out.'

He emptied the wine bottle into his glass.

'And the wine,' he added.

'So,' said Johnny, 'you're going to try to "do better" tonight?'

'Yes. My conscience isn't rebelling in quite the way I expected. I'm not trying to punish Mary by going to bed with Julia – I'm just looking for a little tenderness. I think Mary would almost be relieved if she knew. It's a burden to someone like her not being able to give me what I need.'

'You're really doing her a favour,' said Johnny.

'Yes,' said Patrick, 'I don't like to boast about it, but I'm helping her out. She won't need to feel guilty about abandoning me.'

'If only more people had your sense of generosity,' said Johnny.

'I think quite a lot of people do,' said Patrick. 'Anyway, these philanthropic impulses run in my family.'

'All I feel like saying,' said Johnny, 'is that there's no point to your free fall unless it produces some insight. This is the time for Thomas to develop secure attachment. If you can make it through to his third birthday without destroying your marriage or making Mary feel depressed, that would be a great achievement. I think Robert is already well grounded. Anyway, he has that amazing talent for mimicry which he uses to play with whatever weighs on his mind.'

Before Patrick had time to respond, he heard the screen door swing open and snap back again on its magnetic strip. Both men fell silent and waited to see who was coming out of the house.

'Julia,' said Patrick, as she came into view, swishing across the grey grass, 'come and join us.'

'We've all been wondering what you're up to,' said Julia. 'Are you baying at the moon, or working out the meaning of life?'

'Neither,' said Patrick, 'there's too much baying in this valley already, and we worked out the meaning of life years ago: "Walk tall and spit on the graves of your enemies". Wasn't that it?'

'No, no,' said Johnny. 'It was "love thy neighbour as thyself".'

'Oh, well, given how much I love myself, it amounts to pretty much the same thing.'

'Oh, darling,' said Julia, resting her hands on Patrick's shoulders, 'are you your own worst enemy?'

'I certainly hope so,' said Patrick. 'I dread to think what would happen if somebody else turned out to be better at it than me.'

Johnny ground his crackling, splitting cigar into the ashtray.

'I might head for bed,' he said, 'while you decide whose grave to spit on.'

'Eenee, meenee, minee, mo,' said Patrick.

'Do you know, Lucy's generation don't say, "Catch a nigger by the toe" any more; they say, "Catch a tiger by the toe". Isn't it sweet?'

'Have they rewritten "Rock a bye, Baby" as well? Or is the cradle still allowed to fall?' asked Patrick. 'God,' he added, looking at Johnny, 'it must be difficult for you hearing a person's unconscious breaking through every sentence.'

'I try not to hear it,' said Johnny, 'when I'm on holiday.'

'But you don't succeed.'

'I don't succeed,' smiled Johnny.

'Has everyone gone to bed?' asked Patrick.

'Everyone except Kettle,' Julia replied. 'She wanted to have a little heart-to-heart; I think she's in love with Seamus. She's been to tea in his cottage for the last two afternoons.'

'She *what*?' said Patrick.

'She's stopped talking about Queen Mary's widowhood and started talking about "opening up to one's full potential".'

'That bastard. He's going to try to get Mary disinherited as well,' said Patrick. 'I'm going to have to kill him.'

'Wouldn't it be more efficient to kill Kettle before she changes her will?' asked Julia.

'Good thinking,' said Patrick. 'My judgement was clouded by emotion.'

'What is this?' said Johnny. 'An evening with the Macbeths? What about just letting her open to her full potential?'

'Jesus,' said Patrick, 'who have you been reading recently? I thought you were a realist, not a human-potential moron who claims to see El Dorados of creativity in every flower arrangement. Even in the hands of a psychotherapeutic genius, Kettle's peak would be joining a tango class in Cheltenham, but with Seamus her "full potential" is to be fully ripped off.'

'The potential which Kettle hasn't realized – and she's not alone,' said Johnny, 'has nothing to do with hobbies, or even achievements, it's to do with being able to enjoy anything at all.'

'Oh, that potential,' said Patrick. 'You're right, of course, we all need to work on that.'

Julia grazed his thigh discreetly with her fingernails. Patrick felt a half-erection creep its way into the most inconvenient possible position among the folds of his underwear. Not particularly wanting to struggle with his trousers in front of Johnny, he waited confidently for the problem to disappear. He didn't have to wait long.

Johnny got to his feet and said good night to Patrick and Julia.

'Sleep well,' he added, starting out towards the house.

'One may be too busy opening up to one's full potential,' said Patrick in a racy version of his Kettle voice.

As soon as they heard Johnny entering the house, Julia climbed astride Patrick's lap, facing him with her hands dangling lightly over his shoulders.

'Does he know?' she asked.

'Yes.'

'Is that a good idea?'

'He won't tell anyone.'

'Maybe, but now it's too late for us not to tell anyone. I can't believe we're already into who knows what, that's all. We've only just been to bed together and it's already a problem of knowledge.'

'It's always a problem of knowledge.'

'Why?'

'Because there was this garden, right? And this apple tree . . .'

'Oh, honestly, that has nothing to do with it. That's a different kind of knowledge.'

'They came together. In the absence of God, we have the omniscience of gossip to keep us preoccupied with who knows what.'

'I'm not in fact preoccupied with who knows what, I'm preoccupied with how we feel for each other. I think you want it to be about knowledge because you're more at home in your head than in your heart. Anyhow, you didn't have to tell Johnny.'

'Whatever,' said Patrick, suddenly drained of all desire to prove a point or win an argument. 'I often think there should be a superhero called Whateverman. Not an action hero like Superman or Spiderman, but an inaction hero, a hero of resignation.'

'Is there a comma between "Whatever" and "Man"?'

'Only when he can be bothered to speak, which, believe me, isn't often. When someone screams, "There's a meteor headed straight for us! It's the end of all life on Earth!", he says, "Whatever, man," with a comma in between. But when he is invoked, during an episode of ethnic cleansing, or paranoid schizophrenia, as in, "This is a job for Whateverman", it's all in one word.'

'Does he have a cloak?'

'God, no. He wears the same old jeans and T-shirt year in year out.'

'And this fantasy is all in the service of not admitting that you were wrong to tell Johnny.'

'It was wrong if it upset you,' said Patrick. 'But when my oldest friend asked me what was going on, it would have been glib to leave out the most important fact.'

'Poor darling, you're just too—'

'Authentic,' Patrick interrupted. 'That's always been my trouble.'

'Why don't you bring some of that authenticity upstairs?' asked Julia, leaning forwards and giving Patrick a long slow kiss.

He was grateful that she made it impossible for him to answer her question. He wouldn't have known what to say. Was she mocking his shallow disembodied presence the night before? Or hadn't she noticed? The problem of other minds. Christ, he was at it again. They were kissing. Get into it. Picture of himself getting into it. No, not the picture, the thing in itself. Whatever that was. Who was to say that authenticity lay in being oblivious to the reflective aspect of the mind? He was speculative. Why suppress that in favour of what was, in the end, just a picture of authenticity, a cliché of into-it-ness?

Julia broke off the kiss.

'Where have you gone?' she asked.

'I was lost in my head,' he admitted. 'I think I was thrown by your request for me to bring my authenticity upstairs – there's just so much of it, I'm not sure I can manage.'

'I'll help,' said Julia.

They untangled themselves and walked back into the house, holding hands, like a couple of moon-struck teenagers.

When they reached the landing and were about to slip into Julia's bedroom, they heard stifled giggling from Lucy's bedroom, followed by a crescendo of hushing. Transformed from furtive lovers into concerned parents, they walked down the corridor with a new authority. Julia tapped gently on the door and immediately pushed it open. The room was dark, but light from the corridor fell across a crowded bed. All of Lucy's indispensable soft toys, her white rabbit and her blue-eyed dog and, incredibly, the chipmunk she had chewed religiously since her third birthday, were scattered in various buckled postures across the bedspread, and replaced, inside the bed, by a live boy.

'Darling?' said Julia.

The children made no sound.

'It's no use pretending to be asleep. We heard you down the corridor.'

'Well,' said Lucy, sitting up suddenly, 'we're not doing anything wrong.'

'We didn't say you were,' said Julia.

'This is the most outrageous subplot,' said Patrick. 'Still, I don't see why they shouldn't sleep together if they want to.'

'What's a subplot?' asked Robert.

'Another part of the main story,' said Patrick, 'reflecting it in some more or less flagrant way.'

'Why are *we* a subplot?' asked Robert.

'You're not,' said Patrick. 'You're a plot in your own right.'

'We've got so much to talk about,' said Lucy, 'we just couldn't wait until tomorrow.'

'Is that why you two are still up?' asked Robert. 'Because you've got so much to talk about. Is that why you said we were a subplot?'

'Listen, forget I ever said it,' said Patrick. 'We're all each other's subplots,' he added, trying to confuse Robert as much as possible.

'Like the moon going round the earth,' said Robert.

'Exactly. Everyone thinks they're on the earth, even when they're on somebody else's moon.'

'But the earth goes round the sun,' said Robert. 'Who's on the sun?'

'The sun is uninhabitable,' said Patrick, relieved that they had travelled so far from the original motive of his comment. 'Its only plot is to keep us going round and round.'

Robert looked troubled and was about to ask another question when Julia interrupted him.

'Can we return to our own planet for a second?' she asked. 'I suppose I don't mind you sharing a bed, but remember we're going to Aqualand tomorrow, so you must go straight to sleep.'

'What else would we do?' said Lucy, starting to giggle. 'Smudging?'

She and Robert made sounds of extravagant revulsion and collapsed in a heap of limbs and laughter.

9

PATRICK ORDERED ANOTHER DOUBLE espresso and watched the waitress weave her way back to the bar, only momentarily transfixed by a vision of her sprawled across one of the tables, gripping its sides while he fucked her from behind. He was too loyal to linger over the waitress when he was already involved in a fantasy about the girl in the black bikini on the other side of the cafe, her eyes closed and her legs slightly parted, absorbing the beams of the morning sun, still as a lizard. He might never recover from the look of intense seriousness with which she had examined her bikini line. An ordinary woman would have reserved that expression for a bathroom mirror, but she was a paragon of self-absorption, running her finger along the inside edge of her bikini, lifting it and realigning it still closer to the centre, so that it interfered as little as possible with the total nudity which was her real object. The mass of holiday-makers on the Promenade Rose, shuffling forward to claim their coffin-sized plot of beach, might as well not have existed; she was too fascinated by the state of her tan, her wax job, her waistline, too in love with herself to notice them. He was in love with her too. He was going to die if he didn't have her. If he was going to be lost, and it looked as if he was, he wanted to be lost inside her, to drown in the little pool of her self-love – if there was room.

Oh, no, not that. Please. A piece of animated sports equipment had just walked up to her table, put his pack of red Marlboros and his mobile phone next to her mobile phone and pack of Marlboro Lights, kissed her on the lips and sat down, if that was the right term for the muscle-bound bouncing with which he eventually settled into the chair next to hers. Heartbreak. Disgust. Fury. Patrick skimmed over the ground of his immediate emotions and then forced himself upwards into the melancholy sky of resignation. Of course she was spoken for a million times over. In the end it was a good thing. There could be no real dialogue between those who still thought that time was on their side and those who realized that they were dangling from its jaws, like Saturn's children, already half-devoured. Devoured. He could feel it: the dull efficiency of a praying mantis tearing arcs of flesh from the still living aphid it has clamped between its forelegs; the circular hobbling of a wildebeest, reluctant to lie down with the lion who hangs confidently from his neck. The fall, the dust, the last twitch.

Yes, in the end it was a good thing that Bikini Girl was spoken for. He lacked the pedagogic patience and the particular kind of vanity which would have enabled him to opt for the cheap solution of being a youth vampire. It was Julia who had got him used to sex during her fortnight's stay, and it was among the time refugees of her blighted generation that he must look for lovers. With the possible exception, of course, of the waitress who was now weaving her way back towards him. There was something about the shop-worn sincerity of her smile which suited his mood. Or was it the stubborn pout of the labial mould formed by her jeans? Should he get a shot of brandy to tip into his espresso? It was only ten thirty in the morning, but there were already several misty-cold glasses of beer blazing among the round tables. He only had two days of holiday left. They might as well be debauched. He ordered the brandy. At least that way she would be back soon. That's how he liked to think of her, weaving back and forth on his behalf, tirelessly attending to his clumsy search for relief.

He turned towards the sea, but the harsh glitter of the water blinded him and, while he shielded his eyes from the sun, he found himself imagining all the people on that body-packed curve of blond sand, shining with protective lotions, playing with bats and balls, lolling in the placid bay, reading on their towels and mattresses, all being blasted by a fierce wind and blown into a fine veil of sparkling sand, and the collective murmur, pierced by louder shouts and sharper cries, falling silent.

He must rush down that beach to shelter Mary and the children from ruin, give them a few more seconds of life with the decomposing shield of his own body. He struggled so hard to get away from his roles as a father and a husband, only to miss them the moment he succeeded. There was no better antidote to his enormous sense of futility than the enormous sense of purpose which his children brought to the most obviously futile tasks, such as pouring buckets of sea water into holes in the sand. Before he managed to break away from his family, he liked to imagine that once he was alone he would become an open field of attention, or a solitary observer training his binoculars on some rare species of insight usually obscured by the mass of obligations that swayed before him like a swarm of twittering starlings. In reality solitude generated its own roles, not based on duty but on hunger. He became a cafe voyeur, drunk with desire, or a calculating machine compulsively assessing the inadequacy of his income.

Was there any activity which didn't freeze into a role? Could he listen without being a listener, think without being a thinker? No doubt there was a flowing world of present participles, of listening and thinking, rushing along beside him, but it was part of the grim allegorical tinge of his mentality that he sat with his back to this glittering torrent, staring at a world of stone. Even his affair with Julia seemed to have *The Sorrows of Adultery* carved on its plinth. Instead of thrilling him with his own audacity, it reminded him of how little he had left. After they had started sleeping together, his days were spent sprawled on a pool-side lounger, feeling that he might as well have been splayed in a roadside ditch, discouraging the excitement of some hungry rats, rather than turning down the demands of his adorable children. His guilt-fuelled bouts of charm towards Mary were as flagrant as his row-picking arguments. The margin of freedom he had gained with Julia was soon filled with the concrete of another role. She was his mistress, he was her married man. She would struggle to get him away, he would struggle to keep her in the mistress slot without tearing his family apart. They were already in a perfectly structured situation, with ultimately opposed interests. Its currency was deception: of Mary, of each other, and of themselves. It was only in the immediate greed of a bed that they could find any common ground. He was amazed by the amount of defeat and inconvenience that already surrounded his affair with Julia. The only sane action would be to end it straight away, to define it as a summer fling and not try to elaborate it into a love affair. The terrible thing was that he had already lost control of the situation. He only felt well when he was in bed with her, when he was inside her, when he was coming inside her. Kneeling on the floor, that had been good, when she had sat in the armchair with her knees up and her legs spread. And the night of the thunder storm, the air awash with free ions, when she stood in the window, gasping at the lightning, and he stood behind her and . . . and here came his brandy, thank God.

He smiled at the waitress. What was the French for 'How about it, darling?' Something, something, something, *chérie*. He'd better stick to the French for 'Same again' – stay on safe ground. Yes, he was lost because he liked everything about Julia: the smell of tobacco on her breath, the taste of her menstrual blood. He couldn't rely on revulsion of any sort to set him free. She was kind, she was careful, she was accommodating. He was going to have to rely on the machine of their situation to grind them down, as he knew it would.

'*Encore la même chose,*' he called to the waitress, swirling his finger over his empty glass while she unloaded her tray at a nearby table. She nodded. She was the waitress, and he was the waiter waiting for the waitress. Everyone had their role.

He could feel the *fin de saison*, the lassitude of the beaches and restaurants, the sense that it was time to get back to school and to work, back to the big cities; and among the residents, relief at the subsiding numbers, the fading heat. All his guests had left Saint-Nazaire. Kettle had left in triumph, knowing she would be the first to return. She had signed up for Seamus's Basic Shaman workshop and then, in a kind of shopper's euphoria, decided to stay on for the Chi Gong course given by a pony-tailed martial artist whose photograph she pored over whenever there was someone to watch her. Seamus had given her a book called *The Power of Now*, which she kept face down beside her deck chair, not as reading material, obviously, but as a badge of allegiance to the power that now ran Saint-Nazaire. She had taken him up for the simple reason that it was the most annoying thing she could think of doing. It occupied the time when she was not criticizing Mary for the way she brought up the children. Mary had learned to walk away, to make herself unavailable for half-days at a time. Kettle had never known what to do with those fallow periods until she decided to become a fan of Seamus's Transpersonal Foundation. *The Power of Now* only disappeared when Anne Whitling, an old friend of Kettle's, wearing her own vast straw hat with an Isadora Duncan-length scarf

trailing dangerously behind it, talked her way down the coast
from one of the fashionable Caps. Her profound inability to listen to anyone else was unhappily married to a hysterical concern
about what other people thought of her. When Thomas started
babbling excitedly to Mary about the hose that was coiled next
to the pool house, Anne said, 'What's he saying? What's he saying? If he's saying my nose is too big, I'm going to commit.' This
charming abbreviation, which Patrick had never heard before,
made him imagine bloodstained articles about men's fear of com-
mitment. Should he commit to his marriage? Or commit to Julia?
Or just commit?

How could he go on feeling so awful? And how could he
stop? Stealing a picture from his senile mother was one obvious
way to cheer himself up. The last two valuable paintings she
owned were a pair of Boudins, making up complementary views
of the beach at Deauville, and worth approximately two hundred thousand pounds. He had to rap himself over the knuckles
for assuming that he would inherit the Boudins in 'the normal
course of events'. Only three days ago, just after waving an exhilarating farewell to Kettle, he had received another of Eleanor's
faint, painstaking, pencil-written notes, saying that she wanted
the Boudins sold and the money used to build Seamus's sensory-
deprivation annex. Things just weren't moving along fast enough
for the Kubla Khan of the mindless realms.

He could imagine himself in some distant past thinking he
ought to 'keep the Boudins in the family', feeling sentimental
about those banked-up clouds, the atmosphere of a lost yet vividly present world, the cultural threads radiating from those
Normandy beaches. Now they might as well have been two cash
dispensers in the wall of his mother's nursing home. If he was going to have to walk away from Saint-Nazaire, it would put a spring
in his step to know that the sale of the Boudins and the sale of the
London flat and a preparedness to move to Queen's Park would

allow him to save Thomas from the converted cupboard in which he now slept and offer him an ordinary-sized children's bedroom in a terraced house on a main road, no more than a two-hour traffic jam from his brother's school. Anyway, the last thing he needed was a view of a beach at the other end of France when he could so easily admire the carcinogenic inferno of Les Lecques through the amber lens of his second cognac. 'The sea meets the sky here as well, thank you very much, Monsieur Boudin,' he muttered to himself, already a little light-headed.

Did Seamus know about the note? Had he written it himself? Whereas Patrick was simply going to ignore Eleanor's request to make the gift of Saint-Nazaire absolute in her own lifetime, he was going to make a more drastic refusal in the case of the Boudins: steal them. Unless Seamus had written evidence that Eleanor wanted to give the paintings to the Foundation, any contest would come down to his word against Seamus's. Luckily, Eleanor's post-stroke signature looked like an incompetent forgery. Patrick felt confident that he could run legal circles around the visionary Irishman, even if he was unable to win a popularity contest against him when it was judged by his own mother. It was really, he assured himself, as he briskly ordered a *'dernier cognac'*, like a man with better things to do than get blind drunk before lunch, really just a question of how to unhook these two oily ATMs from the wall.

The light on the Promenade Rose rained down on him like a shower of hot needles. Even behind his dark glasses his eyeballs ached. He was really quite ... the coffee and the brandy ... a little jet-engine whistle. 'Walkin' on the beaches / Lookin' at the peaches / Na, na-na, na-na-na-na-na'. Where was that from? Press Retrieve. Nothing happens, as usual. Gerard Manley Hopkins? He cackled wildly.

He must have a cigar. Must have, must have, must have, on a

must-have basis. When was a cigar just a cigar? Before you must
have it.

With any luck, he should arrive back at the Tahiti Beach
(Irish accent) just in toyem for a syphilized battle of whine. 'God
bless Seamus,' he added piously, making a puking sound at the
foot of a squat bronze lamppost. Puns: the symptom of a schizoid personality.

Here was the *tabac*. The red cylinder. Whoops. '*Pardon, Madame*.' What was it with these big, tanned, wrinkly French women
with chunky gold jewellery, orange hair and caramel-coloured
poodles? They were *everywhere*. Unlock the glass cabinet. '*Celui-là*,'
pointing to a Hoyo de Monterey. The little guillotine. Snip. Do
you have something more serious at the back of the shop? *Un
vrai guillotine. Non, non, Madame, pas pour les cigars, pour les clients!*
Snap.

More hot needles. Hurry to the next patch of pine shade.
Maybe he should have one more teeny-weeny brandy before going back to his family. Mary and the boys, he loved them so
much, it made him want to cry.

He stopped at Le Dauphin. Coffee, cognac, cigar. Just as well
to get these chores out of the way, then he'd be free to enjoy the
rest of the day. He lit his cigar and as the thick smoke trickled
back out of his mouth he felt he was being shown a pattern, like
a rug unrolling in a rug shop. He had taken Mary, a good woman,
and made her into an instrument of torture, a weird echo of Eleanor forty years ago: never available, always exhausted by her
dedication to an altruistic project which didn't include him. He
had achieved this by the ironic device of rejecting the sort of
woman who would have made a bad mother, like Eleanor, and
choosing one who was such a good mother that she was incapable of letting one drop of her love escape from her children. He
could see that his obsession with not having enough money was
only the material form of his emotional privation. He had known

these facts for years, but just at that moment he felt that his grasp of them was especially subtle and clear and that his understanding gave him complete mastery of the situation. A second mouthful of heavy blue Cuban smoke drifted into the air. He was entranced by the sense of his own detachment, as if he had been set free by an instinctual expertise, like a seabird that breaks into flight just before a wave crashes onto the rock where it was perched.

The feeling passed. With only orange juice for breakfast, the six espressos and four glasses of brandy were having a bar brawl in his stomach. What was he doing? He had given up smoking. He flung the cigar towards the gutter. Whoops. '*Pardon, Madame.*' My God, it was the same woman, or almost the same woman. He might have set fire to her poodle. The newspaper headlines didn't bear thinking about . . . *Anglais intoxiqué* . . . *incendie de caniche* . . .

He must call Julia. He could live without her as long as he knew that she couldn't live without him. That was the deal the furiously weak made between their permanent disappointment and their temporary consolations. He looked at it with some disgust but knew that he would sign the contract anyway. He must make sure she was waiting for him, missing him, longing for him and expecting him in her flat on Monday night.

The nearest phone booth, a doorless and piss-scented wastepaper basket, was smouldering in full sunlight on the next corner. The blue plastic burnt his hand as he dialled the number.

'I can't come to the phone at the moment, but please leave a message . . .'

'Hello? Hello? It's Patrick. Are you hiding behind your machine? . . . OK, I'll call you tomorrow. I love you.' He'd almost forgotten to say that.

So, she wasn't in. Unless she was in bed with another man, sniggering at his tentative phone message. If he had one thing to say to the world, it was this: never, never have a child without first getting a reliable mistress. And don't be deceived by the false horizons – 'when the breastfeeding is over; when he spends the whole night in his own bed; when he goes to university'. Like a team of run-away horses, the empty promises hauled a man over shattered stone and giant cactuses while he prayed for the tangled reins to snap. It was all over, there was no comfort in marriage, just duty and obligation. He sank down on the nearest bench, needing to pause before he saw his family again. The cerulean huts and parasols of the Tahiti Beach were already in view, tunnelling deep into his memory. He had been Thomas's age when he first went there and Robert's when his memories became most intense: those pedalo rides which he expected to grind up on African beaches; jumping up and down on the sandcastles carefully assembled for him by foreign au pairs; being allowed to order his own drinks and ice creams as his chin cleared the wooden counter for the first time. As a teenager, he had taken books to the beach. They helped to hide his bulging trunks while he stared from behind his wraparound shades at the first blush of topless sunbathing to pass over the pale sands of Les Lecques. Since then the Tahiti had grown thinner and thinner, until the whole beach was nearly abolished by the sea. In his twenties, he had watched the municipality rebuild it with thousands of tons of imported pebbles. Every Easter, sand was dredged from the bay and spread over the artificial beach by teams of bulldozers, and every winter storms clawed it back into the bay.

He leant forward and rested his chin on his hands. The initial impact of the coffee and brandy was dying out, leaving him only with a doomed nervous energy, like a flung stone bouncing over the water a few times before sinking beneath its surface. He looked wearily at the simulacrum of the original beach, if 'original' was the word for the beach he had known when he was the same age as his children were now. He let this pitifully local definition melt away, and tumbled back through geological time to the perfect boredom of the first beach, with its empty rock pools and its simple molecules not knowing what to do with themselves for billions of years on end. Can anyone think of anything to do other than jostle around? Rows of blank faces, like asking a group of old friends to suggest a new restaurant on a Sunday night. Seen from this primal shore, the emergence of human life looked like Géricault's *Raft of the Medusa*, greenish ghosts drowning in a frigid ocean of time.

He really needed another drink to recover from the chaos of his imagination. And some food. And some sex. He needed to get grounded, as Seamus would say. He needed to rejoin his own species, the rows and rows of belching animals on the beach with only a razor blade or a wax job between them and a great thick pelt; paying with agonizing back pains for their pretentious upright posture, but secretly longing to hobble along with their knuckles dragging in the sand, squealing and grunting, fighting and fucking. Yes, he needed to get real. Only consideration for the white-haired old lady with swollen ankles further down the bench prevented him from raining punches on his clenched pectorals and letting out a territorial bellow. Consideration and, of course, his growing sense of liverish gloom and midday hangover.

He hauled himself up and scraped his way along the last few hundred yards to the Tahiti. Swaying towards him over the smooth pink concrete, an almost naked girl with overpoweringly perfect breasts and a diamond nestling in her navel, locked her eyes onto his and smiled, raising both her arms, ostensibly to wrap her long blonde hair into a loose coil above her head, but really to simulate the way her limbs would be arranged if she were lying on a bed with her arms thrown back. Oh, God, why was life so badly organized? Why couldn't he just hoist her onto a hot car bonnet and tear off that turquoise excuse for a bikini bottom? She wanted it, he wanted it. Well, anyway, he wanted it. She probably wanted exactly what she had, the power to disturb every heterosexual man – and let's not forget our lesbian colleagues, he added with mayoral unction – who she scythed through as she strolled back and forth between her depressing boyfriend and her nippy little car. She walked by, he staggered on. She might as well have chopped off his genitals and chucked them in the sand. He could feel the blood running down his legs, hear the dogs squabbling over the unexpected meat. He wanted to sit down again, to lie down, to bury himself deep underground. He was finished as a man. He envied the male spider who was eaten straight after fertilizing the female, rather than consumed bit by bit like his human counterpart.

He paused at the head of the broad white ladder that led down to the Tahiti Beach. He could see Robert running back and forth with a bucket, trying to fill a leaking moat. Thomas was lying in his mother's arms, sucking his thumb, holding his raggie and watching Robert with his strange objective gaze. They were happy because they had the undivided attention of their mother, and he was unhappy because he had her undivided inattention. That, at least, was the local reason, but hardly the original beach of his unhappiness. Never mind the original beach. He had to step down onto this one and be a father.

'Hello, darling,' said Mary, with that permanently exhausted smile in which her eyes didn't participate. They inhabited a harder world in which she was trying to survive the ceaseless demands of her sons, and the destructive effect on a solitary nature of spending years without a moment of solitude.

'Hi,' said Patrick. 'Shall we have lunch?'

'I think Thomas is about to fall asleep.'

'Right,' said Patrick, sinking down onto his lounger. There was always a good reason to frustrate his desires.

'Look,' said Robert, showing Patrick a swelling on his eyelid, 'I got a mosquito bite.'

'Don't be too hard on mosquitoes,' sighed Patrick, 'only the pregnant females whine, whereas women never stop whining, even after they've had several children.'

Why had he said that? He seemed to be full of zoological misogyny today. If anyone was whining it was him. It certainly wasn't true of Mary. He was the one who suffered from a seething distrust of women. His sons had no reason to share it. He must try to pull himself together. The least he could do was contain his depression.

'I'm sorry,' he said, 'I don't know why I said that. I'm feeling awfully tired.'

He smiled apologetically all round.

'It looks as if you need some help with that moat,' he suggested to Robert, picking up a second bucket.

They walked back and forth, pouring sea water into the sand until Thomas fell asleep in his mother's arms.

AUGUST 2002

IO

FROM THE BLUE PADDLING pool where he had been playing contentedly a moment before, Thomas suddenly dashed across the sand, glancing over his shoulder to see if his mother was following him. Mary pushed her chair back and bolted after him. He was so fast now, faster every day. He was already on the top step and only had to cross the Promenade Rose to reach the traffic. She leapt up three steps at a time and just caught him as he reached the corner of the parked car that hid him from the drivers cruising along the seaside road. He kicked and wriggled as she lifted him in the air.

'Never do that,' she said, almost in tears. 'Never do that. It's *so* dangerous.'

Thomas gurgled with laughter and excitement. He had discovered this new game yesterday when they arrived back at the Tahiti Beach. Last year he used to double back if he got more than three yards away from her.

As Mary carried him from the road to the parasol he shifted into another mode, sucking his thumb and patting her face affectionately with his palm.

'Are you all right, Mama?'

'I'm upset that you ran into the road.'

'I'm going to do something so dangerous,' said Thomas proudly. 'Yes, I am.'

Mary couldn't help smiling. Thomas was so charming.

How could she say she was sad when she was happy the next minute? How could she say she was happy when a minute later she wanted to scream? She had no time to draw up a family tree of every emotion that rushed through her. She had spent too long in a state of shattering empathy, tuned in to her children's vagrant moods. She sometimes felt she was about to forget her own existence completely. She had to cry to reclaim herself. People who didn't understand thought that her tears were the product of a long-suppressed and mundane catastrophe, her terminal exhaustion, her huge overdraft or her unfaithful husband, but they were in fact a crash course in the necessary egotism of someone who needed to get a self back in order to sacrifice it again. She had always been like that. Even as a child she only had to see a bird land on a branch in order for its wild heartbeat to replace her own. She sometimes wondered if her selflessness was a distinction or a pathology. She had no final answer to that either. Patrick was the one who worked in a world where judgements and opinions had to be given with an air of authority.

She sat Thomas down in the stacked plastic chairs of his place at the table.

'No, Mama, I don't want to sit in the double chairs,' said Thomas, climbing down and smiling mischievously as he set off towards the steps again. Mary recaptured him immediately and lifted him back into the chairs.

'No, Mama, don't pick me up, it's really unbearable.'

'Where do you pick up these phrases?' Mary laughed.

Michelle, the owner, came over with their grilled *dorade* and looked at Thomas reproachfully.

'*C'est dangereux, ça,*' she scolded him.

Yesterday Michelle had said she would have spanked her

children for running towards the road like that. Mary was always getting useless advice. She couldn't spank Thomas under any circumstances. Apart from the nausea she felt at the idea, she thought that punishment was the perfect way of masking the lesson it was supposed to enforce; all the child remembered was the violence, replacing the parent's justified distress with his own.

Kettle was a supreme source of useless advice, fed by the deep wells of her own uselessness as a mother. She had always tried to smother Mary's independent identity. It was not that she had treated Mary as a doll – she was too busy being one herself to do that – but as a kind of venture-capital fund: someone who was initially worthless, but who might one day pay off, if she married a big house or a big name. She had made it clear that marrying a barrister who was about to lose a medium-sized house abroad fell short of the bonanza she had in mind. Kettle's disappointment in the adult Mary was only the sequel to the disappointment she felt at her birth. Mary was not a boy. Girls who weren't boys were such a let-down. Kettle pretended that Mary's father was desperate for a boy, whereas the desperation had really belonged to her own father, a soldier who preferred trench warfare to female company and only agreed to the minimum necessary contact with the weaker sex in the hope of producing a male heir. Three daughters later he retired to his study.

Mary's father, on the contrary, had been delighted with her just as she was. His shyness intermeshed with hers in a way that set them both free. Mary, who hardly spoke for the first twenty years of her life, loved him for never making her feel that her silence was a failure. He understood that it came from a kind of over-intensity, a superabundance of impressions. The gap between her emotional life and social convention was too wide for her to cross. He had been the same way when he was young, but gradually learnt to present something that was not quite himself to the world. Mary's violent authenticity brought him back to his own core.

Mary remembered him vividly but her memories were embalmed by his early death. She was fourteen when he died of cancer. She was 'protected' from his illness by an ineffectual secrecy which made the situation more worrying than it was anyway. The secrecy had been Kettle's contribution, her substitute for sympathy. After Henry died, Kettle told Mary to 'be brave'. Being brave meant not asking for sympathy now either. There would have been no point in asking for it, even if the opportunity had not been blocked. Their experiences were essentially so different. Mary was utterly lost in loss, lost in imagining her father's suffering, lost in the madness of knowing that only he could have understood her feelings about his death. At the same time, confusingly, so much of their relationship had been spent in silent communion that there seemed to be no reason for it to stop. Kettle only appeared to be sharing the same bereavement. She was in fact suffering from the latest instalment of her inevitable disappointment. It was so unfair. She was too young to be a widow, and too old to start again on acceptable terms. It was in the wake of her father's death that Mary had got the full measure of her mother's emotional sterility and learnt to despise her. The crust of pity which she had formed since then had grown thinner when she had children of her own. It was now in constant danger of being torn apart by fresh eruptions of fury.

Kettle's most recent contribution had been to apologize for not getting Thomas a present for his second birthday. She had searched 'high and low' (translation: rung Harrods) 'for some of those marvellous reins you used to have as a child'. After Harrods let her down, she was too tired to look for anything else. 'They're bound to come back into fashion,' she said, as if she might give Thomas a pair when he was twenty or thirty, or whenever the world came to its senses and started stocking child reins again.

'I suppose Granny's a great disappointment to you, not getting you any reins,' she said to Thomas.

'No, I don't want any reins,' said Thomas, who had taken to ritually contradicting the latest statement he heard. Kettle, not knowing this, was astonished.

'Nanny used to swear by them,' she resumed.

'And I used to swear at them,' said Mary.

'You didn't, as a matter of fact,' said Kettle. 'Unlike Thomas, you weren't encouraged to swear like a drunken sailor.'

It was true that the last time they had visited Kettle in London, Thomas had said, 'Oh, no! Bloody fucking hell, my washing machine is on again,' and then pretended to turn it off by pressing the disconnected bell next to Kettle's fireplace.

He had heard Patrick say 'bloody fucking hell' that morning, after reading a letter from Sotheby's. The Boudins, it turned out, were fakes.

'What a waste of moral effort,' said Patrick.

'It wasn't a waste. You didn't know they were fakes before you decided not to steal them.'

'I know, that's just it: it would have been such an easy decision if I had known. "Steal from my own mother? Never!" I could have thundered right at the beginning, instead of spending a year wondering whether to be some kind of intergenerational Robin Hood, correcting an imbalance with my virtuous crime. My mother managed to make me hate myself for being honourable,' said Patrick, clasping his head between his hands. 'How conflicted was that? And how unnecessary.'

'What's Dada talking about?' asked Thomas.

'I'm talking about your fucking grandmother's fake paintings.'

'No, she's not my fucking grandmother,' said Thomas, shaking his head solemnly.

'Seamus is not the first person to have bamboozled her into

parting with the little money that *my* fucking grandmother left her. Some art dealer in Paris pulled off that facile trick thirty years ago.'

'No, she's not your fucking grandmother,' said Thomas, 'she's my fucking grandmother.'

Property was another thing Thomas had taken up recently. For a long time he had no sense of owning things, now everything belonged to him.

Mary was alone with Thomas for the first week of August. Patrick was detained in London by a difficult case which she suspected should be called Julia versus Mary, but was pretending to be called something else. How could she say she was jealous of Julia when the next moment she was not? Sometimes, in fact, she was grateful to her. She didn't want Patrick to be taken away, nor did she think he would be. Mary was both naturally jealous and naturally permissive, and the only way these two sides of her could collaborate was by cultivating the permissiveness. That way Patrick never really wanted to leave her, and so her jealousy was satisfied as well. The flow chart looked simple enough, except for two immediate complications. First, there were the times when she was overwhelmed with nostalgia for the erotic life they had shared before she became a mother. Her passion had peaked, naturally, when it was organizing its own extinction, during the time when she was trying to get pregnant. Secondly, she was angered when she felt that Patrick was deliberately worsening their relations in order to invigorate his adultery. There it was: he needed sex, she couldn't provide it, he was going to look elsewhere. Infidelity was a technicality, but disloyalty introduced a fundamental doubt, a terminal atmosphere.

It was the first time Robert had been away from home for more than a night. He was devastatingly relaxed on his first evening at his friend Jeremy's when they spoke on the telephone. Of course she was pleased, of course it was a sign of his confidence in his parents' love that he felt the love was there even when they were not. Still, it was strange to be without him. She could remember him at Thomas's age, when he still ran away in order to be chased and still hid in order to be found. Even then he had been more introspective than Thomas, more burdened. He had been, on the one hand, the inhabitant of a pristine paradise that Thomas would never know, and on the other hand, a prototype. Thomas had benefited from learned mistakes and the more precise hopes that followed them.

'I've had enough now,' said Thomas, starting to climb down from his chairs.

Mary waved at Michelle but she was serving another customer. She held back a plate of chips for this moment. If Thomas saw them earlier he ate no fish, if he saw them now he stayed for a second five-minute sitting. Mary couldn't catch Michelle's attention and Thomas continued his descent.

'Do you want some chips, darling?'

'No, Mama, I don't. Yes, I do want some chips,' Thomas corrected himself.

He slipped and bumped his chin against the table top.

'Mama take you,' he said, spreading his arms out.

She lifted him up and sat him on her lap, rocking him gently. Whenever he was hurt he reverted to calling himself 'you', although he had discovered the proper use of the first person singular six months ago. Until then, he had referred to himself as 'you' on the perfectly logical grounds that everyone else did. He also referred to others as 'I', on the perfectly logical grounds that that was how they referred to themselves. Then one week 'you want it' turned into 'I want it'. Everything he did at the moment – the fascination with danger, the assertion of ownership, the ritual contradiction, the desire to do things for himself – was about this explosive transition from being 'you' to being 'I', from seeing himself through his parents' eyes to looking through his own.

Just for now, though, he was having a grammatical regression, he wanted to be 'you' again, his mother's creature.

'It's so difficult because your will is what gets you through life,' Sally had said last night. 'Why would you want to break your child's will? That's what our mothers wanted to do. That's what it meant to be "good" – being broken.'

Sally, Mary's American friend, was her greatest ally; also a mother showered in useless advice, also determined to give her children uncompromised support, to roll the boulder of her own upbringing out of the way so that they could run free. This task was surrounded by hostile commentary: stop being a doormat; don't be a slave to your children; get your figure back; keep your husband happy; get back 'out there'; go to a party, spending your whole time with your children drives you literally mad; increase your self-esteem by handing your children over to someone else and writing an article saying that women should not feel guilty about handing their children over to someone else; don't spoil your children by giving them what they want; let the little tyrants cry themselves to sleep, when they realize that crying is useless they'll stop; anyway, children love boundaries. Below this layer came the confusing rumours: never use paracetamol, always use paracetamol, paracetamol stops homeopathy from working, homeopathy doesn't work, homeopathy works for some things but not for others; an amber necklace stops their teeth hurting; that rash could be an allergy to cow's milk, it could be an allergy to wheat, it could be an allergy to the air quality, London has become five times more polluted in the last ten years; nobody really knows, it'll probably just go away. Then there were the invidious comparisons and the plain lies: my daughter sleeps all through the night; she hasn't needed nappies since she was three weeks old; his mother breast-fed him till he was five; we're so lucky, they've both got guaranteed places at the Acorn; her best friend at school is Cilla Black's granddaughter.

When all these distractions could be ignored, Mary tried to hack through the dead wood of her own conditioning, through the overcompensation, through the exhaustion and the irritation and the terror, through the tension between dependency and independence which was alive in her as well as her children, which she had to recognize but could give no time to, and get back, perhaps, to the root of an instinct for love, and try to stay there and to act from there.

She felt that Sally was roped to the same cliff face as her, and that they could rely on each other. Sally had sent through a fax last night but Mary hadn't had time to read it yet. She had torn it from the fax machine and squeezed it into her rucksack. Perhaps when Thomas had a sleep – when he had a sleep, that moment into which the rest of life was supposed to be artfully crammed. By the time it came around, she was usually too desperate for sleep herself to break away from his rhythm and do anything different.

The chips had already lost their power to hold Thomas and he was climbing back down the chairs. Mary took his hand and let him lead her back to the steps he had dashed up earlier. They wandered down the Promenade Rose together hand in hand.

'It's lovely and smooth on my feet,' said Thomas. 'Oh,' he suddenly stopped in front of a row of wilted cactuses, 'what's that called?'

'It's some kind of cactus, darling. I don't know the specific name.'

'But I want to know the specific name,' said Thomas.

'We'll have to look it up in my book when we get home.'

'Yes, Mama, we'll . . . Oh! What's that boy doing?'

'He's got a water pistol.'

'For watering the flowers.'

'Well, yes, that would be a good use for it.'

'It's for watering the flowers,' he informed her.

He loosened his hand and walked ahead of her. Although they were constantly together, she often didn't get to look at him for hours on end. He was either too close for her to see the whole of him, or she was focused on the dangerous elements in the situation and had no time to appreciate the rest. Now she could see him whole, without anxiety, looking adorable with his hooped blue T-shirt and khaki trousers and his determined walk. His face was astonishingly beautiful. She sometimes worried about the kind of attention it would attract, and the kind of impact he would get used to having. She could remember when he had first opened his eyes in the hospital. They were blazing with an inexplicably strong sense of intention; a drive to make sense of the world, in order to house another kind of knowledge which he already had. Robert had arrived with a completely different atmosphere, a sense of emotional intensity, of trouble that needed working out.

'Oh,' said Thomas pointing, 'what's that funny man doing?'

'He's putting on his mask and snorkel.'

'It's my mask and snorkel.'

'Well, it's very nice of you to let him use it.'

'I let him use it,' said Thomas. 'He can use it, Mama.'

'Thank you, darling.'

He marched on. He was being munificent now, but in about ten minutes his energy would collapse and everything would start to go wrong.

'Shall we go back to the beach and have a little rest?'

'I don't want a little rest. I want to go to the playground. I love the playground so much,' he said, breaking into a run.

The playground was uninhabitable at this time of day, its dangerous climbing frame led to a metal slide hot enough to fry an egg on. Next to it, a plastic pony squeaked unbearably on a coiled spring. When they arrived at the wooden gate, Mary reached out and swung it open for Thomas.

'No, Mama, I do it,' he said with a sudden wail of misery.

'OK, OK,' said Mary.

'No, I do it,' said Thomas, pulling open with some difficulty the gate, made heavier by a metal plaque displaying eight play-ground rules, four times as many rules as rides. They made the transition to a pink rubber surface masquerading as tarmac. Thomas climbed the curved bars up to the platform above the slide, and then dashed over to the other opening, opposite a fire-man's pole which he couldn't possibly get down on his own. Mary hurried around the climbing frame to meet him. Would he really jump? Was he really going to misjudge his capacities to that extent? Was she pumping fear into a situation where only play was needed? Was it an instinct to anticipate disaster, or was every other mother in the world more relaxed than her? Was it worth pretending to be relaxed, or was pretence always a bad thing? Once Mary was standing beside the pole, Thomas moved back to the slide and quickly pulled himself down. He tipped over at the end of his run and banged his head on the edge. The shock fused with his exhaustion to produce a long moment of silence; his face flushed and he let out a long scream, his pink tongue quivering in his mouth, and his eyes thickly glazed with tears. Mary felt, as usual, that a javelin had been flung into her chest. She picked him up in her arms and held him close, reas-suring them both.

'Raggie with a label,' he sobbed. She handed him a Harrington square with the label still on it. A raggie without a label was not just unconsoling but doubly upsetting because of its tantalizing resemblance to the ones which still had labels.

She walked back swiftly to the beach, carrying him in her arms. He shuddered and grew quiet, clasping Raggie and suck-ing his thumb with the same hand. The adventure was over, the exploration had gone to its limit and ended the only way it could, involuntarily. She laid him down on a mattress under a parasol and curled up next to him, closing her eyes and lying completely still. She heard him suck his thumb more intensely as he settled, and then she could tell from the change in his breathing that he had fallen asleep. She opened her eyes.

Now she had an hour, perhaps two, in which to answer letters, pay her taxes, keep in touch with her friends, revive her intellect, take some exercise, read a good book, think of a brilliant money-making scheme, take up yoga, see an osteopath, go to the dentist and get some sleep. Sleep, remember sleep? The word had once referred to great haunches of unconsciousness, six, eight, nine-hour slabs; now she fought for twenty-minute scraps of disturbing rest, rest which reminded her that she was fundamentally done in. Last night she was kept awake by an overwhelming terror that some harm would come to Thomas if she fell asleep. She was rigid with resistance all night, like a sentry who knows that death is the penalty for nodding off on his watch. Now she really had to get some muddling, hangover-like afternoon sleep, soaked in unpleasant dreams, but first she was going to read Sally's fax, as a sign of her independence, which she often felt was even less well established than Thomas's, since she couldn't test its limits as wildly as he could. It was a practical fax, as Sally had warned her, with the dates and times of her arrival at Saint-Nazaire, but then at the end Sally added, 'I came across this quotation yesterday, from Alexander Herzen. "We think the purpose of a child is to grow up because it does grow up. But its purpose is to play, to enjoy itself, to be a child. If we merely look to the end of the process, the purpose of life is death."'

Yes, that was what she had wanted to say to Patrick when they had been alone with Robert. Patrick had been so concerned with shaping Robert's mind, with giving him a transfusion of scepticism, that he had sometimes forgotten to let him play, enjoy himself and be a child. He let Thomas follow his own course, partly because he was preoccupied with his own psychological survival, but also because Thomas's desire for knowledge outstripped any parental ambition. With him she thought, as she closed her eyes after a last glance at Thomas's sleeping face, it was so clear that playing and enjoying himself were identical with learning to master the world around him.

II

'WHERE HAS MY WILLIE gone?' said Thomas, lying on his blue towel after his bath.

'It's disappeared,' said Mary.

'Oh! There it is, Mama,' he said, uncrossing his legs.

'That's a relief,' said Mary.

'It certainly is a relief,' said Thomas.

After playing in his bath he was reluctant to get back into the padded cell of a nappy. Pyjamas, the dreadful sign that he was expected to go to sleep, sometimes had to wait until he was asleep to be put on. Any sense that Mary was in a hurry made him take twice as long to go to bed.

'Oh, no! My willie's disappeared again,' said Thomas. 'I really am upset about it.'

'Are you, darling?' said Mary, noticing him experiment with the phrase she had used yesterday when he threw a glass on the kitchen floor.

'Yes, Mama, it's driving me crazy.'

'Where can it have gone?' asked Mary.

'I don't believe it,' he said, pausing for her to appreciate the gravity of the loss. 'Oh, there it is!' He gave a perfect imitation of the reassured cheerfulness with which she rediscovered a milk bottle or a lost shoe.

He started to jump up and down and then dropped onto the bed, rolling among the pillows.

'Be careful,' said Mary, watching him bounce too near the metal guards that surrounded the edge of the bed.

It was hard to stay ready for a sudden catch, to keep scanning for sharp corners and hard edges, to let him go to the limit of his adventure. She really wanted to lie down now, but the last thing she should do was to show any sign of exasperation or impatience.

'I am an acrobat at the circus,' said Thomas, trying to do a forward roll but keeling over. 'Mama say, "Be careful, little monkey."'

'Be careful, little monkey,' Mary repeated her line obediently. She must get him a director's chair and a megaphone. He was always being told what to do, now it was his turn.

She felt drained by the long day, most of all by visiting Eleanor in her nursing home. Mary had tried to mask her sense of shock when she arrived with Thomas in Eleanor's room. All of Eleanor's upper teeth were missing from one side of her mouth and only three dangled like black stalactites from the other. Her hair, which she used to have washed every other day, was reduced to a greasy chaos stuck to her now visibly bumpy skull. As Mary leant over to kiss Eleanor, she was assailed by a stench that made her want to reach for the portable changing mat she carried in her rucksack. She must restrain her maternal drive, especially in the presence of a proven champion of maternal self-restraint.

Eleanor's decay was underlined by her loss of equality with Thomas. Last year, neither of them could talk properly or walk steadily; Eleanor had lost enough teeth to leave her with roughly the same number as Thomas had gained; her new need for incontinence pads matched his established need for nappies. This year, everything had changed. Thomas wouldn't need nappies for much longer, Eleanor needed more than she was currently using; only his back molars still had to work their way through, her back molars would soon be the only teeth she had left; he was getting so fast that his mother could hardly keep up, Eleanor could hardly keep herself up in her chair and would soon be bedridden. Mary paused on top of the icy slopes of potential conversation. The already strained assumption that they shared an enthusiasm for Thomas's progress now looked like a covert insult. It was no use reminding her of Robert either, her former ally, now the disciple of his father's hostility.

'Oh, no!' said Thomas to Eleanor. 'Alabala stole my halumbalum.'

Thomas, who was so often stuck with adults in a traffic jam of incomprehensible syllables, sometimes answered back with a little private language of his own. Mary was used to this sweet revenge and also intrigued by the emergence of Alabala, a recent creation who seemed to be falling into the classic role of doing naughty things to and for Thomas, and was accompanied by his conscience, a character called Felan. He looked up at Eleanor with a smile. It was not returned. Eleanor stared at Thomas with horror and suspicion. What she saw was not the ingenuity of a child but the harbinger of her worst fear: that soon, on top of being unable to make herself understood, she would not be able to understand anybody else. Mary moved in quickly.

'He doesn't only talk nonsense,' she said. 'One of his favourite phrases at the moment – I think you'll detect Patrick's influence –' she tried another complicit smile, 'is "absolutely unbearable".'

Eleanor's body lurched forward a couple of inches. She gripped the wooden arms of her chair and looked at Mary with furious concentration.

'Absolute-ly un-bearable,' she spat out, and then fell back, adding a high, faint, 'Yes.'

Eleanor turned again towards Thomas, but this time she looked at him with a kind of greed. A moment ago, he seemed to be announcing the storm of gibberish that would soon enshroud her, but now he had given her a phrase which she understood perfectly, a phrase she couldn't have managed on her own, describing exactly how she felt.

Something similar happened when Mary read out a list of audio books that Eleanor might want sent from England. Eleanor's method for choosing the books bore no obvious relation to their authors or categories. Mary droned through the titles of works by Jane Austen and Proust, Jeffrey Archer and Jilly Cooper, without any signs of interest from Eleanor. Then she read out the title *Ordeal of Innocence* and Eleanor started nodding her head and flapping her hands acquisitively, as if she were splashing water onto her chest. *Harvest of Dust* elicited the same surges of excitement. Stimulated by these unexpected communications, Eleanor remembered the note she had written earlier, and handed it to Mary with her shaking, liver-spotted hand.

Mary made out the faint words, in pencil-written block capitals, 'WHY SEAMUS DOES NOT COME?'

Mary suspected the reason, but could hardly believe it. She hadn't expected Seamus to be so flagrant. His opportunism always seemed to be blended with the genuine delusion that he was a good man, or at least a strong desire to be mistaken for one. And yet here he was, only a fortnight after the final transfer of Saint-Nazaire to the Foundation, dropping his benefactor like a sack on a skip.

She remembered what Patrick had said when he finally used the power of attorney his mother had given him to sign over the house: 'These people who want to crawl unburdened to their graves just don't make it. There is no second childhood, no licence for irresponsibility.' He then got blind drunk.

Mary looked at Eleanor's face. It was impacted with misery.

Her eyes were veiled like the eyes of a recently dead fish, but in her case the dullness seemed to stem from the effort of staying disconnected from reality. Mary could see now that her missing teeth were really a suicidal gesture, with the violent passivity of a hunger strike. They could so easily have been replaced, it must have taken great stubbornness to stay in the vortex of self-neglect, week after week, as they fell out, one by one, ignoring the medical profession, the antidepressants, the nursing home and the remains of her own will to live.

Mary felt pierced by a sense of tragedy. Here was a woman who had abandoned her family for a vision and for a man, and now the man and the vision had abandoned her. She could remember Eleanor telling her, when she could still speak adequately, that she and Seamus had known each other in 'previous lifetimes'. One of these previous lifetimes had taken place on something called a 'skelig', some kind of Irish seaside mound, which Seamus had taken Eleanor to see early in his financial courtship, on that unforgettable, blustery day when he took her hand and said, 'Ireland needs you.' Once Eleanor realized, in a 'past-life recall', that she had lived as Seamus's wife on the very skelig they visited, during the Dark Ages, when Ireland was a beacon of Christianity in that muddle of pillage and migration, her immediate family, with whom she had a relatively shallow past, began to slip from view. And once Seamus visited Saint-Nazaire, he realized that France needed him even more than Ireland needed Eleanor. The house had been a convent in the seventeenth century, and a second 'past-life recall' established that Eleanor was (it seemed obvious once you were told) the mother superior. The noun, Mary remembered thinking, had stayed stuck in front of the adjective ever since. Seamus, amazingly, was the abbot of a local monastery at exactly the same time. And so they had been thrown together again, this time in a 'spiritual friendship' which had been misinterpreted and caused a great scandal in the area.

When Eleanor told her all this, in an oppressive parody of girls' talk, Mary decided not to argue. Eleanor believed more or less anything, as long as it was untrue. It was part of her charitable nature to rush belief to the unbelievable, like emergency aid. She clearly needed to inhabit these historical novels to make up for the disappointment of a passion which was not being acted out in the bedroom (it had evolved too much for that) but was having a thrilling enough time at the Land Registry. It had all seemed so ridiculous to Mary at the time; now she wished she could stick back the peeling wallpaper of Eleanor's credulity. Under the dreadful sincerity of the original confession was that need to be needed which Mary recognized so well.

'I'll ask him,' she said, covering Eleanor's hand gently with her own. Although she hadn't seen him yet, she knew that Seamus was in his cottage. 'Perhaps he's been ill, or in Ireland.'

'Ireland,' Eleanor whispered.

When they were walking back to the car, Thomas stopped and shook his head. 'Oh, dear,' he said. 'Eleanor is not very well.'

Mary loved his straightforward sympathy for suffering. He hadn't yet learned to pretend that it wasn't going on, or to blame the person who was having it. He fell asleep in the car and she decided she might as well go straight to Seamus's cottage.

'Well, now, that's a terrible thing,' said Seamus. 'I thought with the family being here and everything, that Eleanor wouldn't want to see me so much. And, to be honest with you Mary, the Pegasus Press have been breathing down my neck. They want to put my book in their spring catalogue. I've got so many ideas, it's just getting them down. Do you think *Drumbeat of my Heart* or *Heartbeat of my Drum* is better?'

'I don't know,' said Mary. 'It depends which one you mean, I suppose.'

'That's good advice,' said Seamus. 'Talking of drums, we're very pleased with your mother's progress. She's taken to the soul-retrieval work like a duck to water. I just got an email from her saying she wants to come to the autumn intensive.'

'Amazing,' said Mary. She was nervous that the monitor wouldn't work. The green light seemed to be winking in the usual way, but she had never used it in the car before.

'Soul retrieval is something I think Eleanor could benefit from immensely. I'm just thinking aloud now,' said Seamus, swivelling excitedly in his chair and blocking Mary's view of a leathery old Inuit woman, with a pipe dangling from her mouth, that radiated from his computer screen. 'If your mother were to lead a ceremony with Eleanor at the centre of the circle, that could be hugely powerful with all the, you know, connections.' He spread the fingers of both his hands and intermeshed them tenderly.

Poor Seamus, thought Mary, he wasn't really a bad man, he was just a complete idiot. She sometimes became a little competitive with Patrick about who had the most annoying mother. Kettle gave nothing away, Eleanor gave everything away; the results were indistinguishable for the family, except that Mary had 'expectations', made fantastically remote by the robustness of her meticulously selfish mother, who thought of nothing but her own comfort, rushed to the doctor every time she sneezed and 'treated' herself to a holiday once a month to get over the disappointment of the last one. Patrick's disinheritance had nudged him ahead in the bad-mother stakes, but perhaps Seamus was planning to eliminate that advantage by taking Kettle's money as well. Was he, after all, really a bad man doing a brilliant impersonation of an idiot? It was hard to tell. The connections between stupidity and malice were so tangled and so dense.

'I'm seeing more and more connections,' said Seamus, twisting his fingers around each other. 'To be honest with you, Mary, I don't think I'll write another book. It can do your head in.'

'I bet,' said Mary. 'I couldn't even begin to write a book.'

'Oh, I've done the beginning,' said Seamus. 'In fact, I've done several beginnings. Perhaps it's all beginnings, do you know what I mean?'

'With each new heartbeat,' said Mary. 'Or drumbeat.'

'That's right, that's right,' said Seamus.

Thomas's waking cry burst through the monitor. Mary was relieved to know that she was in range.

'Oh, dear, I'm going to have to leave.'

'I'll definitely try to see Eleanor in the next few days,' said Seamus, accompanying her to the door of his cottage. 'I really appreciate what you said about the heartbeat and being in the moment – it's given me a lot of ideas.'

He opened the door, setting off a tinkling of chimes. Mary looked up and saw three Chinese pictographs clustered around a dangling brass rod.

'Happiness, Peace and Prosperity,' said Seamus. 'They're inseparable.'

'I'm sorry to hear that,' said Mary. 'I was rather hoping to get the first two on their own.'

'Ah, but what is prosperity?' said Seamus, walking with her towards the car. 'Ultimately, it's having something to eat when you're hungry. That's the prosperity that was denied to Ireland, for instance, during the 1840s, and that's still denied to millions of people around the world.'

'Gosh,' said Mary. 'There's not a lot I can do about the Irish in the 1840s. But I could give Thomas his "ultimate prosperity" – or can I go on calling it "lunch"?'

Seamus threw back his head and let out a guffaw of wholesome laughter.

'I think that would be simpler,' he said, giving Mary's back an unwelcome rub.

She opened the door and took Thomas out of his car seat.

'How is the little man?' said Seamus.

'He's very well,' said Mary. 'He has a lovely time here.'

'Well, I'm sure that's down to your excellent mothering,' said Seamus, his hand by now burning a hole in the back of her T-shirt. 'But I'd also say that with the soul work, it's very important to create a safe environment. That's what we do here. Now, maybe Thomas is picking that up, you know, at some level.'

'I expect he is,' said Mary, reluctant to deny Thomas a compliment, even when it was really intended by Seamus for himself. 'He's very good at picking things up.'

She managed to stand out of Seamus's range, holding Thomas in her arms.

'Ah,' said Seamus, framing the two of them with a large parenthetical gesture, 'the mother-and-child archetype. It makes me think of my own mother. She had the eight of us to look after. At the time I think I was preoccupied with little ways of getting more than my fair share of the attention.' He chuckled indulgently at the memory of this younger, less enlightened self. 'That was definitely a big dynamic in my family; but looking back from where I'm standing now, what amazes me is how she went on giving and giving. And you know, Mary, I've come to the conclusion that she was tapping into a universal source, into that archetypal mother-and-child energy. Do you know what I mean? I want to put something about that in my book. It all ties in with the shamanic work – at some level. It's just getting it down. I'd welcome any thoughts about that: moments when you've felt supported by something beyond the level of, you know, personal sacrifice.'

'Let me think about it,' said Mary, suddenly realizing where Seamus had learned his little ways of getting mothers to hand over their resources to him. 'In the meantime, I really must make Thomas some lunch.'

'Of course, of course,' said Seamus. 'Well, it's been grand talking to you, Mary. I really feel that we've connected.'

'I feel I've learned a lot as well,' said Mary.

She now knew, for instance, that his feeble promise to 'try to visit Eleanor in the next few days' meant that he would not visit her today, or tomorrow, or the next day. Why would he waste his 'little ways' on a woman who only had a couple of fake Boudins to her name?

She carried Thomas into the kitchen and put him down on the counter. He took his thumb out of his mouth and looked at her with a subtle expression which hovered between seriousness and laughter.

'Seamus is a very funny man, Mama,' he said.

Mary burst out laughing.

'He certainly is,' she said, kissing him on the forehead.

'He certainly is a very funny man!' said Thomas, catching her laughter. He scrunched up his eyes in order to laugh more seriously.

No wonder she was tired after seeing Eleanor and Seamus on the same day, no wonder it was difficult to extort any more vigilance from her aching body and her blanched mind. Something had happened today; she hadn't quite got the measure of it, but it was one of those sudden dam bursts which were the only way she ever ended a long period of conflict. She had no time to work it out while Thomas was still bouncing naked in the middle of the bed.

'That was a very big jump,' said Thomas, climbing to his feet again. 'You certainly are impressed, Mama.'

'Yes, darling. What would you like to read tonight?'

Thomas stopped in order to concentrate on a difficult task.

'Let's talk reasonably about lollipops,' he said, retrieving a phrase from an old book of Patrick's which had got stuck down in Saint-Nazaire.

'Dr Upping and Dr Downing?'

'No, Mama, I don't want to read that.'

Mary took *Babar and Professor Grifiton* from the shelf and climbed over the guard onto the bed. They had a ritual of reviewing the day, and Mary threw out the usual question, 'What did we do today?' Thomas stopped bouncing as she had hoped.

Thomas lowered his voice and shook his head solemnly.

'Peter Rabbit has been eating my grapes,' he said.

'No!' said Mary, shocked.

'Mr McGregor will be very angry with Seamus.'

'Why Seamus? I thought it was Peter Rabbit who took the grapes.'

'No, Mama, it was Seamus.'

Whatever it was that Thomas was 'picking up', it wasn't the sense of a 'safe environment' that Seamus had boasted about creating for 'the soul work'. It was the atmosphere of theft. If Seamus was prepared to treat Eleanor with so little ceremony, when she had set off the prosperity chime in his life with such a resounding tinkle, why would he bother to honour her promises to his defeated rivals? His imagination was teeming with competing siblings, and he had adopted Patrick and Mary for the purposes of triumphing over them in an archaic contest for which neither of them had received his commando training. What was the point of an old woman who couldn't even buy him a sensory-deprivation tank? And what was the point of her descendants cluttering up his Foundation during August?

12

'BUT I DON'T UNDERSTAND, said Robert, watching Mary pack. 'Why do we have to leave?'

'You know why,' said Mary.

He sat on the edge of the bed, his shoulders rounded and his hands wedged under his thighs. If there had been time, she would have sat beside him and hugged him and let him cry again, but she had to get on with the packing while Thomas was sleeping.

Mary hadn't slept for the last two days, equally tormented by the atmosphere of loss and the longing to leave. Houses, paintings, trees, Eleanor's teeth, Patrick's childhood and her children's holidays: to her tired mind they all seemed to be piled up like the wreckage from a flood. She had spent the last seven years watching Patrick's childhood like a rope inching through his clenched hands. Now she wanted to get the hell out. It was already too late to stop Robert from identifying with Patrick's sense of injustice, but she could still save Thomas from getting tangled in the drama of disinheritance. The family was being split in half and it could only come back together if they left.

Patrick had gone to say goodbye to Eleanor. He had promised not to make any irrevocably bitter speeches in case he never saw her again. If he had enough warning of her death, he would doubtless fly down to hold her hand, but it was unrealistic to think that the rest of them would be checking into the Grand Hôtel des Bains to mount a deathbed vigil in the nursing home. Mary had to admit that she looked forward to Eleanor dropping out of their lives altogether.

'Would we get the house if we killed Seamus?' asked Robert.

'No,' said Mary, 'it would go to the next director of the Foundation.'

'That's so unfair,' said Robert. 'Unless I became the director. Yes! I'm a genius!'

'Except that you would have to direct the Foundation.'

'Oh, yeah, that's true,' said Robert. 'Well, maybe Seamus will repent.' He adopted a thick Irish accent. 'I can only apologize, Mary. I don't know what came over me, trying to steal the house from you and the little ones, but I've come to moi senses now and I want you to know that even if you can find it in your heart to forgive me for the agony I've caused you, I shall never be able to forgive myself.' He broke down sobbing.

She knew his fake sobbing was close to being real. For the first time since Thomas was born she felt that Robert was the one who needed her most. His great strength was that he was even more interested in playing with what was going on than he was in wasting his time trying to control it – although he did quite a lot of that as well. His playfulness had collapsed for a few days and been replaced entirely by wishing and longing and regretting. Now she saw it coming back. She could never quite get used to the way he pieced together impersonations out of the things he overheard. Seamus had become his latest obsession, and no wonder. She was too exhausted to do anything but give him a laborious smile and fold the swimming trunks she had unpacked for him less than a week before. Everything had happened so fast. On the day he arrived with Robert, Patrick had found a note asking if Kevin and Anette could have 'some space' in the house. Seamus had dropped in the next morning at breakfast to get his answer.

'I hope I'm not interrupting,' he called out.

'Not at all,' said Patrick. 'It's good of you to come so quickly. Would you like some coffee?'

'I won't, thank you, Patrick. I've really been abusing the caffeine lately in an attempt to get myself going with the writing, you know.'

'Well, I hope you don't mind if I go ahead and abuse some caffeine without you.'

'Be my guest,' said Seamus.

'Is that what I am?' asked Patrick, like a greyhound out of the slips. 'Or are you in fact my guest during this one month of the year? That's the crux of the matter. You know that the terms of my mother's gift included letting us have the house for August, and we're not going to put up with having your friends billeted on us.'

'Well, now, "terms" is a very legalistic way of putting it,' said Seamus. 'There's nothing in writing about the Foundation providing you with a free holiday. I have a genuine sympathy for the trouble you've had in accepting your mother's wishes. That's why I've been prepared to put up with a lot of negativity from your side.'

'We're not discussing the trouble I've had with my mother's wishes, but the trouble you're having with them. Let's not stray from the subject.'

'They're inseparable.'

'Everything looks inseparable to a moron.'

'There's no need to get personal. They're inseparable because they both depend on knowing what Eleanor wanted.'

'It's obvious what she wanted. What isn't clear is whether you can accept the part that doesn't suit you.'

'Well, I have a more global vision than that, Patrick. I see the problem in holistic terms. I think we all need to find a solution together, you and your family, and Kevin and Anette, and me. Perhaps we could do a ritual expressing what we bring to this community and what we expect to take from it.'

'Oh, no, not another ritual. What is it with you people and rituals? What's wrong with having a conversation? When I spent my teenage years in what has become your cottage, there were two bedrooms. Why don't you put your friends up in your own spare room?'

'That's now my study and office space.'

'God forbid they should invade your private space.'

Thomas wriggled down from Mary's arms and started to explore. His desire to move made her even more aware of how paralysed the rest of them had become. She took no pleasure in seeing Patrick frozen in a kind of autumnal adolescence: dogmatic and sarcastic, resentful of his mother's actions, still secretly thinking of Seamus's cottage as the teenage den in which he spent half a dozen summers of semi-independence. Only Thomas, because he hadn't been given any coordinates on this particular grid, could slip to the floor and let his mind flow wherever it wanted. Seeing him get away gave Mary a certain remoteness from the scene being played out by Patrick and Seamus, even though she could feel a sullen violence taking over from Seamus's usual inane affability.

'Did you know,' said Patrick, addressing Seamus again, 'that among the caribou herdsmen of Lapland, the top shaman gets to drink the urine of the reindeer that has eaten the magic mushrooms, and his assistant drinks the urine of the top shaman, and so on, all the way down to the lowest of the low who scramble in the snow, pleading for a splash of twelfth-generation caribou piss?'

'I didn't know that,' said Seamus flatly.

'I thought it was your special field,' said Patrick, surprised.

'Anyhow, the irony is that the premier cru, the first hit, is much the most toxic. Poor old top shaman is reeling and sweating, trying to get all the poison out, whereas a few damaged livers later, the urine is harmless without having lost its hallucinogenic power. Such is the human attachment to status that people will sacrifice their peace of mind and their precious time in order to pickaxe their way towards what turns out to be a thoroughly poisonous experience.'

'That's all very interesting,' said Seamus, 'but I don't see what it has to do with our immediate problem.'

'Only this: that out of what I admit is pride, I am not prepared to be at the bottom of the pissing hierarchy in this "community".'

'If you don't want to be part of this community, you don't have to stay,' said Seamus quietly.

There was a pause.

'Good,' said Patrick. 'Now at least we know what you really want.'

'Why don't *you* go away,' shouted Robert. 'Just leave us alone. This is my grandmother's house, and we have more right to be here than you do.'

'Let's calm down,' said Mary, resting a hand on Robert's shoulder. 'We aren't going to leave in the middle of the children's holidays, whether we come here next year or not. We could compromise over your friends, perhaps. If you sacrifice your office for a week, we could put them up for the last week of our stay. That seems fair enough.'

Seamus faltered between the momentum of his anger and his desire to look reasonable.

'I'll have to get back to you on that,' he said. 'To be honest with you, I'm going to have to process some of the negative feelings I'm having at the moment, before I can come to a decision.'

'You process away,' said Patrick, getting up to bring the conversation to an end. 'Be my guest. Do a ritual.'

He moved round the table, and spread his arms as if to herd Seamus out of the house, but then he came to a halt.

'By the way,' he said, leaning close, 'Mary tells me that you've dropped Eleanor now that she's given you the house. Is that true? After all she's done for you, you might pop in on her.'

'I don't need any lectures from you on the importance of my friendship with Eleanor,' said Seamus.

'Listen, I know she's not great company,' said Patrick, 'but that's just part of the treasure trove of things you have in common.'

'I've had just about enough of your hostile attitude,' said Seamus, his face flushing crimson. 'I've tried to be patient—'

'Patient?' Patrick interrupted. 'You've tried to billet your sidekicks on us and you've tossed Eleanor on the scrap heap because there's nothing more you can screw out of her. Anyone who thinks that "patient" is the word to describe that sort of thing should be doing English as a foreign language rather than signing a book contract.'

'I don't have to stand for these insults,' said Seamus. 'Eleanor and I created this Foundation, and I know that she wouldn't want anything to undermine its success. What's so tragic, in my opinion, is that you don't see how central the Foundation is to your mother's life's purpose, and you don't realize what an extraordinary woman she is.'

'You're so wrong,' said Patrick. 'I couldn't wish for a more extraordinary mother.'

'It's fairly obvious where all this is heading,' said Mary. 'Let's take some time to cool off. I don't see any point in more acrimony.'

'But, darling,' said Patrick, 'acrimony is all we've got left.'

It was certainly all he had left. She knew that it would fall on her to rescue a holiday from the wreckage left by Patrick's disdain. The expectation that she would be tirelessly resourceful and at the same time completely sympathetic to Patrick was not one she could either put up with or disappoint.

As she hoisted Thomas into her arms, she felt again the extent to which motherhood had destroyed her solitude. Mary had lived alone through most of her twenties and stubbornly kept her own flat until she was pregnant with Robert. She had such a strong need to distance herself from the flood of others. Now she was very rarely alone, and if she was, her thoughts were commandeered by her family obligations. Neglected meanings piled up like unopened letters. She knew they contained ever more threatening reminders that her life was unexamined.

Solitude was something she had to share with Thomas for the moment. She remembered a phrase Johnny once quoted about the infant being 'alone in the presence of its mother'. That had stayed with her, and sitting with Thomas after the row between Patrick and Seamus, while he played with his favourite hose, holding it sideways and watching the silvery arc of water splash to the ground, Mary could feel the pressure to encourage him to be useful, to water the plants and to keep the mud from splattering his trousers, but she didn't give in to it, seeing a kind of freedom in the uselessness of his play. He had no outcome in mind, no project or profit, he just liked watching the water flow.

It would have made perfect sense for her to make room for nostalgia now that the departure she had longed for seemed inevitable, but she found herself looking at the garden and the view and the cloudless sky with a cold eye. It was time to go.

Back in the house, she went to her own room for a moment's rest, and found Patrick already sprawled on the bed with a glass of red wine beside him.

'You weren't very friendly this morning,' he said.

'What do you mean?' said Mary. 'I wasn't unfriendly. You were wrapped up in arguing with Seamus.'

'Well, the Thermopylae buzz is wearing off,' said Patrick.

She sat down on the edge of the bed and stroked his hand absently.

'Do you remember, back in the Olden Days, when we used to go to bed together in the afternoon?' asked Patrick.

'Thomas has only just gone to sleep.'

'You know that's not the real reason. We're not grinding our teeth with frustration, promising we'll jump into bed the moment we get the chance: it isn't even a possibility.' Patrick closed his eyes. 'I feel as if we're shooting down a gleaming white tunnel . . .' he said.

'That was yesterday, on the way from the airport,' said Mary.

'A bone with the marrow sucked out,' Patrick persevered. 'Nothing is ever the same again, however often you repeat that magical phrase to the waitress in the cocktail bar.'

'Never, in my case,' said Mary.

'Congratulations,' said Patrick, falling abruptly silent, his eyes still closed.

Was she being unsympathetic? Should she be giving him a charity blow job? She felt that these pleas for attention were timed to be impossible, so as to keep him self-righteously un-faithful. Patrick would have been horrified if she had started to make love to him. Or would he? How could she find out while she was incapable of taking any sexual initiative? The whole thing had died for her, and she couldn't blame his affair for the collapse. It had happened the moment Thomas was born. She couldn't help marvelling at the strength of the severance. It had the authority of an instinct, redirecting her resources from the spent, enfee-bled, damaged Patrick to the thrilling potential of her new child. The same thing had happened with Robert, but only for a few months. This time her erotic life was subsumed in intimacy with Thomas. Her relationship with Patrick was dead, not without guilt and duty turning up at the funeral. She sank down on the bed next to him, stared at the ceiling for a few seconds of empty intensity and then closed her eyes as well. They lay on the bed together, floating in shallow sleep.

'Oh, God,' said Mary to Robert, getting up from the floor where she had been kneeling next to the open suitcase, 'I still haven't cancelled Granny and Sally.'

'I must say it's frightfully disappointing,' said Robert in his Kettle voice.

'Let's see if you're right,' said Mary, sitting down next to him to dial her mother's number.

'Well, I must say it *is* disappointing,' said Kettle, making Mary cover the mouthpiece while she tried to suppress her laughter. 'Perfect,' she whispered to Robert. He raised his arms in triumph.

'Why don't you come anyway?' said Mary to her mother. 'Seamus seems to enjoy your company even more than we do. Which is saying a lot,' she added after too long a pause.

Sally said she would come to see them all in London instead, and then took the view that it was 'great news'.

'To an outsider that place looks like a beautiful bell jar with the air being sucked out. You have to get out before you blow up.'

'She's happy for us,' said Mary.

'Well, gee,' said Robert, 'I hope she loses her house so we can be happy for her.'

When Patrick returned, he put a piece of paper on top of the suitcase Mary was struggling to close and sank down onto the chair by the door. She picked the paper up and saw that it was one of Eleanor's faint pencil-written notes.

> *My work here is over. I want to come home.*
> *Please find a nursing home in Kensington?*

She gave the note to Robert.

'It's difficult to know which sentence gave me most pleasure,' said Patrick. 'Eleanor's tiny store of unshamanic capital will be dismembered in rather less than a year if she moves to Kensington. After that, if she has the bad taste to stay alive, guess who will be expected to keep her vegetating in the Royal Borough?'

'I like the question mark,' said Mary.

'Eleanor's real genius is for putting our emotional and moral impulses into total conflict. Again and again she makes me hate myself for doing the right thing, she makes virtue into its own punishment.'

'I suppose we have to protect her from the horror of knowing that Seamus was really only interested in her money.'

'Why?' said Robert. 'It serves her right.'

'Listen,' said Patrick, 'what I saw today was someone who is terrified. Terrified of dying alone. Terrified that her family will abandon her, as Seamus has done. Terrified that she's fucked up, that she's been sleepwalking through a replica of her mother's behaviour. Terrified by the impotence of her convictions in the face of real suffering, terrified of everything. If we agree to her request, she can switch from philanthropy to family. Essentially, neither of them works any more, but the switch might give her a little relief before she settles back into hell.'

Nobody spoke.

'Let's hope that it's purgatory rather than hell,' said Mary.

'I'm not very up on these things,' said Patrick, 'but if purgatory is a place where suffering refines you rather than degrades you, I see no sign of it.'

'Well, maybe it can be purgatory for us at least.'

'I don't understand,' said Robert. 'Is Granny going to come and live with us?'

'Not in the flat,' said Mary. 'In a nursing home.'

'And we're going to have to pay?'

'Not yet,' she replied.

'But that way Seamus wins completely,' said Robert. 'He gets the house and we get the cripple.'

'She's not a cripple,' said Mary, 'she's an invalid.'

'Oh, sorry,' said Robert, 'that makes all the difference. Lucky us.' He put on his compère voice. 'Today's lucky winners, the Melrose family from London, will be taking home our fabulous first prize. This amazing *invalid* can't speak, can't walk *and* she can't control her bowels.' Robert made the sound of delirious applause, and then changed to a solemn but consoling tone. 'Bad luck, Seamus,' he said, putting his arm around an imaginary contestant, 'you played well, but in the end, they beat you in the Slow Death round. You won't be going home empty-handed, though, because we're giving you this private hamlet in the South of France, with thirty acres of gorgeous woodland, a giant swimming pool and several garden areas for the kiddies to play in . . .'

'That was amazing,' said Mary. 'Where did that pop up from?'

'I don't think Seamus knows yet,' said Patrick. 'She made me read a postcard saying that he was going to come and see her after the family had left. So he still hasn't seen her yet.'

'And did she look as if that might change her mind?'

'No,' said Patrick. 'She smiled when she gave me the note.'

'The mechanical smile, or the radiant one?'

'Radiant,' said Patrick.

'It's worse than we thought,' said Mary. 'She's not just running away from the truth about Seamus's motives, she's making another sacrifice. The only thing she had left to give him was her absence. It's unconditional love, the thing people usually keep for their children, if they can do it at all. In this case the children are the sacrifice.'

'There's an awful Christian stench to it as well,' said Patrick. 'Being useful and affirming her worthlessness at the same time – all in the service of wounded pride. If she stays here she has to pay attention to Seamus's betrayal, but this way we're the ones who are betrayed. I can't get over her stubbornness. There's nothing like doing God's will to make people pig-headed.'

'She can't speak or move,' said Mary, 'but look at the power she has.'

'Yeah,' said Patrick. 'All this chattering that takes place in between is nothing compared to the crying and groaning that takes place at either end of life. It drives me crazy: we're controlled by one wordless tyrant after another.'

'But where are we going for our holidays next year?' asked Robert.

'We can go anywhere,' said Patrick. 'We're no longer prisoners of this Provençal perfection. We're jumping out of the postcard, we're hitting the road.' He sat down next to Robert on the bed. 'Bogotá! Blackpool! Rwanda! Let your imagination roam. Picture the fugitive Alaskan summer breaking out among the potholes of the tundra. Tierra del Fuego is nice at this time of year. No competition for the beaches there, except from those hilarious, blubbery sea lions. We've had enough of the predictable pleasures of the Mediterranean, with its pedalos and its *pizzas au feu de bois*. The world is our oyster.'

'I hate oysters,' said Robert.

'Yeah, I slipped up there,' said Patrick.

'Well, where do you want to go?' asked Mary. 'You can choose anywhere you like.'

'America,' said Robert. 'I want to go to America.'

'Why not?' said Patrick. 'That's where Europeans traditionally go when they've been evicted.'

'We're not being evicted,' said Mary, 'we're finally getting free.'

AUGUST 2003

7

13

WOULD AMERICA BE JUST like he'd imagined it? Along with the rest of the world, Robert had lived under a rain of American images most of his life. Perhaps the place had already been imagined for him and he wouldn't be able to see anything at all.

The first impression that came his way, while the plane was still on the ground at Heathrow, was a sense of hysterical softness. The flow of passengers up the aisle was blocked by a red-haired woman sagging at the knees under her own weight.

'I cannot go there. I cannot get in there,' she panted. 'Linda wants me to sit by the window, but I cannot fit in there.'

'Get in there, Linda,' said the enormous father of the family.

'Dad!' said Linda, whose size spoke for itself.

That certainly seemed typical of something he had seen before in London's tourist spots: a special kind of tender American obesity; not the hard-won fat of a gourmet, or the juggernaut body of a truck driver, but the apprehensive fat of people who had decided to become their own airbag systems in a dangerous world. What if their bus was hijacked by a psychopath who hadn't brought any peanuts? Better have some now. If there was going to be a terrorist incident, why go hungry on top of everything else?

Eventually, the Airbags dented themselves into their seats. Robert had never seen such vague faces, mere sketches on the immensity of their bodies. Even the father's relatively protuberant features looked like the remnants of a melted candle. As she squeezed into her aisle seat, Mrs Airbag turned to the long queue of obstructed passengers, a brown smudge of tiredness radiating from her faded hazel eyes.

'Thank you for your patience,' she groaned.

'It's sweet of her to thank us for something we haven't given her,' said Robert's father. 'Perhaps I should thank her for her agility.'

Robert's mother gave him a warning look. It turned out they were in the row behind the Airbags.

'You're going to have to put the armrests down for takeoff,' Linda's father warned her.

'Mom and me are sharing these seats,' giggled Linda. 'Our tushes are expanding!'

Robert peeped through the gap in the seats. He didn't see how they were going to get the armrests down.

After meeting the Airbags, Robert's sense of softness spread everywhere. Even the hardness of some of the faces he saw on that warm and waxy arrival afternoon, in the flag-strewn mineral crevasses of mid-town Manhattan, looked to him like the embittered softness of betrayed children who had been told to expect everything. For those who were prepared to be consoled there was always something to eat; a pretzel stall, an ice-cream cart, a food-delivery service, a bowl of nuts on the counter, a snack machine down the corridor. He felt the pressure to drift into the mentality of grazing cattle, not just ordinary cattle but industrialized cattle, neither made to wait nor allowed to.

In the Oak Bar, Robert saw a row of men as pale and spongy as mushrooms, all standing on the broad stalks of their khaki trousers in front of the cigar cabinet. They seemed to be playing at being men. They sniggered and whispered, like schoolboys who were expecting to be caught out, to be made to remove the cushions they had stuffed under their pastel button-down shirts, and unpeel the plastic caps which made them look as if they were already bald. Watching them made Robert feel so grown up. He saw the old lady on the next table drape her powdered lips over the edge of her cocktail glass and suck the pink liquid expertly into her mouth. She looked like a camel trying to hide its braces. In the convex reflection of the black ceramic bowl in the window he saw people come and go, yellow cabs surge and slip, the spinning wheels of the park carriages approaching until they grew as small as the wheels of a wristwatch, and disappeared.

The park was bright and warm, crowded with sleeveless dresses and jackets hooked over shoulders. Robert felt the heightened alertness of arrival being eroded by exhaustion, and the novelty of New York overlaid by the sense that he had seen this new place a thousand times before. Whereas the London parks he knew seemed to insist on nature, Central Park insisted on recreation. Every inch was organized for pleasure. Cinder paths looped among the little hills and plains, past a zoo and a skating rink, quiet zones, sports fields and a plethora of playgrounds. Headphoned rollerbladers pursued a private music. Teenagers scaled small mounds of bronze-grey rocks. A flute player's serpentine music echoed damply under the arch of a bridge. As it faded behind them, it was replaced by the shrill mechanical tooting of a carousel.

'Look, Mama, a carousel!' said Thomas. 'I want to go on it. I can't resist doing that, actually.'

'OK,' said Robert's father with a tantrum-avoiding sigh.

Robert was delegated to take Thomas for a ride, sitting on

the same horse as him and fastening a leather belt around his waist.

'Is this a real horse?' said Thomas.

'Yes,' said Robert. 'It's a huge wild American horse.'

'You be Alabala and say it's a wild American horse,' said Thomas.

Robert obeyed his brother.

'No, Alabala!' said Thomas sharply, waving his index finger. 'It's a carousel horse.'

'Whoops, sorry,' said Robert as the carousel set in motion.

Soon it was going fast, almost too fast. Nothing about the carousel in Lacoste had prepared him for these rearing snorting horses, their nostrils painted red and their thick necks twisted out ambitiously towards the park. He was on a different continent now. The frighteningly loud music seemed to have driven all the clowns on the central barrel mad, and he could see that instead of being disguised by a painted sky studded with lights, heavily greased rods were revolving overhead. Along with the violence of the ride, this exposed machinery struck him as typically American. He didn't really know why. Perhaps everything in America would show this genius for being instantly typical. Just as his body was being tricked by a second afternoon, every surprise was haunted by this sense of being exemplary.

Soon after they left the carousel, they came across a vibrant middle-aged woman bent over her lapdog.

'Do you want a cappuccino?' she asked, as if it must be a tremendous temptation. 'Are you ready for a cappuccino? Come on! Come on!' She clapped her hands together ecstatically.

But the dog strained backwards on his leash, as if to say, 'I'm a Dandie Dinmont, I don't drink cappuccino.'

'I think that's a clear "no",' said Robert's father.

'Shh . . .' said Robert.

'I mean,' said Thomas, removing his thumb from his mouth

as he reclined in his stroller, 'I think that's a clear no.' He chuck-led. 'I mean, it's incredible. The little doggie doesn't want a cap-puccino!' He put his thumb back in his mouth and played with the smooth label of his raggie.

After another five minutes his parents were ready to head back to the hotel, but Robert caught a glimpse of some water and ran forward a little further.

'Look,' he said, 'a lake.'

The landscaping created the impression that the far shore of the lake lapped against the base of a double-towered West Side skyscraper. Under the gaze of this perforated cliff, T-shirted men hauled metal boats past reedy islands, girlfriends photo-graphed each other laughing among the oars, immobile children bulged in blue life jackets.

'Look,' said Robert, not quite able to express how astonish-ingly typical it all seemed.

'I want to go on the lake,' said Thomas.

'Not today,' said Robert's father.

'But I want to,' he screamed, tears instantly beading his eyelids.

'Let's go for a run,' said Robert's father, grabbing the stroller and sprinting down an avenue of bronze statues, Thomas's pro-tests gradually replaced by cries of 'Faster!'

By the time they caught up with him, Robert's father was bent double over the handles of the stroller, getting his breath back.

'The selection committee must have been based in Edin-burgh,' he gasped, nodding at the giant statues of Robert Burns and Walter Scott, stooped beneath the weight of their genius. A little further on a much smaller sprightly Shakespeare sported a period costume.

The Churchill Hotel where they were staying had no room service, and so Robert's father went out to buy a kettle and some 'basic provisions'. When he got back, Robert could smell the fresh whiskey on his breath.

'Jesus,' said his father, fishing a box out of his shopping bag, 'you go out to buy a kettle and you come back with nothing less than a Travel Smart Hot Beverage Maker.'

Like Linda's and Mom's unconstrained tushes, phrases seemed to feel entitled to take up as much room as they could. Robert watched his father unloading tea and coffee and a bottle of whiskey from a brown-paper bag. The bottle had already been drunk from.

'Look at these filthy curtains,' said his father, seeing Robert calculating the proportion of the bottle that was already empty. 'The reason why the rest of New York is breathing lovely clean air is that we've got these special pollution filters in our room sucking all the dirt out of the atmosphere. Sally said that the decoration in this place "grows on you" – that's exactly what I'm worried about. Try not to touch any of the surfaces.'

Robert, who had been excited to be staying in any hotel at all, started to look sceptically at his surroundings. A Chinese carpet in mouse's-underbelly pink, with a medal-lioned picto-gram at the centre, gave way to the greasy French provincial up-holstery of the sofa and armchair. Above the sofa, against the buttercup walls, an Indian tapestry of women dancing rigidly by a well, with some cows in the foreground, stood opposite a big painting of two ballerinas, one in a lemon-yellow and the other in a rose-pink tutu. The bath was as cratered as the moon. The chrome had greyed on the taps and the enamel was stained. If you didn't really need a bath before getting in it, you certainly would afterwards. The view from his parents' room, where Thomas was bouncing up and down on the bed shouting, 'Look at me! I'm an astronaut!', gave onto a rusty air-conditioning system that throbbed a few feet beneath the ill-fitting window. From the drawing room, where he was going to sleep on the sofa bed with

Thomas (or, knowing Thomas, where his father was going to sleep after Thomas had taken over his mother's bed), there was a perfect view of the sheet rock that covered the neighbouring skyscraper.

'It's like living in a quarry,' said his father, splashing a couple of inches of whiskey into a glass. He strode over to the window and pulled down the grey plastic blind. The pole holding the blind crashed down onto the drawing room's air-conditioning unit with a hollow clang.

'Bloody hell,' he said.

Robert's mother burst out laughing. 'It's only for a few nights,' she said. 'Let's go out to dinner. Thomas isn't going to get back to sleep for ages. He had three hours on the plane. What about you, darling?' she asked Robert.

'I want to motor on. Can I have a Coca-Cola?'

'No,' said his mother, 'you're quite excited enough already.'

'Apple and cinnamon flavour,' muttered Robert's father, as he continued to unpack the shopping. 'I couldn't find any oats that taste of oats or apples that taste of apples, only oats that taste of apples. And cinnamon, of course, to blend with the toothpaste. A less sober man might end up brushing his teeth with oats, or having a bowl of toothpaste for breakfast – without noticing. It's enough to drive you mad. If there aren't any additives they boast about that too. I saw a packet of camomile tea that said "Caffeine Free". Why would camomile have any caffeine in it?' He took out the last package.

'Morning Thunder,' said Robert's mother. 'Isn't Thomas enough morning thunder already?'

'That's your trouble, darling, you think Thomas can substitute for everything: tea, coffee, work, social life . . .' He let the list hurtle on in silence, and then quickly buried the remark in more general commentary. 'Morning Thunder is very literary, it just has added quotations.' He cleared his throat and read out loud, '"*Born often under another sky, placed in the middle of an always moving scene, himself driven by an irresistible torrent which draws all about him, the American has no time to tie himself to anything, he grows accustomed only to change, and ends by regarding it as the natural state of man. He feels the need of it, more he loves it; for the instability, instead of meaning disaster to him, seems to give birth only to miracles all about him.*" – Alexis de Tocqueville.

'So you see,' he said, ruffling Robert's hair, 'wanting to "motor on" is in perfect keeping with the mood of this country, at least in 1840, or whatever.'

Thomas clambered onto a table whose protective circle of glass was about a foot less wide than the table itself, leaving the mulberry polyester tablecloth exposed at the edges.

'Let's go out to a restaurant,' said Robert's mother, lifting him gently into her arms.

Robert felt the sense of almost violent silence in the lift, made up of the things that his parents were not saying to each other, but also caused by the aroma of mental illness surrounding the knobbly headed lift operator who informed them with pride, rather than the apologies Robert felt they deserved, that the lift had been installed in 1926. Robert liked some things to be old – dinosaurs, for instance, or planets – but he liked his lifts brand new. The family's longing to escape the red velveteen cage was explosive. While the madman jerked a brass lever back and forth, the lift lurched around in the vicinity of the ground floor and finally came to rest only an inch or two below the lobby.

In the fading light, they walked over glittering pavements, steam surging from corner drains and giant grilles replacing the paving stones for feverishly long stretches. Robert refused to give in to the cowardice of avoiding them altogether, but he walked on them reluctantly, trying to make himself lighter. Gravity had never seemed so grave.

'Why do the pavements glitter?' he asked.

'God knows,' said his father. 'It's probably the added iron, or the crushed quotations. Or maybe they've just had the caffeine sucked right out of them.'

Apart from a few yellowing newspaper articles displayed in the window, and a handwritten sign saying GOD BLESS OUR TROOPS, Venus Pizza gave no hint of the disgusting food that was being prepared indoors. The ingredients of the salads and pizzas seemed to fit in with the unreflecting expansion which Robert had been noticing since Heathrow. A list would start out reasonably enough with feta and tomato and then roll over the border into pineapple and Swiss cheese. Smoked chicken burst in on what had seemed to be a seafood party, and 'all the above' were served with French fries and onion rings.

'Everything is "mouthwatering",' said Robert; 'What does that mean? That you need a huge glass of water to wash away the taste?'

His mother burst out laughing.

'It's more like a police report on what they found in someone's dustbin than a dish,' his father complained. 'The suspect was obviously a tropical-fruit freak with a hearty love of Brie and shellfish,' he muttered in an American accent.

'I thought French fries were called Freedom fries now,' said Robert.

'It's cheaper to write GOD BLESS OUR TROOPS than reprint a hundred menus,' said his father. 'Thank goodness Spain joined the coalition of the willing, otherwise we'd be saying things like, "Mine's a Supreme Court omelette with some Freedom fries on the side." English muffins will probably survive the purge, but I wouldn't go round asking for Turkish coffee after the way they behaved. I'm sorry.' Robert's father sank back into the booth. 'I had such a love affair with America, I suppose I feel jilted by its current incarnation. Of course it's a vast and complex society, and I have great faith in its powers of self-correction. But where are they? What happened to rioting? Satire? Scepticism?'

'Hi!' The waitress wore a badge saying KAREN. 'Have you guys made a menu selection? Oh,' she sighed, looking at Thomas, 'you are gorgeous.'

Robert was mesmerized by the strange hollow friendliness of her manner. He wanted to set her free from the obligation to be cheerful. He could tell she really wanted to go home.

His mother smiled at her and said, 'Could we have a Vesuvio without the pineapple chunks or the smoked turkey or . . .' She started laughing helplessly. 'I'm sorry . . .'

'Mummy!' said Robert, starting to laugh as well.

Thomas scrunched up his eyes and rocked back and forth, not wanting to be left out. 'I mean,' he said, 'it's incredible.'

'Maybe we should approach this from the other direction,' said Robert's father. 'Could we have a pizza with tomato, anchovy and black olives.'

'Like the pizzas in Les Lecques,' said Robert.

'We'll see,' said his father.

Karen tried to master her bewilderment at the poverty of the ingredients.

'You want mozzarella, right?'

'No thanks.'

'How about a drizzle of basil oil?'

'No drizzle, thank you.'

'OK,' she said, hardened by their stubbornness.

Robert slid across the Formica table and rested his head sideways on the pillow of his folded arms. He felt he had been trapped all day in an argument with his body: confined on the plane when he was ready to run around, and running around now when he should have been in bed. In the corner a television with the sound turned down enough to be inaudible, but too little to be silent, radiated diagonally into the room. Robert had never seen a baseball game before, but he had seen films in which the human spirit triumphed over adversity on a baseball field. He thought he could remember one in which some gangsters tried to make a sincere baseball star deliberately lose a game, but at the last moment, just when he was about to throw the whole thing away and the groans of disappointment from the crowd seemed to express the whole unsatisfactoriness of a world in which there was nothing left to believe in, he went into a trance and remembered when he had first hit a ball a long way, into the middle of a wheat field in the middle of America. He couldn't betray that amazing slow-motion sky-bound feeling from his childhood, and he couldn't betray his mother who always wore an apron and told him not to lie, and so he hit the ball right out of the stadium, and the gangsters looked a bit like Karen when she took the pizza order, only much angrier, but his girlfriend looked proud of him, even though the gangsters were standing either side of her, because she was basically like his mother with much more expensive peach-coloured clothes, and the crowd went crazy because there was something to believe in again. And then there was a car chase and the gangsters, whose reflexes were not honed by a lifetime in sports and whose bad character turned into bad driving on a crucial bend, crashed their car and exploded.

In the game on television the gangsters seemed to be having much more success and the ball hardly got hit at all. Every few minutes advertisements interrupted the play and then the words WORLD SERIES in huge gold letters spun out of nowhere and glinted on the screen.

'Where's our wine?' said his father.

'Your wine,' Robert's mother corrected him.

He saw his father clench his jaw and swallow a remark. When

Karen arrived with the bottle of red wine, his father started drinking decisively, as if the remark he had not made was stuck in his throat. Karen gave Robert and Thomas huge glasses of ice stained with cranberry juice. Robert sipped his drink listlessly. The day had been unbearably long. Not just the pressurized biscuit-coloured staleness of the flight, but the Immigration formalities as well. His father, who had joked that he was going to describe himself as an 'international tourist' on the grounds that that was how President Bush pronounced 'international terrorist', managed to resist the temptation. He was nevertheless taken into a side room by a black female Immigration officer after having his passport stamped.

'She couldn't understand why an English lawyer was born in France,' he explained in the taxi. 'She clasped her head and said, "I'm just trying to get a concept of your life, Mr Melrose." I told her I was trying to do the same thing and that if I ever wrote an autobiography I'd send her a copy.'

'Oh,' said Robert's mother, 'so that's why we waited an extra half-hour.'

'Well, you know, when people hate officialdom, they either become craven or facetious.'

'Try craven next time, it's quicker.'

When the pizzas finally arrived Robert saw that they were hopeless. As thick as nappies, they hadn't been adjusted to the ninety per cent reduction in ingredients. Robert scraped all the tomato and anchovy and olives into one corner and made two mouthfuls of miniature pizza. It was not at all like the delicious, thin, slightly burnt pizza in Les Lecques but somehow, because he had thought it might be, he had opened a trap door into the summers he used to have and would never have again.

'What's wrong?' asked his mother.

'I just want a pizza like the ones in Les Lecques.' He was assailed by injustice and despair. He really didn't want to cry.

'Oh, darling, I so understand,' she said, touching his hand. 'I know it seems far-fetched in this mad restaurant, but we're going to have a lovely time in America.'

'Why is Bobby crying?' said Thomas.

'He's upset.'

'But I don't want him to cry,' said Thomas. 'I don't want him to!' he screamed, and started crying himself.

'Fucking hell,' said Robert's father. 'I knew we should have gone to Ramsgate.'

On the way back to the hotel, Thomas fell asleep in his stroller.

'Let's cut to the chase,' said Robert's father, 'and not pretend we're going to sleep with each other. You take both of the boys into the bedroom and I'll take the sofa bed.'

'Fine,' said Robert's mother, 'if that's what you want.'

'There's no need to introduce exciting words like "want". It's what I'm realistically anticipating.'

Robert fell asleep immediately, but woke up again when the red digits on the bedside clock said 2:11. His mother and Thomas were still asleep but he could hear a muffled sound from the drawing room. He found his father on the floor in front of the television.

'I put my back out unfolding that fucking sofa bed,' he said, doing push-ups with his hips still pressed to the carpet.

The bottle of whiskey was on the glass table, three-quarters empty next to a ravaged sheet of Codis painkillers.

'I'm sorry about the Venus Pizza,' said his father. 'After going there, and shopping at Carnegie Foods and watching a few hours of this delinquent network television, I've come to the conclusion that we should probably fast during our holiday here. Factory farming doesn't stop in the slaughterhouse, it stops in our bloodstreams, after the Henry Ford food missiles have hurtled out of their cages into our open mouths and dissolved their growth hormones and their genetically modified feed into our increasingly wobbly bodies. Even when the food isn't "fast", the bill is instantaneous, dumping an idle eater back on the snack-crowded streets. In the end, we're on the same conveyor belt as the featherless, electrocuted chickens.'

Robert found his father vaguely frightening, with his bloodshot eyes and the sweat stains on his shirt, twisting the corkscrew of his own talk. Robert knew that he wasn't being communicated with, but allowed to listen to his father practising speeches. All this time while he had been asleep, his father had been pacing up and down a mental courtroom, prosecuting.

'I liked the Park,' said Robert.

'The Park's nice,' his father conceded, 'but the rest of the country is just people in huge cars wondering what to eat next. When we hire a car you'll see that it's really a mobile dining room, with little tables all over the place and cup holders. It's a nation of hungry children with real guns. If you're not blown up by a bomb, you're blown up by a Vesuvio pizza. It's absolutely terrifying.'

'Please stop,' said Robert.

'I'm sorry. I just feel . . .' His father suddenly seemed lost. 'I just can't sleep. The Park is great. The city is breathtakingly beautiful. It's just me.'

'Is whiskey going to be part of the fast?'

'Unfortunately,' said his father, imitating the mischievous way that Thomas liked to say that word, 'the whiskey is something *very* pure and can't reasonably be included in the war against corruption.'

'Oh,' said Robert.

'Or war *on* corruption, as they would say here. War on terror; war on crime; war on drugs. I suppose if you're a pacifist here you have to have a war on war, or nobody would notice.'

'Daddy,' Robert warned him.

'I'm sorry, I'm sorry.' He grabbed the remote control. 'Let's turn off this mind-shattering rubbish and read a story.'

'Excellent,' said Robert, jumping onto the sofa bed. He felt he was pretending to be more cheerful than he was, a little bit like Karen. Perhaps it was infectious, or something in the food supply.

14

'OH, PATRICK, WHY WEREN'T we told that the lovely life we had was going to end?' said Aunt Nancy, turning the pages of the photograph album.

'Weren't you told that?' said Patrick. 'How maddening. But then again, it didn't end for the people who might have told you. Your mother just ruined it by trusting your stepfather.'

'Do you know the worst thing about that – I'm going to use the word "evil" – '

'Popular word these days,' murmured Patrick.

'– man?' Nancy continued, only briefly closing her eyelids to refuse admittance to Patrick's distracting remark. 'He used to grope me in the back of Mummy's car while she was at home dying of cancer. He had Parkinson's by then, so he had a shaky grip, if you know what I'm saying. After Mummy died, he actually asked me to marry him. Can you believe that? I just laughed, but sometimes I think I should have accepted. He only lasted two more years, and I might have been spared the sight of the little nephew's removal men carrying my dressing table out of my bedroom, while I lay in bed, on the morning of Jean's death. I said to the brutes in blue overalls, "What are you doing? Those are my hairbrushes." "We were told to take everything," they grunted, and then they threw me out of bed, so they could load that on the van as well.'

'It might have been even more traumatic to marry someone you loathed and found physically disgusting,' said Patrick.

'Oh, look,' said Nancy, turning a page of the album, 'here's Fairley, where we spent the beginning of the war, while Mummy was still stuck in France. It was the most divine house on Long Island. Do you know that uncle Bill had a one-hundred-and-fifty-acre garden; I'm not talking about woods and fields, there were plenty of those as well. Nowadays people think they're God almighty if they have a ten-acre garden on Long Island. There was *the* most beautiful pink marble throne in the middle of the topiary garden where we used to play grandmother's footsteps. It used to belong to the Emperor of Byzantium . . .' She sighed. 'All lost, all the beautiful things.'

'The thing about things is that they just keep getting lost,' said Patrick. 'The Emperor lost his throne before Uncle Bill lost his garden furniture.'

'Well, at least Uncle Bill's children got to sell Fairley,' Nancy flared up. 'They didn't have it stolen.'

'Listen, I'm the first to sympathize. After what Eleanor did, we're the most financially withered branch of the family,' said Patrick. 'How long were you separated from your mother?' he asked, as if to introduce a lighter note.

'Four years.'

'Four years!'

'Well, we went to America two years before the war started. Mummy stayed in Europe trying to get the really good things out of France and England and Italy, and she only made it to America two years after the Germans invaded. She and Jean escaped via Portugal and when they arrived I remember that her shoe trunk had fallen overboard from the fishing boat they hired to get them across to New York. I thought that if you could get away from the Germans and only lose a trunk with nothing in it but shoes, you weren't having such a bad war.'

'But how did you feel about not seeing her all that time?'

'Well, you know, I had the oddest conversation with Eleanor a couple of years before she had her stroke. She told me that when Mummy and Jean arrived at Fairley, she rowed out to the middle of the lake and refused to talk to them because she was so angry that Mummy had abandoned us for four years. I was shocked because I couldn't remember anything about it. I mean, that would have been a big deal in our young lives. But all I remember is Mummy's shoes getting lost.'

'I guess everybody remembers what's important to them,' said Patrick.

'She told me that she hated Mummy,' said Nancy. 'I mean, I didn't know that was *genetically* possible.'

'Her genes probably just stood by horrified,' said Patrick. 'The story Eleanor always told me was that she hated your mother for sacking the two people she loved and depended on: her father and her nanny.'

'I tied myself to the car when Nanny was being driven away,' said Nancy competitively.

'Well, there you have it – didn't you feel a little gene-defying twinge . . .'

'No! I blamed Jean. He was the one who persuaded Mummy that we were too old to have a nanny.'

'And your father?'

'Well, Mummy said that she just couldn't afford to keep him any more. Every week he would drive her crazy with some new extravagance. In the run-up to Ascot, for instance, he didn't just buy a racehorse, he bought a stable of racehorses. Do you know what I'm saying?'

'Those were the days,' said Patrick. 'I'd love to be in a position to be irritated by Mary buying a couple of dozen racehorses, rather than getting in a blind panic when Thomas needs a new pair of shoes.'

'You're exaggerating.'

'It's the only extravagance I can still afford.'

The telephone rang, drawing Nancy into a study next to her library, and leaving Patrick on the soft sofa dented by the weight of the red leather album, with 1940 stamped in gold on its spine.

The image of Eleanor rowing out to the middle of the lake and refusing to talk to anyone fused in Patrick's imagination with her present condition, bedridden and cut off from the rest of the world.

The day after she had settled into her thickly carpeted, over-heated, nursing tomb in Kensington, Patrick was rung by the director.

'Your mother would like to see you straight away. She thinks she's going to die today.'

'Is there any reason to believe she's right?'

'There's no medical reason as such, but she is very insistent.'

Patrick hauled himself out of his chambers and went over to see Eleanor. He found her crying from the unspeakable frustration of having something so important to say. After half an hour, she finally gave birth to, 'Die today,' delivered with all the stunned wonder of recent motherhood. After that, hardly a day passed without a death promise emerging from half an hour's gibbering, weeping struggle.

When Patrick complained to Kathleen, the perky Irish nurse in charge of Eleanor's floor, she clasped his forearm and hooted, 'She'll probably outlive us all. Take Dr MacDougal on the next floor. When he was seventy, he married a lady half his age – she was a lovely lady, so friendly. Well, the next year, it was quite tragic really, he got the Alzheimer's and moved in here. She was ever so devoted, came to see him every day. Anyway, if she didn't get breast cancer the following year. She was dead three years after marrying him, and he's still upstairs, *going strong.*'

After a final hoot of laughter, she left him standing alone in the airless corridor next to the locked dispensary.

What depressed him even more than the inaccuracy of Eleanor's predictions was the doggedness of her self-deception and her spiritual vanity. The idea that she had any special insight into the exact time of her death was typical of the daydreams that ruled her life. It was only in June, after she had fallen over and broken her hip, that she began to take a more realistic attitude about the degree of control she could have over her death.

Patrick went to visit her in the Chelsea and Westminster Hospital after her fall.

Eleanor had been given morphine for breakfast, but her restlessness was unsubdued. The desperate need to get out of bed, which had produced several falls, bruising her right temple purple-black, leaving her nose swollen and red, staining her right eyelid yellow and eventually fracturing her hip, made her, even now, reach for the bar on the side of her Evans Nesbit Jubilee bed and try to pull herself up with those flabby white arms bruised by fresh puncture marks Patrick could not help envying. A few clear phrases reared up like Pacific islands from a mumbling moaning ocean of meaningless syllables.

'I have a rendezvous,' she said, making a renewed surge towards the end of the bed.

'I'm sure whoever you have to meet will come here,' said Patrick, 'knowing that you can't move.'

'Yes,' she said, collapsing back on the bloodstained pillows for a moment, but lurching forwards again and wailing, 'I have a rendezvous.'

She was not strong enough to stay up for long, and soon resumed a slow writhing motion on the bed, and the long haul through another stretch of murmurous, urgent nonsense. And then 'No longer' appeared, not attached to anything else. She ran her hands down her face in exasperation, looking as if she wanted to cry but was being let down by her body in that respect as well.

At last she managed it.

'I want you to kill me,' she said, gripping his hand surprisingly hard.

'I'd love to help,' said Patrick, 'but unfortunately it's against the law.'

'No longer,' shouted Eleanor.

'We're doing all we can,' he said vaguely.

Looking for solace in practicality, Patrick tried to give his mother a sip of pineapple juice from the plastic glass on her bedside table. He eased his hand under the top pillow and lifted her head, tipping the juice gently towards her peeling lips. He felt himself being transformed by the tenderness of the act. He had never treated anyone so carefully except his own children. The flow of generations was reversed and he found himself holding his useless, treacherous, confused mother with exquisite anxiety. How to lift her head, how to make sure she didn't choke. He watched her roll the sip of juice around her mouth, an alarmed and disconnected look on her face, and he willed her to succeed while she tried to remind her throat how to swallow.

Poor Eleanor, poor little Eleanor, she wasn't well at all, she needed help, she needed protection. There was no obstacle, no interruption to his desire to help her. He was amazed to see his argumentative, disappointed mind overwhelmed by a physical act. He leant over further and kissed her on the forehead.

A nurse came in and saw the glass in Patrick's hand.

'Did you give her some of the Thicken Up?' she asked.

'Some what?'

'Thicken Up,' she said, tapping a tin of that name.

'I don't think my mother wants to thicken up,' said Patrick. 'You haven't got a tin called "Waste Away", have you?'

The nurse looked shocked, but Eleanor smiled.

'Aste way,' she echoed.

'She had a very good breakfast this morning,' the nurse persevered.

'Orce,' said Eleanor.

'Forced?' Patrick suggested.

She turned her wild-eyed face towards him and said, 'Yes.'

'When you get back to the nursing home, you can stop eating if you want to,' said Patrick. 'You'll have more control over your fate.'

'Yes,' she whispered, smiling.

She seemed to relax for the first time. And so did Patrick. He was going to guard his mother from having more horrible life imposed on her. Here at last was a filial role he could throw himself into.

Patrick looked at Nancy's other photograph albums, over a hundred identical red-leather volumes dated from 1919 to 2001, ranged in the shelves directly in front of him. The rest of the room was lined with decorative blocks of leather books and, lower down, glossy books on the art of decoration. Even the two doors, one into the hall and the other into the study where Nancy was talking on the phone, did not interrupt the library theme. Their backs were crowded with the spines of false books resting on trompe l'œil shelves perfectly aligned with the real shelves, so that when the doors were closed the room generated an impressive claustrophobia. The blast of resentment and nostalgia coming from Nancy, undiminished since he last saw her eight years before, made Patrick all the more determined not to live in the has-been world enshrined in the wall of albums – let alone in the might-have-been realm where Nancy's imagination burnt even more ferociously. There seemed little point in trying to give her a bracing lecture on the value of staying contemporary when she wouldn't even stick to the past as it was, but preferred a version cleansed of the injustice which had been done to her nearly forty years earlier. The afterglow of plutocracy was no more alluring to him than a pile of dirty dishes after a dinner party. Something had died, and its death was tied in with the tenderness he had felt for Eleanor when he helped her drink that glass of pineapple juice in hospital.

Seeing his aunt made him marvel again at how different she was from her sister. And yet their attitudes of extreme worldliness and extreme unworldliness had a common origin in a sense of maternal betrayal and financial disappointment. The blame had been reattributed to her stepfather by Nancy, while Eleanor had tried to unload the sense of betrayal onto Patrick. Unsuccessfully, he now liked to think, although after only a few hours with his aunt he felt like a recovering alcoholic who has been given a cocktail shaker for his birthday.

The tall clear windows looked onto a broad lawn sloping down to an ornamental pond and spanned by a wooden Japanese bridge. From where he sat he could see Thomas trying to hang over the side of the bridge, gently restrained by Mary while he pointed at the exotic waterfowl rippling across the bright coin of water. Or perhaps there were koi carp giving depth to the Japanese theme. Or some samurai armour gleaming in the mud. It was dangerous to underestimate Nancy's decorative thoroughness. Robert was writing his diary in the little pond-side pagoda.

Several shelves of unreadable classics creaked open and Nancy strode back into the room.

'That was our rich cousin,' she said, as if invigorated by contact with money.

'Which one?'

'Henry. He says you're going to his island next week.'

'That's right,' said Patrick. 'We're just paw whi-te trash throwin' oursef on the cha-ri-tee of our American kin.'

'He wanted to know if your children were well behaved. I told him they hadn't broken anything yet. "How long have they been there?" he asked. When I said you arrived about two hours ago, he said, "Oh, for God sakes, Nancy, what kind of a sample is that? I'm ringing back tomorrow for a full report." I guess not everybody has the world's most important collection of Meissen figurines.'

'I don't suppose he will either, after Thomas has been to stay.'

'Don't say that!' said Nancy. 'Now you're making me nervous.'

'I didn't know Henry had become so pompous. I haven't seen him in at least twenty years; it was really very hospitable of him to let us come. As a teenager he belonged to that familiar type, the complacent rebel. I suppose the rebel was defeated by the army of Meissen figurines. Who can blame him for surrendering? Imagine the gleaming hordes of porcelain milkmaids clearing the brow of the hill and flooding the bowl of the valley, and poor Henry with only a rolled-up portfolio statement to beat them off.'

'You get awfully carried away by your imagination,' said Nancy.

'Sorry,' said Patrick. 'I haven't been in court for three weeks. The speeches pile up . . .'

'Well, your ancient aunt is going to have a rest now. We're going to Walter's and Beth's for tea, and I'd better be on top form for that. Don't let the children walk on the grass barefoot, or go into the woods at all. I'm afraid this part of Connecticut is a Lyme disease hot spot, and the ticks are just dreadful this year. The gardener tries to keep the poison ivy out of the garden, but he can't control the woods. Lyme disease is just horrible. It's recurring and if it goes untreated it can destroy your life. There's a little boy who lives in the village here and he's really not at all well. He has psychotic fits and things. Beth just takes the antibiotics round the clock. She "self-medicates". She says it's safer to assume you're always in danger.'

'Grounds for perpetual war,' said Patrick. '*Tout ce qu'il y a de plus chic.*'

'Well, if you want to put it that way.'

'I think I do. Not necessarily to her face.'

'Necessarily *not* to her face,' Nancy flared up. 'She's one of my oldest friends and besides, she's the most powerful of the Park Avenue women and it's not a good idea to cross her.'

'I wouldn't dream of it,' said Patrick.

After Nancy had left, Patrick walked over to the drinks tray and, so as not to leave a dirty glass, drank several gulps of bourbon from a bottle of Maker's Mark. He sank back into an armchair and stared out of the window. The impenetrable New England countryside looked pretty enough, but was in fact packed with more dangers than a Cambodian swamp. Mary already had several pamphlets on Lyme disease – named after a Connecticut town only a few miles away – and so there was no need to rush out and tell the family.

'It's safer to assume you're always in danger.' Some verbal tic made him want to say, 'It's safer to assume you're safe unless you're in danger', but he was quickly won over by the plausibility of paranoia. In any case, he now felt in danger all the time. Danger of liver collapse, marital breakdown, terminal fear. Nobody ever died of a feeling, he would say to himself, not believing a word of it, as he sweated his way through the feeling that he was dying of fear. People died of feelings all the time, once they had gone through the formality of materializing them into bullets and bottles and tumours. Someone who was organized like him, with utterly chaotic foundations, a quite strongly developed intellect and almost nothing in between desperately needed to develop the middle ground. Without it, he split into a vigilant day mind, a bird of prey hovering over a landscape, and a helpless night mind, a jellyfish splattered on the deck of a ship. 'The Eagle and the Jellyfish', a fable Aesop just couldn't be bothered to write. He guffawed with abrupt, slightly deranged laughter and got up to take another gulp of bourbon from the bottle. Yes, the middle ground was now occupied by a lake of alcohol. The first drink centred him for about twenty minutes and then the rest brought his night mind rushing over the landscape like the dark blade of an eclipse.

The whole thing, he knew, was a humiliating Oedipal drama. Despite the superficial revolution in his relations with Eleanor, a local victory of compassion over loathing, the underlying impact she had made on his life remained undisturbed. His fundamental sense of being was a kind of free fall, a limitless dread, a claustrophobic agoraphobia. Doubtless there was something universal about fear. His sons, despite their lavish treatment from Mary, had moments of fear, but these were temporary afflictions, whereas Patrick felt that fear was the ground he stood on, or the groundlessness he fell into, and he couldn't help connecting this conviction with his mother's absolute inability to concentrate on another human being. He had to remind himself that the defining characteristic of Eleanor's life was her incompetence. She wanted to have a child and became a lousy mother; she wanted to write children's stories and became a lousy writer; she wanted to be a philanthropist and gave all her money to a self-serving charlatan. Now she wanted to die and she couldn't do that either. She could only communicate with people who presented themselves as the portals to some bombastic generalization, like 'humanity' or 'salvation', something the mewling, puking Patrick must have been unable to do. One of the troubles with being an infant was the difficulty of distinguishing incompetence from malice, and this difficulty sometimes returned to him in the drunken middle of the night. It was now beginning to invade his view of Mary as well.

Mary had been a devoted mother to Robert, but after the absorption of the first year she had resurfaced as a wife, if only because she wanted another child. With Thomas, perhaps because she knew that he was her last child, she seemed to be trapped in a Madonna and Child force field, preserving a precinct of purity, including her own rediscovered virginity. Patrick was in the unenviable role of Joseph in this enduring, unendurable Bethlehem. Mary had completely withdrawn her attention from him and the more he requested it the more he appeared in the light of an imposturous rival to his younger son. He had turned elsewhere, to Julia, and once that had collapsed, to the oblivious embrace of alcohol. He must stop. At his age he either had to join the resistance or become a collaborator with death. There was no room to play with self-destruction once the juvenile illusion of indestructibility had evaporated.

Oh dear, he'd made rather too much progress with the Maker's Mark. The logical thing to do was to take this bottle upstairs and pour the rest of it into the depleted bottle of bourbon hidden in his rucksack, and then nip into town to buy another one for Nancy's drinks table. He would, of course, have to make convincing inroads into the new bottle so that it resembled the old bottle before he had almost finished it. Practically anything was less complicated than being a successful alcoholic. Bombing Third World countries – now there was an occupation for a man of leisure. 'It's all right for some,' he muttered, weaving his way across the room. He was arguably just a teeny-weeny bit too drunk for this time of day. His thoughts were cracking up, going staccato, getting overtrumped just as he was about to pick up the trick.

Check: family in the garden. Check: silence in the hall. Run up the stairs, close the door, get the rucksack, decant the bourbon – all over his hand. Hide the empty on top of cupboard. Car keys. Down and out. Tell family? Yes. No. Yes. No! Get in car. Ding ding ding. Fucking American car safety ding ding. Safer to assume sudden violent death. Police no please no police, p-l-e-a-s-e. Slip away over crunchy nutritious gravel. Cruise control, out of control. Suggestible suggestions. Jump the tracks, get out of the syllable cruncher and into, into the sunlit death-trap countryside. Better pave the whole thing over. Angry posses of ordinary citizens with chain saws and concrete mixers. 'We've lived in fear for long enough! We've got a right to protect our families! It says in the Bible, "The wild places shall be made tame. And the people shall have dominion over the ticks."'

He was drifting along in his silvery blue Buick LeSabre, screaming in a hillbilly accent. He couldn't stop. He couldn't stop anything. He couldn't stop the car, he couldn't stop drinking, he couldn't stop the Koncrete Klux Klan. A bright red Stop sign slipped by as he merged quietly with the main road into town. He parked next to the Vino Veritas liquor store. The car had somehow locked itself, just to be on the safe side. Ding ding ding. Keys still in the ignition. He arched backwards trying to ease the dull pain in his lower back. Eroded vertebrae? Swollen kidneys? 'We have to think our way out of the box of our habitual dichotomies,' he purred, in the smug tones of a self-help tape. 'It's not an *either* vertebrae *or* kidneys situation, it's a *both* kidneys *and* vertebrae situation. Think outside the box! Be creative!'

And here, straight ahead of him, across the railway tracks, down among the playing fields, was another *both and* situation. Both the exuberant sentimentality of American family life unfolding among the brightly coloured tubes and slides and swings of a playground, with its soft wood-chip landing sites and, on a large area of grass beyond the chain-link fence, two pot-bellied policemen training an Alsatian to tear apart any sick fucks who thought to disturb the peace and prosperity of New Milton. One policeman held the dog by the collar, the other stood at the far end of the green with a huge padded arm guard. The Alsatian streaked across the grass, leapt onto the padded arm and shook his head savagely from side to side, his growling just audible through the humid air pierced by the cries of children and the sonic solicitude of safety-conscious cars. Did the children feel safer, or just feel that it was safer to assume they were always in danger? A Botero-shaped family munching soft buns at a round-cornered picnic table looked on as the first policeman hurried across the green and tried to detach the keen young Alsatian from his colleague's arm. The second policeman was by now floundering on the grass trying to persuade the dog that he was not a sick fuck but one of the good guys.

Vino Veritas had three sizes of Maker's Mark. Not sure which one he was supposed to replace, Patrick bought all three.

'Better be safe than sorry,' he explained to the salesman.

'You'd better believe it,' said the salesman with a fervour that catapulted Patrick back into the parking lot.

He was already in another phase of drunkenness. Sweatier, sadder, slower. He needed *both* another drink *and* a huge amount of coffee, so that he could stand up at Walter and Beth's, or indeed anywhere. He was in fact certain, he might as well admit it, that the smallest bottle of Maker's Mark was not the one he had to replace. He hadn't been able to resist buying the baby bottle to complete the family. Ding ding ding. He unpeeled the red faux-wax cap and uncorked the bottle. As the bourbon slipped down his throat, he pictured a flaming beam crashing through the floors and ceilings of a building, spreading fire and wreckage. What a relief.

The Better Latte Than Never coffee shop lived up to the maddening promise of its name. Patrick sailed past the invitation to a skinny caramel grande vanilla frapuccino in a transparent plastic cup jam-packed with mouthwatering ice and strawberry-flavoured whipped cream, and ordered some black coffee. He moved along the assembly line.

'Have a great one!' said Pete, a heavy-jawed blond beast in an apron, sliding the coffee across the counter.

Old enough to remember the arrival of 'Have a nice day', Patrick could only look with alarm on the hyperinflation of 'Have a great one'. Where would this Weimar of bullying cheerfulness end? 'You have a profound and meaningful day now,' he simpered under his breath as he tottered across the room with his giant mug. 'Have a blissful one,' he snapped as he sat at a table. 'You all make sure you have an all-body orgasm,' he whispered in a Southern accent, 'and make it last.' Because you deserve it. Because you owe it to yourself. Because you're a unique and special person. In the end, there was only so much you could expect from a cup of coffee and an uneatable muffin. If only Pete had confined himself to realistic achievements. 'Have a cold shower,' or 'Try not to crash your car.'

He was back in the inflammatory, deranged drunkenness he had lost in the hot parking lot. Yes yes yes. After a few gallons of coffee there'd be no stopping him. Across the room, a voluptuous medical student in a pink cardigan and faded jeans was working on her computer. Her mobile phone was on the slate ledge of the Heat and Glow fireplace, next to the Walkman and the complicated drink. She sat on her chair with her knees raised and her legs wide open as if she had just given birth to her Hewlett Packard, *The Pathology of Disease* squashing some loose notes on the edge of the table. He must have her, on a must-have basis. She was so relaxed in her body. He stared at her and she looked back at him with a calm even gaze. She smiled. It was absolutely terrifying how perfect she was. He looked away and smiled bashfully at his kneecap. He couldn't bear her being friendly. It made him want to cry. She was practically a doctor, she could probably completely save him. His sons would miss him at first, but they'd get over it. Anyway, they could come and stay. She was obviously an incredibly warm and loving person.

The Oedipal vortex had him caught like a dead leaf in its compulsory spin, wanting one consolation after another. Some languages kept the ideas of desire and privation apart, but English forced them into the naked intimacy of a single syllable: want. Wanting love to ease the want of love. The war on want which made one want more. Whiskey was no better at looking after him than his mother had been, or his wife had become, or the pink cardigan would be if he lurched across the room, fell to his knees and begged her for mercy. Why did he want to do that? Where was the Eagle now? Why wasn't he coolly registering the feeling of attraction and reabsorbing it into a sense of his present state of mind, or beyond that, into the simple fact of being alive? Why rush naively towards the objects of his thoughts, when he could stay at their source? He closed his eyes and slumped in his chair.

So, here he was in the magnificence of the inner realm, no longer chasing after pink cardigans and amber bottles, but watching thoughts flick open like so many fans in a hot crowded room. He was no longer jumping into the painted scenes, but noticing the flicking, noticing the heat, noticing that drunkenness gave a certain predominance to images in his otherwise predominantly verbal mind, noticing that the conclusion he was looking for was not blackout and orgasm, but knowledge and insight. The trouble was that even when the object of pursuit changed, the anguish of pursuit remained. He found himself hurtling towards a vacuum rather than hurtling away from it. Big deal. In the end he was better off galloping after the syrupy mirage of a hot fuck. He opened his eyes. She was gone. Want in both directions. Directions delusions anyway. A universe of want. Infinite melancholy.

The scraping chair. Late. Family. Tea. Try not to think. Think: don't think. Madness. Ding ding ding. Cruise control, out of control. Please stop thinking. Who's asking? Who's being asked?

When he drew up to the house, the Others were arranged around Nancy's car in a tableau of reproach and irritation.

'You wouldn't believe what happened to me in New Milton,' he said, wondering what he would say if anybody asked.

'We were about to leave without you,' said Nancy. 'Beth can't stand people being late; they just drop right off her guest list.'

'A slobbering thought,' said Patrick. 'I mean sobering thought,' he corrected himself. Neither version was heard above the sound of crunching gravel and slamming doors. He climbed into the back of Nancy's car and slumped next to Thomas, wishing he had the baby bottle of Maker's Mark to nurse him through tea. During the journey he dozed superficially until he felt the car slow down and come to a halt. When he clambered out he found himself surrounded by unpunctuated woodland. The Berkshire Hills rolled off in every direction, like a heavy swell in a green and yellow ocean, with Walter and Beth's white clapboard ark cresting the nearest wave. He felt seasick and land-bound at the same time.

'Unbelievable,' he muttered.

'I know,' said Nancy. 'They pretty much own the view.'

The tea party unfolded for Patrick in an unreliable middle distance. One moment he felt as glazed over as an aquarium on television, the next he was drowning. There were maids in uniform with eyeball aching white shoes. A small Hispanic butler. Sweet brown cinnamony iced tea. Park Avenue gossip. People laughing about something Henry Kissinger had said at dinner on Thursday.

Then the garden tour began. Walter went ahead, sometimes unlocking his arm from Nancy's in order to clip an impertinent shoot with the secateurs he held in his suede-gloved hand. He certainly wouldn't be doing any gardening if it hadn't been done already. He bore the same relation to the gardening as a mayor to the housing development on which he cuts the inaugural ribbon. Beth followed with Mary and the children. She was persistently modest about the garden and sometimes downright dissatisfied. When she came to a topiary deer that stood on the edge of a flower bed, she said, 'I hate it! It looks like a kangaroo. I pour vinegar on it to try to kill it off. The climate here is impossible: we're up to our waists in snow until the middle of May, and two weeks later we're living in Vietnam.'

Patrick dragged behind the rest of the party, trying to pretend he was in a horticultural trance, leaning over to stare blindly at a nameless flower, hoping he looked like the shade of Andrew Marvell rather than a stale drunk who dreaded being drawn into conversation. The vast lawn turned into a box maze, a topiary zoo (from which the doomed kangaroo was excluded) and finally a lime grove.

'Look, Dada! A *sanglier*!' said Thomas, pointing to a curly haired, heavy snouted bronze boar, with legs that looked too delicate to bear the weight of its pendulous belly and massive tusked head.

'Yes, darling,' said Patrick.

Wild boar had always been French for Patrick and he was heartbroken that they were French for Thomas as well. How could he have retained that word over the whole year? Was he thinking of the wild boar at Saint-Nazaire trotting across the garden to eat the fallen figs, or snuffling among the vines at night, looking for ripe grapes? No, he wasn't. *Sanglier* was just a word for the animal in the statue. He had already turned his back on it and was running down the lime grove pretending to be an aeroplane. Patrick's heartbreak was all his own, and even that was hollow. He no longer felt a corrosive nostalgia for Saint-Nazaire; its loss just clarified the real failure: that he couldn't be the sort of father he wanted to be, a man who had transcended his ancestral muddle and offered his children unhaunted love. He had made it out of what he thought of as Zone One, where a parent was doomed to make his child experience what he had hated most about his life, but he was still stuck in Zone Two, where the painstaking avoidance of Zone One blinded him to fresh mistakes. In Zone Two giving was based on what the giver lacked. Nothing was more exhausting than this deficiency-driven, overcompensating zeal. He dreamt of Zone Three. He sensed that it was there, just over the hill, like the rumour of a fertile valley. Perhaps his present chaos was the final rejection of an unsustainable way of being. He must stop drinking, not tomorrow but later this afternoon when the next opportunity arose.

Strangely excited by this glint of hope, Patrick continued to hang back. The tour drifted on. A stone Diana stood at the far end of the grove, eternally hunting the bronze boar at the other end. Behind the house, a springy wood-chip path meandered through an improved wood. Patches of light shivered on the denuded ground between the broad trunks of oaks and beeches. Beyond the wood they passed a hangar where huge fans, consuming enough electricity to run a small village, kept agapanthus warm in the winter. Next to the hangar was a hen house somewhat larger than Patrick's London flat, and so strangely undefiled that he couldn't help wondering if these were genetically modified hens which had been crossed with cucumbers to stop them from defecating. Beth walked over the fresh sawdust, under the red heat lamps, and discovered three speckled brown eggs in the laying boxes. Every plate of scrambled eggs must cost her several thousand dollars. The truth was that he hated the very rich, especially since he was never going to be one of them. They were all too often only the shrill pea in the whistle of their possessions. Without the editorial influence of the word 'afford', their desires rambled on like unstoppable bores, relentless and whimsical at the same time. They could give the appearance of generosity to all sorts of emotional meanness – 'Do borrow the fourth house we never get round to using. We won't be there ourselves, but Carmen and Alfonso will look after you. No, really, it's no trouble at all, and besides it's about time we got our money's worth out of those two. We pay them a fortune and they never do a stroke of work.'

'What are you muttering about?' said Nancy, who was clearly annoyed that Patrick had underperformed as an admiring guest.

'Oh, nothing,' said Patrick.

'Isn't this hen house divine?' she prompted him.

'It would be a privilege to live here,' said Patrick, catching up abruptly with his social duties.

When the garden tour ended, with a gift of eggs, the visit ended as well. On the way back to Nancy's, Patrick was confronted by his decision not to go on drinking. It was all very well to decide not to drink when he had no choice, but in a few minutes he would be able to climb into the Buick's private liquor store. What did it matter if he started stopping tomorrow? He knew that it somehow mattered completely. If he went on now he would be hung over tomorrow morning and the whole day would begin with a poisonous legacy. But more than that, he wanted to cultivate the faint hope he had felt in the garden. If he stopped tomorrow it would be from an excess of shame, a nastier and less reliable motivation. What, on the other hand, was Zone Three? His mind was occluded by tension; he couldn't reconstruct the hope.

Back in Nancy's library, he stared out of the window, feeling that he was being stared at in turn by the bottle of bourbon he had replaced on the drinks tray. It would be so much neater to bring it down to the level the empty one had started at. Just as he was about to give in, Nancy came into the room and sank with a theatrical sigh into the armchair opposite him.

'I feel we haven't really talked about Eleanor,' she said. 'I think I'm frightened of asking because I was so shocked when I last saw her.'

'You heard about the fall?'

'No!'

'She broke her hip and went into hospital. When I went to see her she started asking me to kill her. She hasn't stopped asking me since. Every time I go . . .'

'Oh, come on,' said Nancy, 'I really don't think that's fair! I mean, it's all too Greek. There must be some special Furies for children who kill their parents.'

'Yeah,' said Patrick. 'Wormwood Scrubs.'

'Oh, God,' said Nancy, twisting in her chair. 'It's so complicated. I mean, I know I wouldn't want to go on living if I couldn't speak, or move, or read, or watch a movie.'

'I have no doubt that helping her to die would be the most loving thing to do.'

'Well, I don't want you to misinterpret me, but maybe we should rent an ambulance and drive her to Holland.'

'Arriving in Holland isn't in itself fatal,' said Patrick.

'Oh, please, let's not talk about it any more. I find it too upsetting. I really couldn't bear it if I ended up like that.'

'Do you want a drink?' asked Patrick.

'Oh, no. I don't drink,' said Nancy. 'Didn't you know? I watched it destroy Daddy's life. But do help yourself if you want one.'

Patrick imagined one of his children saying, 'I watched it destroy Daddy's life.' He noticed that he was leaning forward in his chair.

'I might help myself by not having one,' he said, sinking back and closing his eyes.

15

MARY COULD HARDLY BELIEVE that Patrick and Robert were in one thinly carpeted motel room and she and Thomas were in another, with plastic wraps on the plastic glasses, and Sanitized For Your Protection sashes on the plastic loo seats, and a machine down the corridor whose shuddering ejaculations of ice reminded her unwillingly of the state of her marriage. She could hear the steady hum of the freeway thickening in the early morning. It was the perfect soundtrack to the quick, slick flow of her anxiety. At about four in the morning a phrase had started clicking like a metronome she was too tired to reach out and stop: 'Interstate—inner state, interstate—inner state.' Sleeplessness was the breeding ground of these sardonic harmonies; ice machine— marriage; interstate—inner state. It was enough to drive you mad. Or was it enough to stop you from going mad? Making connections. She could hardly believe that her family was haemorrhaging more money in order to have a horrible time in one of America's migratory nowheres. So much road and so few places, so much friendliness and so little intimacy, so much flavour and so little taste. She longed to get the children back home to London, away from the thin rush of America and back to the density of their ordinary lives.

Patrick had kept up the tradition of getting them thrown out of somewhere rather lovely quite a long time before the end of the holidays. Saint-Nazaire last year, Henry's island this year. Of course she was delighted that he had stopped drinking, but the effect in the first week was to make him behave like other people when they were blind drunk: explosive, irascible, despairing. All the boils were being lanced at once, the kidney dishes overflowing. Henry was certainly a nightmare, but he was also some sort of relation and, above all, a host who was providing a playground for the children, with its own harbour and beaches and sailing boats and motor boats and, to Thomas's undying amazement, its own petrol pump.

'I mean, it's unbelievable, Henry has his own petrol pump!' Thomas said several times a day, opening his palms and shaking his head. Robert was in a statistical frenzy of acres and bedrooms, totting up the immensity of Henry's domain, but both boys were mainly having a wonderful time dashing briefly into the freezing water and going out in Henry's speedboats, riding the wake behind the big ferries which served the public islands.

The only thing which went wrong was everything else. During the first lunch Henry asked Mary to remove Thomas from the dining room when his monologue on the moral necessity of increasing Israel's nuclear-strike capacity was interrupted by Thomas's impersonation of a petrol pump.

'The Syrians are filling their pants right now and they're right to be . . .' Henry was saying gleefully.

'Bvvvv,' said Thomas. 'Bvvvv . . .'

'I'm sure you're familiar with the phrase, "Children should be seen and not heard",' said Henry.

'Who isn't?' said Mary.

'I've always thought it was too liberal,' said Henry, craning his neck out of his shirt to emphasize his bon mot.

'You'd rather not see him either?' said Mary, suddenly furious. She picked Thomas up and carried him out of the room rapidly, Henry's unmolested monologue resuming its flow behind her.

'When Admiral Yamamoto had finished his attack on Pearl Harbor, he had the wisdom to be more apprehensive than triumphant. "Gentlemen," he said, "we have roused a sleeping dragon." It is that thought that should be uppermost in the minds of the world's international terrorists and their state sponsors. With an arsenal of tactical nuclear weapons, not just a deterrent nuclear shield, Israel will send a clear message to the region that it stands shoulder to shoulder . . .'

She burst onto the lawn picturing Henry as one of those unknotted balloons Thomas liked to watch swirling flatulently around the room until it suddenly flopped to the ground in wrinkled exhaustion.

'I'm letting go of a balloon, Mama,' said Thomas, spinning his hand in tight circles.

'How did you know I was thinking about a balloon?' said Mary.

'I did know that,' said Thomas, tilting his head to one side and smiling.

These borderless moments happened often enough for Mary to get used to them, but she couldn't quite shake off her surprise at how precise they were.

By silent agreement the two of them walked away from the house to the little rocky beach at the foot of the lawn. Mary sat down on a small patch of silvery white sand among rocks festooned with beaded black seaweed.

'Will you look after me for a long time?' asked Thomas.

'Yes, darling.'

'Until I'm fourteen?'

'As long as you want me to,' she said. 'As long as I can . . .' she added. He had asked her the other day if she was going to die and she had said, 'Yes, but not for a long time, I hope.' His discovery of her mortality blew away the dust which had dimmed the menace of it in her own mind and made it glare at her again with all its root horror restored. She loathed death for making her let him down. Why couldn't he play a little longer? Why couldn't he feel safe a little longer? She had recovered her balance to some extent, attributing his interest in death to the transition from infancy to childhood, but also wondering if Patrick's impatience with that transition was making it happen sooner than necessary. Robert had been through the same sort of crisis when he was five; Thomas was only three.

Thomas sat down on her lap and sucked his thumb, fingering the smooth label of his raggie with the other hand. He was minutes away from sleep. Mary sat back on her heels and made herself calm. She could do things for Thomas that she couldn't do for herself or anyone else, not even Robert. Thomas needed her for his protection, that was obvious enough, but she needed him for her sense of virtue. When she felt gloomy he made her want to be cheerful, when she was drained he made her find new wells of energy, when she was exasperated she searched for a deeper patience. She sat there as still as the rocks around her and waited while he dropped off.

However hot the day became, the sea here was a refrigerator throwing off a sceptical little breeze. She liked the feeling that Maine was basically inhospitable, that it would soon shake out its summer visitors, like a dog on a beach. In the chink between two winters the northern light sparkled hungrily on the sea. She imagined it stretched out like a gaunt El Greco saint. The thought made her want to paint again. She wanted to make love again. She wanted to think again, if she was going to start making lists, but somehow she had lost her independence. Her being was fused with Thomas's. She was like someone whose clothes had been stolen while she was having a swim, and now she didn't know how to get out of this tiring beautiful pool.

After Thomas had been asleep for five minutes she was able to move to a more comfortable position. She sat against the bank at the bottom of the lawn and placed him lengthwise between her legs, as if he was still being born, still the wrong way round. She formed a canopy with his raggie to protect him from the sun, and leant back and closed her eyes and tried to rest, but her thoughts looped back tightly enough onto Kettle's remote style of mothering and the part it played in producing her own fanatical availability. She thought of her nanny, her kind, dedicated nanny, solving one little problem after the next, inhabiting a nursery world without sex or art or intoxicants or conversation, just practical kindness and food. Of course looking after a child made her feel like the nanny who had looked after her when she was a child. And of course it made her determined to be unlike Kettle who had failed to look after her. Personality seemed to her at once absurd and compulsive: she remained trapped inside it even when she could see through it. Her thoughts on mothers and mothering twisted around, following the thread of a knot they couldn't untie.

For some reason, sitting by this black sea with its slightly chill breeze made her feel she could see everything very clearly. Thomas was asleep and nobody else knew exactly where she was. For the first time in months nobody knew how to make any demands on her and in that sudden absence of pressure she could appreciate the family's tropical atmosphere of unresolved dependency. Eleanor like a sick child pleading with Patrick to 'make it stop'; Thomas like a referee pushing his parents apart if Patrick ever tried to get close to her indifferent body; Robert keeping his diary, keeping his distance. She was at the eye of the storm, with her need to be needed making her appear more self-sufficient than she really was. In reality she couldn't survive on the glory of satisfying other people's unreasonable demands. Her passion for self-sacrifice sometimes made her feel like a prisoner who meekly digs the trench for her own execution. Patrick needed a revolution against the tyranny of dependency, but she needed one against the tyranny of self-sacrifice. Although she was overstretched and monopolized, an appeal to her best instincts only drove her further into the trap. The protests which might be expected to come from Robert's sibling rivalry came instead from the relatively unstable Patrick. It was bad luck that she had become disgusted by the slightest sign of need in Patrick at a time when he had Thomas as well as Eleanor to stimulate his own sense of helplessness. Patrick accused her of overindulging Thomas, but if Thomas was ready to do without certain maternal comforts, Patrick must be even readier. Perhaps he was no longer ripe but rotten. Perhaps a psychic gangrene had set in and it was the smell of corruption that revolted her.

That evening she excused herself from dinner and stayed with Thomas, leaving Patrick and Robert to face the roused dragon of Henry's table talk on their own. Even before dinner, as she sat on the faded pink cushions of the window seat, the panes of the bay window around her bleeding and glittering in the sea-reflected evening light, with the children behaving beautifully and Patrick smiling over a glass of mineral water, she knew she couldn't stand more than a few minutes of Henry's address to the nation. He was on a whirlwind tour of foreign policy, heading east from Israel, through the Stans and the Formers, and on his way to the People's Republics. She had a dreadful feeling that he intended to get to North Korea before bedtime. No doubt he had a cunning plan to nuke North Korea before it nuked South Korea and Japan. She didn't want to hear it.

After his bath, Thomas wanted to climb into her bed and she didn't have the heart to refuse him. They snuggled up together reading *The Wind in the Willows*. Thomas fell asleep as Rat and Mole started to drift down the river after their picnic. When Patrick came into the room she realized that she had also dropped off with the book on her lap and her reading glasses still on.

'I so nearly had a fight with Henry,' said Patrick, striding into the room with his clenched fists still looking for a destination.

'Oh dear, what was it this evening?' she asked.

Patrick was always saying that their erotic, conversational and social lives were over, that they were just parental bureaucrats. Well, here she was, shattered and abruptly woken, but ready for a lively conversation.

'North Korea.'

'I knew it.'

'You always know everything. No wonder you felt you could miss dinner.'

Everything she said was wrong. No matter what she did, Patrick felt abandoned. She tried again.

'I mean, I just had a feeling before dinner that North Korea would be next.'

'That's what Henry thinks: North Korea is next. You should form a coalition.'

'Did you argue with him, or are you going to have to argue with me instead?'

'We relied heavily on the democratic miracle of agreeing to disagree. Henry hates free speech but, partly as a result of that, he isn't free to say so. He banged on about how lucky we were not to live in a country where you could be shot for holding the wrong opinions.'

'He wants to shoot you.'

'Exactly.'

'Great. That'll make our holiday more fun.'

'More fun? Don't you have to be having fun in the first place to have more fun?'

'I think the children are having fun.'

'Oh, well, that's all that matters,' said Patrick with rigid piety. 'I did hint to Henry,' he continued, pacing up and down at the end of the bed, 'that I felt the present administration's foreign policy was made up of projection. That America is the rogue state with a fundamentalist president, and several thousand times the weapons of mass destruction of all other nations combined, et cetera, et cetera.'

'How did that go down?' Mary wanted to keep him going, keep the aggression political.

'Incredulous laughter. A lot of neck-craning. False smiles. Reminded me of "a certain event which played no small part in our lives over here". I said that 9/11 was one of the most shocking things in history, but that its exploitation, what I'd like to call 9/12, was just as shocking in its own way. The tracer bullet was the use of the word "war" on the following day. War is an activity between nation states. A word the British government spent thirty years carefully avoiding in its struggle with the IRA. Why give the standing of a nation state to a few hundred homicidal maniacs, unless you're going to use them as the pretext to make war with some real nation states? Henry said, "I think that's a distinction that would be lost on Joe Six-Pack. We had a war to sell to the American public." That was the trouble with our conversation – my accusations are his assumptions, selling war to the American public, testing new weapons, stimulating the military-industrial complex, using public money to demolish a country which the cabinet's pet corporations benefit from rebuilding and so forth. He loves it all, so he can't be caught making hollow apologies.'

'How was Robert?'

'An excellent junior counsel,' said Patrick. 'He made the no-proven-links point and played pretty skilfully with the idea of "innocent lives". He asked Henry whether innocence was exclusively American. Again, the trouble is that for Henry the answer is really "Yes", so it's hard to get him on the run. He didn't bother to pretend much, except about free speech.'

'How did he answer Robert?'

'Oh, he just said that he could see that I'd "trained" him. He obviously thought we were the tag team from hell. The thing that ruffled him was my last bombing mission, in which I said that a really "developed" nation, as opposed to a merely powerful one, might bother to imagine the impact of two per cent of the world's population consuming fifty per cent of its resources, of the rapid extinction of every species of non-American culture and so forth. I got a little bit carried away and also said that the death of nature was a high price to pay for adding the few last curlicues of convenience to the lives of the very rich.'

'It's amazing he didn't throw us out,' said Mary.

'Don't worry, I'll try again tomorrow. I'll get him in the end. I can see now what upsets him. Politics is an exciting game, but money is sacred.'

She could tell that Patrick was serious. His sense of tension was so extreme that he had to destroy something, and this time it wasn't going to be himself.

'Do you mind not getting us thrown out for a couple of days? I've only just finished unpacking.' She tried to sound breezy.

'And you're comfortably installed with your lover as usual,' said Patrick.

'God, for a man who claims not to suffer from jealousy . . .'

'I don't suffer from jealousy, I suffer from rage. It's more fundamental. Loss produces anger first, possessiveness afterwards.'

'Before the rage, there's anxiety,' said Mary, feeling she knew what she was talking about. 'Anyway, I think you move through all three, even if one is usually dominant. It's not like shopping, you can't just opt for rage.'

'You'd be surprised.'

'I know you prefer anger because you think it's less humili-ating.'

'I don't prefer anger,' shouted Patrick, 'but I get it anyway.'

'I mean prefer it to the neighbouring emotions.'

Thomas, disturbed by Patrick's shouting, shifted in the bed and muttered to himself inaudibly.

'You're straying from the point,' said Patrick, more quietly. 'As usual we can't sleep together because you're in bed with our three-year-old son.'

'We can sleep together,' sighed Mary, 'I'll move him over to the side.'

'I want to make love to a woman, not a sighing heap of guilt and resignation,' hissed Patrick, in an ineffective whisper.

Thomas sat up blearily.

'No, Dada, you stop talking nonsense!' he shouted. 'And Mama, stop upsetting Dada!'

He collapsed back on the pillow and fell asleep again, his work done. A silence fell over the room, which Patrick was the first to interrupt.

'I wasn't talking nonsense . . .' he began.

'Oh, for God's sake,' said Mary. 'You don't have to win an argument with him as well. Can't you hear what he's saying? He wants us to stop arguing, not for you to start arguing with him.'

'Sure,' said Patrick in his suddenly bored way. 'I'll go to his bed, although I don't know why I call it "his" bed. I might as well stop pretending and call it mine.'

'You don't have to . . .'

'No – I do have to,' said Patrick and ducked out of the room.

He had abandoned her abruptly, but failed to transfer his sense of abandonment to her. She felt relieved, angry, guilty, mournful. The cloudscape of her emotional life was so rolling and rapid that she couldn't help marvelling at, sometimes envying, people who were 'out of touch with their feelings'. How did they do it? Right now she wouldn't mind knowing.

Her bedroom had a terrace built above the bay window of the drawing room where she had been sitting before dinner. She walked up to the French windows and imagined herself throwing them open, contemplating the stars, having an epiphany.

It wasn't going to happen. Her body had started its landslide towards sleep. She took one last glance out of the window and wished she hadn't. A thin streak of cloud was crossing the moon in a way that reminded her of the elision in *Un Chien Andalou* between the same image and a razor blade slicing open an eyeball. Her vision was the end of vision. Was she blinded by something she couldn't see, or blinded by seeing something she couldn't bear to look at? She was too tired to work anything out. Her thoughts were just threats, sleep just the rubble of wakefulness.

She got into bed and was covered by a thin layer of broken rest. Soon afterwards, she was disturbed by hearing Patrick slink back into the room. She could feel him staring at her to see if she was awake. She gave nothing away. He eventually settled on the other side of Thomas, who lay in the middle like the sword placed between the unmarried in a medieval bed. Why couldn't she reach out to Patrick? Why couldn't she make a nest of pillows for Thomas on one side of the bed and stay with Patrick on the other? She had no charity left for Patrick. In fact, for the first time in her marriage she could picture herself and the children living alone in the flat while Patrick was off somewhere, anywhere, being miserable.

The next day she was shocked by her coldness, but she soon got used to it.

She had always known it was there, the alternative to the warmth which struck everyone as so typical. Now she took it up like a hermit moving into a cave. She resisted Patrick's rashes of nervous charm without effort. It was too tiring to move back and forth to the jumpy rhythm of his moods. She might as well stay where she was. He was going to ruin their holiday, but first he wanted to make her agree that fighting with Henry was a sign of his splendid integrity rather than his uncontrollable irritation. She refused. By that evening it was clear that Patrick's agreement to disagree with Henry was in peril.

'It's going to be tough to make conversation if you don't stop attacking everything I say,' said plain-speaking Henry. 'Let's stick to talking family.'

'That proven formula for goodwill and unity,' said Patrick with one of his short barking laughs.

'You're as bad as Yasser Arafat,' said Henry. 'You think peace and defeat are the same thing. I'm just trying to extend some hospitality here. You don't have to accept it, if you've got an ideological problem with that.' Henry chuckled at the word 'ideological', which for him was as inherently comic as the word 'bottom' to an exuberant four-year-old.

'That's right,' said Patrick, 'we don't.'

'But we'd like to,' said Mary quickly.

'Speak for yourself,' said Patrick.

'I am,' she said, 'and unlike you I'm also trying to speak for the children.'

'Are you? Only this morning Thomas was saying that Henry is "a very funny man" and, as you know, Robert's nickname for him is "Hitler". I doubt you're even speaking for yourself after you were thrown out of lunch yesterday.'

That had been that. They left the next morning. She expected Patrick to be stubborn and proud and destructive, but she hadn't yet forgiven him for including the children in his final explosive charge.

The ice machine in the motel corridor produced another juddering emission of cubes just the other side of the thin bedroom wall. The interstate's mosquito whine had given way to a hornet drone. Thomas stirred beside her and then, with his usual prompt transition to full desire, he sat up and said, 'I want you to read me a story.' She obediently picked up the copy of *The Wind in the Willows* which they had started reading in Maine.

'Do you remember where we were?' asked Mary.

'Ratty was saying to Moley that he was a plain pig,' said Thomas, rounding his eyes in amazement. 'But, actually, he's a rat.'

'That's right,' laughed Mary. Rat and Mole were on their way back to River Bank in the gathering darkness of a December afternoon. Mole had just smelt the traces of his old home and was overwhelmed by longing and nostalgia. Rat had pressed on to River Bank, his own home, assuming Mole would want to go there as well. Then Mole broke down and told Rat about his homesickness. Mary reread the sentence they had finished with the night before.

'The Rat stared straight in front of him, saying nothing, only patting Mole gently on the shoulder. After a time he muttered gloomily, "I see it all now! What a pig I've been! A pig – that's me! Just a pig – a plain pig!"'

'I mean . . .' Thomas began.

There was a knock on the door. Mary put the book down and asked who it was.

'Bobby!' said Thomas. 'I knew it was you because – well, because it is you!'

Robert sat down on the bed with his shoulders slumped, ignoring his brother's reasoning.

'I hate this place,' he said.

'I know,' said Mary, 'but we'll move on this morning.'

'Again,' groaned Robert. 'We've been to three motels since the Prosecuting Attorney got us thrown off that brilliant island. We might as well get a mobile home.'

'I'm going to ring Sally after breakfast and ask her if we could go to Long Island a few days earlier than planned.'

'I don't want to go to Long Island, I want to go home,' said Robert.

'Moley smells his home and he wants it,' said Thomas, leaning forward to support his brother's case.

They agreed that if they couldn't go straight to Long Island, they would tell Patrick they wanted to go back to England.

'No more magic of the open road,' said Robert. 'Please.'

When she rang Sally there was no answer in Long Island. Eventually she found her in New York.

'We had to come back to the city because our water tank burst and flooded the apartment downstairs. Our neighbours are suing us, so we're suing the plumbers who only put the tank in last year. The plumbers are suing the tank company for defective design. And the residents are suing the building, even though they're all on vacation, because the water was cut off for two days instead of two hours, which caused them a lot of mental stress in Tuscany and Nantucket.'

'Gosh,' said Mary. 'What's wrong with mopping up and getting a new water tank?'

'That is *so* English,' said Sally, delighted by Mary's quaint stoicism.

Mary explained at breakfast that there wasn't really room in the New York apartment, but Sally said they were welcome to all squeeze in somehow.

'I don't want to squeeze in,' said Robert, 'I want to fly out.'

'We're on an aeroplane now,' said Thomas, thrusting his arms out like wings, 'and Alabala is in the cockpit!'

'Oh-oh,' said Robert, 'we'd better catch the next flight.'

'He's on the next flight as well,' said Thomas, as surprised as anyone by Alabala's resourcefulness.

'How did he manage that?' said Robert.

Thomas glanced sideways for a moment to look for the explanation.

'He used his ejector seat,' he said, making an ejector-seat noise, 'and then Felan stopped the next plane and Alabala got on!'

'There's the little matter of our unrefundable tickets,' said Patrick.

'We could have bought new ones with the money we've spent in these disgusting motels,' said Robert.

'You've taught him to argue too well,' said Mary.

'There's no one to argue with, is there?' said Patrick. 'I think we're all sick of America by now.'

16

AFTER HER FALL, ELEANOR'S ceaseless pleas for death had forced Patrick to look into the legalities of euthanasia and assisted suicide. Once again, as with his own disinheritance, he became the legal servant of his mother's repulsive demands. Superficially, there was something more attractive about getting rid of Eleanor than there had been about losing Saint-Nazaire, but then the obscenity of what he was being asked to do would break through the stockade of practicalities with Jacobean vigour. Even if a nursing home was not the usual setting for a *Revenger's Tragedy*, he felt the perils of usurping God's monopoly on vengeance just as keenly as he would have in the catacombs of an Italian castle. He tried to pull himself together, to examine his motives scrupulously. The dead were not dogged enough to make ghosts without the guilt of the living. His mother was like a rock fall blocking a mountain pass. Perhaps he could clear her out of the way, but if his intentions were murderous, her ghost would haunt the pass for ever.

He decided to have nothing to do with organizing her death. Asking him to help her die was the last and nastiest trick of a woman who had always insisted, from the moment he was born, that she was the one who needed cheering up. And then he would visit Eleanor again and see that the cruellest thing he could do was to leave her exactly where she was. He tried to remain angry so he could forbid himself to help, but compassion tortured him as well. The compassion was far harder to bear and he came to think of his vengefulness as a relatively frivolous state of mind.

'Go on, do yourself a favour, get homicidal,' he muttered to himself as he dialled the number of the Voluntary Euthanasia Society.

Before going to America, he kept his research secret. He didn't tell Mary because they never discussed anything important without having a row. He didn't tell Julia because his affair with her was in the final stages of its decay. In any case, secrecy was essential in a country where helping someone to die could be punished with fourteen years' imprisonment. He read articles in the papers about nurses sent to jail for generous injections. The Voluntary Euthanasia Society, despite its promising name, was unable to help. It was a campaigning organization trying to change the legislation. Patrick could remember reading about Arthur Koestler and his wife using the plastic bags provided by Exit to asphyxiate themselves in their house in Montpelier Square. The lady who answered the phone at the Voluntary Euthanasia Society had no knowledge of an organization called Exit. She couldn't even comment on most of his questions, because her advice might be construed as suicide 'counselling', an offence under the same statute that punished assisting and aiding. She hadn't heard of an organization called Dignitas either and couldn't tell him how to get in touch with it. The Everlasting was not the only one to have 'fixed his canon 'gainst self-slaughter', Patrick couldn't help thinking as the fruitless conversation dragged to a close. Directory Inquiries, careless of the legal consequences, gave him the number of Dignitas a few minutes later.

He rang Switzerland, his pulse racing. The calm voice which

answered the phone in German turned out to speak English as well, and promised to send some information. When Patrick pressed him on the legal points, he said that it was not a matter of euthanasia, administered by the doctor, but of assisted suicide administered by the patient. The barbiturate would be prescribed if a Swiss doctor was convinced that it was warranted and that the suicide was entirely voluntary. If Patrick wanted to make progress while he waited for the membership forms to arrive, he should get a letter of consent from Eleanor and a doctor's report on her condition. Patrick pointed out that his mother could no longer write and he doubted that she could give herself an injection either.

'Can she sign?'

'Just.'

'Can she swallow?'

'Just.'

'So, maybe we can help.'

Patrick felt a surge of excitement after his telephone call to Switzerland. Signing and swallowing, those were the keys to the kingdom, the code for the missile launch. There wasn't much time before Eleanor lost them. He dreaded the precious barbiturate dribbling uselessly down her shining chin. As to her signature, it now formed an Alpine silhouette reminiscent of Thomas's earliest stabs at writing. Patrick paced up and down the drawing room of his flat. He was 'working at home', and had waited for Robert to go to school and for Mary to take Thomas to Holland Park before carrying on with his secret research. Now the whole flat was his to bounce around; there was nobody to be efficient for, nobody to be friendly to. Just as well, since he couldn't stop pacing, couldn't stop repeating, 'Sign and swallow, sign and swallow,' like a chained parrot in the corner of an overstuffed room. He felt increasingly tense, having to pause and breathe out slowly to expel the feeling that he was about to faint. There was a sinister,

knife-grinding quality to his excitement. He was going to give
Eleanor exactly what she wanted. But should he be wanting it
quite so much as well?

He recognized the signature of his murderous longings and
felt duly troubled. What seemed new, but then admitted that it
had been there all along, was his own desire for a glass of barbiturate. 'To cease upon the midnight with no pain' – rearranged a
little, it might almost be the chemical name for that final drink:
Sismidnopin.

'Oh, my God! You've got a bottle of Sismidnopin! Can I have
some?' he suddenly squealed as he reached the end of the corridor and spun round to pace back again. His thoughts were all
over the place, or rather they were in one place dragging everything towards them. He imagined a modest little protest march,
starting out in Hampstead with a few ethical types trying to ban
unnecessary suffering, and then swelling rapidly as it flowed
down to Swiss Cottage, until soon every shop was closed and
every restaurant empty and all the trains stood still and the petrol pumps were unattended, and the whole population of London was flowing towards Whitehall and Trafalgar Square and
Parliament Square, cursing unnecessary suffering and screaming
for Sismidnopin.

'Why should a dog, a cat have death,' he wailed front stage,
'and she . . .'. He forced himself to stop. 'Oh, shut up,' he said,
collapsing on a sofa.

'I'm just trying to help my old mum,' he cajoled himself in a
new voice. 'She's a bit past her sell-by date, to be honest. Not enjoying life as much as she used to. Can't even watch the old goggle
box. Eyes gone. No use reading to her, just gets her agitated.
Every little thing frightens her, even her own happy memories.
Terrible situation, really.'

Who was talking? Who was he talking to? He felt taken over.

He breathed out slowly. He was feeling way too tense. He

was going to give himself a heart attack, finishing off the wrong person by mistake. He could see that he was breaking into fragments because the simplicity of his situation – son asked to kill mother – was unbearable; and the simplicity of her situation – person dreads every second of her existence – was more unbearable still. He tried to stay with it, to think about what didn't bear thinking about: Eleanor's experience. He felt her writhing on the bed, begging for death. He suddenly burst into tears, all his evasions exhausted.

The rivalry between revenge and compassion ended during that morning in his flat, and he was left with a more straightforward longing for everyone in his family to be free, including his mother. He decided to press ahead with getting a medical report before his trip to America. There was little point in applying to the nursing home's doctor, whose entire mission was to keep patients alive despite their craving for a lethal injection. Dr Fenelon was Patrick's family doctor, but he had not taken care of Eleanor before. He was a sympathetic and intelligent man whose Catholicism had not yet stood in the way of useful prescriptions and rapid specialist appointments. Patrick was used to thinking of him as grown up and was bewildered to hear him speak of his ethics classes at Ampleforth, as if he had allowed a priest to spray his teenage sketch of the world with an Infallible fixative.

'I still believe that suicide is a sin,' said Dr Fenelon, 'but I no longer believe that people who want to commit suicide are being tempted by the Devil, because we now know that they're suffering from a disease called depression.'

'Listen,' said Patrick, trying to recover as unobtrusively as possible from finding the Devil on the guest list, 'when you can't move, can't speak, can't read, and know that you're losing control of your mind, depression is not a disease, it's the only reasonable response. It's cheerfulness that would require a glandular dysfunction, or a supernatural force to explain it.'

'When people are depressed, we give them antidepressants,' Dr Fenelon persevered.

'She's already on them. It's true that they gave a certain enthusiasm to her loathing of life. It was only after she started taking them that she asked me to kill her.'

'It can be a great privilege to work with the dying,' Dr Fenelon began.

'I don't think she's going to start working with the dying,' Patrick interrupted. 'She can't even stand up. If you mean that it's a great privilege for you, I have to say that I'm more concerned about her quality of life than yours.'

'I mean,' said the doctor, with more equanimity than Patrick's sarcasm might have deserved, 'that suffering can have a transfiguring effect. One sees people, after an enormous struggle, breaking through to a kind of peacefulness they've never known before.'

'There has to be some sense of self to experience the peacefulness – that's precisely what my mother is losing.'

Dr Fenelon sat back in his buttoned leather chair with a sympathetic nod, exposing the crucifix he kept on the shelf behind him. Patrick had often noticed it before, but it now seemed to be mocking him with its brilliant inversion of glory and suffering, making the thing it was natural to be disgusted by into the central meaning of life, not just the mundane meaning of forcing a person to reflect more deeply, but the entirely mysterious meaning of the world being redeemed from sin because Jesus got on the wrong side of the law two thousand years ago. What did it mean that the world had been redeemed from sin? It obviously didn't mean that there was any less sin. And how was Christ's nasty, kinky execution supposed to be responsible for this redemption which, as far as Patrick could tell, hadn't taken place? Until then he had only been dazzled by the irrelevance of Christianity in his own life, but now he found himself loathing it for threatening to cheat Eleanor of a punctual death. After some more schoolboy reminiscences, Dr Fenelon agreed to compile a report on Eleanor's condition. What use was made of it was none of his affair, he assured himself, and made an appointment to meet Patrick at the nursing home two days later.

Patrick went to tell his mother the good news and prepare her for the doctor's visit.

'I want . . .' she howled, and then half an hour later, 'Swiss . . . land.'

Patrick braced himself for his impatience with his mother's impatience.

'Everything is going as fast as possible,' he answered smoothly.

'You . . . ook . . . like . . . my . . . son,' Eleanor managed eventually.

'There's a simple explanation for that,' said Patrick. 'I am your son.'

'No!' said Eleanor, sure of her ground at last.

Patrick left with the even more pressing sense that Eleanor would soon be too senile to consent.

When he took Dr Fenelon into Eleanor's fetid room the next day, she was in a state of hysterical cheerfulness which Patrick had never seen before but immediately understood. She thought that she had to be on best behaviour, to win the doctor over, to show him that she was a good girl who deserved a favour. She stared at him adoringly. He was her liberator, her angel of death. Dr Fenelon asked Patrick to stay, to help him understand Eleanor's incoherent speech. He was impressed by the good quality of her reflexes, the absence of bed sores and the general condition of her skin. Patrick looked away from the white wrinkled expanse of her belly, feeling that he really shouldn't be allowed to see so much of his mother, and certainly didn't want to. He was driven mad by her eagerness. Why couldn't she manifest the misery he had spent the last week labouring to put into words?

She never tired of letting him down. He imagined the unbearably upbeat report that Dr Fenelon would be dictating on his return to the surgery. That evening he composed a letter of consent but he couldn't face seeing his mother again straight away. In any case, Fenelon's report wouldn't arrive before the family left on their American holiday and so Patrick resolved to let the whole thing drop until his return.

In America he tried not to think about a situation he could make no progress with, but he knew that the secret of his macabre project was alienating him from the rest of his family. After sobering up, he clung to his somewhat drunken vision of Zone Three in Walter and Beth's garden. Whenever he tried to define Zone Three, he could only think of it as a generosity that was not based on compensation or duty. Even though he could not quite describe it, he clung to this fragile intuition of what it might mean to be well.

It was only on the plane back to England that he finally told Mary what was going on. Thomas was asleep and Robert was watching a movie. At first Mary said nothing beyond sympathizing with the trouble Patrick had been through. She didn't know whether to voice her suspicion that Patrick had been so busy examining his own motives that he might not have looked carefully enough at Eleanor's. Wanting to die was one of the most commonplace things about life, but dying was something else. Eleanor's demands for help were not an offer to clear herself out of the way, but the only way she had left to keep herself at the centre of her family's attention. And did she really understand that she would have to do the killing herself? Mary felt sure that Eleanor was imagining an infinitely wise doctor with a gaze as deep as a mountain lake, leaning over to give her a fatal goodnight kiss, not a tumbler of bitter barbiturates she had to hoist to her own lips. Eleanor was the most childish person Mary knew, including Thomas.

'She won't do it,' she finally said to Patrick. 'She won't swallow. You'll have to get some special air ambulance, and take her to see the Swiss doctors, and get the prescription, and then she won't do it.'

'If she makes me take her to Switzerland for nothing, I'll kill her,' said Patrick.

'I'm sure that would suit her perfectly,' said Mary. 'She wants death taken out of her hands, not put into them.'

'Whatever,' said Patrick with an impatient sigh. 'But I have to treat her as if she really meant the only thing she ever manages to say.'

'I'm sure she's sincere about wanting to die,' said Mary. 'I'm just not sure she's up to it.'

From within the hub of his headphones, Robert sensed that his parents were having a heated conversation. He took off his headset and asked them what they were talking about.

'Just about Granny – how we can help her,' said Mary.

Robert put his headphones back on. As far as he was concerned Eleanor was just someone who was not yet dead. His parents no longer took him or Thomas to see her because they said it was too disturbing. It was an effort for him to remember, ages ago, being close to her, and it wasn't an effort that seemed worth making. Sometimes, in the presence of his other grandmother, his indifference to Eleanor was taken by surprise and, in contrast to the tight little knot of Kettle's selfishness, he would remember Eleanor's softness and the great aching bruise of her good intentions. Then he would forget how unfair it was that Eleanor had cheated them of Saint-Nazaire and feel how unfair it was for Eleanor being Eleanor – not just her dire circumstances, but being who she was. In the end it was unfair on everyone being who they were because they couldn't be anyone else. It wasn't even that he wanted to be anybody else, it was just a horrible thought that he couldn't be, in an emergency. He took off his headphones again, as if they were the thing that was limiting him. The comedy about the talking dog who became President of the United States wasn't that good anyway. Robert switched channels to the map. It showed their plane hovering near the Irish coast, south of Cork. Then it expanded to show London and Paris and the Bay of Biscay. The next scale included Casablanca and Djibouti and Warsaw. How long was this informational feast going to go on? Where were they in relation to the moon? The only thing anybody wanted to know finally came up: 52 minutes to arrival. They were flying through seven fat hours, pumped full of darkening time zones. Speed; height; temperature; local time in New York; local time in London. They told you everything, except the local time on the plane. Watches just couldn't keep up with those warped, enriched minutes. They ought to flip their dials round and say NOW until they could get back on the ground and start counting distinctly again.

He longed to get back on the ground as well, back home to London. Losing Saint-Nazaire had made London into his total home. He had heard about children who pretended they had been adopted and that their real parents were much more glamorous than the dreary people they lived with. He had done something similar with Saint-Nazaire, pretending it was his real home. After the shock of losing it, he had gradually relaxed into the knowledge that he really belonged among the sodden billboards and giant plane trees of his native city. Compared to the density of New York, London's backward glance at the countryside and the rambling privacy of its streets seemed to be the opposite of what a city was for, and yet he longed to get back to the greasy black mud of the parks, the rained-out playgrounds and paddocks of dead leaves, the glance at his scratchy school uniform in the hall mirror, the clunk of the car door on the way to school. Nothing seemed more exotic than the depth of those feelings.

A stewardess told Mary she must wake Thomas for the landing. Thomas woke up and Mary gave him a bottle of milk. Halfway through, he unplugged the bottle and said, 'Alabala is in the cockpit!' His eyes rounded as he looked up at his brother. 'He's going to land the plane!'

'Oh-oh,' said Robert, 'we're in trouble.'

'The captain says, "No, Alabala, you are *not* allowed to land the plane," said Thomas, thumping his thigh, "but Felan is allowed to land the plane."

'Is Felan in there too?'

'Yes, he is. He's the co-pilot.'

'Really? And who's the pilot?'

'Scott Tracy.'

'So this is an International Rescue plane?'

'Yes. We have to rescue a pentatenton.'

'What's a pentatenton?'

'Well, it's a hedgehog, actually, and it's fallen in the river!'

'In the Thames?'

'Yes! And it doesn't know how to swim, so Gordon Tracy has to rescue it with Thunderbird 4.'

Thomas thrust out his hand and moved the submarine through the muddy waters of the Thames.

Robert hummed the theme tune from *Thunderbirds*, drumming on the armrest between them.

'Perhaps you could get her to sign the letter of consent,' said Patrick.

'OK,' said Mary.

'At least we can assemble all the elements . . .'

'What elements?' asked Robert.

'Never mind,' said Mary. 'Look, we're about to land,' she said, trying to infuse the glinting fields, congested roads and small crowds of reddish houses with an excitement they were unlikely to generate on their own.

On the day of their arrival, the Dignitas membership form and Dr Fenelon's report emerged from the heap of letters in the hall. Sprawled exhausted on the black sofa, Patrick read through the Dignitas brochures.

'All the people in the cases they quote have agonizing terminal diseases or can only move one eyelid,' he commented. 'I'm worried she may just not be ill enough.'

'Let's get everything together and see what they think about her case,' said Mary.

Patrick gave her the letter of consent he had written before leaving for America and she set off with it to the nursing home. In the upper corridor the cleaners had wedged open the doors to air the rooms. Through the doorway Eleanor looked quite calm, until she detected another presence entering the room and stared with a kind of furious blankness in the direction of the newcomer. When Mary announced who she was, Eleanor grabbed the side rail of her barred bed and tried to heave herself up, making desperate mumbling sounds. Mary felt that she had interrupted Eleanor's communion with some other realm in which things were not quite as bad as they were on planet Earth. She suddenly felt that both ends of life were absolutely terrifying, with a quite frightening stretch in between. No wonder people did what they could to escape.

There was no point in asking Eleanor how she was, no point in trying to make conversation, and so Mary plunged in with a summary of what had been going on with the rest of them. Eleanor seemed horrified to be placed within the coordinates of her family. Mary quickly moved on to the purpose of her visit, suggesting that she read the letter out loud.

'If you feel it's what you want to say, you can sign it,' she said.

Eleanor nodded.

Mary got up and closed the door, glancing down the corridor to check that there were no nurses on their way. She pulled her chair close to Eleanor's bed and placed her chin over the hand rail, holding the letter on Eleanor's side of the bars. She began to read with surprising nervousness.

I have had several strokes over the last few years, each one leaving me more shattered than the last. I can hardly move and I can hardly speak. I am bedridden and incontinent. I feel uninterrupted anguish and terror and frustration at my own immobility and uselessness. There is no prospect of improvement, only of drifting into dementia, the thing I dread most. I can already feel my faculties betraying me. I do not look on death with fear but with longing. There is no other liberation from the daily torture of my existence. Please help me if you can.

yours sincerely,

'Do you think that's fair?' asked Mary, trying not to cry.

'No . . . es,' said Eleanor with great difficulty.

'I mean a fair description.'

'Es.'

They gripped each other's hands for a while, saying nothing. Eleanor looked at her with a kind of dry-eyed hunger.

'Do you want to sign it?'

'Sign,' said Eleanor, swallowing hard.

When Mary broke out into the streets, along with her sense of physical relief at getting away from the smell of urine and boiled cabbage, and the waiting-room atmosphere in which death was the delayed train, she felt grateful that there had been a moment of communication with Eleanor. In that gripped hand she had felt not just an appeal but a determination that made her wonder if she was right to doubt Eleanor's preparedness to commit suicide. And yet there was something fundamentally lost about Eleanor, a sense that she had neither engaged in the mundane realm of family and friendship and politics and property, nor had she engaged with the realm of contemplation and spiritual fulfilment; she had simply sacrificed one to the other. If she belonged to the tribe who always heard the siren call of the choice they were about to lose, she was bound to feel an absolute need to stay alive once suicide had been perfectly organized for her. Salvation would always be elsewhere. Suddenly it would be more spiritual to stay alive – to learn patience, remain in the refining fires of suffering, whatever. More dreadful life would be imposed on her and it would inevitably seem more spiritual to die – to be reunited with the source, stop being a burden, meet Jesus at the end of a tunnel, whatever. The spiritual, because she had never committed herself to it any more effectively than to the rest of life, was subject to endless metamorphosis without losing its theoretical centrality.

When Mary got home, Thomas ran out into the hall to greet her. He wrapped his arms around her thigh with some difficulty, due to the Hoberman sphere, a multicoloured collapsible dodecahedron frame, which he had allowed to close around his neck and wore as a spiky helmet. His hands were clad in a pair of socks and he was holding a battery-operated propeller fan of fairy lights acquired on a visit to the Chinese State Circus on Blackheath.

'We're on Earth, aren't we, Mama?'

'Most of us,' said Mary, thinking of the look she had glimpsed on Eleanor's face through the open door of her room.

'Yes, I did know that,' said Thomas wisely. 'Except astronauts who are in outer space. And they just float about because there's no gravity!'

'Did she sign?' said Patrick, appearing in the doorway.

'Yes,' said Mary, handing him the letter.

Patrick sent the letter and membership form and doctor's

report to Switzerland and waited for a couple of days before ringing to find out if his mother's application was likely to be successful.

'In this case I think we will be able to help,' was the answer he received. He stubbornly refused to get involved with his emotions, letting panic and elation and solemnity lean on the doorbell while he only glanced at them from behind closed curtains, pretending not to be at home. He was helped by the storm of practical demands which enveloped the family during the next week. Mary told Eleanor the news and was answered with a radiant smile. Patrick arranged a flight for the following Thursday. The nursing home was told that Eleanor was moving, without being told where. A consultation was booked with a doctor in Zurich.

'We could all go on Wednesday to say goodbye,' said Patrick.

'Not Thomas,' said Mary. 'It's been too long since he's seen her and the last time he made it very clear that he was upset. Robert can still remember her when she was well.'

None of Mary's close friends could look after Thomas on Wednesday afternoon and she was finally forced to ask her mother.

'Of course I'll do anything I can to help,' said Kettle, feeling that if ever there was a time to make all the right noises, it was now. 'Why don't you drop him off at lunchtime? Amparo can make him some lovely fish fingers and you can all come to tea after you've said goodbye to poor old Eleanor.'

When Wednesday came round Mary brought Thomas to the door of her mother's flat.

'Your mother is not here,' said Amparo.

'Oh,' said Mary, surprised and at the same time wondering why she was surprised.

'She go out to buy the cakes for tea.'

'But she'll be back soon . . .'

'She has lunch with a friend and then she come back, but don't you worry, I look after the little boy.'

Amparo reached out her child-greedy, ingratiating hands. Thomas had met her only once before and Mary handed him over with some reluctance but above all with a sense of terminal boredom. Never again, she would never ask her mother to help again. The decision seemed as irrevocable and overdue as a slab of cliff falling into the sea. She smiled at Amparo and handed over Thomas, not reassuring him too much in case it made him think there was something troubling about his situation.

The thing to do is the thing to do, thought Thomas, heading towards the disconnected bell beside the fireplace in the drawing room. He liked to stand on the small chair and press the bell and then let in whoever came to the fireplace-door. By the time Amparo had said goodbye to Mary and caught up with him, he was welcoming a visitor.

'It's Badger!' he said.

'Who is this Badger?' said Amparo with precautionary alarm.

'Mr Badger is not in the habit of smoking cigarettes,' said Thomas, 'because they make him grow bigger and smaller. So he smokes cigars!'

'Oh, no, my darling, you must not smoke,' said Amparo. 'It's very bad for you.'

Thomas climbed onto the small chair and pressed the bell again.

'Listen,' he said, 'there's somebody at the door.'

He leapt down and ran around the table. 'I'm running to open the door,' he explained, coming back to the fireplace.

'Be careful,' said Amparo.

'It's Lady Penelope,' said Thomas. 'You be Lady Penelope!'

'Would you like to help me with the hoovering?' said Amparo.

'Yes, m'lady,' said Thomas in his Parker voice. 'You'll find a thermos of hot chocolate in your hat box.' He howled with plea-sure and flung himself on the cushions of the sofa.

'Oh, my God, I just tidy this,' wailed Amparo.

'Build me a house,' said Thomas, pulling the cushions onto the floor. 'Build me a house!' he shouted when she started to put them back. He lowered his head and frowned severely. 'Look, Amparo, this is my grumpy face.'

Amparo caved in to his desire for a house and Thomas crawled into the space between two cushions and underneath the roof of a third.

'Unfortunately,' he remarked once he had settled into posi-tion, 'Beatrix Potter died a long time ago.'

'Oh, I'm sorry, darling,' said Amparo.

Thomas hoped that his parents would live for a very long time. He wanted them to be immortalized. That was a word he had learnt in his *Children's Book of Greek Myths*. Ariadne was im-mortalized when she was turned into a star by Dionysus. Im-mortalized meant that she lived for ever – except that she was a star. He didn't want his parents to turn into stars. What would be the point of that? Just twinkling away.

'Just twinkling away,' he said sceptically.

'Oh, my God, you come with Amparo to the bathroom.'

He couldn't understand why Amparo stood him by the loo and tried to pull his trousers down.

'I don't want to do peepee,' he said flatly and started to walk away. The truth was that Amparo was quite difficult to have a conversation with. She didn't seem to understand anything. He decided to go on an expedition. She trailed behind him, witter-ing on.

'No, Amparo,' he said, turning on her, 'leave me alone!'

'I can't leave you, darling. You have to have an adult with you.'

'No! I!' said Thomas. 'You are frustrating me!'

Amparo bent double with laughter. 'Oh, my God,' she said. 'You know so many words.'

'I have to talk, otherwise my mouth gets clogged up with bits and pieces of words,' said Thomas.

'How old are you now, darling?'

'I'm three,' said Thomas. 'How old did you think I was?'

'I thought you were at least five, you're such a grown-up boy.'

'Hum,' said Thomas.

He saw that there was no prospect of shaking her off and so he decided to treat her the way his parents treated him when they wanted to bring him under control.

'Shall I tell you an Alabala story?' he said.

They were back in the drawing room. He sat Amparo down on an armchair and climbed into his cushion cave.

'Once upon a time,' he began, 'Alabala was in California and he was driving along with his mummy and there was an earthquake!'

'I hope this story has a happy ending,' said Amparo.

'No!' said Thomas. 'You don't interrupt me!' He sighed and began again. 'And the ground opened up and California fell into the sea, which was not very convenient, as you can imagine. And there was a huge tidal wave, and Alabala said to his mummy, "We can surf to Australia!" And so they did, and Alabala was allowed to drive the car.' He searched the ceiling for inspiration and then added with all the naturalness of suddenly remembering. 'When they arrived on the beach in Australia, Alan Razor was there giving a concert!'

'Who is Alan Razor?' asked Amparo, completely lost.

'He's a composer,' said Thomas. 'He has helicopters and violins and trumpets and drills, and Alabala played in the concert.'

'What did he play?'

'Well, he played a hoover, actually.'

When Kettle returned from her lunch, she found Amparo

clutching her sides, thinking she was helpless with laughter at the thought of a hoover being played at a concert, but in fact hysterical at having her idea of what children should be like disrupted by being with Thomas.

'Oh, dear,' she panted, 'he's really an amazing little boy.'

While the two women struggled not to look after him, Thomas was at last able to have some time to himself. He decided that he never wanted to be an adult. He didn't like the look of adults. Anyway, if he became an adult what would happen to his parents? They would become old, like Eleanor and Kettle.

The intercom buzzed and Thomas leapt to his feet.

'I'll answer it!' he said.

'It's too high up,' said Kettle.

'But I want to!'

Kettle ignored him and pressed the intercom to let the others into the building. Thomas screamed in the background.

'What was that screaming about?' asked Mary when she arrived in the flat.

'Granny wouldn't let me press the button,' said Thomas.

'It's not a child's toy,' said Kettle.

'No, but he's a child playing,' said Mary. 'Why not let him play with the intercom?'

Kettle thought of rising above her daughter's argumentative style, but decided against it.

'I can't do anything right,' she said, 'so we might as well assume I'm wrong – then there won't be any need to point it out. I've only just come in, so I'm afraid tea isn't ready. I rushed home from a lunch that I couldn't get out of.'

'Yes,' laughed Mary. 'We saw you gazing through the shop windows when we were trying to park the car. Don't worry, I won't ask you to help with the children again.'

'I'll make the tea, if you like,' said Amparo, offering Kettle the opportunity to stay with her family.

'It's all right,' snapped Kettle. 'I'm still capable of making a pot of tea.'

'Am I being childish?' said Thomas, approaching his father.

'No,' said Patrick. 'You're being a child. Only grownups can be childish, and my God, we take advantage of the fact.'

'I see,' said Thomas, nodding wisely.

Robert was slumped in an armchair feeling despondent. He'd had enough of both his grandmothers to last him a lifetime.

Kettle tottered back in, laying the tray down with a groan of relief.

'So, how was your mother?' she asked Patrick.

'She only spoke two words,' he answered.

'Did they make any sense?'

'Perfect sense: "Do nothing."'

'You mean she doesn't want to . . . to go to Switzerland?' asked Kettle, emphasizing a code she knew the children were excluded from.

'That's right,' said Patrick.

'That's a bit of a muddle,' said Kettle.

Mary felt the effort she was putting into avoiding her favourite word: 'disappointment'.

'It's something we're all entitled to feel ambivalent about,' said Patrick. 'Mary saw it all along. I suppose she was less invested in the results, or just clearer. Anyhow, I intend to take this last instruction very seriously indeed. I will do nothing.'

'Do nothing!?' said Thomas. 'I mean, how do you do nothing? Because if you *do* nothing, you do something!'

Patrick burst out laughing. He picked up Thomas and put him on his knee and kissed the top of his head.

'I shan't be visiting her again,' said Patrick. 'Not out of spite, but out of gratitude. She's made us a gift and it would be ungracious not to accept it.'

'A gift?' said Kettle. 'Aren't you reading rather too much into those two words.'

'What else is there to do but read too much into things?' said Patrick breezily. 'What a poor, thin, dull world we'd live in if we didn't. Besides, is it possible? There's always more meaning than we can lay our hands on.'

Kettle was transfixed by several kinds of indignation at once, but Thomas filled the silence by jumping off his father's knee and shouting, 'Do nothing! Do nothing!' as he circled the table laden with cakes and tea.

AT LAST

I

'SURPRISED TO SEE ME?' said Nicholas Pratt, planting his walking stick on the crematorium carpet and fixing Patrick with a
look of slightly aimless defiance, a habit no longer useful but too
late to change. 'I've become rather a memorial-creeper. One's
bound to at my age. It's no use sitting at home guffawing over
the ignorant mistakes of juvenile obituarists, or giving in to the
rather monotonous pleasure of counting the daily quota of ex-
tinct contemporaries. No! One has to "celebrate the life": there
goes the school tart. They say he had a good war, but I know
better!—that sort of thing, put the whole achievement in perspective. Mind you, I'm not saying it isn't all very moving. There's
a sort of swelling orchestra effect to these last days. And plenty
of horror, of course. Padding about on my daily rounds from
hospital bed to memorial pew and back again, I'm reminded of
those oil tankers that used to dash themselves onto the rocks
every other week and the flocks of birds dying on the beaches
with their wings stuck together and their bewildered yellow eyes
blinking.'

Nicholas glanced into the room. 'Thinly attended,' he murmured, as if preparing a description for someone else. 'Are those
people your mother's religious friends? Too extraordinary. What

colour would you call that suit? Aubergine? *Aubergine* à *la crème d'oursin?* I must go to Huntsman and get one knocked up. What do you mean, you have no Aubergine? Everyone was wearing it at Eleanor Melrose's. Order a mile of it straight away!

'I suppose your aunt will be here soon. She'll be an all too familiar face amidst the Aubergines. I saw her last week in New York and I'm pleased to say I was the first to tell her the tragic news about your mother. She burst into tears and ordered a *croque monsieur* to swallow with her second helping of diet pills. I felt sorry for her and got her asked to dinner with the Blands. Do you know Freddie Bland? He's the smallest billionaire alive. His parents were practically dwarfs, like General and Mrs. Tom Thumb. They used to come into the room with a tremendous fanfare and then disappear under a console table. Baby Bland has taken to being serious, the way some people do in their senile twilight. She's decided to write a book about Cubism, of all ridiculous subjects. I think it's really part of her being a perfect wife. She knows what a state Freddie used to get into over her birthday, but thanks to her new hobby, all he has to do now is get Sotheby's to wrap up a revolting painting of a woman with a face like a slice of watermelon by that arch fake Picasso, and he knows she'll be over the moon. Do you know what Baby said to me? At breakfast, if you please, when I was almost defenceless.' Nicholas put on a simpering voice:

'"Those divine birds in late Braque are really just an excuse for the sky."

'"Such a good excuse," I said, choking on my first sip of coffee, "so much better than a lawn mower or a pair of clogs. It shows he was in complete control of his material."

'Serious, you see. It's a fate I shall resist with every last scrap of my intelligence, unless Herr Doktor Alzheimer takes over, in which case I'll have to write a book about Islamic art to show that the towel-heads have always been much more civilized than us, or a fat volume on how little we know about Shakespeare's mother and her top-secret Catholicism. Something serious.

'Anyhow, I'm afraid Aunt Nancy rather bombed with the Blands. It must be hard to be exclusively social and entirely friend-less at the same time. Poor thing. But do you know what struck me, apart from Nancy's vibrant self-pity, which she had the nerve to pretend was grief? What struck me about those two girls, your mother and your aunt, was that they are, were—my life is spent wobbling between tenses—completely American. Their father's connection with the Highlands was, let's face it, entirely liquid and after your grandmother sacked him he was hardly ever around. He spent the war with those dimwits the Windsors in Nassau; Monte Carlo after the war; and finally foundered in the bar of White's. Of the tribe who are blind drunk every day of their lives from lunch until bedtime, he was by far the most charming, but frustrating I think as a father. At that level of drunkenness one's essentially trying to embrace a drowning man. The odd eruption of sentimentality for the twenty minutes the drink took him that way was no substitute for the steady flow of self-sacrificing kindness that has always inspired my own efforts as a father. With what I admit have been mixed results. As I'm sure you know, Amanda hasn't spoken to me for the last fifteen years. I blame her psychoanalyst, filling her never very brilliant little head with Freudian ideas about her doting Papa.'

Nicholas's rotund style of delivery was fading into an increas-ingly urgent whisper, and the knuckles of his blue-veined hands were white from the effort of holding himself upright. 'Well, my dear, we'll have another little chat after the ceremony. It's been marvellous finding you on such good form. My condolences and all that, although if ever there was a "merciful release," it was in the case of your poor mother. I've become something of a Flor-ence Nightingale in my old age, but even the Lady with the Lamp had to beat a retreat in the face of that terrifying ruin. It's bound to act as a brake on the rush to get me canonized but I prefer to pay visits to people who can still enjoy a bitchy remark and a glass of champagne.'

He seemed about to leave but then turned back. 'Try not to be bitter about the money. One or two friends of mine who've made a mess of that side of things have ended up dying in National Health wards and I must say I've been very impressed by the humanity of the mostly foreign staff. Mind you, what is there to do with money except spend it when you've got it or be bitter about it when you haven't? It's a very limited commodity in which people invest the most extraordinary emotions. What I suppose I really mean is *do* be bitter about the money; it's one of the few things it can do: siphon off some bitterness. Do-gooders have sometimes complained that I have too many bêtes noires, but I need my bêtes noires to get the noire out of me and into the bêtes. Besides, that side of your family has had a good run. What is it now? Six generations with every single descendant, not just the eldest son, essentially idle? They may have taken on the camouflage of work, especially in America, where everyone had to have an office, if only to swivel about with their shoes on the desk for half an hour before lunch, but there's been no necessity. It must be rather thrilling, although I can't speak from experience, for you and your children, after this long exemption from competition, to get stuck in. God knows what I would have made of my life if I hadn't divided my time between town and country, between home and abroad, between wives and mistresses. I have divided time and now doth time divide me, what? I must take a closer look at these religious fanatics your mother surrounded herself with.'

Nicholas hobbled off with no pretence that he expected any response other than silent fascination.

When Patrick looked back on the way that illness and dying had torn apart Eleanor's flimsy shamanic fantasies, Nicholas's 'religious fanatics' seemed to him more like credulous draft-dodgers. At the end of her life Eleanor had been thrown into a merciless crash-course in self-knowledge, with only a 'power animal' in one hand and a rattle in the other. She had been left with the steepest practice of all: no speech, no movement, no sex, no drugs, no travel, no spending, hardly any food; just alone in silent contemplation of her thoughts. If contemplation was the word. Perhaps she felt that her thoughts were contemplating her, like hungry predators.

'Were you thinking about her?' said a soft Irish voice. Annette rested a healing hand on Patrick's forearm and tilted her understanding head to one side.

'I was thinking that a life is just the history of what we give our attention to,' said Patrick. 'The rest is packaging.'

'Oh, I think that's too stark,' said Annette. 'Maya Angelou says that the meaning of our lives is the impact we have on other people, whether we make them feel good or not. Eleanor always made people feel good, it was one of her gifts to the world. Oh,' she added with sudden excitement, gripping Patrick's forearm, 'I only made this connection on the way in: we're in Mortlake crematorium to say farewell to Eleanor, and guess what I took to read to her on the last occasion I saw her? You'll never guess. *The Lady of the Lake*. It's an Arthurian whodunit, not very good actually. But that says it all, doesn't it? Lady of the lake—Mortlake. Given Eleanor's connection with water and her love of the Arthurian legends.'

Patrick was stunned by Annette's confidence in the consoling power of her words. He felt irritation being usurped by despair. To think that his mother had chosen to live among these resolute fools. What knowledge was she so determined to avoid?

'Who can say why a crematorium and a bad novel should have vaguely similar names?' said Patrick. 'It's tantalizing to be taken so far beyond the rational mind. I tell you who would be very receptive to that sort of connection: you see the old man over there with the walking stick. Do tell him. He loves that kind of thing. His name is Nick.' Patrick dimly remembered that Nicholas loathed this abbreviation.

'Seamus sends his best,' said Annette, accepting her dismissal cheerfully.

'Thank you.' Patrick bowed his head, trying not to lose control of his exaggerated deference.

What was he doing? It was all so out of date. The war with Seamus and his mother's Foundation was over. Now that he was an orphan everything was perfect. He seemed to have been waiting all his life for this sense of completeness. It was all very well for the Oliver Twists of this world, who started out in the enviable state it had taken him forty-five years to achieve, but the relative luxury of being brought up by Bumble and Fagin, rather than David and Eleanor Melrose, was bound to have a weakening effect on the personality. Patient endurance of potentially lethal influences had made Patrick the man he was today, living alone in a bedsit, only a year away from his latest visit to the Suicide Observation Room in the Depression Wing of the Priory Hospital. It had felt so ancestral to have delirium tremens, to bow down, after his disobedient youth as a junkie, to the shattering banality of alcohol. As a barrister he was reluctant nowadays to kill himself illegally. The alcohol felt deep, humming down the bloodline. He could still remember, when he was five, taking a donkey ride among the palm trees and the packed red-and-white flowerbeds of Monte Carlo's Casino Gardens, while his grandfather sat on a green bench shaking uncontrollably, clamped by sunlight, a stain spreading slowly through the pearl-grey trousers of his perfectly cut suit.

Lack of insurance forced Patrick to pay for his own stay in the Priory, exhausting all his funds in a thirty-day gamble on recovery. Unhelpfully short from a psychiatric point of view, a month was still long enough for him to become immediately infatuated with a twenty-year-old patient called Becky. She looked like Botticelli's Venus, improved by a bloody trellis of razor cuts crisscrossing its way up her slender white arms. When he first saw her in the lounge of the Depression Wing, her radiant unhappiness sent a flaming arrow into the powder keg of his frustration and emptiness.

'I'm a self-harming resistant depressive,' she told him. 'They've got me on eight different kinds of pills.'

'Eight,' said Patrick admiringly. He was down to three himself: the daytime antidepressant, the nighttime antidepressant, and the thirty-two oxazepam tranquillizers a day he was taking to deal with the delirium tremens.

Insofar as he could think at all on such a high dose of oxazepam, he could think only of Becky. The next day, he heaved himself off his crackling mattress and slouched to the Depression Support Group in the hope of seeing her again. She was not there, but Patrick could not escape from joining the circle of tracksuited depressives. 'As to sports, let our wear do it for us,' he sighed, slumping down in the nearest chair.

An American called Gary kicked off the sharing with the words, 'Let me give you a scenario: suppose you were sent to Germany for work, and suppose a friend you hadn't heard from in a long time called you up and came to visit with you from the States . . .' After a tale of shocking exploitation and ingratitude, he asked the group what he should say to this friend. 'Cut them out of your life,' said the bitter and abrasive Terry, 'with friends like that, who needs enemies?'

'Okay,' said Gary, relishing his moment, 'and suppose I told you that this "friend" was my mother, what would you say then? Why would that be so different?'

Consternation raced through the Group. A man, who had been feeling 'completely euphoric' since his mother had come over on Sunday and taken him out to buy a new pair of trousers, said that Gary should never abandon his mother. On the other hand, there was a woman called Jill who had been 'for a long walk by the river I wasn't supposed to come back from—well, put it this way, I did come back *very wet*, and I said to Dr. Pagazzi, who I love to bits, that I thought it had something to do with my mother, and he said, "We're not even going to go there."' Jill said that, like her, Gary should have nothing to do with his mother. At the end of the session, the wise Scottish moderator tried to shield the group from this downpour of self-centred advice.

'Someone once asked me why mothers are so good at pushing our buttons,' he said, 'and the answer I gave was, "Because they put them there in the first place."'

Everyone nodded gloomily, and Patrick asked himself, not for the first time, but with renewed desperation, what it would mean to be free, to live beyond the tyranny of dependency and conditioning and resentment.

After the Support Group, he saw a caved-in, illicitly smoking, barefooted Becky go down the staircase beyond the laundry. He followed her and found her crumpled on the stairs, her giant pupils swimming in a pool of tears. 'I hate this place,' she said. 'They're going to throw me out because they say I've got a bad attitude. But I only stayed in bed because I'm so *depressed*. I don't know where I'm going to go, I can't face going back to my parents.'

She was screaming to be saved. Why not run away with her to the bedsit? She was one of the few people alive who was more suicidal than him. They could lie on the bed together, Priory refugees, one convulsing while the other slashed. Why not take her back and let her finish the job for him? Her bluest veins to bandage, her whitening lips to kiss. No no no no no. He was too well, or at least too old.

These days he could only remember Becky with deliberate effort. He often watched his obsessions pass over him like so many blushes, and by doing nothing about them, watched them fade. Becoming an orphan was a thermal on which this new sense of freedom might continue to rise, if only he had the courage not to feel guilty about the opportunity it presented.

Patrick drifted towards Nicholas and Annette, curious to see the outcome of his matchmaking.

'Stand by the graveside or the furnace,' he heard Nicholas instructing Annette, 'and repeat these words, "Goodbye, old thing. One of us was bound to die first and I'm delighted it was you!" That's my spiritual practice, and you're welcome to adopt it and put it into your hilarious "spiritual tool box".'

'Your friend is absolutely priceless,' said Annette, seeing Patrick approaching. 'What he doesn't realize is that we live in a loving universe. And it loves you too, Nick,' she assured Nicholas, resting her hand on his recoiling shoulder.

'I've quoted Bibesco before,' snapped Nicholas, 'and I'll quote him again: "To a man of the world, the universe is a suburb".'

'Oh, he's got an answer to everything, hasn't he?' said Annette. 'I expect he'll joke his way into heaven. St. Peter loves a witty man.'

'Does he?' said Nicholas, surprisingly appeased. 'That's the best thing I've heard yet about that bungling social secretary. As if the Supreme Being would consent to spend eternity surrounded by a lot of nuns and paupers and par-boiled missionaries, having his lovely concerts ruined by the rattle of spiritual tool boxes and the screams of the faithful, boasting about their crucifixions! What a relief that an enlightened command has finally reached the concierge at the Pearly Gates: "For Heaven's sake, send Me a conversationalist!"'

Annette looked at Nicholas with humorous reproach.

'Ah,' he said, nodding at Patrick, 'I never thought I'd be so grateful to see your impossible aunt.' He lifted his stick and waved it at Nancy. She stood in the doorway looking exhausted by her own haughtiness, as if her raised eyebrows might not be able to stand the strain much longer.

'Help!' she said to Nicholas. 'Who are these peculiar people?'

'Zealots, Moonies, witch-doctors, would-be terrorists, every variety of religious lunatic,' explained Nicholas, offering Nancy his arm. 'Avoid eye contact, stick close to me and you may live to tell the tale.'

Nancy flared up when she saw Patrick. 'Of all the days *not* to have the funeral,' she said.

'Why?' he asked, confused.

'It's Prince Charles's wedding. The only other people who might have come will be at Windsor.'

'I'm sure you'd be there as well, if you'd been invited,' said Patrick. 'Don't hesitate to nip down with a Union Jack and a cardboard periscope if you think you'd find it more entertaining.'

'When I think how we were brought up,' wailed Nancy, 'it's too ridiculous to think what my sister did with . . .' She was lost for words.

'The golden address book,' purred Nicholas, gripping his walking stick more tightly as she sagged against him.

'Yes,' said Nancy, 'the golden address book.'

2

NANCY WATCHED HER INFURIATING nephew drift towards his mother's coffin. Patrick would never understand the fabulous way that she and Eleanor had been brought up. Eleanor had stupidly rebelled against it, whereas it had been ripped from Nancy's prayerfully clasped hands.

'The golden address book,' she sighed again, locking arms with Nicholas. 'I mean, for example, Mummy only ever had one car accident in her entire life, but even then, when she was hanging upside down in the buckled metal, she had the Infanta of Spain dangling next to her.'

'That's very in-depth, I must say,' said Nicholas. 'A car accident can get one tangled up with all sorts of obscure people. Picture the commotion at the College of Heralds if a drop of one's blood landed on the dashboard of a lorry and mingled with the bodily fluids of the brute whose head had been dashed against the steering wheel.'

'Do you always have to be so facetious?' snapped Nancy.

'I do my best,' said Nicholas. 'But you can't pretend that your mother was a fan of the common man. Didn't she buy the entire village street that ran along the boundary wall of the Pavillon

Colombe, in order to demolish it and expand the garden? How many houses was that?'

'Twenty-seven,' said Nancy, cheering up. 'They weren't all demolished. Some of them were turned into exactly the right kind of ruin to go with the house. There were follies and grottos, and Mummy had a replica made of the main house, only fifty times smaller. We used to have tea there, it was like something out of *Alice in Wonderland*.' Nancy's face clouded over. 'There was a horrible old man who refused to sell, although Mummy offered him far too much for his poky little house, and so there was an inward bulge following the line of the old wall, if you see what I'm saying.'

'Every paradise demands a serpent,' said Nicholas.

'He did it just to annoy us,' said Nancy. 'He put a French flag on the roof and used to play Edith Piaf all day long. We had to smother him in vegetation.'

'Maybe he liked Edith Piaf,' said Nicholas.

'Oh, don't be funny! Nobody could like Edith Piaf at that volume.'

Nicholas sounded sour to Nancy's sensitive ear. So what if Mummy hadn't wanted ordinary people pressing up against her property? It was hardly surprising when everything else was so divine. Fragonard had painted *Les Demoiselles Colombe* in that garden, hence the necessity for having Fragonards in the house. The original owners had hung a pair of big Guardis in the drawing room, hence the authenticity of getting them back.

Nancy couldn't help being haunted by the splendour and the wreckage of her mother's family. One day she was going to write a book about her mother and her aunts, the legendary Jonson Sisters. She had been collecting material for years, fascinating bits and pieces that just needed to be organized. Only last week, she had sacked a hopeless young researcher—the tenth in a succession of greedy egomaniacs who wanted to be paid in advance—

but not before her latest slave had discovered a copy of her grandmother's birth certificate. According to this wonderfully quaint document, Nancy's grandmother had been 'Born in Indian Country'. How could the daughter of a young army officer, born at this unlikely address, have guessed, as she tottered about among the creaky pallet beds and restless horses of an adobe fort in the Western Territories, that her own daughters would be tottering along the corridors of European castles and filling their houses with the debris of failed dynasties—splashing about in Marie Antoinette's black marble bath, while their yellow Labradors dozed on carpets from the throne room of the imperial palace in Peking? Even the lead garden tubs on the terrace of the Pavillon Colombe had been made for Napoleon. Gold bees searching through silver blossoms, dripping in the rain. She always thought that Jean had made Mummy buy those tubs to take an obscure revenge on Napoleon for saying that his ancestor, the great duc de Valençay, was 'a piece of shit in a silk stocking'. What she liked to say was that Jean kept up the family tradition, minus the silk stocking. Nancy gripped Nicholas's arm even more tightly, as if her horrid stepfather might try to steal him as well.

If only Mummy hadn't divorced Daddy. They had such a glamorous life in Sunninghill Park, where she and Eleanor were brought up. The Prince of Wales used to drop in all the time, and there were never fewer than twenty people staying in the house, having the best fun ever. It was true that Daddy had the bad habit of buying Mummy extremely expensive presents, which she had to pay for. When she said, 'Oh, darling, you shouldn't have,' she really meant it. She grew nervous of commenting on the garden. If she said that a border needed a little more blue, a couple of days later she would find that Daddy had flown in some impossible flower from Tibet which bloomed for about three minutes and cost as much as a house. But before the drink took over,

Daddy was handsome and warm and so infectiously funny that the food often arrived shaking at the table, because the footmen were laughing too much to hold the platters steadily.

When the Crash came, lawyers flew in from America to ask the Craigs to rack their brains for something they could do without. They thought and thought. They obviously couldn't sell Sunninghill Park. They had to go on entertaining their friends. It would be too cruel and too inconvenient to sack any of the servants. They couldn't do without the house in Bruton Street for overnight stays in London. They needed two Rolls-Royces and two chauffeurs because Daddy was incorrigibly punctual and Mummy was incorrigibly late. In the end they sacrificed one of the six newspapers that each guest received with their breakfast. The lawyers relented. The pools of Jonson money were too deep to pretend there was a crisis; they were not stock-market speculators, they were industrialists and owners of great blocks of urban America. People would always need hardened fats and dry-cleaning fluids and somewhere to live.

Even if Daddy had been too extravagant, Mummy's marriage to Jean was a folly that could be explained only by the resulting title—she was definitely jealous of Aunt Gerty being married to a grand duke. Jean's role in the Jonson story was to disgrace himself, as a liar and a thief, a lecherous stepfather and a tyrannical husband. While Mummy lay dying of cancer, Jean threw one of his tantrums, screaming that doubt was being cast on his honour by her will. She was leaving him her houses and paintings and furniture only for his lifetime and then on to her children, as if he couldn't be trusted to leave them to the children himself. He knew perfectly well that they were Jonson possessions . . . and on and on; the morphine, the pain, the screaming, the indignant promises. She changed her will and Jean went back on his word and left everything to his nephew.

God, how Nancy loathed Jean! He had died almost forty

years ago, but she wanted to kill him every day. He had stolen everything and ruined her life. Sunninghill, the Pavillon, the Palazzo Arichele, all lost. She even regretted the loss of some of the Jonson houses she would never have inherited, not unless lots of people had died, that is, which would have been a tragedy, except that at least she would have known how to live in them properly, which was more than could be said of some people she could name.

'All the lovely things, all the lovely houses,' said Nancy, 'where have they all gone?'

'Presumably the houses are where they've always been,' said Nicholas, 'but they're being lived in by people who can afford them.'

'But that's just it, I should be able to afford them!'

'Never use a conditional tense when it comes to money.'

Really, Nicholas was being impossible. She certainly wasn't going to tell him about her book. Ernest Hemingway had told Daddy that he really ought to write a book, because he told such funny stories. When Daddy protested that he couldn't write, Hemingway sent a tape-recorder. Daddy forgot to plug the thing in, and when the spools didn't go round, he lost his temper and threw it out of the window. Luckily, the woman it landed on didn't take any legal action and Daddy had another marvellous story, but the whole incident had made Nancy superstitious about tape-recorders. Maybe she should hire a ghost writer. Exorcized by a ghost! That would be original. Still, she had to give the poor ghost an idea of how she wanted it done. It could be theme by theme, or decade by decade, but that seemed to her a stuffy egg-head bookworm kind of approach. She wanted it done sister by sister; after all, the rivalry between them was quite the dynamic force.

Gerty, the youngest and most beautiful of the three Jonson Sisters, was definitely the one Mummy was most competitive with. She married the Grand Duke Vladimir, nephew of the last Tsar of Russia. 'Uncle Vlad', as Nancy called him, had helped to assassinate Rasputin, lending his Imperial revolver to Prince Yussupov for what was supposed to be the final kill, but turned out to be only the middle stage between poisoning the energetic priest with arsenic and drowning him in the Neva. Despite many pleas, the Tsar exiled Vladimir for his part in the assassination, making him miss the Russian Revolution and the chance to get bayoneted, strangled or shot by Russia's new Bolshevik masters. Once in exile, Uncle Vlad went on to assassinate himself by drinking twenty-three dry martinis before lunch every day. Thanks to the Russian whimsy of smashing a glass after drinking from it, there was hardly a moment's silence in the house. Nancy had Daddy's copy of a forgotten memoir by Uncle Vlad's sister, the Grand Duchess Anna. It was inscribed in purple ink to 'my dear brother-in-law', although he was in fact her brother's sister-in-law's husband. The inscription seemed to Nancy somehow typical of the generous inclusiveness that had enabled that amazing family to straddle two continents, from Kiev to Vladivostok. Before Uncle Vlad's marriage to Gerty in Biarritz, his sister had to perform the blessing that would traditionally have been performed by their parents. It was a moment they dreaded because it reminded them of the horrifying reason for the absence of their family. The grand duchess described her feelings in *The Palace of Memory*:

> Through the window I could see the great waves pounding the rocks; the sun had gone down. The grey ocean at that moment looked to me as ruthless and indifferent as fate, and infinitely lonely.

Gerty decided to convert to the Russian Orthodox religion, in order to be closer to Vladimir's people. Anna went on:

Our cousin, the Duke of Leuchtenberg, and I were
her sponsors. The ceremony was a long and wearisome one, and I felt sorry for Gerty, who did not understand a word of it.

If her pet ghost could write as well as that, Nancy felt sure she
would have a bestseller on her hands. The eldest Jonson Sister was
the richest of all: bossy, practical Aunt Edith. While her flighty
younger sisters jumped into the pages of an illustrated history
book, holding hands with the remnants of some of the world's
greatest families, sensible Aunt Edith, who preferred her antiques
to arrive in a crate, made a consolidating marriage to a man whose
father, like her own, had been on the list of the hundred richest
men in America in 1900. Nancy spent the first two years of the
war living with Edith, while Mummy tried to get some of her really valuable things into storage in Switzerland before joining her
daughters in America. Edith's husband, Uncle Bill, struck an original note by paying with his own money for the presents he gave
his wife. One birthday present was a white clapboard house with
dark green shutters and two gently curved wings, on a slope of
lawn above a lake, at the centre of a ten-thousand-acre plantation.
She loved it. That was the sort of useful tip that they never gave
you in books called *The Art of Giving*.

Patrick glanced at his unhappy aunt, still complaining to Nicholas
by the entrance. He couldn't help thinking of the favourite dic-
tum of the moderator from his Depression Group, 'Resentment
is drinking the poison, and hoping that someone else will die'.
All the patients had impersonated this sentence in more or less
convincing Scottish accents at least once a day.

If he was now standing beside his mother's coffin with uneasy detachment, it was not because he had cherished his aunt's

'golden address book'. As far as Patrick was concerned, the past
was a corpse waiting to be cremated, and although his wish was
about to be granted in the most literal fashion, in a furnace only
a few yards from where he was standing, another kind of fire was
needed to incinerate the attitudes which haunted Nancy; the psychological impact of inherited wealth, the raging desire to get rid
of it and the raging desire to hang on to it; the demoralizing effect
of already having what almost everyone else was sacrificing their
precious lives to acquire; the more or less secret superiority and
the more or less secret shame of being rich, generating their characteristic disguises: the philanthropy solution, the alcoholic solution, the mask of eccentricity, the search for salvation in perfect
taste; the defeated, the idle, and the frivolous, and their oppo-
nents, the standard-bearers, all living in a world that the dense
glitter of alternatives made it hard for love and work to penetrate.
If these values were in themselves sterile, they looked all the more
ridiculous after two generations of disinheritance. Patrick wanted
to distance himself from what he thought of as his aunt's virulent
irrelevance, and yet there was a fascination with status running
down the maternal line of his family that he had to understand.

He remembered going to see Eleanor just after she had
launched her last philanthropic project, the Transpersonal Foundation. She had decided to renounce the frustration of being a
person in favour of the exciting prospect of becoming a Transper-
son; denying part of what she was, the daughter of one bewildered family and the mother of another, and claiming to be what
she was not, a healer and a saint. The impact of this adolescent
project on her ageing body was to produce the first of the dozen
strokes which eventually demolished her. When Patrick went
down to see her in Lacoste after that first stroke, she was still
able to speak fluently enough, but her mind had become entirely
suspicious. The moment they were alone together in her bedroom, with the tattered curtains under full sail in the evening

breeze, she clasped his arm and hissed to him urgently. 'Don't tell anybody my mother was a duchess.'

He nodded conspiratorially. She relaxed her grasp and searched the ceiling for the next worry.

Nancy's instructions, without even a stroke to justify them, would have been the exact opposite. Tell nobody? Tell everybody! Behind the cartoon contrasts of Nancy's worldliness and Eleanor's otherworldliness, Nancy's bulk and Eleanor's emaciation, there was a common cause, a past that had to be falsified, whether by suppression or selective glorification. What was that? Were Eleanor and Nancy individuals at all, or were they just part of the characteristic debris of their class and family?

Eleanor had taken Patrick to stay with her Aunt Edith in the early 1970s when he was twelve. While the rest of the world was worrying about the OPEC crisis, stagflation, carpet bombing and whether the effects of LSD were permanent, eternal or temporary, they found Edith living in a style which made no concession whatsoever to the fifty years since Live Oak had been given to her. The forty black servants made the slaves in *Gone With the Wind* look like extras on a film set. On the evening that Patrick and Eleanor arrived, Moses, one of the footmen, asked if he could be excused in order to go to his brother's funeral. Edith said no. There were four people at dinner and Moses was needed to serve the hominy grits. Patrick didn't mind if the servant who brought the quail, or the one who took the vegetables around, served the hominy grits as well, but there was a system in place and Edith was not going to allow it to be disrupted. Moses, in white gloves and a white coat, stepped forward silently, tears pouring down his cheeks, and offered Patrick his first taste of grits. He never knew if he would have liked them.

Later, beside a crackling fire in her bedroom, Eleanor raged against her aunt's cruelty. The scene over dinner had been too resonant for her; she could never disentangle the taste of the grits from Moses's tears, or indeed her mother's perfect taste from her own childhood tears. Eleanor's sense that her sanity was rooted in the kindness of servants meant that she would always be on Moses's side. If she had been articulate, this loyalty might have made her political; as it was it made her charitable. Most of all she raged against the way her aunt made her feel as if she were still twelve years old, as she had been when she was a passionate but mute guest at the beginning of the war, staying at Fairley, Bill and Edith's place on Long Island. His mother was hypnotized by the memory of being Patrick's age. Her arrested development always rigorously shadowed his efforts to grow up. In his early childhood she had been preoccupied by how much her nanny meant to her, while failing to provide him with a similar paragon of warmth and trustworthiness.

Looking up from his mother's coffin, Patrick saw that Nancy and Nicholas were planning to approach him again, their instinct for social hierarchy turning a bereaved son into the temporary top dog at his mother's funeral. He rested a hand on Eleanor's coffin, forming a secret alliance against misunderstanding.

'My dear,' said Nicholas, apparently refreshed by some important news, 'I hadn't realized, until Nancy enlightened me, what a serious partygoer your Mama used to be, before she took up her "good works".' He seemed to poke the phrase aside with his walking stick, clearing it from his path. 'To think of shy, religious little Eleanor at the Beistegui Ball! I didn't know her then, or I would have felt compelled to shield her from that stampede of ravenous harlequins.' Nicholas moved his free hand artistically through the air. 'It was a magical occasion, as if the gilded layabouts in one of Watteau's paintings had been released from their enchanted prison and given an enormous dose of steroids and a fleet of speedboats.'

'Oh, she wasn't all that shy, if you know what I'm saying,' Nancy corrected him. 'She had any number of beaux. You know your mother could have made a dazzling marriage.'

'And saved me the trouble of being born.'

'Oh, don't be so silly. You would have been born anyway.'

'Not quite.'

'When I think,' said Nicholas, 'of all the impostors who claim to have been at that legendary party, it's hard to believe that I knew someone who was there and chose never to mention it. And now it's too late to congratulate her on her modesty.' He patted the coffin, as an owner might pat a winning racehorse. 'Which shows the pointlessness of that particular affectation.'

Nancy spotted a white-haired man in a black pinstriped suit and a black silk tie walking down the aisle.

'Henry!' she said, staggering back theatrically. 'We needed some Jonson reinforcements.' Nancy loved Henry. He was so rich. It would have been better if the money had been hers, but a close relation having it was the next best thing.

'How are you, Cabbage?' she greeted him.

Henry kissed Nancy hello, without looking especially pleased to be addressed as 'Cabbage'.

'My God, I didn't expect to see you,' said Patrick. He felt a wave of remorse.

'I didn't expect to see you either,' said Henry. 'Nobody communicates in this family. I'm over here for a few days staying at the Connaught, and when they wheeled in *The Times* with my breakfast this morning, I saw that your mother had died and that there was a ceremony here today. Fortunately, the hotel got me a car straight away and I was able to make it.'

'I haven't seen you since you kindly had us to stay on your island,' said Patrick, deciding to plunge in. 'I think I was rather a nightmare. I'm sorry about that.'

'I guess nobody enjoys being unhappy,' said Henry. 'It always spills over. But we mustn't let a few foreign-policy differences get in the way of the really important things.'

'Absolutely,' said Patrick, struck by how kind Henry was being. 'I'm so glad you've made it here today. Eleanor was very fond of you.'

'Well, I loved your mother. As you know, she stayed with us at Fairley for a couple of years at the beginning of the war and so naturally we became very close. She had an innocent quality that was really attractive; it drew you in and at the same time it kept you at a certain distance. It's hard to explain, but whatever you feel about your mother and this charity she got involved with, I hope you know that she was a good person with the best intentions.'

'Yes,' said Patrick, accepting the simplicity of Henry's affection for a moment, 'I think "innocent" is exactly the right word.' He marvelled again at the effect of projection: how hostile Henry had seemed to him when Patrick was hostile towards everyone; how considerate he seemed now that Patrick had no argument with him. What would it be like to stop projecting? Was it possible at all?

As he turned to leave, Henry reached out and touched Patrick's shoulder.

'I'm sorry for your loss,' he said, with a formality that was by then infused with emotion. He nodded to Nancy and Nicholas.

'Excuse me,' said Patrick, looking back at the entrance of the crematorium, 'I have to say hello to Johnny Hall.'

'Who's he?' asked Nancy, sensing obscurity.

'You may well ask,' scowled Nicholas. 'He wouldn't be anybody at all, if he wasn't my daughter's psychoanalyst. As it is, he's a fiend.'

3

PATRICK WALKED AWAY FROM his mother's coffin, aware that unless he rushed back hysterically, he had stood beside her for the last time. He had seen the cold, damp contents of the coffin the night before, when he paid a visit to Bunyon's funeral parlour. A friendly, blue-suited woman with short white hair had greeted him at the door.

'Hello, love, I heard a taxi and I thought it was you.'

She guided him downstairs. Pink and brown diamond carpet like the bar of a country house hotel. Discreet advertisements for special services. A framed photograph of a woman kneeling by a black box from which a dove was only too pleased to be set free. Bolting upwards in a blur of white wings. Did it return to the Bunyon's dovecote and get recycled? Oh, no, not the black box again. 'We can release a dove for you on the day of your funeral'. Gothic script seemed to warp every letter that passed through the door of the funeral parlour, as if death were a German village. There were stained-glass windows, electrically lit, on the stairs down to the basement.

'I'll leave you with her. If there's anything you need, don't hesitate. I'll be upstairs.'

'Thank you,' said Patrick, waiting for her to turn the corner before stepping into the Willow Chapel.

He closed the door behind him and glanced hurriedly into the coffin, as though his mother had told him it was rude to stare. Whatever he was looking at, it was not the 'her' he had been promised with solemn cosiness a few minutes before. The absence of life in that familiar body, the rigid and rectified features of the face he had known before he even knew his own, made all the difference. Here was a transitional object for the far end of life. Instead of the soft toy or raggie that a child uses to cope with its mother's absence, he was being offered a corpse, its scrawny fingers clutching an artificial white rose whose stiff silk petals were twisted into position over an unbeating heart. It had the sarcasm of a relic, as well as the prestige of a metonym. It stood for his mother and for her absence with equal authority. In either case, it was her final appearance before she retired into other people's memory.

He had better take another look, a longer look, a less theoretical look, but how could he concentrate in this disconcerting basement? The Willow Chapel turned out to be under a busy pavement, pierced by the declamatory brightness of mobile-phone talk and tattooed by clicking heels. A rumbling taxi emerged from the general traffic and splashed a puddle onto the paving stones above the far corner of the ceiling. He was reminded of the Tennyson poem he hadn't thought of for decades, 'Dead, long dead, / Long dead! / And my heart is a handful of dust, / And the wheels go over my head, / And my bones are shaken with pain, / For in a shallow grave they are thrust, / Only a yard beneath the street, / And the hoofs of the horses beat, beat, / The hoofs of the horses beat, / Beat into my scalp and my brain, / With never an end to the stream of passing feet.' He could see why Bunyon's had chosen to call this room the Willow Chapel rather than the Coal Cellar or the Shallow Grave. 'Hello, love,

your mum's in the Coal Cellar,' muttered Patrick. 'We could release a dove in the Shallow Grave, but it would have no chance
whatever of escape.' He sat down and rocked his torso over his
folded arms. His entrails were in torment, as they had been since
hearing about his mother's death three days ago. No need for
ten years of psychoanalysis to work out that he felt 'gutted'. He
was doing what he always did under pressure, observing everything, chattering to himself in different voices, circling the unacceptable feelings, in this case conveniently embedded in his
mother's coffin.

She had left the world with screeching slowness, sliding inch
by inch into oblivion. At first he could not help enjoying the
comparative quiet of her presence, but then he noticed that he
was clinging to the urban noises outside in order not to be drawn
into the deep pit of silence at the centre of the room. He must
take a closer look, but first he really had to turn down the lights
that were glaring through chrome grids in the low polystyrene
ceiling. They bleached the glow of the four stout candles impaled on brass stands at the corners of the coffin. He dimmed
the spotlights and restored some of the ecclesiastical pomposity
to the candles. There was one more thing he had to check. A pink
velvet curtain partitioned the room; he had to know what was
behind it before he could pay attention to his mother. It turned
out to hide a storage area packed with equipment: a grey metal
trolley with sensible wheels, some no-nonsense rubber tubes and a
huge gold crucifix. Everything needed to embalm a Christian.
Eleanor had expected to meet Jesus at the end of a tunnel after
she died. The poor man was a slave to his fans, waiting to show
crowds of eager dead the neon countryside that lay beyond the
rebirth canal of earthly annihilation. It must be hard to be chosen
as optimism's master cliché, the Light at the End of the Tunnel,
ruling over a glittering army of half-full glasses and silver-lined
clouds.

Patrick let the curtain drop reluctantly, acknowledging that he had run out of distractions. He edged towards the coffin, like a man approaching a cliff. At least he knew that this coffin contained his mother's corpse. Twenty years ago, when he had been to see his father's remains in New York, he was shown into the wrong room. 'In loving memory of Hermann Newton'. He had done everything he could to opt out of that bereavement process, but he was not going to evade this one. A cool dry part of his mind was trying to bring his emotions under its aphoristic sway, but the stabbing pain in his guts undermined its ambitions, and confused his defences.

As he stared into the coffin, he felt the encroachment of an agitated animal sadness. He wanted to linger incredulously by the body, still giving it some of the attention it had commanded in life: a shake, a touch, a word, an enquiring gaze. He reached out and put his hand on her chest and felt the shock of its thinness. He leant over and kissed her on the forehead and felt the shock of its coldness. These sharp sensations lowered his defences further, and he was overwhelmed by an expanding rush of sympathy for the ruined human being in front of him. During its fleeting life, this vast sense of tenderness reduced his mother's personality to a detail, and his relationship with her to a detail within a detail.

He sat down again and leant forward over his crossed legs and folded arms to give himself some faint relief from the pain in his stomach. And then he suddenly made a connection. Of course, how strange—how determined. Aged seven, going on his first trip alone abroad with his mother, a few months after his parents' divorce. His first flash of Italy: the white number plates, the blue bay, the ochre churches. They were staying at the Excelsior in Naples, on a waterfront buzzing with waspish motorcycles and humming with crowded trams. From the balcony of their magnificent room, his mother pointed to the street urchins crouched on the roofs, or clinging to the backs of the trams. Patrick, who thought they were in Naples on holiday, was alarmed to hear that Eleanor had come there to save these poor children. There was a marvellous man, a priest called Father Tortelli, who never tired of picking up lost Neapolitan boys and giving them shelter in the refuge that Eleanor had been bankrolling from London. She was now going to see it for the first time. Wasn't it exciting? Wasn't it a good thing to be doing? She showed Patrick a photograph of Father Tortelli: a small, tough, fifty-year-old man in a black shirt who looked as if he was no stranger to the boxing ring. His bearish arms were locked around the fragile, sharp-boned shoulders of two sun-tanned boys in white vests. Father Tortelli was protecting them from the streets, but who was protecting them from Father Tortelli? Not Eleanor. She was providing him with the means to fill his refuge with ever-growing numbers of orphans and runaways. After lunch that day, Patrick had an attack of violent gastro-enteritis, and instead of leaving him in luxurious neglect while she went to look after the other children, his mother was made to stay with him and hold his hand while he screamed with pain in the green marble bathroom.

No amount of stomach ache could make her stay now. Not that he wanted her to stay, but his body had a memory of its own which it continued to narrate without any reference to his current wishes. What was it that had driven Eleanor to furnish children for her husband and for Father Tortelli, and why was the drive so strong that, after the collapse of her marriage, she immediately replaced a father with a Father, a doctor with a priest? Patrick had no doubt that her motives were unconscious, as unconscious as the somatic memory that had taken him over in the last three days. What could he do but drag these fragments out of the dark and acknowledge them?

After a quiet knock, the door opened and the attendant leant into the room.

'Just to make sure everything is all right,' she whispered.

'Maybe it is,' said Patrick.

The journey back to his flat had a mildly hallucinatory quality, surging through the rainy night in a fluorescent bus, freshly flooded by so many fierce impressions and remote memories. There were two Jehovah's Witnesses on board, a black man handing out leaflets and a black woman preaching at the top of her voice. 'Repent of your sins and take Jesus into your heart, because when you die it will be too late to repent in the grave and you'll burn in the fires of Hell . . .'

A red-eyed Irishman in a threadbare tweed jacket started shouting in counterpoint from a back seat. 'Shut up, you fuckin' bitch. Go suck Satan's cock. You're not allowed to do this, whether you're Muslim, or Christian, or Satanic.' When the man with the leaflets headed for the upper deck, he persisted, investing his accent with a sadistic Southern twang, 'I can see you, Boy. How do you think you'd look with your head under your arm, Boy. If you don't shut that bitch up, I'll adjust your face for you, Boy.'

'Oh, do shut up yourself,' said an exasperated commuter.

Patrick noticed that his stomach pains had gone. He watched the Irishman sway in his seat, his lips continuing to argue silently with the Jehovah's Witness, or with some Jesuit from his youth. Give us a boy till the age of seven and we'll have him for life. Not me, thought Patrick, you won't have me.

As the bus pushed haltingly towards his destination, he thought about those brief but pivotal nights in the Suicide Observation Room, unpeeling one sweat-soaked T-shirt after another, throwing off the sauna of the bedclothes only to shudder in the freezer of their absence; turning the light on and off, pained by the brightness, alarmed by the dark; a poisonous headache lurching around his skull like the lead in a jumping bean. He had brought nothing to read except *The Tibetan Book of the Dead*, hoping to find its exotic iconography ridiculous enough to purge any fantasies he might still cling to about consciousness continuing after death. As it turned out, he found his imagination seduced by a passage from the introduction to the *Chonyid Bardo*, 'O nobly born, when thy body and thy mind were separating, thou must have experienced a glimpse of the Pure Truth, subtle, sparkling, bright, dazzling, glorious and radiantly awesome, in appearance like a mirage moving across a landscape in springtime in one continuous stream of vibrations. Be not daunted thereby, nor terrified, nor awed. That is the radiance of thine own true nature. Recognize it.'

The words had a psychedelic authority that overpowered the materialist annihilation he longed to believe in. He struggled to restore his faith in the finality of death, but couldn't help seeing it as a superstition among superstitions, no more bracingly rational than the rest. The idea that an afterlife had been invented to reassure people who couldn't face the finality of death was no more plausible than the idea that the finality of death had been invented to reassure people who couldn't face the nightmare of endless experience. His delirium tremens collaborated with the poets of the *Bardo* to produce a sensation of seething electrocution as he was goaded towards the abattoir of sleep, terrified that the slaughter of his rational mind would present him with a 'glimpse of the Pure Truth'.

Memories and phrases loomed and flitted like fog banks on a night road. Thoughts threatened him from a distance, but disappeared as he approached them. 'Drowned in dreams and burning to be gone'. Who had said that? Other people's words. Had he already thought 'other people's words'? Things seemed far away and then, a moment later, repetitious. Was it like fog, or was it more like hot sand, something he was labouring through and trying not to touch at the same time? Cold and wet, hot and dry. How could it be both? How could it be other than both? Similes of dissimilarities—another phrase that seemed to chase itself like a miniature train around a tight circuit. Please make it stop.

A scene that kept tumbling back into his delirious thoughts was his visit to the philosopher Victor Eisen after Victor's near-death experience. He had found his old Saint-Nazaire neighbour in the London clinic, still strapped to the machines that had flat-lined a few days earlier. Victor's withered yellow arms emerged limply from an institutional dressing gown, but as he described what had happened his speech was as rapid and emphatic as ever, saturated by a lifetime of confident opinions.

'I came to a riverbank and on the other side was a red light which controlled the universe. There were two figures either side of it, who I knew to be the Lord of Time and the Lord of Space. They communicated to me directly through their thoughts, without using any speech. They told me that the fabric of Time-Space was torn and that I had to repair it, that the fate of the universe depended on me. I had a tremendous sense of urgency and purpose and I was on my way to fulfil my task when I felt myself being dragged back into my body and I very reluctantly returned.'

For three weeks Victor was won over by the feeling of authenticity that accompanied his vision, but then the habits of his public atheism and the fear that the logical reductions enshrined in his philosophical work might be invalidated made him squeeze his new sense of openness back into the biological crisis he was suffering at the time. He decided that the pressing mission he had been sent on by the controller of the universe was an allegory of a brain running out of oxygen. His mind had been failing, not expanding.

As he lay sweating in that narrow room, thinking about Victor's need to decide what everything meant, Patrick wondered if he would if he could ever make his ego light enough to relax in not having to settle the meaning of things. What would that feel like?

In the meantime, the Suicide Observation Room lived up to its majestic name. In it, he saw that suicide had always formed the unquestioned backdrop to his existence. Even before he had taken to carrying around a copy of *The Myth of Sisyphus* in his overcoat pocket, making its first sentence the mantra of his early twenties, Patrick had greeted the day with the basic question, 'Can anyone think of a good reason not to kill himself?' Since he lived at the time in a theatrical solitude, crowded with mad and mocking voices, he was not likely to get an affirmative answer. Elaborate postponement was the best he could hope for, and in the end the obligation to talk proved stronger than the desire to die. During the next twenty years the suicidal chatter died down to an occasional whisper on a coastal path, or in a quiet chemist. When it returned in full force, it took the form of a grim monologue rather than a surreal chorus. The comparative simplicity of the most recent assault made him realize that he had only ever been superficially in love with easeful death and was much more deeply enthralled by his own personality. Suicide wore the mask of self-rejection; but in reality nobody took their personality more seriously than the person who was planning to kill himself on its instructions. Nobody was more determined to stay in charge at any cost, to force the most mysterious aspect of life into their own imperious schedule.

His month in the Priory had been a crucial period of his life, transforming the crisis that had led to the breakdown of his marriage and the escalation of his drinking. It was disquieting to think how close he had come to running away after only three days, lured by Becky's departure. Before leaving, she had found him in the lounge of the Depression Wing.

'I was looking for you. I'm not meant to speak to anyone,' she said in a mock whisper, 'because I'm a bad influence.'

She gave him a little folded note and a light kiss on the lips before hurrying out of the room.

This is my sister's address. She's away in the States, so I'll be there alone, if you feel like running away from this fucking place and doing something CRAZY. Love Becks.

The note reminded him of the jagged CRAZYs he used to doodle in the margins of his O-level chemistry notes after smoking a joint during the morning break at school. It was out of the question to visit her, he told himself, as he called a minicab service listed in the payphone booth under the back stairs. Was this what they meant by powerless?

'Just don't!' he muttered, closing the door of his minicab firmly to show how determined he was not to pursue a bloodstained festival of dysfunction. He gave the driver the address on Becky's note.

'Well, you must be all right if they let you out,' said the jaunty driver.

'I let myself out. I couldn't afford it.'

'Bit pricey, is it?'

Patrick didn't answer, glazed over with desire and conflict.

'Have you heard the one about the man who goes into the psychiatrist's office?' asked the driver, setting off down the drive and smiling in the rear-view mirror. 'He says, "It's been terrible, Doctor, for three years I thought I was a butterfly, and that's not all, it gets worse: for the last three months I thought I was a moth." "Good God," says the psychiatrist, "what a difficult time you've been having. So, what made you come here today and ask for help?" "Well," says the man, "I saw the light in the window and I felt drawn to it, so I just flew in."'

'That's a good one,' said Patrick, sinking deeper into Becky's imagined nakedness, while wondering how long his latest dose of oxazepam would last. 'Do you specialize in Priory patients because of your sunny temperament?'

'You say that,' said the driver, 'but last year for about four months I literally couldn't get out of bed, literally couldn't see the point in anything.'

'Oh, I'm sorry,' said Patrick.

From Hammersmith Broadway to the Shepherd's Bush round-about, they talked about the causeless weeping, the suicidal day-dreams, the excruciating slowness, the sleepless nights and the listless days. By the time they reached Bayswater, they were best friends and the driver turned round to Patrick and said with the full blast of his restored cheerfulness, 'In a few months you'll be looking back on what you've just been through and saying, "*What* was all that about? What was all that fuss and aggravation about?" That's what happened to me.'

Patrick looked back down at Becky's note. She had signed herself with the name of a beer. Becks. He started to whisper hoarsely under his breath, in a Marlon Brando as Vito Corleone voice, 'The one who comes to you and asks for a meeting, and has the same name as a well-known brand of beer—*she's* the one that wants you to have a relapse . . .'

Not the voices, he mustn't let them kick off. 'It starts off with a little Marlon Brando impersonation,' sighed Mrs. Mop, 'and the next thing you know . . .'

'Shut up!' Patrick interrupted.

'What?'

'Oh, not you. I'm sorry.'

They turned into a big square with a central garden. The driver drew up to a white stucco building. Patrick leant sideways and looked out of the window. Becky was on the third floor, beautiful, available and mentally ill.

To think of the things he'd done for a little intimacy, earth flying over his shoulder as he dug his own grave. There were the good women who gave him the care he had never had. They had to be tortured into letting him down, to show that they couldn't really be trusted. And then there were the bad women who saved time by being untrustworthy straight away. He generally alternated between these two broad categories, enchanted by some variant which briefly masked the futility of defending the decaying fortress of his personality, while hoping that it would obligingly rearrange itself into a temple of peace and fulfilment. Hoping and moping, moping and hoping. With only a little detachment, his love life looked like a child's wind-up toy made to march again and again over the precipice of a kitchen table. Romance was where love was most under threat, not where it was likely to achieve its highest expression. If a candidate was sufficiently hopeless, like Becky, she took on the magnetism of the obviously doomed. It was embarrassing to be so deluded, and even more embarrassing to react to the delusion, like a man running away from his own looming shadow.

'I know this sounds a little bit *crazy*, for want of a better word,' said Patrick with a snort of laughter, 'but do you think you could drive me back? I'm not ready yet.'

'Back to the Priory?' said the driver, no longer quite as sympathetic to his passenger.

He doesn't want to know about those of us who have to go back, thought Patrick. He closed his eyes and stretched out in the back seat. 'Talk would talk and go so far askance . . . something, something . . . You don't want madhouse and the whole thing there.' The whole thing there. The wonderful inarticulacy of it, expanding with threat and contracting with ostensive urgency.

On the drive back, Patrick started to feel chest pains which even the violence of his longing for pathological romance could no longer explain. His hands were shaking and he could feel the sweat breaking out on his forehead. By the time he reached Dr. Pagazzi's office, he was hallucinating mildly and apparently trapped in a two-dimensional space with no depth, like an insect crawling around a window pane, looking for a way out. Dr. Pagazzi scolded him for missing his four o'clock dose of oxazepam, saying that he might have a heart attack if he withdrew too fast. Patrick lifted the dull plastic tub in his shaking hand and knocked back three oxazepam.

The next day he 'shared' his near escape with the Depression Group. It turned out that all of them had nearly run away, or had run away and come back, or thought about running away much of the time. Some, on the other hand, dreaded leaving, but they only seemed superficially opposite to the ones who wanted to run away: everyone was obsessed with how much therapy they needed before they could begin a 'normal life'. Patrick was surprised by how grateful he felt for the sense of solidarity with the other patients. A lifelong habit of being set apart was briefly overturned by a wave of goodwill towards everyone in the group.

Johnny Hall had taken an unassuming seat near the back of the room. Patrick worked his way round the far end of the pew to join his old friend.

'How are you bearing up?' said Johnny.

'Pretty well,' said Patrick, sitting down next to him. 'I have a strange feeling of excitement which I wouldn't admit to anyone except you and Mary. I felt rather knocked out for the first few days, but then I had what I think your profession would call an "insight". I went to the funeral parlour yesterday evening and sat with Eleanor's body. I connected . . . I'll tell you later.'

Johnny smiled encouragingly. 'Christ,' he said, after a pause, 'Nicholas Pratt. I didn't expect to see him.'

'Neither did I. You're so lucky to have an ethical reason not to talk to him.'

'Doesn't everybody?'

'Quite.'

'I'll see you afterwards at the Onslow,' said Johnny, leaving

Patrick to the usher who had come up to him and was standing by expectantly.

'We can start whenever you're ready, sir,' said the usher, somehow hinting at the queue of corpses that would pile up unless the ceremony got going right away.

Patrick scanned the room. There were a few dozen people sitting in the pews facing Eleanor's coffin.

'Fine,' he said, 'let's begin in ten minutes.'

'Ten minutes?' said the usher, like a young child who has been told he can do something really exciting when he's twenty-one.

'Yes, there are still people arriving,' said Patrick, noticing Julia standing in the doorway, a spiky effusion of black against the dull morning: black veil, black hat, stiff black silk dress and, he imagined, softer black silk beneath. He immediately felt the impact of her mentality, that intense but exclusive sensitivity. She was like a spider's web, trembling at the slightest touch, but indifferent to the light that made its threads shine in the wet grass.

'You're just in time,' said Patrick, kissing Julia through her scratchy black veil.

'You mean late as usual.'

'No; just in time. We're about to kick off, if that's the phrase I'm looking for.'

'It's not,' she said, with that short husky laugh that always got to him.

The last time they had seen each other was in the French hotel where their affair had ended. Despite their communicating rooms, they could think of nothing to say to each other. Sitting through long meals, under the vault of an artificial sky, painted with faint clouds and garlands of tumbling roses, they stared at a flight of steps that led down to the slapping keels of a private harbour, ropes creaking against bollards, bollards rusting into stone quays; everything longing to leave.

'Now that you're not with Mary, you don't need me. I was . . . structural.'

'Exactly.'

The single word was perhaps too bare and could only be out-stripped by silence. She had stood up and walked away without further comment. A gull launched itself from the soiled balus-trade and clapped its way out to sea with a piercing cry. He had wanted to call her back, but the impulse died in the thick carpet lengthening between them.

Looking at him now, the freshly bereaved son, Julia decided she felt utterly detached from Patrick, apart from wanting him to find her irresistible.

'I haven't seen you for such a long time,' said Patrick, looking down at Julia's lips, red under the black net of her veil. He remained inconveniently attracted to almost all the women he had ever been to bed with, even when he had a strong aversion to a revival on all other grounds.

'A year and a half,' said Julia. 'Is it true that you've given up drinking? It must be hard just now.'

'Not at all: a crisis demands a hero. The ambush comes when things are going well, or so I'm told.'

'If you can't speak personally about things going well, they haven't changed that much.'

'They have changed, but my speech patterns may take a while to catch up.'

'I can't wait.'

'If there's an opportunity for irony . . .'

'You'll take it.'

'It's the hardest addiction of all,' said Patrick. 'Forget heroin. Just try giving up irony, that deep-down need to mean two things at once, to be in two places at once, not to be there for the catas-trophe of a fixed meaning.'

'Don't!' said Julia, 'I'm having enough trouble wearing nicotine patches and still smoking at the same time. Don't take away my irony,' she pleaded, clasping him histrionically, 'leave me with a little sarcasm.'

'Sarcasm doesn't count. It only means one thing: contempt.'

'You always were a quality freak,' said Julia. 'Some of us like sarcasm.'

Julia noticed that she was playing with Patrick. She felt a small tug of nostalgia, but reminded herself sternly that she was well rid of him. Besides, she had Gunther now, a charming German banker who spent the middle of the week in London. It was true that he was married, as Patrick had been, but in every other way he was the opposite: slick, fit, rich and disciplined. He had opera tickets, and bookings in caviar bars and membership of nightclubs, organized by his personal assistant. Sometimes he threw caution to the winds and put on his ironed jeans and his zip-up suede jacket and took her to jazz clubs in unusual parts of town, always, of course, with a big, reassuring, silent car waiting outside to take them back to Hays Mews, just behind Berkeley Square, where Gunther, like all his friends, was having a swimming pool put into the sub-basement of his triple mews house lateral conversion. He collected hideous contemporary art with the haphazard credulity of a man who has friends in the art world. There were artistic black-and-white photographs of women's nipples in his dressing room. He made Julia feel sophisticated, but he didn't make her want to play. The thought simply didn't enter her head when she was with Gunther. He had never struggled to give up irony. He knew, of course, that it existed and he pursued it doggedly with all the silliness at his command.

'We'd better find a seat,' said Patrick. 'I'm not quite sure what's going on; I haven't even had time to look at the order of service.'

'But didn't you organize it?'

'No. Mary did.'

'Sweet!' said Julia. 'She's always so helpful, more like a mother than your own mother really.'

Julia felt her heart rate accelerate; perhaps she had gone too far. She was amazed that her old competition with that paragon of self-sacrifice had suddenly burst out, now that it was so out of date.

'She was, until she had children of her own,' said Patrick amiably. 'That rather blew my cover.'

From fearing that he would take offence, Julia found herself wishing he would stop being so maddeningly calm.

Organ music purred into life.

'Well, real or not, I have to burn the remains of the only mother I'll ever have,' said Patrick, smiling briskly at Julia and setting off down the aisle to the front row where Mary was keeping a seat for him.

4

MARY SAT IN THE front pew of the crematorium staring at Eleanor's coffin, mastering a moment of rebellion. Wondering where Patrick was, she had looked back and seen him bantering flirtatiously with Julia. Now that nothing serious depended on her cultivated indifference, she felt a thud of exasperation. Here she was again, being helpful, while Patrick, in one of the more legitimate throes of his perpetual crisis, bestowed his attention on another woman. Not that she wanted more of his attention; all she wanted from Patrick was for him to be a little freer, a little less predictable. To be fair, and she sometimes wished she could stop being so fair, that's what he wanted as well. She had to remind herself that separation had made them grow closer. No longer hurled together or driven apart by their habitual reactions, they had settled into a relatively stable orbit around the children and around each other.

Her irritation was further blunted when a second backward glance yielded a grave smile from Erasmus Price, her own tiny concession to the consolations of adultery. She had started her affair with him in the South of France, where Patrick had insisted on renting a house during the final disintegration of their marriage, compulsively circling back to the area around his childhood home in Saint-Nazaire. Mary protested against this extravagance in vain; Patrick was in the last phase of his drinking, stumbling around the labyrinth of his unconscious, unavailable for discussion.

The Prices, whose own marriage was falling apart, had sons roughly the same age as Robert and Thomas. Despite these promising symmetries, harmony eluded the two families.

'Anybody who is amazed that "a week is a long time in politics",' said Patrick on the second day, 'should try having the Prices to stay. It turns out to be a fucking eternity. Do you know how he got his wacky name? His father was in the middle of editing the sixty-five-volume Oxford University Press *Complete Works of Erasmus* when his mother interrupted him with the news that she had given birth to a son. "Let's call him Erasmus," he cried, like a man inspired, "or Luther, whose crucial letter to Erasmus I was re-reading only this morning." Given the choice . . .' Patrick subsided.

Mary ignored him, knowing that he was just setting up that day's pretext for more senseless drinking. After Patrick had passed out and Emily Price had gone to bed, Mary sat up late, listening to Erasmus's troubles.

'Some people think that the future belongs to them and that they can lose it,' he said on the first evening, staring into his wine-dark glass, 'but I don't have that sense at all. Even when the work is going well, I wouldn't mind if I could painlessly and instantly expire.'

Why was she drawn to these gloomy men? As a philosopher, at least Erasmus, like Schopenhauer, could make his pessimism into a world view. He cheered up at the mention of the German philosopher.

'My favourite remark of his was the advice he gave to a dying friend: "You are ceasing to be something you would have done better never to become."'

'That must have helped,' said Mary.

'A real nostalgia-buster,' he whispered admiringly.

According to Erasmus his marriage was irreparable; the puzzle for Mary was that it existed at all. As a guest, Emily Price had three main drawbacks: she was incapable of saying please, incapable of saying thank you and incapable of saying sorry, all the while creating a surge in the demand for these expressions. When she saw Mary applying sunblock to Thomas's sharp pale shoulders, she hurried over and scooped the white cream out of Mary's cupped hand, saying, 'I can't see it without wanting to take some.' By her own account, the same hunger had haunted the birth of her eldest son: 'The moment I saw him, I thought: *I want another one.*'

Emily complained about Cambridge, she complained about her husband and about her sons, she complained about her house, she complained about France and the sun and the clouds and the leaves and the wind and the bottle tops. She couldn't stop; she had to bail out the flooding dinghy of her discontent. Sometimes she set false targets with her complaining: Cambridge was hell, London was great, but when Erasmus applied for a job at London University, she made him withdraw. At the time, she had said that he was too cowardly to apply, but on holiday with the Melroses she admitted the truth. 'I only wanted to move to London so I could complain about the air quality and the schools.'

Patrick was momentarily jolted out of his stupor by the challenge of Emily's personality.

'She could be the centrepiece of a Kleinian Conference—"Talk About Bad Breasts".' He giggled sweatily on the bed while Mary cultivated patience. 'She had a difficult start in life,' he sighed. 'Her mother wouldn't let her use the biros in their house, in case they ran out of ink.' He fell off the bed laughing, knocked his head on the bedside table and had to take a handful of codeine to deal with the bump.

When Mary abandoned tolerance, she did it vehemently. She could feel Emily's underlying sense of privation like the blast from a furnace, but she somehow made the decision to put aside her characteristic empathy, to stay with the annoying consequences and not to feel the distressing causes of Emily's behaviour, especially after Erasmus's clumsy pass, which she hadn't entirely rejected, on the second evening of their endless conversation about marital failure. For a week, they kept each other afloat with the wreckage from their respective marriages. On their return to England it took them two months to admit the futility of trying to build an affair out of these sodden fragments—just long enough for Mary to struggle loyally through Erasmus's latest work, *None the Wiser: Developments in the Philosophy of Consciousness*.

It was the presence of *None the Wiser* on Mary's bedside table that alerted Patrick to his wife's laborious romance.

'You couldn't be reading that book unless you were having an affair with the author,' he guessed through half-closed eyes.

'Believe me, it's virtually impossible even then.'

He gave in to the relief of closing his eyes completely, a strange smile on his lips. She realized with vague disgust that he was pleased to have the huge weight of his infidelity alleviated by her trivial contribution to the other side of the scales.

After that, there was what her mother would have called an 'absolutely maddening' period, when Patrick only emerged from his new blackout bedsit in order to lecture or interrogate her about consciousness studies, sometimes with the slow sententious precision of drunkenness, sometimes with its visionary fever, all delivered with the specious fluency of a man used to pleading a case in public.

'The subject of consciousness, in order to enter the realm of science, must become the object of consciousness, and that is precisely what it cannot do, for the eye cannot perceive itself, cannot vault from its socket fast enough to glimpse the lens. The language of experience and the language of experiment hang like oil and water in the same test tube, never mingling except from the violence of philosophy. The violence of philosophy. Would you agree? Whoops. Don't worry about that lamp, I'll get you a new one.

'Seriously, though, where do you stand on microtubules? Microtubular bells. Are you For or Against? Do you think that a theory of extended mind can base itself confidently in quantum non-locality? Do you believe that two linked particles conceived in the warm spiralling quantum womb of a microtubule could continue to inform each other as they rush through vast fields of interstellar darkness; still communicating despite the appearance of *icy separation*? Are you For, or Against? And what difference would it make to experience if these particles did continue to resonate with each other, since it is not particles that we experience?'

'Oh, for God's sake shut up.'

'Who will rid us of the Explanatory Gap?' he shouted, like Henry II requesting an assassin for his troublesome priest. 'And is that gap just a product of our misconstrued discourse?' He ploughed on, 'Is reality a consensual hallucination? And is a nervous breakdown in fact a *refusal to consent*? Go on, don't be shy, tell me what you think.'

'Why don't you go back to your flat and pass out there? I don't want the children seeing you in this state.'

'What state? A state of philosophical enquiry? I thought you would approve.'

'I've got to collect the boys. Please go home.'

'How sweet that you think of it as my home. I'm not in that happy position.'

He would leave, abandoning the consciousness debate for a slamming door. Even 'fucking bitch' had a welcome directness after the twisted use he made of abstract phrases like 'property dualism' to express his shattered sense of home. She felt less and less guilty about his stormy departures. She dreaded Robert and Thomas asking her about their father's moods, his glaring silences, his declamatory introversion, the spectacle of his clumsiness and misery. The children in fact saw very little of him. He was 'away on business' for the last two months of his drinking and for his month in the Priory. With his unusual talent for mimicry, Robert still managed to impersonate the concerns that Erasmus wrote books about and Patrick used to make veiled attacks on his wife.

'Where do thoughts come from?' he muttered, pacing up and down pensively. 'Before you decide to move your hand where does the decision live?'

'Honestly, Bobby,' said Thomas, letting out a short giggle. 'I expect Brains would know.'

'Well, Mr. Tracy,' stammered Robert, bobbing up and down on imaginary strings, 'when you move your hand, your . . . your brain tells you to move your hand, but what tells your brain to tell your hand?'

'That's a real puzzle, Brains,' said Robert, switching to Mr. Tracy's basso profundo.

'Weh-well, Mr. Tracy,' he returned to the stammering scientist, 'I've invented a machine that may be able to s-solve that puzzle. It's called the Thinkatron.'

'Switch it on, switch it on!' shouted Thomas, swishing his raggie in the air.

Robert made a loud humming sound that gradually grew more threatening.

'Oh, no, it's going to blow up!' warned Thomas. 'The Thinkatron is going to blow up!'

Robert flung himself on the floor with the sound of a huge explosion.

'Gee, Mr. Tracy, I guess I must have o-o-overloaded the primary circuits.'

'Don't worry, Brains,' said Thomas magnanimously, 'I'm sure you'll work it out. But seriously,' he added to Mary, 'what is the "consciousness debate" that Dada gets so angry about?'

'Oh, God,' said Mary, desperate for someone close to her who didn't want to talk about consciousness. She thought she could put Thomas off by making the subject sound impenetrably learned. 'It's really the philosophical and scientific debate about whether the brain and the mind are identical.'

'Well, of course not,' said Thomas taking his thumb out of his mouth and rounding his eyes, 'I mean, the brain is part of the body and the mind is the outer soul.'

'Quite,' said Mary, amazed.

'What I don't understand,' said Thomas, 'is why things exist.'

'What do you mean? Why there's something rather than nothing?'

'Yes.'

'I have no idea, but it's probably worth staying surprised by that.'

'I am surprised by it, Mama. I'm really surprised.'

When she told Erasmus what Thomas had said about the mind being the 'outer soul', he didn't seem as impressed as she had been.

'It's rather an old-fashioned view,' he commented, 'although the more modern point of view, that the soul is the inner mind, can't be said to have got us anywhere by simply inverting the relationship between two opaque signifiers.'

'Right,' said Mary. 'Still, don't you think it's rather extraordinary for a six-year-old to be so clear about that famously tricky subject?'

'Children often say things that seem extraordinary to us precisely because the big questions are not yet "famously tricky" for them. Oliver is obsessed with death at the moment and he's also only six. He can't bear it, it hasn't become part of How It Is; it's still a scandal, a catastrophic design flaw; it ruins everything. We've got used to the fact of death—although the experience is irreducibly strange. He hasn't found the trick of putting a hood on the executioner, of hiding the experience with the fact. He still sees it as pure experience. I found him crying over a dead fly lying on the windowsill. He asked me why things have to die and all I could offer him was tautology: because nothing lasts for ever.'

Erasmus's need to take a general and theoretical view of every situation sometimes infuriated Mary. All she had wanted was a little compliment for Thomas. Even when she finally told him that she felt there was no point in carrying on with their affair, he accepted her position with insulting equanimity, and then went on to admit that he had 'recently been toying with the Panpsychist approach', as if this unveiling of the wild side of his intellect might tempt her to change her mind.

Mary had decided not to take the children to Eleanor's funeral, but to leave them with her mother. Thomas had no memory of Eleanor and Robert was so steeped in his father's sense of betrayal that the occasion would be more likely to revive faded hostility than to relieve a natural sense of sadness and loss. They had all been together for the last time about two years before in Kew Gardens, during the bluebell season, soon after Eleanor had come back from Saint-Nazaire to live in England. On their way to the Woodland Walk, Mary pushed Eleanor's wheelchair through the twisting Rhododendron Dell, hemmed in by walls of outrageous colour. Patrick hung back, gulping down the odd miniature of Johnnie Walker Black Label in moments of feigned fascination with a sprawling pink or orange blossom, while Robert and Thomas explored the gigantic bushes ranged against the slopes on either side. When a golden pheasant emerged onto the path, its saffron-yellow and blood-red feathers shining like enamel, Mary stopped the wheelchair, astonished. The pheasant crossed the hot cinder with the bobbing majesty of an avian gait, the price of a strained talent, like the high head of a swimming dog. Eleanor, crumpled in her seat, wearing old baby-blue flannel trousers and a maroon cardigan with big flat buttons and holes at the elbow, stared at the bird with the alarmed distaste that had taken up residence in her frozen features. Patrick, determined not to talk to his mother, hurried past muttering that he'd 'better keep an eye on the boys'.

Eleanor gestured frantically to Mary to come closer and then produced one of her rare whole sentences.

'I can never forget that he's David's son.'

'I don't think it's his father who haunts him these days,' said Mary, surprised by her own sharpness.

'Haunts . . .' said Eleanor.

Mary was thrusting the wheelchair through the dappled pot-holes of the Woodland Walk by the time Eleanor was able to speak again.

'Are . . . you . . . all . . . right?'

She asked the same question again and again, with mounting agitation, ignoring the haze of bluebells, mingled with the yellow stalks of wild garlic, under the shifting and swelling shade of the oaks. She was trying to save Mary from Patrick, not out of any insight into her circumstances, but in order to save herself, by some retroactive magic, from David. Mary's attempts to give an affirmative answer tormented Eleanor, since the only answer she could accept was: 'No, I'm not all right! I'm living in hell with a tyrannical madman, just as you did, my poor darling. On the other hand, I sincerely believe that the universe will save us, thanks to the awesome shamanic powers of the wounded healer that you truly are.'

For some reason Mary couldn't quite bring herself to say

this, and yet there was still a troubling sisterhood between the two women. Mary recognized certain features of Eleanor's upbringing all too easily: the intense shyness, the all-important nanny, the diffident sense of self, the masochistic attraction to difficult men. Eleanor was the cautionary tale of these forces, a warning against the worthlessness of self-sacrifice when there was almost no self to sacrifice, of dealing with being lost by getting more lost. Above all, she was a baby, not a 'big baby' like so many adults, but a small baby perfectly preserved in the pickling jar of money, alcohol and fantasy.

Since that colourful day in Kew, neither of the boys had been taken to see their grandmother in her nursing home. Patrick stopped visiting her as well, after her excruciating flirtation with assisted suicide two years before. Only Mary persevered, sometimes with the scant dutiful reminder that Eleanor was, after all, her mother-in-law; sometimes with the more obscure conviction that Eleanor was out of balance with her family and that the work of redressing that balance must start straight away, whether Eleanor was able to participate or not. It was certainly strange, as the months wore on, to be talking into space, hoping that she was doing some good, while Eleanor stared ever more rigidly and blankly at the ceiling. And in the absence of any dialogue, she often ran aground on her contempt for Eleanor's failure to protect her child.

She could remember Eleanor describing the first few weeks after she returned from hospital with the infant Patrick. David was so tormented by his son's crying that he ordered her to take the noisy brat to the remotest room in the attic. Eleanor already felt exiled enough in David's beloved Cornwall, at the end of a headland overlooking an impenetrably wooded estuary, and she could hardly believe, as she was thrown out of her bedroom too suddenly to put on her slippers, or to collect a blanket for the baby, that there was a further exile available, a small cold room in the big cold house. For her the building was already sodden with melancholy horror. She had married David in the Truro registry office when she was heavily pregnant with their first child. Overestimating his medical skills, he had encouraged her to have the child at home. Without the incubator that she needed, Georgina died two days later. David sailed his boat out into the estuary, buried her at sea, and then disappeared for three days to get drunk. Eleanor stayed in bed, bleeding and abandoned, staring at the grey water through the bay window of her bedroom. After Georgina's death, she had refused to go to bed with David. One evening he punched her in the back of the knees as she was going upstairs. When she fell, he twisted her arm behind her back and raped her on the staircase. Just as she thought she was finally disgusted enough to leave him, she found that she was pregnant.

Up in the attic with the new rape-born baby in her arms, she felt hysterically unconfident. Looking at the narrow bed she was gripped by the fear that if they lay down on it together, she would roll over and asphyxiate him, and so she chose the wooden chair in the corner, next to the empty fireplace, and sat up all night, clutching him in her arms. During those nights in the wooden chair, she was sucked down into sleep again and again, and then woken abruptly by sensing the baby's body sliding down her nightdress towards the precipice of her knees. She would catch him at the last moment, terrified that his soft head was about to crash onto the hard floor; and yet unable to go to the bed they both longed for, in case she crushed him to death.

The days were a little better. The maternity nurse came in to help, the housekeeper bustled about in the kitchen, and with David out sailing and drinking, the house took on a superficially cheerful atmosphere. The three women fussed over Patrick and when Eleanor was resting back in her own bedroom she almost forgot about the dreadful nights; she almost forgot about the death of Georgina when she closed her eyes and could no longer see the stretch of grey water outside her window, and when she fed the baby from her breasts and they fell asleep together, she almost forgot about the violence that had brought him into the world.

But then one day, three weeks after they came back from hospital, David stayed behind. He was in a dangerous mood from the start; she could smell the brandy in his coffee and see the furious jealousy in his looks. By lunchtime, he had wounded everyone in the house with his cutting remarks, and all the women were anxious, feeling him pacing around, waiting for the chance to hurt and humiliate them. Nevertheless, they were surprised when he strode into the kitchen, carrying a battered leather bag and wearing a surgeon's ill-fitting green pyjamas. He ordered them to clear a space on the scrubbed oak table, unfolded a towel, took out a wooden case of surgical instruments from the bag and opened it next to the towel. He asked for a saucepan of boiling water, as if everything had already been agreed and everyone knew what was going on.

'What for?' said the housekeeper, the first to wake from the trance.

'To sterilize the instruments,' David answered in the tone of a man explaining something very obvious to someone very stupid. 'The time has come to perform a circumcision. Not, I assure you,' he added, as if to allay their innermost fears, 'for religious reasons,' he allowed himself a fleeting smile, 'but for medical ones.'

'You've been drinking,' Eleanor blurted out.

'Only a beaker of surgical spirit,' he quipped, a little giddy from the prospect of the operation; and then, no longer in the mood for fun, 'Bring me the boy.'

'Are you sure it's for the best?' asked the maternity nurse.

'Do not question my authority,' said David, throwing everything into it: the older man, the doctor, the employer, the centuries

733

of command, but also the paralysing dart of his psychological presence, which made it seem life-threatening to oppose him.

His credentials as a murderer were well established in Eleanor's imagination. Late at night, when he was down to one listener, amongst the empty bottles and crushed cigars, David was fond of telling the story of an Indian pig-sticking hunt he had been on in the late nineteen-twenties. He was thrilled by the danger of galloping through the high grass with a lance, chasing a wild boar whose tusks could ruin a horse's legs, throw a rider to the ground and gore him to death. Impaling one of these fast, tough pigs was also a terrific pleasure, more involving than a long-distance kill. The only blemish on the expedition was that one of the party was bitten by a wild dog and developed the symptoms of rabies. Three days from the nearest hospital, it was already too late to help, and so the hunters decided to truss up their foaming and thrashing friend in one of the thick nets originally intended for transporting the bodies of the dead pigs, and to hoist him off the ground, tying the corners of the net to the branches of a big jacaranda tree. It was challenging, even for these hard men, to enjoy the sense of deep relaxation that follows a day of invigorating sport with this parcel of hydrophobic anguish dangling from a nearby tree. The row of lanterns down the dinner table, the quiet gleam of silver, the well-trained servants, the triumph of imposing civilization on the wild vastness of the Indian night, seemed to have been thrown into question. David could only just make out, against a background of screams, the splendid tale of Archie Montcrieff driving a pony and trap into the Viceroy's ballroom. Archie had worn an improvised toga and shouted obscenities in 'an outlandish kind of Cockney Latin', while the pony manured the dance floor. If his father hadn't been such a friend of the Viceroy's he might have had to resign his commission, but as it was, the viceroy admitted, privately of course, that Archie had raised his spirits during 'another damned dull dance'.

When the story was finished, David rose from the table muttering, 'This noise is intolerable,' and went into his tent to fetch his pistol. He walked over to the rabies victim and shot him in the head. Returning to the dumbfounded table, he sat down with a 'feeling of absolute calm' and said, 'Much the kindest thing to do.' Gradually, the word spread around the table: much the kindest thing to do. Rich and powerful men, some of them quite high up in government, and one of them a judge, couldn't help agreeing with him. With the silencing of the screams and a few pints of whisky and soda, it became the general view by the end of the evening that David had done something exceptionally courageous. David would almost smile as he described how he had brought everyone at the table round, and then in a fit of piety, he would sometimes finish by saying that although at the time he had not yet set eyes on a copy of *Gray's Anatomy*, he really thought of that pistol shot as the beginning of his 'love affair with medicine'.

Eleanor felt obliged to hand over the baby to him in the kitchen in Cornwall. The baby screamed and screamed. Eleanor thought there must be dogs whimpering in their kennels a hundred miles away, the screams were so loud and high. All the women huddled together crying and begging David to stop and to be careful and to give the baby some local anaesthetic. They knew this was no operation, it was an attack by a furious old man on his son's genitals; but like the chorus in a play, they could only comment and wail, without being able to alter the action.

'I wanted to say, "You've already killed Georgina and now you want to kill Patrick,"' Eleanor told Mary, to show how bold she would have been if she had said anything at all. 'I wanted to call the police!'

Well, why didn't you? was all that Mary could think, but she said nothing about Eleanor saying nothing; she just nodded and went on being a good listener.

'It was like . . .' said Eleanor, 'it was like that Goya painting of Saturn devouring his son.' Brought up surrounded by great paintings, Eleanor had experienced a late-adolescent crush on the History of Art, rudely guillotined by her disinheritance, and replaced by a proclivity for bright dollops of optimistic symbolism. Nevertheless, she could still remember, when she was twenty, driving through Spain in her first car, and being shocked, on a visit to the Prado, by the black vision of those late Goyas.

Mary was struck by the comparison, because it was unusual for Eleanor to make that sort of connection, and also because she knew the painting well, and could easily visualize the gaping mouth, the staring eyes and the ragged white hair of the old god of melancholy, mad with jealousy and the fear of usurpation, as he fed on the bleeding corpse of his decapitated child. Watching Eleanor plead for exoneration made Mary realize that her mother-in-law could never have protected anyone else when she was so entranced by her own vulnerability, so desperate to be saved. Later in her marriage, Eleanor did manage to get police protection for herself. It was in Saint-Nazaire, just after she learned about her mother's death and, not yet knowing the content of the will, was expecting to get control of a world-class fortune. She had to fly to Rome later that morning for the funeral, and David sat opposite her at the breakfast table, brooding about the possible consequences of his wife's increased independence.

'You're looking forward to getting your hands on all that lovely money,' he said, walking round to her side of the table. She got up, sensing danger. 'But you're not going to,' he added, grabbing her and pressing his thumbs expertly into her throat, 'because I'm going to kill you.'

Almost unconscious, she had managed to knee him in the balls with all her remaining strength. In the reflex of pain, he let go long enough for her to slide across the table and bolt out of the house. He pursued her for a while, but the twenty-three-year age difference took its toll on his tired body and she escaped into the woods. Convinced that he would follow by car, she struggled through the undergrowth to the local police station, and arrived scratched, bleeding and in tears. The two gendarmes who drove her back to the house stood guard over a proud and sulky David while she packed her bags for Rome. She left with relief, but without Patrick, who stayed behind with only the flimsy protection of yet another terrified nanny—they lasted, on average, about six weeks. Eleanor might have been out of reach, but once he had given the nanny a munificent day out, and sent Yvette home, David had the consolation of torturing his son without any interference from the gendarmerie.

In the end, Eleanor's betrayal of the maternal instinct that ruled Mary's own life formed an absolute barrier to the liking she could feel for her. She could remember her own sons at three weeks old: their hot silky heads burrowing their way back into the shelter of her body to soften the shock of being born. The thought of handing them over, before their skin could bear the roughness of wool, to be hacked at with knives by a cruel and sinister man required a level of treachery that blinded her imagination.

No doubt David had searched hard among the foolish and the meek to find a woman who could put up with his special tastes, but once his depravity was on full display, how could Eleanor escape the charge of colluding with a sadist and a paedophile? She had invited children from other families to spend their holidays in the South of France and, like Patrick, they had been raped and inducted into an underworld of shame and secrecy, backed by convincing threats of punishment and death. Just before her first stroke, Eleanor received a letter from one of those children, saying that after a lifetime of insomnia, self-harm, frigidity, promiscuity, perpetual anxiety and suicide attempts, she had started to lead a more normal life, thanks to seven years of therapy, and had finally been able to forgive Eleanor for not protecting her during the summer she stayed with the Melroses. When she showed the letter to Mary, Eleanor dwelt on the injustice of being made to feel guilty about a category of behaviour she had not even known existed, although it was going on in the bedroom next to hers.

And yet how ignorant could she really have been? The year before the arrival of the letter that so dismayed Eleanor, Patrick had received a letter from Sophie, an old au pair, who had heroically stayed with the Melroses for more than two years, more than twenty times the average endurance shown by the parade of incredulous young foreign women who passed through the house. In her letter, Sophie confessed to decades of guilt about the time she had spent looking after Patrick. She used to hear screams down the corridor of the house in Lacoste, and she knew that Patrick was being tormented, not merely punished or frustrated, but she was only nineteen at the time and she hesitated to intervene. She also confessed that she was terrified of David and, despite being genuinely fond of Patrick and feeling some pity for Eleanor, longed to get away from his grotesque family.

If Sophie knew that something was terribly wrong, how could Eleanor not have known? It was common enough to ignore what was seemingly impossible to ignore, but Eleanor stuck to her blindness with uncommon tenacity. Through all her programmes of self-discovery and shamanic healing, she avoided acknowledging her passion for avoidance. If she had ever discovered her real 'power animals', Mary suspected they would have been the Three Monkeys: See No Evil, Hear No Evil, Speak No Evil. Mary also suspected that these grim vigilantes had been killed off by one of her strokes, flooding her all at once with the fragments of knowledge that she had kept sealed off from one another, like the cells of a secret organization. In a parody of wholeness, the fragments converged when it was too late to make them cohere.

Eleanor was entirely confined to the nursing home for the last two years of her life, rarely leaving her bed. For the first year, Mary went on assuming that at least one of the threads holding Eleanor to her tormented existence was concern for her family, and she continued to reassure her that they were well. Later, she began to see that what really trapped Eleanor was not the strength of her attachments, but rather their weakness: without anything substantial to 'let go' of, she was left with only the volatility of her guilt and confusion. Part of her was aching to die, but she could never find the time; there was no gap between the proliferating anxieties; the desire to die collided instantly with the dread of dying, which in turn gave birth to a renewed desire.

For the second year, Mary was largely silent. She went into the room and wished Eleanor well. What else was there to do?

The last time she had seen her mother-in-law was two weeks ago. By then Eleanor had achieved a tranquillity indistinguishable from pure absence. Gaunt and drawn, her face seemed incapable of any deliberate change. Mary could remember Eleanor telling her, in one of those alienating confidential chats, that she knew exactly when she was going to die. The mysterious source of this information (Astrology? Channelling? A morbid guru? A drumming session? A prophetic dream?) was never unveiled, but the news was delivered with the slightly boastful serenity of pure fantasy. Mary felt that the certainty of death and the uncertainty of both its timing and its meaning were fundamental facts of life. Eleanor, on the other hand, knew exactly when she was going to die and that her death was not final. By the end, as far as Mary could tell, this conviction had deserted Eleanor, along with all the other features of her personality, as if a sandstorm had raged through her, ripping away every sign of comfort and leaving a smooth and sterile landscape under a dry blank sky.

Still, Eleanor had died on Easter Sunday, and Mary knew that nothing could have pleased her more. Or would have pleased her more, had she known. Perhaps she did know, even though her mind appeared to be fixed in a realm removed from anything as mundane as a calendar. Even then there was still no way of knowing whether that was the day she had been expecting to die.

Mary adjusted her position on the uncomfortable crematorium bench. Where was a convincing and practical theory of consciousness when you really needed it? She glanced back a few rows at Erasmus, but he appeared to have fallen asleep. As she turned back to the coffin a few feet in front of her, Mary's speculations collapsed abruptly. She found herself imagining, with a vividness she couldn't sustain while it was still going on, how it had felt for Eleanor during those two last brutal years, having her individuality annihilated, faculty by faculty, memory by memory.

Her eyes blurred with tears.

'Are you all right?' whispered Patrick, as he sat down next to her.

'I was thinking about your mother,' she said.

'A highly suitable choice,' Patrick murmured, in the voice of a sycophantic shopkeeper.

For some reason Mary started to laugh uncontrollably, and Patrick started laughing too, and they both had to bite their lower lips and keep their shoulders from shaking too wildly.

5

HOPING TO MASTER HIS fit of grief-stricken laughter, Patrick breathed out slowly and concentrated on the dull tension of waiting to begin. The organ sighed, as if bored of searching for a decent tune, and then meandered on resignedly. He must pull himself together: he was here to mourn his mother's death, a serious business.

There were various obstructions in his way. For a long time the feeling of madness brought on by the loss of his French home had made it impossible to get over his resentment of Eleanor. Without Saint-Nazaire, a primitive part of him was deprived of the imaginary care that had kept him sane as a child. He was certainly attached to the beauty of the place, but much more deeply to a secret protection that he dare not renounce in case it left him utterly destroyed. The shifting faces formed by the cracks, stains and hollows of the limestone mountain opposite the house used to keep him company. The line of pine trees along its ridge was like a column of soldiers coming to his rescue. There were hiding places where nobody had ever found him, and vine terraces to jump down, giving him the feeling he could fly when he had to flee. There was a dangerous well where he could drown rocks and clods of earth, without drowning himself. The most heroic connection of all was with the gecko that had taken custody of his soul in a moment of crisis and dashed out onto the roof, to safety and to exile. How could it ever find him again, if Patrick wasn't there any more?

On his last night in Saint-Nazaire there was a spectacular storm. Sheet lightning flickered behind ribbed banks of cloud, making the dark bowl of the valley tremble with light. At first, fat tropical raindrops dented the dusty ground, but soon enough, rivulets guttered down the steep paths, and little waterfalls flowed from step to step. Patrick wandered outside into the warm heavy rain, feeling mad. He knew that he had to end his magical contract with this landscape, but the electric air and the violent protest of the storm renewed the archaic mentality of a child, as if the same thick piano wires, hammered by thunder and pelting rain, ran through his body and the land. With water streaming down his face there was no need for tears, no need to scream with the sky cracking overhead. He stood in the drive, among the milky puddles and the murmur of new steams and the smell of the wet rosemary, until he sank to the ground, weighed down by what he was unable to give up, and sat motionless in the gravel and the mud. Forked lightning landed like antlers on the limestone mountain. In that sudden flash, he made out a shape on the ground between him and the wall that ran along the edge of the drive. Concentrating in the murky light, he saw that a toad had ventured out into the watery world beyond the laurel bushes, where Patrick imagined it had been waiting all summer for the rain, and was now resting gratefully on a bar of muddy ground between two puddles. They sat in front of each other, perfectly still.

Patrick pictured the white corpses of the toads he used to see each spring, at the bottom of the stone pools. Around their spent bodies, hundreds of soft black tadpoles clung to the grey-green algae on the walls, or wriggled across the open pond, or overflowed into the runnels that carried the water from pool to pool, between the source and the stream in the crease of the valley. Some of the tadpoles slipped limply down the slope; others swam frantically against the current. Robert and Thomas spent hours each Easter holiday, removing the little dams that formed overnight, and, when the covered part of the channel was blocked and the grass around the lower pond flooded, airlifting the stranded tadpoles in their cupped hands. Patrick could remember doing the same thing as a child, and the sense of giant compassion that he used to feel as he released them back into the safety of the pond through his flooding fingers.

In those days there had been a chorus of frogs during the spring nights, and during the day, sitting on the lily pads in the crescent pond, bullfrogs blowing their insides out like bubble gum; but in the system of imaginary protection that the land used to allow him, it was the lucky tree frogs that really counted. If only he could touch one of them, everything would be all right. They were hard to find. The round suckers on the tips of their feet meant that they could hang anywhere in the tree, camouflaged by the bright green of a new leaf or an unripe fig. When he did see one of these tiny frogs, fixed to the smooth grey bark, its brilliant skin stretched over a sharp skeleton, it looked to him like pulsing jewellery. He would reach out his index finger and touch it lightly for good luck. It might have only happened once, but he had thought about it a thousand times.

Remembering that charged and tentative gesture, he now looked with some scepticism at the warty head of the sodden toad in front of him. At the same time, he remembered his A-level Arden edition of *King Lear* with its footnote about the jewel in the head of the toad, the emblem of the treasure hidden in the midst of ugly, muddy, repulsive experience. One day he would live without superstition, but not yet. He reached out and touched the head of the toad. He felt some of the same awe he had felt as a child, but the resurgence of what he was about to lose gave the feeling a self-cancelling intensity. The mad fusion of mythologies created an excess of meaning that might at any moment flip into a world with no meaning at all. He drew away and, like someone returning to the familiar compromises of his city flat after a long exotic journey, recognized that he was a middle-aged man, sitting eccentrically in his muddy driveway in the middle of a thunderstorm, trying to communicate with a toad. He got up stiffly and slouched back to the house, feeling realistically miserable, but still kicking the puddles in defiance of his useless maturity.

Eleanor had given Saint-Nazaire away, but at least she had provided it in the first place, if only as a massive substitute for herself, a motherland that was there to cover for her incapacities. In a sense its loveliness was a decoy, the branches of almond blossom reaching into a cloudless sky, the unopened irises, like paintbrushes dipped in blue, the clear amber resin bleeding from the gunmetal bark of the cherry trees—all of that was a decoy, he must stop thinking about it. A child's need for protection would have assembled a system out of whatever materials came to hand, however ritual or bizarre. It might have been a spider in a broom cupboard, or the appearance of a neighbour across the well of a block of flats, or the number of red cars between the front door and the school gates, that took on the burden of love and reassurance. In his case, it had been a hillside in France. His home had stretched from the dark pinewood at the top of the slope, all the way to the pale bamboo that grew beside the stream at its foot. In between were terraces where vine shoots burst from twisted stumps that spent the winter looking like rusted iron, and olive trees rushed from green to grey and grey to green in the combing wind. Halfway down the slope were the cluster of houses and cypresses and the network of pools where he had experienced the most horror and negotiated the most far-fetched reprieves. Even the steep mountainside opposite the house was colonized by his imagination, and not only with the army of trees marching along its crest. Later on, its rejection of human encroachment became an image of his own less reliable aloofness.

Nobody could spend their whole life in a place without missing it when they left. Pathetic fallacies, projections, substitutions and displacements were part of the inevitable traffic between any mind and its habitual surroundings, but the pathological intensity he had brought to these operations made it vital for him to see through them. What would it be like to live without consolation, or the desire for consolation? He would never find out, unless he uprooted the consolatory system that had started on the hillside at Saint-Nazaire and then spread to every medicine cabinet, bed and bottle he had come across since; substitutes substituting for substitutes: the system was always more fundamental than its contents, and the mental act more fundamental still. What if memories were just memories, without any consolatory or persecutory power? Would they exist at all, or was it always emotional pressure that summoned images from what was potentially all of experience so far? Even if that was the case, there must be better librarians than panic, resentment and dismembering nostalgia to search among the dim and crowded stacks.

Whereas ordinary generosity came from a desire to give something to someone, Eleanor's philanthropy had come from a desire to give everything to anyone. The sources of the compulsion were complex. There was the repetition syndrome of a disinherited daughter; there was a rejection of the materialism and snobbery of her mother's world; and there was the basic shame at having any money at all, an unconscious drive to make her net worth and her self-worth converge in a perfect zero; but apart from all these negative forces, there was also the inspiring precedent of her great-aunt Virginia Jonson. With a rare enthusiasm for an ancestor, Eleanor used to tell Patrick all about the heroic scale of Virginia's charitable works; how she made so much difference to so many lives, showing that ardent selflessness which is often more stubborn than open egotism.

Virginia had already lost two sons when her husband died in 1901. Over the next twenty-five years she demolished half the Jonson fortune with her mournful philanthropy. In 1903 she endowed the Thomas J. Jonson Memorial Fund with twenty million dollars and in her will with another twenty-five million, at a time when these were sums of a rare vastness, rather than the typical Christmas bonus of a mediocre hedge-fund manager. She also collected paintings by Titian, Rubens, Van Dyck, Rembrandt, Tintoretto, Bronzino, Lorenzo di Credi, Murillo, Velasquez, Hals, Le Brun, Gainsborough, Romney and Botticelli, and donated them to the Jonson Wing of the Cleveland Museum of Art. This cultural legacy was what interested Eleanor least, perhaps because it resembled too closely the private acquisitive frenzy taking place in her own branch of the Jonson family. What she really admired were Virginia's Good Works, the hospitals and YMCAs she built, and above all, the new town she created on a four-hundred-acre site, in the hope of clearing Cleveland's slums by giving ideal housing to the poor. It was named Friendship, after her summer place in Newport. When it was completed in 1926, Virginia addressed a 'Greeting' to its first residents in the *Friendship Messenger*.

> Good morning. Is the sun a little brighter, there in Friendship? Is the air a little fresher? Is your home a little sweeter? Is your housework somewhat easier? And the children—do you feel safer about them? Are their faces a little ruddier; are their legs a little sturdier? Do they laugh and play a lot louder in Friendship? Then I am content.

To Eleanor, there had been something deeply moving about this Queen Victoria of Ohio, a little woman with a puffy white face, always dressed in black, always reclusive, seeking no personal glory for her charitable acts, driven by deep religious convictions, still naming streets and buildings after her dead sons right up to the end—her Albert had his Avenue and her Sheldon had his Close in the safer, child-friendly precincts of Friendship.

At the same time, the coolness of relations between the Jonson sisters and their Aunt Virginia showed that in the opinion of her nieces she had not struck the right balance between the civic-minded and the family-minded. If anyone was going to give away Jonson money, the sisters felt that it should be them, rather than the daughter of a penniless clergyman who had married their uncle Thomas. They were each left a hundred thousand dollars in Virginia's will. Even her friends did better. She endowed a trust with two and a half million dollars to provide annuities for sixty-nine friends for the rest of their lives. Patrick suspected that Virginia's talent for annoying Eleanor's mother and her aunts was the unacknowledged source of Eleanor's admiration for her great-aunt. She and Virginia stood apart from the dynastic ambitions of wealth. For them, money was a trust from God that must be used to do good in the world. Patrick hoped that during her frantic silence in the nursing home, Eleanor had been dreaming, at least some of the time, of the place she might occupy next to the great Jonson philanthropist who had Gone Before.

Virginia's meanness to the Jonson Sisters was no doubt underpinned by the knowledge that her brother-in-law would leave each of them with a huge fortune.

Nevertheless, by their generation, the thrill of being rich was already shadowed by the shocks of disinheritance and the ironies of philanthropy. The 1929 Crash came two years after Virginia's death. The poor became destitute, and the white middle classes, who were much poorer than they used to be, fled the inner city for the half-timbered cosiness of Friendship, even though Virginia had built it in memory of a husband who was 'a friend to the Negro race'.

Eleanor's friendship was with something altogether vaguer than the Negro race. 'Friend to the neoshamanic revival of the Celtic Twilight' seemed less likely to yield concrete social progress. During Patrick's childhood, her charitable focus had resembled Virginia's Good Works much more closely, except that it was devoted overwhelmingly to children. He had often been left alone with his father while Eleanor went to a committee meeting of the Save the Children Fund. The absolute banishment of irony from Eleanor's earnest persona created a black market for the blind sarcasm of her actions. Later, it was Father Tortelli and his Neapolitan street urchins who were the targets of her evasive charity. Patrick could not help thinking that this passion for saving all the children of the world was an unconscious admission that she could not save her own child. Poor Eleanor, how frightened she must have been. Patrick suddenly wanted to protect her.

When Patrick's childhood had ended and the inarticulate echoes of her own childhood faded, Eleanor stopped supporting children's charities, and embarked on the second adolescence of her New Age quest. She showed the same genius for generalization that had characterized her rescue of children, except that her identity crisis was not merely global, but interplanetary and cosmic as well, without sinking one millimetre into the resistant bedrock of self-knowledge. No stranger to 'the energy of the universe', she remained a stranger to herself. Patrick could not pretend that he would have applauded any charitable gift involving all his mother's property, but once that became inevitable, it was a further pity that it had all gone to the Transpersonal Foundation.

Aunt Virginia would not have approved either. She wanted to

bring real benefits to fellow human beings. Her influence on Eleanor had been indirect but strong and, like all the other strong influences, matriarchal. The Jonson men sometimes seemed to
Patrick like those diminutive male spiders that quickly discharge
their only important responsibility before being eaten by the much
larger females. The founder's two sons left two widows: Virginia,
the widow of good works, and Eleanor's grandmother, the widow
of good marriages, whose second marriage to the son of an English
earl launched her three daughters on their dazzling social and mat-
rimonial careers. Patrick knew that Nancy had been intending to
write a book about the Jonsons for the last twenty years. Without
any tiresome show of false modesty, she had said to him, 'I mean,
it would be much better than Henry James and Edith Wharton
and those sort of people, because it *really* happened.'

Men who married Jonson women didn't fare much better
than the founder's sons. Eleanor's father and her uncle Vladimir
were both alcoholics, emasculated by getting the heiress they
thought they wanted. They ended up sitting together in White's,
nursing their wounds over a luxurious drink; divorced, discarded,
cut off from their children. Eleanor was brought up wondering
how an heiress could avoid destroying the man she married, unless he was already too corrupt to be destroyed, or rich enough
to be immune. She had chosen from the first category in marrying David, and yet his malice and pride, which were impressive
enough to begin with, were still magnified by the humiliation of
depending on his wife's money.

Patrick was not one of the Jonson castrati by marriage, but
he knew what it was to be born into a matriarchal world, given
money by a grandmother he scarcely knew, and cut off by a
mother who still expected him to look after her. The psychological impact of these powerful women, generous from an im-
personal distance, treacherous up close, had furnished him with
one basic model of what a woman should look like and how she

would in fact turn out to be. The object of desire generated by this combination was the Hiso Bitch—Hiso was an acronym for high society invented by a Japanese friend of his. The Hiso Bitch had to be a reincarnation of a Jonson Sister: glamorous, intensely social, infinitely rich in the pursuit of pleasure, embedded among beautiful possessions. As if this was not enough (as if this was not too much) she also had to be sexually voracious and morally disoriented. His first girlfriend had been an embryonic version of the type. He still thought sometimes about kneeling in front of her, in the pool of light from the reading lamp, the shining folds of her black silk pyjamas gathered between her splayed legs, a trickle of blood running down her proffered arm, the gasp of pleasure, whispering, 'Too much too much,' the film of sweat on her angular face, the syringe in his hand, her first fix of cocaine. He did his best to addict her, but she was a vampire of a different sort, feeding off the despairing obsession of the men who surrounded her, draining ever more socially assured admirers in the hope of acquiring their sense of belonging, even as she trivialized it in their eyes by making herself seem the only thing worth having and then walking away.

In his early thirties his compulsive search for disappointment brought him Inez, the Sistine Chapel of the Hiso Bitch. She insisted that every one of her cartload of lovers was exclusive to her, a condition she failed to secure from her husband, but successfully extorted from Patrick, who left the relatively sane and generous woman he was living with in order to plunge into the hungry vacuum of Inez's love. Her absolute indifference to the feelings of her lovers made her sexual receptiveness into a kind of free-fall. In the end the cliff he fell off was as flat as the one Gloucester was made to leap off by his devoted son: a cliff of blindness and guilt and imagination, with no beetling rocks at its base. But she did not know that and neither did he.

With her curling blonde hair and her slender limbs and her

beautiful clothes, Inez was alluring in an obvious way, and yet it was easy enough to see that her slightly protruding blue eyes were blank screens of self-love on which a small selection of fake emotions was allowed to flicker. She made rather haphazard impersonations of someone who has relationships with others. Based on the gossip of her courtiers, a diet of Hollywood movies and the projection of her own cunning calculations, these guesses might be sentimental or nasty, but were always vulgar and melodramatic. Since she hadn't the least interest in the answer, she was inclined to ask, 'How *are* you?' with great gravity, at least half a dozen times. She was often exhausted by the thought of how generous she was, whereas the exhaustion really stemmed from the strain of not giving away anything at all. 'I'm going to buy six thoroughbred Arab stallions for the Queen of Spain's birthday,' she announced one day. 'Don't you think it's a good idea?'

'Is six enough?' asked Patrick.

'You don't think six is enough? Do you have any idea how much they cost?'

He was amazed when she did buy the horses, less surprised when she kept them for herself and bored when she sold them back to the man she had bought them from. However maddening she was as a friend, it was in the cut and thrust of romance that her talents excelled.

'I've never felt this way before,' she would say with troubled profundity. 'I don't think anybody has really understood me until now. Do you know that? Do you know how important you are to me?' Tears would well up in her eyes as she hardly dared to whisper, 'I don't think I've ever felt at home until now,' nestling in his strong, manly arms.

Soon afterwards he would be left waiting for days in some foreign hotel where Inez never bothered to show up. Her social secretary would call twice a day to say that she had been delayed but was really on her way now. Inez knew that this tantalizing absence was the most efficient way to ensure that he would think of nothing but her, while leaving her free to do the same thing at a safe distance. His mind might wander almost anywhere if she was lying in his arms talking nonsense, whereas if he was nailed to the telephone, haemorrhaging money and abandoning all his other responsibilities, he was bound to think of her constantly. When they did eventually meet up, she would hurry to point out how unbearable it had all been for her, ruthlessly monopolizing the suffering generated by her endlessly collapsing plans.

Why would anyone allow himself to be annihilated by such shallowness, unless a buried image of a careless woman was longing for outward form? Lateness, let-down, longing for the unobtainable: these were the mechanisms that turned a powerful matriarchal stimulant into a powerful maternal depressant. Bewildering lateness, especially, took him directly into an early despair, waiting in vain on the stairs for his mother to come, terrified that she was dead.

Patrick suddenly experienced these old emotions as a physical oppression. He ran his fingers along the inside of his collar to make sure that it was not concealing a tightening noose. He couldn't bear the lure of disappointment any longer, or for that matter the lure of consolation, its Siamese twin. He must somehow get beyond both of them, but first he had to mourn his mother. In a sense he had been missing her all his life. It was not the end of closeness but the end of the longing for closeness that he had to mourn. How futile his longing must have been for him to disperse himself into the land at Saint-Nazaire. If he tried to imagine anything deeper than his old home, he just pictured himself standing there, straining to see something elusive, shielding his eyes to watch a dragonfly dip into the burning water at noon, or starlings twisting against the setting sun.

He could now see that the loss of Saint-Nazaire was not an

obstacle to mourning his mother but the only possible means to do so. Letting go of the imaginary world he had put in her place released him from that futile longing and took him into a deeper grief. He was free to imagine how terrified Eleanor must have been, for a woman of such good intentions, to have abandoned her desire to love him, which he did not doubt, and be compelled to pass on so much fear and panic instead. At last he could begin to mourn her for herself, for the tragic person she had been.

6

PATRICK HAD LITTLE IDEA what to expect from the ceremony. He had been on a business trip to America at the time of his mother's death and pleaded the impossibility of preparing anything to say or read, leaving Mary to take over the arrangements. He had only arrived back from New York yesterday, just in time to go to Bunyon's funeral parlour, and now that he was sitting in a pew next to Mary, picking up the order of service for the first time, he realized how unready he was for this exploration of his mother's confusing life. On the front of the little booklet was a photograph of Eleanor in the sixties, throwing her arms out as if to embrace the world, her dark glasses firmly on and no breathalyser test results available. He hesitated to look inside; this was the muddle, the pile-up of fact and feeling he had been trying to outmanoeuvre since the end of Eleanor's flirtation with assisted suicide two years ago. She had died as a person before her body died, and he had tried to pretend that her life was over before it really was, but no amount of anticipation could cheat the demands of an actual death, and now, with a combination of embarrassment and fear and evasiveness, he leant forward and slipped the order of service back onto the shelf in front of him. He would find out what was in it soon enough.

He had gone to America after receiving a letter from Brown and Stone LLP, the lawyers for the John J. Jonson Corporation, known affectionately as 'Triple J'. They had been informed by 'the family'—Patrick now suspected that it was Henry who had told them—that Eleanor Melrose was incompetent to administer her own affairs, and since she was the beneficiary of a trust created by her grandfather, of which Patrick was the ultimate beneficiary, measures should be taken to procure him a U.S. power of attorney in order to administer the money on his mother's behalf. All this was news to Patrick and he was freshly astonished by his mother's capacity for secrecy. In his amazement he failed to ask how much the trust contained and he got onto the plane to New York not knowing whether he would be put in charge of twenty thousand dollars or two hundred thousand.

Joe Rich and Peter Zirkovsky met him in one of the smaller oval-tabled, glass-sided conference rooms of Brown and Stone's offices on Lexington Avenue. Instead of the sulphurous yellow legal pads he was expecting, he found lined cream paper with the name of the firm printed elegantly on the top of each page. An assistant photocopied Patrick's passport, while Joe examined the doctor's letter testifying to Eleanor's incapacity.

'I had no idea about this trust,' said Patrick.

'Your mother must have been keeping it as a nice surprise,' said Peter with a big lazy smile.

'It might be that,' said Patrick tolerantly. 'Where does the income go?'

'Currently we're sending it to . . .' Peter flicked over a sheet of paper, 'the Association Transpersonel at the Banque Populaire de la Côte d'Azur in Lacoste, France.'

'Well, you can stop that straight away,' said Patrick.

'Whoa, slow down,' said Joe. 'We're going to have to get you a power of attorney first.'

'That's why she didn't tell me about it,' said Patrick, 'because she's continuing to subsidize her pet charity in France while I pay for her nursing-home fees in London.'

'She may have lost her competence before she had a chance to change the instructions,' said Peter, who seemed determined to furnish Patrick with a loving mother.

'This letter is fine,' said Joe. 'We're going to have to get you to sign some documents and get them notarized.'

'How much money are we talking about?' asked Patrick.

'It's not a large Jonson trust and it's suffered in the recent stock-market corrections,' said Joe.

'Let's hope it behaves incorrigibly from now on,' said Patrick.

'The latest valuation we have,' said Peter, glancing down at his notes, 'is two point three million dollars, with an estimated income of eighty thousand.'

'Oh, well, still a useful sum,' said Patrick, trying to sound slightly disappointed.

'Enough to buy a country cottage!' said Peter in an absurd impersonation of an English accent. 'I gather house prices are pretty crazy over there.'

'Enough to buy a second room,' said Patrick, eliciting a polite guffaw from Peter, although Patrick could in fact think of nothing he wanted more than to separate the bed from the sit.

Walking down Lexington Avenue towards his hotel in Gramercy Park, Patrick began adjusting to his strange good fortune. The long arm of his great-grandfather, who had died more than half a century before Patrick was born, was going to pluck him out of his cramped living quarters and get him into a place where there might be room for his children to stay and his friends to visit. In the meantime it would pay for his mother's nursing home. It was puzzling to think that this complete stranger was going to have such a powerful influence on his life. Even his benefactor had inherited his money. It had been his father who had founded the Jonson Candle Company in Cleveland, in 1832.

By 1845 it was one of the most profitable candle companies in the country. Patrick could remember reading the founder's uninspiring explanation for his success: 'We had a new process of distilling cheap greases. Our competitors were using costly tallow and lard. Candles were high and our profits were large for a number of years.' Later, the candle factory diversified into paraffin, oil treatment and hardening processes, and developed a patented compound that became an indispensable ingredient in dry cleaning around the world. The Jonsons also bought buildings and building sites in San Francisco, Denver, Kansas City, Toledo, Indianapolis, Chicago, New York, Trinidad and Puerto Rico, but the original fortune rested on the hard-headedness of the founder who had 'died on the job', falling through a hatchway in one of his own factories, and also on those 'cheap greases' which were still lubricating the life of one of his descendants a hundred and seventy years after their discovery.

John J. Jonson, Jr., Eleanor's grandfather, was already sixty by the time he finally married. He had been travelling the world in the service of his family's burgeoning business, and was only recalled from China by the death of his nephew Sheldon in a sledging accident at St Paul's School. His eldest nephew, Albert, had already died from pneumonia at Harvard the year before. There were no heirs to the Jonson fortune and Sheldon's grieving father, Thomas, told his brother it was his duty to marry. John accepted his fate and, after a brief courtship of a general's daughter, got married and moved to New York. He fathered three daughters in rapid succession, and then dropped dead, but not before creating a multitude of trusts, one of which was meandering its way down to Patrick, as he had discovered that afternoon.

What did this long-range goodwill mean, and what did it say about the social contract that allowed a rich man to free all of his descendents from the need to work over the course of almost

two centuries? There was something disreputable about being
saved by increasingly remote ancestors. When he had exhausted
the money given to him by a grandmother he scarcely knew, money
arrived from a great-grandfather he could never have known. He
could feel only an abstract gratitude towards a man whose face
he would not have been able to pick out from a heap of sepia
daguerreotypes. The ironies of the dynastic drive were just
as great as the philanthropic ironies generated by Eleanor, or
her great-aunt Virginia. No doubt his grandmother and his great-
grandfather had hoped to empower a senator, enrich a great art
collection or encourage a dazzling marriage, but in the end they
had mainly subsidized idleness, drunkenness, treachery and
divorce. Were the ironies of taxation any better: raising money
for schools and hospitals and roads and bridges, and spending it
on blowing up schools and hospitals and roads and bridges in
self-defeating wars? It was hard to choose between these vari-
ously absurd methods of transferring wealth, but just for now he
was going to cave in to the pleasure of having benefited from
this particular form of American capitalism. Only in a country
free from the funnelling of primogeniture and the levelling of
égalité could the fifth generation of a family still be receiving
parcels of wealth from a fortune that had essentially been made
in the 1830s. His pleasure coexisted peacefully with his disapproval, as he walked into his dim and scented hotel, which resembled the film set of an expensive Spanish brothel, with the
room numbers sewn into the carpet, on the assumption that the
guests were on all fours after some kind of near overdose and
could no longer find their rooms as they crawled down the obscure corridors.

The phone was ringing when he arrived in the velvet jewel
box of his room, bathed in the murky urine light of parchment
lampshades and presumptive hangover. He groped his way to
the bedside table, clipping his shin on the bowed legs of a chair

designed to resemble the virile effeminacy of a matador's jacket, with immense epaulettes jutting out proudly from the top of its stiff back.

'Fuck,' he said as he answered the phone.

'Are you all right?' said Mary.

'Oh, hi, sorry, it's you. I just got impaled on this fucking matador chair. I can't see anything in this hotel. They ought to hand out miner's helmets at the reception.'

'Listen, I've got some bad news.' She paused.

Patrick lay back on the pillows with a clear intuition of what she was going to say.

'Eleanor died last night. I'm sorry.'

'What a relief,' said Patrick defiantly. 'Amongst other things . . .'

'Yes, other things as well,' said Mary and she gave the impression of accepting them all in advance.

They agreed to talk in the morning. Patrick had a fervent desire to be left alone matched only by his fervent desire not to be left alone. He opened the minibar and sat on the floor cross-legged, staring at the wall of miniatures on the inside of the door, shining in the dazzling light of the little white fridge. On shelves next to the tumblers and wine glasses were chocolates, jellybeans, salted nuts, treats and bribes for tired bodies and discontented children. He closed the fridge and closed the cupboard door and climbed carefully onto the red velvet sofa, avoiding the matador chair as best he could.

He must try not to forget that only a year ago hallucinations had been crashing into his helpless mind like missiles into a besieged city. He lay down on the sofa, clutching a heavily embroidered cushion to his already aching stomach, and slipped effortlessly into the delirious mentality of his little room in the Priory. He remembered how he used to hear the scratch of a metal nib, or the flutter of moth wings on a screen door, or the swish of a carving knife being sharpened, or the pebble clatter of a retreating wave, as if they were in the same room with him, or rather as if he was in the same place as them. There was a broken rock streaked with the hectic glitter of quartz that quite often lay at the foot of his bed. Blue lobsters explored the edges of the skirting board with their sensitive antennae. Sometimes it was whole scenes that took him over. He would picture, for instance, brake lights streaming across a wet road, the smoky interior of a car, the throb of familiar music, a swollen drop of water rushing down the windscreen, consuming the other drops in its path, and feel that this atmosphere was the deepest thing he had ever known. The absence of narrative in these compulsory waking dreams ushered in a more secretive sense of connection. Instead of trudging across the desert floor of ordinary succession, he was plunged into an oceanic night lit by isolated flares of bioluminescence. He surfaced from these states, unable to imagine how he could describe their haunting power to his Depression Group and longing for his breakfast oxazepam.

He could have all that back with a few months of hard drinking, not just the quicksilver swamps of early withdrawal with their poisonous, fugitive, shattering reflections, and the discreet delirium of the next two weeks, but all the group therapy as well. He could still remember, on his third day in the Alcohol and Addiction Group, wanting to dive out of the window when an old-timer had dropped in to share his experience, strength and hope with the trembling foals of early recovery. A well-groomed ex-meths drinker, with white hair and a smoker's orange fingers, he had quoted the wisdom of an even older-timer who was 'in the rooms' when he first 'came round': 'Fear knocked at the door!' (Pause) 'Courage answered the door!' (Pause) 'And there was nobody there!' (Long pause). He could also have more of the Scottish moderator from the Depression Group, with his cute mnemonic for the power of projection: 'you've got what you spot and you spot what you've got'. And then there were the 'rock bottoms' of the other patients to reconsider, the man who woke next to a girlfriend he couldn't remember slashing with a kitchen knife the night before; the weekend guest surrounded by the hand-painted wallpaper he couldn't remember smearing with excrement; the woman whose arm was amputated when the syringe she picked up from the concrete floor of a friend's flat turned out to be infected with a flesh-eating superbug; the mother who abandoned her terrified children in a remote holiday cottage in order to return to her dealer in London and countless other stories of less demonstrative despair—moments of shame that precipitated 'moments of clarity' in the pilgrim's progress of recovery.

All in all, the minibar was out. His month in the Priory had worked. He knew as deeply as he knew anything that sedation was the prelude to anxiety, stimulation the prelude to exhaustion and consolation the prelude to disappointment, and so he lay on the red velvet sofa and did nothing to distract himself from the news of his mother's death. He stayed awake through the night feeling unconvincingly numb. At five in the morning, when he calculated that Mary would be back from the school run in London, he called her flat and they agreed that she would take over the arrangements for the funeral.

The organ fell silent, interrupting Patrick's daydream. He picked up the booklet again from the narrow shelf in front of him, but before he had time to look inside, music burst out from the speakers in the corners of the room. He recognized the song just before the deep black cheerful voice rang out over the crematorium.

> *Oh, I got plenty o' nuthin',*
> *An' nuthin's plenty fo' me.*
> *I got no car, got no mule, I got no misery.*
> *De folks wid plenty o' plenty*

Got a lock on dey door,
'Fraid somebody's a-goin' to rob 'em
While dey's out a-makin' more.
What for?

Patrick looked round and smiled mischievously at Mary. She smiled back. He suddenly felt irrationally guilty that he hadn't yet told her about the trust, as if he were no longer entitled to enjoy the song, now that he didn't have quite as much *nuthin'* as before. *More. / What for?* was a rhyme that deserved to be made more often.

Oh, I got plenty o' nuthin',
An' nuthin's plenty fo' me.
I got de sun, got de moon,
Got de deep blue sea.
De folks wid plenty o' plenty,
Got to pray all de day.
Seems wid plenty you sure got to worry
How to keep de debble away,
A-way.

Patrick was entertained by Porgy's insistence on the sinfulness of riches. He felt that Eleanor and aunt Virginia would have approved. After all, before they became masters of the universe, usurers were consigned to the seventh circle of Hell. Under a rain of fire, their perpetually restless hands were a punishment for hands that had made nothing useful or good in their lifetime, just exploited the labour of others. Even from the less breezy position of being one of the *folks wid plenty o' plenty*, and at the cost of buying into the fantasy that folks with *plenty o' nuttin'* didn't also have to worry about keeping the *Debble* away, Eleanor would have endorsed Porgy's views. Patrick renewed his concentration for the final part of the song.

> *Never one to strive*
> *To be good, to be bad—*
> *What the hell! I is glad*
> *I's alive!*
>
> *Oh, I got plenty o' nuthin',*
> *An' nuthin's plenty fo' me.*
> *I got my gal, got my song,*
> *Got Hebben de whole day long.*
> *(No use complainin'!)*
> *Got my gal, got my Lawd, got my song!*

'Great choice,' Patrick whispered to Mary with a grateful nod. He picked up the order of service again, finally ready to look inside.

7

HOW NAUSEATING, THOUGHT NICHOLAS, a Jew being sentimental on behalf of a Negro: you lucky fellows, you've got plenty o'
nuthin', whereas we're weighed down with all this international
capital and these wretched Broadway musical hits. When an idea
is floundering, Nicholas said to himself, practising for later, song-
writers always wheel out the celestial bodies. *De things dat I prize, /
Like de stars in de skies, / All are free.* No surprises there—one couldn't
expect to get much rent from a hydrogen bomb several million
light-years away. It was hard enough persuading a merchant banker
to cough up a decent rent for one's lovely Grade II listed Queen
Anne dower house in Shropshire, without asking him to drive to
the moon for the weekend. Talk about too far from London, and
nothing to do when one got there, except bounce around while the
oxygen runs out. There was such a thing as the way of the world.
Sixty per cent of the *Titanic's* first-class passengers survived;
twenty-five percent of the second-class passengers, and no one
from steerage. That was the way of the world. 'Sure is grateful,
boss,' simpered Nicholas under his breath, 'I got de deep blue sea.'

Oh, God, what was going on now? The ghastly 'Spiritual Tool
Box' was going up to the lectern. He could hardly bear it. What
was he doing here? In the end, he was just as sentimental as silly

old Ira Gershwin. He had come for David Melrose. In many ways David had been an obscure failure, but his presence had possessed a rare and precious quality: pure contempt. He bestrode middle-class morality like a colossus. Other people laboured through the odd bigoted remark, but David had embodied an absolute disdain for the opinion of the world. One could only do one's best to keep up the tradition.

For Erasmus the most interesting lines were undoubtedly, *Never one to strive / To be good, to be bad—/ What the hell! I is glad / I's alive!* Nietzsche was there, of course, and Rousseau (inevitably), but also the Diamond Sutra. Porgy was unlikely to have read any of them. Nevertheless, it was legitimate to think in terms of the pervasive influence of a certain family of ideas, of non-striving and of a natural state that preceded rule-based morality and in some sense made it redundant. Maybe he could see Mary after the funeral. She had always been so receptive. He sometimes thought about that.

Thank goodness there were people who were happy with nothing, thought Julia, so that people like her (and everyone else she had ever met), could have *more*. It was virtually impossible to think of a sentence that made a positive use of that dreadful word 'enough', let alone one that started raving about 'nothing'. Still, the song was rather perfect for Patrick's dotty mother, as well as being an upbeat disinheritance anthem. Hats off to Mary, as usual. Julia sighed with admiration. She assumed that Patrick had been feeling too 'mad' to do anything practical, and that Mother Mary had been asked to step in.

Really, thought Nancy, it was too ridiculous to turn to the Gershwin brothers when one's own godfather was the divine Cole Porter. Why had Mummy wasted him on indifferent Eleanor when Nancy, who really appreciated his glamour and wit, might have had him all to herself? Not that *Porgy and Bess* didn't have its glamorous side. She had gone to a big New York opening with Hansie and Dinkie Guttenburg and had the best time ever, going backstage to congratulate everybody. The real stars weren't at all overawed by meeting a ferociously handsome German prince with a severe stutter, but you could tell that some of the little chorus girls didn't know whether to curtsy, start a revolution, or poison his wife. She would definitely include that scene in her book, it was such a coming together of everything fun, unlike this drab funeral. Really, Eleanor was letting the family down and letting herself down as well.

Annette was stunned, as she walked down the aisle towards the lectern, by the appropriateness, the serendipity and the synchronicity of that wonderful, spiritual song. Only yesterday she had been sitting with Seamus at their favourite power point on the terrace at Saint-Nazaire (actually they had decided that it was the heart chakra of the entire property, which made perfect sense when you thought about it), celebrating Eleanor's unique gifts with a glass of red wine, and Seamus had mentioned her incredibly strong connection with the African-American people. He had been privileged to be present at several of Eleanor's past-life regressions and it turned out that she had been a runaway slave during the American Civil War, trying to make her way to the abolitionist North with a young baby in her arms. She'd had the most terrible time of it, apparently, only travelling at night, in the dead of winter, hiding in ditches and living in fear for her life. And now, the very next day, at Eleanor's funeral, a man who was obviously the descendant of a slave was singing those marvellous lyrics. Perhaps—Annette almost came to a halt, overwhelmed by further horizons of magical coincidence—perhaps he was the very baby Eleanor had carried to freedom through the ditches and the night, grown into a splendid man with a deep and resonant voice. It was almost unbearably beautiful, but she had a task to perform and with a regretful tug she extracted herself from the amazing dimension to which her train of thought had transported her, and stood squarely at the lectern, unfolding the pages she had been carrying in the pocket of her dress. She fingered the amber necklace she had bought at the Mother Meera gift shop when she had gone for *darshan* with the avatar of Talheim. Feeling mysteriously empowered by the silent Indian woman whose gaze of unconditional love had x-rayed her soul and set her off on the healing path she was still following today, Annette addressed the group of mourners in a voice torn between an expression of pained tenderness and the need for an adequate volume.

'I'm going to start by reading a poem that I know was close to Eleanor's heart. I introduced her to it, actually, and I know how much it spoke to her. I am sure that many of you will be familiar with it. It's "The Lake Isle of Innisfree" by William Butler Yeats.' She started reading in a loud lilting whisper.

> *I will arise and go now, and go to Innisfree,*
> *And a small cabin build there, of clay and wattles made;*
> *Nine bean rows will I have there, a hive for the honey bee,*
> *And live alone in the bee-loud glade.*

Whereas it was sophisticated enough to order nine oysters, thought Nicholas, there was something utterly absurd about nine bean rows. Oysters naturally came in dozens and half-dozens—for all he knew, they grew on the seabed in dozens and half-dozens—and so there was something understandably elegant about ordering nine of them. Beans, on the other hand, came in vague fields and profuse heaps, making the prissy precision of nine ridiculous. At the very least it conjured up a dissonant vision of an urban allotment in which there was hardly likely to be room for a clay and wattle cabin and a bee-loud glade. No doubt the Spiritual Tool Box thought that 'Innisfree' was the climax of Yeats's talent, and no doubt the Celtic Twilight, with its wilful innocence and its tawdry effects, was perfectly suited to Eleanor's other-worldly worldview, but in reality the Irish Bard had only emerged from an entirely forgettable mauve mist when he became the mouthpiece for the aristocratic ideal. '*Surely among a rich man's flowering lawns, / Amid the rustle of his planted hills, / Life overflows without ambitious pains; / And rains down life until the basin spills.*' Those were the only lines of Yeats worth memorizing, which was just as well since they were the only ones he could remember. Those lines inaugurated a meditation on the 'bitter and violent' men who performed great deeds and built great houses, and of what happened to that greatness as it turned over time into mere privilege: '*And maybe the great-grandson of that house, / For all its bronze and marble, 's but a mouse.*' A risky line if it weren't for all the great mouse-infested houses one had known. That was why it was so essential, as Yeats was suggesting, to remain bitter and angry, in order to ward off the debilitating effects of inherited glory.

Annette's voice redoubled its excruciated gentleness for the second stanza.

And I shall have some peace there, for peace comes dropping slow,
Dropping from the veils of the morning to where the cricket sings;
There midnight's all a-glimmer, and noon a purple glow,
And evening full of the linnet's wings.

Peace comes dropping slow, thought Henry, how beautiful. The lines lengthening with the growing tranquillity, and the deepening jet lag, and his head dropping slow, dropping slow onto his chest. He needed an espresso, or the veils of mourning were going to shroud his mind entirely. He was here for Eleanor, Eleanor on the lake at Fairley, alone in a rowing boat, refusing to come back in, everybody standing on the shore shouting, 'Come back! Your mother's here! Your mother's arrived!' For a girl who was too shy to look you in the eye, she could be as stubborn as a mule.

Where the cricket sings, thought Patrick, is where you live with Seamus in my old home. He imagined the shrill grating coming from the grass and the gradual build-up, cicada by cicada, of pulsing waves of sound, like auditory heat shimmering over the dry land.

Mary was relieved that *plenty o' nuthin'* seemed to have gone down well with Patrick, and she felt that the make-believe simplicity of 'Innisfree' was a charming reminder of Eleanor's yearning to exclude the dark complexities of life at any price. What Mary couldn't relax about was the address she had asked Annette to make. And yet what could she do? There was no point in denying that side of Eleanor's life and Annette was better qualified than anyone else in the room to talk about it. At least it would give Patrick something to rant about for the next few days. She listened to Annette's singsong, cradle-rocking delivery of the final stanza of 'Innisfree' with growing dread.

> *I will arise and go now, for always night and day*
> *I hear the lake water lapping with low sounds by the shore;*

While I stand on the roadway, or on the pavements grey,
I hear it in the deep heart's core.

Annette closed her eyes and reached again for her amber
necklace. '*Om namo Matta Meera,*' she murmured, re-empowering
herself for the speech she was about to make.

'All of you will have known Eleanor in different ways, and
many of you for much longer than me,' she began with an understanding smile. 'I can only talk about the Eleanor that I knew,
and while I try to do justice to the wonderful woman that she
was, I hope you will hold the Eleanor that you knew in what
Yeats calls *the deep heart's core*. But at the same time, if I show you
a side of her that you didn't know, all I would ask is that you let
her in, let her in and let her join the Eleanor that each of you is
holding in your heart.'

Oh, Jesus, thought Patrick, let me out of here. He imagined
himself disappearing through the floor with a shovel and some
bunk-bed slats, the theme music of *The Great Escape* humming in
the air. He was crawling under the crematorium through fragile
tunnels, when he felt himself being dragged backwards by
Annette's maddening voice.

'I first met Eleanor when a group of us from the Dublin Wom-
en's Healing Drum Circle were invited down to Saint-Nazaire,
her wonderful house in Provence, which I'm sure many of you
are familiar with. As we were coming down the drive in our
minibus, I caught my first glimpse of Eleanor sitting on the wall
of the big pond, with her hands tucked under her thighs, for all
the world like a lonely young child staring down at her dangling
shoes. By the time we arrived in front of the pond she was liter-

ally greeting us with open arms, but I never lost that first impression of her, just as I think she never lost a connection to the child-like quality that made her believe so passionately that justice could be achieved, that consciousness could be transformed and that there was goodness to be found in every person and every situation, however hidden it might seem at first sight.'

Of course consciousness can be transformed, thought Erasmus, but what is it? If I pass an electric current through my body, or bury my nose in the soft petals of a rose, or impersonate Greta Garbo, I transform my consciousness; in fact it is impossible to stop transforming consciousness. What I can't do is describe what it is *in itself*: it's too close to see, too ubiquitous to grasp and too transparent to point to.

'Eleanor was one of the most generous people it has been my privilege to know. You only had to hint that you needed something and if it was in her power to provide it, she would leap at the opportunity with an enthusiasm that made it look as if it was a relief to her rather than to the person who was asking.'

Patrick imagined the simple charm of the dialogue.
    Seamus: I was thinking that it would be, eh, consciousness-
       raising, like, to own a private hamlet surrounded by
       vines and olive groves, somewhere sunny.
    Eleanor: Oh, how amazing! I've got one of those. Would
       you like it?
    Seamus: Oh, thank you very much, I'm sure. Sign here and
       here and here.
    Eleanor: What a relief. Now I have nothing.

'Nothing,' said Annette, 'was too much trouble for her. Service to others was her life's purpose, and it was awe-inspiring to see the lengths she would go to in her quest to help people achieve their dreams. A torrent of grateful letters and postcards used to arrive at the Foundation from all over the world. A young Croatian scientist who was working on a "zero-energy fuel cell"—don't ask me what that is, but it's going to save the planet—is one example. A Peruvian archaeologist who had uncovered amazing evidence that the Incas were originally from Egypt and continued to communicate with the mother civilization through what he called "solar language". An old lady who had been working for forty years on a universal dictionary of sacred symbols and just needed a little extra help to bring this incredibly valuable book to completion. All of them had received a helping hand from Eleanor. But you mustn't think that Eleanor was only concerned with the higher echelons of science and spirituality, she was also a marvellously practical person who knew the value of a kitchen extension for a growing family, or a new car for a friend living in the depths of the country.'

What about a sister who was running out of cash? thought Nancy grumpily. First they had taken away her credit cards, and then they had taken away her chequebook, and now she had to go in person to the Morgan Guaranty on Fifth Avenue to collect her monthly pocket money. They said it was the only way to stop her running up debts, but the best way to stop her running up debts was to give her more money.

'There was a wonderful Jesuit gentleman,' Annette continued, 'well, he was an ex-Jesuit actually, although we still called him Father Tim. He had come to believe that Catholic dogma was too narrow and that we should embrace all the religious traditions of the world. He eventually became the first Englishman to be accepted as an *ayahuascera*—a Brazilian shaman—among one of the most authentic tribes in Amazonia. Anyhow, Father Tim wrote to Eleanor, who had known him in his old Farm Street days, saying that his village needed a motor-boat to go down to the local trading post, and of course she responded with her usual impulsive generosity, and sent a cheque by return. I shall never forget the expression on her face when she received Father Tim's reply. Inside the envelope were three brightly coloured toucan feathers and an equally colourful note explaining that in recognition of her gift to the Ayoreo people, a ritual had been performed in Father Tim's far-away village inducting her into the tribe as a "Rainbow Warrior". He said that he had refrained from mentioning that she was a woman, since the Ayoreo took a "somewhat unreconstructed view of the gentler sex, not unreminiscent of that taken by old Mother Church", and that he would have "suffered the fate of St. Sebastian" if he "admitted to his ruse." He said that he intended to confess on his deathbed, so as to help move the tribe forward into a new era of harmony between the male and female principles, so necessary to the salvation of the world. Anyhow,' sighed Annette, recognizing that she had drifted from her written text, but taking this to be a sign of inspiration, 'the effect on Eleanor was quite literally magical. She wore the toucan feathers around her neck until they sadly disintegrated, and for a few weeks she told all and sundry that she was an Ayoreo Rainbow Warrior. She was for all the world like the little girl who goes to a new school and comes home one day transformed because she has made a new best friend.'

Although arrested development was his stock in trade and he made a habit of shutting down his psychoanalytic ear when he was not working, Johnny could not help being struck by the ferocious tenacity of Eleanor's resistance to growing up. He was as guilty as anyone of over-quoting good old Eliot's 'Human kind cannot bear very much reality', but he felt that in this case the evasiveness had been uninterrupted. He could remember first meeting Eleanor when Patrick invited him to Saint-Nazaire for the school holidays. Even then she had a habit of lapsing into baby talk, very disconcerting for adolescents distancing themselves from childhood. The tragedy was that five or perhaps ten years of decent five-day-a-week analysis could have mitigated the problem significantly.

'That was the sort of breadth that Eleanor showed in her kindness to others,' said Annette, sensing that it would soon be time to draw her remarks to a conclusion. She put aside a couple of pages she had failed to read during her Amazonian improvisation, and looked down at the last page to remind herself what she had written. It struck her as a little formal now that she had entered into a more exploratory style, but there were one or two things embedded in the last paragraph that she must remember to say.

Oh, please get on with it, thought Patrick. Charles Bronson was having a panic attack in a collapsing tunnel, Alsatians were barking behind the barbed wire, searchlights were weaving over the breached ground, but soon he would be running through the woods, dressed as a German bank clerk and heading for the railway station with some identity papers forged at the expense of Donald Pleasance's eyesight. It would all be over soon, he just had to keep staring at his knees for a few minutes longer.

'I would like to read you a short passage from the *Rig Veda*,' said Annette. 'It quite literally leapt at me from the shelf when I was in the library at the Foundation, looking for a book that would evoke something of Eleanor's amazing spiritual depths.' She resumed her singsong reading voice.

> *She follows to the goal of those who are passing on beyond, she is the first in the eternal succession of the dawns that are coming,—Usha widens bringing out that which lives, awakening someone who was dead ... What is her scope when she harmonizes with the dawns that shone out before and those that now must shine? She desires the ancient mornings and fulfils their light; projecting forwards her illumination she enters into communion with the rest that are to come.*

'Eleanor was a firm believer in reincarnation, and not only did she regard suffering as the refining fire that would burn away the impediments to a still higher spiritual evolution, but she was also privileged to have something very rare indeed: a specific vision of how and where she would be reincarnated. At the Foundation we have what we call an "Ah-ha Box" for those little epiphanies and moments of insight when we think, "Ah-ha!" We all have them, don't we? But the trouble is that they slip away during the course of a busy day and so Seamus, the Chief Facilitator of the Foundation, invented the Ah-ha Box so that we could write down our thoughts, pop them in the box and share them in the evening.'

Annette felt the lure of anecdote and digression, resisted for a few seconds, and then caved in. 'We used to have a trainee shaman with a shall I say "challenging" personality, and he was in the habit of having about a dozen Ah-ha moments a day. Many of them turned out to be covert, or not so covert, attacks on other people in the Foundation. Well, one evening when we had all waded through at least ten of his so-called epiphanies, Seamus said, in his incomparably humorous way, "You know, Dennis, one man's Ah-ha moment is another man's Ho-ho moment." And I remember Eleanor simply cracking up. I can still see her now. She covered her mouth because she thought it would be unkind to laugh too much, but she couldn't help herself. I don't think any portrait of Eleanor would be complete without that naughty giggle and that quick, trusting smile.

'Anyhow,' said Annette, recovering her sense of direction for a final assault, 'as I was saying: one day, after her first stroke but before she moved into the French nursing home, we found this amazing note from Eleanor in the Ah-ha Box. The note said that she had been on a vision quest and she had seen that she would be returning to Saint-Nazaire in her next lifetime. She would come back as a young shaman and Seamus and I would be very old by then, and we would hand the Foundation back to her as she had handed it to us in what she called a "seamless continuity". And I would like to end by asking you to hold that phrase, "seamless continuity", in your minds, while we sit here for a few moments in silence and pray for Eleanor's swift return.'

Standing behind the lectern, Annette lowered her head, exhaled solemnly and shut her eyes.

8

MARY THOUGHT THAT 'SWIFT RETURN' was going a bit far. She glanced nervously at the coffin, as if Eleanor might fling off the lid and hop out at any moment, throwing open her arms to embrace the world, with the awkward theatricality of the photograph on the order of service. Sensing Patrick's radiant embarrassment, she regretted asking Annette to make an address, but it was hard to think of anyone who could have spoken instead. Eleanor's slash and burn social life had destroyed continuity and deep friendship, especially after the lonely years of dementia and the fractured relationship with Seamus.

Mary had asked Johnny to read a poem and she had even been desperate enough to get Erasmus to read a passage. Nancy, the only alternative, had been hysterical with self-pity and unclear about when she was getting in from New York. The rather strained choice of readers was balanced (or made worse) by the familiarity of the passages she had chosen. Two great biblical staples were coming up next, and she now felt that it was intolerably boring of her to have picked them. On the other hand, nobody knew anything about death, except that it was unavoidable, and since everyone was terrified by that uncertain certainty, perhaps the opaque magnificence of the Bible, or even the vague

Asiatic immensities that Annette obviously preferred, were better than a wilful show of novelty. Besides, Eleanor had been a Christian, amongst so many other things.

As soon as Annette sat down it would be Mary's turn to replace her at the front of the room. The truth was, she was feeling slightly mad. She got up with a reluctance that cunningly disguised itself as a feeling of unbearable urgency, squeezed past Patrick without looking him in the eye and made her way to the lectern. When she told people how nervous she was about any kind of public appearance, they said incredibly annoying things like, 'Don't forget to breathe.' Now she knew why. First she felt that she was going to faint and then, as she started to read the passage she had rehearsed a hundred times, she felt that she was choking as well.

> *Though I speak with the tongues of men and angels, and*
> *have not love, I am become a sounding brass, or a tinkling*
> *cymbal. And though I have the gift of prophecy, and*
> *understand all mysteries and all knowledge; and though I*
> *have all faith, so that I could remove mountains, and have*
> *not love, I am nothing. And though I bestow all my goods to*
> *feed the poor, and though I give my body to be burned and*
> *have not love, it profiteth me nothing.*

Mary felt a scratching sensation in her throat, but she tried to persevere without coughing.

> *Love suffereth long, and is kind; love envieth not: love*
> *vaunteth not itself, is not puffed up, doth not behave itself*
> *unseemly, seeketh not her own, is not easily provoked,*
> *thinketh no evil, rejoiceth not in iniquity, but rejoiceth in*
> *the truth; beareth all things, believeth all things, hopeth all*
> *things, endureth all things. Love never faileth:*

Mary cleared her throat and turned her head aside to cough. Now she had ruined everything. She couldn't help feeling that there was a psychological connection between this part of the passage and her coughing fit. When she had read it yet again this morning, it had struck her as the zenith of false modesty: love boasting about not boasting, love unbelievably pleased with itself for not being puffed up. Until then, it had seemed to be an expression of the highest ideals, but now she was so tired and nervous she couldn't quite shake off the feeling that it was one of the most pompous things ever written. Where was she? She looked at the page with a kind of swimming panic. Then she spotted where she had left off, and pressed forward, feeling that her voice did not quite belong to her.

> *but whether there be prophecies, they shall fail; whether there be tongues, they shall cease; whether there be knowledge, it shall vanish away. For we know in part, and we prophesy in part. But when that which is perfect is come, then that which is in part shall be done away.*
>
> *When I was a child, I spake as a child, I understood as a child: but when I became a man, I put away childish things. For now we see through a glass, darkly; but then face to face: now I know in part; but then shall I know even as also I am known.*
>
> *And now abideth faith, hope, love, these three; the greatest of these is love.*

Erasmus had not listened to Mary's reading of St. Paul's Epistle to the Corinthians. Ever since Annette's address, he had been lost in speculation about the doctrine of reincarnation and whether it deserved to be called 'literally nonsensical'. It was a phrase that reminded him of Victor Eisen, the Melrose family's philosopher friend of the sixties and seventies. In philosophical

discussions, after a series of vigorous proofs, 'literally nonsensical' used to rush out of him like salt from a cellar that suddenly
loses its top. Although he was now a rather faded figure without
any enduring work to his name, Eisen had been a fluent and con-
ceited public intellectual during Erasmus's youth. In his eagerness to dismiss, which in the end may have secured his own
dismissal, he would certainly have found reincarnation 'literally
nonsensical': its evidence-free, memory-free, discarnate narrative failed to satisfy the Parfittian criteria of personal identity.
Who is being reincarnated? That was the devastating question,
unless the person who was asked happened to be a Buddhist. For
him the answer was 'Nobody'. Nobody was reincarnated because
nobody had been incarnated in the first place. Something much
looser, like a stream of thought, had taken human form. Neither
a soul nor a personal identity was needed to precipitate a human
life, just a cluster of habits clinging to the hollow concept of independent existence, like a crowd of grasping passengers sinking
the lifeboat they imagined would save them. In the background
was the ever-present opportunity to slip away into the glittering
ocean of a true nature that was not personal either. From this
point of view, it was Parfitt and Eisen who were literally nonsensical. Still, Erasmus had no problem with a rejection of reincarnation on the grounds that there was no good reason to believe that
it was true—as long as the implicit physicalism of such a rejection
was also rejected! The correlation between brain activity and consciousness could be evidence, after all, that the brain was a receiver
of consciousness, like a transistor, or a transceiver, and not the
skull-bound generator of a private display. The . . .

Erasmus's thoughts were interrupted by the sensation of a
hand resting on his shoulder and shaking him gently. His neighbour, after securing his attention, pointed to Mary, who stood in
the aisle looking at him significantly. She gave him what he felt

was a somewhat curt nod, reminding him that it was his turn to read. He rose with an apologetic smile and, crushing the toes of the woman who had shaken him on the shoulder, made his way towards the front of the room. The passage he had to read was from Revelations—or Obfuscations, as he preferred to call them. Reading it over on the train from Cambridge, he had felt a strange desire to build a time machine so that he could take the author a copy of Kant's *Critique of Pure Reason*.

Erasmus put on his reading glasses, flattened the page against the slope of the lectern, and tried to master his longing to point out the unexamined assumptions that riddled the famous passage he was about to read. He might not be able to infuse his voice with the required feeling of awe and exaltation, but he could at least eliminate any signs of scepticism and indignation. With the inner sigh of a man who doesn't want to be blamed for what's coming next, Erasmus set about his task.

> *Then I saw a new heaven and a new earth, for the first heaven and the first earth had passed away, and the sea was no more.*

Nancy was still furious with the clumsy oaf who had stepped on her toes and now, on top of that, he was proposing to take the sea away. No more sea meant no more seaside, no more Cap d'Antibes (although it had been completely ruined), no more Portofino (unbearable in the summer), no more Palm Beach (which was not what it used to be).

> *And I saw the holy city, new Jerusalem,*

Oh, no, not another Jerusalem, thought Nancy. Isn't one enough?

*coming down out of heaven from God, prepared as a bride
adorned for her husband; and I heard a great voice from the
throne saying, 'Behold, the dwelling of God is with men. He
will dwell with them and they shall be his people, and God
himself will be with them; he will wipe away every tear
from their eyes, and death shall be no more neither shall
there be mourning nor crying nor pain any more, for the
former things have passed away.'*

All these readings from the Bible were getting on Nancy's
nerves. She didn't want to think about death—it was depressing.
At a proper funeral there were amazing choirs that didn't usually sing at private events, and tenors who were practically impossible to get hold of, and readings by famous actors or
distinguished public figures. It made the whole thing fun and
meant that one hardly ever thought about death, even when the
readings were exactly the same, because one was struggling to
remember when some tired-looking person had been chancellor
of the exchequer, or what the name of their last movie was. That
was the miracle of glamour. The more she thought about it, the
more furious she felt about Eleanor's dreary funeral. Why, for
instance, had she decided to be cremated? Fire was something
one dreaded. Fire was something one insured against. The Egyp-
tians had got it right with the pyramids. What could be cosier
than something huge and permanent with all one's things tucked
away inside (and other people's things as well! Lots and lots of
things!) built by thousands of slaves who took the secret of the
construction with them to unmarked graves. Nowadays one would
have to make prohibitive social-security payments to teams of
unionized construction workers. That was modern life for you.
Nevertheless, some sort of big monument was infinitely preferable to an urn and a handful of dust.

And he who sat upon the throne said, 'Behold, I make all things new.' Also he said, 'Write this, for these words are trustworthy and true.' And he said to me, 'It is done. I am the Alpha and the Omega, the beginning and the end. To the thirsty I will give water without price from the fountain of the water of life. He who conquers shall have this heritage, and I will be his God and he will be my son.'

Johnny couldn't help being reminded by all these readings of a paper he had written in his opinionated youth, called 'Omnipotence and Denial: The Lure of Religious Belief.' He had made the simple point that religion inverted everything that we dread about human existence: we're all going to die (we're all going to live for ever); life is terribly unfair (there will be absolute and perfect justice); it's horrible being downtrodden and powerless (the meek shall inherit the earth); and so on. The inversion had to be complete; it was no use saying that life was pretty unfair but not quite as unfair as it sometimes seemed. The pallor of Hades may have been its doom: after making the leap of believing that consciousness did not end with death, a realm of restless shadows pining for blood, muscle, battle and wine must have seemed a thin prize. Achilles said that it was preferable to be a slave on earth than king in the underworld. With that sort of endorsement an afterlife was headed for extinction. Only something perfectly counterfactual could secure global devotion. In his paper Johnny had drawn parallels between this spectacular denial of the depressing and frightening aspects of reality and the operation of the unconscious in the individual patient. He had gone on to make more detailed comparisons between various forms of mental illness and what he imagined to be their corresponding religious discourse, with the disadvantage of knowing nothing about the religious half of the comparison. Feeling

that he might as well solve all the world's problems in twelve
thousand words, he had tied in political repression with personal
repression, and made all the usual points about social control.
The underlying assumption of the paper was that authenticity
was the only project that mattered and that religious belief necessarily stood in its way. He was now faintly embarrassed by the
lack of subtlety and self-doubt in his twenty-nine-year-old self.
Still in training, he hadn't yet had a patient, and was therefore
much more certain about the operation of the human psyche
than he was today.

Mary had asked him to read a long poem by Henry Vaughan
that he had never come across before. She told him that it fitted
perfectly with Eleanor's view that life was an exile from God,
and death a homecoming. Other, more enjoyable poems had
seemed conventional or irrelevant by contrast, and Mary had
decided to stay loyal to Eleanor's metaphysical nostalgia. As far
as Johnny was concerned, giving a religious status to these moods
of longing was just another form of resistance. Wherever we
came from and wherever we were going (and whether those ideas
meant anything at all) it was the bit in between that counted. As
Wittgenstein had said, 'Death is not an event in life: we do not
live to experience death.'

Johnny smiled vaguely at Erasmus as they crossed paths in
the aisle. He balanced his copy of *The Metaphysical Poets* on the
ledge of the lectern and opened it on the page he had marked
with a taxi receipt. His voice was strong and confident as he read.

> *Happy those early days, when I*
> *Shin'd in my Angel-infancy!*
> *Before I understood this place*
> *Appointed for my second race,*
> *Or taught my soul to fancy aught*
> *But a white celestial thought;*

When yet I had not walk'd above
A mile or two from my first Love,
And looking back—at that short space—
Could see a glimpse of His bright face;
When on some gilded cloud or flower
My gazing soul would dwell an hour,
And in those weaker glories spy
Some shadows of eternity;
Before I taught my tongue to wound
My Conscience with a sinful sound,
Or had the black art to dispense
A several sin to ev'ry sense,
But felt through all this fleshly dress
Bright shoots of everlastingness.

Nicholas had started to feel that special sense of claustrophobia he associated with being trapped in chapel at school. Wave after wave of Christian sentiment without even the consolation of an overdue Latin translation tucked furtively in his hymnal. He cheered himself up with his own version of the Christian story: God sent his only begotten son to Earth in order to save the poor, and it was a complete washout, like all half-baked socialist projects; but then the Supreme Being came to his senses and sent Nicholas to save the rich, and it came to pass that it was an absolute *succès fou*. No doubt with its deplorable history of torture, Inquisition, religious wars, crushing dogma, as well as its altogether more forgivable history of sexual impropriety and worldly self-indulgence, the Roman Catholic Church would look on this crucial development as a heresy; but a heresy was only the prelude to a new Protestant religious order. 'Nicholism' would sweep through what his ghastly American investment adviser called the 'high-net-worth community'. The great question, as always, was what to wear. As the Arch Plutocrat of the Church for the Redemption of Latter-Day Riches one had to cut a dash. Nicholas's imagination wandered back to the page's outfit he had worn as a ten-year-old boy at a very grand royal wedding—the silk breeches, the silver buttons, the buckled shoes . . . he had never felt quite as sure of his own importance since that day.

Johnny renewed his efforts at intonation for the final stanza.

> O how I long to travel back,
> And tread again that ancient track!
> That I might once more reach that plain
> Where first I left my glorious train;
> From whence th' enlighten'd spirit sees
> That shady City of Palm-trees.
> But ah! my soul with too much stay
> Is drunk, and staggers in the way!
> Some men a forward motion love,
> But I by backward steps would move;
> And when this dust falls to the urn,
> In that state I came, return.

Complete rubbish, thought Nicholas, to imply that one returned to the place from which one came. How could it be the same after one's immensely colourful contribution, and how could one's attitude to it be the same after passing through this Vale of Invitations and Sardonic Laughter? He glanced down at the order of service. It looked as if that poem by Vaughan was the last reading. At the bottom of the page there was a note inviting everyone to join the family at the Onslow Club for a drink after the ceremony. He would love to get out of it, but in a moment of reckless generosity he had promised Nancy that he would accompany her. He also had a four o'clock appointment to visit a dying friend at the Chelsea and Westminster Hospital and so it was in fact conveniently nearby. Thank goodness he had booked a car for the day; with distances of that kind (about six hundred yards) one always had to put up with the ill temper of cab drivers who were drifting around the Fulham Road dreaming of a fare to Gatwick or Penzance. He must keep a firm hold on his car; otherwise Nancy would commandeer it for her own purposes. He could easily totter out of the hospital, suffering from the 'compassion burn-out' he knew sometimes afflicted the most heroic nurses, only to find that his car was in Berkeley Square where Nancy was trying to bamboozle a Morgan Guaranty employee into giving her some cash. Her cousin Henry, who had unexpectedly turned up today, had once told him that when he and Nancy were children she had been known as 'the Kleptomaniac'. Little things used to disappear—special hairbrushes, childish jewellery, cherished piggy banks—and turn up in the magpie's nest of Nancy's bedroom. Parents and nannies explained, pedantically at first and then with growing anger, that stealing was wrong, but the temptation was too strong for Nancy and she was expelled from a series of boarding schools for theft and lying. Ever since Nicholas had known her, she had been locked into a state of covetousness, a sense of how much better she would have used, and how much more she deserved, the fabulous possessions belonging to her friends and family. She resisted envying things which belonged to people she didn't know at all, but only to distance herself from her maid, who filled the kitchen with prurient babble about the lives of soap-opera stars. Her recounting of their commonplace 'tragedies' was used to soothe what had been excited by earlier stories of unmerited rewards and ludicrous lifestyles.

Celebrities were all very well for the masses, but what counted for Nicholas was what he called 'the big world', namely the minuscule number of people whose background, looks, or talent to amuse made them worth having to dinner. Nancy belonged to the big world by birth and could not be exiled from that paradise by her perfectly ghastly personality. One had to be loyal to something, and since it offered more scope for treachery than anything except politics, Nicholas was loyal to the big world.

He watched Patrick with a predator's vigilance, hoping for a sign that the ceremony was finally over. Suddenly, the sound system swelled back to life with the brassy opening strains of 'Fly Me to the Moon'.

> *Fly me to the moon*
> *Let me play among the stars*
> *Let me see what spring is like*
> *On a-Jupiter and Mars*

Here we go again, thought Nicholas, off to the bloody moon. Frank Sinatra's voice, oozing with effortless confidence, drove him to distraction. It reminded him of the kind of fun he had not been having in the fifties and sixties. No doubt Eleanor had imagined she was enjoying herself when she lowered the record needle onto a Frank Sinatra single, whizzing round at a giddy forty-five rpm, its discarded sleeve, among the lipstick-smeared glasses of gin and the overflowing ashtrays, displaying a photograph of that sly undistinguished face grinning from the upper reaches of a sky-blue suit.

He continued to stare at Patrick and Mary in the hope that they would leave. Then he saw, to his horror, that it was not Eleanor's son but her coffin that was on the move, sliding forward on steel rollers towards a pair of purple velvet curtains.

> *In other words, hold my hand*
> *In other words, baby, kiss me*

The coffin receded behind the closing curtains and disappeared. Mary got up at last and led the way down the aisle, followed closely by Patrick.

Fill my heart with song
And let me sing for ever more
You are all I long for
All I worship and adore
In other words, please be true
In other words, I love you

Finding himself unexpectedly agitated by the sight of Eleanor's coffin being mechanically swallowed, Nicholas lurched hastily into the aisle, interposing himself between Mary and Patrick. He hobbled forwards, his walking stick reaching eagerly ahead of him, and burst through the doorway into the chill London spring.

9

PATRICK STEPPED INTO THE pallid light, relieved that his mother's funeral was over, but oppressed by the party that still lay ahead. He walked up to Mary and Johnny, who stood under the barely blossoming branches of a cherry tree.

'I don't feel like talking to anyone for a while—except you, of course,' he added politely.

'You don't have to talk to us either,' said Johnny.

'Perfect,' said Patrick.

'Why don't you go ahead with Johnny?' asked Mary.

'Well, if that's all right. Can you . . .'

'Cope with everything,' suggested Mary.

'Exactly.'

They smiled at each other, amused by how typical they were both being.

As Patrick walked to Johnny's car, a plane roared and whistled overhead. He glanced back at the Italianate building he had just left. The campanile encasing the furnace chimney, the low arches of the brick cloister, the dormant rose garden, the weeping willow and the mossy benches formed a masterpiece of decent neutrality.

'I think I'll get cremated here myself,' said Patrick.

'No need to rush,' said Johnny.

'I was going to wait until I died.'

'Good thinking.'

A second plane screeched above them, goading the two men into the muffled interior of the car. Through the railings, beside the Thames, joggers and cyclists bobbed along, determined to stay alive.

'I think my mother's death is the best thing to happen to me since . . . well, since my father's death,' said Patrick.

'It can't be quite that simple,' said Johnny, 'or there would be merry bands of orphans skipping down the street.'

The two men fell silent. Patrick was not in the mood to banter. He felt the presence of a new vitality that could easily be nullified by habit, including the habit of seeming to be clever. Like everyone else, he lived in a world where the same patterns of emotion were projected again and again against the walls of an airless chamber, but just for the moment, he felt the absurdity of mistaking that flickering scene for life. What was the meaning of a feeling he had had forty years ago, let alone one he had refused to have? The crisis was not in the past but in clinging to the past; trapped in a decaying mansion on Sunset Boulevard, forced to watch home movies by a wounded narcissist. Just for the moment he could imagine tiptoeing away from Gloria Swanson, past her terrifying butler, and out into the roar of the contemporary streets; he could imagine the whole system breaking down, without knowing what would happen if it did.

At the little roundabout beyond the crematorium gates, Patrick saw a sign for the Townmead Road Re-Use and Recycling Centre. He couldn't help wondering if Eleanor was being recycled. Poor Eleanor was already muddled enough without being dragged through the dull lights and the dazzling lights and multicoloured mandalas of the Bardo, being challenged by crowds of wrathful deities and hungry ghosts to achieve the transcendence she had run away from while she was alive.

The road ran beside the hedge-filled railings of the Mortlake Cemetery, past the Hammersmith and Fulham Cemetery, across Chiswick Bridge, and down to the Chiswick Cemetery on the other side. Acre upon acre of gravestones mocking the real-estate ambitions of riverside developers. Why should death, of all nothings, take up so much space? Better to burn in the hollow blue air than claim a plot on that sunless beach, packed side by side in the bony ground, relying on the clutching roots of trees and flowers for a vague resurrection. Perhaps those who had known good mothering were drawn to the earth's absorbing womb, while the abandoned and betrayed longed to be dispersed into the heartless sky. Johnny might have a professional view. Repression was a different kind of burial, preserving trauma in the unconscious, like a statue buried in the desert sand, its sharp features protected from the weather of ordinary experience. Johnny might have views on that as well, but Patrick preferred to remain in silence. What was the unconscious anyway, as against any other form of memory, and why was it given the sovereignty of a definite article, turning it into a thing and a place when the rest of memory was a faculty and a process?

The car climbed the narrow, battered flyover that straddled the Hogarth roundabout. A temporary measure that just wouldn't go away, it had been crying out for replacement ever since Patrick could remember. Perhaps it was the transport equivalent of smoking: never quite the right day to give it up—there's going to be a rush hour tomorrow morning . . . the weekend is coming up . . . let's do this thing after the Olympics . . . 2020 is a lovely round number, a perfect time for a fresh start.

'This dodgy flyover,' said Patrick.

'I know,' said Johnny, 'I always think it's going to collapse.'

He hadn't meant to talk. An inner monologue had broken the surface. Better sink back down, better make a fresh start.

Making a fresh start was a stale start. There was nothing to make and nothing to start, just a continuous breaking out of appearances from potential appearances, like speech from an inner monologue. To be on an equal plane with that articulation: that was freshness. He could feel it in his body, as if in every moment he might cease to be, or continue to be, and that by continuing he was renewed.

'I was just thinking about repression,' said Patrick, 'I don't think that trauma does get repressed, do you?'

'I think that's now the right view,' said Johnny.

'Trauma is too strong and intrusive to be forgotten. It leads to disassociation and splitting off.'

'So, what does get repressed?' asked Patrick.

'Whatever challenges the accommodations of the false self.'

'So there's still plenty of work for it to do.'

'Tons,' said Johnny.

'But there could be no repression at all, no secret burial; just life radiating through us.'

'Theoretically,' said Johnny.

Patrick saw the familiar concrete facade and aquarium-blue windows of Bupa Cromwell Hospital.

'I remember spending a month in there with a slipped disc, just after my father died.'

'And I remember bringing you some extra painkillers.'

'I salute its ambitious wine list and its action-packed Arabic television channels,' said Patrick, waving majestically at the post-brutalist masterpiece.

The traffic flowed smoothly across the Gloucester Road and down towards the Natural History Museum. Patrick reminded himself to keep quiet. All his life, or at least since he could talk, he had been tempted to flood difficult situations with words.

When Eleanor lost the power to speak and Thomas had not yet acquired it, Patrick discovered a core of inarticulacy in himself that refused to be flooded with words, and which he had tried to flood with alcohol instead. In silence he might see what it was he kept trying to obliterate with talk and drink. What was it that couldn't be said? He could only grope for clues in the darkness of the pre-verbal realm.

His body was a graveyard of buried emotion; its symptoms were clustered around the same fundamental terror, like that rash of cemeteries they had just passed, clustered around the Thames. The nervous bladder, the spastic colon, the lower-back pain, the labile blood pressure that leapt from normal to danger-ously high in a few seconds, at the creak of a floorboard or the thought of a thought, and the imperious insomnia that ruled over them all pointed to an anxiety deep enough to disrupt his instincts and take control of the automatic processes of his body. Behaviours could be changed, attitudes modified, mentalities transformed, but it was hard to have a dialogue with the somatic habits of infancy. How could an infant express himself before he had a self to express, or the words to express what he didn't yet have? Only the dumb language of injury and illness was abundantly available. There was screaming of course, if it was allowed.

He could remember, when he was three years old, standing beside the swimming pool in France looking at the water with apprehensive longing, wishing he knew how to swim. Suddenly he felt himself being hoisted off the ground and thrown high in the air. With the slowness of horror, when the density of impres-sions registered by the panic-stricken mind makes time thicken, he used all the incredulity and alarm that rushed into his thrash-ing body to distance himself from the lethal liquid he had been warned so often not to fall into by accident, but soon enough he plunged down into the drowning pool, kicking and beating the thin water until at last he broke the surface and sucked in some air before he sank back down again. He fought for his life in a chaos of jerks and gulps, sometimes taking in air and sometimes water, until finally he managed to graze his fingers on the rough stone edge of the pool and he gave in to sobbing as quietly as possible, swallowing his despair, knowing that if he made too much noise his father would do something really violent and unkind.

David sat in his dark glasses smoking a cigar, angled away from Patrick, a jaundiced cloud of pastis on the table in front of him, extolling his educational methods to Nicholas Pratt: the stimulation of an instinct to survive; the development of self-sufficiency; an antidote to maternal mollycoddling; in the end, the benefits were so self-evident that only the stupidity and sheepishness of the herd could explain why every three-year-old was not chucked into the deep end of a swimming pool before he knew how to swim.

Robert's curiosity about his grandfather had prompted Patrick to tell him the story of his first swimming lesson. He felt that it would be too burdensome to tell his son about David's beatings and sexual assaults, but at the same time wanted to give Robert a glimpse of his grandfather's harshness. Robert was completely shocked.

'That's so horrible,' he said. 'I mean a three-year-old would think he was dying. In fact, you could have died,' he added, giving Patrick a reassuring hug, as if he sensed that the threat was not completely over.

Robert's empathy overwhelmed Patrick with the reality of what he had taken to be a relatively innocuous anecdote. He could hardly sleep and when he did he was soon woken by his pounding heart. He was hungry all the time but could not digest anything he ate. He could not digest the fact that his father was a man who had wanted to kill him, who would rather have drowned him than taught him to swim, a man who boasted of shooting someone in the head because he had screamed too much, and might shoot Patrick in the head as well, if he made too much noise.

At three of course Patrick would have been able to speak, even if he was forbidden to say what was troubling him. Earlier than that, without the sustenance of narrative, his active memory disintegrated and disappeared. In these darker realms the only clues were lodged in his body, and in one or two stories his mother had told him about his very early life. Here again his father's intolerance of screaming was pivotal, exiling Patrick and his mother to the freezing attic of the Cornish house during the winter he was born.

He sank a little deeper into the passenger seat. As he recognized that he had gone on expecting to be suffocated or dropped, he felt the suffocation and vertigo of the expectations themselves, and if he asked himself whether infancy was destiny, he felt the suffocation and the vertigo of the question. He could feel the weight of his body and the weight on his body. It was like a restraining wall, buckled and sweating from the pressure of the hillside behind it—the only means of access, and at the same time a ferocious guard against the formless miseries of infancy. This was what Johnny might want to call a pre-Oedipal problem, but whatever name was given to a nameless unease, Patrick felt that his tentative new vitality depended on a preparedness to dig into that body of buried emotion and let it join the flow of contemporary feeling. He must pay more attention to the scant evidence that came his way. A strange and upsetting dream had woken him last night, but now it had slipped away and he couldn't get it back.

He understood intuitively that his mother's death was a crisis strong enough to shake his defences. The sudden absence of the woman who had brought him into the world was a fleeting opportunity to bring something slightly new into the world instead. It was important to be realistic: the present was the top layer of the past, not the extravaganza of novelty peddled by people like Seamus and Annette; but even something slightly new could be the layer underneath something slightly newer. He mustn't miss his chance, or his body would keep him living under its misguided heroic strain, like a Japanese soldier who has never been told the news of surrender and continues to booby-trap his patch of jungle and prepare for the honour of a self-inflicted death.

Nauseating as it was to upgrade his father's cruelty to the 'front of the plane' in homicidal class, he felt an even greater reluctance to renounce his childhood view of his mother as the co-victim of David's tempestuous malice. The deeper truth that he had been a toy in the sadomasochistic relationship between his parents was not, until now, something he could bear to contemplate. He clung to the flimsy protection of thinking that his mother was a loving woman who had struggled to satisfy his needs, rather than acknowledging that she had used him as an extension of her lust for humiliation. How self-serving was the story of the freezing attic? It certainly reinforced the picture of Eleanor as a fellow refugee escaping with burns on her back and a baby in her arms from the incendiary bombs of David's rage and self-destruction. Even when Patrick found the courage to tell her that he had been raped by his father, she had rushed to say, 'Me too.' Falling over herself to be a victim, Eleanor seemed indifferent to the impact that her stories might be having at any other level. Suffocated, dropped, born of rape as well as born to be raped—what did it matter, as long as Patrick realized how difficult it had been for her and how far she was from having collaborated with their persecutor. When Patrick asked why she didn't leave, she had said she was afraid that David would kill her, but since he had already twice tried to kill her when they were living together, it was hard to see how living apart would have made it more likely. The truth, which made his blood pressure shoot up as he admitted it, was that she craved the extreme violence of David's presence, and that she threw her son into the bargain. Patrick wanted to stop the car and get out and walk; he wanted a shot of whisky, a shot of heroin, a revolver shot in the head—kill the screaming man, get it over with, be in charge. He let these impulses wash over him without paying them too much attention.

The car was turning into Queensbury Place, next to the Lycée Francais de Londres, where Patrick had spent a year of bilingual delinquency when he was seven years old. At the prize-giving ceremony in the Royal Albert Hall, there was a copy of *La Chèvre de Monsieur Seguin* on his red plush seat. He soon became obsessed with the story of the doomed and heroic little goat, lured into the high mountains by the riot of Alpine flowers ('Je me languis, je me languis, je veux aller a la montagne'). Monsieur Seguin, who has already lost six goats to the wolf, is determined not to lose another and locks the hero in the woodshed, but the little goat climbs out through the window and escapes, spending a day of ecstasy on slopes dotted with red and blue and yellow and orange flowers. Then, as the sun begins to set, he suddenly notices among the lengthening shadows the silhouette of the lean and hungry wolf, sitting complacently in the tall grass, contemplating his prey. Knowing he is going to die, the goat nevertheless determines to fight until the dawn ('pourvu que je tienne jusqu'à l'aube'), lowers his head and charges at the wolf's chest. He fights all night, charging again and again, until finally, as the sun rises over the grey crags of the mountain opposite, he collapses on the ground and is destroyed. This story never failed to move Patrick to tears as he read it every night in his bedroom in Victoria Road.

That was it! Last night's strange dream: a hooded figure

striding among a herd of goats, pulling their heads back and slit-
ting their throats. Patrick had been one of the goats on the outer
edge of the herd and with a sense of doom and defiance worthy
of his childhood hero he reached up and tore out his own larynx
so as not to give the assassin the satisfaction of hearing him
scream. Here was another form of violent silence. If only he had
time to work it all out. If only he could be alone, this knot of
impressions and connections would untangle at his feet. His
psyche was on the move; things that had wanted to be hidden
now wanted to be revealed. Wallace Stevens was right: 'Freedom
is like a man who kills himself / Each night, an incessant butcher,
whose knife / Grows sharp in blood.' He was longing for the
splendours of silence and solitude, but instead he was going to a
party.

Johnny turned into Onslow Gardens and sped along the suddenly empty stretch of street.

'Here we are,' he said, slowing down to look for a parking
space close to the club.

IO

KETTLE HAD EXPLAINED TO Mary her principled stand against attending Eleanor's funeral.

'It would be sheer hypocrisy,' she told her daughter. 'I despise disinheritance, and I think it's wrong to go to someone's funeral boiling with rage. The party's a different matter: it's about supporting you and Patrick. I'm not pretending it doesn't help that it's just round the corner.'

'In that case you could look after the boys,' said Mary. 'We feel exactly the same way about their coming to the cremation as you feel about going. Robert disconnected from Eleanor years ago and Thomas never really knew her, but we still want them to come to the party, to mark the occasion for them in a lighter way.'

'Oh, well, of course, I'd be delighted to help,' said Kettle, immediately determined to get her revenge for being burdened with an even more troublesome responsibility than the one she had been trying to evade.

As soon as Mary had dropped the boys off at her flat, Kettle got to work on Robert.

'Personally,' she said, 'I can't ever forgive your *other* grandmother for giving away your lovely house in France. You must miss it terribly; not being able to go there in the holidays. It was really more of a home than London, I suppose, being in the countryside and all that.'

Robert looked rather more upset than she had intended.

'How can you say that? That's a horrible thing to say,' said Robert.

'I was just trying to be sympathetic,' said Kettle.

Robert walked out of the kitchen and went to sit alone in the drawing room. He hated Kettle for making him think that he should still have Saint-Nazaire. He didn't cry about missing it anymore, but he still remembered every detail. They could take away the place but they couldn't take away the images in his mind. Robert closed his eyes and thought about walking back home late one evening with his father through the Butterfly Wood in a high wind. The sound of creaking branches and calling birds was torn away and dissolved among the hissing pines. When they came out of the wood it was nearly night, but he could still make out the gleaming vine shoots snaking through the ploughed earth, and he saw his first shooting star incinerated on the edge of the clear black sky.

Kettle was right: it was more of a home than London. It was his first home and there could only ever be one, but he held it now in his imagination and it was even more beautiful than ever. He didn't want to go back and he didn't want to have it back, because it would be such a disappointment.

Robert had started to cry when Kettle came briskly into the drawing room with Thomas behind her.

'I asked Amparo to get a film for you. If you've got over your tantrum you could watch it with Thomas; she says her grandchildren absolutely love it.'

'Look, Bobby,' said Thomas, running over to show Robert the DVD case, 'it's a flying carpet.'

Robert was furious at the injustice of the word 'tantrum', but he quite wanted to see the film.

'We're not allowed to watch films in the morning,' he said.

'Well,' said Kettle, 'you'll just have to tell your father you were playing Scrabble, or something frightfully intellectual that he would approve of.'

'But it's not true,' said Thomas, 'because we're going to see the film.'

'Oh, dear, I can't get anything right, can I?' said Kettle. 'You'll be pleased to hear that silly old Granny is going out for a while. If you can face the treat I've gone to the trouble of organizing, just tell Amparo and she'll put it on for you. If not, there's a copy of the *Telegraph* in the kitchen—I'm sure you can get the crossword puzzle done by the time I'm back.'

With this triumphant sarcasm, Kettle left her flat, a martyr to her spoilt and oversensitive grandsons. She was going to the Patisserie Valerie to have coffee with the widow of our former ambassador to Rome. If the truth be told, Natasha was a frightful bore, always going on about what James would have said, and what James would have thought, as if that mattered anymore. Still, it was important to stay in touch with old friends.

Transport by Ford limousine was all part of the Bunyon's Bronze Service package that Mary had selected for the funeral. Neither the four vintage Rolls-Royces of the Platinum Service, nor the four plumed black horses and glass-sided carriage of the High Victorian Service, offered any serious competition. There was room for three other people in the Ford limo. Nancy had been Mary's first dutiful choice but Nicholas Pratt had a car and driver of his own and had already offered Nancy a lift. In the end, Mary shared the car with Julia, Patrick's ex-lover; Erasmus, her own ex-lover; and Annette, Seamus's ex-lover. Nobody spoke until the car was turning, at a mournful pace, onto the main road.

'I hate bereavement,' said Julia, looking at the mirror in her small powder compact, 'it ruins your eyeliner.'

'Were you fond of Eleanor?' asked Mary, knowing that Julia had never bothered with her.

'Oh, it's nothing to do with her,' said Julia, as if stating the obvious. 'You know the way that tears spring on you, in a silly film, or at a funeral, or when you read something in the paper: not really brought on by the thing that triggers them, but from accumulated grief, I suppose, and life just being so generally maddening.'

'Of course,' said Mary, 'but sometimes the trigger and the grief are connected.'

She turned away, trying to distance herself from the routine frivolity of Julia's line on bereavement. She glimpsed the pink flowers of a magnolia protesting against the black-and-white half-timbered facade of a mock-Tudor side street. Why was the driver going by Kew Bridge? Was it considered more dignified to take the longer route?

'I didn't put on my eyeliner this morning,' said Erasmus, with the studied facetiousness of an academic.

'You can borrow mine if you like,' said Annette, joining in.

'Thank you for what you said about Eleanor,' said Mary, turning to Annette with a smile.

'I only hope I was able to do justice to a very special lady,' said Annette.

'God yes,' said Julia, reapplying her eyeliner meticulously. 'I do wish this car would stop moving.'

'She was certainly someone who wanted to be good,' said Mary, 'and that's rare enough.'

'Ah, intentionality,' said Erasmus, as if he were pointing out a famous waterfall that had just become visible through the car window.

'Paving the road to Hell,' said Julia, moving on to the other eye with her greasy black pencil.

'Aquinas says that love is "desiring another's good",' Erasmus began.

'Just desiring another is good enough for me,' interrupted Julia. 'Of course one doesn't want them to be run over or gunned down in the street—or not often, anyway. It seems to me that Aquinas is just stating the obvious. Everything is rooted in desire.'

'Except conformity, convention, compulsion, hidden motivation, necessity, confusion, perversion, principle.' Erasmus smiled sadly at the wealth of alternatives.

'But they just create other kinds of desire.'

'If you pack every meaning into a single word, you deprive it of any meaning at all,' said Erasmus.

'Well, even if you think Aquinas is a complete genius for saying that,' said Julia, 'I don't see how "desiring another's good" is the same as desiring others to think you're a goody-goody.'

'Eleanor didn't just want to be good, she was good,' said Annette. 'She wasn't just a dreamer like so many visionaries, she was a builder and a mover and shaker who made a practical difference to lots of lives.'

'She certainly made a practical difference to Patrick's life,' said Julia, snapping her compact closed.

Mary was driven mad by Julia's presumption that she was more loyal than anyone to Patrick's interests. Her fidelity to his infidelity was an act of aggression towards Mary that Julia wouldn't have allowed herself without Erasmus's presence and Patrick's absence. Mary decided to keep a cold silence. They were already in Hammersmith and she was easily furious enough to last until Chelsea.

When Nancy invited Henry to join her in Nicholas's car, he pointed out that he had a car of his own.

'Tell him to follow us,' said Nicholas.

And so Henry's empty car followed Nicholas's full car from the crematorium to the club.

'One knows so many more dead people than living ones,' said Nicholas, relaxing into an abundance of padded black leather while electronically reclining the passenger seat towards Nancy's knees so as to lecture his guests from a more convenient angle, 'although, in terms of sheer numbers, all the people who have ever existed cannot equal the verminous multitude currently clutching at the surface of our once beautiful planet.'

'That's one of the problems with reincarnation: who is being reincarnated if there are more people now than the sum of the people who have ever existed?' said Henry. 'It doesn't make any sense.'

'It only makes sense if lumps of raw humanity are raining down on us for their first round of civilization. That, I'm afraid, is all too plausible,' said Nicholas, arching his eyebrow at his driver and giving a warning glance to Henry. 'It's your first time here, isn't it, Miguel?'

'Yes, Sir Nicholas,' said Miguel, with the merry laugh of a man who is used to being exotically insulted by his employer several times a day.

'It's no use telling you that you were Queen Cleopatra in a previous lifetime, is it?'

'No, Sir Nicholas,' said Miguel, unable to control his mirth.

'What I don't understand about reincarnation is why we all forget,' complained Nancy. 'Wouldn't it have been more fun, when we first met, to have said, "How are you? I haven't seen you since that perfectly ghastly party Marie-Antoinette gave in the Petit Trianon!" Something like that, something fun. I mean, if it's true, reincarnation is like having Alzheimer's on a huge scale, with each lifetime as our little moment of vivid anxiety. I know that my sister believed in it, but by the time I wanted to ask her about why we forget, she *really* did have Alzheimer's, and so it would have been tactless, if you know what I'm saying.'

'Rebirth is just a sentimental rumour imported from the vegetable kingdom,' said Nicholas wisely. 'We're all impressed by the resurgence of the spring, but the tree never died.'

'You can get reborn in your own lifetime,' said Henry quietly. 'Die to something and go into a new phase.'

'Spare me the spring,' said Nicholas. 'Ever since I was a little boy, I've been in the high summer of being me, and I intend to go on chasing butterflies through the tall grass until the abrupt and painless end. On the other hand, I do see that some people, like Miguel, for instance, are crying out for a complete overhaul.'

Miguel chuckled and shook his head in disbelief.

'Oh, Miguel, isn't he awful?' said Nancy.

'Yes, madam.'

'You're not supposed to agree with her, you moron,' said Nicholas.

'I thought Eleanor was a Christian,' said Henry, who disliked Nicholas's servant-baiting. 'Where does all this Eastern stuff come from?'

'Oh, she was just generally religious,' said Nancy.

'Most people who are Christian at least have the merit of not being Hindu or Sufi,' said Nicholas, 'just as Sufis have the merit of not being Christian, but religiously speaking, Eleanor was like one of those amazing cocktails that make you wonder what motorway collision could have first combined gin, brandy, tomato juice, crème de menthe, and Cointreau into a single drink.'

'Well, she was always a nice kid,' said Henry stoutly, 'always concerned about other people.'

'That can be a good thing,' admitted Nicholas, 'depending on who the other people are, of course.'

Nancy rolled her eyeballs slightly at her cousin in the back seat. She felt that families should be allowed to say horrible things to one another, but that outsiders should be more careful. Henry looked longingly back at his empty car. Even Nicholas needed to take a rest from himself. As his car sped past Bupa Cromwell Hospital everyone fell silent by mutual consent and Nicholas closed his eyes, gathering his resources for the social ordeal that lay ahead.

After the film, Thomas sat on a cushion and pretended to be riding his own flying carpet. First of all he visited his mother and father, who were at his grandmother's funeral. He had seen photographs of his dead grandmother that made him think he could remember her, but then his mother had told him that he last saw her when he was two and she was living in France and so he realized that he had made up the memory from the photograph. Unless in fact he had a very dim memory of her and the photograph had blown on the tiny little ember of his connection with his granny, like a faint orange glow in a heap of soft grey ash, and for a moment he really could remember when he had sat on his granny's lap and smiled at her and patted her wrinkly old face— his mother said he smiled at her and she was really pleased.

The flying carpet shot on to Baghdad, where Thomas jumped off and kicked the evil sorcerer Jafar over the parapet and into the moat. The princess was so grateful that she gave him a pet leopard, a turban with a ruby in the middle and a lamp with a very powerful and funny genie living in it. The genie was just expanding into the air above him when Thomas heard the front door opening and Kettle greeting Amparo in the hall.

'Have the boys been good?'

'Oh, yes, they love the film, just like my granddaughters.'

'Well, at least I've got that right,' sighed Kettle. 'We must hurry; I have a cab waiting outside. I was so exhausted by my friend's complaining that I had to hail a taxi the moment I got out of the patisserie.'

'Oh, dear, I'm so sorry,' said Amparo.

'It can't be helped,' said Kettle stoically.

Kettle found Thomas cross-legged on a cushion next to the big low table in the middle of the drawing room and Robert stretched on the sofa staring at the ceiling.

'I'm riding on a flying carpet,' said Thomas.

'In that case, you won't need the silly old taxi I've got for us to go to the party.'

'No,' said Thomas serenely, 'I'll find my own way.'

He leant forward and grabbed the front corners of the cushion, tilting sideways to go into a steep left turn.

'Let's get a move on,' said Kettle, clapping her hands together impatiently. 'It's costing me a fortune to keep this taxi waiting. What are you doing staring at the ceiling?' she snapped at Robert.

'Thinking.'

'Don't be ridiculous.'

The two boys followed Kettle into the frail old-fashioned cage of a lift that took them to the ground floor of her building. She seemed to calm down once she told the taxi driver to take them to the Onslow Club, but by then both Robert and Thomas felt too upset to talk. Sensing their reluctance, Kettle started to interrogate them about their schools. After dashing some dull questions against their proud silence, she gave in to the temptation of reminiscing about her own schooldays: Sister Bridget's irresistible charm towards the parents, especially the grander ones, and her high austerity towards the girls; the hilarious report in which Sister Anna had said that it would take 'divine intervention' to make Kettle into a mathematician.

Kettle carried on with her complacent self-deprecation as the taxi rumbled down the Fulham Road. The brothers withdrew into their private thoughts, only emerging when they stopped outside the club.

'Oh, look, there's Daddy,' said Robert, lunging out of the taxi ahead of his grandmother.

'Don't wait for me,' said Kettle archly.

'Okay,' said Thomas, following his brother into the street and running up to his father.

'Hello, Dada,' he said, jumping into Patrick's arms. 'Guess what I've been doing? I've been watching *Aladdin*! Not *bin* Laden but *A*-laddin.' He chuckled mischievously, patting both Patrick's cheeks at once.

Patrick burst out laughing and kissed him on the forehead.

II

AS HE ARRIVED AT the entrance of the Onslow Club, with Thomas still in his arms and Robert walking by his side, Patrick heard the distant but distinct sound of Nicholas Pratt disgorging his opinions on the pavement behind him.

'A celebrity these days is somebody you've never heard of,' Nicholas boomed, 'just as "*j'arrive*" is what a French waiter says as he hurries away from you in a Paris cafe. Margot's fame belongs to a bygone era: one actually knows who she is! Nevertheless, to write five autobiographies is going too far. Life is life and writing is writing and if you write as Margot does, like a glass of water on a rainy day it can only dilute the effect of whatever it was you *used* to do well.'

'You are awful,' said Nancy's admiring voice.

Patrick turned around and saw Nancy, her arm locked in Nicholas's, with a rather demoralized-looking Henry walking on her other side.

'Who is that funny man?' asked Thomas.

'He's called Nicholas Pratt,' said Patrick.

'He's like Today in a *very* grumpy mood,' said Thomas.

Patrick and Robert both laughed as much as Nicholas's proximity allowed.

'She said to me,' Nicholas continued in his coy simpering voice, '"I know it's my fifth book, but there always seems to be more to say." If one says nothing in the first place, there always *is* more to say: there's everything to say. Ah, Patrick,' Nicholas checked himself, 'how thrilling to be introduced, at my advanced age, to a new club.' He peered with exaggerated curiosity at the brass plaque on a white stucco pillar. 'The Onslow Club, I don't remember ever hearing it mentioned.'

He's the last one, thought Patrick, watching Nicholas's performance with cold detachment, the last of my parents' friends left alive, the last of the guests who used to visit Saint-Nazaire when I was a child. George Watford and Victor Eisen and Anne Eisen are dead, even Bridget, who was so much younger than Nicholas, is dead. I wish he would drop dead as well.

Patrick lazily retracted his murderous desire to get rid of Nicholas. Death was the kind of boisterous egomaniac that needed no encouragement. Besides, being free, whatever that might mean, couldn't depend on Nicholas's death, or even on Eleanor's.

Still, her death pointed to a post-parental world that Nicholas's presence was obstructing. His perfectly rehearsed contempt was a frayed cable connecting Patrick to the social atmosphere of his childhood. Patrick's one great ally during his troubled youth had always loathed Nicholas. Victor Eisen's wife, Anne, felt that the nimbus of insanity surrounding David Melrose's corruption had made it seem inevitable, whereas Nicholas's decadence was more like a stylistic choice.

Nicholas straightened up and took in the children.

'Are these your sons?'

'Robert and Thomas,' said Patrick, noticing a strong reluctance to put the increasingly burdensome Thomas down on the pavement next to his father's last living friend.

'What a pity David isn't here to enjoy his grandsons,' said Nicholas. 'He would have ensured at the very least that they didn't spend the whole day in front of the television. He was very worried about the tyranny of the cathode-ray tube. I remember vividly when we had seen some children who were practically giving birth to a television set, he said to me, "I dread to think what all that radiation is doing to their little genitals."'

Patrick was lost for words.

'Let's go inside,' said Henry firmly. He smiled at the two boys and led the party indoors.

'I'm your cousin Henry,' he said to Robert. 'You came to stay with me in Maine a few years back.'

'On that island,' said Robert. 'I remember. I loved it there.'

'You must come again.'

Patrick pressed ahead with Thomas, while Nicholas, like a lame pointer following a wounded bird, hobbled after him across the black-and-white tiles of the entrance hall. He could tell that he had unsettled Patrick and didn't want to lose the chance to consolidate his work.

'I can't help thinking how much your father would have enjoyed this occasion,' panted Nicholas. 'Whatever his drawbacks as a parent, you must admit that he never lost his sense of humour.'

'Easy not to lose what you never had,' said Patrick, too relieved that he could speak again to avoid the mistake of engaging with Nicholas.

'Oh, I disagree,' said Nicholas. 'He saw the funny side of *everything.*'

'He only saw the funny side of things that didn't have one,' said Patrick. 'That's not a sense of humour, just a form of cruelty.'

'Well, cruelty and laughter,' said Nicholas, struggling to take off his overcoat next to the row of brass hooks on the far side of the hall, 'have always been close neighbours.'

'Close without being incestuous,' said Patrick. 'In any case, I have to deal with the people who have come to mourn my mother, however much you may miss my other amazing parent.'

Taking advantage of the tangle that had briefly turned Nicholas's overcoat into a straitjacket, Patrick doubled back to the entrance of the club.

'Ah, look, there's Mummy,' he said, at last releasing Thomas onto the chequerboard floor and following him as he ran towards Mary.

'I hate to sound like Greta Garbo, but "I want to be alone",' said Patrick in a ludicrous Swedish accent.

'Again!' said Mary. 'Why don't these feelings come over you when you *are* alone? That's when you phone up to complain that you don't get invited to parties anymore.'

'That's true, but it's not my mother's after-funeral sandwiches that I have in mind. Listen, I'll just whizz around the block, as if I was having a cigarette, and then I promise I'll come back and be totally present.'

'Promises, promises,' said Mary, with an understanding smile.

Patrick saw Julia, Erasmus and Annette coming in behind Mary and felt the stranglehold of social responsibility. He wanted to leave more than ever but at the same time realized that he wouldn't be able to. Annette spotted Nicholas across the hall.

'Poor Nick, he's got into a real muddle with his overcoat,' she said, rushing to his rescue.

'Let me help you with that.' She pulled at Nicholas's sleeve and released his twisted shoulder.

'Thank you,' said Nicholas. 'That fiend, Patrick, saw that I was trussed up like a turkey and simply walked away.'

'Oh, I'm sure he didn't mean to,' said Annette optimistically.

Having parked his car, Johnny arrived and added to the weight of guests forcing Patrick back into the hall. As he was pushed inside by the collective pressure, Patrick saw a half-familiar grey-haired woman stepping into the club with an air of tremendous determination and asking the hall porter if there was a party for Eleanor Melrose's funeral.

He suddenly remembered where he had seen her before. She had been in the Priory at the same time as him. He met her when he was about to leave on his abortive visit to Becky. She had surged up to him at the front door, wearing a dark green sweater and a tweedy skirt, and started to talk in an urgent and over-familiar way, blocking his path to the exit.

'You leaving?' she asked, not pausing for an answer. 'I must say I don't envy you. I love it here. I come here for a month every year, does me the world of good, gets me away from home. The thing is, I absolutely loathe my children. They're monsters. Their father, whose guts I loathe, never disciplined them, so you can imagine the sort of horrors they've turned into. Of course I've had my part to play. I mean, I lay in bed for ten months not uttering a single syllable and then when I did start talking I couldn't stop because of all the things that had piled up during the ten months. I don't know what you're in here for officially, but I have a feeling. No, listen to me. If I have one word of advice it's "Amitriptyline". It's absolutely wonderful. The only time I was happy was when I was on it. I've been trying to get hold of it ever since, but the bastards won't give me any.'

'The thing is I'm trying to stop taking anything,' said Patrick.

'Don't be so stupid; it's the most marvellous drug.'

She followed him out onto the steps after his cab arrived. '*Amitriptyline*,' she shouted, as if he'd been the one to tell her about it, 'you lucky thing!'

He had not followed her fierce advice and taken up Amitriptyline; in fact in the next few months he had given up the oxazepam and the antidepressants and stopped drinking alcohol altogether.

'It's so weird,' said Patrick to Johnny as they climbed the stair-case to the room designated for the party, 'a woman arrived just now who was in the Priory at the same time as me last year. She's a complete loony.'

'It's bound to happen in a place like that,' said Johnny.

'I wouldn't know, being completely normal,' said Patrick.

'Perhaps too normal,' said Johnny.

'Just too damn normal,' said Patrick, pounding his fist into his palm.

'Fortunately, we can help you with that,' said Johnny, in the voice of a wise paternalistic American doctor, 'thanks to Xywyz, a breakthrough medication that only employs the last four let-ters of the alphabet.'

'That's incredible!' said Patrick, wonder-struck.

Johnny dashed through a rapid disclaimer: 'Do not take Xy-wyz if you are using water or other hydrating agents. Possible side-effects include blindness, incontinence, aneurism, liver fail-ure, dizziness, skin rash, depression, internal haemorrhaging and sudden death.'

'I don't care,' wailed Patrick, 'I want it anyway. I gotta have it.'

The two men fell silent. They had been improvising little sketches for decades, since the days when they smoked ciga-rettes and later joints on the fire escape during breaks at school.

'She was asking about this party,' said Patrick, as they reached the landing.

'Maybe she knew your mother.'

'Sometimes the simplest explanations are the best,' Patrick conceded, 'although she might be a funeral fanatic having a manic episode.'

The sound of uncorking bottles reminded Patrick that it was only a year since Gordon, the wise Scottish moderator, had in-terviewed him before he joined the Depression Group for daily sessions. Gordon drew his attention to 'the alcoholic behind the alcohol'.

'You can take the brandy out of the fruitcake,' he said, 'but you're still left with the fruitcake.'

Patrick, who had spent the night in a state of seething hallucination and cosmic unease, was not in the mood to agree with anything.

'I don't think you can take the brandy out of the fruitcake,' he said, 'or the eggs out of the soufflé, or the salt out of the sea.'

'It was only a metaphor,' said Gordon.

'*Only* a metaphor!' Patrick howled. 'Metaphor is the whole problem, the solvent of nightmares. At the molten heart of things everything resembles everything else: that's the horror.'

Gordon glanced down at Patrick's sheet to make sure he had taken his latest does of oxazepam.

'What I'm really asking,' he persevered, 'is what have you been self-medicating for, at the end of the day, if not depression?'

'Borderline personality, narcissistic rage, schizoid tendencies . . .' Patrick suggested some plausible additions.

Gordon roared with therapeutic laughter. 'Excellent! You've come in with some self-knowledge under your belt.'

Patrick glanced down the stairwell to make sure the Amitriptyline woman wasn't nearby.

'I saw her twice,' he told Johnny, 'once at the beginning of my stay and once in the middle, when I was starting to get better. The first time she lectured me on the joys of Amitriptyline, but the second time we didn't even talk, I just saw her delivering the same speech to someone from my Depression Group.'

'So, she was a sort of Ancient Mariner of Amitriptyline.'

'Exactly.'

Patrick remembered his second sighting of her very clearly,

because it had taken place on the pivotal day of his stay. A raw clarity had started to take over from the withdrawal and delirium of his first fortnight. He spent more and more time alone in the garden, not wanting to drown in the chatter of a group lunch, or spend anymore time in his bedroom than he already did. One day he was sitting on the most secluded bench in the garden when he suddenly started to cry. There was nothing in the patch of pasty sky or the partial view of a tree that justified his feeling of aesthetic bliss; no wood pigeons thrummed on the branch, no distant opera music drifted across the lawn, no crocuses shivered at the foot of the tree. Something unseen and unprovoked had invaded his depressive gaze, and spread like a gold rush through the ruins of his tired brain. He had no control over the source of his reprieve. He had not reframed or distanced his depression; it had simply yielded to another way of being. He was crying with gratitude but also with frustration at not being able to secure a supply of this precious new commodity. He felt the depths of his own psychological materialism and saw dimly that it stood in his way, but the habit of grasping at anything that might alleviate his misery was too strong, and the sense of gratuitous beauty that had shimmered through him disappeared as he tried to work out how it could be captured and put to use.

And then the Amitriptyline woman appeared wearing the same green sweater and tweedy skirt that he had first seen her in. He remembered thinking that she must have come with a small suitcase.

'But the bastards won't give me any . . .' she was saying to Jill, a tearful member of Patrick's Depression Group.

Jill had run sobbing out of that morning's session, after her suggestion that the group treat the word 'God' as an acronym for Gift of Desperation had been greeted by the bitter and abrasive Terry with the words, 'Excuse me while I vomit.'

Anxious to avoid conversation with the two women, Patrick bolted behind the dark lateral branches of a cedar tree.

'You lucky thing . . .' The Amitriptyline speech continued on its inevitable course.

'But I haven't been given any,' Jill protested, clearly feeling the presence of God, as tears welled up in her eyes again.

'The last time I saw her, I got stuck behind a cedar tree for twenty minutes,' Patrick explained to Johnny, as they walked into a pale blue room with high French windows overlooking a placid communal garden. 'When I saw her coming, I dashed behind a tree while they took over the bench I'd been sitting on.'

'Serves you right for abandoning your depression buddy,' said Johnny.

'I was having an epiphany.'

'Oh, well . . .'

'It all seems so far away.'

'The epiphany or the Priory?'

'Both,' said Patrick, 'or at least they did until that woman turned up.'

'Maybe insight comes when you need to get out of the madhouse. The loony downstairs might be a catalyst.'

'Anything might be a catalyst,' said Patrick. 'Anything might be evidence, anything might be a clue. We can never afford to relax our vigilance.'

'Fortunately we can help with that,' Johnny slipped again into his American doctor's voice, 'thanks to Vigilante. Fought over by fighter pilots, presiding over presidents, terrifying terrorists, the busy-ness behind the business of America. *Vigilante: "Keeping Our Leaders on the Job Around the Clock."*' Johnny's voice switched to a rapid murmur. 'Do not take Vigilante if you are suffering from high blood pressure, low blood pressure, or normal blood pressure. Consult your physician if you experience chest pains, swollen eyelids, elongated ears . . .'

Patrick tuned out of the disclaimer and looked around at the almost empty room. Nancy was already deep in a plate of sandwiches at the far end of a long table loaded with too much food for the small party of mourners. Henry was standing next to her, talking to Robert. Behind the table was an exceptionally pretty waitress, with a long neck and high cheekbones and short black hair. She gave Patrick a friendly open smile. She must be an aspiring actress between auditions. She was absurdly attractive. He wanted to leave with her straight away. Why did she seem so irresistible? Did the table of almost untouched food make her seem generous as well as lovely? What was the proper approach on such an occasion? My mother just died and I need cheering up? My mother never gave me enough to eat but you look as if you could do much better? Patrick let out a short bark of private laughter at the absurdity of these tyrannical impulses, the depth of his dependency, the fantasy of being saved, the fantasy of being nourished. There was just too much past weighing down on his attention, taking it below the waterline, flooding him with primitive, pre-verbal urges. He imagined himself shaking off his unconscious, like a dog just out of the sea. He walked over to the table, asked for a glass of sparkling water and gave the waitress a simple smile with no future. He thanked her and turned away crisply. There was something hollow about the performance; he still found her utterly adorable, but he saw the attraction for what it was: his own hunger, with no interpersonal implications whatsoever.

He was reminded of Jill from his Depression Group, who had complained one day that she had 'a relationship problem—well, the problem is that the person I have a relationship with doesn't know that we have a relationship'. This confession had elicited peals of derisive laughter from Terry.

'No wonder you're in treatment for the ninth time,' said Terry.

Jill hurried from the room, sobbing.

'You're going to have to apologize for that,' said Gordon.

'But I meant it.'

'That's why you have to apologize.'

'But I wouldn't mean it if I apologized,' Terry argued.

'Fake it to make it, man,' said Gary, the American whose opportunistic tourist of a mother had created such a flurry during Patrick's first Group session.

Patrick wondered if he was faking it to make it—a phrase that had always filled him with disgust—by turning away so resolutely from a woman he would rather have seduced. No, it was the seduction that would have been faking it, the Casanova complex that would have forced him to disguise his infantile yearnings with the appearance of adult behavior: courtesy, conversation, copulation, commentary—elaborate devices for distancing him from the impotent baby whose screams he could not bear to hear. The glory of his mother's death was that she could no longer get in the way of his own maternal instincts with her presumptive maternal presence and stop him from embracing the inconsolable wreck that she had given birth to.

12

AS THE ROOM BEGAN to fill, Patrick was drawn out of his private thoughts and back into his role as host. Nicholas walked past him with haughty indifference to join Nancy at the far end of the room. Mary came over with the Amitriptyline woman in tow, followed closely by Thomas and Erasmus.

'Patrick,' said Mary, 'you should meet Fleur, she's an old friend of your mother's.'

Patrick shook hands with her politely, marvelling at her whimsical French name. Now that she had taken off her overcoat he could see the green sweater and tweed skirt he recognized from the Priory. Bright red lipstick in the shape of a mouth shadowed Fleur's own mouth, about half an inch to the right, giving the impression of a circus clown caught in the middle of removing her make-up.

'How did you know . . .' Patrick began.

'Dada!' said Thomas, too excited not to interrupt. 'Erasmus is a real philosopher!'

'Or at any rate a realist philosopher,' said Erasmus.

'I know, darling,' said Patrick, ruffling his son's hair. Thomas hadn't seen Erasmus for a year and a half, and clearly the category of philosopher had come into focus during that time.

'I mean,' said Thomas, looking very philosophical, 'I always think the trouble with God is: Who created God? And,' he added, getting into the swing of it, 'who created whoever created God?'

'Ah, an infinite regress,' said Erasmus sadly.

'Okay, then,' said Thomas, 'who created infinite regress?' He looked up at his father to check that he was arguing philosophically.

Patrick gave him an encouraging smile.

'He's frightfully clever, isn't he?' said Fleur. 'Unlike my lot: they could hardly string a sentence together until they were well into their teens, and then it was only to insult me—and their father, who deserved it of course. Absolute monsters.'

Mary slipped away with Thomas and Erasmus, leaving Patrick stranded with Fleur.

'That's teenagers for you,' said Patrick, with resolute blandness. 'So, how did you know Eleanor?'

'I adored your mother. I think she was one of the very few good people I ever met. She saved my life really—I suppose it must have been thirty years ago—by giving me a job in one of the charity shops she used to run for the Save the Children Fund.'

'I remember those shops,' said Patrick, noticing that Fleur was gathering momentum and didn't want to be interrupted.

'I was thought by some people,' Fleur motored on, 'well, by everyone except your mother really, to be unemployable, because of my episodes, but I simply had to get out of the house and *do* something, so your mother was an absolute godsend. She had me packing up second-hand clothes in no time. We used to send them off to the shop we thought they'd do best in, keeping the really good ones for our shop in Launceston Place, just round the corner from your house.'

'Yes,' said Patrick quickly.

'We used to have such fun,' Fleur reminisced, 'we were like a couple of schoolgirls, holding up the clothes and saying, "Richmond, I think," or "*Very* Cheltenham." Sometimes we'd both shout, "Rochdale!" or, "Hemel Hempstead!" at exactly the same time. Oh, how we laughed. Eventually your mother trusted me enough to put me on the till and let me run the shop for the whole day, and that, I'm afraid, is when I had one of my episodes. We had a fur coat in that morning—it was the time when people started to get paint thrown at them if they wore one—an amazing sable coat—I think that's what tipped me over the edge. I was gripped by a need to do something really glamorous, so I shut up the shop and took all the money from the till and put on the sable coat—it wasn't very suitable at the height of June, but I had to wear it. Anyway, I went out and hailed a cab and said, "Take me to the Ritz!"'

Patrick looked around the room anxiously, wondering if he would ever get away.

'They tried to take my coat off me,' Fleur accelerated, 'but I wouldn't hear of it, and so I sat in the Palm Court in a heap of sable, drinking champagne cocktails and talking to anyone who would listen, until a frightfully pompous head waiter asked me to leave because I was being "a nuisance to the other guests"! Can you imagine the rudeness of it? Well, anyway, the money I'd taken from the till turned out not to be enough for the enormous bill and so the wretched hotel insisted on keeping the coat, which turned out to be very inconvenient because the lady who had given it to us came back and said she'd changed her mind . . .'

By now Fleur was falling over herself to keep up with her thoughts. Patrick tried to catch Mary's eye, but she seemed to be deliberately ignoring him.

'All I can say is that your mother was absolutely marvellous. She went and paid the bill and rescued the coat. She said she was used to it because she was always clearing her father's bar bills in grand places, and she didn't mind at all. She was an absolute saint and let me go on running the shop when she was away, saying that she was sure I wouldn't do it again—which I'm afraid to say I did, more than once.'

'Would you like a drink?' asked Patrick, turning back towards the waitress with renewed longing. Perhaps he should run away with her after all. He wanted to kiss the pulse in her long neck.

'I shouldn't really but I'll have a gin and tonic,' said Fleur, hardly pausing before she continued. 'You must be very proud of your mother. She did an enormous amount of practical good, the only sort of good there *is* really—touched on hundreds of lives, threw herself into those shops with tremendous energy—I firmly believe she could have been an entrepreneur, if she had needed the money—the way she used to set off to the Harrogate Trade Fair with a spring in her step.'

Patrick smiled at the waitress and then looked down at the tablecloth bashfully. When he looked up again she was smiling at him with sympathy and laughter in her eyes. She clearly understood everything. She was wonderfully intelligent as well as impossibly lovely. The more Fleur talked about Eleanor, the more he wanted to start a new life with the waitress. He took the gin and tonic from her tenderly and handed it on to the loquacious Fleur, who seemed to be saying, 'Well, do you?' for reasons he couldn't fathom.

'Do I what?' he asked.

'Feel proud of your mother?'

'I suppose so,' said Patrick.

'What do you mean, you "suppose so"? You're worse than my children. Absolute monsters.'

'Listen, it's been a great pleasure to meet you,' said Patrick, 'and I expect we'll talk again, but I probably ought to circulate.'

He moved away from Fleur unceremoniously and, wanting to look as if he had a firm intention, walked towards Julia, who stood alone by the window drinking a glass of white wine.

'Help!' said Patrick.

'Oh, hi,' said Julia, 'I was just staring out of the window vacantly, but not so vacantly that I didn't see you flirting with that pretty waitress.'

'Flirting? I didn't say a word.'

'You didn't have to, darling. A dog doesn't have to say a word when it sits next to us in the dining room making little whimpering sounds while strings of saliva dangle down to the carpet; we still know what it wants.'

'I admit that I was vaguely attracted to her, but it was only after that grey-haired lunatic started talking to me that she began to look like the last overhanging tree before the roar of the rapids.'

'How poetic. You're still trying to be saved.'

'Not at all; I'm trying not to want to be saved.'

'Progress.'

'Relentless forward motion,' said Patrick.

'So who is this lunatic who forced you to flirt with the waitress?'

'Oh, she used to work in my mother's charity shop years ago. Her experience of Eleanor was so different from mine, it made me realize that I'm not in charge of the meaning of my mother's life, and that I'm deluded to think that I can come to some magisterial conclusion about it.'

'Surely you could come to some conclusion about what it means to you.'

'I'm not even sure if that's true,' said Patrick. 'I've been noticing today how inconclusive I feel about both my parents. There isn't any final truth; it's more like being able to get off on different floors of the same building.'

'It sounds awfully tiring,' Julia complained. 'Wouldn't it be simpler to just loathe their guts?'

Patrick burst out laughing.

'I used to think that I was detached about my father. I thought that detachment was the great virtue, without the moral condescension built into forgiveness, but the truth is that I feel everything: contempt, rage, pity, terror, tenderness and detachment.'

'Tenderness?'

'At the thought of how unhappy he was. When I had sons of my own and felt the strength of my instinct to protect them, I was freshly shocked that he had deliberately inflicted harm on his son, and then the hatred returned.'

'So you've pretty much abandoned detachment.'

'On the contrary, I just recognize how many things there are to be detached about. The incandescent hatred and the pure terror don't invalidate the detachment, they give it a chance to expand.'

'The StairMasters of detachment,' said Julia.

'Exactly.'

'I wonder if I'm allowed to smoke out here,' said Julia, opening the French windows and stepping outside. Patrick followed her onto the narrow balcony and sat on the edge of the white stucco balustrade. As she took out her packet of Camel Blue, his eyes traced the elegant profile he had often studied from a neighbouring pillow, now set against the restrained promise of the still-leafless trees. He watched Julia kiss the filter of her cigarette and suck the swaying flame of her lighter into the tightly packed tobacco. After the first immense drag, smoke flowed over her upper lip, only to be drawn back through her nose into her expanding lungs and eventually released, at first in a single thick stream and then in the little puffs and misshapen rings and drifting walls formed by her smoky words.

'So, have you been working out especially hard on your Inner StairMaster today?'

'I've felt a strange mixture of elation and free-fall. There's something cool and objective about death compared to the savage privacy of dying which my mother's illness forced me to imagine over the last four years. In a sense I can think about her clearly for the first time, away from the vortex of an empathy that was neither compassionate nor salutary, but a kind of understudy to her own horror.'

'Wouldn't it be even better not to think about her at all?' said Julia with a second languorous gulp of cigarette smoke.

'No, not today,' said Patrick, suddenly repelled by Julia's enamelled surface.

'Oh, of course, not today—of all days,' said Julia, sensing his defection. 'I just meant eventually.'

'The people who tell us to "get over it" and "get on with it" are the least able to have the direct experience that they berate navel-gazers for avoiding,' said Patrick, in the prosecuting style he adopted when defending himself. 'The "it" they're "getting on with" is a ghostly re-enactment of unreflecting habits. Not thinking about something is the surest way to remain under its influence.'

'It's a fair cop, guv,' said Julia, disconcerted by Patrick's sincerity.

'What would it mean to be spontaneous, to have an unconditioned response to things—to anything? Neither of us is in a position to know, but I don't want to die without finding out.'

'Hmm,' said Julia, clearly not tempted by Patrick's obscure project.

'Excuse me,' said a voice behind them.

Patrick looked round and saw the beautiful waitress. He had forgotten that he was in love with her, but now it all came back to him.

'Oh, hi,' he said.

She scarcely acknowledged him, but kept her eyes fixed on Julia.

'I'm sorry but you're not allowed to smoke out here,' she said.

'Oh, dear,' said Julia, taking a drag on her cigarette, 'I didn't know. It's funny, because it is outside.'

'Well, technically it's still part of the club and you can't smoke anywhere in the club.'

'I understand,' said Julia, continuing to smoke. 'Well, I'd better put it out then.' She took another long suck on her almost finished cigarette, dropped it on the balcony and ground it underfoot before stepping back indoors.

Patrick waited for the waitress to look at him with complicity and amusement, but she returned to her post behind the long table without glancing in his direction.

The waitress was useless. Julia was useless. Eleanor was useless. Even Mary in the end was useless and would not prevent him from returning to his bedsit alone and without any consolation whatever.

It was not the women who were at fault; it was his omnipotent delusion: the idea that they were there to be useful to him in the first place. He must make sure to remember that the next time one of the pointless bitches let him down. Patrick let out another bark of laughter. He was feeling a little bit mad. Casanova, the misogynist; Casanova, the hungry baby. The inadequacy at the rotten heart of exaggeration. He watched a modest veil of self-disgust settle on the subject of his relations with women, trying to prevent him from going deeper. Self-disgust was the easy way out, he must cut through it and allow himself to be unconsoled. He looked forward to the austere demands of that word, like a cool drink after the dry oasis of consolation. Back in his bedsit unconsoled, he could hardly wait.

It was getting cold on the balcony and Patrick wanted to get back indoors, but he was prevented by his reluctance to join Kettle and Mary, who were standing just the other side of the French windows.

'I see that you and Thomas are still practically glued to each other,' said Kettle, casting an envious glance at her grandson draped comfortably around his mother's neck.

'Nobody can hope to ignore their children as completely as you did,' sighed Mary.

'What do you mean? We always . . . communicated.'

'Communicated! Do you remember what you said to me when you telephoned me at school to tell me that Daddy had died?'

'How awful it all was, I suppose.'

'I couldn't speak I was so upset, and you told me to *cheer up*. To *cheer up*! You never had any idea who I was and you still don't.'

Mary turned away with a growl of exasperation and walked towards the other end of the room. Kettle greeted the inevitable outcome of her spite with an expression of astonished incomprehension. Patrick hovered on the balcony waiting for her to move away, but watched instead as Annette came up to engage her in conversation.

'Hello, dear,' said Annette, 'how are you?'

'Well, I've just had my head bitten off by my daughter, and so just for the moment I'm in a state of shock.'

'Mothers and children,' said Annette wisely, 'maybe we should have a workshop on that dynamic and tempt you back to the Foundation.'

'A workshop on mothers and children would tempt me to stay away,' said Kettle. 'Not that I need much encouragement to stay away; I think I've finished with shamanism.'

'Bless you,' said Annette. 'I won't feel that I've finished until I'm totally connected to the source of unconditional love that inhabits every soul on this planet.'

'Well, I've set my sights rather lower,' said Kettle. 'I think I'm just relieved not to be shaking a rattle, with my eyes watering from all that wretched wood smoke.'

Annette let out a peal of tolerant laughter.

'Well, I know Seamus would love to see you again and that he thought you'd especially benefit from our "Walking with the

Goddess" workshop, "stepping into the power of the feminine". I'm going to be participating myself.'

'How is Seamus? I suppose he's moved into the main house now.'

'Oh, yes, he's in Eleanor's old bedroom, lording it over all of us.'

'The bedroom Patrick and Mary used to be in, with the view of the olive groves?'

'Oh, that's a glorious view, isn't it? Mind you, I love my room, looking out on the chapel.'

'That's my room,' said Kettle. 'I always used to stay in that room.'

'Isn't it funny how we get attached to things?' laughed Annette. 'And yet, in the end, even our bodies aren't really our own; they belong to the Earth—to the Goddess.'

'Not yet,' said Kettle firmly.

'I tell you what,' said Annette, 'if you come to the Goddess workshop, you can have your old room back. I don't mind moving out; I'm happy anywhere. Anyway, Seamus is always talking about "moving from the property paradigm to the participation paradigm", and if the facilitators at the Foundation don't do it, we can't expect anyone else to.'

Patrick's primary objective was to get off the balcony without drawing attention to himself, and so he suppressed the desire to point out that Seamus had been moving in the opposite direction, from participating in Eleanor's charity to occupying her property.

Kettle was clearly confused by Annette's kind offer of her old bedroom. Her loyalty to her bad mood was not easily shaken and yet it was hard to see what she could do except thank Annette.

'That's unusually kind of you,' she said dismissively.

Patrick seized his chance and bolted off the balcony, passing behind Kettle's back with such decisiveness that he knocked her into Annette's clattering cup of tea.

'Mind out,' snapped Kettle before she could see who had barged into her. 'Honestly, Patrick,' she added when she saw the culprit.

'Oh, dear, you're covered in tea,' said Annette.

Patrick did not pause and only called 'Sorry' over his shoulder as he crossed the room at a quick pace. He continued out onto the landing and, without knowing where he was going, cantered down the staircase with a light hand on the banister, like a man who had been called away on urgent business.

13

MARY SMILED AT HENRY from across the room and started to move in his direction, but before she could reach his side Fleur surged up in front of her.

'I hope I haven't offended your husband,' she said. 'He walked away from me very abruptly and now he seems to have stormed out of the room altogether.'

'It's a difficult day for him,' said Mary, fascinated by Fleur's lipstick, which had been reapplied, mostly to the old lopsided track around her mouth but also to her front teeth.

'Has he had mental-health problems?' said Fleur. 'I only ask because—God knows!—I've had my fair share and I've grown rather good at telling when other people have a screw loose.'

'You seem quite well now,' said Mary, lying virtuously.

'It's funny you should say that,' said Fleur, 'because this morning I thought, "There's no point in taking your pills when you feel so well." I feel very, very well, you see.'

Mary recoiled instinctively. 'Oh, good,' she said.

'I feel as if something amazing is going to happen to me today,' Fleur went on. 'I don't think I've ever achieved my full potential—I feel as if I could do anything—as if I could raise the dead!'

'That's the last thing anyone would expect at this party,' said Mary, with a cheerful laugh. 'Do ask Patrick first if it's Eleanor you've got in mind.'

'Oh, I'd love to see Eleanor again,' said Fleur, as if endorsing Mary's candidate for resurrection and about to perform the necessary operation.

'Will you excuse me?' said Mary. 'I've got to go and talk to Patrick's cousin. He's come all the way from America and we didn't even know he was coming.'

'I'd love to go to America,' said Fleur, 'in fact, I might fly there later this afternoon.'

'In a plane?' said Mary.

'Yes, of course . . . Oh!' Fleur interrupted herself. 'I see what you mean.'

She stuck out her arms, thrust her head forwards and swayed from side to side, with an explosion of laughter so loud that Mary could sense everyone in the room looking in her direction.

She reached out and touched Fleur's outstretched arm, smiling at her to show how much she had enjoyed sharing their delightful joke, but turning away firmly to join Henry, who stood alone in the corner of the room.

'That woman's laugh packs quite a punch,' said Henry.

'Everything about her packs a punch, that's what I'm worried about,' said Mary. 'I feel she may do something very crazy before we all get home.'

'Who is she? She's kind of exotic.'

Mary noticed how distinct Henry's eyelashes were against the pale translucence of his eyes.

'None of us has ever met her. She just turned up unexpectedly.'

'Like me,' said Henry, with egalitarian gallantry.

'Except that we know who you are and we're very pleased to see you,' said Mary, 'especially since not a lot of people have turned up. Eleanor lost touch with people; her social life was very disintegrated. She had a few little pockets of friendship, each assuming that there was something more central, but in fact there was nothing in the middle. For the last two years, I was the only person who visited her.'

'And Patrick?'

'No, he didn't go. She became so unhappy when she saw him. There was something she was dying to say but couldn't. I don't just mean in the mechanical sense that she couldn't speak in the last two years. I mean that she never could have said what she wanted to tell him, even if she had been the most articulate person in the world, because she didn't know what it was, but when she became ill she could feel the pressure of it.'

'Just horrible,' said Henry. 'It's what we all dread.'

'That's why we must drop our defences while it's still a voluntary act,' said Mary, 'otherwise they'll be demolished and we'll be flooded with nameless horror.'

'Poor Eleanor, I feel so sorry for her,' said Henry.

They both fell silent for a while.

'At this point the English usually say, "Well, this is a cheerful subject!" to cover their embarrassment at being serious,' said Mary.

'Let's just stick with the sorrow,' said Henry with a kind smile.

'I'm really pleased you came,' she said. 'Your love for Eleanor was so uncomplicated, unlike everyone else's.'

'Cabbage,' said Nancy, grabbing Henry's arm, with the exaggerated eagerness of a shipwrecked passenger who discovers that she is not the only member of her family left alive, 'thank God! Save me from that dreadful woman in the green sweater! I can't believe my sister ever knew her—socially. I mean, this really is the most extraordinary gathering. I don't feel it's really a Jonson occasion at all. When I think of Mummy's funeral, or Aunt Edith's. Eight hundred people turned up at Mummy's, half the

French cabinet, and the Aga Khan, and the Windsors; *everybody* was there.'

'Eleanor chose a different path,' said Henry.

'More like a goat track,' said Nancy, rolling her eyes.

'Personally, I don't give a damn who comes to my funeral,' said Henry.

'That's only because you know that it'll be solid with senators and glamorous people and sobbing women!' said Nancy. 'The trouble with funerals is that they're so last-minute. That's where memorials come in, of course, but they're not the same. There's something so dramatic about a funeral, although I can't abide those open caskets. Do you remember Uncle Vlad? I still have nightmares about him lying there in that gold and white uniform looking all *gaunt*. Oh, God, wagon formation,' cried Nancy, 'the green goblin is staring at me again!'

Fleur was feeling a sense of irrepressible pleasure and potency as she scanned the room for someone who had not yet had the benefit of her conversation. She could understand all the currents flowing through the room; she only had to glance at a person to see into the depths of their soul. Thanks to Patrick Melrose, who was distracting the waitress by getting her telephone number, Fleur had been able to mix her own drink, a glass full of gin with a splash of tonic, rather than the other way round. What did it matter? Mere alcohol could not degrade her luminous awareness. After taking a gulp from her lipstick-smudged tumbler, she walked up to Nicholas Pratt, determined to help him understand himself.

'Have you had mental-health problems?' she asked Nicholas, fixing him with an intrepid stare.

'Have we met?' said Nicholas, gazing icily at the stranger who stood in his path.

'I only ask because I have a feeling for these things,' Fleur went on.

Nicholas hesitated between the impulse to utterly destroy this batty old woman in a moth-eaten sweater, and the temptation to boast about his robust mental health.

'Well, have you?' insisted Fleur.

Nicholas raised his walking stick briefly, as if about to nudge Fleur aside, only to replant it more firmly in the carpet and lean into its full support. He inhaled the frosty, invigorating air of contempt flooding in from the window smashed by Fleur's impertinent question; contempt that always made him, though he said it himself, even more articulate than usual.

'No, I have not had "mental-health problems",' he thundered. 'Even in this degenerate age of confession and complaint we have not managed to turn reality entirely on its head. When the vocabulary of Freudian mumbo-jumbo is emptied onto every conversation, like vinegar onto a newspaper full of sodden chips, some of us choose not to *tuck in*.' Nicholas craned his head forward as he spat out the homely phrase.

'The sophisticated cherish their "syndromes",' he continued, 'and even the most simple-minded fool feels entitled to a "complex". As if it weren't ludicrous enough for every child to be "gifted", they now have to be ill as well: a touch of Asperger's, a little autism; dyslexia stalks the playground; the poor little gifted things have been "bullied" at school; if they can't confess to being abused, they must confess to being abusive. Well, my dear woman,' Nicholas laughed threateningly, '—I call you "my dear" from what is no doubt known as *Sincerity Deficit Disorder*, unless some ambitious quack, landing on the scalding, sarcastic beaches of the great continent of irony, has claimed the inversion of surface meaning as *Potter's Disease* or *Jones's Jaundice*—no, my *dear* woman, I have not suffered from the slightest taint of mental illness. The modern passion for pathology is a landslide that has been forced to come to a halt at some distance from my eminently sane feet. I have only to walk towards that heap of refuse for it to part, making way for the impossible man, the man who is entirely well; psychotherapists scatter in my presence, ashamed of their sham profession!'

'You're completely off your rocker,' said Fleur, discerningly. 'I thought as much. I've developed what I call "my little radar" over the years. Put me in a room full of people and I can tell straight away who has had *that* sort of problem.'

Nicholas experienced a moment of despair as he realized that his withering eloquence had made no impact, but like an expert tango dancer who turns abruptly on the very edge of the dance floor, he changed his approach and shouted, 'Bugger off!' at the top of his voice.

Fleur looked at him with deepening insight.

'A month in the Priory would get you back on your feet,' she concluded, 're-clothe you in your rightful mind, as the hymn says. Do you know it?' Fleur closed her eyes and started to sing rapturously, ' "Dear Lord and Father of mankind / Forgive our foolish ways / Re-clothe us in our rightful minds . . ." Marvellous stuff. I'll have a word with Dr. Pagazzi, he's quite the best. He can be rather severe at times, but only for one's own good. Look at me: I was mad as a hatter and now I'm on top of the world.'

She leant forward to whisper confidentially to Nicholas.

'I feel very, very well, you see.'

There were professional reasons for Johnny not to engage with Nicholas Pratt, whose daughter had been a patient of his, but the sight of that monstrous man bellowing at a dishevelled old woman pushed his restraint beyond the limits he had imposed on himself until now. He approached Fleur and, with his back turned to Nicholas, asked her quietly if she was all right.

'All right?' laughed Fleur. 'I'm extremely well, better than ever.' She struggled to express her sense of abundance. 'If there were such a thing as being too well, I'd be it. I was just trying to help this poor man who's had more than his fair share of mental-health problems.'

Reassured that she was unharmed, Johnny smiled at Fleur and started to withdraw tactfully, but Nicholas was by now too enraged to let such an opportunity pass.

'Ah,' he said, 'here he is! Like an exhibit in a courtroom drama, brought on at the perfect moment: a practising witch-doctor, a purveyor of psycho-*paralysis,* a guide to the catacombs, a guide to the sewers; he promises to turn your dreams into nightmares and he keeps his promises religiously,' snarled Nicholas, his face flushed and the corners of his mouth flecked with tired saliva. 'The ferryman of Hell's second river won't accept a simple coin, like his proletarian colleague on the Styx. You'll need a fat cheque to cross the Lethe into that forgotten under world of dangerous gibberish where toothless infants rip the nipples from their mothers' milkless breasts.'

Nicholas seemed to be labouring for breath, as he unrolled his vituperative sentences.

'No fantasy that you invent,' he struggled on, 'could be as re-pulsive as the fantasy on which his sinister art is based, polluting the human imagination with murderous babies and incestuous children . . .'

Nicholas suddenly stopped speaking, his mouth working to take in enough air. He rocked sideways on his walking stick be-fore staggering backwards a couple of steps and crashing down against the table and onto the floor. He caught the tablecloth as he fell and dragged half a dozen glasses after him. A bottle of red wine toppled sideways and its contents gurgled over the edge of the table and splashed onto his black suit. The waitress lunged forward and caught the bucket of half-melted ice that was slid-ing towards Nicholas's supine body.

'Oh, dear,' said Fleur, 'he got himself too worked up. "Hoisted by his own petard", as the saying goes. This is what happens to people who won't ask for help,' she said, as if discussing the case with Dr. Pagazzi.

Mary leant over to the waitress, her mobile phone already open.

'I'm going to call an ambulance,' she said.

'Thanks,' said the waitress. 'I'll go downstairs and warn reception.'

Everyone in the room gathered around the fallen figure and looked on with a mixture of curiosity and alarm.

Patrick knelt down beside Nicholas and started to loosen his tie. Long after it could have been helpful, he continued to loosen the knot until he had removed the tie altogether. Only then did he undo the top button of Nicholas's shirt. Nicholas tried to say something but winced from the effort and closed his eyes instead, disgusted by his own vulnerability.

Johnny acknowledged a feeling of satisfaction at having played no active part in Nicholas's collapse. And then he looked down at his fallen opponent, sprawled heavily on the carpet, and somehow the sight of his old neck, no longer festooned with an expensive black silk tie, but wrinkled and sagging and open at the throat, as if waiting for the final dagger thrust, filled him with pity and renewed his respect for the conservative powers of an ego that would rather kill its owner than allow him to change.

'Johnny?' said Robert.

'Yes,' said Johnny, seeing Robert and Thomas looking up at him with great interest.

'Why was that man so angry with you?'

'It's a long story,' said Johnny, 'and one that I'm not really allowed to tell.'

'Has he got psycho-paralysis?' said Thomas. 'Because paralysis means you can't move.'

Johnny couldn't help laughing, despite the solemn murmur surrounding Nicholas's collapse.

'Well, personally, I think that would be a brilliant diagnosis; but Nicholas Pratt invented that word in order to make fun of psychoanalysis, which is what I do for a job.'

'What's that?' said Thomas.

'It's a way of getting access to hidden truths about your feelings,' said Johnny.

'Like hide and seek?' said Thomas.

'Exactly,' said Johnny, 'but instead of hiding in cupboards and behind curtains and under beds, this kind of truth hides in symptoms and dreams and habits.'

'Can we play?' said Thomas.

'Can we stop playing?' said Johnny, more to himself than to Thomas and Robert.

Julia came up and interrupted Johnny's conversation with the children.

'Is this the end?' she said. 'It's enough to put one off having a temper tantrum. Oh, God, that religious fanatic is cradling his head. That would definitely finish me off.'

Annette was sitting on her heels next to Nicholas, with her hands cupped around his head, her eyes closed and her lips moving very slightly.

'Is she praying?' said Julia, flabbergasted.

'That's nice of her,' said Thomas.

'They say one should never speak ill of the dead,' said Julia, 'and so I'd better get a move on. I've always thought that Nicholas Pratt was perfectly ghastly. I'm not a particular friend of Amanda's, but he seems to have ruined his daughter's life. Of course you'd know more about that than I do.'

Johnny had no trouble staying silent.

'Why don't you stop being so horrible?' said Robert passionately. 'He's an old man who's really ill and he might hear what you're saying, and he can't even answer back.'

'Yes,' said Thomas, 'it's not fair because he can't answer back.'

Julia at first seemed more bewildered than annoyed, and when she finally spoke it was with a wounded sigh.

'Well, you know it's time to leave a party when the children start to mount a joint attack on your moral character.'

'Could you say goodbye to Patrick for me?' she said, kissing Johnny abruptly on both cheeks and ignoring the two boys. 'I can't quite face it after what's happened—to Nicholas, I mean.'

'I hope we didn't make her angry,' said Robert.

'She made herself angry, because it was easier for her than being upset,' said Johnny.

Only seconds after her departure, Julia was forced back into the room by the urgent arrival of the waitress, two ambulance men and an array of equipment.

'Look!' said Thomas. 'An oxygen tank and a stretcher. I wish I could have a go!'

'He's over here,' said the waitress unnecessarily.

Nicholas felt his wrist being lifted. He knew his pulse was being taken. He knew it was too fast, too slow, too weak, too strong, everything wrong. A rip in his heart, a skewer through his chest. He must tell them he was not an organ donor, or they would steal his organs before he was dead. He must stop them! Call Withers! Tell them to *put a stop to it at once*. He couldn't speak. Not his tongue, they mustn't take his tongue. Without speech, thoughts plough on like a train without tracks, buckling, crashing, ripping everything apart. A man asks him to open his eyes. He opens his eyes. Show them he's still compos mentis, compost mentis, recycled parts. No! Not his brain, not his genitals, not his heart, not fit to transplant, still writhing with self in an alien body. They were shining a light in his eyes, no, not his eyes; please don't take his eyes. So much fear. Without a regiment of words, the barbarians, the burning roofs, the horses' hooves beating down on fragile skulls. He was not himself any more; he was under the hooves. He could not be helpless; he could not be humiliated; it was too late to become somebody he didn't know—the intimate horror of it.

'Don't worry, Nick, I'll be with you in the ambulance,' a voice whispered in his ear.

It was the Irish woman. With him in the ambulance! Gouging his eyes out, fishing around for his kidneys with her nimble fingers, taking a hacksaw out of her spiritual tool box. He wanted to be saved. He wanted his mother; not the one he had actually had, but the real one he had never met. He felt a pair of hands grip his feet and another pair of hands slip around his shoulders. Hung, drawn and quartered: publicly executed for all his crimes. He deserved it. Lord have mercy on his soul. Lord have mercy.

The two ambulance men looked at each other and on a nod lifted both ends of Nicholas at once and placed him on the stretcher they had spread out beside him.

'I'm going with him in the ambulance,' said Annette.

'Thank you,' said Patrick. 'Will you call me from the hospital if there's any news?'

'Surely,' said Annette. 'Oh, it's a terrible shock for you,' she said, giving Patrick an unexpected hug. 'I'd better go.'

'Is that woman going with him?' asked Nancy.

'Yes, isn't it kind of her?'

'But she doesn't even know him. I've known Nicholas for ever. First it's my sister and now it's practically my oldest friend. It's too impossible.'

'Why don't you follow her?' said Patrick.

'There is one thing I could do for him,' said Nancy, with a hint of indignation, as if it was a bit much to expect her to be the only person to show any real consideration. 'Miguel, his poor driver, is waiting outside without the least idea of what's happened. I'll go and break the news to him, and take the car on to the hospital, so it's there if Nicholas needs it.'

Nancy could think of at least three places she might stop on the way. The examination was bound to take ages, in fact Nicholas might already be dead, and it would help to take poor Miguel's mind off the dreadful situation if he drove her around all afternoon. She had no cash for taxis, and her swollen feet were already bulging out of the ruthlessly elegant inside edges of her two-thousand-dollar shoes. People said she was incorrigibly extravagant, but the shoes would have cost two thousand dollars *each*, if she hadn't bought them parsimoniously in a sale. She had no prospect of getting any cash for the rest of the month, punished by her beastly bankers for her 'credit history'. Her credit history, as far as she was concerned, was that Mummy had written a lousy will that allowed her evil stepfather to steal all of Nancy's money. Her heroic response had been to spend as if justice had been done, as if she were restoring the natural order of the world by cheating shopkeepers, landlords, decorators, florists, hairdressers, butchers, jewellers and garage owners, by withholding tips from coat-check girls, and by engineering rows with staff so that she could sack them without pay.

On her monthly trip to the Morgan Guaranty—where Mummy had opened an account for her on her twelfth birthday—she collected fifteen thousand dollars in cash. In her reduced circumstances, the walk to Sixty-ninth Street was a Venus flytrap flushed with colour and shining with adhesive dew. She often arrived home with half her month's money spent; sometimes she counted out the entire sum and, seeming mystified by the missing two or three thousand, managed to walk away with a pink marble obelisk or a painting of a monkey in a velvet jacket, promising to come back that afternoon, marking another black spot in the complex maze of her debt, another detour on her city walks. She always gave her real telephone number, with one digit changed, her real address, one block uptown or downtown, and an entirely false name—obviously. Sometimes she called herself Edith Jonson, or Mary de Valençay, to remind herself that she had nothing to be ashamed of, that there had been a time when she could have bought a whole city block, never mind a bauble in one of its shops.

By the middle of the month she was invariably flat broke. At that point she fell back on the kindness of her friends. Some had her to stay, some let her add her lunches and her dinners to their tabs at Jimmy's or Le Jardin, and others simply wrote her a large cheque, reflecting that Nancy had barged to the front of the queue again and that the victims of floods, tsunamis and earthquakes would simply have to wait another year. Sometimes she created a crisis that forced her trustees to release more capital in order to keep her out of prison, driving her income inexorably lower. For Eleanor's funeral, she was staying with her great friends the Tescos, in their divine apartment in Belgrave Square, a lateral conversion across five buildings on two floors. Harry Tesco had already paid for her air ticket—first class—but she was going to have to break down sobbing in Cynthia's little sitting room before going to the opera tonight, and tell her the terrible pressure she was under. The Tescos were as rich as God and it really made Nancy quite angry that she had to do anything so humiliating to get more money out of them.

'You couldn't drop me off on the way, could you?' Kettle asked Nancy.

'It's Nicholas's private car, dear, not a limo service,' said Nancy, appalled by the indecency of the suggestion. 'It's really too upsetting when he's so ill.'

Nancy kissed Patrick and Mary goodbye and hurried away.

'It's St Thomas' Hospital, by the way,' Patrick called after her. 'The ambulance man told me it's the best place for "clot-busters".'

'Has he had a stroke?' asked Nancy.

'Heart attack, they could tell from the cold nose—the extremities go cold.'

'Oh, don't,' said Nancy, 'I can't bear to think about it.'

She set off down the stairs with no time to waste: Cynthia had made her an appointment at the hairdresser's using the magic words, 'charge it to me'.

When Nancy had left, Henry offered the aggrieved Kettle a lift. After only a few minutes of complaint about the rudeness of Patrick's aunt, she accepted, and said goodbye to Mary and the children. Henry promised to call Patrick the next day, and accompanied Kettle downstairs. To their surprise they found Nancy still standing on the pavement outside the club.

'Oh, Cabbage,' she said with a wail of childish frustration, 'Nicholas's car has gone.'

'You can come with us,' said Henry simply.

Kettle and Nancy sat in the back of the car in hostile silence. Up in front Henry told the driver to go to Princes Gate first, then on to St Thomas' Hospital and finally back to the hotel. Nancy suddenly realized what she had done by accepting a ride. She had forgotten about Nicholas altogether. Now she was going to have to borrow money from Henry to catch a taxi back to the hairdresser's from some godforsaken hospital in the middle of nowhere. It was enough to make you scream.

Nicholas's fall, the commotion that followed, the arrival of the ambulance men and the dispersal of some of the guests had all eluded Erasmus's attention. When Fleur had burst into song in the middle of her conversation with Nicholas, the words 'reclothe us in our rightful minds' sent a little shock through him, like a piercing dog whistle, inaudible to the others but pitched perfectly for his own preoccupations, it recalled him to his true

master, insisting that he leave the muddy fields of inter-subjectivity
and the intriguing traces of other minds for the cool ledge of the
balcony where he might be allowed, for a few moments, to think
about thinking. Social life had a tendency to press him up against
his basic rejection of the proposition that an individual identity
was defined by turning experience into an ever more patterned
and coherent story. It was in reflection and not in narrative that
he found authenticity. The pressure to render his past in anecdote, or indeed to imagine the future in terms of passionate as-
pirations, made him feel clumsy and false. He knew that his
inability to be excited by the memory of his first day at school,
or to project a cumulative and increasingly solid self that wanted
to learn the harpsichord, or longed to live in the Chilterns, or
hoped to see Christ's blood streaming in the firmament, made
his personality seem unreal to other people, but it was precisely
the unreality of the personality that was so clear to him. His
authentic self was the attentive witness to a variety of inconstant
impressions that could not, in themselves, enhance or detract
from his sense of identity.

Not only did he have an ontological problem with the generally unquestioned narrative assumptions of ordinary social life
but he also, at this particular party, found himself questioning
the ethical assumption, shared by everyone except Annette (and
not shared by Annette for reasons that were in themselves prob-
lematic), that Eleanor Melrose had been wrong to disinherit her
son. Setting aside for a moment the difficulties of judging the
usefulness of the Foundation she had endowed, there was an
undeniable potential Utilitarian merit to the wider distribution
of her resources. Mrs. Melrose might at least count on John Stu-
art Mill and Jeremy Bentham and Peter Singer and R. M. Hare
to look sympathetically on her case. If a thousand people, over
the years, emerged from the Foundation having discovered, by
whatever esoteric means, a sense of purpose that made them

into more altruistic and conscientious citizens, would the benefit to society not outweigh the distress caused to a family of four
people (with one barely conscious of the loss) who had expected
to own a house and turned out not to? In the maelstrom of per-
spectives could a sound moral judgment be made from any other
point of view but that of the strictest impartiality? Whether
such a point of view could ever be established was another question to which the answer was almost certainly negative. Nevertheless, even if Utilitarian arithmetic, based on the notion of an
unobtainable impartiality, were set aside on the grounds that
motivation was desire-based, as Hume had argued, the auton-
omy of an individual's preferences for one kind of good over another still offered a strong ethical case for Eleanor's philanthropic
choice.

There had been a widespread sense of relief when Fleur accompanied Nicholas's stretcher downstairs and appeared to have
left the party, but ten minutes later she reappeared resolutely in
the doorway. Seeing Erasmus leaning on the balustrade staring
pensively down at the gravel path, she immediately expressed
her alarm to Patrick.

'What's that man doing on the balcony?' she asked sharply,
like a nanny who despairs of leaving the nursery for even a few
minutes. 'Is he going to jump?'

'I don't think he was planning to,' said Patrick, 'but I'm sure
you could persuade him.'

'The last thing we need is another death on our hands,' said
Fleur.

'I'll go and check,' said Robert.

'Me too,' said Thomas, dashing through the French windows.

'You mustn't jump,' he explained, 'because the last thing we
need is another death on our hands.'

'I wasn't thinking of jumping,' said Erasmus.

'What were you thinking about?' asked Robert.

'Whether doing some good to a lot of people is better than doing a lot of good to a few,' Erasmus replied.

'The needs of the many outweigh the needs of the few. Or the one,' said Robert solemnly, making a strange gesture with his right hand.

Thomas, recognizing the allusion to the Vulcan logic of *Star Trek II,* made the same gesture with his hand.

'Live long and prosper,' he said, smiling uncontrollably at the thought of growing pointed ears.

Fleur strode onto the balcony and addressed Erasmus without any trivial preliminaries.

'Have you tried Amitriptyline?' she asked.

'I've never heard of him,' said Erasmus. 'What's he written?'

Fleur realized that Erasmus was much more confused than she had originally imagined.

'You'd better come inside,' she said coaxingly.

Glancing into the room Erasmus noticed that the majority of the guests had left and assumed that Fleur was hinting tactfully that he should be on his way.

'Yes, you're probably right,' said Erasmus.

Fleur reflected that she had a real talent for dealing with people in extreme mental states and that she should probably be put in charge of the depression wing of a psychiatric hospital, or indeed of a national policy unit.

As he went indoors, Erasmus decided not to get entangled in more incoherent social life, but simply to say goodbye to Mary and then leave immediately. As he leant over to kiss her, he wondered if a person of the predominantly narrative type would desire Mary because he had desired her in the past, and whether he would be imagining that fragment of the past being transported, as it were, in a time machine to the present moment. This fantasy reminded him of Wittgenstein's seminal remark that 'nothing is more important in teaching us to understand the concepts we have than constructing fictitious ones'. In his own case, his desire, such as it was, had the character of an inconsequential present-tense fact, like the scent of a flower.

'Thank you for coming,' said Mary.

'Not at all,' mumbled Erasmus, and after squeezing Mary's shoulder lightly, he left without saying goodbye to anyone else.

'Don't worry,' said Fleur to Patrick, 'I'll follow him at a discreet distance.'

'You're his guardian angel,' said Patrick, struggling to disguise his relief at getting rid of Fleur so easily.

Mary followed Fleur politely onto the landing.

'I haven't got time to chat,' said Fleur, 'that poor man's life is in danger.'

Mary knew better than to contradict a woman of Fleur's strong convictions. 'Well, it's been a pleasure to meet such an old friend of Eleanor's.'

'I'm sure she's guiding me,' said Fleur. 'I can feel the connection. She was a saint; she'll show me how to help him.'

'Oh, good,' said Mary.

'God bless you,' Fleur called out as she set off down the stairs at a cracking pace, determined not to lose track of Erasmus's suicidal progress through the streets of London.

'What a woman!' said Johnny, watching through the doorway as Fleur left. 'I can't help feeling that somebody should be following her rather than the other way round.'

'Count me out,' said Patrick, 'I've had an overdose of Fleur. It's a wonder she was ever allowed out of the Priory.'

'She looks to me as if she's just at the beginning of a manic episode,' said Johnny. 'I imagine she was enjoying it too much and decided not to take her pills.'

'Well, let's hope she changes her mind before she "saves" Erasmus,' said Patrick. 'He might not survive if she rugby tackles him on a bridge, or leaps on him while he's trying to cross the road.'

'God!' said Mary, laughing with relief and amazement. 'I wasn't sure she was ever going to leave. I hope Erasmus made it round the corner before she got outside.'

'I'm going to have to leave myself,' said Johnny. 'I've got a patient at four o'clock.'

He said goodbye to everyone, kissing Mary, hugging the boys, and promising to call Patrick later.

Suddenly the family was alone, apart from the waitress, who was clearing up the glasses and putting the unopened bottles back into a cardboard box in the corner.

Patrick felt a familiar combination of intimacy and desolation, being together and knowing they were about to part.

'Are you coming back with us?' asked Thomas.

'No,' said Patrick, 'I have to go and work.'

'Please,' said Thomas, 'I want you to tell me a story like you used to.'

'I'll see you at the weekend,' said Patrick.

Robert stood by, knowing more than his brother but not enough to understand.

'You can come and have dinner with us if you like,' said Mary.

Patrick wanted to accept and wanted to refuse, wanted to be alone and wanted company, wanted to be close to Mary and to get away from her, wanted the lovely waitress to think that he led an independent life and wanted his children to feel that they were part of a harmonious family.

'I think I'll just . . . crash out,' he said, buried under the debris of contradictions and doomed to regret any choice he made. 'It's been a long day.'

'Don't worry if you change your mind,' said Mary.

'In fact,' said Thomas, 'you should change your mind, because that's what it's for!'

14

AS HE LABOURED UP to his bedsit, a miniature roof conversion with sloping walls on the fifth floor of a narrow Victorian building in Kensington, Patrick seemed to regress through evolutionary history, growing more stooped with each flight, until he was resting his knuckles on the carpet of the top landing, like an early hominid that has not yet learned to stand upright on the grasslands of Africa and only makes rare and nervous expeditions down from the safety of the trees.

'Fuck,' he muttered, as he got his breath back and raised himself to the level of the keyhole.

It was out of the question to invite that adorable waitress back to his hovel, although her telephone number was nestling in his pocket, next to his disturbingly thumping heart. She was too young to have to squeeze herself out from under the corpse of a middle-aged man who had died in the midst of trying to justify her wearisome climb to his inadequate flat. Patrick collapsed onto the bed and embraced a pillow, imagining its tired feathers and yellowing pillowcase transformed into her smooth warm neck. The anxious aphrodisiac of a recent death; the long gallery of substitutes substituting for substitutes; the tantalizing thirst for consolation: it was all so familiar, but he reminded himself grimly that he had come back to his non-home, now that he was alone at last, in order to be unconsoled. This flat, the bachelor pad of a non-bachelor, the student digs of a non-student, was as good a place as he could wish for to practise being unconsoled. The lifelong tension between dependency and independence, between home and adventure, could be resolved only by being at home everywhere, by learning to cast an equal gaze on the raging self-importance of each mood and incident. He had some way to go. He only had to run out of his favourite bath oil to feel like taking a sledgehammer to the bath and begging a doctor for a Valium script.

Nevertheless, he lay on the bed and thought about how determined he was: a Tomahawk whistling through the woods and thudding into its target, a flash of nuclear light dissolving a circle of cloud for miles around. With a groan he rolled slowly off the bed and sank into the black armchair next to the fireplace. Through the window on the other side of the flat he could see slate roofs sloping down the hill, the spinning metal chimney vents glinting in the late-afternoon sun and, in the distance, the trees in Holland Park, their leaves still too tight-fisted to make their branches green. Before he rang the waitress—he took out the note and found that she was called Helene—before he rang Mary, before he went out for a long sedative dinner and tried to read a serious book, under the dim lighting and over the maddening music, before he pretended that he thought it was important to keep up with current affairs and switched on the news, before he rented a violent movie, or jerked off in the bath because he couldn't face ringing Helene after all, he was going to sit in this chair for a while and show a little respect for the pressures and intimations of the day.

What exactly had he been mourning? Not his mother's death— that was mainly a relief. Not her life—he had mourned her suffering and frustration years ago when she started her decline into dementia. Nor was it his relationship with her, which he had long regarded as an effect on his personality rather than a transaction with another person. The pressure he had felt today was something like the presence of infancy, something far deeper and more helpless than his murderous relationship with his father. Although his father had been there with his rages and his scalpels, and his mother had been there with her exhaustion and her gin, this experience could not be described as a narrative or a set of relationships, but existed as a deep core of inarticulacy. For a man who had tried to talk his way out of everything he had thought and felt, it was shocking to find that there was something huge that he had failed to mention at all. Perhaps this was what he really had in common with his mother, a core of inarticulacy, magnified in her case by illness, but in his case hidden until he heard the news of her death. It was like a collision in the dark in a strange room; he was groping his way round something he couldn't remember being there when the lights went out. Mourning was not the word for this experience. He felt frightened but also excited. In the post-parental realm perhaps he could understand his conditioning as a single fact, without any further interest in its genealogy, not because the historical perspective was untrue, but because it had been renounced. Someone else might achieve this kind of truce before their parents died, but his own parents had been such enormous obstructions that he had to be rid of them in the most literal sense before he could imagine his personality becoming the transparent medium he longed for it to be.

The idea of a voluntary life had always struck him as extravagant. Everything was conditioned by what had gone before; even his fanatical desire for some margin of freedom was conditioned by the drastic absence of freedom in his early life. Perhaps only a kind of bastard freedom was available: in the acceptance of the inevitable unfolding of cause and effect there was at least a freedom from delusion. The truth was that he didn't really know. In any case he had to start by recognizing the degree of his unfreedom, anchored in this inarticulate core that he was now at last embracing, and look on it with a kind of charitable horror. Most of his time had been spent in reaction to his conditioning, leaving little room to respond to the rest of life. What would it be like to react to nothing and respond to everything? He might at least inch in that direction. As he had been trying to tell an unreceptive Julia, he was less persuaded than ever by final judgements or conclusions. He had long suffered from Negative Incapability, the opposite of that famous Keatsian virtue of being in mysteries, uncertainties and doubts without reaching out for facts and explanations—or whatever the exact phrase was—but now he was ready to stay open to questions that could not necessarily be answered, rather than rush to answers that he refused to question. Maybe he could respond to everything only if he experienced the world as a question, and perhaps he continually reacted to it because he thought that its nature was fixed.

The phone on the little table next to him started to ring and Patrick, dragged out of his thoughts, stared at it for a while as if he had never seen one before. He hesitated and then finally picked it up just before his answerphone message cut in.

'Hello,' he said wearily.

'It's me, Annette.'

'Oh, hi. How are you? How's Nicholas?'

'I'm afraid I've got terrible news,' said Annette. 'Nicholas didn't make it. I'm so sorry, Patrick, I know he was an old family friend. He actually stopped breathing in the ambulance. They tried to revive him when we got to the hospital, but they couldn't get him back. I think all those electrodes and adrenalin are so frightening. When a soul is ready to go, we should let it go gently.'

'It's difficult to find a legal formulation for that approach,' said Patrick. 'Doctors have to pretend that they think more life is always worth having.'

'I suppose you're right, legally,' sighed Annette. 'Anyway, it must be overwhelming for you, and on the day of your mother's funeral.'

'I hadn't seen Nicholas for years,' said Patrick. 'I suppose I was lucky to get a last glimpse of him when he was on top form.'

'Oh, he was an amazing man,' said Annette. 'I've never met anyone quite like him.'

'He was unique,' said Patrick, 'at least I hope so. It would be rather terrifying to find a village full of Nicholas Pratts. Anyhow, Annette,' Patrick went on, realizing that his tone was not quite right for the occasion, 'it was very good of you to go with him. He was lucky to be with someone spontaneously kind at the time of his death.'

'Oh, now you're making me cry,' said Annette.

'And thank you for what you said at the funeral. You reminded me that Eleanor was a good person as well as an imperfect mother. It's very helpful to see her from other points of view than the one I've been trapped in.'

'You're welcome. You know that I loved her.'

'I do. Thank you,' said Patrick again.

They ended the conversation with the improbable promise to talk soon. Annette was flying back to France the next day and Patrick was certainly not going to call her in Saint-Nazaire. Nevertheless he said goodbye with a strange fondness. Did he really think that Eleanor was a good person? He felt that she had made the question of what it meant to be good central—and for that he was grateful.

Patrick took in the news that Nicholas was dead. He pictured him, back in the sixties, in a Mr. Fish shirt, making venomous conversation under the plane trees in Saint-Nazaire. He imagined himself as the little boy he had been at that time, shattered and mad at heart, but with a ferocious, heroic persona, which had eventually stopped his father's abuses with a single determined refusal. He knew that if he was going to understand the chaos that was invading him, he would have to renounce the protection of that fragile hero, just as he had to renounce the illusion of his mother's protection by acknowledging that his parents had been collaborators as well as antagonists.

Patrick sank deeper into the armchair, wondering how much of all this he could stand. Just how unconsoled was he prepared to be? He covered his stomach with a cushion as if he expected to get hit. He wanted to leave, to drink, to dive out of the window into a pool made of his own blood, to cease to feel anything forever straight away, but he mastered his panic enough to sit back up and let the cushion drop to the floor.

Perhaps whatever he thought he couldn't stand was made up partly or entirely of the thought that he couldn't stand it. He didn't really know, but he had to find out, and so he opened himself up to the feeling of utter helplessness and incoherence that he supposed he had spent his life trying to avoid, and waited for it to dismember him. What happened was not what he had expected. Instead of feeling the helplessness, he felt the helplessness and compassion for the helplessness at the same time. One followed the other swiftly, just as a hand reaches out instinctively to rub a hit shin, or relieve an aching shoulder. He was after all not an infant, but a man experiencing the chaos of infancy welling up in his conscious mind. As the compassion expanded he saw himself on equal terms with his supposed persecutors, saw his parents, who appeared to be the cause of his suffering, as unhappy children with parents who appeared to be the cause of their suffering: there was no one to blame and everyone to help, and those who appeared to deserve the most blame needed the most help. For a while he stayed level with the pure inevitability of things being as they were, the ground zero of events on which skyscrapers of psychological experience were built, and as he imagined not taking his life so personally, the heavy impenetrable darkness of the inarticulacy turned into a silence that was perfectly transparent, and he saw that there was a margin of freedom, a suspension of reaction, in that clarity.

Patrick slid back down in his chair and sprawled in front of the view. He noticed how his tears cooled as they ran down his cheeks. Washed eyes and a tired and empty feeling. Was that what people meant by peaceful? There must be more to it than that, but he didn't claim to be an expert. He suddenly wanted to see his children, real children, not the ghosts of their ancestors' childhoods, real children with a reasonable chance of enjoying their lives. He picked up the phone and dialled Mary's number. He was going to change his mind. After all, that's what Thomas said it was for.